THE COLLECTED STORIES

OF

MACHADO DE ASSIS

THE COLLECTED STORIES

OF

MACHADO DE ASSIS

Joaquim Maria Machado de Assis

Translated by

MARGARET JULL COSTA

AND

ROBIN PATTERSON

LIVERIGHT PUBLISHING CORPORATION

A division of W. W. Norton & Company

Independent Publishers Since 1923

NEW YORK | LONDON

For information about permission to reproduce selections from this book,
write to Permissions, Liveright Publishing Corporation, a division of
W. W. Norton & Company, Inc., 500 Fifth Avenue, New York, NY 10110

For information about special discounts for bulk purchases, please contact
W. W. Norton Special Sales at specialsales@wwnorton.com or 800-233-4830

Manufacturing by LSC Communcations, Harrisonburg
Book design by Ellen Cipriano
Production manager: Anna Oler

ISBN 978-0-87140-496-1

Liveright Publishing Corporation, 500 Fifth Avenue, New York, N.Y. 10110
www.wwnorton.com

W. W. Norton & Company Ltd., 15 Carlisle Street, London W1D 3BS

1 2 3 4 5 6 7 8 9 0

CONTENTS

MISCELLANEOUS PAPERS *(1882)*

UNDATED STORIES *(1884)*

RELICS FROM AN OLD HOUSE *(1906)*

FOREWORD

JOAQUIM MARIA MACHADO DE ASSIS wrote short stories throughout his career, publishing seven collections between 1870 and 1906, interspersed with his nine novels. Critics like to divide the novels into two sets, seeing the first four as slender and "romantic" (the author's own term) and the last five as complex, ironic masterpieces. We can't do anything like this with these stories, although we may say that with the years the continuing lightness of touch is applied to darker subjects. This is certainly the impression the full set of stories gives. We move from young love and shallow social ambition to suicide and slavery, from portraits of manners to deep philosophical questions. But even this impression calls out for some correction. There are early stories about memory and late stories about youth, and it is hard to think of anything darker than the early piece "Brother Simão" (1870), where a monk dies filled with loathing for humanity because of a lie told to him long ago. So perhaps the firmer truth is that as we read the stories we get better at registering the darkness, at seeing through the light, so to speak.

Machado's short stories resemble those of Chekhov in their talent for saying too little (that is, just enough), but his closest literary companion, if we are looking for comparisons, is his almost exact contemporary Henry James, and especially in his longer pieces, where he appears as a great master of the form that James called "our ideal, the beautiful and blest nouvelle." In this respect, we might think especially of "The Woman in Black," "The Blue Flower," and "The Alienist."

But more than either of these writers, Machado constantly engages in an open playfulness with the reader. In the stories as in the novels, his style of wit belongs with that of Henry Fielding or Laurence Sterne, whose work he knew well. We could also cite the excellent company he could not know he would come to keep, that of Vladimir Nabokov and Italo Calvino.

Machado has generally been well served by translators, although many of his stories have not until now appeared in English versions. But no one has caught the ease and grace of his prose as Margaret Jull Costa and Robin Patterson have. This achievement is important not only because it allows us actually to see a style traveling from one language to another but because the apparently casual movement of Machado's writing, so well rendered here, allows all kinds of implications to arise as if of their own accord.

In one story, a single narrator tells us both that "there are no mysteries for an author who can scrutinize every nook and cranny of the human heart" and that one of his characters "had a series of thoughts that remained hidden from the author of this story." In others we meet imagined readers who are "less canny," "less demanding," or "more experienced," and in "Miss Dollar," the first story in *The Collected Stories of Machado de Assis*, the author goes to town on this topic.

The narrator thinks melancholy readers will imagine the female of the title as "a pale, slender Englishwoman" and devotes a whole paragraph to creating this pre-Raphaelite possibility. The description ends, "Her voice should be like the murmurings of an aeolian harp, her love a swoon, her life a contemplation, her death a sigh." The next sentence begins, "All very poetic, but nothing like the heroine of this story." The narrator offers "a robust American girl" as an alternative, more in keeping with the currency of her name, no doubt, and also a well-off middle-aged English lady, who will arrive in Brazil and marry the reader—or at least the reader who imagines her in this incarnation. The "more astute reader" will have none of these fantasies, of course, and will be sure that Miss Dollar is "Brazilian through and through," although still as rich as her name makes her sound.

None of this is true, the narrator now tells us, meaning none of this matches the fiction he has in mind, because Miss Dollar is "a little Italian greyhound bitch." And the story is not about her anyway, but about the man who finds her when she is advertised as lost, and who falls in love with her owner.

Machado teases his readers, but he also relies on them to be his accomplices; and sometimes he makes our complicity distinctly uncomfortable. In the last story in this volume, "The Tale of the Cabriolet" (1906), a slave arrives at the church of São José in Rio de Janeiro and asks the priest to perform the last rites at a nearby house. The man seems "quite distraught" about the news he is carrying, and the narrator comments:

> Anyone reading this with a darkly skeptical soul will inevitably ask if the slave was genuinely upset, or if he simply wanted to pique the curiosity of the priest and the sacristan. I'm of the view that anything is possible in this world and the next. I believe he was genuinely upset, but then again I don't *not* believe that he was also eager to tell some terrible tale.

The sacristan in fact spends the rest of the story sniffing out the tale for himself, not because he is a gossip or a meddler but because he loves tales. "With him it was a case of art for art's sake." And with us? With Machado himself? Aren't we looking for tales, terrible or not? How far are we from being upset?

The wit and grace of Machado's writing never diminish in these stories, and the scene is almost always the same. We are watching the bourgeoisie of Rio Janeiro at play, and occasionally trying to be serious. They misunderstand each other, they get married, they worry about dying, there is the occasional violent murder. Money and the business of keeping up appearances are large questions. The characters read Hugo and Feydeau, Dumas *père* and Dumas *fils*, and indeed the general tone is that of nineteenth-century Paris as reconstructed in so many Latin American locations of that time. Machado is gently mocking this class that believes only in borrowed culture, or in what the Brazilian critic Roberto Schwarz calls "misplaced ideas," but he is not advocating any kind of nativism.

When the chief character of "The Alienist," refusing distinguished positions offered to him by the king of Portugal, refers to the Brazilian city of Itaguaí as "my universe," we laugh because he seems to have made his world so small. But then we may also feel that his grandiose claim for his hometown and the exclusive fascination of others with the culture of Europe are simply rival forms of provincialism. There is a third way. We can take all

culture, local and international, as our own, and this is the practice suggested by Machado's own allusions, as it is by those of Jorge Luis Borges,
writing a little later in a neighboring Latin American country. "We cannot
confine ourselves to what is Argentine in order to be Argentine," Borges
says, and Machado might add that we don't have to believe that Paris is the
capital of the world in order to read French literature.

In "Father Against Mother," first published in 1905, near the end of
Machado's life, the stage belongs not to the bourgeoisie but to a lower social
sector, that of a man who has been a clerk in a store, a bookkeeper to a
notary, an office boy, and a postman, and is now a slave catcher. This was
"one of the trades of the time," the narrator says, and of course "not . . . a
very noble profession." This understatement has considerable force because
the story has already informed us in some detail about "certain . . . implements" of slavery:

> There was the neck iron, the leg iron, and the iron muzzle. The
> muzzle covered the mouth as a way of putting a stop to the vice
> of drunkenness among slaves. It had only three holes, two to see
> through and one to breathe through, and was fastened at the back
> of the head with a padlock.

Nothing very noble here, just ingenious mechanical cruelty. The idea
of putting a stop to vice must be rank hypocrisy, but Machado continues to
imitate the voice of moral piety:

> [T]he muzzle also did away with the temptation to steal, because
> slaves tended to steal their master's money in order to slake their
> thirst, and thus two grave sins were abolished, and sobriety and
> honesty saved. The muzzle was a grotesque thing, but then human
> and social order cannot always be achieved without the grotesque,
> or, indeed, without occasional acts of cruelty.

The same tone is present when the narrator remarks that slave catchers
are "helping the forces who defend the law and private property," and that
their trade therefore may be said to have "a different sort of nobility, the
kind implicit in retrieving what is lost."

Slavery was finally abolished in Brazil in 1888, by which time Machado had published four of his seven volumes of stories. The slave trade itself had ended in 1850. Slaves are everywhere in these works, a fact of life, and not often commented on. We can be sure Machado has little sympathy for the woman who complains of her "feckless slaves," or the man who alternately smashes plates over his slaves' heads and calls them by "the sweetest, most endearing names." There is a slave who is "more brother than slave as regards devotion and affection." But generally the slaves are just slaves, part of a sub-jugated work force taken for granted. Is Machado endorsing the institution of slavery? No, he is evoking a world and leaving the judgment of that world to the reader's conscience. And in "Father Against Mother" he is slyly hoping we will *not* share the opinions offered.

But then after evoking the horrible instruments and the fragile justifi-cations for their use, he invites us to think of both the slave catcher and a caught slave as human beings capable of love and distress. The slave catcher and his wife are very much in love and desperately want to have a child. At last they have a son, but then they have no money—the trade is not going well. They are evicted from their house, and the man is about to leave his son at the foundling hospital, when he sees and arrests a runaway female slave. He is the father named in the title, and she is the mother. I won't reveal the plot further, since the point is to signal the incredible poise and moral reach of Machado's narrator. We don't exactly feel sympathy for the man, but we are tempted to something like it, even if our minds are still full of the thought of those horrible implements described at the story's start. Of course the system doesn't excuse him, but he didn't invent the self-serving regime of "human and social order" that everyone is so happy to take as a norm.

Roberto Schwarz calls the story "How to Be a Bigwig," first published in 1881, "the key to [Machado's] mature satirical style." This story has no apparent darkness, and the reader's role is essential. The work is pure dia-logue, so we don't even have Machado's narrator as an unreliable playmate or misinformant. A father decides to have a chat with his son, who has just turned twenty-one. The boy has "a private income and a college degree," he could do almost anything. "[P]olitics, the law, journalism, farming, industry, commerce, literature, or the arts" all await him if he wants them. Which-ever he chooses, the father says, he will need a very particular second career, "just in case the others fail entirely, or do not quite meet [your] ambitions." This career is that of a bigwig. The boy doesn't understand, and the father explains. The bigwig is a man of "measure and reason," who fits the role so perfectly because he has nothing in his mind that might compete with the steady, empty gravity of his comportment. There are people who have ideas and conceal them, but it is far better, the father says, to have no ideas at all, and he finds in his son "the perfect degree of mental vacuity required by such a noble profession." We note the phrase that occurs also in this story: it is important to waste a lot of time in the company of others, because "solitude is the workshop of ideas." A good habit is to go into bookstores to chat, rather than to read or buy anything, and a proper mastery of clichés is invaluable. "Publicity" is to be wooed, the young man's future speeches are to be packed with ready-made phrases, and above all, the father says, "whatever you do, never go beyond the boundaries of enviable triteness." He adds, "I forbid you to arrive at any conclusions that have not already been reached by others." The son thinks this is all going to be quite difficult, and the father agrees. The father, very pleased with himself, compares the advice he has just given to his son with Machiavelli's instructions in *The Prince*.

Clearly Machado's mature style involves a mockery of this complacent, cynical advisor and his passive, all too obedient client. But then we think perhaps the father is a satirist himself, mocking the world he lives in, and trying to provoke his son into the very thinking he says he should avoid. Does he really need to compliment him on his mental vacuity? And what about the son? Could he be playing a waiting game, aghast at his father's nonsense but not sure what to do? What if all three of these interpretative possibilities are in play? I doubt whether many of us can juggle them all at once, but there is nothing in the story that will allow us finally to choose among them. And the readings I have just suggested do not even include the one that is hiding in plain sight: the father may be sincere and also quite right. His views and the world he evokes are regrettable affairs, but since when did regret do away with the truth?

Machado's stories—delicate, funny, elusive, never bitter, often near to unacknowledged horrors—teach us how to read: how to read the stories themselves and how to read their often too complacent world, perhaps even more subtly than his novels teach their related lessons. We might think, in conclusion, of the masterpiece called "Midnight Mass" (1894), which begins with the voice of a man saying, "I've never quite understood a conversation

I had with a lady many years ago, when I was seventeen and she was thirty." We think we already know this story, simply by learning the sexes and ages in question. In one sense we do. It is all about mutual desire and embarrassment and missed implications. But then we remember that the narrator is saying he doesn't understand it even now, and we wonder if we really are wiser than he is. What does it mean when nothing happens, and that same nothing lingers unforgettably in your life?

Michael Wood

INTRODUCTION

M UCH HAS BEEN MADE OF Joaquim Maria Machado de Assis's humble
beginnings, and yet he, apparently, thought his own life to be of little
interest and insisted that what counted was his work. Of course, in general
terms, he's right, but, given his evolution from a poorly educated child of
impoverished parents to Brazil's greatest writer and pillar of the establishment, a brief biographical note would not seem out of place. His paternal
grandparents were mulattos and freed slaves. His father, also a mulatto, was
a painter and decorator, his mother a washerwoman, a white Portuguese
immigrant from the Azores. Both parents, however, could read and write,
which was not common among working-class people at the time.

Machado was born in 1839 and brought up for the first ten years of his
life on a country estate on the outskirts of Rio owned by the widow of a senator, Maria José de Mendonça Barroso Pereira, who became his godmother.
Machado also had a sister, but she died when only four years old. Although
he did go to school, he was far from being a star pupil. It seems, however,
that Machado helped during mass at the estate's chapel, and was befriended
by the priest, Father Silveira Sarmento, who may also have taught him
Latin. Machado's mother died of tuberculosis when Machado was only ten.
He then moved with his father to another part of Rio, and his father remar-
ried. Some biographers say that his stepmother, Maria Inês da Silva, looked
after him, and that Machado attended classes in the girls' school where she
worked as a cook. Some say that he learned French in the evenings from a

French immigrant baker. Others describe Machado as showing a precocious interest in books and languages. What is certain is that he published his first sonnet in 1854, when he was fifteen, in the *Periódico dos Pobres* (the *Newspaper of the Poor*). A year later, he became a regular visitor to a rather eccentric bookshop in central Rio owned by journalist and typographer Francisco de Paula Brito (the shop is mentioned in "A Strange Thing"), which was a meeting place for all kinds of people, including artists and writers.

At seventeen, Machado was taken on as an apprentice typographer and proofreader at the Imprensa Nacional, where the writer Manuel Antônio de Almeida encouraged him to pursue a career in literature. Only two years later, the poet Francisco Otaviano invited him to work as writer and editor on the *Correio Mercantil*, an important newspaper of its day and one that is often mentioned in these stories. He wrote two operas and several plays, none of which met with great success, but he loved the theater and became involved in Rio's theater world from a very young age. Indeed, by the time he was twenty-one, he was already a well-known figure in intellectual circles. He worked as a journalist on other newspapers and founded a literary circle called Arcádia Fluminense. During all this time he read voraciously in numerous languages—it is said that, as well as modern literature, he set himself the lifetime goal of reading all of the universal classics in their original language, including ancient Greek. He built up an extensive library, bequeathed to the Brazilian Academy of Letters (of which he was cofounder and first president) upon his death. Between the ages of fifteen and thirty, he wrote prolifically: poetry, plays, librettos, short stories, and newspaper columns, as well as translations from French and Spanish and all or most of Dickens's *Oliver Twist*. It would appear that his reported ill health, notably the epilepsy described by several of his biographers, did not in any way hold him back.

In 1867 he was decorated at the young age of twenty-eight by the emperor with the Order of the Rose and subsequently appointed to a position in the Ministry of Agriculture, Commerce, and Public Works. He went on to become head of a department, serving in that same ministry for over thirty years, until just three months before his death. The job, although demanding, left him ample time to write, and write he did: nine novels, nine plays, more than two hundred stories, five collections of poems, and more than six hundred *crônicas*, or newspaper columns. He also found time to marry, his wife proving crucial both to his happiness and to the expansion of his literary knowledge. Carolina Augusta Xavier de Novais, the sister of a close friend, was five years older than Machado; they fell in love almost instantly and were soon married, despite her family disapproving of her marrying a mulatto. Carolina was extremely well educated and introduced him to the work of many English-language writers. They remained happily married for thirty-five years, and when she died in 1904, at the age of seventy, Machado fell into a deep depression. He wrote only one novel after her death, *Memorial de Aires* (1908), and his last collection of stories, *Relíquias de Casa Velha* (*Relics from an Old House*), published in 1906, is prefaced by a very tender sonnet dedicated to her. On his death in 1908, he was given a state funeral. And yet his occupation on his death certificate was given as "Civil servant," and when his final work, *Memorial de Aires*, was published later that year, it went almost unnoticed.

That, very briefly, was his life, but, as Machado so rightly said, his writing *was* his life. He is probably best known to the English-language reader for three novels: *Memórias Póstumas de Brás Cubas* (1881; published in English as *The Posthumous Memoirs of Brás Cubas* or *Epitaph of a Small Winner*), *Quincas Borba* (1891; published in English as *Philosopher or Dog?*), and *Dom Casmurro* (1899). And while these are remarkable, groundbreaking works, his stories are often just as remarkable, running the full gamut of subject matter and emotion. This edition brings together, for the first time in English, all of the stories contained in the seven collections published in his lifetime, from 1870 to 1906: *Rio Tales, Midnight Tales, Miscellaneous Papers, Undated Stories, Assorted Stories, Collected Pages*, and *Relics from an Old House*. He wrote at least another 129 stories that remained unpublished in book form until after his death. Most of the stories were originally published in daily newspapers—principally *Gazeta de Notícias*—or in magazines—*Jornal das Famílias, A Estação*, and *Almanaque Brasileiro Garnier*—with longer stories being published in serial form, chapter by chapter. Machado was responsible for selecting the stories included in each of these seven collections, so what we have here are the stories that Machado himself considered to be his best.

The stories are predominantly set in Rio de Janeiro, then the capital of the Brazilian Empire. (Dom Pedro I had been proclaimed emperor of Brazil following independence from Portugal in 1822.) There are the occasional sorties to places a day or two's journey from the city, such as Petrópolis, the fashionable summer capital in the mountains just north of the city. Other

Brazilian towns, cities, and provinces get an occasional mention, but usually only as places that characters disappear to or return from, and vague references to "the North," "the South," and "the interior" abound. Machado himself scarcely traveled beyond the immediate environs of the city, and while his characters do travel widely, including to Europe and especially Paris, we, the readers, bid farewell to them on the quayside and only hear about their distant exploits secondhand.

The city itself is often simply a stage set, almost an outdoor drawing room for his characters—although street names and landmarks are mentioned frequently, there is almost nothing in terms of physical description, and there are only the most fleeting references to its tropical climate. Machado is, of course, describing the city to its own inhabitants, and so the street names he mentions are signposts indicating social status, and the landmarks are the places familiar to the city's upper classes: the Passeio Público, which were elegant gardens on the shoreline of the bay between the city center and the opulent suburbs of Glória and Catete; the Jardim Botânico, the magnificent botanical gardens a short ride out of the city on the other side of Corcovado Mountain; and, most frequently of all, Rua do Ouvidor, the long, narrow street of fashionable shops, theaters, and cafés—"the Via Dolorosa of long-suffering husbands," as Machado describes it in "The Lapse." Occasional references are made to the city's less salubrious quarters—the port areas of Saúde and Gamboa, and the former Valongo slave market.

In some cases, Machado is describing a city that no longer existed, for Rio, with its burgeoning population, was in the midst of an intense transformation from colonial backwater to imperial metropolis, and many of the stories are set several decades earlier. Events are often given a specific date—not least in the collection mischievously entitled *Undated Stories*—and geographical signposts are also in some cases historical ones. To a contemporary reader, of course, all of this would have been much clearer than it is to us; reading the stories today, we should simply bear in mind that the Rio the narrator presents as such a concrete and real world is often nothing of the sort.

Political considerations as well as artistic license may have encouraged Machado to place his stories at a discreet distance in time. During most of Machado's lifetime, Brazil was ruled by a constitutional, although often authoritarian, monarchy that was prone to factionalism and abrupt shifts in political favor. The last of these shifts led to the overthrow of the monarchy itself in 1889, precipitated by the abolition of slavery the previous year. The importation of slaves had been banned, at least in theory, in 1850, and, in 1871, a year after the publication of the first collection of these stories, the "Law of the Free Womb" (or "Law of September 28," as Machado more discreetly refers to it) granted freedom to all children born to slaves after that date, thus making the eventual abolition of slavery inevitable, even if it took another seventeen years to come about. Machado rarely confronts the issue head-on. ("The Cane" and "Father Against Mother," both written after abolition, are notable exceptions.) Casual references to slaves abound; sometimes these are fond, sometimes cruel, but most often (and shockingly, to a modern reader) they simply pass without comment as a feature of everyday life. Machado was criticized by some of his contemporaries for not writing more openly about the evils of slavery. And yet, for the grandson of freed slaves writing for a predominantly slave-owning elite, we are left in little doubt about what a controversial and sensitive subject it was for Machado, or where his sympathies lay.

Other historical events and controversies are also noticeable by their near-absence. The earliest of these stories was written in the immediate aftermath of the War of the Triple Alliance (1864–70), a long and bloody conflict between Paraguay on one side, and Brazil, Argentina, and Uruguay on the other. And yet, perhaps precisely because memories of it were so raw, Machado refers to it only in passing in a handful of stories. Much later, however, "Maria Cora," first published in 1898, deals more explicitly with the then-recent, and bloody, civil war of 1893–95 between the new republic and Federalist rebels based in the southern state of Rio Grande do Sul. Machado, characteristically, dwells on the absurdity of the dispute.

To return to the stories themselves, some critics, perhaps somewhat dismissively, describe the early stories as belonging to Machado's "romantic phase," and while some of the plots could be viewed as such, the coolly ironic voice in which they are told already seems strikingly modern. In fact, that voice may have had its origins in two books that seem to have been a major influence on Machado's own writing: Laurence Sterne's *Tristram Shandy* and Xavier de Maistre's *Voyage Around My Room*. For example, in the very first story in this collection, "Miss Dollar," Machado spends the initial pages playing with our expectations as to what kind of heroine he is about to introduce to us. "Ernesto What's-His-Name" opens as follows: "That young man standing over there on the corner of Rua Nova do Conde and Campo da Aclamação at ten o'clock at night is not a thief, he's not even a philosopher." And we immediately become the eager listeners, plunged into speculations about a character we know nothing about. As readers, we are both fully aware that this is a fiction and simultaneously drawn in as gullible readers. Machado was passionately interested in chess and was himself a brilliant player. In his stories, too, he is very much the grand master, placing his pieces on the board and then seeing what happens, how those pieces react and interact.

Our narrator is often unromantically unreliable, too, claiming that he can't tell us a character's name or doesn't know it or has forgotten, or declaring that what happened next was quite simply indescribable and then going on to describe it in detail. The first-person narrators are no better in this respect and, like us, have faulty memories and cannot necessarily be trusted.

One of Machado's main themes is obsession, and it is a strong presence from the earliest stories to the last. Some characters are merely obsessed with themselves, with losing their looks or their money; others are obsessed with the past or with rereading the same books over and over, or accumulating as much money as possible, or, in the marvelous Swiftian short story–cum–novella "The Alienist," with imposing a particular psychological theory on society as a whole. Obsession also veers into outright madness in "Second Life" and the even more chilling "The Secret Cause." Jealousy, too—another form of obsession—raises its ugly head in many stories; in some cases the characters land safely on the other side of a bout of jealousy, while others are left standing amid the debris of a marriage.

The repeated, seemingly erudite, references—Dante, Shakespeare, Rabelais, Homer, Charles Lamb, Horace, Pascal, Molière, Milton, Heine, Hegel, Descartes, to name but a few—are part of that thread of sly humor running through his work. Is the assumption that we, the readers, are equally erudite or is he just playing with us, as he appears to be with the often slightly inaccurate quotations with which he sprinkles the stories? Not to mention the Latin tags—*ab ovo, abyssum abyssus, Eheu! Fugaces . . .*— usually left incomplete for us, supposedly, to fill in the blank.

More erudition, serious or otherwise, is on display in the stories that seem to spring straight from Machado's fertile imagination, spurred on by his own extensive reading. These take us to sixteenth-century Japan ("The Bonze's Secret") and an ethereally exotic Thailand ("The Academies of Siam"), to the times of the Ptolemies ("An Alexandrian Tale") and the sons

of Noah ("In the Ark"), and even to the end of time itself, for an imagined encounter between Prometheus and Ahasuerus ("Life!"). The world of
books and his imagination were for Machado a very real complement to that
of the city and people around him, and they frequently collided, perhaps
most vividly in "A Visit from Alcibiades," where our unnamed narrator sits
down after dinner to read a chapter of Plutarch and accidentally summons
up the physical presence of the ancient Greek statesman himself, leading to
an incident requiring the attention of the Rio chief of police.

Often there are references to the process of writing itself. He mocks the
use of literary references in "Much Heat, Little Light." Nouns and adjectives
chase each other around the clergyman's head in "The Canon, or the Metaphysics of Style." Both verbosity and literary theory are lampooned in "How
to be a Bigwig," and a composer despairs at his loss of creative inspiration in
"Fame." Machado doesn't just tell us his stories—he pulls back the curtain
and invites us to watch his own process of invention.

The overall tone of the stories is one of ironic distance, an assumption
that we share the author's bemused fascination with the foibles and fates of
these strange creatures, real or imagined. And while Machado gives us many
male characters in all their flawed variety, there are possibly even more notable female characters, some faithful unto death and utterly decent, some
infinitely vain, some maligned or scheming or flirtatious or indolent. Many
of the stories appear to be filled with a kind of nostalgia for the past, as if the
present were unsatisfactory or too shallow and transient, and yet the past
is seen as something both irretrievable and inscrutable. One of Machado's
most famous stories, "Midnight Mass," begins: "I've never quite understood
a conversation I had with a lady many years ago, when I was seventeen and
she was thirty." Machado's characters are often still puzzling over some past
event, or hoping to set the record straight or to revive long-lost feelings.
There are a few happy endings and happy marriages, but the stories abound
in thwarted ambitions or loves unspoken or unrequited, even, in one story
("The Mirror"), a loss of all sense of identity, which can only be retrieved
by the narrator standing in front of a mirror in his lieutenant's uniform to
remind himself that he does exist.

Machado is also a brilliant stylist, but not in any flamboyant way. He
writes in a Portuguese that is deceptively simple and straightforward, but
he chooses his words with great precision, and has a superb ear for how
people speak, whether it be a jaded old man, a frivolous young woman,

or a ten-year-old boy. Machado's translator needs to remain very alert if he or she is to capture every nuance. For example, in "Much Heat, Little Light," he describes Luís Tinoco's literary efforts thus: "He bespattered his borrowed ideas with a selection of allusions and literary names, which was the full extent of his erudition . . ." The Portuguese word we have translated as "bespattered" (*"respingava"*) means "splashed," but carries within it notions of "soiling" and "staining," which the English version must reflect. The translator must also resist normalizing oddity, for Machado does sometimes say some very odd things. In "The Holiday," for example, the young narrator says: "And yet even so, my schoolfellows still came to peer inside my mind." The translation has to respect the oddness of those schoolboys peering into someone's mind.

Machado sprang from the romantic-realist school of literature in Brazil, and his early stories were clearly written for the largely female readership of magazines and newspapers. His contemporaries, and Brazilians today, consider him to be Brazil's greatest writer largely because of the stories and novels he published from 1881 onward, when he brought out, within a year of each other, both *The Posthumous Memoirs of Brás Cubas* and *Miscellaneous Papers*. For whatever reason, from that point on, his writing took a radically different path from that of his contemporaries. In the case of his short stories, we see a greater inventiveness in form and subject matter, frequently delving into the wilder reaches of his imagination in a way that is often thought to prefigure magical realism—"The Most Serene Republic" (*Miscellaneous Papers*), "The Canon, or the Metaphysics of Style" (*Assorted Stories*), and "Canary Thoughts" (*Collected Pages*) being but three examples. Other stories, particularly in the final collection, *Relics from an Old House*, have their feet more firmly rooted in reality, with a mature and almost elegiac tone. This is not to denigrate the earlier stories, which, if more conventional, are, by turns, touching and funny and satirical, and always hold the reader's attention, perhaps because of that alluring, coaxing, and often unreliable narrator.

It is difficult fully to measure the influence of Machado de Assis in other Latin American countries, or indeed elsewhere, but the first English translation of three of his short stories did not appear until 1921, and it was another thirty years before English translations of *The Posthumous Memoirs of Brás Cubas* (under the title *Epitaph of a Small Winner*) and *Dom Casmurro* were published. Other translations followed, including somewhat wider selections of his short stories (but never the complete collections), and it was not until the 1990s that eminent American and British writers began to take notice, notably Susan Sontag, Philip Roth, Harold Bloom, and Salman Rushdie. One could put this belated recognition down to a certain parochialism among British and American publishers and readers, or to a twentieth-century disdain for so much that was handed down from the nineteenth (ironical in Machado's case, given that he prefigured so much of what we think of as quintessentially "twentieth" century), but whatever the reason, we can at least take comfort that his precocious genius is being recognized now.

One reason for this may be that his stories bear witness to a desire to map the human psyche in all its endless variety. Is there perhaps a self-portrait in "The Tale of the Cabriolet," the last story in the last collection, published two years before his death? Machado introduces us to a sacristan who is obsessed (yet another one) with hearing and collecting other people's stories, not in order to approve or disapprove or to gossip about them, but for the sheer pleasure of the story itself, however mundane, bizarre, or terrible. This sounds very much like Machado himself, an avid and, yes, obsessive collector of other people's lives. As the narrator in "The Blue Flower" says: "There are no mysteries for an author who can scrutinize every nook and cranny of the human heart."

Margaret Jull Costa and Robin Patterson

RIO TALES

(1870)

MISS DOLLAR

I

FOR THE PURPOSES OF THIS story it would be handy if the reader were kept waiting a very long time before finding out who Miss Dollar was. On the other hand, if there were no such introduction, the author would be obliged to make long digressions, which would certainly fill up the pages, but without moving the action along at all. I have no alternative, therefore, but to introduce you to Miss Dollar now.

If you, the reader, are male and of a melancholy bent, imagine, then, that Miss Dollar is a pale, slender Englishwoman, somewhat fleshless and bloodless, with very large blue eyes and long, fair hair waving in the wind. The girl in question should be as delicate and ideal as one of Shakespeare's creations; she should be the very opposite of the roast beef of Olde England, which sustains the United Kingdom's liberty. This Miss Dollar should know Tennyson's poems by heart and have read Lamartine in the original French; if she knows Portuguese, she should delight in reading Camões's sonnets and Gonçalves Dias's *Cantos*. Milky tea should be her chief sustenance, along with a few sweets and biscuits to stave off hunger. Her voice should be like the murmurings of an aeolian harp, her love a swoon, her life a contemplation, her death a sigh.

All very poetic, but nothing like the heroine of this story.

Let us suppose that the reader is not given to such daydreams and bouts of melancholy; let us, then, imagine a totally different Miss Dollar. This one will be a robust American girl, with rosy cheeks, a curvaceous figure, bright, sparkling eyes, in short, a round, ripe, real woman. Fond of good food and good wine, this Miss Dollar—as is only natural when the stomach calls— would prefer a decent lamb chop to a page of Longfellow, and she will never understand why people find sunsets so poetic. She will be a good mother according to the doctrine laid down by certain religious scholars, namely: fertile and ignorant.

The reader who is past his second youth and sees before him only a hopeless old age will not be of the same opinion. For him, the only Miss Dollar truly worthy of being described in these pages would be a good Englishwoman in her fifties, with a few thousand pounds sterling to her name and who, arriving in Brazil in search of a subject for a novel, ends up living a novel, by marrying the reader in question. This Miss Dollar would be incomplete unless she wore spectacles with green-tinted lenses and wore her thick, graying hair parted in the middle. White lace gloves and a linen hat in the shape of a gourd would add the finishing touch to this magnificent foreigner.

A more astute reader will say that the heroine of the story neither is nor ever was English, but, rather, Brazilian through and through, and that the name, Miss Dollar, merely suggests that the young woman in question is very rich.

This would be an excellent contribution if it were true; unfortunately, neither that nor any of the others is true. The Miss Dollar of the story is not a romantic girl, nor a sturdy mature woman, nor an aging novelist, nor a wealthy Brazilian. Here the proverbial perspicacity of readers is found wanting, for Miss Dollar is a little Italian greyhound bitch.

Such a heroine will immediately cause certain people to lose interest in the story: a grave error. Despite being only a little greyhound bitch, Miss Dollar was lucky enough to see her name in the newspapers before she even entered this story. The following promise-filled lines appeared in the small ads section of O *Jornal do Commercio* and O *Correio Mercantil*:

> Lost last night, 30th: a little Italian greyhound bitch. Answers to the name of Miss Dollar. Anyone finding her and bringing her to Rua de Matacavalos, No. . . . will receive a reward of 200 mil-réis.

Miss Dollar has a collar around her neck with a padlock bearing the following words: *De tout mon coeur.*

Anyone in urgent need of two hundred *mil-réis* and lucky enough to read that advertisement would have spent the day scouring the streets of Rio de Janeiro in case they spotted the escapee, Miss Dollar. Any greyhound that appeared on the horizon was pursued tenaciously until the pursuer was able to ascertain that it was not the sought-after animal. This hunt for the two hundred *mil-réis*, however, proved completely useless, given that, on the day the advertisement appeared, Miss Dollar was already lodging in the house of a man who lived in the Cajueiros district and was a collector of dogs.

II

No one could ever say precisely what it was that drove Dr. Mendonça to collect dogs; some said it was quite simply a passion for that symbol of fidelity or servility, others that Mendonça's adoration of dogs was simply his revenge on his fellow man, whom he found utterly repugnant.

Whatever the reasons, the truth is that no one had a finer or more varied collection than he. They were of all breeds, sizes, and colors. He cared for them as if they were his children, and if one of them died, he would be plunged into grief. One might almost say that, in Mendonça's mind, the dogs were as important as love itself, and, as the saying goes: without dogs, the world would be a wilderness.

The superficial reader will conclude that our Mendonça was an eccentric, but he wasn't. Mendonça was the same as other men, and liked dogs in much the same way as others like flowers. Dogs were his roses and violets, and he nurtured them just as carefully. He liked flowers, too, but he preferred to see them on the plants on which they were born; cutting a sprig of jasmine or caging a canary seemed to him equally murderous acts.

Mendonça was a good-looking thirty-four-year-old, with a frank, distinguished manner. He had studied medicine and had, for some time, practiced as a doctor. His clinic had been doing very well until the city was struck by an epidemic. Dr. Mendonça invented an elixir against the illness, and this proved so successful that it earned him a couple of thousand *mil-réis*. He still practiced medicine, but only in an amateur capacity. He had enough money for himself and his family, his family consisting of the aforementioned dogs.

On the memorable night when Miss Dollar got lost, Mendonça was returning home when he was fortunate enough to find the stray greyhound in the Largo do Rocio. The dog started following him, and Mendonça, realizing that the dog had no apparent owner, took her with him back to Cajueiros.

As soon as they arrived, he submitted the dog to a careful examination. Miss Dollar was a real beauty; she had the slender, graceful form of her noble breed, and her velvety brown eyes, so bright and serene, seemed to express her utter contentment with the world. Mendonça studied her closely. He read the words on the padlock on the collar and became convinced that the animal must be greatly loved by her owner, whoever that was.

"If the owner doesn't turn up, she stays with me," he said, delivering Miss Dollar into the hands of the houseboy in charge of the dogs.

The houseboy was given the task of feeding Miss Dollar, while Mendonça planned a golden future for his new guest, whose progeny would live on in the house.

Mendonça's plan lasted as long as dreams usually last, a single night. While reading the newspaper the next day, he came upon the advertisement transcribed above, promising a reward of two hundred *mil-réis* to anyone who returned the lost dog. The size of the reward and his own passion for dogs told him the scale of the grief of Miss Dollar's master or mistress. With considerable sadness, he decided to return the dog. He hesitated for a few moments, but what finally convinced him were his feelings of honesty and compassion, which were the dominant features of that particular soul. And since he found it hard to let go of the dog, however recently acquired, he decided to return her to the owner himself and made the necessary preparations to do so. He had breakfast, and, having made sure that Miss Dollar had done likewise, they both set off to Matacavalos.

Since the Barão do Amazonas had not yet won the Battle of Riachuelo, which was the name later given to Rua de Matacavalos, the street still bore its traditional name, which meant nothing of any great importance.

The house indicated in the advertisement was rather a fine one, suggesting that its inhabitants were fairly wealthy. Before Mendonça had even knocked on the door, Miss Dollar, recognizing her home, began to jump up and down with joy and utter a few happy, guttural barks which—were there such a thing as canine literature—would have been a hymn of gratitude.

A houseboy came to the door, and Mendonça explained that he had come to return the lost greyhound. A big smile appeared on the houseboy's face, and he ran inside to give the good news. Taking advantage of the slightly open door, Miss Dollar pushed her way in and raced up the stairs. His duty done, Mendonça was just about to leave when the houseboy returned, asking him to go upstairs to the drawing room.

The room was deserted. Some owners of elegantly furnished rooms often allow time for these to be admired by visitors before coming to welcome them. This may have been the custom in that house, but not on this occasion, because no sooner had the doctor entered the room than an old lady emerged from an adjoining room, clutching Miss Dollar in her arms and smiling broadly.

"Do sit down," she said, pointing to a chair.

"I won't stay long," said the doctor, sitting down. "I just came to bring you the dog, which has been with me since yesterday."

"You can't imagine how upset we've been since Miss Dollar went missing."

"Oh, I can, senhora. I, too, am a lover of dogs, and if one of mine were ever to go missing, I would feel its absence deeply. Your Miss Dollar—"

"Forgive me," said the old lady, "she isn't mine. She belongs to my niece."

"Oh, I see."

"Here she comes now."

Mendonça got to his feet as the niece in question came into the room. She was a young woman of about twenty-eight and in the full flower of her beauty, one of those women who look set for a late but imposing old age. The dark silk of her dress emphasized her intensely white skin. Her dress rustled as she walked, enhancing still further her majestic stature and comportment. The bodice of her dress had a very modest neckline, but one could sense beneath the silk a beautiful marble torso sculpted by a divine sculptor. Her naturally wavy brown hair was arranged in a very simple, homely way—which is the best of all known fashions—and it gracefully adorned her forehead, like a crown bestowed on her by nature. There was not so much as a touch of pink on her cheeks to provide some contrast or harmony with the extreme whiteness of her skin. She had a small, somewhat imperious mouth, but her eyes were her most striking feature: imagine two emeralds swimming in milk.

Mendonça had never seen green eyes before, although he had been told that they existed, and knew by heart the famous lines by Gonçalves Dias in his poem on the subject, but, up until then, such eyes were what the phoenix had been for the ancients. One day, talking to some friends about precisely this, he had said that if ever he met a pair of green eyes, he would flee from them in terror.

"But why?" asked one of his companions, somewhat taken aback.

"Green is the color of the sea," answered Mendonça, "and just as I avoid storms at sea, so will I avoid the storms caused by such eyes."

I leave it to the reader to judge this eccentric idea of Mendonça's, who is becoming increasingly "precious" in Molière's sense of the word.

III

Mendonça bowed respectfully to the new arrival, and she gestured to him to sit down again.

"I am so grateful to you for returning my poor dog, who means so very much to me," said Margarida, also sitting down.

"I thank God it was me who found her, because she could have fallen into the hands of someone who might not have returned her."

Margarida beckoned to Miss Dollar, who jumped off the old lady's lap and went and placed her front paws on her owner's knees. Margarida and Miss Dollar exchanged a long, affectionate look. While this lasted, the young woman played with one of the greyhound's ears, thus giving Mendonça the chance to admire her exquisite fingers armed with very sharp nails.

However, although Mendonça was greatly enjoying being there, he realized that any further delay would be both strange and humiliating, for it might seem that he was waiting to receive the reward. In order to avoid such an inelegant interpretation, he gave up the pleasure of talking and looking at the young woman and got to his feet, saying:

"Well, my mission has been accomplished . . ."

"But—" began the old lady.

Mendonça understood the threat that lay behind that word. He said:

"The joy that I have restored to this household is the best reward I could possibly hope for. Now, if you'll excuse me . . ."

The two women understood his intentions, and the young woman repaid his courtesy with a smile, while the older woman, channeling all her remaining bodily strength into her fingers, fondly clasped his hand.

Mendonça left, feeling deeply impressed by the very interesting Margarida. What he mainly noticed, apart from her beauty—which was of the very first order—was a certain sad seriousness in her eyes and in her manner. If that was her nature, then it fit well with the doctor's own personality; if it was the result of some episode in her life, then it was the page of a novel calling for analysis by a pair of skillful eyes. In truth, her only defect, as far as Mendonça was concerned, was the color of her eyes, not because it was unattractive, but because he did not like green eyes. This dislike, it must be said, was more literary than anything else. Mendonça had become attached to the words he had once spoken and that we quoted earlier, and it was these words that fueled his dislike. Now, don't take against him or me: Mendonça was an intelligent, educated man with plenty of common sense; he also had a markedly romantic bent; despite this, though, he also had an Achilles' heel. In that respect, he was like most other men, for there are Achilleses out there who are one vast heel from head to toe. Mendonça's weak point was this: the love of a nicely turned phrase was enough to distort his affections; he would willingly sacrifice a promising situation to a well-honed sentence.

When he spoke to a friend about the lost greyhound and his conversation with Margarida, Mendonça remarked that he could really come to like her if only she didn't have green eyes. His friend gave a slightly sarcastic laugh and said:

"Doctor, I cannot understand such prejudice. I've even heard tell that green eyes are the sign of a kind heart. Besides, the color of someone's eyes is irrelevant, what matters is the look in those eyes. They could be as blue as the sky and as treacherous as the sea."

This anonymous friend's remark had the virtue of being as poetic as Mendonça's, and so it took deep root in the latter's consciousness. He did not, like Buridan's ass, remain caught, undecided, between a pile of hay and a pail of water; the ass might hesitate, but Mendonça did not. He suddenly recalled the Spanish Jesuit Tomás Sánchez's views about probable opinions and so opted for the most probable.

A serious-minded reader will doubtless find all this business about green eyes and their probable qualities quite childish. He will thereby prove that he has little practical experience of the world. Illustrated almanacs delight in describing the eccentricities and flaws of great men, who are nevertheless admired by all humanity, whether for their scholarship or for their courage in battle. The reader should not, therefore, create a special category in which to pigeonhole our doctor. Let us accept him along with his ridiculous notions; after all, who does not have such notions? The ridiculous provides a kind of ballast for the soul when it enters the sea of life; indeed, some make the entire voyage with no other cargo.

To make up for these weaknesses, Mendonça had, as I have mentioned, other sterling qualities. Adopting his friend's opinion as the most probable, Mendonça decided that the key to his future might lie in Margarida's hands, and he duly came up with a plan for their joint happiness: a house out in the wilds, with a view of the sea to the west, so that they could watch the sunset together. Margarida and he, united by love and by the Church, would drain the entire cup of celestial happiness, drop by drop. Mendonça's dream also contained other details that we need not mention here. He thought about this plan for some days and, on a few occasions, even walked down Rua de Matacavalos, but since, alas, he never once saw Margarida or her aunt, he abandoned these walks and returned to his dogs.

His collection of dogs was a veritable gallery of illustrious men. The most esteemed among them was called Diogenes; there was also a greyhound who answered to the name of Caesar, a spaniel called Nelson, a terrier called Cornelia, and Caligula, a huge mastiff, who was the very image of the great monster produced by Roman society. When he was surrounded by these people, all of whom were famous for different reasons, Mendonça felt that he was stepping back into history, and this provided him with a means of forgetting about the rest of the world.

IV

One day, Mendonça was standing outside Carceler's patisserie, where he had been enjoying an ice cream with a friend of his, when he saw a carriage drive past; inside the carriage were two ladies who looked very like the two ladies from Rua de Matacavalos. Mendonça looked so startled that his friend asked:

"Whatever's wrong?"

"Nothing. I thought I recognized those ladies. Did you see them, Andrade?"

"No, I didn't."

The carriage turned into Rua do Ouvidor, where the two friends also happened to be heading. It had stopped just beyond Rua da Quitanda, outside a shop, where the ladies had presumably gotten out and gone in. Mendonça did not actually see them getting out, but he saw the carriage and suspected it was the same one. He quickened his pace without saying anything to Andrade, who merely did the same, filled with the natural curiosity of a man sensing some hidden secret.

Moments later, they were standing at the shop door, where Mendonça was able to see that these were indeed the two ladies from Rua de Matacavalos. With the air of someone about to buy something, he went boldly in. The aunt was the first to recognize him. Mendonça bowed respectfully, and both women gladly acknowledged his greeting. Miss Dollar was at Margarida's side, and she, thanks to the extraordinary instinct bestowed by Nature on dogs and other courtesans of fortune, leapt with glee as soon as she saw Mendonça and even placed her two front paws on his belly.

"It seems that Miss Dollar has fond memories of you," said Dona Antônia (for this was the name of Margarida's aunt).

"So it would seem," said Mendonça, stroking the greyhound and looking up at Margarida.

At that moment, Andrade came into the shop too.

"Ah, I only just realized it was you," he said, addressing both ladies.

And he shook their hands, or, rather, squeezed Dona Antônia's hand and just the tips of Margarida's fingers.

Mendonça had not expected this, and was glad to be presented with a means of deepening his superficial acquaintance with that family.

"Would you be kind enough to introduce me to these ladies?" he said to Andrade.

"You mean you don't know them?" asked Andrade in amazement.

"Well, he both does and doesn't know us," replied the aunt, smiling. "So far, the only one to introduce us has been Miss Dollar."

Dona Antônia told Andrade about the dog who had been lost and found.
"In that case," said Andrade, "allow me to introduce you now."

When the formal introductions were over, the clerk brought Margarida her purchases, and the two ladies said goodbye, asking the two young men to come and visit them.

I have not set down a single word spoken by Margarida in the conversation transcribed above, because she said only two words to each of the men.

"Good day," she said, offering each of them the tips of her fingers, before leaving and climbing back into the carriage.

The young men also left and continued along Rua do Ouvidor in silence. Mendonça was thinking about Margarida, and Andrade was wondering how he could wheedle his way into Mendonça's confidence. Vanity has as many forms as that fabled creature Proteus. Andrade's vanity consisted in making himself the confidant of other people, for it seemed to him that he could obtain through trust what could otherwise only be achieved through indiscretion. It wasn't hard for him to discover Mendonça's secret, and by the time they had reached the corner of Rua dos Ourives, Andrade knew everything.

"Now," said Mendonça, "you'll understand why I need to go to her house. I need to see her and find out if I can—"

"Of course," cried Andrade, "to find out if you can be loved. And why not? But I'll tell you now, it won't be easy."

"Why?"

"Margarida has already rejected five proposals of marriage."

"She clearly didn't love those suitors," said Mendonça with the air of a mathematician alighting on the solution to a problem.

"She was passionately in love with the first one," said Andrade, "and not exactly indifferent to the last."

"Presumably something happened to prevent the marriages."

"No, not at all. Are you surprised? I must admit I am. She's a very strange young woman. If you feel you have the strength to be the Columbus of that world, then set off across the seas with your armada; but watch out for some mutinous passions, which are the fierce sailors of such voyages of discovery."

Pleased with this historical-allegorical allusion, Andrade glanced at Mendonça, who was too absorbed in thoughts of Margarida to hear what his friend had said. Andrade made do with his own contentment and smiled the smug smile of a poet who has just written the last line of a poem.

V

Some days later, Andrade and Mendonça went to Margarida's house, and spent half an hour there in polite conversation. Further visits followed, with Mendonça visiting rather more often than Andrade. Dona Antônia was always the friendlier of the two women, and only after some time did Margarida emerge from the Olympian silence in which she usually enfolded herself.

Indeed, how could she resist, for, although he was no frequenter of salons, Mendonça proved to be the perfect person to entertain those two seemingly mortally bored ladies. The doctor played the piano rather well; he was a lively conversationalist; and he knew the thousands of bits of trivia women tend to find amusing when they cannot or do not wish to discourse on the lofty subjects of art, history, and philosophy. It did not take him long to become a good friend of the family.

After their first few visits, Mendonça learned from Andrade that Margarida was a widow. Mendonça could not conceal his astonishment.

"But you've always talked about her as if she were a spinster," he said.

"No, I didn't explain myself well, and all those marriage proposals she turned down came after she was widowed."

"How long has she been a widow?"

"Three years."

"That explains everything," said Mendonça after a pause. "She wants to remain faithful unto the grave, an Artemis for our own age."

Unconvinced by this reference to Artemis, Andrade smiled at his friend's remark, and when Mendonça insisted, he replied:

"I told you before that she was passionately in love with her first suitor and not entirely indifferent to the last, either."

"Then I really don't understand."

"Neither do I."

From that point on, Mendonça began to court the widow assiduously, but she received his first loving glances with such supreme disdain that he almost abandoned the whole enterprise; however, while she appeared to be refusing his love, she did not refuse him her esteem and treated him with great affection as long as he looked at her precisely as everyone else did.

Love rejected is love multiplied. Each rebuff only increased Mendonça's passion. He even began to neglect fierce Caligula and elegant Julius Caesar. His two slaves noticed a profound change in his habits. They assumed he must be worried about something, and this suspicion was confirmed when Mendonça came home one day and kicked Cornelia in the nose, when that most interesting of terriers, mother to two Gracchi, rushed to celebrate the doctor's return home.

Andrade was not unaware of his friend's suffering and tried to console him. In such cases, consolation is as sought-after as it is useless; Mendonça heard Andrade's words and confided all his sorrows to him. Andrade mentioned to Mendonça that an excellent way of putting an end to passion was to leave home and set off on a journey. To this Mendonça answered with a quotation from La Rochefoucauld: "Absence diminishes mediocre passions and increases great ones, just as the wind extinguishes candles and fans fires."

This quote had the effect of silencing Andrade, who believed about as much in constancy as he did in Artemises, but he did not want to question either the authority of the great moralist or Mendonça's resolve.

VI

Three months passed. Mendonça's courtship did not advance one step, but the widow continued to treat him in the same friendly fashion. And this was mainly what kept the doctor kneeling at the feet of that obdurate woman, for he had still not abandoned all hope of winning her heart.

Some serious-minded reader will be wishing that Mendonça were a less regular visitor to the house of a lady exposed to the calumnies of the world. The doctor did consider this, but assuaged his conscience with the presence of an individual whom we have not named before because of his relative unimportance to the plot, and this was none other than Senhora Dona Antônia's son, the apple of her eye. His name was Jorge, and he got through two hundred *mil-réis* a month without ever having earned a penny himself, and thanks entirely to his mother's generosity. He spent more time at the barber's than a woman in the declining days of the Roman Empire might have spent being primped and preened by her maids. He never missed a play at the Teatro Alcazar; he rode fine horses and, with bounty beyond measure, stuffed the pockets of certain notorious ladies and various other obscure parasites. He wore size-E gloves and size-36 boots, two qualities which he threw in the faces of the less elegant of his friends, who wore size-40 boots and size H gloves. Mendonça felt that the presence of this overgrown child made the situation safe. He hoped this would satisfy the world or rather the city's idle gossips, but would this be enough to seal the lips of those idlers?

Margarida seemed as indifferent to what the world might say as she was to the young man's assiduous courtship of her. Was she perhaps indifferent to everything in the world? No, she loved her aunt, adored Miss Dollar, enjoyed good music, and read novels. She dressed well, although without being a slave to fashion; she never waltzed and, at most, would dance a quadrille at the parties to which she was invited. She did not talk much, but when she did, she expressed herself well. She was graceful and animated, but neither pretentious nor ostentatious.

Whenever Mendonça arrived, Margarida would welcome him with evident pleasure, and even though he was accustomed to this, he was always taken in. Margarida really did enjoy his company, but she appeared not to give his presence the degree of importance that would have warmed his heart. She enjoyed his company much as one enjoys a lovely sunny day, but without falling in love with the sun.

Such a situation could not possibly go on for very long. One night, making an effort of which he would never have thought himself capable, Mendonça asked Margarida this indiscreet question:

"Were you happy with your husband?"

Margarida frowned in disbelief, then fixed her eyes on those of the doctor, which seemed to continue silently to ask that question.

"Yes," she said after a few moments.

Mendonça said not a word; this was not the answer he had expected. He had put too much trust in the apparent intimacy that reigned between them, and he wanted somehow to find out what lay behind the widow's imperviousness. His gambit failed; Margarida grew very serious, and only the arrival of Dona Antônia saved him from this awkward situation. Shortly afterward, Margarida's usual good mood was restored, and the conversation resumed its usual lively, amicable tone. When Jorge joined them, the conversation grew still livelier. Dona Antônia, with the eyes and ears of a mother, thought her son the wittiest creature in the world; but the truth is that there wasn't a more frivolous fellow in all Christendom. His mother laughed at everything her son said, and he alone was quite capable of filling up the conversation with anecdotes and by mimicking the sayings and manners he had picked up at the theater. Mendonça watched all this and tolerated the boy with a show of angelic resignation.

By livening up the conversation, Jorge's arrival made the hours speed by. At ten o'clock, the doctor left, accompanied by Dona Antônia's son, who was off to have supper somewhere. Mendonça declined Jorge's invitation to join him, and said goodbye to him in Rua do Conde, on the corner of Rua do Lavradio.

That same night, Mendonça resolved to take a decisive step: he would write Margarida a letter. Anyone who knew the widow would have thought this a bold move, and, given the precedents described above, it was positive madness. Nevertheless, the doctor did not hesitate to put pen to paper, confident that he could express himself far better in writing than in person. He dashed off the letter with febrile impatience; the following morning, immediately after breakfast, he put the letter inside a novel by George Sand and ordered the houseboy to deliver it to Margarida.

She unwrapped the book and put it down on the living room table; half an hour later, she returned and picked up the book, intending to read it. As soon as she did so, the letter fell out. She opened it and read the following:

> *Whatever the cause of your indifference, I respect it and do not intend to rebel against it. However, while I cannot rebel, do I not have the right to complain? You must be aware that I love you, just as I am aware of your indifference, but however great that indifference, it cannot compare with the deep, urgent love that has filled my heart at a time when I felt I had long since left behind me such youthful passions. I will not describe to you the sleepless nights and tears, the hopes and disappointments, the sad pages of this book which fate has placed in the hands of man so that two souls might read it. None of that is of any interest to you.*
>
> *I dare not ask you about your indifference toward me personally, but why do you extend that indifference to so many others? Having reached an age when passion is the norm, and being, as you are, blessed*

by heaven with a rare beauty, why do you wish to hide away from the world and deny nature and your heart their undeniable rights? Forgive me for asking such an audacious question, but I find myself faced by an enigma that my heart longs to decipher. I wonder sometimes if you are tortured by some great grief, and wish I could be the doctor of your heart; I confess that I would love to restore to you some lost illusion, which is, after all, an inoffensive enough ambition.

If, however, your indifference is merely an expression of perfectly legitimate pride, then forgive me for daring to write to you when your eyes expressly forbade me to. Tear up this letter, which has value neither as a memento nor as a weapon.

The letter was entirely composed of such thoughts; the cold, measured words conveyed none of his own fiery feelings. The reader cannot have failed to notice, though, the innocence with which Mendonça asked for an explanation that Margarida would probably not give.

When Mendonça told Andrade he had written to Margarida, Andrade burst out laughing.

"Was I wrong to do so?" asked Mendonça.

"You've ruined everything. The other suitors also began by writing a letter, and it was tantamount to writing the death certificate of their love."

"Oh, well, if the same thing happens again, I'll just have to accept it," said Mendonça with an almost casual shrug. "But I wish you would stop talking about those other suitors. I'm not a suitor in that same sense."

"I thought you wanted to marry her."

"I do, if possible," said Mendonça.

"That is what all the others wanted too; you would marry and enter into the sweet possession of the wealth it would fall to you to share and which comes to considerably more than one hundred *contos*. My dear fellow, I don't mention the other suitors in order to offend you, for I was one of the suitors she sent packing."

"You?"

"Yes, but, don't worry, I was neither the first nor even the last."

"And you wrote her a letter."

"As did the others, and, like them, I never received a reply, or rather, I did: she returned my letter to me. Anyway, now that you've written to her, just wait for her response, and you'll see that I've been telling you the truth. You're lost, Mendonça. You've made a real blunder."

Andrade was the kind of man who insisted on describing the very darkest side of any situation, on the pretext that one ought to tell one's friends the truth. Having painted a suitably gloomy picture, he said goodbye to Mendonça and left.

Mendonça went home, where he spent another sleepless night.

VII

Andrade was wrong; the widow did reply to the doctor's letter, but only to say:

> I forgive you everything; however, what I will not forgive is a second letter. There is no cause for my indifference; it is purely a matter of temperament.

The meaning of this letter was even more gnomic than the way in which it was expressed. Mendonça read it several times, in an attempt to fathom it out, but to no avail. He did reach one conclusion: there was clearly some hidden reason for Margarida's fear of marriage. Then he came to another conclusion, that Margarida would, in fact, forgive him if he wrote to her again.

The first time Mendonça returned to Rua de Matacavalos, he was dreading having to speak to Margarida; she, however, saved him from any awkwardness by talking as if nothing had happened between them. There was no opportunity for Mendonça to talk to her about the letters because Dona Antônia was with them all the time, something for which he was very grateful, since he had no idea what he would say were he left alone with Margarida.

Days later, Mendonça wrote a second letter to the widow and by the same method. The letter was returned to him unopened. Mendonça then regretted have disobeyed Margarida's orders and resolved, once and for all, never to return to the house in Rua de Matacavalos. Besides, he lacked the courage to go there; it was so awkward being with someone who could never return his love.

A month went by, and his feelings for the widow had diminished not one iota. He loved her as passionately as before, and, just as he had thought, absence only increased his love, just as the wind fans a fire. In vain he tried to lose himself in books or in Rio's busy social life; he even began writing an article on the theory of hearing, but his pen kept being distracted by his heart, and what he wrote emerged as a mixture of frayed nerves and sentiment. At the time, Renan's *The Life of Jesus* was at the height of its fame, and Mendonça filled his study with all kinds of pamphlets written on the subject and immersed himself in the mysterious drama of Judea. He did all he could to occupy his mind with other thoughts and to forget about the elusive Margarida, but this proved impossible.

One morning, Dona Antônia's son came to call, for two reasons: to ask him why he no longer visited Matacavalos and to show off his new trousers. Mendonça approved of the trousers and excused his absence, saying that he had been terribly busy. Jorge was not the sort of fellow to detect the truth lying hidden behind those indifferent words. Seeing Mendonça surrounded by a horde of books and pamphlets, Jorge asked if he was studying to become a deputy. He was, wasn't he?

"No, not at all," said Mendonça.

"True. My cousin always has her nose in a book too, and I'm pretty sure she has no such ambitions, either."

"Your cousin?"

"Oh, you've no idea. All she does is read. She shuts herself up in her room and spends whole days reading."

Given what Jorge said, Mendonça imagined that Margarida was perhaps a woman of letters, even a poet, who spurned men's love in favor of the muses' fond embrace. This was a completely baseless supposition and the child of a mind blinded by love. There are various reasons for reading a great deal without one necessarily having any truck with the muses.

"My cousin never used to read so much. It's a new fad of hers," said Jorge, taking from his cigar case a magnificent Havana cigar worth three *tostões*, and offering another to Mendonça. "Here," he went on, "smoke this—it's from Bernardo's shop—and tell me if you can find a better cigar anywhere."

Once the cigars were smoked, Jorge took his leave, bearing with him the promise that the doctor would visit Dona Antônia's house as soon as possible.

Two weeks later, Mendonça returned to Matacavalos.

He found Andrade and Dona Antônia in the drawing room, where they received him almost with cries of hallelujah. Mendonça did indeed resemble someone who has just emerged from his tomb, for he was thinner and paler, and his melancholy mood had imprinted on his face a look of sadness and weariness. He claimed to have been overwhelmed by work, then began chatting away as gaily as ever. That gaiety, of course, was entirely forced. After a quarter of an hour, his face resumed its sad expression. During that time, Margarida did not appear; for some reason, Mendonça had not asked after her, but, when there was still no sign of her, he asked if she was ill. Dona Antônia told him that Margarida was a little unwell.

Margarida's unwellness lasted about three days; it was merely a headache, which her cousin Jorge attributed to her reading too much.

After a few more days, Margarida surprised Dona Antônia with an unusual request: she wanted to go and spend some time in the countryside.

"Are you bored with the city?" asked her aunt.

"Yes, a little," answered Margarida, explaining that she fancied spending a couple of months in the country.

Since Dona Antônia could deny her niece nothing, she agreed to that rural retreat, and they began preparations. Mendonça learned of this plan when he was out for a stroll one night and met Jorge, who was on his way to the theater. Jorge considered the plan a stroke of great good fortune, because it would rid him of the one obligation he had in the world, namely having to dine with his mother.

Mendonça was not in the least surprised by this decision, for all Margarida's decisions were beginning to seem to him inevitable.

When he returned to his house, he found a note from Dona Antônia, which said:

> We have to leave Rio for a few months; I hope you will not let us go without coming to say goodbye. We set off on Saturday, and there is something I would like you to do for me.

Mendonça drank a cup of tea and settled down to sleep. But he couldn't sleep. He tried to read, but he couldn't do that, either. It was still quite early, and so he went out for a walk. His steps led him to Matacavalos. Dona Antônia's house was dark and silent; everyone must already be asleep. Mendonça walked on, then stopped by the railings surrounding the garden. From there he could see Margarida's bedroom window, almost at ground level and giving onto the garden. A lamp was burning, which meant that Margarida must still be awake. Mendonça took a few more steps; the garden gate was open. Mendonça could feel his heart beating furiously. A suspicion entered his mind. It happens to even the most trusting of souls; besides, perhaps his suspicion was right. Not that Mendonça had any rights over the widow; he had been firmly rebuffed. If he had any duty toward her, it was to withdraw in silence.

Mendonça did not want to overstep the boundary set for him; one of the servants had doubtless simply forgotten to close the garden gate. He persuaded himself that the open gate was mere chance and, with some effort, he walked on. Then he stopped and thought again; some demon was propelling him through that gate. He went back and very cautiously entered the garden.

He had only gone a few feet when Miss Dollar emerged out of the darkness, barking, having apparently slipped out of the house unnoticed. Mendonça bent down and stroked her, and the dog seemed to recognize him, for she stopped barking and began licking him instead. The shadow of a woman appeared on the wall of Margarida's bedroom; she had come over to the window to see what all the noise was about. Mendonça shrank back among the bushes growing by the railings, and Margarida, seeing no one, went back into her room.

After a few minutes, Mendonça came out of his hiding place and went over to Margarida's window. He was accompanied by Miss Dollar. Even if he'd been taller, he would not have been able to see into the young woman's room. As soon as Miss Dollar reached that point, she trotted lightly up the stone steps connecting the garden and the house; the door to Margarida's room was in the corridor immediately beyond; that door stood open. Mendonça followed Miss Dollar and when he set foot on the last step, he heard Miss Dollar scampering about in the room and repeatedly running to the door barking, as if to warn Margarida that a stranger was approaching.

Mendonça was about to go farther when a slave came into the garden, attracted by the barking; he peered about him, but, seeing nothing and no one, withdrew. Margarida went to the window and asked what the matter was; the slave reassured her, saying that there was no one out there.

As Margarida turned away from the window, Mendonça appeared at her bedroom door. She shuddered and turned still paler; then, her eyes aflame with all the indignation a heart can muster, she asked in a tremulous voice:

"What are you doing here?"

It was then, and only then, that Mendonça realized the baseness of his actions, or, to be more exact, his madness. He seemed to see in Margarida his own conscience reproaching him for such undignified behavior. The poor young man did not even try to excuse himself; his response was simple and honest:

"I know I have behaved contemptibly," he said. "I have no reasonable explanation. I was mad, and only now do I see how wrong my actions were. I do not ask you to forgive me, Dona Margarida; I do not deserve to be forgiven; I deserve only scorn. Goodbye!"

"Oh, I understand perfectly, sir," said Margarida. "By discrediting my name, you wish to make me do what your heart could not persuade me to. That is not the act of a gentleman!"

"I assure you that such a thing could not be further from my thoughts."

Margarida slumped down in a chair, apparently crying. Mendonça made as if to go into the room, for, until then, he had not moved from the doorway. Margarida looked up at him with tear-filled eyes and gestured imperiously for him to leave.

Mendonça obeyed. Neither of them slept that night. Both were bent beneath the weight of shame, but to be fair to Mendonça, his shame was far greater than hers; and the pain of one could not compare to the remorse of the other.

VIII

The following day Mendonça was at home, smoking cigar after cigar, something he usually reserved for special occasions, when a carriage drew up outside his house and out stepped Dona Antônia. This visit seemed to Mendonça to presage no good. However, she dispelled all his fears as soon as she came into the house.

"I believe," said Dona Antônia, "that, given my great age, it is safe for me to visit a bachelor on my own."

Mendonça tried to smile at this joke, but failed. He invited the good lady to take a seat and he sat down, too, waiting for her to explain the reason for her visit.

"I wrote to you yesterday," she said, "asking you to come and see me

today. Then I decided to come and see you instead, fearing that, for whatever reason, you might not come to Matacavalos."

"You had a favor to ask of me."

"No, not all," she replied, smiling. "That was just an excuse. What I
want is to tell you something."

"What?"

"Do you know who did not get out of bed today?"

"Dona Margarida?"

"Exactly. She woke up feeling rather under the weather and saying that
she had slept badly. And I think I know the reason," added Dona Antônia,
smiling mischievously at Mendonça.

"What would that be?"

"Don't you know?"

"No."

"Margarida loves you."

Mendonça leapt out of his chair as if propelled by a spring. Dona Antônia's words were so unexpected that he thought he must be dreaming.

"She loves you," Dona Antônia said again.

"I don't think she does," answered Mendonça after a silence. "You must
be mistaken."

"Mistaken!" said Dona Antônia.

She then told Mendonça that, curious to know what lay behind Margarida's sleepless nights, she had gone into her niece's room and found Margarida's personal diary, written in imitation of all those many heroines in
novels; and there she had read what she had just told him.

"But if she loves me," said Mendonça, feeling his soul filling up with a
whole world of hope, "if she loves me, why then does she reject me?"

"The diary explains precisely why. Margarida was unhappily married;
her husband was only interested in her money. She became convinced that
she would never be loved for herself, but only for her wealth. She attributes
your love to greed. Now do you believe me?"

Mendonça began to protest his innocence.

"There's no need," said Dona Antônia, "I believe in the sincerity of your
love. I have for a long time, but how to convince a suspicious heart?"

"I don't know."

"Nor do I," she said, "but that is what has brought me here today. I'm asking you to see if you can make my Margarida happy again, if you can make her believe in your love."

"I don't think that's possible."

Mendonça considered telling Dona Antônia about what had happened the previous night, but decided not to.

Dona Antônia left shortly afterward.

Mendonça's situation may have been clearer, but it was also more complicated. It would have been possible to do something before last night's scene, but not after; Mendonça felt that now it would be impossible to achieve anything.

Margarida's illness lasted two days, after which she got out of bed, feeling slightly low in spirits, and the first thing she did was to write to Mendonça asking him to visit her.

Mendonça was most surprised to receive this invitation, and he obeyed immediately.

"After what happened three days ago," Margarida said, "you will understand that I cannot remain at the mercy of idle gossip. You say you love me, well, then, our marriage is inevitable."

Inevitable! The word left a bitter taste in the doctor's mouth, but he could hardly protest. He remembered, too, that he was loved, and while this thought made him smile, the accompanying thought, that Margarida suspected his motives, instantly put paid to any momentary flicker of pleasure.

"As you wish," he said.

When, that same day, Margarida told her aunt the news, Dona Antônia was amazed at the speed with which their marriage had been arranged. She assumed the young man had performed some miracle. Later, though, she noticed that bride and groom looked more as if they were about to attend a funeral than a marriage. She asked her niece about this, but received no satisfactory answer.

The wedding was a modest, sober affair. Andrade was best man, Dona Antônia was matron of honor, and Jorge asked a friend of his from the theater, a priest, to conduct the ceremony.

Dona Antônia wanted the newlyweds to continue living in the house with her. And the first time Mendonça found himself alone with Margarida, he said:

"I married you in order to save your reputation, but I do not want such an accident of fate to oblige another person to love me. I am, however, your friend. Until tomorrow."

And with that, Mendonça left the room, leaving Margarida caught between her own view of him and the impression made on her by those words.

There could not have been an odder situation than that of those two newlyweds separated by a chimera. The happiest day of their lives was becoming a day of unhappiness and loneliness; the formality of the wedding was simply the prelude to the most absolute divorce. With a little less skepticism on the part of Margarida and some rather more gentlemanly behavior on his, they would have been spared the grim ending to this comedy of the heart. We had best leave to the reader's imagination the torments of their wedding night.

However, time, which always has the last word, will overcome what man's mind cannot. Time persuaded Margarida that her suspicions had been entirely groundless, and when her heart concurred, their still very recent marriage became a real marriage.

Andrade knew nothing of all this; whenever he met Mendonça, he would call him the Columbus of love. Like anyone who only rarely has a good idea, Andrade, having come up with this bon mot, would repeat it ad nauseam.

Husband and wife are still married and have promised to remain so until death do them part. Andrade has joined the diplomatic service and looks set to become one of our most eminent representatives abroad. Jorge continues to be a dedicated reveler; and Dona Antônia is preparing to bid farewell to this world.

As for Miss Dollar, the indirect cause of all these events, she was knocked down by a carriage one day when she ran out into the street. She died shortly afterward. Margarida could not help but shed a few tears over the noble creature, who was buried on her country estate, with a gravestone bearing this simple inscription:

MISS DOLLAR

LUÍS SOARES

———

I

"BY EXCHANGING DAY FOR NIGHT," Luís Soares would say, "we are restoring Nature's empire and correcting the work of society. The heat of the sun is telling mankind to rest and sleep, while the relative cool of the night is the proper season in which we should live. Since I am independent in all my actions, I do not wish to submit to an absurd law imposed on me by society: I will stay awake at night and sleep during the day."

Unlike many governments, Soares carried out this program with a scrupulousness worthy of a noble mind. For him, dawn was dusk and dusk was dawn. He slept for twelve hours during the day, that is, from six in the morning until six in the evening. He breakfasted at seven and dined at two in the morning, but eschewed supper. Supper for him was a cup of hot chocolate brought to him by his servant at five in the morning when he came home. Soares would down the chocolate, smoke a couple of cigars, exchange a few puns with his servant, read a page or two of a novel, then go to bed.

He never read newspapers. He considered the newspaper the most pointless thing in the world, after politics, poems, and mass. This doesn't mean that Soares was an atheist as regards religion, politics, and poetry. No, he was simply indifferent. He greeted all "matters of importance" with the same grimace of disgust as he would at the sight of an ugly woman. He could have turned out to be a truly nasty piece of work, instead, though, he was merely an utterly useless individual.

Thanks to the large fortune left him by his father, Soares was able to lead the life he led, avoiding any kind of work and following the instincts of his nature and the caprices of his heart. "Heart" is perhaps something of an exaggeration. It was doubtful that Soares had one. He himself said so. Whenever a lady begged him to love her, Soares would reply:

"My dear little woman, I was born with the great advantage of having no heart and no brain. What others call reason and sentiment are complete mysteries to me. I don't understand them because I don't feel them."

Soares would add that Fortune had supplanted Nature by placing a large quantity of money in his cradle. He forgot, however, that, although generous, Fortune also makes certain demands and requires some effort on the part of her godchildren. Fortune is not like the daughters of Danaus. When she sees that the barrel of water is drying up, she will take her pitchers elsewhere. Soares did not know this. He thought his wealth would be constantly reborn like the heads of the Hydra. He spent money left, right, and center, and the wealth his father had accumulated through hard work slipped from his hands like birds eager to fly free.

When he least expected it, he found that he was poor. One morning, or, rather, one evening, Soares saw written on a piece of paper the fateful words that had appeared on the wall at Belshazzar's feast. It was a letter given to him by his servant, who explained that Soares's banker had delivered it at midnight. The servant spoke as his master lived, calling midday midnight.

"I've told you before," said Soares, "I only receive letters from friends or from—"

"Some young woman, yes, I know. That's why I haven't given you the other letters that your banker has been bringing you for a whole month now. Today, though, he insisted that I had to give you this one."

Soares sat down on the bed and asked his servant in a tone that was half joking, half angry:

"Are you his servant or mine?"

"Master, the banker said you were in grave danger."

"What danger?"

"I don't know."

"Show me the letter."

The servant handed him the letter.

Soares opened it and read it twice. According to the letter, he now had only six *contos de réis* to his name. For Soares, this was almost nothing.

For the first time in his life, he experienced a deep emotion. It had never occurred to him that he might run out of money; he had never imagined that he would one day find himself in the same position as any other man who needs to work for a living.

He listlessly ate his breakfast, then went out. He went to the Alcazar. When his friends saw his downcast face, they asked if he had suffered some disappointment in love. Soares replied that he was ill. The local courtesans felt it would be in good taste to appear equally sad. There was general consternation.

One of his friends, José Pires, suggested a visit to Botafogo to drive away Soares's melancholy mood. Soares agreed. Alas, a trip to Botafogo was too run-of-the-mill to distract him. Then they thought of visiting Corcovado, an idea that was immediately accepted and acted upon.

But can anything distract a young man in Soares's position? The visit to Corcovado proved equally futile, leaving him so fatigued that, on the return journey, he fell sound asleep.

When he woke, he sent for Pires to come and speak to him urgently. An hour later, a carriage pulled up outside the door: it was Pires, but he was accompanied by a dark-complexioned young woman who answered to the name of Vitória. The two walked into Soares's living room talking loudly, in the casual manner of family members.

"I thought you were ill," Vitória said to the master of the house.

"No, I'm not," he replied, "but what are you doing here?"

"That's a good one!" said José Pires. "She came because she's my boon companion, of course. Did you want to talk to me about something in particular?"

"I did."

"Well, let's find a quiet corner somewhere. Vitória can stay here, leafing through your albums."

"I certainly will not," said the young woman. "If that's how it is, I'd better leave. On just one condition: that you both come to my house afterwards. We're having big supper party tonight."

"Agreed!" said Pires.

Vitória departed, and the two young men were left alone.

Pires was a frivolous, gossipy type. As soon as he sensed a bit of tittle-tattle, he would do his best to find out all the details. He felt flattered that Soares should confide in him and sensed that he was about to tell him something important. He therefore adopted a suitably earnest air. He settled himself comfortably in an armchair, rested his chin on the handle of his cane, and began the attack with these words:

"Right, here we are alone. What did you want to tell me?"

Soares told him everything; he read out the banker's letter; he laid bare to Pires his utter poverty. He said that he could see no possible solution, even confessing frankly that he had spent long hours contemplating suicide.

"Suicide!" exclaimed Pires. "You must be insane!"

"Insane!" retorted Soares. "Well, I can see no other way out of this particular cul-de-sac. Besides, it's only half a suicide, given that poverty is half a death."

"I agree that poverty is not a pleasant thing, and I even think . . ."

Pires broke off there. An idea had just crossed his mind, the idea that Soares might end their conversation by asking him for money. Pires had one firm belief: never lend money to friends. After all, he would say, you don't lend blood.

Soares failed to notice this sudden pause, and said:

"Living like a pauper after being so rich, it's just impossible."

"What do you want from me, then?" asked Pires, who felt it would be best to take the bull by the horns.

"Advice."

"Useless advice, given that you've already made a decision."

"Possibly, but I must confess it's not so easy to leave life, and however good or bad life is, it's always hard to die. On the other hand, revealing my poverty to the people who have always known me as a rich man is a humiliation too far. What would you do in my place?"

"Well," began Pires, "there are various different possibilities . . ."

"For example."

"First possibility: go to New York and make a fortune."

"No good. I'd rather stay in Rio de Janeiro."

"Second possibility: marry a rich woman."

"That's easy enough to say, but who?"

"Look around. Didn't you have a cousin who was in love with you?"

"I don't think she is anymore, and, besides, she's not rich. She only has thirty *contos*, barely enough for a year."

"That's a good principle in life."

"Thank you. What else?"

"Third and best possibility: go to your uncle, wheedle your way into his affections, tell him you repent of your old ways, ask him for a job, and see if he'll make you his sole heir."

Soares said nothing, but this seemed to him a good idea.

"You like that third possibility, don't you?" asked Pires, laughing.

"It's not at all bad, although I know it will be a long, hard process. Then again, I don't have much choice."

"Good," said Pires, getting up. "You just have to be sensible. It will require some sacrifice on your part, but, remember, this is the only way you're going to get a fortune quickly. Your uncle is not a well man and could kick the bucket any day now. Make good use of your time. And now let's go to Vitória's supper party."

"No, I'm not going," said Soares, "I need to get used to my new life."

"Fine. Goodbye, then."

"Look, I told you all this in strictest confidence. It's our secret."

"I'll be as silent as the grave," said Pires, going down the stairs.

The following day, though, all their young friends knew that Soares was about to withdraw from the world . . . because he had run out of money. Soares himself saw this in his friends' faces. They all seemed to be saying: What a shame! That'll put a dent in our social life!

Pires never again visited him.

II

The name of Soares's uncle was Major Luís da Cunha Vilela, and he was, indeed, an old and ailing man, although this was no guarantee that he would die soon, for Major Vilela maintained a strict regime which kept him alive. Well into his sixties now, he was, by turns, jovial and stern. He loved to laugh, but was implacable when it came to bad habits. A constitutionalist by necessity, in his heart he was an absolutist. He mourned the loss of the old ways and constantly criticized the new. He had, after all, been the last man to stop wearing his hair in a pigtail.

Major Vilela lived in Catumbi with his niece Adelaide and another, more elderly female relative. He led a very patriarchal life. Caring little or nothing about what went on in the outside world, he dedicated himself entirely to his household, where a few friends and certain neighboring families occasionally came to visit and spend the evenings. The major was always cheerful, even when prostrated by his rheumatism. Fellow rheumatics will find this hard to believe, but I can confirm that this is true.

One morning—fortunately a morning on which the major was entirely free of pain, and was laughing and joking with his two female relatives— Soares turned up at his uncle's door.

When the major saw the visiting card bearing his nephew's name, he thought it must be a joke. His nephew was the last person he would expect to visit him. He hadn't seen him for two years, and a year and a half had passed between his last two visits. However, such was the seriousness with which the houseboy announced that Senhor Luís was waiting in the parlor that the major finally believed him.

"What do you make of it, Adelaide?"

Adelaide did not respond.

The major went straight to the parlor.

Soares had pondered how best to approach his uncle. Falling on his knees before him would be too dramatic; falling into his arms would require a spontaneity he did not possess; besides, Soares could not bear to feel or feign an emotion he did not have. He considered beginning a conversation that had nothing to do with his real reason for being there, and slowly moving toward an admission that he was ready to change his ways. The disadvantage of this approach was that any reconciliation would inevitably be preceded by a sermon, something he could well do without. He had still not yet chosen one of the many alternatives that came into his head when the major appeared at the door to the parlor.

The major stood there silently, regarding his nephew with a stern, interrogative eye.

Soares hesitated for a moment, but since he did not stand to benefit from prolonging the situation, on a natural impulse he went over to his uncle and held out his hand.

"Uncle," he said, "you need not say anything. The look in your eyes says it all. I was a sinner and I repent of my sins. Here I am."

The major took his hand, which Soares kissed with as much respect as he could muster. Then the major went over to a chair and sat down. Soares remained standing.

"If you sincerely do repent, then I open to you both my door and my heart. If your repentance is insincere, then you can leave now. I haven't been to the theater for a very long time, and I don't like actors."

Soares assured him that he was entirely sincere. He admitted that he had been a crazed dissolute, but now that he had reached the age of thirty, it was time to grow up. He saw now that his uncle had been right all along. He had initially dismissed his uncle's views as the curmudgeonly grumblings of old age, but such levity was only to be expected in a lad brought up to live a life of excess. Luckily, he had seen the light, and his ambition was now to live like any other decent man, his first step being to take on some public position that would oblige him to work and become a serious citizen. It was just a matter of finding such a position.

As he listened to the speech of which I give only an extract above, the major was trying to plumb the depths of Soares's mind. Was he being sincere? He concluded that the lad's words were indeed truly heartfelt, so much so that he thought he saw a tear in his eyes, although no tear, not even a pretend one, actually appeared.

When Soares finished speaking, the major held out his hand and clasped the hand held out to him by the young man.

"I believe you, Luís. And I'm glad that you have at last repented. The life you led was neither life nor death; life is more dignified and death more peaceful than the existence you were blithely frittering away. You come here now like a prodigal son. You will have the best place at the table. My family is your family."

The major continued in this vein, and Soares stood quietly listening to his uncle's speechifying. He told himself that this was merely one example of the misery yet to come, and would be discounted from his sins.

The major finally led the young man into the dining room, where lunch awaited them.

Adelaide and the elderly female relative were both there. Senhora Antônia de Moura Vilela received Soares with loud exclamations of delight, which Soares found genuinely embarrassing. As for Adelaide, she merely nodded in his direction, without actually looking at him. He returned her nod.

The major noted the coldness of her welcome, but merely snickered in a way peculiar to him, as if he knew the cause.

They sat down at the table, and lunch was interspersed with the major's jokes, Senhora Antônia's recriminations, Soares's explanations and Adelaide's silence. When the meal was over, the major gave Soares permission to smoke, a concession that the young man resisted at first, then accepted. The ladies left the room, and the two men sat on alone at the table.

"So you're willing to work?"

"Yes, Uncle."

"Well, I'll see if I can find a job for you. What kind of work would you prefer?"

"Whatever you decide, Uncle, just as long as I'm working."

"Fine, tomorrow I'll write a letter of recommendation for you to present to a couple of ministers. Let's just hope you find a post easily. I want to see you working hard and seriously; I want to see you make a man of yourself. Dissipation produces nothing but debts and disappointments. Do you have any debts?"

"No, none," said Soares.

He was lying. He had a relatively small debt with his tailor, but he was hoping to pay that off before his uncle found out.

The following day, the major wrote the promised letter, which Soares took to one of the ministers, and, a month later, he was fortunate enough to be employed in an office earning a good wage.

To be fair to the lad, he made an enormous sacrifice in changing his habits, and to judge by his previous record, no one would have thought him capable of such a sacrifice. However, both change and sacrifice could be explained by his desire to resume his life of dissipation. This was merely a rather long parenthesis in Soares's existence. He was hoping to close the parenthesis and return to the sentence he had begun, in other words, living with Aspasius and carousing with Alcibiades.

His uncle suspected none of this, but he was afraid Soares might be tempted to backslide, either because he was seduced by memories of his former dissipations or had grown bored with the monotony and weariness of work. In order to prevent disaster, he decided to encourage Soares's political ambitions, thinking that politics would be the perfect remedy for that particular patient, as if it were a well-known fact that Lovelace and Turgot can easily coexist in the same head.

Soares did not discourage the major. He said it was only natural that he should go into politics, even saying that he had occasionally dreamed of having a seat in the Chamber of Deputies.

"I'll see what I can do," said his uncle. "But, first, you need to study political science and the history of our government; above all, though, you need to continue being what you are now: a serious young man."

No sooner said than done, for Soares immediately plunged into his reading and began earnestly studying the debates in the Chamber of Deputies.

Soares did not live with his uncle, but spent any nonworking hours at his house, returning home after a patriarchal tea, very different from the slap-up suppers he had known before.

I shan't deny that there may not have been a thread linking the two phases of Luís Soares's life, or that the emigrant from fashionable society did not make the occasional return visit to his homeland. These forays were, however, so secret that no one knew of them, possibly not even the inhabitants of said homeland, with the exception of the chosen few who welcomed the expatriate. This was unusual, because in that land, naturalized citizens are not thought of as foreign, unlike in England, which denies the queen's subjects the right to choose another country.

Soares occasionally met up with Pires. The convert's confidant proved his former friendship by offering him a Havana cigar and recounting a few of the triumphs he had enjoyed in the war of love, in which the fool imagined himself to be a consummate general.

Major Vilela's nephew had been employed for five months, and, so far, his bosses had no reason to complain. Such devotion was worthy of a better cause. On the outside, Luís Soares was a monk, but scratch the surface and you would find the devil.

And that devil could spy in the distance a possible conquest . . .

III

Cousin Adelaide was twenty-four years old, and, in the full flower of her youth, her beauty had the capacity to make men feel they might die of love for her. She was tall and well proportioned; she had a classically shaped head; her brow was broad and clear, her eyes dark and almond-shaped, and her nose slightly aquiline. Anyone studying her for a few moments would feel that she contained all the energies, both of the passions and of the will.

The reader will doubtless remember the cool greeting exchanged by Adelaide and her cousin; you will also recall that Soares had told his friend Pires that he had once been loved by his cousin. Put those two things together. Adelaide's coolness stemmed from a painful memory; Adelaide *had* loved her cousin, not with the usual cousinly love, which tends to emerge out of long familiarity rather than from any sudden attraction. She had loved him with all the vigor and warmth of her soul; but, by then, he was already beginning to visit other regions of society and was indifferent to her affections. A friend who knew this secret asked him one day why he did not marry Adelaide, to which Soares answered coldly:

"No one with a fortune like mine would marry, but if I did, I would need to marry someone who had a still larger fortune. Adelaide's wealth is only a fifth of mine; for her, it would be a really lucrative deal, but not for me."

The friend who heard this reply gave further proof of his friendship by going to Adelaide and telling her what Soares had said. This was a tremendous blow, not only because it proved beyond a doubt he did not love her, but because it did not even give her the right to respect him. Soares's confession was a corpus delicti. The officious confidant was perhaps hoping to pick up the spoils, but as soon as Adelaide heard his treacherous words, she immediately despised the traitor too.

The incident went no further.

Soares's return to his uncle's house left Adelaide in a very painful situation; she was forced to have dealings with a man she could not respect. For his part, Soares also felt inhibited, not because he regretted the words he had spoken that day, but because of his uncle, who knew nothing about the affair. The uncle did in fact know, but Soares assumed he didn't. The major knew of Adelaide's passion and knew, too, that her cousin had rejected her. He may not have known the actual words repeated to her by Soares's friend, but he knew the gist; he knew that, as soon as he had felt he was loved, the lad had begun to loathe his cousin, and she, seeing herself repulsed, had begun to loathe him too. He had assumed initially that Soares's absence from the house was due to her presence there.

Adelaide was the daughter of one of the major's brothers, an extremely rich and extremely eccentric man, who had died ten years before, leaving his daughter in the care of the major. Her father had been a great traveler and, it transpired, had spent a large part of his fortune on his travels. When he died, his only child, Adelaide, was left with a mere thirty *contos*, which her uncle preserved intact as her future dowry.

Soares coped as best he could with the strange situation in which he found himself. He never conversed with his cousin, or only enough not to arouse his uncle's suspicions. She did the same.

But who can control their heart? Adelaide felt her old affection for Soares beginning to resurface. She tried to fight these feelings, but the only way to stop a plant from growing is to tear it out by the roots. The roots were still there. Despite all her efforts, love gradually took the place of hate, and if she had suffered greatly before, that suffering was now multiplied tenfold. A battle began between pride and love. She kept her suffering to herself, though, and said not a word.

Luís Soares noticed that when his fingers touched hers, she was clearly very moved, and would first blush, then turn pale. Soares was an experienced sailor in the seas of love: he knew its calms and its storms. He realized that his cousin had fallen in love with him again. This discovery brought him no joy; on the contrary, it annoyed him intensely. He was afraid that if his uncle learned of his niece's feelings, then he would suggest that Soares marry her, and a refusal to do so would doubtless compromise his hoped-for inheritance. Soares's ideal was to inherit without having to marry. Giving me wings, he thought, but binding my feet is tantamount to condemning me to prison. That is the fate of a domesticated parrot, one I do not aspire to.

His fears proved to be justified. The major discovered the cause of his niece's sadness and decided to resolve the situation by proposing that Soares marry her.

Soares could not openly refuse without compromising the edifice of his fortune.

"This marriage," his uncle told him, "completes my happiness. At a stroke, I bring together two people I love, and I can then die in peace, taking no sorrows with me into the next world. You'll accept, won't you?"

"I will, Uncle, but I must just say that marriage is based on love, and I do not love my cousin."

"But you will. Get married first . . ."

"I wouldn't want to disillusion her."

"What do you mean, 'disillusion her'?" said his uncle, smiling. "I like to hear you speaking so poetically, but marriage is not poetry. I agree that it's always best if, before marrying, two people already feel some mutual esteem, but I think you do. As for flaming passions, my dear nephew, such things are fine in poetry and even in prose, but in life, which is neither prose nor poetry, marriage demands only respect and a certain conformity of character and upbringing."

"You know I would never disobey an order from you."

"I'm not ordering you to do anything; I'm merely making a suggestion. You say you don't love your cousin, fine, but do your best to love her and give me the pleasure of seeing you married. But don't delay, because it won't be long before I shuffle off this mortal coil."

Soares agreed. Unable to resolve the problem, he postponed it. The major was pleased with the arrangement and consoled his niece with the promise that she would one day marry her cousin. This was the first time he had broached the subject, and Adelaide did not conceal her surprise, a surprise that proved most flattering to the major's powers of discernment.

"Just because I'm old, you think I can no longer see with my heart. Well, I see everything, Adelaide, even those things that try to remain hidden."

She could not hold back her tears, and when he tried to console her by offering her some hope, she shook her head, saying:

"No, there is no hope!"

"Leave it to me," said the major.

While her uncle's kindness was entirely spontaneous and born of the love he bore for his niece, she realized that his intervention could give her cousin the impression that she was begging him for his affection like someone asking for alms.

This was her woman's pride speaking, preferring suffering to humiliation. When she put these objections to her uncle, he smiled kindly and tried to reassure her.

A few days passed and nothing happened. Soares was enjoying the respite given him by his uncle. Adelaide resumed her air of cold indifference, and Soares, knowing the reason for this coldness, responded to that show of pride with a wry smile. Twice Adelaide caught that scornful look. What further proof did she need that he remained as indifferent to her as before? She noted, too, that whenever they found themselves alone, he was always the first to leave the room. No, he hadn't changed.

"He doesn't love me, he never will!" she told herself.

IV

One morning, Major Vilela received the following letter:

> *My valiant Major. I arrived back from Bahia today and I'll drop round this evening to see you and embrace you. Prepare a fine supper, for I don't imagine you will receive me as if I were just anyone. And don't forget the* vatapá. *Your friend, Anselmo.*

"Excellent!" said the major. "Anselmo is coming to see us, Cousin Antônia, tell the cooks to prepare a *vatapá*."

The Anselmo who had just arrived from Bahia was Anselmo Barroso de Vasconcelos. He was a rich landowner and a veteran of the War of Independence. Despite his seventy-eight years, he was still strong and capable of great deeds. He had been a close friend of Adelaide's father, who had introduced him to the major, with whom he remained friends after her father died. Anselmo had been with his friend until his final moments and had mourned his passing as he would a brother's. Those tears cemented the friendship between him and the major.

Anselmo arrived that evening full of talk and jokes and as lively as if he were about to embark on his second youth. He embraced everyone and kissed Adelaide, whom he complimented on her growing beauty.

"Now, don't laugh at me," he told her, "I was your father's greatest friend and, alas, poor friend, he died in my arms."

Soares, who was finding the life he led at his uncle's house stultifyingly dull, was delighted to meet this talkative old man, who was a veritable firework. Anselmo, however, seemed not to take to the major's nephew. When the major learned this, he said:

"I'm sorry to hear that, because Soares is a very serious lad."

"Too serious, if you ask me. A lad who never smiles . . ."

Some incident or other, I'm not sure what, prevented Anselmo from finishing his sentence.

After supper, Anselmo said to the major:

"What date is it tomorrow?"

"The fifteenth."

"Of which month?"

"Oh, come on, now. Of December!"

"Right. Tomorrow, the fifteenth of December, I need to have a meeting with you and your relatives. If the steamship had been a day late, I would have been in real trouble."

The following day, the meeting Anselmo had asked for took place. Present were the major, Soares, Adelaide, and Dona Antônia, the deceased man's only relatives.

"It's ten years to the day that this young woman's father died," said Anselmo, indicating Adelaide. "As you know, Dr. Bento Varela was my best friend, and I returned his affection until the very last moment of his life. As you also know, he was an eccentric genius, and he lived an equally eccentric life. He was always coming up with new projects, each more grandiose than the last, each more impossible than the last, and none of them was ever brought to fruition, because no sooner had his creative spirit come up with one idea than it was already planning another."

"That's true," said the major.

"Bento died in my arms, and, as a final proof of his friendship, he gave me a letter, which, he said, I should open only in the presence of his family members ten years after his death. Were I to die, the obligation would fall on my heirs, or, if they were not available, then on the major, Senhora Dona Adelaide, or anyone connected to him by blood. And if none of the above was alive, a notary had been charged with carrying out that duty. I had put all this in my will, which I will now have to revise. The letter I mentioned is here in my pocket."

There was a murmur of curiosity.

Anselmo took from his pocket a letter bearing a black wax seal.

"Here it is," he said. "Unopened. I don't know what it says, but I can more or less guess what it contains because of certain circumstances that I will reveal to you now."

Those present grew still more attentive.

"Before he died," Anselmo went on, "my dear friend gave me part of his fortune, I mean the larger part, because Adelaide received only thirty *contos*. I received from him three hundred *contos*, which I have kept intact until today, and which I must distribute according to the instructions in this letter."

General gasps of surprise were followed by a faint shiver of anxiety. What would they be, these mysterious instructions left by Adelaide's father? Dona Antônia remembered that, as a girl, she had been the dead man's sweetheart, and, for a moment, she flattered herself with the idea that, at the gates of death, the crazy old man might perhaps have thought of her.

"That's so typical of my brother Bento," said the major, taking a pinch of snuff. "He always was a man for mysteries, surprises, and extravagant ideas, not to mention his other sins, if, that is, he committed any . . ."

Everyone was all ears as Anselmo opened the letter and read it out.

My dear, kind Anselmo. I want you to do me one last favor. You already have in your possession the larger portion of my fortune, and I would say the better portion apart, that is, from my dear daughter Adelaide. Keep those three hundred contos for ten years, and at the end of that period, read this letter out to my relatives.

If, by then, my daughter Adelaide is still alive and married, then give her that fortune. If she is not married, then give it to her anyway, but on one condition, that she marry my nephew Luís Soares, the son of my sister Luísa; I love him dearly and, even though he himself is rich, I want him to have my daughter's fortune. Should she refuse to meet this condition, then the entire fortune is yours.

When Anselmo finished reading, an amazed silence filled the room, an amazement shared by Anselmo himself, who had known nothing of the letter's contents until then.

Soares was staring at Adelaide, who was, in turn, staring down at the floor.

When the silence continued, Anselmo decided to break it.

"Like you," he said, "I had no idea what was in this letter; fortunately it has arrived in time for my late friend's final wish to be granted."

"Indeed," said the major.

On hearing this, Adelaide very slowly looked up, and her eyes met her cousin's eyes. His were filled with contentment and tenderness, and she gazed into those eyes for some moments. On his lips there appeared a smile, which was no longer a mocking smile. She smiled scornfully back at him as if at the bowings and scrapings of a courtier.

Anselmo got to his feet.

"Now that you know everything," he said to the two cousins, "I hope you will resolve the matter, and since there can be no doubt as to the result, I give you my heartfelt congratulations. Meanwhile, if you'll excuse me, I have other people to see."

With his departure, the party broke up. Adelaide retired to her room with Dona Antônia. Uncle and nephew remained in the room.

"Luís," said his uncle, "you are the most fortunate man in the world."

"Do you think so, Uncle?" said Soares, trying to conceal his joy.

"I do. Not only do you have a young woman who is madly in love with you. Suddenly an unexpected fortune falls into her lap, and she can only have that fortune if she marries you. Even the dead are working in your favor."

"I can assure you, Uncle, that money has nothing to do with it, and if I agree to marry my cousin it will be for other reasons entirely."

"I know that wealth is not essential, but it has some value. It's better to have three hundred *contos* than thirty; it's three figures, not two. However, I will not advise you to marry her if you feel no affection for her, and I'm not talking here about the kind of passions you spoke of. However much money is involved, a bad marriage is still a bad marriage."

"I'm sure you're right, Uncle. That's why I haven't yet given my answer, and why I won't do so as yet. If I do become fond of my cousin, then I am ready to accept that unexpected wealth."

As the reader will have guessed, Soares was firmly resolved to marry. Instead of waiting for his uncle to die, it seemed to him a far better idea to gain immediate possession of that large sum of money, something that seemed to him all the easier, given that a voice from the grave was demanding it.

Soares was counting, too, on Adelaide's deep respect for her father. This, together with the love she felt for him, should produce the desired effect.

That night, he slept very little. He dreamed of the Orient. His imagination created a harem carpeted with the finest Persian rugs and redolent of all of Arabia's finest perfumes; the most beautiful women in the world reclined on soft divans. In the middle of the room a Circassian beauty was dancing to the sound of an ivory tambourine. Then an angry eunuch burst into the room, wielding an Ottoman sword, which he plunged into Soares's chest, at which point Soares awoke from the nightmare and was unable to go to sleep again.

He got up earlier than usual and went for a walk until it was time for breakfast and the office.

V

Luís had a plan.

He would gradually lower his defenses, pretending to succumb to Adelaide's charms. Such sudden wealth meant that he had to be discreet. The transition had to be slow. He had to be a diplomat.

Readers will have realized that, despite a certain astuteness on Soares's part, he had not fully grasped the situation, and, besides, he was, by nature, indecisive and fickle.

He had hesitated about marrying Adelaide when his uncle had first spoken to him about it and when it was certain that he would, later on, inherit the major's fortune. He had said then that he had no desire to be a parrot. The situation was the same now; he was prepared to accept a fortune in exchange for a prison cell. It's true that if this decision appeared to contradict the first, it could be because he was growing weary of the life he was leading. And, of course, this time he would not have to wait for the money, it would be given to him as soon as he married.

"Three hundred *contos*," he thought, "that would make me even richer than I was. I can't wait to hear what my friends will say!"

Believing his happiness to be assured, Soares began his siege of the castle, a castle that had already surrendered.

He now constantly tried to catch her eye and, when he did, his eyes would ask her for the very thing he had rejected before, the young woman's heart. When, at the table, their hands touched, Soares took pains to maintain that contact, and when she hurriedly withdrew her hand, he was not discouraged. When he found himself alone with her, he did not run away as he had before, but addressed a few words to her, to which Adelaide would respond coolly and politely.

"She's obviously playing hard to get," thought Soares.

Once, he went a step further, entering the room unseen when Adelaide was playing the piano. When she finished playing, he was standing behind her.

"Beautiful!" he exclaimed. "Allow me to kiss those inspired hands."

She gave him a very somber look, then picked up the handkerchief she had placed on the piano and left the room without saying a word.

This episode demonstrated to Soares the difficult nature of the enterprise, but he remained confident, not because he thought himself capable of great things, but out of a sort of trust in his own good fortune.

"It's hard to swim upstream," he said, "but it can be done. No heroes were made without a battle."

However, further disappointments followed, and had he not been driven on by the thought of all that money, he would have laid down his arms.

One day, he decided to write her a letter. It occurred to him that it would be very difficult to tell her of his feelings face-to-face, but that, however much she loathed him personally, she would at least read a letter.

Adelaide sent the letter back with the houseboy who had delivered it.

The second letter suffered the same fate. When he sent a third, the houseboy refused to take it.

Luís Soares suffered a moment of disillusionment. His indifference was beginning to turn to hate; if he did marry her, he would probably treat her as his mortal enemy.

The situation was becoming ridiculous, or, rather, it had been for a long time, but Soares hadn't noticed. To put a stop to this absurd state of affairs, he decided to make one final bold move. He seized the first opportunity that appeared, and made an open declaration of his feelings to her, full of pleadings and sighs and possibly tears. He admitted he'd been wrong, mistaken, but now he was utterly repentant. He had finally fallen under her spell.

"Fallen under my spell?" she said. "I don't understand. What do you mean?"

"You know perfectly well, the spell of your beauty, your love. Please don't imagine that I'm lying. I'm so deeply in love that I would even be capable of committing a crime."

"A crime?"

"Isn't suicide a crime? Of what value is life to me without your love? Please, speak!"

She looked at him for a few moments without uttering a word.

He knelt down.

"Be it death or happiness," he said, "I want to receive it on my knees."

Adelaide smiled and said very slowly:

"Three hundred *contos*. That's a very high price to pay for a miserable wretch."

And with that, she turned her back on him.

Soares froze. For a few moments he remained in that same position, his

eyes fixed on Adelaide as she walked away. He bowed his head beneath the
weight of such humiliation. He had not foreseen such a cruel revenge on her
part. Not a hateful word, not a flicker of anger, only calm disdain, a quiet,
lofty scorn. Soares had suffered greatly when he lost his fortune, but now
that his pride had been so bruised, his pain was infinitely greater.

Poor lad!

Adelaide went inside. It seems she had expected such a scene, because,
on entering the house, she immediately went in search of her uncle, and
told him that, however much she venerated her father's name, she could not
obey his wishes and would not marry.

"I thought you loved him," said the major.

"I did love him."

"Do you love someone else?"

"No."

"Then explain yourself."

Adelaide gave him a frank account of Soares's behavior ever since he'd
come to their house, the sudden change in him, his intentions, the scene in
the garden. The major listened attentively, tried to excuse his nephew, but,
deep down, he believed Soares to be a bad man.

Once Soares was feeling calmer, he went into the house and said goodbye to his uncle until the next day, pretending he had some urgent business
to attend to.

VI

Adelaide gave Anselmo a detailed account of the events that prevented her
from fulfilling the conditions in the posthumous letter entrusted to him.
Since she had to refuse, her father's fortune should revert to Anselmo; she
was perfectly content with what she had.

Anselmo would not give up, however, and before he accepted her
refusal, he wanted to see what he himself could make of Luís Soares.

When Soares saw Anselmo enter the house, he suspected it had something to do with the marriage. Anselmo was a very keen judge of character and, despite Soares's downcast look of victimhood, he saw at once that
Adelaide was right.

And that was that. Anselmo prepared to leave for Bahia and announced his departure to the major's family.

However, when they were all gathered together in the parlor on the eve of Anselmo's departure, he spoke these words:

"You're getting stronger and fitter by the day, Major. I think you would benefit from a trip to Europe. And this young lady here would like to see Europe too, and despite her age, I believe Senhora Dona Antônia would enjoy it as well. For my part, I'm prepared to give up Bahia and come with you. What do you say?"

"We'll need to think about it," said the major.

"Think? If you think about it, you'll never go. What do *you* say, Adelaide?"

"I'll do whatever my uncle says," answered Adelaide.

"Besides," said Anselmo, "now that Dona Adelaide is in possession of a large fortune, she'll want to see the beautiful things other countries have to offer in order to better appreciate the beauty of our own . . ."

"That's all very well," said the major, "but when you say a large fortune . . ."

"Three hundred *contos*."

"That belongs to you."

"To me? Do you think me a thief? What do I care for the dying fantasy of a generous friend? The money belongs to this young woman, his legitimate heir, not to me. I have enough already."

"That's very generous of you, Anselmo!"

"How could I be otherwise?"

They all agreed on the trip to Europe.

Luís Soares heard all this without saying a word, but was cheered by the idea that he might be able to tag along with his uncle. The following day he suffered a cruel disappointment. The major said that, before he left, he would recommend him to the minister.

Soares still hoped that he might be able to accompany the family. Was this pure greed for his uncle's fortune, a desire to see new places, or just to have his revenge on his cousin? It was perhaps all those things.

He clung to these hopes until the very last moment. Then the family left without him.

Abandoned, with no future hopes or prospects other than the daily grind of work, not to mention his humiliated, wounded amour propre, Soares resolved to take the sad, cowardly way out.

One night, his servant heard a shot ring out in Soares's bedroom; when he went in, he found a corpse.

Pires learned of Soares's death from someone he met in the street and immediately hurried to Vitória's house, where she was seated at her dressing table.

"Have you heard?" he asked.

"Heard what?"

"Soares has shot himself."

"When?"

"Just now."

"Poor man! Is it serious?"

"It is. Are you going out?"

"I'm going to the Alcazar."

"Oh, yes, they're doing *Bluebeard* tonight, aren't they?"

"Yes."

"I'll come with you, then."

And he started humming a tune from *Bluebeard*.

And that was all Luís Soares received from his closest friends by way of a funeral oration.

THE WOMAN IN BLACK

I

THE FIRST TIME Dr. Estêvão Soares spoke to Deputy Meneses was in the Teatro Lírico at the time of the memorable battle between the *lagruístas* and the *chartonistas*, supporters, respectively, of the singers Emilie La Grua and Anne Charton Demeur. A mutual friend introduced them, and they parted at the end of the evening, exchanging visiting cards and saying that if ever they could be of service to each other, etc., etc.

Just two months later, they met again.

Estêvão Soares had to go to the house of a government minister to sort out some paperwork for a provincial relative of his, and there he met Meneses, who was just coming out of a meeting.

They were both genuinely pleased to meet each other again, and Meneses managed to make Estêvão promise to come to his house a few days later.

The minister in question dealt with the young doctor's request very quickly, but when Estêvão was ready to leave, he was faced by a heavy downpour, with the rain beginning to run in torrents down the street.

He looked to left and right for an empty cab, but in vain; all the carriages that passed were occupied.

There was only one empty carriage, apparently waiting for someone, presumably the deputy.

A few minutes later, that representative of the nation appeared and was surprised to find the doctor still at the door.

"It's raining so heavily," said Estêvão, "I can't really leave and so I've been waiting here in case an empty cab came by."

"You'll be lucky, but, please, allow me to offer you a seat in my carriage."

"I hate to put you to any trouble . . ."

"It's no trouble at all. It's a pleasure. I'll drop you at your house. Where do you live?"

"Rua da Misericórdia."

"Fine, get in."

Estêvão still hesitated for a moment, but he could hardly refuse without seeming to be spurning the worthy gentleman's generous offer.

They got into the carriage.

However, instead of telling the driver to take them to Rua da Misericórdia, the deputy shouted:

"Home, João!"

Estêvão looked at him in surprise.

"I know," said Meneses, "you're surprised to see me break my promise, but I'd just like you to see where I live, so that you'll know where to come when you visit me—soon, I hope."

The carriage set off in the torrential rain.

Meneses was the first to break the brief silence, saying to his young friend:

"I hope the novel of our friendship will not end at the first chapter."

Although already conscious of the deputy's solicitous manner, Estêvão was completely taken aback to hear him speak of the novel of their friendship. The reason for this was simple. The friend who had introduced them at the theater had said to him the following day:

"Meneses is a real misanthrope, a skeptic; he believes in nothing and respects no one. In politics as in society, he plays a purely negative role."

Despite his real liking for the deputy, it was with these words in mind that Estêvão spoke to him for the second time, and he was astonished by everything about him, by Meneses's manner and by his words and the affectionate nature these seemed to reveal.

He replied to the deputy with equal frankness.

"Why should we end at the first chapter?" he asked. "A friend is never something to be scorned, but welcomed like a gift from the gods."

"From the gods!" said Meneses, laughing. "I see you are a pagan."

"Somewhat, yes, but in the good sense of the word," answered Estêvão, also laughing. "My life is a little like Odysseus's life."

"I hope you at least have an Ithaca, your homeland, and a Penelope, your wife."

"Neither one nor the other."

"Then we will get along famously."

And with that, the deputy turned away to watch the rain streaming down the carriage window.

A few minutes passed, during which Estêvão was at liberty to study his traveling companion.

Meneses turned around then and began another topic of conversation.

When the carriage entered Rua do Lavradio, Meneses said to the doctor:

"This is where I live. My house is just here. Promise you'll come and visit me occasionally."

"I'll come tomorrow."

"Good. And how is your medical practice going?"

"Oh, I'm only just starting," said Estêvão, "and I don't have much work as yet, but I hope to make something of it eventually."

"The colleague who introduced us told me that you're a young man of great merit."

"Well, I certainly hope to make a contribution to society."

Ten minutes later, the carriage stopped outside a house in Rua do Lavradio.

They both got out and went inside.

Meneses showed Estêvão his study, which was furnished with two long bookshelves.

"This is my family," said the deputy, showing him the books. "History, philosophy, poetry, and a few books on politics. This is where I work and study. Whenever you come here, this is where I'll receive you."

Promising to return the following day, Estêvão went downstairs to the carriage, which was waiting to take him to Rua da Misericórdia.

When he arrived home, Estêvão was saying to himself:

"In what way is this man a misanthrope? A misanthrope would be gruff and rude, unless, of course, he has proved more fortunate than Diogenes and found in me the honest man he's been looking for."

II

Estêvão was a serious fellow. He had talent, ambition, and a desire for knowledge, all powerful weapons in the hands of a man aware of his own potential. His life had been one of deep, constant, uninterrupted study since he was sixteen years old. When Estêvão enrolled in medical school, he did so rather reluctantly, not wishing to disobey his father. His true vocation was for mathematics. What does it matter? he thought when he learned of his father's intentions for him: I will study medicine *and* mathematics. And he did indeed find time for both, and even found time to study literature, so that the principal works of antiquity and those of contemporary writers were as familiar to him as treatises on surgical operations and hygiene.

All this studying brought with it a certain diminution in his health. At twenty-four, Estêvão was thinner than he had been at sixteen; he was very pale and his head jutted forward slightly from his long habit of reading. However, these vestiges of intellectual dedication had not affected the regularity and harmony of his features, nor had his eyes lost any of their brightness and expressiveness despite long hours bent over books. He possessed, besides, a natural elegance; not that he was a dandy; his elegance lay in his manner, his attitude, his smile, his clothes, all of which were combined with a certain rigor, which was the cornerstone of his character. While he may often have broken the rules of fashion, no one could ever have accused him of breaking the code of the gentleman.

He had lost his parents when he was only twenty, but had enough common sense to continue alone on his journey into the world. Studying became his refuge and his support. He knew nothing of love. He had been so focused on filling his mind that he had forgotten he had a heart. Do not, however, infer from this that Estêvão was a positivist. On the contrary, his soul still had the two wings nature had given him in all their grace and strength. He would often break out of the prison of the flesh to fly up into the heavens, in search of some obscure, uncertain, ill-defined ideal. When he returned from these ecstasies, he would recover from them by burying himself in books, in search of some scientific truth. Newton was his antidote to Goethe.

Apart from this, Estêvão did have some rather unusual ideas. His friend, a priest of about thirty, was a keen disciple of François Fénelon and admirer of his *Adventures of Telemachus*. Now, this priest would often tell Estêvão that he lacked only one thing in order to be complete, and that was to marry. He would say:

"When you have a beloved and loving wife by your side, you will be a complete and happy man. You will then divide your time between the two loftiest things given to us by nature, our intelligence and our heart. On that day, I want to be the one to bind you together in matrimony . . ."

"In that case, Father Luís," Estêvão would say, "bring me both wife and blessing."

The priest would smile at this answer, and since that smile seemed to Estêvão to beg another question, he would go on:

"If I ever find a woman as complete as I would like, I promise that I will marry. However, as you yourself would say: all human works are imperfect, and I certainly wouldn't argue with you there, Father Luís; allow me, therefore, to walk alone with my own imperfections."

A heated debate would then ensue, which would grow livelier and livelier until the point when Estêvão would conclude thus:

"Father Luís, a girl who leaves aside her dolls in order to learn by heart a few ill-chosen books; who interrupts a lesson in order to hear a description of a love scene; who, as regards art, knows only Paris fashion figurines; who cannot wait to go to a ball, and who, before she falls in love with a man, first makes sure his tie is correct and his boots a perfect fit; Father Luís, this girl could easily become a splendid ornament to a salon or even a fecund mother, but she could never be a wife."

This statement had the defect of all absolute rules, which is why Father Luís would always say:

"You're quite right, but I'm not telling you to marry the rule; look for the exception to that rule and take her to the altar, where I will be waiting to perform the marriage ceremony."

Such were Estêvão's views on love and women, and these feelings came to him in part from nature, but also from books. He demanded the intellectual and moral perfection of an Héloïse, taking the exception to prove the rule. He was intolerant of any venial sins, not even recognizing them as such. There are no venial sins, he would say, when it comes to manners and love.

Estêvão's own family had contributed to this rigidity of spirit. Until his twentieth year, he had seen the sanctity of love sustained by domestic virtue. His mother, who had died when she was thirty-eight, had loved her husband to the last, and survived him by only a few months. Estêvão knew that his parents' love for each other had been ardent and keen when they were engaged and during the early years of their marriage too; but in the later years of their marriage, which he had witnessed, he had seen a calm, solicitous, trusting love, full of devotion and respect, practiced almost as a religion, free from recriminations or resentments, and as deep as it had been on the very first day. Estêvão's parents died beloved and happy in the tranquil serenity of marital duty.

To Estêvão's mind, the love that founds a family should be just that and nothing else. This was only right and proper, but Estêvão's intolerant views began with his conviction that the last family had died with his own family, and with it the last tradition of love. What would it take to bring down that system, even momentarily? The tiniest of things: a smile and two eyes.

However, when those two eyes did not appear, Estêvão devoted most of his time to his scientific studies, filling any free moments with distractions that required little concentration.

He lived alone; he had a slave, who was the same age as him and had been brought up in his father's house, and who was more brother than slave as regards devotion and affection. He had a few friends and, now and then, they would visit him and he, them. Among these was the young Father Luís, whom Estêvão called the Plato of the cassock.

Naturally kind and affectionate, generous and chivalrous, devoid of any rancorous or hateful feelings, an enthusiast for all things good and true, this was Dr. Estêvão Soares at the age of twenty-four.

We have already said something about his physical appearance; we need only add that he had a handsome head, thick brown hair, bright, observant brown eyes, and a naturally curly mustache that stood out in marked contrast to his pale face. He was also tall and had an admirable pair of hands.

III

Estêvão Soares visited Meneses the following day.

The deputy was expecting him and received him as if he were an old friend. Estêvão had unwittingly arranged to visit at a time that prevented Meneses from attending the Chamber, not that he minded; he simply didn't go. However, he was delicate enough not to mention this to Estêvão.

Meneses was in his study when the houseboy announced the doctor's arrival. He went to greet him at the door.

"As punctual as a king," he said gaily.

"Of course. I wouldn't want you to think I'd forgotten."

"I'm grateful to you."

They both sat down.

"I'm grateful because I was afraid you might have misunderstood me and that my feelings of friendship for you might not merit any consideration on your part . . ."

Estêvão was about to protest.

"Forgive me," Meneses went on, "I see that I was wrong, and that's why I'm so grateful. At forty-seven, I'm no longer a boy, and for someone of your age, friendship with a man like me is no longer of any value."

"Old age, when it's respectable, should be respected, and loved when it's lovable. Besides, you're not old. True, your hair is turning gray, but it's more as if you were embarking on a second youth."

"Is that how I seem to you?"

"You not only seem so, you are."

"Whatever the truth of the matter," said Meneses, "the fact is that we can be friends. How old are you?"

"Twenty-four."

"Goodness, young enough to be my son. Are your parents still alive?"

"They both died four years ago."

"And I seem to recall you telling me you were single . . ."

"Yes, I am."

"So you're free to concentrate solely on science?"

"Science is my wife."

"Yes, your intellectual wife, but that can't be enough for a man like you. There's plenty of time for that, though; you're still young."

As they spoke, Estêvão was studying and observing Meneses, whose face was lit by the light coming in through one of the windows. There was something austere about his head, with its mane of graying, elegantly disheveled hair. His eyes were dark and rather dull, but one could sense they had once been lively and passionate. His grizzled side-whiskers were like those worn by Lord Palmerston, at least according to the engravings. His face was unlined, apart from a single crease between his eyebrows, a sign of concentration rather than a trace left by time. He had a high forehead, and his chin and cheekbones were slightly prominent. You could tell that in his first youth he must have been handsome, and that in old age he would look imposing and august. He smiled occasionally, and that smile, even though his face was not that of an old man, made a very strange impression; it was like a shaft of moonlight falling on an ancient ruin. His smile was pleasant, but devoid of joy.

There was something impressive and attractive about him, and Estêvão felt more and more drawn to this man who sought his company and held out the hand of friendship to him.

The conversation continued in the same affectionate tone in which it had begun; the first encounter between friends is the very opposite of the first encounter between lovers; in the latter, silence speaks volumes; in the former, you inspire and gain each other's confidence by a frank exposition of feelings and ideas.

They did not talk about politics. Estêvão made a brief allusion to Meneses's duties as a deputy, but it was a passing comment to which the deputy paid no attention.

After an hour, Estêvão got up to leave; he had to go and see a patient.

"That is the most sacred of reasons, otherwise I would keep you here longer."

"I'll come again, though."

"You certainly will, and I'll return the visit occasionally too. If, that is, you're not fed up with me after two weeks . . . Look, come in the evening; have supper with me; once I've finished at the Chamber, I'm completely free."

Estêvão agreed to all these proposals.

And he did go back and twice had supper with the deputy, who also visited him at home; they went to the theater together and became on good terms with the various families of their acquaintance. After a month, they were old friends. They had both taken careful note of each other's character and feelings. Meneses liked the doctor's seriousness and good sense; he respected him and accepted his prejudices, applauding the generosity of his ambitions. For his part, the doctor saw in Meneses a man who combined the austerity of experience with a gentlemanly amiability, being modest in his manners, cultivated, and sensitive. He found not a trace of the misanthropy he had been warned about. It's true that, on occasions, Meneses did seem more disposed to listen than to speak, and, at such times, his gaze grew still and somber, as if he were contemplating his own consciousness, rather than looking at any external object. Such moments did not last, however, and Meneses soon reverted to his usual self.

"He's not a misanthrope," thought Estêvão, "but there is some kind of drama going on inside him."

This idea took on a certain verisimilitude when, one night at the Teatro Lírico, Estêvão drew Meneses's attention to a woman dressed in black, who was sitting in a box on the first level.

"I don't know that woman," said Estêvão, "do you?"

Meneses looked up at the box, studied the woman for a few moments, then said:

"No, I don't."

The conversation went no further, but the doctor noticed that the woman looked at Meneses twice more, and that Meneses did the same, and that their eyes met.

At the end of the performance, the two friends walked over to the side corridor where the woman in black had been sitting. Estêvão was curious—the curiosity of an artist: he wanted to see her from close up. The door to her box was shut. Had she already left? It was impossible to know. Meneses walked by without looking. When they reached the landing of the stairs leading down to the exit onto Rua dos Ciganos, they were both stopped by the great crush of people. Shortly afterward, they heard someone's hurrying footsteps, and Meneses immediately took Estêvão's arm and continued on down the stairs despite having to push his way through the throng.

Estêvão understood, although he had seen nothing.

For his part, Meneses gave nothing away.

As soon as they were free of the crowd, the deputy launched into a lively conversation with the doctor.

"What effect does it have on you, pushing past all those elegant ladies, through that confusion of silks and perfumes?"

Estêvão replied distractedly, and Meneses continued the conversation in the same vein. Five minutes later, the incident at the theater was entirely forgotten.

IV

One day, Estêvão Soares was invited to a ball at the house of an old friend of his father's.

It was a large and glittering company, and, although Estêvão led a quiet existence, he knew quite a number of people there. He did not dance, but he looked, talked, laughed a little, and left.

When he had arrived at the ball, his heart had been utterly free; when he left, however, it was—to adopt the language of the poets of Arcadia— pierced by an arrow, love's arrow.

Love? To be honest, that word cannot be used to describe the feeling experienced by Estêvão; it was not yet love, but it could quite easily become love. For the moment, it was a feeling of sweet, gentle fascination; one of the guests had made on him the same impression that fairies make on wandering princes or exiled princesses, at least according to what we read in fairy tales.

The woman in question was not a maiden; she was a widow of thirty-four, very beautiful, gracious and kind. This was the first time Estêvão had seen her; at least, he could not recall having seen her before. They had talked for half an hour, and he was so enchanted by Madalena's manners, voice, and beauty that, when he reached home, he was unable to sleep.

Like the good doctor he was, he noted the symptoms of this hypertrophy of the heart called love and did his best to combat the nascent illness. He read a few pages of a mathematics book, or, rather, he ran his eyes over the pages, because as soon as he started to read, his mind left the book and went off to find the widow.

Tiredness succeeded where Euclid failed and, toward dawn, Estêvão Soares finally fell asleep.

He dreamed of the widow.

He dreamed he was holding her in his arms, that he was showering her with kisses, that she was his wife in the eyes of the Church and society.

When he woke, he remembered the dream and smiled.

"Get married!" he said. "That's all I need. How could I, with my naturally shy, ambitious character, how could I possibly be happily married? I'll think no more about it. I'll never see that woman again, and that's that."

He began getting dressed.

Breakfast was brought to him, and he ate rapidly because it was late, then went out to see a few patients.

As he passed Rua do Conde, he remembered that Madalena had told him that this was the street where she lived, but where exactly? She had told him the number, but he had been so entranced by her voice that he had failed to retain this information.

Since no one could help him, he decided to continue on his way.

The following day, though, he made a point of walking twice up and down Rua do Conde to see if he could find the charming widow. He found nothing, but just as he was about to take a cab and return home, he bumped into the family friend at whose house he had met Madalena.

Estêvão had already considered approaching him, but had immediately rejected the thought, because asking him where the widow lived might betray his intentions.

That was the word Estêvão used—betray.

After greeting the doctor and exchanging a few words with him, the man said goodbye, announcing that he was going to visit Madalena.

Estêvão trembled with satisfaction.

He watched his friend from a distance and saw him go into a house.

"So that's where she lives," he thought.

And he walked briskly away.

When he got home, he found a letter perfumed with sandalwood; the address was written in a neat, elegant, but unfamiliar hand.

He broke the seal.

This is what the letter said:

> We're having tea at my house tomorrow. It would give us great
> pleasure if you would care to spend a few hours with us. Madalena C.

Estêvão read and reread the note; he even made as if to raise it to his lips, but, ashamed of what seemed to him mere weakness, he simply gave the letter a peremptory sniff and put it in his pocket.

Estêvão was something of a fatalist.

"If I hadn't gone to that ball, I wouldn't have met that woman and I wouldn't be feeling as I do now, and I would have avoided either a misfortune or a joy, because both those things could come from this chance encounter. To be or not to be, as Hamlet said. Should I go to her house? It's only polite, after all. Yes, I must, but I will go prepared for everything. I must break with these ideas and resume my former tranquil existence."

He was still thinking all this when Meneses arrived at his house. He had come to take Estêvão out to supper, and they left together. On the way, Estêvão asked Meneses a few strange questions.

For example:

"Do you believe in fate, my friend? Do you think there is a good god and a bad god constantly engaged in a power struggle over our lives?"

"Fate is will," answered Meneses. "Each man makes his own fate."

"And yet we do have presentiments. Sometimes we have an inkling of events in which we did not even take part. Do you not think perhaps that some beneficent god is telling us these things?"

"You're speaking like a pagan, and I don't believe any of it. I do believe that my stomach is empty and that the best thing we can do is to have supper right here in the Hotel de Europa rather than going back to Rua do Lavradio."

They went into the hotel.

Various deputies were there, talking politics, and they all gathered around Meneses. Estêvão listened and responded, but without once forgetting the widow, the letter, and the smell of sandalwood.

There were some interesting contrasts between the general conversation and Estêvão's thoughts.

For example, a deputy would say:

"The government is overreaching itself, and the provinces can't take much more of it. Principle has been tossed out of the window. In my province alone, some subdelegates have been dismissed simply because they're relatives of mine; my son-in-law, who was director of finances, was thrown out and the post given to some dandy who's related by marriage to the Valadar family. I tell you I'm really going to lay into the opposition tomorrow."

Estêvão was looking at the deputy who was speaking, but in his head, he was saying this:

"Madalena really is beautiful, unbelievably beautiful. She has extraordinary eyes. Her hair is gorgeous too; everything about her is fascinating. I would be happy to have her as my wife, but who knows? And yet I feel that I *will* love her. It's irresistible. I have to love her. But what about her? What does she mean by that invitation? Does she love me?"

Estêvão was so immersed in these ideal thoughts, so distracted, that, when a deputy asked him if he didn't also find the whole situation grim and hopeless, he replied:

"Oh, yes, gorgeous!"

"Ah," said the deputy, "I see you're on the side of the ministers!"

Estêvão smiled, but Meneses frowned. He had understood everything.

V

When they left, the deputy said to the doctor:

"My friend, you've been disloyal to me . . ."

"Whatever do you mean?" asked Estêvão, half serious and half joking, not having understood the deputy's remark.

"Because," Meneses went on, "you have a secret you're not telling me."

"Me?"

"Yes, a secret love."

"Why do you say that?"

"I noticed just now that, while everyone else was discussing politics, you were thinking about a woman, a *gorgeous* woman."

Seeing that he had been found out, Estêvão did not deny it.

"It's true. I was thinking about a woman."

"And will I be the last to know?"

"Know what? There's no love, nothing. I happened to meet a woman who made a real impression on me, and I'm still thinking about her now. But it may well go no further than that. That's it. It's an unfinished chapter; a novel of which there is only the first page. I really think it will be difficult for me to fall in love."

"Why?"

"I don't know. I find it hard to believe in love."

Meneses looked hard at Estêvão and smiled, shaking his head:

"Look, leave disbelief to those who have already been disappointed in love; you're young and as yet know nothing of such disappointments. No one can be a skeptic at your age. Besides, if the woman is pretty, I wager you'll end up telling me a very different story."

"Possibly," said Estêvão.

And at the same time, he thought about Meneses's words, words that reminded him of what had happened at the Teatro Lírico.

Meanwhile, Estêvão duly went to Madalena's house. He was as meticulously dressed and perfumed as if he were going to visit his fiancée. What would come of that encounter? Would he emerge a free man or a slave? Estêvão could not help thinking that perhaps she loved him already, and the invitation seemed to him irrefutable proof of this. As he got into a cab, he began to build all kinds of castles in the air.

At last, he reached her house.

VI

Madalena was alone in the room with her small son.

No one else.

It was half-past nine.

"Am I too early?" he asked.

"You could never be too early."

Estêvão bowed, and Madalena went on:

"The reason I'm alone is because I felt a little unwell earlier and sent messages putting off the handful of people I'd invited."

"But I didn't receive a message . . ."

"That is because I didn't send you one. It was the first time I'd invited you, and I certainly didn't want to drive away such a distinguished gentleman."

Madalena's words were not even believable as the feeblest of excuses.

Estêvão realized at once that there must be some hidden motive.

Could it be love?

Estêvão thought that it was, and he was sorry, because, despite everything, he had imagined a more discreet, less precipitate passion. However pleasing this was, he did not want to be the object of her desires, and felt terribly embarrassed to be there with a woman with whom he was beginning to fall in love and who perhaps loved him. What could he say to her? It was the first time he had found himself in such a situation. There is every reason to think that, at the time, Estêvão would have preferred to be a hundred leagues from there, and yet, however far away he was, he would still be thinking about her.

Madalena was extraordinarily beautiful, and yet her face revealed her to be someone who has suffered greatly. She was tall and strong, and had a beautiful neck, magnificent arms, large brown eyes, and a mouth made for love.

At that moment, she was wearing a black dress. Black suited her.

Estêvão gazed on her with love and adoration; he heard her speak and felt enchanted and overwhelmed by a feeling he could not explain.

It was a mixture of love and fear.

Madalena was tactful and solicitous. She spoke of his many merits and his burgeoning reputation, and urged him to come and visit her occasionally.

At half-past ten, tea was served, and Estêvão stayed until eleven o'clock.

By the time he left, he was completely besotted. Madalena had yoked him to her cart, and the poor boy had no wish to cast off that yoke.

As he walked home, his head was full of plans: he could see himself married to her, beloved and loving, provoking envy everywhere, and, more importantly, happy in himself.

When he reached his house, he thought he should write a letter to send to Meneses the next day. He wrote five and tore all of them up.

Finally, he wrote this very simple note:

> *My friend, you were quite right; at my age, no one is a skeptic; we believe. I believe and I am in love. I never would have thought it possible, but it's true. I am in love. Would you like to know who I'm in love with? I will take you to her house. You'll find her very pretty—because she is!*

The letter said many more things, but they were all basically a gloss on the same idea.

Estêvão went back to Madalena's house, and became a regular, assiduous visitor.

The widow treated him so kindly that it was impossible to doubt the feelings that lay behind that kindness. That at least is what Estêvão thought. She was nearly always alone, and he delighted in listening to her talk. They were growing closer and closer.

On only his second visit, Estêvão spoke to her about Meneses and asked permission to introduce her to him. She said she would be delighted to receive any of his friends, but asked him to postpone any introductions for the moment. He accepted everything Madalena asked or thought and so said nothing more.

As was only natural, when his visits to the widow grew more frequent, his visits to his friend became less so.

Meneses did not complain; he understood and said to Estêvão:

"Don't apologize, that's the way things are. Friendship must give way to love. I just want you to be happy."

One day, Estêvão asked his friend why he no longer believed in love, and if he had suffered some great misfortune.

"No, not at all," said Meneses.

Then, realizing that the doctor deserved his confidence and might not believe him, he added:

"No, why deny it? I did suffer a great misfortune. I, too, loved, but did not find sweetness and dignity in love. Anyway, it's a personal tragedy of which I prefer not to speak. I have to accept it."

VII

"When would you like me to introduce you to my friend Meneses?" Estêvão asked Madalena one night.

"Oh, yes, that's right. Well, one of these days. I see you are a great friend of his."

"Yes, we're very close."

"True friends?"

"Yes, true friends."

Madalena smiled, continuing to play with her son's hair, and planting a kiss on his forehead.

The boy laughed gaily and hugged his mother.

The idea of becoming the child's honorary father surfaced in Estêvão's mind. He looked at him, called to him, stroked him, and kissed him on exactly the same spot where Madalena's lips had rested.

Estêvão could play the piano and, at Madalena's request, he would sometimes play something for her.

In these and other amusements the hours passed; love, however, did not progress one step.

They could have been two volcanoes ready to erupt, but, so far, there was no sign of this.

Estêvão found the situation very awkward, discouraging, and painful, but whenever he considered taking decisive action, this was precisely when he revealed himself at his most craven and cowardly.

It was the first time he had been in love, and he didn't even know what words to choose.

One day, he resolved to write to her.

"That's the best way," he thought. "A letter is eloquent and has the great advantage of keeping a certain distance."

He went into his study and began a letter.

He spent an hour on this, lingering long over every sentence. He wanted to avoid being classified as either foolish or sensual. He didn't want the letter to suggest any frivolous or bad feelings; he wanted to show himself as pure as he was.

Ah, but how often events intervene. Estêvão was still rereading and correcting the letter when a good friend of his arrived. His name was Oliveira and he was said to be Rio de Janeiro's foremost dandy.

He entered, carrying a roll of paper.

Estêvão immediately hid his letter.

"Hello, Estêvão," said Oliveira. "What were you writing just now? Something libelous or a love letter?"

"Neither," Estêvão replied tartly.

"I have some news for you."

"What?"

"I've become a writer."

"Really?"

"Yes, and I have come to read you my first comedy."

"Oh, please, no!" cried Estêvão, getting up.

"You must hear at least a few scenes, my friend. Are you not going to encourage me in my new career? Come on, just a couple of scenes. That's not much to ask."

Estêvão sat down again.

The playwright went on:

"Or perhaps you'd prefer to hear a speech from my tragedy entitled *Brutus's Dagger* . . ."

"No, no, I'd rather hear the comedy—much less bloodthirsty. Come on, then, on with it."

Oliveira unfurled the roll of paper, sorted out the various pages, and began to read what follows in a slow, nasal voice:

Scene I

CÉSAR (*entering stage right*)
JOÃO (*entering stage left*)

CÉSAR

Why's the door closed! Is the mistress up already?

JOÃO

Yes, she is, but she's not feeling well.

CÉSAR

What's wrong with her?

JOÃO

She's . . . she's not feeling well.

CÉSAR

Oh, I see. (*To himself*) The usual thing. (*To João*) So what's today's remedy, then?

JOÃO

Today's remedy? (*After a pause*) I don't know.

CÉSAR

Never mind. Off you go.

Scene II

CÉSAR, FREITAS (*entering stage right*)

CÉSAR

Good day, Mr. Advocate . . .

FREITAS

. . . An advocate in pursuit of lost causes. They're the only kind that interest me, after all, trying to pursue a cause that isn't lost would be absurd. How's my client?

CÉSAR

João tells me she's feeling unwell.

FREITAS

Too unwell even to see you?

CÉSAR

Yes, even me. But why are you looking at me like that? Are you jealous?

FREITAS

No, it's not jealousy, it's admiration. Normally, no one really suits the name they were given, but in your case, Senhor César, you cannot, God bless you, deny that yours is a significant name, and that you are trying to be in the world of love what that other Caesar was on the battlefield.

CÉSAR

Is this how advocates usually speak?

FREITAS

Occasionally. (*Going to sit down*) Are you surprised?

CÉSAR (*taking out his cigar case*)

Yes, I'm surprised . . . Would you care for a cigar?

FREITAS

Thank you, no, I'll take a pinch of snuff instead. (*Takes out his snuff box*) Will you join me?

CÉSAR

No, thank you.

FREITAS (*sitting down*)

My client's case is going swimmingly. The other party is calling for a ten-day adjournment, but I'm going to—

CÉSAR

That's fine, Senhor Freitas, you can spare me the rest, unless you choose not to bore me with legal jargon. In short, she's going to win?

FREITAS

Of course. If she can prove that—

CÉSAR

She's winning, that's what matters.

FREITAS

How could she not, given that I'm involved . . .

CÉSAR

So much the better.

FREITAS

I can't recall ever having lost a case; that is, I did lose one, but only because, on the very eve of victory, my client said he wanted to lose. No sooner said than done. I proved the opposite of what I'd already proved, and lost . . . or, rather, won, because losing like that is the same as winning.

CÉSAR

You are the doyen of advocates.

FREITAS (*modestly*)

You're too kind . . .

CÉSAR

What about conscience, though?

FREITAS

Whose conscience?

CÉSAR

Yours, of course!

FREITAS

Mine! Oh, that always wins too.

CÉSAR (*getting up*)

Really?

FREITAS (*remaining seated*)

Do you have a case you'd like to bring?

CÉSAR

No, no, not at all, but when I have, rest assured I will knock at your
door . . .

FREITAS

I am at your disposal, sir.

VIII

Estêvão brought the reading to an abrupt halt, which greatly upset the novice poet. This poor candidate to the muses tried to plead with him, but
Estêvão would not be moved, and the only concession he made was a promise to read the play later.

Oliveira had to content himself with this, but would not leave until he
had recited from memory a speech by the protagonist of his tragedy, long,
complicated verses topped off with a stanza of lyric poetry, in the style of
Victor Hugo's "Les Djinns."

Then he left.

Meanwhile, time had passed.

Estêvão reread his letter and still wanted to send it, but his poet friend's
interruption had proved useful, for, on rereading the letter yet again, Estêvão
found it cold and empty; the language was very passionate, but in no way did
it describe the fire in his heart.

"It's pointless," he said, tearing the letter into pieces, "the human tongue will always be impotent when it comes to expressing certain feelings of the soul; what I wrote was so cold, and quite different from what I actually feel. I'm condemned to say nothing or to say it badly. When I'm with her, I feel too weak, too feeble . . ."

Estêvão went over to the window just as a former colleague of his was walking past in the street below, arm in arm with a woman, a very pretty woman, whom he had married the month before.

They both looked so happy and content.

Estêvão contemplated the scene sadly and adoringly. Marriage was no longer the impossibility he had spoken of when he had only ideas, not feelings. Now it was something that could become a reality.

The couple who had just passed gave him new energy.

"I need to put an end to this," he said, "I must go to her and tell her that I love her, adore her, and want to be her husband. She will love me, if she doesn't already, but, yes, she does love me . . ."

And he got dressed, ready to go out.

As he was pulling on his gloves and glancing at the clock, the houseboy brought him a letter.

It was from Madalena.

> *I do hope, my dear doctor, that you will come and see me today. Yesterday, I waited for you in vain. I need to talk to you.*

Estêvão was in such a hurry to leave and wanted so urgently to be with Madalena that he only finished reading this note when he was halfway down the stairs.

What he didn't want to lose was that glimmer of courage.

He left.

When he reached Madalena's house, she was standing at the window, watching for him. She welcomed him warmly, as she always did. Estêvão apologized as best he could for failing to appear on the previous evening, adding that it had pained him deeply not to be there.

What better opportunity to throw in the bombshell of a frank and passionate declaration of love? He hesitated for a few seconds longer, then, screwing up all his courage, he was about to go on, when she said to him:

"I wanted to see you in order to tell you something important, something that I could only tell a man of honor like yourself."

Estêvão turned pale.

"Do you know where I saw you for the first time?"

"At the ball."

"No, it was before that. At the Teatro Lírico."

"Ah!"

"You were with your friend Meneses."

"Yes, we did go there a few times."

Madalena then launched into a long explanation, to which he listened unblinking, but, at the same time, turning paler still and feeling deeply troubled. Her final words were:

"As you see, sir, such things can only be confided to a great soul. Small souls could not understand them. If I deserve anything, and if this confidence can be repaid with a kind act, then I ask you to do as I request."

The doctor covered his eyes with his hand and said only:

"But—"

At that moment, Madalena's little boy came into the room; she got up and led him by the hand to where Estêvão Soares was sitting.

"If not for me, then for the sake of this innocent child!"

The child, all uncomprehending, threw himself into Estêvão's arms. Estêvão kissed him on the forehead and said to the widow:

"If I hesitated, it was not because I doubted the truth of what you have just told me, but because it is a very difficult mission you entrust me with. I promise, though, that I will carry it out to the best of my ability."

IX

Estêvão left Madalena's house with unsteady step and clouded gaze and filled with all kinds of contradictory feelings. His conversation with Madalena had been a long ordeal, and that final promise a decisive, mortal blow. Estêvão left there like a man who has just murdered his own burgeoning hopes; he walked aimlessly, he needed both to breathe fresh air and to be in a darkened room, to be alone and, at the same time, in the midst of a vast crowd.

On the way, he met Oliveira, the novice poet.

He recalled that Oliveira's reading of his play had prevented him from sending the letter and thereby spared him the saddest of disappointments.

He found himself embracing the poet with all his heart.

Oliveira returned his embrace, and, when he could finally detach himself from the doctor's arms, said:

"Thank you, my friend. Such a show of enthusiasm is most affecting. I have always thought of you as a great judge of literature, and the proof that you have just given me is both a consolation and an encouragement; it consoles me for what I have already suffered, and encourages me to embark on new ventures. If Torquato Tasso—"

Feeling a speech threatening, and especially given his friend's misinterpretation of his embrace, Estêvão resolved to continue on his way and to abandon the poet.

"I'm sorry, I'm in a hurry. Goodbye."

"Goodbye and thank you!"

Estêvão reached his own house and flung himself down on the bed. No one ever knew this—and only the walls of his room were witnesses—but the truth is that Estêvão wept bitter tears.

So what was it that Madalena had told him and asked of him?

The widow was not a widow; she was Meneses's wife. She had traveled down from the North a few months before her husband, who only came to Rio to carry out his duties as a deputy. Meneses, who loved her madly and whose love was requited with equal fervor, had accused her of being unfaithful, citing a letter and a portrait as evidence. She had denied this, but explained herself very badly. Her husband left and sent her off to the capital.

Madalena accepted the situation with resignation and courage; she neither complained nor begged; she did as her husband ordered.

And yet Madalena was not guilty of the crime, which was only a crime in appearance; she was condemned because she had behaved honorably. The letter and the portrait did not belong to her; they had, imprudently and fatally, been left in her safekeeping. Madalena could have told her husband everything, but that would have meant breaking a promise, and she did not want that. She preferred the domestic storm to fall only on her.

Now, however, the need to keep the secret had passed. Madalena had received word from the North, in which her friend, on her deathbed, asked her to destroy both the letter and the portrait or to return them to the man who had given them to her. This was enough to justify Madalena's confession.

Madalena could have sent the letter to her husband, or asked to meet him, but she was afraid. She knew it would be useless, because Meneses could be very rigid.

She had seen Estêvão one night at the theater in company with her husband; she had made inquiries and learned that they were friends; she was
asking him, then, to mediate between them, to save her and restore a family's happiness.

It was not, therefore, only Estêvão's love that was wounded, it was his
amour propre too. He realized at once that he had been invited to that
house for one reason alone. It's true that the letter had only arrived the
day before, but this had merely hastened the resolution of the situation.
Madalena would doubtless have asked him to perform some similar service
even if she hadn't received the letter.

Had it been any other man, Estêvão would have refused to help the
"widow," but it was his friend, a man to whom he owed both esteem and the
duties of friendship.

And so he accepted that cruel mission.

"So be it," he said, "I have to drive the woman I love into the arms of
another, and, even worse, far from taking pleasure in being able to restore
domestic harmony, I find myself in the dreadful position of being in love
with my friend's wife, and for that there is only one solution—to go far
away . . ."

Estêvão stayed at home for the rest of that day.

He considered writing to the deputy and telling him everything, then
thought it would be better to talk to him face-to-face. This would be more
difficult, but more effective if he was to keep his promise.

However, he put this off until the following day, or, rather, the same
day, since the night did not interrupt the flow of time, given that he did not
sleep a wink.

X

The poor lover left his bed as the sun was rising.

He wanted to read the newspapers and asked for them to be brought
to him.

He was just setting them aside, having read all he wanted, when he suddenly saw his own name in the *Jornal do Commercio*.

It was a commissioned article, a puff, entitled *A Masterpiece*.

This is what the article said:

It is with pleasure that we announce to the nation the imminent appearance of an excellent new comedy written by a young writer from Rio de Janeiro called Antônio Carlos de Oliveira.

This robust talent, long unrecognized, is finally about to enter the sea of public life, and to this end he wanted to try his hand at writing a substantial work.

We understand that only days ago, the author, at the request of his many friends, read the play in the house of Dr. Estêvão Soares, before an illustrious audience, who applauded loudly and proclaimed Senhor Oliveira as a future Shakespeare.

Dr. Estêvão Soares was kind enough to ask to read the play again, and yesterday, when he met Senhor Oliveira in the street, he embraced him warmly, to the general amazement of numerous passersby.

Coming from such a fine judge of literature, this embrace speaks volumes about Senhor Oliveira's talent.

We are ourselves keen to read Senhor Oliveira's play and are sure that it will make the fortune of any theater that puts it on.

A Lover of Literature

Despite all the other emotions churning inside him, this article enraged Estêvão. There could be no doubt that the author of the article must also be the author of the play. His embrace had been misinterpreted, and the so-called poet had used it to his advantage. If he had at least omitted Estêvão's name, that might have excused the writer's foolish vanity, but his name was there as an accomplice to the play.

Setting aside the newspaper, Estêvão decided to write a letter of protest and was just about to do so, when he received a note from Oliveira.

This is what the note said:

Dear Estêvão,

A friend of mine decided to write something about my play. I told him I had read the play to you, and explained that, despite your keen desire to hear the whole thing, you had to rush off to tend to a patient. Despite this, the aforementioned friend decided to reveal all in today's Jornal do Commercio, *very slightly tampering with the truth. Forgive him: he meant well.*

Yesterday, I arrived home, feeling so proud of your embrace that I wrote an ode, my lyric vein rising to the surface after the comic and the tragic. Here it is—in draft form. If it's no good, simply tear it up.

The letter bore yesterday's date.

The ode was very long, and Estêvão didn't even bother to read it, but hurled it down.

The ode began thus:

Leave your mountain peak, O muse!
Come, inspire the poet's lyre;
Fill with light my bold brow,
And let us send into eternity,
On the wings of a resounding ode,
The encouraging embrace of friendship!

I sing not of Achilles' lofty deeds
Nor do I hail the clamorous beat
Of martial drums on battlefields!
No, another matter inspires my pen.
I sing not of the death-dealing sword,
I sing of the embrace that gives life and glory!

XI

As promised, Estêvão set off immediately in search of Meneses. Instead of coming straight to the point, he wanted, initially, to sound him out as regards his past. It was the first time he had touched on the matter. Meneses, all unsuspecting, was merely taken a little by surprise; however, such was his confidence in his friend that he could refuse him nothing.

"I've always thought," Estêvão said, "that there must have been some kind of drama in your life. This may be a mistake on my part, but I can't get the idea out of my head."

"Yes, there was a drama of sorts, one that was booed off the stage. No, don't smile. That's the truth. What do you imagine it might have been?"

"I've no idea, I imagine . . ."

"You expect drama from a politician?"

"Why not?"

"I'll tell you. I both am and am not a politician. I didn't enter public life out of any kind of vocation; I entered it as one enters a tomb: in order to sleep better. Why did I do this? Because of the drama you speak of."

"A woman, perhaps . . ."

"Yes, a woman."

"Perhaps," said Estêvão, attempting a smile, "even a wife?"

Meneses trembled and looked at his friend, alarmed and suspicious now.

"Who told you that?"

"I was merely asking a question."

"Yes, it was my wife, but I'll say no more. You're the first person to have wheedled so much out of me. The past is past, it's dead: *parce sepultis*."

"Possibly," said Estêvão, "and what if I belonged to a philosophical sect intent on reviving the dead, even a dead past . . . ?"

"Your words either mean a great deal or nothing at all. What are you getting at?"

"I don't intend to revive the past, but to repair it, to restore it to its former glory, as is only right. My object is to tell you, my dear friend, that the condemned woman is, in fact, innocent."

When he heard these words, Meneses gave a faint gasp.

Then, springing to his feet, he asked Estêvão to tell him what he knew and how.

Estêvão told him everything.

When he finished, the deputy shook his head in disbelief, the last symptom of incredulity, which is the lingering echo of great domestic catastrophes.

Estêvão, though, was prepared for his friend's objections. He energetically defended the wife, and urged Meneses to do his duty.

Meneses's final response was this:

"My dear Estêvão, Caesar's wife should always be above suspicion. I believe what you say, but what's done is done."

"That's a very harsh principle, my friend."

"But inevitable."

Estêvão left.

When he was alone, Meneses sat, sunk in thought; he believed what

Estêvão had said, and he loved his wife, but he could not believe there could be a return to those happier days.

By refusing to believe, he thought, he could stay in the tomb where he had slept so peacefully.

Estêvão, however, did not give up.

When he got home, he wrote a long letter to the deputy, urging him to go back to his family, which had been so briefly and unnecessarily torn asunder. Estêvão was very eloquent, and it took little to convince Meneses's heart.

The doctor proved himself extremely able in this diplomatic mission. After a few days, the clouds of the past had dissipated and the couple were reunited.

How?

Madalena learned of her husband's intentions, and received a warning that he was about to visit.

Just as the deputy was preparing to leave for her house, he was told that a lady was asking for him.

The lady was Madalena.

Meneses did not even attempt to embrace her, but knelt at her feet.

All was forgotten.

Wanting to celebrate this reconciliation, they invited Estêvão to spend the day with them, for to him they owed their happiness.

Estêvão did not go.

The following day, though, Meneses received this note:

Forgive me, my friend, for not coming to say goodbye to you in person. I have to leave for Minas immediately. I will return in a few months.

I hope you will both be happy and will not forget me.

Meneses rushed to Estêvão's house, where he found him packing for his journey.

Meneses found this urgency very odd and the note still odder, but the doctor said nothing of the real motive for his departure.

When Meneses returned, he told his wife what had happened and asked her if she could understand it.

"No," she answered.

But she had, at last, understood.

"A noble soul," she said to herself.

But she said nothing to her husband, and in this she revealed herself to be a wife concerned for their conjugal peace, and, above all, a woman.

Meneses did not go to the house for many days after this, and left as soon as he could for the North.

His absence upset a number of votes and his departure thwarted many schemes.

However, a man has the right to seek his own happiness, and Meneses's happiness was independent of politics.

AUGUSTA'S SECRET

I

IT'S ELEVEN O'CLOCK in the morning.

Dona Augusta Vasconcelos is reclining on a sofa with a book in her hand. Adelaide, her daughter, is tinkering at the piano.

"Is Papa up yet?" Adelaide asked her mother.

"No," Dona Augusta said, without glancing up from her book.

Adelaide left the piano and went over to her mother.

"But it's so late, Mama," she said. "It's eleven o'clock. Papa does sleep a lot."

Augusta put the book down on her lap and, looking at Adelaide, said:

"That's because he came home very late."

"I've noticed that now Papa's never here to kiss me good night when I go to bed. He's always out somewhere."

Augusta smiled.

"You're still such a country bumpkin," she said. "You go to bed at the same time as the chickens. Things are different here. Your father has things to do at night."

"Is it to do with politics, Mama?" asked Adelaide.

"I don't know," said Augusta.

I began by saying that Adelaide was Augusta's daughter, and this information, so necessary to the story, was no less necessary in reality, because, at first sight, no one would ever have thought they were mother and daughter; Vasconcelos's wife was so young that mother and daughter looked more like sisters.

Augusta was thirty and Adelaide fifteen, but, comparatively speaking, the mother looked even younger than the daughter. She still had all the freshness of a fifteen-year-old, as well as something that Adelaide lacked: an awareness of her own beauty and youth, an awareness that would have been praiseworthy were it not combined with a vanity that was as immense as it was deep. She was of only average height, but nevertheless cut an imposing figure. Her skin was, at once, very pale and very rosy. She had brown hair and green eyes. Her long, shapely hands seemed made for loving caresses. Augusta, however, put her hands to better use, covering them in soft kid gloves.

All of Augusta's graces were there in Adelaide, but in embryonic form. You could tell that, by the time Adelaide was twenty, she would rival Augusta; meanwhile, she still retained certain childish qualities that somewhat masked those natural gifts.

And yet a man could easily have fallen in love with her, especially if he was a poet with a liking for fifteen-year-old virgins, perhaps because she was rather pale, and poets down the ages have always had a weakness for pale women.

Augusta dressed with supreme elegance, and while she did spend a lot of money on clothes, she made the most of those enormous expenditures, if one could describe it as "making the most" of them. To be fair, though, Augusta never haggled, she always paid the asking price for everything. She was proud of this, and felt that to behave otherwise was ridiculous and low-class.

In this, Augusta both shared the sentiments and served the interests of certain traders, who agreed that it would be dishonorable to beat them down on the price of their merchandise.

Whenever they spoke of this, Augusta's draper would tell her:

"Asking one price and then selling the product for a lower price is tantamount to confessing that you intended to swindle your customer."

The draper preferred to do so without confessing to anything.

And again to be fair to Augusta, we must acknowledge that she spared no expense in ensuring that Adelaide was always dressed as elegantly as she herself was.

And this was no small task.

From the age of five, Adelaide had been brought up in the country by some of Augusta's relatives, who were more interested in growing coffee than in spending money on clothes, and Adelaide grew up with those habits and those ideas. This is why arriving in Rio to rejoin her family proved to be a real transformation. She passed from one civilization to another; she lived through several years in the space of one hour. Fortunately for her, she had an excellent teacher in her mother. Adelaide changed, and on the day this story begins, she was already quite different, although still a long way behind her mother.

As Augusta was answering her daughter's curious question about what Vasconcelos actually did at night, a carriage drew up at the front door.

Adelaide ran to the window.

"It's Dona Carlota, Mama," she said.

A few minutes later, Dona Carlota entered the room. To introduce readers to this new character, I need say only that she was like a volume two of Augusta: beautiful, like her; elegant, like her; vain, like her, which is to say that they were the very best of enemies.

Carlota had come to ask Augusta to sing at a concert she was planning to give at home, a concert dreamed up purely as an opportunity to show off her magnificent new dress.

Augusta gladly accepted.

"How's your husband?" she asked Carlota.

"He's gone into town. And yours?"

"He's sleeping."

"The sleep of the just?" asked Carlota with a mischievous smile.

"Apparently," said Augusta.

At this point, Adelaide, who, at Carlota's request, had gone over to the piano to play a nocturne, rejoined them.

Augusta's friend said to her:

"I bet you've already got a sweetheart in your sights."

Greatly embarrassed, Adelaide blushed deeply and said:

"Don't say such things."

"I'm sure you do; either that or you're getting to the age when you certainly will have a sweetheart, and I'm telling you now that he'll be very handsome."

"It's still too early for that," said Augusta.

"Early!"

"Yes, she's only a child. She'll get married when she's ready, but that won't be for a while yet."

"I see," said Carlota, laughing, "you want to prepare her. And I entirely approve, but in that case, don't take her dolls away from her."

"Oh, she's given up dolls already."

"Then it will be very hard to fend off any sweethearts. One thing replaces the other."

Augusta smiled, and Carlota got up to leave.

"Are you going already?" said Augusta.

"Yes, I must. Bye-bye."

"'Bye!"

They exchanged kisses, and Carlota left.

Immediately afterward, two delivery boys arrived: one bearing some dresses and the other a novel, all of which had been ordered the day before. The dresses had cost a fortune, and the book was Ernest-Aimé Feydeau's novel *Fanny*, a satire on society manners.

II

At about one in the afternoon that same day, Vasconcelos rose from his bed.

He was about forty, good-looking, and endowed with a magnificent pair of graying side-whiskers, which gave him the air of a diplomat, something that he was a million miles from being. He had a smiling, expansive face, and positively oozed robust health.

He possessed a decent fortune and did not work, or, rather, he worked very hard at squandering said fortune, with his wife as enthusiastic collaborator.

Adelaide had been quite right about her father; he went to bed late, always woke up after midday, and left again in the evening, only to return the following morning in the early hours, which is to say that he made regular brief visits to the family home.

Only one person had the right to demand that Vasconcelos become a more assiduous visitor, and that was Augusta; but she said nothing. They got on well enough, though, because the husband, as a reward for his wife's tolerant behavior, denied her nothing and every whim of hers was quickly granted.

If Vasconcelos could not accompany her to every outing and every ball, a brother of his stood in for him; Lourenço was a commander of two different orders, an opposition politician, an excellent player of ombre, and, in his few moments of leisure, a most amiable fellow. He was what might be described as "an awkward so-and-so," at least as regards his brother, for while he obeyed his sister-in-law's every order, he would address the occasional admonitory sermon to his brother. Good seed that fell on stony ground.

Anyway, Vasconcelos had eventually woken up, and he woke in a good mood. His daughter was very pleased to see him; he spoke to his wife most affably, and she responded in kind.

"Why do you always wake up so late?" asked Adelaide, stroking his side-whiskers.

"Because I go to bed late."

"But why do you go to bed late?"

"What a lot of questions!" said Vasconcelos, smiling.

Then he went on:

"I go to bed late because my political duties require it. You don't know what politics is: it's something very ugly, but very necessary."

"I *do* know what politics is!" said Adelaide.

"All right, then, tell me."

"In the country, whenever they were beating up the magistrate, they always used to say that the motive was political, which I thought was really odd, because politically speaking, not beating him up would have made much more sense . . ."

Vasconcelos laughed out loud at his daughter's remark, and was just going off to have his breakfast when in came his brother, who could not resist saying:

"A fine time to be having breakfast!"

"Don't you start. I have my breakfast whenever I feel like it. Don't try and pin me down to certain hours and certain meanings. Call it breakfast or lunch, I don't mind, but whatever it is, I'm going to eat it."

Lourenço responded by pulling a face.

When breakfast was over, Senhor Batista arrived. Vasconcelos received him in his private study.

Batista was twenty-five and the typical man-about-town; excellent company at a supper attended by rather dubious guests, but absolutely useless in respectable company. He was witty and quite intelligent, but he had to be in the right situation for these qualities to be revealed. Otherwise, he was handsome, sported a fine mustache, wore expensive shoes, and dressed impeccably; he also smoked like a trooper, but smoked only the finest cigars.

"Only just woken up, have you?" Batista asked as he went into Vasconcelos's study.

"Yes, about three-quarters of an hour ago. I've just finished breakfast. Have a cigar."

Batista took one and sat down in a chair, while Vasconcelos struck a match.

"Have you seen Gomes?" asked Vasconcelos.

"Yes, I saw him yesterday. The big news is that he's given up society life."

"Really?"

"When I asked him why he hadn't been seen for over a month, he told me he was undergoing a transformation, and that the Gomes he was will live on only as a memory. Incredible though it may seem, he appeared to mean it."

"I don't believe him. He's having a joke at our expense. Any other news?"

"None, not unless you've heard any."

"Not a peep."

"Come on! Didn't you go to the Jardim yesterday?"

"Yes, there was a supper on there . . ."

"A family do, eh? I was at the Alcazar. What time did that 'family supper' end?"

"At four in the morning."

Vasconcelos lay down in a hammock, and the conversation continued along the same lines, until a houseboy came to tell Vasconcelos that Senhor Gomes was in the parlor.

"Ah, the man himself!" said Batista.

"Tell him to come up," ordered Vasconcelos.

The houseboy went back downstairs, but Gomes only joined them a quarter of an hour later, having spent some time chatting with Augusta and Adelaide.

"Well, long time no see," said Vasconcelos when Gomes finally entered the room.

"You haven't exactly searched me out," Gomes retorted.

"Excuse me, but I've been to your house twice, and twice they told me you were out."

"That was pure bad luck, because I hardly ever go out now."

"So you've become a hermit, have you?"

"I'm a chrysalis at the moment, and will reemerge as a butterfly," said Gomes, sitting down.

"Poetry, eh? Watch out, Vasconcelos."

This new character, the longed-for, long-lost Gomes, appeared to be about thirty. He, Vasconcelos, and Batista were a trinity of pleasure and dissipation, bound together by an indissoluble friendship. When, about a month before, Gomes stopped appearing in the usual circles, everyone noticed, but only Vasconcelos and Batista really felt his absence. However, they did not try too hard to drag Gomes out of his solitude, in case there was some ulterior motive on his part.

Nevertheless, they greeted Gomes like the prodigal son.

"Where have you been hiding? What's all this business about chrysalises and butterflies? Who do you think you're fooling?"

"No, really, my friends. I'm growing wings."

"Wings!" said Batista, trying not to laugh.

"Only if they're the wings of a sparrow-hawk ready to pounce on its prey . . ."

"No, I'm serious."

And Gomes seemed absolutely genuine.

Vasconcelos and Batista exchanged a sideways glance.

"Well, if it's true, tell us about these wings of yours and where exactly you want to fly," said Vasconcelos, and Batista added:

"Yes, you owe us an explanation, and if we, your family council, think it a good explanation, we will give our approval. If not, there'll be no wings for you, and you'll go back to being what you've always been."

"I second that," said Vasconcelos.

"It's quite simple. I'm growing angel's wings so that I can fly up into the heaven of love."

"Love!" exclaimed his two friends.

"Yes, love," said Gomes. "What have I been up until now? A complete wastrel, a total debauchee, squandering both my fortune and my heart. But is that enough to fill a life? I don't think so."

"I agree, it isn't enough, there needs to be something else, but the difference lies in how . . ."

"Exactly," said Vasconcelos, "exactly. It's only natural that the two of you will think otherwise, but I believe I'm right in saying that without a chaste, pure love, life is a mere desert."

Batista gave a start.

Vasconcelos fixed his eyes on Gomes.

"You're thinking of getting married, aren't you?" he said.

"I don't know about marriage, I only know that I'm in love and hope one day to marry the woman I love."

"Marry!" cried Batista.

And he let out a loud guffaw.

Gomes was so serious, though, and insisted so gravely on his plans for his own regeneration, that the two friends ended up listening with equal seriousness.

Gomes was speaking a strange language, entirely new on the lips of a man who, at any dionysian or aphrodisiac feast, was always the wildest and rowdiest of guests.

"So, you're leaving us, then?" said Vasconcelos.

"Me? Yes and no. You will find me in certain salons, but never again will we meet in theaters or in houses of ill repute."

"*De profundis . . .*" sang Batista.

"May we at least know where and who your Marion is?" asked Vasconcelos.

"She's not a Marion, she's a Virginie. At first I merely felt fond of her, then fondness became love and is now out-and-out passion. I fought it for as long as I could, but lay down my arms in the face of a far more potent force. My great fear was that I would not have a soul worthy to be offered to this gentle creature, but I do, a soul as fiery and pure as it was when I was eighteen. Only the chaste eyes of a virgin could have discovered the divine pearl beneath the mud in my soul. I am being reborn a far better man than I was."

"The boy's clearly insane, Vasconcelos. We should pack him off to the lunatic asylum this minute, and just in case he should suffer some new attack of madness, I'll leave right now."

"Where are you going?" asked Gomes.

"I have things to do, but I'll come and see you shortly. I want to find out if there's still time to haul you out of the abyss."

And with that he left.

III

Once they were alone, Vasconcelos asked:

"So you really are in love?"

"Yes, I am. I knew you'd find that hard to believe; I myself don't quite believe it, and yet it's true. I'm ending up where you began. For better or worse? For better, I think."

"Do you intend to conceal the person's name?"

"I'll conceal it from everyone but you."

"You clearly trust me, then . . ."

Gomes smiled.

"No," he said, "it's a necessary condition. You, above all men, should know the name of my heart's chosen one, for she's your daughter."

"Adelaide?" asked Vasconcelos in astonishment.

"Yes, your daughter."

This revelation was a real bombshell. Vasconcelos had never suspected such a thing.

"Do you approve?" asked Gomes.

Vasconcelos was thinking, and, after a few moments of silence, he said:

"My heart approves of your choice; you're my friend, you're in love, and as long as she loves you . . ."

Gomes was about to speak, but, smiling, Vasconcelos went on:

"But what about society?"

"What society?"

"The society that believes both you and me to be libertines; they're hardly going to approve."

"So that's a no, is it?" said Gomes sadly.

"No, it's not, you fool! It's an objection you could rebut by declaring that society is a great slanderer and famously indiscreet. My daughter is yours, on one condition."

"Which is?"

"Reciprocity. Does she love you?"

"I don't know."

"So you're not sure . . ."

"I really don't know, I only know that I love her and would give my life for her, but I have no idea if my feelings are requited."

"They will be. I'll test the waters. In two days' time, I'll give you my answer. To think you could be my son-in-law . . ."

Gomes's response was to fall into his friend's arms. The scene was verging on the comic when three o'clock struck. Gomes remembered that he'd arranged to meet another friend. Vasconcelos remembered that he had to write some letters.

Gomes left without speaking to the two ladies.

At about four o'clock, Vasconcelos was preparing to go out, when he was told that Senhor José Brito had come to see him.

When he heard this name, the normally jovial Vasconcelos frowned.

Shortly afterward, Senhor José Brito entered his study.

Senhor José Brito was, as far as Vasconcelos was concerned, a specter, an echo from the abyss, the voice of reality—a creditor.

"I wasn't expecting to see you today," said Vasconcelos.

"I'm surprised," answered Senhor José Brito with a kind of piercing calm, "because today is the twenty-first."

"I thought it was the nineteenth," stammered Vasconcelos.

"The day before yesterday it was, but today is the twenty-first. Look," said the creditor, picking up the *Jornal do Commercio* lying on a chair, "Thursday the twenty-first."

"Have you come for the money?"

"Here's the bill of exchange," said Senhor José Brito, taking his wallet out of his pocket and a piece of paper out of the wallet.

"Why didn't you come earlier?" asked Vasconcelos, trying to put off the evil hour.

"I came at eight o'clock this morning," replied the creditor, "and you were asleep; I came at nine, *idem*; I came at ten, *idem*; I came at eleven, *idem*; I came at noon, *idem*. I could have come at one o'clock, but I had to send a man to prison and I couldn't get away any earlier. At three, I had my dinner, and here I am at four o'clock."

Vasconcelos took a puff on his cigar to see if he could come up with some clever way of avoiding making a payment he had not been expecting.

Nothing occurred to him, but then the creditor himself gave him an opening.

"Besides," he said, "the time hardly matters, since I was sure you would pay me."

"Ah," said Vasconcelos, "that explains it. I wasn't expecting you today, you see, and so I don't have the money with me."

"What's to be done, then?" asked the creditor innocently.

Vasconcelos felt a glimmer of hope.

"You could wait until tomorrow."

"Ah, tomorrow I'm hoping to be present at the confiscation of assets from an individual I took to court for a very large debt, so I'm afraid I can't . . ."

"I see, well, in that case, I'll bring the money to your house."

"That would be fine if business worked like that. If we were friends, then obviously I would accept your promise and it would all be settled tomorrow, but I'm your creditor, and my one aim is to protect my own interests. Therefore, I think it would be best if you paid me today."

Vasconcelos smoothed his hair with one hand.

"But I don't have the money!" he said.

"Yes, that must be very awkward for you, but it doesn't upset me in the least; that is, it ought to upset me a little, because you clearly find yourself in a very precarious situation."

"Do I?"

"Indeed. Your properties in Rua da Imperatriz are mortgaged up to the hilt; the house in Rua de São Pedro was sold, and the money from the sale long since spent; your slaves have all left one by one, without you even noticing, and you recently spent a vast amount on setting up house for a certain lady of dubious reputation. You see, I know it all. More than you do yourself."

Vasconcelos was visibly terrified.

The creditor was telling the truth.

"But," said Vasconcelos, "what are we to do?"

"That's easy enough, we double the debt, and you give me a deposit right now."

"Double the debt, but that's—"

"Throwing you a lifeline. I'm really being very reasonable. Come on, say yes. Write me a note for the deposit now and we'll tear up the bill of exchange."

Vasconcelos tried to object, but it was impossible to convince Senhor José Brito.

He signed a note for eighteen *contos*.

When his creditor left, Vasconcelos began thinking seriously about his life.

Up until then, he had spent so wildly and so blindly that he hadn't noticed the abyss he himself had dug beneath his feet.

It had taken the voice of one of his executioners to alert him to this.

Vasconcelos pondered, calculated, and went through all his expenses and his obligations, and saw that he had less than a quarter of his fortune left—a mere pittance if he were to continue living as he had until now.

What to do?

Vasconcelos picked up his hat and went out.

It was growing dark.

After walking for some time, deep in thought, he went into the Alcazar.

It was a way of distracting himself.

There he found the usual people.

Batista came to greet his friend.

"Why the glum face?" he asked.

And for want of a better answer, Vasconcelos replied: "Oh, it's nothing. Someone just stepped on a corn."

However, a chiropodist standing nearby heard this remark and thereafter did not take his eyes off poor Vasconcelos, who was in a particularly sensitive mood that night. In the end, he found the chiropodist's insistent gaze so troubling that he left.

He went to the Hotel de Milão to have supper. However preoccupied he might be, his stomach was still making its usual demands.

In the middle of eating, he suddenly remembered the one thing he should never have forgotten: Gomes's proposal of marriage to his daughter.

It was like a ray of sunshine.

"Gomes is rich," thought Vasconcelos. "That's the best way out of all these problems. Gomes can marry Adelaide, and, since he's my friend, he couldn't possibly deny me what I need. For my part, I will try to get back what I've lost. What a stroke of luck!"

Vasconcelos continued his meal in the best of moods, then returned to the Alcazar, where a few other lads and some members of the female sex helped him to forget his troubles completely.

He returned peacefully home at his regular time of three o'clock in the morning.

IV

The following day, Vasconcelos's first priority was to sound out Adelaide. He wanted to do so, though, when Augusta was not there. Fortunately, she needed to go to Rua da Quitanda to view some new fabrics, and she set off with her brother-in-law, leaving Vasconcelos entirely free.

As readers will already know, Adelaide loved her father deeply, and would do anything for him. She was, moreover, the soul of kindness. Vasconcelos was counting on those two qualities.

"Come here, Adelaide," he said, going into the living room. "How old are you now?"

"Fifteen."

"Do you know how old your mother is?"

"She's twenty-seven, isn't she?"

"No, she's thirty, which means that your mother married when she was just fifteen."

Vasconcelos paused to gauge the effect of these words, but in vain. Adelaide had no idea what he was getting at.

Her father went on:

"Have you considered marriage?"

She blushed deeply and said nothing, but when her father insisted, she answered:

"Oh, Papa, I don't want to marry."

"You don't want to marry? Whyever not?"

"Because I don't want to. I'm happy living here."

"You could marry and still live here."

"Yes, but I don't want to."

"Come on, you're in love with someone, aren't you? Admit it."

"Don't ask me such things, Papa. I'm not in love with anyone."

Adelaide sounded so genuine that Vasconcelos could not doubt her sincerity.

"She's telling the truth," he thought. "I need to try another tack."

Adelaide sat down next to him and said:

"So can we just not talk about this anymore, Papa?"

"We must talk, my dear. You're still a child and can't yet look to the future. Imagine if I and your mother were to die tomorrow. Who would look after you? Only a husband."

"But there's no one I like."

"Not at the moment, but if your fiancé were a handsome lad with a good heart, you would come to like him. I've already chosen someone who loves you deeply, and you'll come to love him too."

Adelaide shuddered.

"I will?" she said. "But who is it?"

"Gomes."

"But I don't love him, Papa."

"Not now, I'm sure, but you can't deny that he's worthy of being loved. In a couple of months you'll be madly in love with him."

Adelaide said not a word. She bowed her head and started playing with one of her thick, dark plaits. She was breathing hard and staring down at the carpet.

"So that's agreed, is it?" asked Vasconcelos.

"But, Papa, what if I was unhappy?"

"That's impossible, my dear. You will be happy and you'll adore your husband."

"Oh, Papa," said Adelaide, her eyes brimming with tears, "please don't make me marry yet."

"Adelaide, a daughter's first duty is to obey her father, and I'm your father. I want you to marry Gomes and you will marry him."

To have their full effect, these words needed to be followed by a quick exit. Vasconcelos knew this and immediately departed, leaving Adelaide in deep despair.

She didn't love anyone. No other love object lay behind her refusal, nor did she feel any particular aversion for her would-be suitor. She merely felt complete indifference.

In the circumstances, marriage could only be a hateful imposition.

But what could Adelaide do? Who could she turn to?

She had only her tears.

As for Vasconcelos, he went up to his study and wrote the following lines to his future son-in-law:

Everything is going well. I give you permission to come and pay court to my daughter, and hope to see you married in a couple of months.

He sealed the letter and sent it off.

Shortly afterward, Augusta and Lourenço returned.

While Augusta disappeared up to her boudoir to change her clothes, Lourenço went looking for Adelaide, who was out in the garden.

Noticing that her eyes were red, he asked her why, but she denied she had been crying.

Lourenço didn't believe his niece and urged her to tell him what was wrong.

Adelaide trusted her uncle, almost because he *was* so direct and gruff. After a few minutes, Adelaide told Lourenço all about the scene with her father.

"So that's why you're crying, little one."

"Yes. How can I avoid getting married?"

"Don't worry, you won't have to. I promise."

Adelaide felt a shiver of joy.

"Do you promise, Uncle, to persuade Papa?"

"Well, persuade or prevail, one or the other, but you won't have to get married. Your father is a fool."

Lourenço went up to see Vasconcelos at precisely the moment when the latter was about to leave.

"Are you going out?" asked Lourenço.

"I am."

"I need to talk to you."

Lourenço sat down, and Vasconcelos, who already had his hat on, stood waiting for him to speak.

"Sit down," said Lourenço.

Vasconcelos sat down.

"Sixteen years ago—"

"You're going an awfully long way back. If you don't shave off half a dozen years, I can't promise to hear you out."

"Sixteen years ago," Lourenço went on, "you got married, but the difference between that first day and today is enormous."

"Of course," said Vasconcelos. "*Tempora mutantur, nos et—*"

"At the time," Lourenço went on, "you said you'd found paradise, a true paradise, and for two or three years you were a model husband. Then you changed completely, and paradise would have become a real hell if your wife were not the cold, indifferent creature she is, thus avoiding some truly terrible domestic scenes."

"But what has this got to do with you, Lourenço?"

"Nothing, and that isn't what I wanted to talk to you about. What I want to do is to stop you sacrificing your daughter on a whim, handing her over to one of your fellow dissolutes."

Vasconcelos sprang to his feet:

"You must be insane," he said.

"No, I'm perfectly sane and prudently advising you not to sacrifice your daughter to a libertine."

"Gomes isn't a libertine. True, he's led the life of many a young man, but he loves Adelaide and is a reformed character. It's a good marriage, and that's why I think we must all accept it. That's what I want, and I'm the one who gives the orders around here."

Lourenço was about to say more, but Vasconcelos had left.

"What can I do?" thought Lourenço.

V

Vasconcelos was not greatly bothered by Lourenço's opposition to his plans. He could, it's true, sow the seeds of resistance in his niece's mind, but Adelaide was easily persuaded and would agree with whoever she happened to be speaking to, and the advice she received one day would easily be overthrown by any contrary advice she was given the following day.

Still, it would be wise to get Augusta's support. Vasconcelos decided to do this as soon as possible.

Meanwhile, he needed to organize his own affairs, and so he found a lawyer, to whom he gave all the necessary documents and information, charging him with providing the necessary guidance and advising him on what measures he could take to oppose any claims made against him because of his debts or his mortgages.

None of this should make you think that Vasconcelos was about to change his ways. He was simply preparing himself to continue life as before.

Two days after his conversation with his brother, Vasconcelos went in search of Augusta, in order to speak frankly with her about Adelaide's marriage.

During that time, the future bridegroom, taking Vasconcelos's advice, was already paying court to Adelaide. If the marriage was not forced on her, it was just possible that she might end up liking the lad. Besides, Gomes was a handsome, elegant fellow and knew how to impress a woman.

Would Augusta have noticed his unusually assiduous presence in the house? That was the question Vasconcelos was asking himself as he went into his wife's boudoir.

"Are you going out?" he asked her.

"No, I'm expecting a visitor."

"Oh, who?"

"Seabra's wife," she said.

Vasconcelos sat down and tried to find a way of beginning the special conversation that had brought him there.

"You're looking very pretty today!"

"Really?" she said, smiling. "Well, I'm no different today than on any other day, and it's odd that you should pick today to say so."

"No, I mean it, you're even prettier than usual, so much so, that I could almost feel jealous."

"Come, now!" said Augusta with an ironic smile.

Vasconcelos scratched his head, took out his watch, wound it up, tugged at his beard, picked up a newspaper, read a couple of advertisements, then threw the paper down on the floor; finally, after a rather long silence, he thought it best to make a frontal assault on the citadel.

"I've been thinking about Adelaide," he said.

"Why's that?"

"She's a young woman—"

"A young woman!" exclaimed Augusta. "She's still a child."

"She's older than you were when you got married."

Augusta frowned slightly.

"What are you getting at?" she asked.

"What I'm getting at is that I want to make her happy by seeing her happily married. Some days ago, a very worthy young man asked me for her hand and I said yes. When I tell you the young man's name, I'm sure you'll approve. It's Gomes. They should marry, don't you think?"

"Certainly not!" retorted Augusta.

"Why not?"

"Adelaide's just a child. She's not old enough or sensible enough yet. She'll marry when the time is right."

"When the time is right? Are you sure the young man will wait that long?"

"Patience," said Augusta.

"Do you have something against Gomes?"

"No. He's a distinguished enough young fellow, but he's not right for Adelaide."

Vasconcelos hesitated before continuing; it seemed to him there was no point in going on. However, the thought of Gomes's fortune gave him courage, and he asked:

"Why isn't he?"

"Are you so very sure he's right for Adelaide?" said Augusta, avoiding her husband's question.

"Yes, I am."

"Well, whether he's right or not, she shouldn't get married now."

"What if she were in love?"

"What does that matter? She'll wait!"

"I have to tell you, Augusta, that we can't let this marriage pass us by. It's an absolute necessity."

"An absolute necessity? I don't understand."

"Let me explain. Gomes has a large fortune."

"So do we."

"That's where you're wrong," said Vasconcelos, interrupting her.

"How so?"

Vasconcelos went on:

"You'd have to find out sooner or later, and I think this is the moment to tell you the truth, and the truth is that we're poor, ruined."

Augusta heard these words, her eyes wide with horror.

"It's not possible!"

"Unfortunately, it is."

A silence fell.

"There, I've got her," thought Vasconcelos.

Augusta broke the silence.

"But if our fortune has gone, I'd have thought you would have something better to do than sit around talking about it; you need to rebuild that fortune."

Vasconcelos gave her a look of utter astonishment, and as if this look were a question, Augusta quickly added:

"Don't look so surprised. I think it's your duty to rebuild our fortune."

"That isn't what surprises me, what I find surprising is that you should put it like that. Anyone would think I was to blame."

"Oh," said Augusta, "I suppose you're going to say that I am."

"If blame there is, then we're both to blame."

"What, me too?"

"Yes, you too. Your wildly extravagant spending sprees have been a major contributor to our downfall; and since I've denied you nothing and still deny you nothing, I take full responsibility. And if that's what you're throwing in my face, then I agree."

Augusta gave an angry shrug and shot Vasconcelos a look of such scorn that it would have been valid grounds for divorce.

Vasconcelos saw the shrug and the look.

"A love of luxury and excess," he said, "will always have the same consequences, which are terrible, but perfectly understandable. The only way of avoiding them is to live more moderately, but that never even occurred to you. After six months of married life, you plunged into the whirlwind of fashion, and your little stream of expenditures became a vast river of profligacy. Do you know what my brother said to me once? He said that the reason you sent Adelaide off to the country was so that you would be free to live with no obligations of any kind."

Augusta had stood up and taken a few steps across the room; she was pale and trembling.

Vasconcelos was continuing this litany of recriminations, when his wife interrupted him, saying:

"And why did you not put a stop to my extravagance?"

"For the sake of domestic harmony."

"Lies!" she cried. "You wanted to live a free and independent life. Seeing me embarking on that life of excess, you thought you could buy my tolerance of your behavior by tolerating mine. That was the only reason. The way you live may be different from mine, but it's far worse. I may have squandered money at home, but you did the same out in the street. There's no point denying it, because I know everything; I know all the names of the succession of rivals you've given me, and I never said a word, and I'm not censuring you now, that would be pointless and too late."

The situation had changed. Vasconcelos had begun as judge and ended up as codefendant. It was impossible to deny, and arguing was risky and futile. He preferred to appear reasonable, even cajoling.

"Given the facts (and I accept that you're right), we are clearly both to blame, and I see no reason to lay all the blame on me. I should rebuild our fortune, I agree. And one way of doing that is to marry Adelaide off to Gomes."

"No," said Augusta.

"Fine, then, we'll be poor and even worse off than we are now; we'll sell everything . . ."

"Forgive me," said Augusta, "but I don't understand why you, a strong young man, who clearly played the larger role in bringing about this disaster, cannot throw yourself into rebuilding our squandered fortune."

"It would take a very long time, and meanwhile life goes on and we keep spending. As I've said, the best way out of this is to marry Adelaide off to Gomes."

"No, I don't want that," said Augusta, "I won't consent to such a marriage."

Vasconcelos was about to respond, but Augusta, having uttered these words, had flounced out of the room.

Vasconcelos followed a few minutes later.

VI

Lourenço knew nothing about this scene between his brother and sister-in-law, and, given Vasconcelos's stubbornness, he had decided to say nothing more; however, since he was very fond of his niece and did not want to see her handed over to a man of whose habits he disapproved, he decided to wait until the situation took a more decisive turn and only then play a more active role.

In order not to waste time, though, and possibly to gain the use of some potentially powerful weapon, Lourenço began an investigation intended to gather detailed information on Gomes.

Gomes, for his part, believed the marriage to be a certainty, and did not waste a moment in his conquest of Adelaide.

He could not fail to notice, however, that for no reason he could ascertain, her mother Augusta was becoming increasingly cold and indifferent, and it occurred to him that she was possibly the source of some opposition.

As for Vasconcelos, discouraged by the discussion in his wife's boudoir, he was hoping for better days and depending, above all, on the sheer force of necessity.

One day, however, exactly forty-eight hours after his argument with Augusta, he asked himself this question:

"Why is Augusta refusing to give Adelaide to Gomes in marriage?"

One question led to another, one deduction led to another, and a painful suspicion took root in Vasconcelos's mind.

"Does she perhaps love him?" he wondered.

Then, as if one abyss attracted another abyss, and one suspicion called to another suspicion, Vasconcelos thought:

"Were they once lovers?"

For the first time, Vasconcelos felt the serpent of jealousy biting his heart.

I say "jealousy" for want of a better word, because I don't know if what he was feeling was jealousy or merely wounded pride.

Could Vasconcelos's suspicions have any basis in fact?

To be honest, no. However vain Augusta might be, she remained faithful to her unfaithful husband, and for two reasons: her conscience and her temperament. Even if she hadn't been convinced of her duty as a wife, she would never break her wedding vows. She was not made for passions, apart from the ridiculous passions aroused by vanity. She loved her own beauty above all things, and her best friend was whoever would tell her she was the most beautiful of women; and yet, while she would give away her friendship, she would never give away her heart, and this is what saved her.

And there you have the truth: But who would tell Vasconcelos? Once he began to suspect that his honor was at risk, Vasconcelos started to review his whole life. Gomes had been a visitor to his house for six years and was free to come and go as he liked. An act of betrayal would be easy enough. Vasconcelos recalled words, gestures, glances, none of which had been of any significance before, but which, now, began to look suspicious.

For two days, Vasconcelos was consumed by these thoughts. He did not leave the house, and whenever Gomes arrived, he would observe his wife with unusual interest; even the coldness with which she received Gomes was, in her husband's eyes, proof of the crime.

Then, on the morning of the third day (Vasconcelos now rose early), his brother came into his study, looking his usual disapproving self.

Lourenço's presence prompted Vasconcelos to reveal everything to him.

Lourenço was a man of good sense and, when necessary, could be supportive too.

He listened to Vasconcelos, and when the latter had finished, he broke his silence with these words:

"This is pure nonsense. If your wife is against the marriage, then it's for some other reason."

"But it's the marriage to Gomes she's objecting to."

"Yes, because you presented Gomes to her as the suitor, but she might well have reacted in the same way if you had suggested someone else. There must be another reason; perhaps Adelaide has spoken to her and asked her to oppose the marriage, because your daughter doesn't love Gomes and can't marry him."

"But she will."

"That's not the only reason she can't marry him, though . . ."

"Go on."

"There's also the fact that the marriage is pure speculation on Gomes's part."

"Speculation?" asked Vasconcelos.

"Just as it is for you," said Lourenço. "You're giving him your daughter because you have your eyes on his fortune; and he will take her because he has his eyes on yours . . ."

"But he—"

"He has nothing. He's ruined like you. I did a little investigating and learned the truth. Naturally, he wants to continue the same dissolute life he has led up until now, and your fortune is a way to do that."

"Are you sure of this?"

"Absolutely."

Vasconcelos was terrified. In the midst of all his suspicions, he had still clung to the hope that his honor would be saved and that the marriage would set him up financially.

Lourenço's revelation put paid to that hope.

"If you want proof, send for him and tell him you're penniless and, for that reason, cannot allow him to marry your daughter. Observe him closely and see what effect your words have on him."

There was no need to summon the suitor. An hour later, he called at the house.

Vasconcelos told him to come straight up to his study.

VII

After an initial exchange of courtesies, Vasconcelos said:

"I was just about to write and ask you to come."

"Why's that?" asked Gomes.

"So that we could talk about . . . about the marriage."

"Ah, is there a problem?"

"I'll explain."

Gomes grew more serious, foreseeing some grave difficulty.

Vasconcelos spoke first.

"There are certain circumstances," he said, "that need to be set out very clearly, so that there can be no room for misunderstanding . . ."

"I agree entirely."

"Do you love my daughter?"

"How often do I have to tell you? Yes, I do."

"And you will love her whatever the circumstances?"

"Yes, unless those circumstances might affect her happiness."

"Let's be frank, then, since, as well as the friend you have always been, you are now almost my son. For us to be discreet would be decidedly indiscreet."

"Indeed," said Gomes.

"I've just found out that my financial affairs are in a parlous state. I have overspent and am basically ruined, and it would be no exaggeration to say that I am now poor."

Gomes did his best not to look shocked.

"Adelaide," Vasconcelos went on, "has no fortune, not even a dowry. All I am giving you is a young woman, although I can promise you that she's a real angel and will make an excellent wife."

Vasconcelos fell silent, his eyes fixed on Gomes, as if, by scrutinizing his face he might discover what was going on in his heart.

Gomes should have responded at once, but, for a few minutes, a deep silence reigned.

Finally, he spoke.

"I appreciate your frankness and I will be equally frank."

"I would expect no less."

"It was certainly not money that prompted my love for your daughter;

I trust you will do me the justice of believing that I am above such base considerations. Besides, on the day when I asked you for the hand of my beloved, I believed myself to be rich."

"Believed?"

"Yes, only yesterday, my lawyer told me the true state of my financial affairs."

"Not good, eh?"

"Oh, if only it were as simple as that. But it seems that for the last six months I have been existing thanks entirely to my lawyer's extraordinary efforts to scrape together some money, because he couldn't bring himself to tell me the truth. And I only found out yesterday!"

"I see."

"Imagine the despair of a man who believes himself to be wealthy and, one day, discovers he has nothing!"

"I don't need to imagine it!"

"I came here today feeling happy, because any happiness I still have resides in this house; but the truth is that I'm poised on the edge of an abyss. Fate has chosen to punish us both at the same moment."

After this explanation, to which Vasconcelos listened unblinking, Gomes tackled the thorniest part of the matter.

"As I say, I appreciate your frankness and I accept your daughter even without a fortune. I have no fortune, either, but I am still strong enough to work."

"You accept her, then?"

"Listen, I accept Dona Adelaide on one condition: that she wait awhile for me to begin my new life. I intend going to the government and asking for a post there, if I can still remember what I learned at school. As soon as I'm properly established, I will come back for her. Do you agree?"

"If she's happy with that," said Vasconcelos, grasping at this one last hope, "then it's decided."

Gomes went on:

"Good, speak to her about this tomorrow, and send me her response. Ah, if only I still had my fortune, then I could prove to you how much I love her."

"Fine, we'll leave it at that."

"I await your response."

And with that they said goodbye.

Vasconcelos was left with this thought:

"The only credible part of what he said is that he now has nothing. But there's no point in waiting: hard on hard never made a brick wall."

As Gomes was going down the stairs, he was saying to himself:

"What I find odd is that he should tell me that he's poor at precisely the moment when I've just discovered my own ruin. But he'll wait in vain: in this case, two halves don't make a whole."

Vasconcelos went downstairs.

His intention was to tell Augusta the result of his conversation with Adelaide's suitor. One thing, however, was still bothering him: Augusta's refusal to agree to Adelaide's marriage without giving any reason.

He was still thinking about this when, as he walked through the hall, he heard voices in the parlor.

It was Augusta talking to Carlota.

He was about to go in when these words reached his ears:

"But Adelaide's still such a child."

It was Augusta's voice.

"A child!" said Carlota.

"Yes. She's not old enough to marry."

"If I were you, I wouldn't stop this marriage, even if it does take place in a few months' time, because Gomes really doesn't seem such a bad fellow."

"Oh, he isn't, but I just don't want Adelaide to marry."

Vasconcelos pressed his ear to the keyhole, anxious not to miss a single word of this dialogue.

"What I don't understand," said Carlota, "is your insistence on her not marrying at all. Sooner or later, she'll have to."

"Yes, but as late as possible," said Augusta.

A silence fell.

Vasconcelos was growing impatient.

"Oh," Augusta went on, "if you knew how I dread Adelaide getting married."

"But why?"

"Why? You seem to have forgotten something, Carlota. What I dread are the children she'll have—my grandchildren! The idea of being a grand-mother, Carlota, is just too awful!"

Vasconcelos breathed a sigh of relief and opened the door.

"Oh!" cried Augusta.

Vasconcelos bowed to Carlota, and, as soon as she left, he turned to his wife and said:

"I overheard your conversation with that woman."

"Well, it wasn't a secret conversation, but what exactly did you hear?"

Vasconcelos smiled and said:

"I heard the reason why you're afraid. I never realized that love of one's own beauty could lead to such egotism. The marriage to Gomes won't now happen, but if Adelaide ever does love someone, I really don't see how we can withhold our consent."

"We'll see," answered Augusta.

The conversation stopped there, because these two consorts were drifting ever further apart; one was thinking about all the noisy pleasures of youth, while the other was thinking exclusively about herself.

The following day, Gomes received a letter from Vasconcelos:

Dear Gomes,

   Something unexpected has happened. Adelaide does not wish to marry. I tried to reason with her, but could not convince her.

                    Yours, Vasconcelos

Gomes folded up the letter and used it to light a cigar, then began thinking this deep thought:

"Where am I going to find an heiress who'll want me as a husband?"

If anyone knows of one, do tell him.

Vasconcelos and Gomes still sometimes meet in the street or at the Alcazar; they talk and smoke and take each other's arm, exactly like the friends they never were or like the rogues they are.

CONFESSIONS OF A YOUNG WIDOW

———————

I

TWO YEARS AGO, I made an unusual decision: I took myself off to Petrópolis in the middle of the month of June—to live. This decision proved fertile ground for conjectures. Even you, in the letters you wrote to me here, squandered your energies on trying to guess or imagine a thousand reasons, each more absurd than the last.

I did not nor could I respond to those letters, in which your evident concern betrayed two simultaneous feelings: the affection of a friend and the curiosity of a woman. It wasn't the right moment to open my heart to you or to unfold to you the various reasons that drove me from Rio, where the operas at the Teatro Lírico, your parties, and Cousin Barros's family gatherings would have provided me with distractions after my husband's recent death.

Indeed, many believed his demise to be the sole reason for my departure. That was the least equivocal version. I let it pass as I did all the others and stayed in Petrópolis. As soon as summer arrived, you came here with your husband, determined not to return to Rio until you had discovered the secret I was refusing to reveal. I remained as silent as the tomb, as inscrutable as the Sphinx. You lay down your weapons and left.

You have addressed me ever since as your Sphinx.

And it's true, I was a Sphinx. And if, like Oedipus, you had answered my riddle with the word "man," you would have uncovered my secret and undone my charm.

But, as they say in novels, let us not anticipate events.

It is time to tell you about this episode in my life.

I prefer to do so in letters rather than face-to-face. Were I with you, I might blush. The heart opens up more easily in letters and shame does not stop certain words from being spoken. Notice that I make no mention of tears, which is a sign that my peace of mind has returned.

My letters will arrive once a week, so that you can read the story as if it were a serial in a weekly magazine.

I give you my word that you will find it both enjoyable and educational.

And a week after my last letter, I will come and embrace you, kiss you, and thank you. I feel a great need to live. The last two years have been a complete blank in the ledger of my life: two years of tedium, inner despair, trampled pride, repressed love.

True, I did read a lot, but only time, absence, and the memory of my deceived heart and my offended dignity could bring me the necessary calm, the calm I feel today.

And that is not all I gained. I also came to know a man whose picture I carry in my mind and who seems now remarkably like so many other men. This is no small thing; and the lesson will prove useful to me and to you and to our less experienced friends. Show them these letters; they are pages from a manuscript which, had I read it before, might have spared me my lost illusions and two years of wasted life.

I must end here. This is merely the preface to my novel, study, or story, or whatever you wish to call it. I'm not really bothered about names, and so have no need to consult any masters of the art.

Whether study or novel, it is a book of truths, an episode simply told, an intimate conversation between two minds, and in the complete confidence of two hearts that esteem and respect each other.

Farewell.

II

This was at the time when my husband was still alive.

Rio was a busy, bustling city then, not the cruelly monotonous place I sense from your letters and from the newspapers to which I subscribe.

My house was a meeting place for a few rather witty young men and some elegant young women. I was, by general consent, the queen-elect, and presided over any family gatherings held in my house. Outside, there were lively theaters, parties with friends, and a thousand other distractions that gave my life certain outward joys, for lack of any inner ones, which are the only truly fruitful joys.

While I may not have been happy, I led an enjoyable enough life.

And here begins my novel.

One day, my husband asked me, as a special favor, if we could put off visiting the Teatro Lírico that night. He said he couldn't go because it was the eve of the departure of the steamer.

A perfectly reasonable request.

Some evil spirit whispered in my ear, for I replied tartly that I absolutely *had* to go to the theater, and that he must go with me. He repeated his request and I repeated my refusal. It did not take much for me to think that somehow my honor was at stake. Now I see that it was either pure vanity on my part or else fate.

I held a certain sway over my husband. My imperious tone would brook no refusal, and my husband finally gave in, and we went to the theater.

There was a very sparse audience, and the singers all had bad colds. At the end of the first act, my husband smiled vengefully and said:

"Just as I thought."

"Meaning what?" I asked with a frown.

"It's dreadful. You made it sound as if coming to the theater tonight were a matter of honor. I can't help thinking that the performance cannot possibly have lived up to your expectations."

"On the contrary, I think it's wonderful."

"Oh, please."

You will understand that I did not wish to admit defeat, but you would be quite right in thinking that I was deeply bored with the opera and with the evening.

With a defeated air, my husband, who tended not to answer back, said nothing more, and moved closer to the front of our box, where he peered through his opera glasses at the few occupied boxes opposite.

I shifted my chair farther back and, leaning against the wall, looked out into the corridor to watch the people passing by.

Directly opposite the door to our box, a man was standing, smoking a cigarette, with his eyes fixed on me. I didn't notice this at first, until I was forced to by the sheer insistence of his gaze. I looked at him to see if he was some acquaintance of ours waiting to be discovered so that he could come and greet us. The fact that he knew us might explain his odd behavior, but I didn't know him at all.

After a few seconds, aware that he had still not taken his eyes off me, I averted my gaze and fixed it instead on the curtain and the audience.

When my husband had finished examining the other boxes, he handed me the opera glasses and joined me at the rear of the box.

We exchanged a few words.

After a quarter of an hour, the orchestra began playing the overture for the second act. I stood up, and my husband moved my chair forward for me, and in that brief interval, I cast a furtive glance out at the corridor.

The man was still there.

I asked my husband to close the door.

The second act began.

Then, in a spirit of curiosity, I waited to see if the watcher would take his place in the stalls. I wanted to get a better look at him among the crowd.

However, he either didn't take his seat or I failed to spot him.

The second act was even more tedious than the first.

In the interval, I again moved my chair to the back of the box, and my husband opened the door, saying that it was too hot.

I glanced out into the corridor.

I saw no one, but a few minutes later, the same man arrived and stood in the same place and stared at me with the same impertinent eyes.

We women are always vain about our looks and want to be admired for our beauty. This is why we're often indiscreet enough to enjoy a man's rather dangerous flattery. There is, however, a form of flattery that irritates and frightens; it irritates because it's impertinent and frightens because it's dangerous. This was the case here.

My admirer's insistence presented me with a dilemma: he was either the victim of a mad passion or possessed of an impudent audacity. Either way, I should clearly not encourage his feelings.

I thought all this during the interval. The third act was about to begin. I waited for my silent pursuer to withdraw and then said to my husband:

"Shall we go?"

"Are you sure?"

"Yes, the opera's wonderful, but I just feel really sleepy."

My husband made so bold as to question this:

"If it's so wonderful, why are you sleepy?"

I did not reply.

We left.

In the corridor, we met the Azevedo family, who were just returning from visiting an acquaintance of theirs in a neighboring box. I paused to embrace the ladies in the party. I told them we were leaving because I had a headache.

We reached the door that opened onto Rua dos Ciganos.

I waited there for some minutes for our carriage to arrive.

And who should appear, leaning in the doorway?

The mysterious stranger.

I was furious.

I covered my face as best I could with my hood and waited for the carriage, which arrived soon afterward.

The mysterious man stood there, as impassive and silent as the door he was leaning against.

During the journey home, I could not stop thinking about that incident. I was only roused from my abstraction when the carriage drew up at the door of our house, in Rua Matacavalos.

I felt ashamed of myself and decided to think no more about the matter.

But would you believe it, Carlota? It took me half an hour to get to sleep, because my imagination insisted on revisiting the corridor, the doorway, and my platonic admirer.

The following day, I thought about it less. A week later, it had been wiped from my memory, and I thanked God for saving me from an obsession that could have proved fatal.

I decided to embrace that divine help and resolved not to go to the theater for some time.

I concentrated on domestic life and, for distraction, relied on getting together with friends in the evening.

Meanwhile, the day of your little girl's birthday was fast approaching. I remembered that, a month before, in order to contribute to the celebrations, I had begun knitting her a little present, which I needed to finish.

One Thursday morning, I asked the maid to bring me my sewing basket and was about to continue my work when, tucked inside a skein of wool, I found a blue envelope containing a letter.

I thought this very odd. There was no name on the envelope. It was sealed and appeared to be waiting to be opened by whoever it was intended for. Who could that be? My husband? I was accustomed to opening any letters addressed to him, and so I did not hesitate. I broke the seal on the envelope and found a pink sheet of paper inside.

The letter said:

> Do not be surprised, Eugênia; this letter is the product of despair
> and that despair is the product of love. I love you—very much. For
> some time now, I have tried to drive away that feeling, to smother it, but
> I can do so no longer. Did you not see me at the Teatro Lírico? A secret,
> inner force led me there. But I have not seen you since. When will I see
> you again? Although, if I do not see you, then I must be patient. How-
> ever, if your heart were to beat for me for just one minute of each day
> that would be enough for a love that seeks neither mere sensual pleasure
> nor public recognition. If I offend you, please forgive this sinner; if you
> could love me, you would make me a god.

I read this letter with tremulous hands and tear-filled eyes; and for some minutes afterward, I was completely lost to the world.

A thousand different, contradictory ideas went through my mind, like those great flocks of black birds that fly across the sky when a storm is approaching.

Could it be love that had made that stranger write to me? Or was it just a trap laid by a calculating seducer? I looked vaguely around me, afraid my husband might come in.

The sheet of paper was there before me, and those mysterious words seemed to me like the eyes of an evil serpent. Without thinking, I crumpled it nervously up in my hands.

If Eve had done the same with the head of the serpent tempting her, there would have been no sin. I, alas, could not be so sure of obtaining the same result, because the serpent I could see and whose head I had crushed, could, like the Hydra of Lerna, sprout many more heads.

Don't be surprised at this mixture of biblical and pagan imagery. At the time, I wasn't thinking, my mind was merely rambling; only long afterward could I think straight.

Two feelings were at work within me: firstly, a kind of terror of the abyss, the deep abyss which I sensed lay behind that letter; secondly, a sense of bitter shame that I was low enough in that stranger's esteem for him to stoop to such measures.

Only when I had calmed down did it occur to me to think what I should have thought right at the start. Who had put that letter there? My first impulse was to summon all the servants. What stopped me was the realization that while I would probably learn nothing from a simple question, everyone would then know about the letter. And what purpose would that serve?

I summoned no one.

I could not help thinking, though, that the letter had been a bold move, which could have failed at every turn; what could have motivated that man to take such a step? Love or the desire to seduce?

Returning to this dilemma, my mind, despite all the dangers involved, wanted to accept that first hypothesis, because it was the one that suited my situation as a married woman and my vanity as a beautiful one.

I tried to find out the truth by reading the letter again: I read it not once, twice, thrice, but five times.

An unhealthy curiosity drew me to it. Finally, I made an effort and resolved to destroy it, promising myself that if a second letter should appear, I would dismiss every servant and slave in the house.

Still clutching the piece of paper, I left the living room and went to my own room, where I lit a candle and burned the letter that was burning my hands and my head.

As the last scrap of paper blackened and crumpled, I heard footsteps behind me. It was my husband.

I spontaneously threw myself into his arms.

Somewhat surprised, he returned my embrace.

However, when my embrace continued, I felt him gently pushing me away, saying:

"That's enough, now. You're suffocating me."

I drew back.

It saddened me to see that the man who could and should save me was incapable of understanding, even instinctively, that I was clinging to him as though to the idea of duty.

Then the feeling clutching at my heart gave way for a moment to a feeling of fear. The ashes from the burned letter were still there on the floor, and there was the candle lit in broad daylight. That should have been enough to prompt a few questions, but he was not even curious enough to ask.

He took a couple of steps about the room, then left.

I felt a single tear roll down my cheek. It wasn't the first bitter tear I would shed, but it was perhaps the first indication of sin.

III

A month passed.

During that time, nothing at home changed. No second letter appeared, and my extreme vigilance proved futile.

I could not forget about the letter, though. Ah, if it were only a matter of not forgetting, but the first words kept resurfacing again and again in my memory, then the others, then all of them. I knew the letter by heart!

Do you remember? One of the things I often used to boast about was my excellent memory. Even that gift proved to be a punishment. Those words distracted me, made my head throb. Why? Ah, Carlota, it's because I found in those words an indefinable charm, a painful charm, because it was accompanied by feelings of remorse—but a charm from which I could not free myself.

It wasn't my heart that was to blame, it was my imagination. My imagination was leading me into perdition; the struggle between duty and the imagination is cruel and dangerous for weak souls. And I was weak. It was the mystery of it all that so captured my imagination.

In the end, time and other diversions deflected my mind from that obsessive thought.

After a month had elapsed, while I had not completely forgotten about the mysterious stranger and his letter, I was at least calm enough to laugh at myself and my fears.

One Thursday night, we had a few visitors, among them many of my female friends, although not your good self. My husband had not yet come home from work, but his absence was neither noticed nor felt, given that, however decent a fellow he was, he was never exactly the life and soul of the party.

We had sung and played and talked amid an atmosphere of frank and generous enjoyment; Amélia Azevedo's uncle was amusing us with his eccentricities; Amélia garnered much applause with her heavenly voice; and we had just reached a pause, waiting for tea to be served.

At that point, my husband arrived.

He was not alone. At his side was a tall, slim, elegant man, whom I did not recognize. In the ensuing silence, my husband stepped forward and introduced him to me.

I heard my husband say that our guest was called Emílio ***.

Only then did I see him properly, and I had to suppress a gasp.

It was *him*!

My gasp was replaced by a look of surprise. No one noticed. He, even less. He fixed his eyes on me and, with a gracious bow, addressed a few flattering, courteous remarks to me.

I replied as best I could.

Further introductions were made, and for ten minutes, an awkward silence reigned.

All eyes were turned on the new arrival. My eyes were turned on him, too, and I could see that everything about him conspired to attract attention: a proud, handsome head, deep, magnetic eyes, elegant, delicate manners, an easy, distinguished air, in marked contrast with the affected, prosaically self-conscious air of the other young men.

My examination of him was necessarily brief. I could not, nor did I want to, meet Emílio's eyes. I lowered my gaze and waited anxiously for the conversation to resume its normal course.

My husband took it upon himself to set the tone. Unfortunately, the new guest was still the subject of the general conversation that followed.

We learned that Emílio was from the provinces, the son of wealthy parents, and had been educated in Europe, whose every corner he had visited.

He had returned to Brazil only recently and, before going back to his provincial roots, had decided to spend a little time in Rio de Janeiro.

That is all we found out. There followed many questions about his travels, and he replied in a most friendly, helpful fashion.

I was the only one who showed no curiosity, because I was struck dumb. I wanted an explanation for that mysterious romance, which had begun in a theater corridor and continued with an anonymous letter and his arrival in my house with my own husband as intermediary.

From time to time, I would glance across at Emílio and find him looking cool and calm, responding politely to the questions put to him and himself recounting, with modest, natural grace, some of his adventures abroad.

An idea occurred to me. Was he really the mysterious man of the theater and the letter? He seemed so at first, but I could have been wrong; I couldn't precisely recall that other man's features, and while it seemed to me that the two creatures were one and the same, could the mistake be explained by some miraculous resemblance?

As I pondered this, time passed, and the conversation continued as if I were not there. Tea was served. Afterward, there was more singing and playing. Emílio listened with almost devout attention and revealed himself to be a man of taste as well as a discreet and attentive conversationalist.

By the end of the evening, he had captivated everyone. My husband was particularly thrilled. He clearly considered himself fortunate to have found a new friend for himself, and another guest for our family gatherings.

Emílio left, promising to return.

When I was alone with my husband, I asked him:

"Where did you meet that man?"

"He's a real gem, isn't he? He was introduced to me at the office a few days ago, and I immediately took a shine to him. He seems to be a good-hearted fellow, plus he's bright, discreet, and sensible. Everyone likes him . . ."

And, seeing me so serious and silent, he broke off and asked:

"Was I wrong to bring him here?"

"Wrong? No, why?"

"No reason. After all, what could possibly be wrong about inviting him? He's such a distinguished young man . . ."

I brought this new hymn of praise to an end by summoning a slave to whom I gave some orders.

Then I withdrew to my room.

My sleep that night was not, believe me, the sleep of the just. What irritated me most was the nervous state I got into after these events. I could no longer entirely brush aside these feelings; they happened against my will, overwhelming me and dragging me with them. It was a curiosity of the heart, which is the first sign of the storms to which our lives and our futures succumb.

I felt as if that man could read my very soul and knew how to choose his moment, a moment when he would be most likely to impress himself on my imagination as an imposing, poetic figure. You, who met him later on, would you not say that, given the circumstances, he did this in order to make an impression on the mind of a woman like me?

Like me, I say. My circumstances were rather special; I may never have spoken to you openly about this, but I'm sure you suspected as much.

Had I been a wife to my husband and had he been a husband to me, I would have been perfectly safe. This was not the case. We entered our marital home like two travelers, perfect strangers, entering an inn, where the wild weather and the lateness of the hour had obliged us to take shelter beneath the same roof.

My marriage, then, was the result of calculation and convenience. Not that I blame my parents. They wanted me to be happy and they died convinced that I was.

I could, despite everything, have found in the husband they gave me an object of happiness for the rest of my days. All I would have needed was for my husband to see in me a twin soul, a kindred spirit. This did not happen. My husband saw marriage as most people do: as a way of obeying the Lord's command in Genesis.

Apart from that, he was always considerate and slept peacefully in the belief that he had done his duty.

Duty! That was my lifeline. I knew that passions did not reign supreme and that our will can triumph over them. In this respect, I was strong enough to repel malevolent thoughts. However, it was not the present that I found so suffocating, so terrifying, it was the future. Up until then, that romance had held a certain sway over my imagination because of the mystery surrounding it; reality, however, would open my eyes. I found consolation in the hope that I would triumph over a guilty love, but in that future, whose proximity I could not gauge, would I be entirely able to resist passion and maintain intact my reason and my conscience? That was the question.

In the midst of all these vacillations, I did not once see my husband reach out his hand to save me. On the contrary, when he found me in the act of burning that letter, and I flung myself into his arms, he, as you will remember, rather abruptly pushed me away.

This is what I thought and felt during the long night that followed Emílio's introduction into our house.

The following day, I woke, feeling weary of heart, but, whether out of inertia or exhaustion, I felt all these painful, tormenting thoughts vanish in the morning light, like real birds of night and solitude.

A bright light illumined my thoughts. It was a repetition of the same idea that kept coming back to me in the midst of all those recent anxieties.

Why be afraid? I told myself. I'm such a sad, fearful creature; and I wear myself out creating mountains, only to collapse, exhausted, in the middle of a vast plain. No obstacle stands in my path as virtuous, rational wife. This man, if he is the same one, is merely a gullible reader of realist novels. It's only the mystery that makes him interesting; seen from closer to, he's sure to be either vulgar or vile.

IV

I won't weary you with a detailed, daily account of events.

Emílio continued to visit our house, always behaving with the same delicacy and gravity, and charming everyone with his genuinely amiable manner, which managed to be distinguished without being affected.

I don't know why my husband was so enthusiastic about this new friendship. Emílio had managed to awaken in him a new enthusiasm for me and for everyone. What caprice of Nature was this?

I often questioned my husband about this very sudden, very public friendship; I tried to plant suspicions in his mind, but he would not be moved.

"What do you want me to say?" he would answer. "I don't know why I like the fellow so much. I just think he's a really fine person, and I can't conceal how much I enjoy his company."

"But you don't even know him," I would object.

"Now, really! I've heard only excellent things about him, and besides, you can see at once that he's a person of distinction."

"Manners can be very deceiving."

"So they say . . ."

I confess, my friend, that I could have forced my husband to exclude Emílio, but when this idea came into my head, for some reason I laughed at my fears and declared myself strong enough to resist whatever might happen.

Moreover, Emílio's behavior encouraged me to lay down my arms. He treated me with utter respect, as he did all the other women, and never once revealed an ulterior motive, some secret thought.

And the inevitable happened. Given his behavior toward me, I could hardly maintain my rigorous indifference to his friendly approaches.

Things evolved in such a way that I even persuaded myself that everything that had happened before had nothing whatsoever to do with him, and the only connection between the two men was a truly remarkable resemblance, which, of course, I could not confirm, because, as I said before, I had been unable to look closely at the man in the theater.

It did not take long for us to become close friends, and I was for him what all the other women were: admiring and admired.

Emílio began to visit not only in the evenings, but during the day, too, at times when my husband was at home, and, later, even when he wasn't.

My husband had usually been the one to bring him to our house, but, at other times, Emílio came in his own carriage, which he himself drove with tremendous grace and elegance. He spent hours and hours at our home, playing the piano and talking.

I must admit that the first time I received him alone, I trembled, but there was no need for such childish fear; Emílio never behaved in a way that confirmed my suspicions. If I still harbored any suspicions, they all melted away.

Two months passed.

One afternoon, I was alone at home; I was waiting for you so that we could go and visit your ailing father. A carriage stopped outside the door. I sent a servant to see who it was. It was Emílio.

I received him as I always did.

I told him we were going to visit your father, and he immediately said that he would leave. I urged him to wait until you arrived, and he did so as if some reason other than politeness kept him there.

Half an hour passed.

We talked about banal subjects. Then, during a brief silence, Emílio got up and went to the window. I stood up as well and walked over to the piano to fetch my fan. When I returned to the sofa, I saw in the mirror that Emílio was looking at me in a very strange way. It was a complete transformation. It was as if his whole soul lay in that gaze.

I shuddered.

I nevertheless made an effort to control myself and sat down again, looking very serious.

Emílio came over to me.

I looked up at him.

His gaze had not changed.

I looked down.

"Are you frightened?" he asked.

I said nothing, but began to tremble again, and my heart was pounding so wildly I thought it might leap from my breast.

Those words contained the same expression as his eyes, and they had the same effect on me as the words in his letter.

"Are you frightened?" he said again.

"Of what?" I asked, trying to smile in order to lighten the situation.

"You looked frightened."

A silence.

"Dona Eugênia," he said, sitting down. "I can no longer hide the secret that has been tormenting me. It would be a pointless sacrifice. Whether it makes me happy or not, I prefer to know where I stand. Dona Eugênia, I love you."

I cannot begin to describe my feelings on hearing those words. I felt myself turn pale, and my hands were like ice. I tried to speak, but I couldn't.

Emílio went on:

"Oh, I know the risk I'm taking. I can see this is a forbidden love. But what can I do? It's fate. I've traveled many leagues, seen so many beauties, and yet my heart never once beat faster. Fate has reserved for me a rare good fortune or, perhaps, a terrible misfortune, that of being loved or spurned by you. I bow to destiny. I will accept whatever answer you give me. What do you say?"

While he was talking, I was able, as I listened, to consider my response. When he finished, I looked up and said:

"What answer do you expect from me?"

"Anything."

"You can expect only one . . ."

"That you don't love me?"

"I cannot and do not love you, nor would I love you if I could or if I wanted to. Please leave."

And with that I stood up.

Emílio did the same.

"I will leave," he said, "but I leave with all the fires of hell burning in my heart."

I shrugged as if this were a matter of indifference to me.

"Oh, I know you don't care. That is what most pains me. I would much prefer your hatred, for, believe me, indifference is the worst possible punishment. However, I will resign myself to it. Such a grave crime should bring with it an equally grave punishment."

And, picking up his hat, he came over to me again.

I stepped back.

"Oh, don't be afraid. Do I make you afraid?"

"Afraid?" I retorted proudly.

"Or is it disgust?" he asked.

"Perhaps," I murmured.

"Just one question," he said. "Do you still have that letter?"

"Ah," I said, "so it was you who wrote that letter."

"It was. And I was the mysterious stranger at the theater too. And the letter?"

"I burned it."

"Just as I thought."

And, bowing coldly, he walked to the door. He had almost reached it, when I saw him hesitate and press one hand to his heart.

I felt a moment of pity, but regardless of whether he was suffering or not, he had to leave. Nevertheless, I took a step toward him and, from a safe distance, asked:

"Would you tell me something?"

He stopped and turned around.

"Of course."

"How could you have pretended to be my husband's friend?"

"It was an unworthy act, I know, but my love is such that it does not even recoil from such unworthy behavior. It's the only love I know. But, forgive me, I will trouble you no further. Goodbye. Forever!"

And he left.

I thought I heard a sob.

I went and sat down on the sofa. Shortly afterward, there was the sound of a carriage moving off down the street.

I don't know how the time between his departure and your arrival passed, but you found me in that same place.

Up until then, I had only read about love. That man seemed to feel the love I'd dreamed of and read about. The idea that Emílio's heart was, at that moment, bleeding, aroused in me an intense feeling of pity. Pity was the first step.

I thought: "Who knows what he might be suffering now? And, after all, it's not his fault. He loves me, he told me so; his love is stronger than reason itself. He is clearly utterly devoted, so much so that he opened his heart to me. He loves me, that is his excuse."

Then I went over all his words in my mind and tried to recall the tone in which he had spoken them. I remembered, too, what I'd said and the tone in which I'd responded to his confession of love.

Perhaps I had been too harsh. I could have maintained my dignity without opening a wound in his heart. If I'd spoken more gently, I might have gained his respect and veneration. Now he will still love me, but he will only remember what happened with a sense of bitterness.

I was still immersed in these thoughts when you came in.

Do you remember commenting on how sad I looked and asking me why? I didn't answer. We went to your father's house, but my sad mood remained.

That night, when my husband asked if Emílio had visited, I said the first thing that came into my head.

"No, he didn't come today."

"Really?" he said. "He must be ill."

"I've no idea."

"I'll go and see him tomorrow."

"Where?"

"At his house."

"Why?"

"Because he might be ill."

"I doubt it. Why not just wait and see?"

I spent a horribly anxious night. The thought of Emílio would not let me sleep. I imagined he would be weeping bitter tears, in despair over his rejected love.

Was this pity? Was it love?

Carlota, it was both those things. What else could it be? I had set off along a fatal path; a strange force was drawing me along. I was weak when I could have been strong. I blame no one but myself.

I'll write more next Sunday.

V

The following afternoon, when my husband returned, I asked after Emílio.

"I took your advice and I didn't go and see him," he said. "But if he doesn't come today, I will."

A day passed with no news of him.

The following day, when he still did not appear, my husband went to his house.

I'll be honest. I myself reminded my husband to go.

I waited anxiously for news.

My husband returned that evening. He looked rather sad. I asked what had happened.

"I don't know. He was in bed. He told me it was just a slight cold, but I think it's more than that."

"But what?" I asked, looking hard at my husband.

"He spoke of leaving for the North. He seems sad, distracted, preoccupied. He talks about hoping to see his parents, but, at the same time, seems afraid he might never see them again. He's afraid he might die on the journey. I don't know what's happened to him, but something has. Perhaps . . ."

"Perhaps what?"

"Perhaps it's some money problem."

This answer troubled me deeply, and played a large part in what happened later.

After a brief silence, I asked:

"What will you do?"

"I'll speak frankly with him. I'll ask him what the problem is and help him if I can. At any rate, I won't let him leave. What do you think?"

"I agree."

All these things contributed greatly to keeping Emílio in my thoughts, and, painful though it is for me to admit it, I could not think of him now without my heart beating faster.

The following night, we had a few friends around, not that I added much to the gaiety of the party. I was sad and disconsolate. I was angry with myself. I imagined I was Emílio's executioner, and found the idea that he was suffering for my sake deeply painful.

However, at around nine o'clock, my husband appeared, arm in arm with Emílio.

There was a general murmur of surprise.

Since Emílio had not been seen for some days, everyone had started asking after him, and then he turned up looking as pale as wax.

I won't tell you what happened that evening. Emílio seemed to be in pain; he wasn't his usual cheerful self; on the contrary, he was so silent and downcast that everyone felt uncomfortable, and I suffered horribly, imagining myself to be the cause of his pain.

I only managed to speak to him once, when we were some way away from the others.

"Forgive me," I said, "if I spoke harshly to you. You must understand my position. You took me by surprise, and I did not have time to consider my answer. I know you have suffered, but, please, do not suffer any more, forget . . ."

"Thank you," he murmured.

"My husband mentioned your plans . . ."

"Yes, to go back to my hometown."

"But you're ill . . ."

"Oh, it will pass."

And when he said this, he gave me such a strange, sinister look that I felt afraid.

"How? How will it pass?"

"There are ways."

"Don't say that."

"What else is left for me here?"

And he closed his eyes and wiped away a tear.

"What's this?" I said. "Are you crying?"

"My last tears."

"Oh, if you knew how it hurts me. Don't cry, I beg you. More than that, I'm begging you to live."

"Oh!"

"I'm ordering you."

"Ordering me? And if I don't obey? If I can't? Do you think one can live with a thorn in one's heart?"

Written down like that, it sounds contrived, but the way in which he said these words was so impassioned, so painful and moving. I listened, completely oblivious to the world. A few people were coming over to join us, and, wanting to put an end to the conversation, I said:

"Do you love me? Only love can issue orders, and love is ordering you to live!"

Emílio's face lit up with joy. I got up, intending to talk to the approaching guests.

"Thank you," he whispered in my ear.

At the end of the evening, when Emílio said goodbye, his eyes aglow with gratitude and love, I was overwhelmed with a strange confusion of feelings: love, remorse, and tenderness.

"Emílio seemed much happier," my husband said.

And I looked at him, unable to respond.

Then I went straight up to bed. I seemed to see in my husband the image of my own conscience.

The following day, I received this letter from Emílio:

> Eugênia. Thank you. I have come back to life, and I owe that entirely to you. Thank you! You made a man of a corpse, now make a god of a man. Please! Please!

I read and reread this letter, and—can you believe it, Carlota?—I kissed it. I showered it with heartfelt kisses, passionately, deliriously. I was in love! In love!

The same struggle was going on inside me, but my feelings were quite different. Before, it had been my heart running away from my reason, now it was my reason running away from my heart.

I could see and feel that it was a crime; but, whether it was fate or simply my own fond nature, I found in the delights of that crime a justification for my error, a way of legitimizing my passion.

When my husband was near me, I felt better and braver . . .

But I'll stop here. I feel a weight on my heart. It's the memory of all those events.

I will write again on Sunday.

VI

A few days passed following the scenes I described in my last letter.

There began a correspondence between Emílio and myself, and after two weeks, I thought only of him.

None of our regular visitors, not even you, would have noticed. We were extremely discreet lovers.

True, people often asked why I was so distracted and melancholy, and this would bring me back to real life, and I would immediately change my behavior.

My husband seemed the person most affected by my sad moods.

I must admit that his solicitude made me feel uncomfortable, and I would often reply rather abruptly, not because I hated him, but because he was the one person I could not bear to be questioned by.

One afternoon, he came home and said:

"Eugênia, I have news for you."

"What's that?"

"You'll be really pleased."

"Tell me, then."

"It's a little trip out."

"Where to?"

"It was my idea, and I've already told Emílio, and he thought it an excellent plan. We'll go to Gávea on Sunday, bright and early. Not that anything's been arranged, of course. That depends on you. What do you say?"

"I approve."

"Good. Carlota can come too."

"And so she should," I added. "As well as a few of my other friends."

Shortly afterward, you all received your invitations.

You'll remember that day. What you don't know is that, on that outing, thanks to the general hubbub and distraction, Emílio and I had a conversation that gave me my first bitter taste of love's sorrow.

"Eugênia," he said, taking my arm, "are you sure you love me?"

"Yes."

"In that case, what I'm asking you—not that it's me asking, but my heart and your heart—is for a noble action that would exalt us both in our own eyes. Is there not some corner of the world where we could live, far from everyone and close to heaven?"

"Do you mean run away together?"

"Yes!"

"No, never!"

"You don't love me, then."

"Yes, I do, and that is crime enough. I don't want to go beyond that."

"Are you rejecting a chance of happiness?"

"I'm rejecting dishonor."

"You don't love me, then."

"What can I say? I do love you, but I want to remain the same woman in your eyes, loving, yes, but also, up to a point, pure."

"A love that stops to think is not true love."

I said nothing. Emílio had spoken these words so scornfully and so woundingly that I felt my heart begin to pound and the blood rush to my face.

The excursion ended badly.

After that scene, Emílio grew very cold toward me, which hurt me. I tried to go back to how things had been before, but failed.

One day, when we were alone, I said:

"Emílio, if I were to run away with you tomorrow, what would you do?"

"I would obey that divine command."

"And afterward?"

"What do you mean, 'afterward'?" asked Emílio, as if bemused by my question.

"Yes, afterward," I went on. "After a while, would you not view me with scorn?"

"Scorn? I don't see—"

"Yes, why not? What else would I deserve?"

"If you'd made that sacrifice for my sake, then it would be cowardly of me to throw it back at you."

"Deep down, though, you would despise me."

"I swear that I would not."

"Well, I would despise myself. I would never forgive myself."

Emílio covered his face with his hands and appeared to be crying. I had been speaking quite confidently until then, and I went over to him and removed his hands from his face.

"What's this?" I said. "Can't you see you're making me cry too?"

He looked at me, his eyes brimming with tears. My eyes, too, were moist.

"Goodbye," he said suddenly. "I'm leaving."

And he took a step toward the door.

"If you promise me that you will live," I said, "then leave; if you have some other, more sinister plan, then stay."

I don't know what he saw in my eyes, but, clasping the hand I held out to him, he kissed it several times (those were our first kisses) and said urgently:

"I'll stay, Eugênia!"

We heard a noise outside. I went to see what it was. It was my husband, who had returned home feeling ill. He had suffered some kind of attack or fainting fit at the office. When he came around, he had still felt very unwell. Some friends had brought him back in a cab.

I ran to the door. My husband looked disheveled and deathly pale. He could only barely walk with the help of his friends.

I was so shocked that I forgot everything else. The doctor who had accompanied my husband immediately prescribed some medication. I was anxious and kept asking everyone if my husband would be all right.

They all assured me that he would.

Emílio seemed cast down by these events. He went over to my husband and squeezed his hand.

When Emílio was about to leave, my husband said:

"Listen, I know you can't be here all the time, but do come and see me every day, if you can."

"Of course," said Emílio, and left.

My husband was in a bad way for the rest of that day and night. I did not sleep, but spent the night in his room.

The following day, I was exhausted. All those conflicting feelings combined with a lack of sleep had left me utterly drained. Unable to go on, I summoned my cousin Elvira and went to bed.

I will close at this point. I am almost at the end of my sad tale.

Until Sunday.

VII

My husband's illness did not last long. He got worse with each day that passed. After a week, the doctors told him frankly that he did not have long to live.

When I received this fateful news, I almost lost my mind. He was still my husband, Carlota, and, despite all, I could not forget that he had been my companion in life and the one safe haven during all my emotional storms.

Finding me in this state of despair, Emílio tried to console me. I made no attempt to conceal from him what a great blow my husband's death would be.

One night, we were all together, me, my cousin Elvira, one of my husband's relatives, and Emílio. We were keeping the patient company. After a long silence, my husband turned to me and said:

"Give me your hand."

And, squeezing my hand hard, he turned his face to the wall, and died.

FOUR MONTHS PASSED. Emílio shared my grief and was a faithful presence at all the funeral ceremonies held for my late husband.

His visits, however, became less frequent, but I thought this was simply natural delicacy on his part.

After those four months, I learned from one of my husband's friends that Emílio was about to leave Rio. I couldn't believe it. I wrote him a letter.

I loved him then, as I had before, only even more so now that I was free.

In my letter I said:

> *Emílio: I understand that you are about to leave Rio. Is that possible? I myself could not believe my ears! You know how much I love you. Now is not the time to celebrate our vows, but it will not be long before the world will grant us the union our love demands. Come and see me and explain in person. Your Eugênia.*

Emílio did come and see me. He assured me that, although he was going away, it was on a matter of business and he would be back shortly. He would be leaving in a week's time.

I asked him to swear this was true, and he swore.

I let him leave.

Four days later, I received the following letter:

I lied, Eugênia. I'm leaving now. I told you a further lie. I will not be coming back. I won't come back because I can't. Marriage to you would be my ideal of happiness were I not a man whose habits make him entirely unsuited for marriage. Goodbye. Forgive me, and wish me a safe journey. Goodbye. Emílio.

You can easily imagine my feelings on reading that letter. It was like a whole castle crumbling into rubble. This was the reward I received for my love, my first love: ingratitude and scorn. It was only right: such a guilty love should not end well; I was being punished by the consequences of my crime.

I wondered, though, how that man, who seemed so deeply in love with me, could reject a woman whose honesty he could guarantee, given that she had resisted the wishes of her own heart. This seemed to me a complete mystery. Now I see that there was nothing mysterious about it: Emílio was a vulgar seducer, and all that distinguished him from the others was that he was slightly more adept.

That is my story. You can imagine how I have suffered over these last two years. Time, though, is a great healer, and I am now cured.

My rejected love and my feelings of remorse for having, in a way, betrayed my husband's trust, hurt me deeply. However, I think I have paid dearly for my crime and believe I have been rehabilitated in the eyes of my conscience.

But will I be rehabilitated in the eyes of God?

And in your eyes? You will tell me that tomorrow, for I will be with you just twenty-four hours after sending this letter.

Goodbye!

STRAIGHT LINE, CURVED LINE

———

I

I T HAPPENED IN PETRÓPOLIS, in 186*. My story, as you see, happened not so very long ago. It is drawn from contemporary records and present-day customs. A few readers may even know some of the characters who will appear in this brief portrait. It wouldn't be so very odd if, tomorrow, on meeting, say, Azevedo, one of my readers might exclaim:

"I've just read a story about you. The author was quite kind and discreet, but the description was so like you and he took so little care to disguise your features, that, as I turned the pages, I kept saying to myself: 'Yes, it's Azevedo to the life.'"

He's a happy man, Azevedo! At the moment when this story begins, he is a happy husband, entirely happy. Just married, possessed of a wife who was the most beautiful woman in Petrópolis society, and possessed, too, of the kindest heart to be found beneath the sun of the Americas, the owner of a couple of well-situated and eminently rentable properties, respected, loved, and untroubled, that is our Azevedo, who, to complete his great good fortune, is a handsome, healthy twenty-six-year-old.

Fortune has also given him a very easy job—doing nothing. He has a degree in law, but has never made any use of it; it's still in the classic tin box in which he brought it from the University of São Paulo. He would occasionally revisit his degree certificate, but only very rarely, and then not again until another long period of time had elapsed. It's not so much a certificate as a relic.

When Ernesto Azevedo left university and went back to the family estate in the province of Minas Gerais, he had a plan: to go to Europe. After a few months, his father agreed to let him go, and Azevedo began preparations for the voyage. He arrived in Rio with the firm intention of taking a berth on the first steamer available, but not everything depends on the will of man. Before embarking, Azevedo went to a dance, and awaiting him there was the net in which he would be caught. And what a net! Twenty years old, a slim, frail, delicate figure, one of those insubstantial creatures who seems to dissolve in the first light of day. Azevedo could not help himself; he fell passionately in love; a month later, he was married, and a week after that, the couple left for Petrópolis.

What house would be home to that handsome, loving, happy couple? The house they chose could not have been more appropriate; it was a light, slender, elegant affair, more of a holiday home than a permanent dwelling; a real little love nest for those two fugitive doves.

Our story begins exactly three months after their departure to Petrópolis. Azevedo and his wife were still as deeply in love as they had been on the first day. Then love took on a new and far greater importance, for—dare I say it, O couples who have only been married for three months—their first child had already appeared on the horizon. And both heaven and earth rejoice when the first ray of sun appears on the horizon. I am not using this image for purely stylistic reasons, it is simply a logical deduction. Anyway, Azevedo's wife was called Adelaide.

And so it was in Petrópolis, one December afternoon in 186*, that Azevedo and Adelaide were sitting in the garden of the house in which they guarded their happiness from the outside world. Azevedo was reading aloud, and Adelaide was listening to him, but it was as if she were listening to a heartbeat, so closely did her husband's voice and the words of the book correspond to her innermost feelings.

After a while, Azevedo stopped and asked:

"Shall we pause there?"

"If you like," said Adelaide.

"Yes, we'd better," said Azevedo, closing the book. "Good things shouldn't be enjoyed all at one sitting. Let's leave a little for tonight. Besides, it's time I moved from the written idyll to the real idyll—and looked at you."

Adelaide, in turn, looked at him and said:

"It's as if we were beginning our honeymoon all over again."

"And we are," added Azevedo, "if marriage is not an eternal honey-moon, what is it? The joining of two existences in order to ponder discreetly the best way of eating cucumbers and cabbages? No, thank you! I believe marriage should be one long falling in love. Don't you think so too?"

"I feel it rather than think it," said Adelaide.

"You feel, and that's enough."

"But that women should feel is only natural, whereas men—"

"Men are men."

"What in women is sentiment, in men is sentimentality. I've been told that ever since I was child."

"Well, they've been lying to you all along," said Azevedo, laughing.

"I hope so!"

"It's true. And never trust people who talk a lot, be they men or women. You have an example close to home. Here's Emília, who is always talking about how independent she is, but how many times has she been married? Twice so far, and she's only twenty-five. She would do better to talk less and marry less."

"She's only joking," said Adelaide.

"All right, but what there can be no joking about is that our three months of marriage feel like three minutes."

"Three whole months!" exclaimed Adelaide.

"How time flies!" said Azevedo.

"Will you always say that?" asked Adelaide, an incredulous look on her face.

Azevedo kissed her and asked:

"Are you beginning to have doubts?"

"No, just a little fear. It's so wonderful to be so happy!"

"You will always be happy and always equally happy. There's no other possibility."

At that moment, they heard a voice coming from the garden gate.

"What's all this talk about possibilities?"

They both looked up to see who it was.

At the garden gate stood a tall, good-looking man, elegantly dressed, wearing yellow gloves and carrying a small whip.

Azevedo did not, at first, appear to recognize him. Adelaide looked from one to the other, bewildered. This, however, lasted no more than a minute, then Azevedo cried:

"It's Tito! Come in, Tito!"

Tito sauntered nonchalantly up the garden path. He embraced Azevedo and bowed graciously to Adelaide.

"This is my wife," said Azevedo, introducing Adelaide to the new arrival.

"I thought as much," said Tito, "and let me take this opportunity to congratulate you."

"Did you not receive a wedding invitation?"

"I did, but I was in Valparaíso."

"Sit down and tell us about your trip."

"That would take a long time," said Tito, taking a seat. "What I can tell you is that I disembarked yesterday in Rio. I tried to find out where you were living and was told that you were in Petrópolis temporarily. I rested a little, then, today, I took the boat from Prainha and here I am. I suspected that a poetic soul like you would want to hide your happiness away in some secret corner of the world. And this really is a little piece of paradise. A garden, pergolas, a light, elegant house, a book. Love poetry too. Bravo! Perfect! *Tityre, tu patulae recubans . . .* I have stumbled upon an idyll. And you, shepherdess, where is your crook?"

Adelaide laughed out loud.

Tito went on:

"You even laugh like a happy shepherdess. And you, Theocritus, what are you up to? Letting the days flow by like the waters of the Paraíba? O fortunate creature!"

"Still the same old Tito!" said Azevedo.

"The same madman, you mean? Do you think he's right, senhora?"

"If you don't mind my saying so, yes, I do."

"No, I don't mind in the least. I even feel rather honored, for it's true, I am an inoffensive madman. But you two really do seem unusually happy. How many months have you been married?"

"It will be three months on Sunday," said Adelaide.

"I was just saying to Adelaide that it seems to me more like three minutes," added Azevedo.

Tito looked at them, smiling, and said:

"Three months or three minutes! There you have the whole truth about life. If you were laid upon a gridiron, like Saint Lawrence, five minutes would seem like five months. And yet still we talk of time. What is time, after all? It's a matter of how we experience it. Months for the unhappy and minutes for the happy!"

"And what happiness, eh?" cried Azevedo.

"Complete and utter bliss, I imagine. Husband to a seraph, in mind and heart, ah, I'm sorry, I forgot you were there, Adelaide . . . but don't blush. You'll hear me say the same thing twenty times a day. I always say what I think. You must be the envy of all our friends."

"I have no idea."

"Of course not. How could you, secluded as you are in this little hide-away of yours? And you're quite right. Being happy in full view of everyone else would mean sharing your happiness, and out of respect for that principle, I really should leave . . ."

And, saying this, Tito stood up.

"Stop talking and stay with us."

"True friends are also true happiness," said Adelaide.

"Ah!"

"It might be good for you to spend a little time at our school and learn the science of marriage," said Azevedo.

"Whatever for?" asked Tito, brandishing his whip.

"In order to get married."

"Hm," said Tito.

"Don't you want to?" asked Adelaide.

"So you haven't changed your mind, then?"

"No," answered Tito.

Adelaide looked curious and asked:

"Do you have a horror of marriage?"

"I simply have no vocation for it," said Tito. "And it is purely a matter of vocation. If you don't have it, don't do it, it's a complete waste of time and fatal for one's peace of mind. That has been my belief for a long time now."

"Your time has perhaps not yet come."

"And it never will," said Tito.

"I seem to remember," said Azevedo, offering his friend a cigar, "that there was a day when you tossed aside your usual theories and fell deeply in love."

"I would hardly describe it as 'deeply in love.' Providence did one day provide me with confirmation of my solitary instincts. I began courting a young lady . . ."

"Oh, yes, it was a funny business."

"What happened?" asked Adelaide.

"Tito went to a dance and saw a young woman. The next day, he went to her house and, just like that, asked for her hand in marriage. She said . . . what was it she said, now?"

"She wrote me a note saying that I was a fool and should leave her alone. She didn't actually use the word 'fool,' but it came to the same thing. Needless to say, that wasn't the response I was hoping for. Anyway, I turned tail and have never been in love since."

"But were you in love on that occasion?" asked Adelaide.

"I don't know if it was love," answered Tito, "it was something . . . But that was a good five years ago. Since then I haven't met anyone who made my heart beat faster."

"So much the worse for you."

"I know," said Tito with a shrug. "But then, while I may not have enjoyed the private pleasures of love, I at least haven't endured the miseries or the disappointments. And that is a great good fortune."

"True love knows nothing of such things," said Adelaide sententiously.

"Really? Look, let's change the subject, shall we? I could deliver a speech on the matter, but I prefer—"

"You must stay here with us," Azevedo broke in. "That's decided."

"No, I can't . . ."

"You can and must stay."

"But I've already told my manservant to get me a room at the Hotel de Bragança . . ."

"Well, tell him otherwise, and stay here."

"I don't want to disturb your peace."

"But you won't."

"Stay!" said Adelaide.

"All right, I'll stay."

"And tomorrow," said Adelaide, "once you've rested, you must tell us the secret of this independence of mind you're so proud of."

"It's no secret," said Tito. "It's this: given the choice between love and a game of ombre, I don't think twice, I always choose ombre. By the way, Ernesto, I met an amazing player of ombre in Chile. He played the boldest gascarola I've ever seen . . . Do you know what a gascarola is, senhora?"

"No," said Adelaide.

"Well, I'll explain."

Azevedo glanced to one side and said:

"Ah, here's Emília."

There at the garden gate was a lady arm in arm with an older man of about fifty.

Dona Emília was what one might call a beautiful woman; she was lofty in stature and lofty in nature too. She was the kind of woman who would impose from on high any feelings of love she might inspire. Her manners and her graces gave her a rather queenly air, which made one feel like leading her to a throne.

She dressed simply but elegantly, a natural elegance that was quite different from being overdressed; indeed, I once came up with this maxim: "There are the elegantly dressed and there are the overdressed."

Her main points of beauty were her beautiful dark eyes, large and bright, her thick brown hair, her nose as straight as Sappho's, her small red mouth, satin cheeks, and the neck and arms of a statue.

As for the older man on her arm, he was, as I said, about fifty years old. He was what we call in Portuguese *chão*—vulgar and coarse, an old rake. Painted and corseted, he was like an ancient ruin rebuilt by modern hands, which gave him that in-between appearance, lacking both the austerity of old age and the freshness of youth. He had clearly been a handsome fellow in his day, but any conquests he may have made in the past would now be but faded memories.

When Emília came into the garden, everyone was already on their feet. She shook Azevedo's hand and went to kiss Adelaide on the cheek. She was just about to sit down in the chair Azevedo offered her, when she noticed Tito, who was standing slightly apart.

They greeted each other rather stiffly. Tito seemed calm and coolly polite, and, afterward, Emília kept her eyes fixed on him, as if summoning up some past memory.

Once the necessary introductions had been made, including Diogo Franco (the name of the old man on Emília's arm), they all sat down.

The first to speak was Emília:

"I wouldn't have come today if it hadn't been for Senhor Diogo's kindness."

Adelaide looked at Diogo and said:

"You're a marvel, Senhor Diogo."

Diogo drew himself up and murmured rather modestly:

"No, really, it was nothing."

"Just wait until you hear. He's not only one marvel, he's two. Did you know, he's going to give me a present?"

"A present!" said Azevedo.

"Yes," Emília went on, "a present he has ordered to be sent from the farthest-flung corners of Europe, a souvenir of his travels there as an adolescent . . ."

Diogo was positively radiant.

"No, really, it's a mere trifle," he said, gazing tenderly at Emília.

"Whatever is it?" asked Adelaide.

"It is . . . can you guess? A white bear!"

"A white bear?"

"Really?"

"It's about to arrive, apparently, but he only told me about it yesterday. Isn't that sweet?"

"A bear!" Azevedo said.

Tito leaned toward his friend and whispered in his ear:

"That will make two of them."

Overjoyed at this response to the news of his present, but quite wrong about the nature of that response, Diogo said:

"No, really, it's nothing. It's just a bear, although I did ask for a truly beautiful one to be sent. You probably can't imagine what a white bear looks like. It's completely white, you know."

"You don't say!" said Tito.

"It's a wonderful beast!" said Diogo.

"I'm sure it is," said Tito. "Just imagine that, a white bear that's completely white." Then, sotto voce, he asked Azevedo: "Who is this man?"

"He's courting Emília; he's fifty years old."

"And what does she do about that?"

"Oh, she just ignores him."

"Is that what she says?"

"Yes, and it's true."

While they were talking, Diogo was playing with the fob-chain on his watch, and the two ladies were chatting. After that last exchange between Azevedo and Tito, Emília turned to Azevedo and asked:

"Is it true, Senhor Azevedo, that you celebrate birthdays in this house and don't invite me?"

"But it was pouring with rain," said Adelaide.

"Ungrateful girl. You know perfectly well that rain doesn't count as an excuse."

"Besides," said Azevedo, "it was a very modest affair."

"Even so, I'm practically family!"

"The thing is, they're still on their honeymoon despite being married for five whole months," said Tito.

"And we'll have none of your sarcasm, thank you," said Azevedo.

"That's very naughty of you, Senhor Tito!"

"Tito?" Emília asked Adelaide quietly.

"Yes."

"Ah, Dona Emília doesn't yet know about our friend Tito," said Azevedo. "I'm almost afraid to tell her."

"Is it so very bad?"

"It might be," said Tito casually.

"Very bad!" exclaimed Adelaide.

"What is it, then?" asked Emília.

"He is a man incapable of love," Adelaide went on. "Indeed, he couldn't be more indifferent to love. In short, he prefers, what was it, now? Oh, yes, he prefers a game of ombre to love."

"Is that what he told you?" asked Emília.

"And I would say it again," said Tito. "But be assured, I say this not because of women, but because of myself. I believe that all women deserve my adoration, but I am so fashioned that all I can offer them is my disinterested esteem."

Emília looked at him and said:

"If that isn't vanity, then it's a disease."

"You'll forgive me when I say that I believe it to be neither a disease nor vanity. It's simply my nature: some people hate oranges, others hate love affairs; now, whether it's the tough skin that's the problem, I really don't know, but that's the way it is."

"He's very hard, isn't he?" said Emília, looking at Adelaide.

"Me? Hard?" said Tito, getting up. "I'm as delicate as silk, a mere baby, a miracle of gentleness . . . It hurts me deeply to be so unlike other men and so impervious to amorous influences, but what can I do? It's not my fault."

"Just you wait," said Azevedo. "Time will change you."

"But when? I'm already twenty-nine."

"Twenty-nine?" said Emília.

"Yes, I turned twenty-nine at Easter."

"You don't look it."

"You're most kind."

The conversation continued in this vein until dinner was announced. Emília and Diogo had already dined and only stayed in order to keep the Azevedos and Tito company, Tito declaring himself to be absolutely starving.

The conversation over dinner touched only on banal topics.

When coffee was served, a servant arrived from the hotel where Diogo was staying; he brought with him a letter for Diogo, with a note on the envelope announcing that it was urgent. Diogo took the letter, read it, and seemed to turn pale, but he, nevertheless, continued to take part in the general conversation. This incident, though, prompted Adelaide to ask Emília:

"When will your eternal inamorato ever set you free, do you think?"

"I have no idea!" said Emília. "He's not a bad man, but he's got into the habit of telling me every week that he feels a burning passion for me."

"Well, if it's only a weekly declaration . . ."

"Yes, that's all it is, and he does have the advantage of being an infallible companion whenever I go out and about and he's a reliable hurdy-gurdy when at home, always churning out the same stories. He's already described to me about fifty times the amorous battles he's fought. His one wish is to travel around the world with me. If the subject comes up in the evening, as it usually does, I order some tea, which is an excellent way of cooling his ardor. He's mad about tea, as mad as he is about me! But what do you make of that white bear? What if he really has sent for a bear?"

"You must accept it."

"How I am going to feed a bear? As if I didn't have enough to do!"

Adelaide smiled and said:

"It sounds to me as if you'll end up falling in love . . ."

"Who with? The bear?"

"No, with Diogo."

At this point, they were standing next to a window. Tito was sitting on the sofa, talking to Azevedo. Diogo was sunk in an armchair, deep in thought.

Emília kept looking at Tito. After a pause, she said to Adelaide:

"What do you make of your husband's friend? He seems dreadfully vain. He says he's never been in love. Is that credible?"

"It might be true."

"I don't believe it for a moment. How can you be so naïve? He's obviously pretending."

"It's true that I don't know much about him."

"As for me, I seem to recognize that face . . . but I can't remember where I know him from."

"He appears genuine enough, but to say what he said really is a bit much."

"Of course . . ."

"What are you smiling at?"

"He reminds me of another such man," said Emília. "It was years ago now. He was always boasting about how he was immune to love. He used to say that, for him, women were like Chinese vases: he admired them, but nothing more. Poor man. He succumbed in less than a month. I saw him kiss the tips of my shoes, Adelaide . . . after which, I sent him packing."

"What did you do?"

"Oh, I can't remember now. Our Lady of Cunning performed the miracle. I avenged our sex and laid low a proud man."

"Well done."

"He was not dissimilar to this gentleman. But let's talk about more important matters. I've just received the latest fashion plates from France . . ."

"And what's new?"

"Oh, lots of things. I'll send them to you tomorrow. There's a really lovely new style of sleeve you must see. I've already ordered a few things to be made up for me in Rio. And there are loads of gorgeous traveling outfits."

"There doesn't seem much point in me ordering anything."

"Why?"

"I hardly leave the house."

"What, not even to dine with me on New Year's Day?"

"Oh, I wouldn't miss that!"

"Well, come, then, and what about this man, Senhor Tito?"

"If he's still here and if you'd like him to come . . ."

"Yes, let him come, why not? I'll keep him on a very short rein. I don't think he can always be so . . . uncivil. I don't know how you put up with him. He sets my nerves on edge!"

"Oh, I don't much care what he says."

"But doesn't it make you indignant, the insulting way he talks about women?"

"Not really."

"You're lucky, then."

"What do you expect me to do with a man who says such things? If I weren't married, I might feel more indignant. If I were free, I might well do to him what you did to that other man. But as it is, I don't honestly care . . ."

"Not even when he says he would always choose a game of cards over love? Putting us lower down the ranks than the queen of spades! And the way he said it too! Such coolness, such indifference!"

"He really is very naughty!"

"He deserves to be punished."

"He does. Why don't you punish him?"

"No, it's not worth it."

"You punished that other man."

"Yes, but it's really not worth it."

"Liar!"

"Why do you say that?"

"Because I can already see that you're half tempted to carry out another act of revenge . . ."

"Me? No!"

"Yes, why not? It's not a crime . . ."

"True, but . . . we'll see."

"Could you?"

"*Could* I?" said Emília with a look of wounded pride.

"Will he kiss the tips of your shoes?"

Emília remained silent for a few moments, then, pointing with her fan at the neat little boots she was wearing, she added:

"Yes, he'll kiss these very boots."

Emília and Adelaide went over to join the men. Tito, who appeared to be deep in conversation with Azevedo, broke off their conversation to address them and Diogo, who was still plunged in thought.

"What's this, Senhor Diogo?" Tito asked. "Are you meditating?"

"Ah, I'm sorry. I was distracted!"

"Poor man," Tito murmured to Azevedo.

Then, turning to the ladies, he asked:

"Does my cigar bother you?"

"Not at all," said Emília.

"So I may continue to smoke?"

"You may," said Adelaide.

"It's a bad habit, but it's my only vice. When I smoke, it's as if I were breathing in eternity. It lifts me up and I'm a changed man. Such a divine invention!"

"They say it's an excellent remedy for those disappointed in love," said Emília in an insinuating tone.

"I wouldn't know. But there's more to it than that. Since the invention of smoking, no one has ever needed to be alone again. A cigar makes for the best possible company. Besides, a cigar is a genuine *Memento homo*, slowly turning, as it does, into dust; it reminds a man of the true and inevitable end of all things. It's a philosophical warning, a *memento mori* that accompanies us everywhere. That, in itself, is a great advance. But I'm boring you with such a tedious speech. You must forgive me . . . I didn't mean to go on so. Indeed, it already seems to me that you're looking at me with such a singular look in your eyes that . . ."

Emília, to whom these words were addressed, answered:

"I couldn't say whether the look is singular or not, but the eyes are definitely mine."

"They're not, I think, your usual eyes. You're perhaps thinking to yourself that I'm strange, eccentric . . ."

"Vain, I would say."

"Remember the seventh commandment: Thou shalt not bear false witness."

"The commandment does specify 'false.'"

"In what way, then, am I vain?"

"Ah, I can't answer that."

"Why? Because you don't want to?"

"No, Because I don't know. It's something one feels, but cannot put a name to. You exude vanity, in your gaze, your words, your looks, but it's impossible to put one's finger on the origin of such an illness."

"That's a shame. I would very much like to hear your diagnosis of my 'illness.' To make up for that, you can hear my diagnosis of yours . . . Your illness stems . . . shall I say it?"

"Do."

"From a touch of resentment."

"Really?"

"Go on," said Azevedo, laughing.

Tito continued:

"Yes, resentment for what I said earlier."

"Ah, there you could not be more mistaken," said Emília, also laughing.

"I'm sure I'm right. But it's entirely unnecessary. I'm not to blame for anything. This is how Nature made me."

"Nature alone?"

"Nature and a little reading. Let me set out the reasons why I cannot love or hope to love anyone: first, I'm not handsome enough . . ."

"Oh, really!" said Emília.

"Thank you for that cry of protest, but I think I'm right. I'm not handsome enough, I'm not—"

"Oh, really!" And it was Adelaide's turn to protest.

"Second, I'm not curious, and love, if we reduce it to its true proportions, is nothing but curiosity; third, I'm not patient, and in any amorous conquest, patience is the chief virtue; fourth and final point: nor am I an idiot, because, if, despite all those defects, I were ever to attempt to love someone, I would be displaying a complete and utter lack of reason. So that is what I am, by nature and by dint of hard work."

"He appears to be sincere, Emília."

"Do you think so?"

"As sincere as the truth," said Tito.

"But when it comes down to it, whether he's sincere or not, why should I care?"

"No reason at all," said Tito.

II

The day after the scenes described above, the sky decided to drench the earth of lovely Petrópolis with its tears.

Tito, who had intended to spend the day visiting the town, was forced to remain in the house. He was the perfect guest, because whenever he felt he was in the way, he would discreetly withdraw, and when he wasn't in the way, he became the most delightful of companions.

Tito combined great joviality with great delicacy; he could make people laugh without ever resorting to impropriety. What's more, he had just returned from a long and picturesque journey with the pockets of his memory (if you'll allow me that image) stuffed with lively anecdotes. He had made the journey in a poetic rather than a dandyish spirit. He was an excellent observer and storyteller, two qualities so indispensable to the traveler, but which are, alas, all too rare. Most people who travel don't know how to look or how to describe what they see.

Tito had traveled all the way up the Pacific coast and had lived in Mexico, as well as several American states. He had then taken the steamer from New York to Europe. He had seen London and Paris. He had been to Spain, where he lived a kind of Figaro life, serenading modern-day Rosinas at their windows, and, as trophies, had brought back several ladies' fans and mantillas. He then moved on to Italy and raised his spirit up to the heights of classical art. He saw the shadow of Dante in the streets of Florence; he saw the souls of the doges hovering nostalgically over the widowed waters of the Adriatic Sea; the land of Raphael, Virgil, and Michelangelo was for him a vibrant source of memories of the past and ideas for the future. He went to Greece, where he evoked the spirit of the lost generations who had imbued art and poetry with a fire that still glowed brightly down the dark centuries.

Our hero traveled farther still, and saw everything with the eyes of one who knows how to look and described everything with the soul of one who knows how to tell a tale. Azevedo and Adelaide spent many a rapt hour.

"All I know of love," he would say, "is that it's a four-letter word, euphonious enough, it's true, but portending struggles and misfortunes. The love of fortunate lovers is full of happiness, because it has the virtue of not looking up at the stars in the sky, but contents itself with a few midnight feasts and the occasional excursion on horseback or by boat."

This was how Tito always spoke. Was he telling the truth, or was this merely the language of convention? Everyone believed the first hypothesis, because this chimed with Tito's jovial, playful nature.

On the first day of his stay in Petrópolis, the rain, as we explained earlier, prevented the various characters in this story from meeting up. They all stayed in their respective houses. The following day, however, proved kinder, and Tito took advantage of the good weather to visit that cheerful mountain resort. Azevedo and Adelaide decided to join him and ordered three of their own horses to be saddled up for that brief outing.

On the way back, they called in to see Emília. The visit lasted only a few minutes. The lovely widow received them as graciously and courteously as a princess. It was the first time Tito had been there, and, whether for this or for some other reason, the mistress of the house paid most attention to him.

Diogo, who was in the process of making his hundredth declaration of love to Emília, and for whom Emília had just poured a cup of tea, did not view kindly the attentions showered on the visitor by the lady of his thoughts. For that and possibly other reasons, the aging Adonis listened very glumly to the conversation.

As the visitors were leaving, Emília invited Tito to come again, saying that he would always be welcome. Tito accepted this offer in a gentlemanly fashion, and then they all left.

Five days after this visit, Emília went to see Adelaide. Tito was not there, and Azevedo, having gone out to deal with some business matter, returned a few minutes later. When, after an hour of conversation, Emília stood up in order to return home, Tito came in.

"I was just about to leave when you arrived," said Emília. "We seem to be at odds in everything."

"That is certainly not my intention," answered Tito. "On the contrary, my one wish is not to be at odds with anyone, and certainly not with you."

"That doesn't appear to be the case."

"Why do you say that?"

Emília smiled and said in a slightly censorious tone:

"You know how it would please me if you were to take up my invitation to visit me, but you have not as yet done so. Did you forget?"

"Yes, I did."

"How charming."

"I'm always very frank. I realize you would prefer a delicate lie, but I know of nothing more delicate than the truth."

Emília smiled.

At this point, Diogo arrived.

"Were you about to leave, Dona Emília?" he asked.

"Yes, I was waiting for your arm to escort me."

"Here it is."

Emília said goodbye to Azevedo and Adelaide. And when Tito bowed to her respectfully, Emília said with icy calm:

"There is someone who is as delicate as the truth, and that is Senhor Diogo. I hope to be able to say the same—"

"Of me?" said Tito, interrupting her. "I'll be there tomorrow."

Emília left, arm in arm with Diogo.

The next day, Tito did indeed go to Emília's house. She waited for him with some impatience, and since she did not know at what hour he would visit, she spent the whole day, from the morning on, waiting. Tito only deigned to appear at dusk.

Emília lived with an old aunt of hers. She was a kind lady, a good friend to her niece, and entirely submissive to her will, which meant that Emília could rest assured that her aunt would always fall in with her every wish.

There was no one else in the room that Tito was shown into. He therefore had more than enough time to examine it at his leisure. It was a small room, but furnished and decorated with great taste. Light, elegant, expensive furniture; four exquisite statuettes—copies of works by James Pradier—an Érard piano, and all arranged in a most interesting and lively way.

Tito spent the first quarter of an hour examining the room and the objects filling it. This examination must have had a great influence on any study he might have wished to make of the young woman's mind. Tell me how you live, and I'll tell you who you are.

That first quarter of an hour passed, and still not a soul appeared and not a sound was heard. Tito began to grow impatient. As we know, he could be somewhat blunt, despite his great delicacy, to which anyone who knew him would attest. It seems, though, that his bluntness, which he almost always exercised on Emília, was perhaps assumed rather than natural. What is certain is that, after half an hour had passed, Tito, irritated by the delay, muttered to himself:

"She's having her revenge!"

And, picking up the hat he had placed on a chair, he was just walking over to the door when he heard a rustle of silk. Looking up, he saw Emília entering the room.

"Were you escaping?"

"Yes, I was."

"Please forgive the delay."

"There's nothing to forgive. I'm sure some serious reason must have prevented you from coming down earlier. As for me, I have no need to ask forgiveness, either. I waited, grew tired of waiting, and would have come back on another occasion. All of which is perfectly normal."

Emília offered Tito a chair, then sat down on a sofa, and, apparently accepting his rebuff, she said:

"You really are a complete original, Senhor Tito."

"I should hope so. You have no idea how I loathe copies. What possible merit is there in doing what everyone else does? I was not born for such imitative tasks."

"But you have already done something that many other people do."

"What's that?"

"You promised me yesterday that you would visit and you have kept that promise."

"Ah, please do not attribute that to any virtue on my part. I could easily not have come, but I did. It was pure chance not choice."

"Well, I choose to thank you anyway."

"That is a way of closing your door to me."

"Why?"

"Because I can't be bothered with such expressions of gratitude, nor do I think they could in any way increase my admiration for you. I often went to visit statues in various European museums, but if they had ever thought to thank me for my visit, I can assure you that I would not have gone back."

These words were followed by a brief silence, which Emília was the first to break.

"Have you known Adelaide's husband for long?"

"Ever since I was a child."

"Oh, so you were once a child."

"And still am."

"That is precisely how long I have known Adelaide. And I've never regretted it."

"Nor have I."

"There was a period," Emília went on, "when we were separated, but that didn't change our friendship one jot. That was at the time of my first marriage."

"Ah, you've been married twice?"

"In two years."

"And why were you widowed the first time?"

"Because my husband died," said Emília, laughing.

"No, my question is this: Why did you become a widow even after the death of your first husband? Could you not have remained married?"

"How?" Emília asked with some amazement.

"By continuing to be the wife of your dead husband. If love ends in the grave, there hardly seems any point in seeking it out."

"You really are a most unusual man."

"Possibly."

"You must be if you fail to see that life cares nothing for such demands of eternal fidelity. Besides, one can preserve the memory of those who die without renouncing life. Now it's my turn to ask you why you're looking at me with such a singular look in your eyes."

"I couldn't say whether that look is singular or not, but the eyes are definitely mine."

"So you think I committed bigamy?"

"No, I don't think anything. But let me give you my final reason for my inability to love."

"I'm all ears."

"I don't believe in fidelity."

"Not at all?"

"Not at all."

"Thank you very much."

"Oh, I know it's hardly polite to say so, but, firstly, I have the courage of my convictions, and secondly, you were the one who provoked me. Alas, it is true: I do not believe in faithful and eternal love. I'll let you into a secret. I did once try to love someone; I threw every fiber of my being into it; I prepared myself to heap all my pride and all my hopes onto the object of my love. What a lesson it taught me! Having encouraged my hopes, the object of my love married someone else, who was no more handsome and no more loving than me."

"What does that prove?" asked Emília.

"It proves that what can and does happen on a daily basis to others happened to me."

"Yes, but—"

"You must forgive me, but I think it's in my blood now."

"Don't say that. Such things do happen, but that doesn't mean it will happen again. Will you allow for no exceptions? You need to go deeper into other people's hearts if you want to find the truth . . . and you will find it."

"Oh, really!" said Tito, bowing his head and tapping the tip of his shoe with his walking stick.

"I can assure you that it's true."

"I doubt it."

"I feel sorry for a creature like you," she went on. "If you've never known love, you've never lived! Is there anything to compare with two souls who adore each other? When love enters your heart, everything is transformed, everything changes, night becomes day, pain becomes pleasure. If you know nothing of these things, you might as well die, because you are the most unfortunate of men."

"I've read as much in books, but I'm still not convinced . . ."

"Have you taken a look around this room?"

"Yes, I looked at one or two things."

"Did you notice that engraving?"

Tito looked at the engraving she was pointing to.

"I think I would be right in saying," he said, "that it represents Love taming the wild beasts."

"Look and learn."

"What, from the engraver?" asked Tito. "That's not possible. I've seen living engravings. I've been the target for many arrows. They can riddle me all over, but I am strong as any Saint Sebastian. I stand firm and do not flinch."

"Such pride!"

"What could vanquish such pride? Beauty? Not even a Cleopatra. Chastity? Not even a Susanna. Even if you were to combine all the finest qualities in one creature, I would not change. That's simply how I am."

Emília stood up and went over to the piano.

"I assume you don't hate music?" she asked, as she opened the lid.

"No, I love music," answered Tito, staying where he was. "Although, when it comes to the exponents of music, I only like the good ones. Hearing someone play badly makes me want to see them hanged."

Emília played the prelude to a symphony. Tito listened with close attention. She really did play divinely.

"So," she said, getting up, "should I be hanged?"

"No, you should be crowned. You play superbly."

"That's another matter on which you are not in the least original. Everyone tells me the same thing."

"Yes, but nor would I deny the light from the sun."

At this point, Emília's aunt came into the room. Emília introduced her to Tito. The conversation took on a more personal, more reserved tone; however, it did not last long, because Tito, suddenly snatching up his hat, announced that he had things to do.

"When will we see you again?"

"Oh, you'll see me."

And with that, he left.

Emília followed him with her eyes for some time from the window. Tito, as if indifferent, did not look back.

Just as Emília left the window, Tito met old Diogo, who was heading toward Emília's house. He appeared to be deep in thought; indeed, so distracted was he that he almost bumped into Tito.

"Where are you off to in this distracted state?" asked Tito.

"Oh, it's you, Senhor Tito. Have you just come from Dona Emília's house?"

"I have."

"That's where I'm going. Poor girl, she must be wondering where I've got to."

"Don't worry, she isn't," said Tito coolly.

Diogo shot him a resentful glance.

A silence ensued, during which Diogo played with his watch chain and Tito blew smoke rings with the smoke from his exquisite cigar. One of these rings ended up in Diogo's face. He coughed and said to Tito:

"Please, Senhor Tito. That's enough!"

"What's wrong, my dear sir?" asked Tito.

"Surely you don't have to blow smoke in my face as well!"

"I'm sorry, I didn't realize. But I don't understand what you mean by 'as well.'"

"Let me explain," said Diogo cheerfully. "Give me your arm."

"Of course."

And they continued walking along like two old friends.

"I'm ready for your explanation."

"Here goes. And I want you to be perfectly frank with me. You know that I'm dying of love for Dona Emília. No, don't argue, just agree. Up until now, everything was going well, then you arrived in Petrópolis."

"Yes, but—"

"Hear me out. You arrived in Petrópolis and, for reasons known only to you and even though I hadn't harmed you in any way, you decided to oust me. Ever since then, you've been paying court to—"

"My dear Senhor Diogo, this is all pure fantasy. I am not paying court to Dona Emília, nor do I intend to. Have you seen me at her house?"

"You've just come from there."

"Well, it's the first time I've visited her."

"How can I be sure?"

"Didn't you hear the way she said goodbye to me yesterday at Azevedo's house? They were hardly the words of a woman who—"

"That proves nothing. Women, and especially that woman, do not always say what they mean . . ."

"So you think she feels something for me?"

"If I didn't, I wouldn't be talking to you."

"Well, it's news to me."

"It's only a suspicion, of course, but she talks of nothing else. She asks me twenty times a day about you and your habits, about your past life and your opinions. As you can imagine, I can only say, 'I don't know,' but I'm beginning to hate you, and you can hardly blame me."

"Is it my fault that she likes me? But, really, Senhor Diogo, there's no need to worry. She doesn't like me, and I don't like her. Carry on regardless and be happy."

"Happy! If only I could be! But I don't believe I can, I'm not made for happiness. Look, Senhor Tito, I love that woman as dearly as life itself. One look from her is worth more to me than a whole year of success and happiness. It's because of her that I've let my business affairs go to pot. Did you not notice the other day that I received a most upsetting letter? Well, I'd lost a lawsuit. And all for what? For her!"

"Does she give you any encouragement?"

"Oh, I don't understand the girl! One day, she's so sweet to me that I'm in seventh heaven; the next, her indifference is enough to plunge me into hell. Today, a smile; tomorrow, a look of disdain. She tells me off for not visiting her, and then, when I do visit, she takes about as much notice of me as she does of Ganymede—Ganymede is the name of a little dog I gave her.

Yes, she cares as much about me as she does for that dog. She does it on purpose. The girl is a complete enigma."

"Well, I won't be the one to solve it, Senhor Diogo. I wish you much happiness. Goodbye."

And the two men parted. Diogo continued on to Emília's house, and Tito to Azevedo's.

Tito had just discovered that he was often in Emília's thoughts, but this caused not the slightest commotion inside him. Why? We will find that out later on. What we must say, though, is that the same suspicions had arisen in Adelaide's mind as in Diogo's. Her close friendship with Emília allowed her to submit Emília to a frank interrogation and to receive an equally frank confession. On the day after the scene just described, Adelaide told Emília her thoughts.

Emília responded with a laugh.

"I don't understand you," said Adelaide.

"It's perfectly simple," said Emília. "If you think me capable of falling in love with a friend of your husband's, you're wrong. No, I don't love him. As I said to you when I first set eyes on him, I am determined to have him at my feet. In fact, if I remember rightly, you were the one who laid down that challenge, a challenge I accepted. I have to avenge our sex. It may be vanity on my part, but I believe I can do what no other woman has done."

"Ah, you cruel creature. So that's it!"

"Absolutely."

"Do you think it's possible?"

"Why not?"

"Remember that a defeat would be twofold . . ."

"I know, but I won't be defeated."

This conversation was interrupted by Azevedo, and Emília gestured to Adelaide to say nothing. It was agreed between them that not even Azevedo should know what was afoot. And Adelaide said nothing to her husband.

III

A week passed.

As we have seen, Tito was exactly as he had been on the very first day. He went for walks, read, talked, and seemed blissfully unaware of the plots

being woven about him. During that time, he made only two visits to Emília's house, once with the Azevedos and once with Diogo. He was the same
on both occasions—cold, indifferent, impassive. No look, however seductive or significant, could shake him; not even the idea that he was much in
Emília's thoughts could spark his interest.

"If he really is incapable of love, why does he not at least engage in one
of those *amours de salon* that so flatter men's vanity?"

This was a question that Emília put to herself, bewildered by the young
man's indifference. She could not understand how Tito could remain so icy
cold when confronted by her charms. This, unfortunately, was how it was.

Weary of working in vain, she decided to take a decisive step. She steered
the conversation onto the sweet pleasures of marriage and bemoaned her
widowed state. The Azevedos were, for her, the image of perfect conjugal
bliss. She presented them to Tito as an incentive for anyone wishing to be
happy on this earth. Neither thesis nor hypothesis, however, could thaw
Tito's coldness.

Emília was playing a dangerous game. She had to decide between her
desire to avenge her sex and what was proper for a woman in her position;
she was, however, a proud creature; and while she was respectful of her own
strict morality, she did not show the same degree of respect for the inconve-
nience that went hand in hand with preserving that moral code. Vanity had
a prodigious influence over her. And so the lovely widow deployed all licit
means to make Tito fall in love with her.

But once he had fallen in love, what would she do? An idle question,
since, once she had him at her feet, she would try to keep him kneeling
there along with old Diogo. That would be the best possible trophy any
proud beauty could aspire to.

One morning, eight days after the scenes described in the previous
chapter, Diogo appeared at the Azevedos' house. They had just finished
breakfast. Azevedo had gone up to his study to finish off some correspondence, and Adelaide was in the downstairs living room.

Diogo entered, looking terribly sad, sadder than she had ever seen him
before. She ran over to him.

"Whatever's wrong?" she asked.

"Ah, senhora, I am the most wretched of men!"

"But why? Come and sit down . . ."

Diogo sat, or, rather, slumped down into the chair Adelaide offered him. She took a seat next to him and encouraged him to tell her his woes.

"What's happened?"

"Two misfortunes," he said. "The first in the form of a verdict. I've lost yet another lawsuit, which is unfortunate, but it's as nothing compared to—"

"You mean there's something worse?"

"Yes, the second misfortune came in the form of a letter."

"A letter?"

"Yes, read this."

Diogo removed from his wallet a small pink letter, smelling of essence of magnolia.

Adelaide read the letter.

When she had finished, Diogo asked:

"What do you make of that?"

"I don't understand," said Adelaide.

"It's from her."

"Yes, and so?"

"It's a letter to him."

"Who?"

"Him! The devil! My rival! Tito!"

"Ah!"

"I cannot tell you what I felt when I picked up that letter. I have never trembled before anything in my life, but when I read that, my head began to spin. It's still spinning now. With every step I take, I feel as if I were about to faint."

"Don't despair," said Adelaide.

"That is precisely why I have come here, in search of consolation, reassurance. I knew you were at home and hoped to find you alone. It's such a shame that your estimable husband is still alive, because the greatest possible consolation would be for you to accept my poor, misunderstood heart."

"Fortunately, he's still alive."

Diogo uttered a sigh and said:

"Fortunately!"

Then, after a silence, he went on:

"I had two reactions: one was to treat them both with utter scorn, but that would only give them still greater freedom and leave me racked with pain and humiliation; the second was to challenge him to a duel; that would be best, I'll kill him or else—"

"Don't talk like that."

"It's vital that one of us is crossed off the list of the living."

"What if you're mistaken?"

"But I'm not mistaken. I'm absolutely sure."

"Sure about what?"

Diogo unfolded the letter and said:

"Listen: *If you have still not understood me then you must lack all insight. Remove your mask, and I will explain myself. I'll be having tea alone this evening. The importunate Diogo will not be troubling me with his usual nonsense. Give me the pleasure of seeing you and admiring you. Emília.*"

"Is that all?"

"Ah, if it were more than that, I would be dead! But I was able to steal the letter and thus prevent that meeting from taking place."

"When was the letter written?"

"Yesterday."

"Calm down. Can you keep a secret? I should not be telling you this, and I'm only doing so because you're upset. I can guarantee that this letter is a trick. It's a way of avenging the female sex, a way of making Tito fall in love. That's all."

Diogo trembled with joy.

"Really?" he asked.

"Yes, it's true, but remember, it's a secret. As I said, I'm only telling you as a way of reassuring you. Don't spoil our joke."

"And this is really true?"

"How many times must I tell you?"

"Oh, what a weight off my mind! I promise you that your secret is safe with me. How very funny. I'm so glad I came to talk to you. Can I tell Dona Emília that I know all about it?"

"No!"

"So I'd better pretend to know nothing."

"Yes."

"Fine."

Diogo was rubbing his hands together and blinking contentedly. He was radiant with happiness. How glorious, what joy, to see his supposed rival fall into the widow's trap!

At this point, the inner door opened, and Tito appeared. He had just gotten up.

"Good morning, Dona Adelaide," he said, then, sitting down and turning to look at Diogo, he added. "Good morning, Diogo. You seem very happy today. Have you won first prize on the lottery?"

"First prize?" said Diogo. "Yes, I have."

"Did you sleep well?" Adelaide asked Tito.

"I slept the sleep of the just, of course. I had very sweet dreams. I dreamed about Senhor Diogo."

"Of me?" murmured Diogo, adding to himself: "Poor man. I feel sorry for him."

"Where's Azevedo?" asked Tito.

"He's gone out."

"Already?"

"Well, it is eleven o'clock."

"Eleven! Yes, I did wake up rather late. I have two visits to make, one to Dona Emília—"

"Oh!" cried Diogo.

"Why so surprised, my friend?"

"Oh, no reason."

"I'll go and ask them to prepare your breakfast," said Adelaide.

The two men were left alone. Tito lit a slender cigar, and Diogo pretended to be thinking his own thoughts, all the while shooting sideways glances at Tito, who, after taking only two puffs on his cigar, turned and asked:

"How's the romance going?"

"What romance?"

"With Emília. Have you managed to convince her of your great consuming passion?"

"I could do with some lessons, actually. Could you teach me?"

"Me? Are you crazy?"

"Oh, I know how experienced you are, modest, but very experienced! Whereas I am a mere apprentice. Indeed, only a short while ago, I was even thinking of challenging you to a duel."

"A duel?"

"Yes, but it was ridiculous idea which I soon rejected."

"Besides, people don't fight duels in Brazil."

"Defending one's honor is normal practice everywhere."

"Bravo, Don Quixote!"

"And I felt my honor had been insulted."

"By me?"

"Yes, but I changed my mind when I realized I was the one insulting you, by proposing to do battle with a past master; me, a mere apprentice . . ."

"A past master at what?"

"At love! I know it's true . . ."

"Stop it! I'm no such thing. You're the master; after all, you're worth one bear, even two. How could you possibly . . . Were you really jealous of me?"

"I was."

"You clearly don't know me. Have you not heard my views on the subject?"

"Sometimes that only makes things worse."

"Worse? How?"

"Women won't let an affront like that go unpunished. And your ideas are an affront to the female sex. I wonder what a suitable punishment would be? But I'll go no further . . ."

"Where are you off to?"

"I'm leaving. Goodbye. And forget about that absurd idea of me challenging you to a duel . . ."

"Of course. But you had a very lucky escape."

"From what?"

"From death. It would have been such a pleasure to stick my sword in that belly of yours, a pleasure comparable only to that of embracing you while you're alive and kicking!"

Diogo gave a forced laugh:

"Thank you very much! And see you again soon!"

"Come back. Where are you off to? Aren't you going to say goodbye to Dona Adelaide?"

"I'll be back shortly," said Diogo, putting on his hat and rushing out.

Tito watched him leave.

"That fellow," he said to himself when alone, "has never had an original thought in his life. He didn't think up that business about vengeful women all by himself. Rather . . . I smell a plot. That suits me fine. The sooner, the better."

A German servant came to tell Tito that his breakfast was ready, and Tito was just about to go in, when Azevedo appeared at the door.

"So there you are! You obviously didn't rise with the sun. You look as if you'd just got up."

"I know, and I'm about to have my breakfast."

They both went into the dining room, where the table was set, and Tito asked:

"Are you having a second breakfast?"

"No."

"Well, you can watch how it's done."

Tito sat down at the table and Azevedo stretched out on a sofa.

"Where did you go?"

"For a walk. I've realized that I need to see and admire what is indifferent to me in order to appreciate fully what fills my heart with true happiness."

"Really? So one can also tire of happiness! As you see, reason is still on my side."

"Perhaps, but despite everything, it seems to me that you are intent on joining the married brigade."

"Me?"

"Yes, you."

"Why?"

"Is it or is it not true?"

"What do you mean, 'true'?"

"All I know is that one afternoon recently, when you fell asleep over a book—I can't remember what book it was now—I heard you talking in your dreams and pronouncing the name 'Emília' with the utmost tenderness."

"Really?" asked Tito, his mouth full.

"Yes. I came to the conclusion that if you were dreaming about her, then she must be on your mind, and that if she's on your mind, then you must love her."

"You concluded wrongly."

"Wrongly?"

"You drew the conclusion of a man who has been married for five months. What does a dream prove?"

"It proves a lot!"

"It proves nothing. You're acting like a superstitious old woman."

"There must be something going on, though. Could you tell me what it is?"

"I could if it weren't for the fact that you're married."

"What has that got to do with it?"

"Everything. You could, unwittingly, be indiscreet. At night, between a kiss and a yawn, husband and wife open their respective bags of confidences to each other. You could, without thinking, ruin everything."

"No, I wouldn't. But that means you do have something to tell me."

"No, nothing."

"You're merely confirming my suspicions. You like Emília, don't you?"

"I certainly don't hate her."

"So you do like her. And she deserves to be liked. She's an excellent lady, uncommonly beautiful and possessed of all the finest qualities. Perhaps you would rather she were not a widow?"

"Yes, because she probably spends much of the day gloating over the two husbands she's already dispatched to the next world, while she waits to dispatch a third . . ."

"She's not like that at all."

"Can you guarantee that?"

"Pretty much."

"Ah, my friend," said Tito, getting up from the table and lighting a cigar, "take the advice of a fool: never guarantee anything, especially when it comes to matters of the heart. If you have to choose between discreet prudence and blind trust, don't hesitate, and let the former be your guide. What can you guarantee about Emília? You know her no better than I do. I've known her for two weeks, and I can read her like a book, and while I certainly wouldn't attribute any malevolent feelings to her, I'm sure she does not possess the rarest of rare qualities that would make her 'the exception.' Do you know something I don't?"

"No, nothing."

"So, you know nothing, do you?" Tito said to himself.

"I'm basing myself purely on my personal observations, and it seems to me that a marriage between you two would be rather a good idea."

"If you mention marriage one more time, I'm leaving."

"Not even the word?"

"No, not the word, the idea, nothing."

"And yet you admire and applaud my marriage . . ."

"I applaud many things in other people, things of which I myself am incapable. It all depends on vocation . . ."

Adelaide appeared at the door of the dining room, and the conversation between the two men came to an abrupt halt.

"I bring you news."

"What news?" asked Tito and Azevedo in unison.

"I've just had a note from Emília . . . She's inviting us to visit her tomorrow, because . . ."

"Because?" asked Azevedo.

"Because she might be going back to Rio in a week or so's time."

"Oh," said Tito with bland indifference.

"You'd better pack your bags," Azevedo said to Tito.

"Why?"

"Aren't you going to follow in the footsteps of the goddess?"

"Don't make fun of me, cruel friend, when there's absolutely no—"

"Come on . . ."

Adelaide smiled at these words.

Half an hour later, Tito went up to the study where Azevedo kept his books. He intended to read Saint Augustine's *Confessions*.

"Why the sudden trip to Rio?" Azevedo asked his wife.

"Do you really want to know?"

"I do."

"All right, but it's a secret. I don't know for sure, but I think it's a strategy."

"A strategy? I don't understand."

"I'll explain. It's a way of ensnaring Tito."

"Ensnaring?"

"You're very slow today! Yes, ensnaring him in the bonds of love . . ."

"Ah!"

"Emília felt she had to do it. It's just a joke. When he declares himself vanquished, she will be avenged for what he said about the female sex."

"Not bad . . . And you're part of this strategy, are you?"

"Only in an advisory capacity."

"So you're plotting against my friend, my alter ego."

"Now, now, don't say a word. You don't want to ruin the plan."

Azevedo laughed long and loud. He was amused by this premeditated punishment of poor Tito.

The visit Tito had said he was due to make to Emília that day did not happen.

However, knowing Emília's intentions, Diogo had gone immediately to her house to await Tito's arrival, and there he spent the whole day, in vain: in vain he dined, in vain he spent the entire afternoon boring Emília and her aunt, and still Tito did not appear.

That evening, however, when Diogo, bored with waiting at Emília's house, was just about to leave, Tito's presence was announced.

Emília trembled, but this went unnoticed by Diogo.

Tito entered the room where Emília, her aunt, and Diogo were all sitting.

"I wasn't expecting you," Emília said.

"That's the way I am. I arrive when least expected. I'm like death or a win on the lottery."

"Tonight, you're a win on the lottery," said Emília.

"And what number is your ticket?"

"Number twelve, for the twelve hours I've had the pleasure of Senhor Diogo's company today."

"Twelve hours!" exclaimed Tito, turning to Diogo.

"And our good friend has yet to tell us a single story . . ."

"Twelve hours!" Tito said again.

"And what's so astonishing about that, sir?" asked Diogo.

"It does seem rather a long time."

"One only counts the hours when one is bored . . . With your permission, I will withdraw . . ."

And, saying this, Diogo picked up his hat to leave, shooting a look of jealous scorn at Emília.

"Why?" she asked. "Where are you going?"

"I am lending wings to the hours," Diogo whispered into Emília's ear. "They will pass quickly now."

"I forgive you and ask you to sit down again."

Diogo did as asked.

Emília's aunt begged to be excused for a few moments, leaving only the three of them.

"So," said Tito, "he didn't tell you a single story."

"Not one."

Emília glanced at Diogo as if to reassure him. Feeling calmer now, Diogo remembered what Adelaide had told him and immediately cheered up.

"After all," he thought, "the joke's on him. I am merely the means to entrap him. Let's all play our part in pulling the rug from under his feet."

"Not a single story," Emília said again.

"Oh, I know plenty of stories," said Diogo insinuatingly.

"Then tell us one of those many stories," said Tito.

"Certainly not! Why don't you tell us one?"

"If you insist . . ."

"Oh, I do, I do," said Diogo, blinking. "Tell us one about jilted bridegrooms, or love's deceits, or hardened voyagers. Go on!"

"No, I'm going to tell you a story about a man and a monkey."

"Oh," said Emília.

"It's very interesting," said Tito. "Listen."

"Forgive me," said Emília, "but let's have tea first."

"Of course."

Tea was served shortly afterward, and when it was over, Tito began his story:

STORY OF A MAN AND A MONKEY

About twenty years ago, not far from the town of *** in the interior of Brazil, there lived a thirty-five-year-old man, whose mysterious life was the subject of much gossip in the surrounding towns and a source of terror to any travelers who happened along the road that passed only a few feet from his house.

The house itself was enough to strike fear into the least timid of hearts. Seen from a distance, it was built so close to the ground that it did not even resemble a house. However, anyone who dared to go closer would see that half of the building was above ground level and half below. While it was very solidly built, it had neither doors nor windows, only a square opening that served as both window and door, through which the mysterious inhabitant came and went.

Few people saw him leave, not just because he rarely did leave, but because he left at very strange times of day. This solitary individual only left his house to go roaming around when the moon was full. He always took with him a large monkey, who answered to the name Caligula.

Monkey and man, man and monkey, were inseparable friends, inside the house and out, when the moon was new.

People had many theories about this mysterious man.

The most widely held theory was that he was a wizard. According to another, he was crazy, and yet another held that he was merely a misanthrope.

This last theory was supported by two facts: first, there was no positive evidence to indicate that the man ever behaved like a wizard or a madman; second, there was his avowed friendship with the monkey and his horror of being seen by other men. Whenever we begin to loathe mankind, we always grow fonder of animals, who have the advantage of neither talking too much nor intriguing against us.

This mysterious man . . . Wait, we need to give him a name: let's call him Daniel. Well, Daniel preferred the company of the monkey and spoke to no one else. Travelers passing by on the road would sometimes hear shrieks coming from both man and monkey; it was the man stroking the monkey.

What did those two creatures live on? One morning, someone saw the monkey leave the house only to return shortly afterward carrying a package in its mouth. The muleteer who witnessed this wanted to find out where the monkey went to fetch that package, which doubtless contained food for those two solitary beings. The following morning, he hid in the wood; the monkey arrived at the usual hour and went over to a tree trunk; higher up the trunk was a large branch, which the monkey threw to the ground. Then, putting his hands inside the trunk, he took out a package identical to the one seen on the previous day, and left.

The muleteer made the sign of the cross, and was so frightened by what he had seen that he told no one.

This went on for three years.

During this time, the man did not age at all. He looked exactly as he had on the first day, with his long reddish beard and mane of shoulder-length hair. Winter and summer, he wore a big, heavy jacket, boots, but no hat.

It was impossible for travelers or neighbors to penetrate that solitary house, but it need not be so for us, dear lady and dear friend.

The house is divided into three rooms, a dining room, a parlor—for visitors—and a bedroom. The bedroom is occupied by the two inhabitants, Daniel and Caligula.

The dining room and the parlor are the same size, the bedroom only half that size. The furniture in the parlor comprises two grubby benches positioned against the wall, and a low table in the middle. The floor is made of wood. On the walls hang two portraits: one of a young woman, the other of an old man. The young woman has a delightful, angelic face. The old man's face inspires respect and admiration. On the other two walls hang, on one side, a knife with an ivory handle, and on the other, a dead hand, withered and yellow.

The dining room contains only a table and two benches.

The furniture in the bedroom consists of a pallet bed, where Daniel sleeps, while Caligula lies on the floor, alongside his master.

So much for the furniture.

Seen from outside, one might think that a man could not even stand upright in those rooms, but because, as I said earlier, the lower half was below ground level, it was in fact, quite large enough.

What kind of life would monkey and man have led during those three years? Who can say?

When Caligula brings the package in the morning, Daniel divides the food into two portions, one for lunch and the other for supper. Then man and monkey sit down facing each other in the dining room and eat those two meals in brotherly companionship.

As I mentioned, when it's a full moon, they sally forth each night until the moon begins to wane. They leave at around ten o'clock and return at around two in the morning. When they enter the house, Daniel takes the dead man's hand off the wall and slaps himself twice. Having done this, he retires to bed, and Caligula goes with him.

One night, in the month of June, at the time of the full moon, Daniel prepared to go out. With one leap, Caligula landed out in the road. Daniel closed the door and the two of them set off.

The moon, entirely full, shed its pale, melancholy light on the vast woods covering the nearby hills, lighting up the vast area of grassland surrounding the house.

All one could hear in the distance was the murmur of a waterfall, and, closer by, the hooting of some owls and the chirping of an endless number of crickets scattered over the plain.

Daniel was walking slowly along, a stick under one arm, accompanied by the monkey, which kept leaping up onto his shoulders, then back onto the ground.

Even without the gloomy nature of that solitary place inhabited only by the man and the monkey, anyone meeting the pair at that hour risked dying of fright. Daniel was extremely tall and thin and cut an equally gloomy figure. His abundant hair and beard made his head seem still larger than it was, and, bareheaded as he was, he looked positively satanic.

On other days, Caligula was just an ordinary monkey, but on those nocturnal walks, he took on the same mysterious, gloomy air as Daniel.

The two had been out for an hour already, and the house was some way off. What could be more natural than for the police to take the opportunity to enter the house and uncover its mystery? The police, however, despite having every means at their disposal, could not bring themselves to investigate what the local people believed to be some diabolical mystery. The police are human, too, and know all there is to know about the human race.

As I was saying, an hour had passed since man and monkey had left the house. Then they began to climb a small hill—

Tito was interrupted by a yawn from Diogo.

"Are you ready for bed?" asked Tito.

"That is precisely where I intend to go."

"But what about the story?"

"Well, it is, of course, a most amusing story. Up until now, we've seen two characters, a man and a monkey, no, what am I saying, we've seen two other characters, a monkey and a man. Fascinating stuff. And just to vary things, I suppose the man will one day go out and leave the monkey on its own."

Diogo uttered these words with almost comic rage, then picked up his hat and left.

Tito burst out laughing.

"Aren't you going to finish the story?" asked Emília.

"Finish it, senhora? I was already struggling to know how to continue . . . It was simply a way of helping you out. The man's obviously a frightful bore."

"No, no, you're wrong."

"Really?"

"He amuses me, although, of course, I find your conversation infinitely more pleasing."

"Now you've just told a falsehood."

"What?"

"You said you found my conversation pleasing, and that's an out-and-out lie."

"Now you're fishing for compliments."

"No, I'm just being honest. I really don't know how you put up with me: I'm rude, tedious, sarcastic, a complete skeptic, in short, a most undesirable conversationalist. You're obviously a very kind person to say such benevolent, friendly things—"

"That's enough of your sarcasm."

"Sarcasm, senhora?"

"Yesterday, my aunt and I took tea alone. Alone!"

"Ah!"

"I was counting on you to come and spend a boring hour or so with us."

"Boring? Let me explain what happened. It was all Ernesto's fault."

"Was it?"

"It's true. He met me in the house of some mutual friends, there were four of us in all, the talk turned to ombre, and we ended up having a game or two. We were there all night. And, as always happens, I won!"

"Did you, now?"

"And they were no mere novices, either, but real masters of the game, especially one of them. Up until eleven o'clock it seemed that fortune was refusing to smile on me, but after that, things turned in my favor, and I began to dazzle. And, believe me, they were dazzled. I have a certificate to prove it, but, what's this, are you crying?"

Emília did indeed have a handkerchief pressed to her eyes. Was she crying? It's true that when she removed the handkerchief, her eyes were moist. She turned away from the light and said:

"Of course not . . . do go on."

"There's nothing more to tell," said Tito.

"I hope you enjoyed yourself . . ."

"Somewhat . . ."

"But letters are meant to be answered. Why did you not respond to mine?" said Emília.

"Your what?"

"The letter I wrote asking you to come and take tea with us."

"I don't remember."

"You don't remember?"

"Or if I did receive that letter, it was at a moment when I didn't have time to read it, and then I must have forgotten and left it somewhere . . ."

"That's quite possible, but it's the last time . . ."

"Do you mean you're never going to invite me to tea again?"

"Yes, that's precisely what I mean. You risk missing out on something better."

"Not at all. You're a charming hostess and I always enjoy coming to your house. I mean it. So you took tea alone? What about Diogo?"

"I got rid of him. Do you imagine he would make for amusing company?"

"Apparently. He's a polite enough fellow, somewhat temperamental, it's true, but since that is a common fault, I hardly feel I can criticize him for that."

"Diogo has been avenged."

"For what, senhora?"

Emília looked hard at Tito and said:

"Oh, nothing."

Then, standing up, she went over to the piano.

"I'm going to play something," she said. "Do you mind?"

"Not at all."

Emília began to play, but the music was so sad that it made Tito feel rather melancholy too. After a time, he interrupted her with these words:

"That's dreadfully sad music!"

"I'm translating my own soul," said the widow.

"Are you sad, then?"

"What do you care about my sadnesses?"

"No, you're right, I don't care about them in the least. But it's nothing I've done, is it?"

Emília got up and went over to him.

"Do you think I can forgive you for snubbing me?"

"What do you mean, 'snubbing' you?"

"By not accepting my invitation."

"But I've already explained—"

"Enough! I'm sorry, too, that Adelaide's husband was involved in that game."

"He left at ten o'clock, and someone else took his place, not a bad player, as it happens."

"Poor Adelaide!"

"But, as I said, he left at ten o'clock."

"He should never have gone in the first place. He should belong entirely to his wife. I know I'm speaking to an unbeliever, but you cannot imagine the sheer bliss of a dutiful domestic life. Two creatures living solely for each other as one person; thinking, breathing, dreaming the same things; finding their horizon in the other's eyes, with no greater ambition, not wanting anything more. Do you know what that is?"

"I do . . . it's marriage viewed from the outside."

"I know someone who could prove that it exists."

"Really? And who is this rare creature?"

"If I tell you, you'll just make fun, so I won't."

"Me? Make fun? No, tell me. I'm curious."

"Don't you believe there could be someone who loves you?"

"It's possible . . ."

"Don't you believe that someone, despite your idiosyncratic nature, could genuinely love you, with a love utterly different from the ordinary love one finds in salons; a love capable of self-sacrifice, of everything? You don't, do you?"

"Yes, I do, but—"

"Well, that person and that love both exist."

"Then there are two of those rare creatures."

"Don't mock. They do exist, you just have to look for them."

"Ah, that would be difficult. You see, I don't have the time. And even if I were to find them, what would be the point? They wouldn't do me any good anyway. That kind of thing is for other men, Diogo, for example . . ."

"Diogo?"

The lovely widow seemed gripped by anger for a moment. Then, after a silence, she said:

"Goodbye. I'm sorry, but I feel unwell."

"I'll see you tomorrow, then!"

And with that, Tito shook Emília's hand and left as blithely and gaily as if he were leaving a birthday party.

Once she was alone, Emília fell into a chair and covered her face with her hands.

She had been sitting like this for about five minutes, when old Diogo reappeared at the door.

"Oh, you're still here?"

"Yes, senhora," said Diogo, approaching. "Unhappily, I am."

"I don't understand."

"I didn't leave, you see. Some hidden demon urged me to commit an infamous act, and I did, but at least I learned something to my advantage: I'm safe now, for I know that you don't love me."

"You heard, then?"

"Everything. And I understood."

"What did you understand, my friend?"

"That you love Tito."

"Ah!"

"I will withdraw, then, but I didn't wish to do so without you knowing that I leave in the knowledge that I am not loved, and before you actually dismiss me."

Emília remained utterly calm as she listened to these words, and while he was speaking, she had time to think about what she should say.

Diogo was about to make his final bow, when the widow addressed him:

"Listen, Senhor Diogo. You heard correctly, but you interpreted what you heard quite wrongly. Because what you think you know—"

"I know, you're going to tell me that it's all part of a trick you're playing on that young man . . ."

"How do you know?"

"Dona Adelaide told me."

"And it's true."

"I don't believe you."

"Why not?"

"Because there were tears in your voice. Your words pierced my heart. If you knew how I suffered!"

The lovely widow could not help but smile at the comically tragic look on Diogo's face. Then, when he seemed plunged in somber thoughts, she said:

"You're quite wrong; in fact, I intend to return to Rio."

"Is that true?"

"Do you really think a man like him could arouse any serious feelings? Never!"

These words were spoken in the tone she usually used to persuade her eternal inamorato. That and another smile were enough to reassure Diogo. A few minutes later, he was positively beaming.

"And to convince you once and for all, I'm going to write a note to Tito . . ."

"I'll deliver it myself," said Diogo, quite wild with contentment.

"Why not!"

"Until tomorrow, then. Sweet dreams, and forgive me if I've behaved badly. Goodbye."

He gallantly kissed Emília's hand and left.

IV

The following day, at noon, Diogo went to see Tito and, after talking about various other matters, he took from his pocket a letter, which he pretended to have forgotten about until then, and to which he appeared to give no great importance.

"What a bombshell!" he said to himself as Tito tore open the envelope. Here is what the letter said:

> I gave you my heart, but you did not want it and even scorned it. You so trampled it underfoot that it has stopped beating. It's dead. I'm not blaming you, for one should not speak of light to the blind. It was entirely my fault. I thought I could bring you happiness and receive equal happiness in return. I was wrong.
>
> You have the honor of withdrawing from the field wearing the laurels of victory. I remain here wounded and defeated. Never mind! Feel free to mock me, I won't deny you that right.
>
> Meanwhile, I must tell you that I recognized you; I never said anything, but I recognized you at once. That first day when I saw you at Adelaide's house, I realized you were the same man who once came to me and threw himself at my feet . . . You were mocking me then, as you

did today. I should have known that. I have paid dearly for my mis-
take. Goodbye, goodbye forever.

Tito glanced repeatedly at Diogo while he was reading this letter. Why
had he agreed to deliver the note? Was it genuine or a forgery? As well
as being unsigned, there had been a clear attempt to disguise the writing.
Could it be another of the old man's ploys to get rid of him? If so, he must
have known what had happened on the previous evening.

Tito reread the letter many times, and when he parted from Diogo, he
said that his response would soon follow.

Diogo left, rubbing his hands with glee.

The letter read by you, the readers, along with our hero was not the
same letter Emília had read to Diogo. In that draft note, she had declared
simply that she was leaving for Rio, adding that among the memories she
would carry away with her from Petrópolis would be that of Tito, and the
impression he had made on her. However, with supremely feminine dexter-
ity, that draft note was not, as you will have seen, the one Emília sent to Tito.

Tito responded to Emília's letter in the following terms:

Madam,

*I have read and reread your letter, and I will not conceal from you
the sadness it awoke in me. Is that really the true state of your heart?
Are you really so in love with me?*

*You say I trampled on your heart. The thought saddens me, although
I cannot confirm that it's true. I cannot remember ever having inflicted
such damage, but then you say that I did, and I must believe you.*

*Reading this letter, you will be thinking that I am the most impudent
gentleman ever to have trodden Brazil's fair soil. You would be mistaken. This is not impudence on my part, but frankness. I regret that it
should have come to this, but I can only tell you the truth.*

*I must confess that I cannot even be sure that the letter I am respond-
ing to was from you. Your writing, of which I saw an example in Dona
Adelaide's scrapbook, is nothing like the writing in the letter, which
is clearly in a disguised hand; it could be from anyone. Besides, there
is no signature.*

*I mention this because an initial doubt was sown in me by the per-
son chosen to deliver the letter. Could you really find no one better for*

*the task than Diogo? I must say that was truly the funniest thing I've
ever seen.*

*But I shouldn't laugh. You opened your heart to me in a way that
inspires compassion not laughter, and that compassion is in no way dis-
respectful to you, because it lacks all irony. It is pure and sincere. I am
sorry I cannot give you the happiness you ask me for, but that is how it is.*

*I should stop now, and yet I find it hard to raise my pen from the
paper. Few men will ever find themselves in the position of being the
pursued, not the pursuer. But I must and will finish here, sending you
my deepest regrets and praying to God that you find a heart less cold
than mine.*

*My writing is disguised as was yours, and, as in your letter, I leave
the signature blank.*

This letter was delivered to the widow that same afternoon. Azevedo
and Adelaide went to visit her that evening, but could not dissuade her from
leaving for Rio. Emília was even rather cold toward Adelaide, who, unable to
understand the reason for such coolness, left feeling somewhat sad.

The following day, Emília and her aunt packed their bags and left for Rio.

Diogo stayed on in Petrópolis, taking his time over packing his own
cases, because, he said, he did not want to be seen departing at the same
time as those two good ladies and for unseemly thoughts about him and
Emília to circulate.

Adelaide was completely bemused by all of this, for, as I said, she felt
sure that both Emília's coldness and her insistence on leaving Petrópolis concealed some incomprehensible secret. Was she hoping by her departure to
draw Tito after her? If so, she was quite mistaken, because Tito did exactly
as he did every day, waking late and eating his breakfast in the best of spirits.

"I suppose you know," Adelaide said to him, "that our friend Emília will
have left for Rio by now?"

"So I heard."

"Why is that, do you think?"

"Ah, that I do not know. They are the lofty secrets of a woman's mind!
Why does the breeze blow from this direction one day and not from over
there? I really don't care, frankly."

When Tito had finished his breakfast, he did, as usual, retire to his
room to read for a couple of hours.

Adelaide was just about to issue some instructions to the servants when she was astonished to see Emília enter the house, accompanied by her maid.

"So you didn't go, after all?" said Adelaide, rushing over to embrace her.

"As you see."

At a gesture from Emília, the servant left the room.

"What happened?" Adelaide asked, seeing her friend's strangely agitated state.

"What happened?" Emília repeated. "The unforeseeable. You're like a sister to me, Adelaide, so I can speak frankly. No one can hear us, can they?"

"No, Ernesto is out and Tito is up in his room. But whatever's wrong?"

"Adelaide," said Emília, her eyes brimming with tears, "I love him!"

"What?"

"As I said, I am utterly, deeply, madly in love with him. I have tried my best to suppress my feelings, but I can't; and when, out of blind prejudice, I tried to hide my love from him, I couldn't, the words just spilled forth . . ."

"But how did it happen?"

"It's as if it were a punishment; I got well and truly burned on the fire I myself started. These feelings didn't just begin today. Something began stirring within me when I saw how steadfastly scornful he remained; at first I felt rather vexed, then I was filled with a desire to triumph, then by an ambition to give way on everything, on condition that I won everything too. In short, I lost all self-control. I was the one madly in love with him and this became abundantly clear in my words, my gestures, everything. And the more indifferent he became, the more my love for him increased."

"Are you serious?"

"You have only to look at me."

"Who would have thought it?"

"It seems impossible to me, too, but it's true."

"And what about him?"

"Oh, he just muttered something noncommittal and left."

"Will he hold out, do you think?"

"I don't know."

"If I'd had even a suspicion this would happen, I would never have suggested that ill-fated plan of ours."

"No, you don't understand. Do you think I regret feeling as I do? No! I feel happy, I feel proud. It's one of those loves that bursts forth and fills one's soul with satisfaction. I should bless you."

"So it's true love, then. Will he never be converted?"

"I don't know, but regardless of whether he will or not, I'm not asking for his conversion, just for a little less indifference and a little more understanding."

"So what are you going to do?" asked Adelaide, feeling her eyes filling with tears too.

There was a moment's silence.

"What you don't know," Emília went on, "is that he is not a complete stranger to me. I met him before I married for the first time. He was the man who asked for my hand in marriage before Rafael . . ."

"Ah!"

"Did you know about that?"

"He did tell us that story, but never mentioned the lady in question. So that was you."

"It was. We both recognized each other, but said nothing."

"Why?"

The answer to this question was provided by Tito, who suddenly came in through the inner door. He had happened to be looking out of the window when Emília arrived and had crept downstairs in order to eavesdrop on her conversation with Adelaide. His surprise at her unexpected return must excuse such indiscretion.

"Why, you ask?" he said. "I will tell you."

"But first of all," said Adelaide, "are you aware that such complete indifference on your part could prove fatal to someone who is not so indifferent to you?"

"You are referring to your friend here, are you?" asked Tito. "Well, I can resolve everything with a simple question."

And, turning to Emília, he held out his hand to her and said:

"Will you accept my hand in marriage?"

Emília gave a yelp of utter joy, but then some remnant of pride, perhaps, or some other feeling, converted that joy into a single word, which she uttered with her voice breaking:

"Yes!" she said.

Tito lovingly kissed her hand, then added:

"But I should temper my generosity; I should say, rather, that I accept *your* hand. Should I or should I not? I'm a touch eccentric and always enjoy turning everything on its head."

"Of course; I'm happy either way. And yet I'm filled with a great sense of remorse. Am I giving you as complete a happiness as the happiness I receive from you?"

"Remorse? Yes, you should feel remorse, but for quite another reason. You feel horribly humiliated at the moment, and I did make you suffer, didn't I? However, when you hear what I have to say, you will agree, I'm sure, that I, too, suffered, and far more bitterly."

"This sounds like something out of a novel," Adelaide said to Tito.

"No, it's pure reality," answered Tito, "prosaic reality. One day, some years ago now, I was fortunate enough to see a young woman, with whom I fell in love. That love was as irresistible as it was sudden. And it was more ardent then than it is now, because, at the time, I was innocent of the ways of the world. I resolved to declare my love and ask for her hand in marriage. I received this note in reply . . ."

"I know," said Emília. "I was that young woman, and I feel utterly humbled. Forgive me!"

"My love forgives you. I never stopped loving you. I was certain that I would find you again one day and I have done my best to make you love me."

"No, really, if you wrote this down, people would say it was a novel," said Adelaide gaily.

"Life is a novel," said Tito.

Half an hour later, Azevedo arrived. Amazed to find Emília there when he had assumed she would be on the train, and even more amazed by the cordial way in which Tito and Emília were chatting away to each other, he asked how all this had happened.

"It's quite simple," answered Adelaide. "Emília came back because she's going to marry Tito."

This reply failed to satisfy Azevedo, and he demanded a further explanation.

"I see," he said at last. "Having failed to get anywhere by following the straight line, Tito decided to see what could be achieved by following the curved line, which sometimes proves to be the shortest route."

"As it has here," said Tito.

Emília dined at their house. That evening, Diogo came to say goodbye, because he had to leave for Rio the next day. Imagine his surprise when he saw Emília there!

"You've come back!"

"Yes," said Emília, laughing.

"Well, I was about to leave, too, but now I won't. Ah, yes, and I've just received a letter from Europe, brought to me by the captain of the *Macedonia*. The bear has arrived!"

"Good, it will be company for you," said Tito.

Diogo pulled a face; then, when he asked what lay behind Emília's sudden return, she explained that she was going to marry Tito.

Diogo did not believe her.

"This is another trick, isn't it?" he said with a wink.

And he not only refused to believe it then, he would not believe it later, either, despite all the evidence. A few days after this, they all left for Rio. Diogo remained unconvinced, but when he arrived at Emília's house one day and saw that the wedding was about to take place, the poor man could no longer deny the facts. This was a huge blow to him, but he nevertheless summoned up the courage to attend the ceremony, at which Azevedo and Adelaide were witnesses. Two months later, the happy bridegroom wrote to Azevedo:

> I must confess that I was playing a dangerous game. I could have lost, but fortunately, I won.

BROTHER SIMÃO

———

I

BROTHER SIMÃO BELONGED TO the Benedictine order of friars. Even though he was only thirty-eight when he died, he looked about fifty. The reason for his premature aging was exactly the same as the one that had led him to join the order when he was thirty, and, as far as we can tell from the fragmentary memoir he left behind, was ample justification for both.

Brother Simão was a suspicious, taciturn man. He would spend whole days in his cell, from which he only emerged at mealtimes and for divine service. He had not a single friend in the whole monastery, because he made it impossible for anyone even to attempt the necessary preliminary stages that both begin and consolidate any friendship.

In a monastery, where the deep communion of souls should be taken for granted, Brother Simão appeared to be the exception to the rule. One of the novices nicknamed him the Bear, and the name stuck, although only among the other novices. And yet, even though Brother Simão's solitary nature was displeasing to the ordained friars, they nevertheless felt a degree of respect, even veneration, for him.

One day, it was reported that Brother Simão had fallen gravely ill. Doctors were called and he was given all the necessary care and attention. The illness, however, proved fatal, and, five days later, Brother Simão died.

During that time, his fellow friars crowded into Brother Simão's cell. He spoke not a word until, when the final moment was approaching, he sat up in bed, beckoned the abbot over to his bedside, and whispered in a strange, muffled voice:

"I die filled with a loathing for humanity!"

The abbot recoiled when he heard these words and the manner in which they were spoken. As for Brother Simão, he fell back on his pillow and passed into eternity.

When all the usual honors had been paid to their dead brother, the other friars asked the abbot what Brother Simão had said that had so frightened him. The abbot told them, crossing himself as he did so. The friars, however, saw in those words only some past secret, which, though grave, was certainly not dreadful enough to instill terror into the abbot's heart. Then the abbot told them what he had thought on hearing those vengeful words and seeing the terrible piercing look that accompanied them. He had felt sure then that Brother Simão was mad, indeed, that he had been mad when he first entered the order. The other friars said that while Brother Simão's silent, solitary habits might well have been symptoms of some mental illness, albeit of a very mild and gentle sort, it seemed impossible that, during the eight years he had spent there, Brother Simão should have shown no further signs of madness. The abbot, however, was unconvinced.

Meanwhile, they began an inventory of the dead man's few possessions, and, among these, they found a roll of papers bound together with a ribbon and bearing this label: *Notes for a memoir to be written by Brother Simão de Santa Águeda, Benedictine friar.*

These papers were a great find for the community, who were all curious to know more. They would finally be able to peer behind the mysterious veil obscuring Brother Simão's past life, and thus perhaps confirm the abbot's suspicions. To this end the papers were duly read by everyone.

For the most part, they were fragments, brief, scant notes, and yet it was clear that, for a time, Brother Simão had, indeed, been mad.

While ignoring the less relevant parts of the *Memoirs*, the author of this account will try to make use of the seemingly least paltry and least obscure fragments.

II

Brother Simão makes no mention of his place of birth or the names of his parents. All we know of his early life is that, having finished his basic education, he was unable to pursue a career in letters as he wished, and was obliged to work as a bookkeeper in his father's business.

At the time, a cousin of his lived with them; her mother and father had both died, leaving her to be cared for, brought up, and maintained by her aunt and uncle, Simão's parents, who, it would seem, had money enough to do so. Her father had been a rich man, but, having lost everything to gambling and unfortunate business dealings, had ended up in absolute poverty.

This orphaned cousin was called Helena; she was beautiful, affectionate, and extremely kindhearted. Simão, who had been brought up with her and lived with her under the same roof, could not resist his cousin's fine qualities or her beauty. They fell in love. And in their dreams for the future, they both assumed they would marry, which is, after all, the most natural of ambitions for two loving hearts.

It did not take long for Simão's parents to find out about their love. Now, even though this is not stated in the friar's notes, it must be said that his parents were uncommonly selfish. They were happy enough to feed Helena, but could not possibly consent to their son marrying a poor orphan like her. They had their sights set on a rich heiress, and had determined that she would marry their son.

One afternoon, when the lad was still filling in the figures in the master ledger, his father came into the office looking simultaneously grave and cheerful, and told his son to stop his work and listen. The boy obeyed. His father said:

"I'm sending you off to the province of ***. I have some letters for my agent there, Amaral, and, since they are extremely important, I prefer not to entrust them to our somewhat lackadaisical postal system. Would you prefer to take the steamer or our brig?"

The question was asked in such a way that allowed for only one answer, and the boy, turning very pale and lowering his eyes, replied:

"I will go wherever you wish, Father."

Inwardly grateful for his son's submissive attitude, which would save him the cost of a steamer ticket, the father was pleased to report to his wife that the boy had made no objections.

That night, the two lovers happened to meet alone in the dining room.

Simão told Helena what had happened. They both wept a few furtive tears, and hoped that his absence would last no more than a month.

Over tea, Simão's father talked about the trip, which he thought would be a matter of only a few days. This reignited the lovers' hopes. The rest of the evening was taken up with the father giving advice to his son on how to behave when at the house of his agent. At ten o'clock, everyone went to their rooms as usual.

The days passed quickly, until, finally, it was time for the brig to depart. Helena emerged from her room, her eyes red with crying. When her aunt asked brusquely what was wrong, Helena said that she had spent too long reading the night before. Her aunt advised her to stop reading so much and to bathe her eyes with mallow water.

As for her uncle, he summoned Simão to his study, gave him a letter for the agent, and embraced him. His trunk and a servant were ready and waiting. The farewell was a sad occasion. His parents shed a few tears, and Helena wept copiously.

As for Simão, his eyes were dry and burning. He did not cry easily, and so suffered all the more.

The brig set sail. As long as land was in sight Simão did not leave the deck, and it was only when, to use Ribeyrolles's picturesque phrase, the walls of that moving prison finally closed about him, that Simão, filled with sadness and a sense of dread, went down to his cabin. A kind of presentiment was telling him that he would never see his cousin again. He felt as if he were being sent into exile.

When he reached his destination, he sought out his father's agent and handed him the letter. Senhor Amaral read the letter, looked at the lad, and, after a silence folded the letter up and said:

"Right, you just have to wait until I've sorted out this business of your father's. In the meantime, you will live with me."

"When can I go back?" asked Simão.

"In a few days' time, unless things prove more complicated than I thought."

That "unless," which appeared as if only incidentally on Amaral's lips, was really the main meat of the matter. The letter from Simão's father read as follows:

My dear Amaral,

For various weighty reasons I am obliged to remove my son from town. Keep him with you for as long as you can. The pretext for the journey is my need to finish off some business I have with you, and that is what you should tell the lad, always assuring him that this will take little or no time at all. I recall that, in your youth, you harbored the rather sad ambition to be a novelist, well, now is your chance to invent as many unforeseen circumstances and occurrences as you wish, with the aim of keeping the boy there until you hear further from me. Yours, etc. . . .

III

Days and more days passed, and the moment to return home never came. The would-be novelist proved to have an extremely fertile imagination and tirelessly invented excuses with which to convince the boy that he must stay.

Meanwhile, since the minds of lovers are no less inventive than those of novelists, Simão and Helena found a means of writing to each other, and thus drew some consolation for that absence from the presence of words and paper. Héloïse was quite right when she said that the art of writing was invented by some lover separated from her love. In their letters, the two sweethearts swore to remain eternally faithful.

After two months of vain hopes and many letters, Helena's aunt came upon one of Simão's letters. It was, I believe, the twentieth. A great storm broke over the household. Her uncle, who was at work, rushed home and was told the news. The result was that ink, pens, and paper were all banished from the house, and a close watch was kept on the poor unhappy girl.

Letters to the wretched exile became few and far between. He wrote long, tear-stained letters asking her why she did not write, but the rigorous controls imposed by his parents had taken on extraordinary proportions, and all of the exile's letters ended up in the hands of his father, who, once he had read and admired his son's passionate words, would have all his ardent epistles burned.

Days and months passed without a single letter from Helena. By then,

Amaral's inventive vein had dried up, and he had run out of excuses for keeping Simão there.

Then Simão received a letter written in his father's hand. The only thing that distinguished it from other missives he had received from his father was its much greater length. When Simão opened the letter and read it, he trembled and turned pale. For in the letter, the honest businessman told him that Helena, the lovely girl whom he had thought to make his daughter when she married Simão, had died. He had copied out some of the death notices that appeared in the newspapers and added a few consoling thoughts from home, finally urging him to take the next boat home.

The final sentence read:

> For although my business dealings there are still not finished, and
> you are unable to marry Helena because God has taken her from us,
> come home, my child, and console yourself by marrying another, the
> daughter of Counselor ***. She's a young woman now and would make
> a very good match. Do not despair. Think of me.

Simão's father had not fully grasped the depth of his son's love for Helena, and even if he had, he lacked the necessary insight to understand it. Such griefs cannot be consoled with a letter or with a marriage. It would have been better to bring the boy home and then tell him the sad news, because that news, set down so coldly, had dealt the lad a mortal blow.

Simão remained physically alive, but spiritually dead, so much so that he himself went in search of a grave. It would be far better if I could let Simão himself explain what he suffered after receiving that letter, but his writings are full of errors, and I would not wish to have to correct those ingenuous and utterly sincere outpourings of grief.

The grave chosen by Simão was a monastery. He wrote back to his father, thanking him for the offer of the counselor's daughter, but saying that, from that day forth, he would dedicate himself to serving God.

His father was astonished. He had never expected his son to demonstrate such resolve. He wrote back at once, hoping to make him change his mind, but in vain.

As for the agent, Amaral—for whom everything was becoming more and more complicated—he allowed Simão to go to the monastery, preferring to keep well out of an affair about which he really knew nothing at all.

IV

Some time after these events, Brother Simão of Santa Águeda was sent on a religious mission to the province where he was born.

He prepared his luggage and set off.

He had been sent to a town in the interior, not to the provincial capital. However, when he arrived in the capital, he felt it his duty to visit his parents. They were greatly diminished both physically and morally, doubtless weighed down by their feelings of sorrow and remorse for having precipitated their son into taking that decision. They had sold their business and now lived off the interest.

They received their son with great excitement and genuine love. After many tears and comforting words, Simão's visit came to an end.

"So what brings you to the capital, Simão?"

"I have a mission to carry out in my role as friar. I have come to preach to the Lord's flock so that they do not stray from the right path."

"Here in the capital?"

"No, in the countryside. I begin in the town of ***."

His aged parents both shuddered, but Simão did not notice. The following day, he left, despite his parents urging him to stay. They noticed that he had not even mentioned Helena, and they did not wish to open old wounds.

Days later, in the town Brother Simão had mentioned, a crowd gathered to hear what he had to say.

The old church was packed with people.

At the appointed hour, Brother Simão entered the pulpit and began to speak. Half of the congregation became bored and left halfway through. The reason for this was simple. Accustomed to the fire-and-brimstone sermons of Pedro Botelho and to the golden words of most other preachers, they could take no pleasure in the friar's gentle, simple, persuasive language, modeled on the parables told by the founder of our religion.

The preacher was about to finish when a couple hurried in; they were husband and wife; he was an honest farmer, earning a decent income from the farm he owned and from his own hard work; she, in turn, was greatly respected for her many virtues, but seemed permanently burdened by a terrible melancholy.

Having dipped their fingers in the stoup and made the sign of the cross, they went and sat in a pew from which they had a clear view of the preacher.

Just then, a scream was heard, and everyone rushed to help the woman, who had fainted. Brother Simão had to stop speaking until the incident had been dealt with. However, when a gap appeared in the crowd gathered around the woman, he saw her face.

It was Helena.

In Brother Simão's manuscript there are eight lines of dots, as if he himself did not know what happened next, for, after recognizing Helena, he continued his sermon, except that the sermon made no sense now; to the general consternation of the congregation, he merely rambled on in a kind of delirium.

V

This delirium lasted for several days. He did get better, though, thanks to the care he received, and appeared to have been restored to health; only the doctor was unconvinced and wanted to continue with the treatment. Brother Simão, however, insisted on going back to the monastery, and no amount of reasoning could stop him.

The reader will assume, quite rightly, that Helena had been forced into marriage by her aunt and uncle.

The shock of seeing Simão again was too much for the poor woman, and she died two months later, to the inconsolable grief of her husband, who genuinely loved her.

On his return to the monastery, Brother Simão grew still more solitary and more taciturn, and remained slightly unhinged.

We already know what happened at his death and the impression this made on the abbot.

For a long period, Brother Simão's cell was kept shut. It was only opened again some time later in order to receive an old lay brother who, on payment of money, had persuaded the abbot to let him end his days among those doctors of the soul. The man was Simão's father, the mother having already died.

During the old man's final years, it was generally believed that he was no less crazy than Brother Simão de Santa Águeda.

MIDNIGHT TALES

(1873)

Author's Preface

Gathered together here are a few stories, quickly jotted down, with the sole intention of not taking up too much of the reader's precious time. By this I do not mean that these tales merit less attention, nor that they lack insight and style. I mean only that these pages, compiled by a kindly publisher, are the most unambitious stories in the world.

I take this opportunity to thank the critics and the public for the generous welcome they gave my first novel, born some time ago now. Work of other kinds has so far prevented me from finishing another, but one will appear in due course.

November 10, 1873
M.A.

THE BLUE FLOWER

Chapter I

RETURN TO BRAZIL

ABOUT SIXTEEN YEARS AGO, Senhor Camilo Seabra disembarked in Rio de Janeiro on his return from Europe. Born in the province of Goiás, he had gone to Europe to study medicine and was returning with his degree in his pocket and a deep sense of longing in his heart. He had been away for eight years, and had seen and admired all the major things that a man can see and admire over there, always assuming he lacks neither taste nor means. He lacked for neither, and if he had possessed, I won't say a lot, but at least a little more common sense, he would have enjoyed the experience far more than he did, and could then, with some justification, have said that he had truly lived.

As he crossed the bar into Brazil's capital city, his face betrayed little patriotic feeling. He looked withdrawn and melancholy, like someone holding back an emotion that was not exactly one of earthly bliss. He cast a jaundiced eye over the city gradually unfolding before him as the ship approached its anchorage. When the moment came to disembark, he did so about as blithely as would a prisoner when entering the prison gates. As the skiff moved away from the ship, on whose mast fluttered the French tricolor, Camilo murmured:

"Farewell, France!"

Then he wrapped himself in a magnificent silence and allowed himself to be rowed ashore.

After such a long absence, the sight of the city did manage to hold his attention a little. However, unlike Ulysses, his soul did not thrill to see his homeland again, but was filled, rather, with dullness and tedium. He was comparing what lay before him with what he had seen during those long years away, and his heart was gripped by an all-pervading sense of loss. He found the nearest convenient hotel and decided to stay for a few days before continuing his journey to Goiás. He dined in sad solitude, his mind full of a thousand recollections of the world he had just left, and, after dinner, in order to give his memory free rein, he lay down on the sofa in his room and began to count off, like beads on a rosary, the many cruel misfortunes that had befallen him.

In his opinion, no mortal had ever been so sorely abused by a hostile fate. The whole of Christian martyrology, all the Greek tragedies, and the Book of Job paled into insignificance beside his own misfortunes.

Let us review some of the cruel facts of our hero's life.

He had been born rich, the son of Comendador Seabra, a landowner in Goiás, who had never himself left his native province. In 1828, a French naturalist had visited Goiás, and become such firm friends with the comendador that the latter chose him and him alone as godfather to his only son, who, at the time, was just one year old. The naturalist, long before he became a naturalist, had committed a few venal poetic sins that had garnered him a certain amount of praise in 1810, but time—the old rag-and-bone man of eternity—had carried them off to the infinite dumping ground of all worthless things. The ex-poet forgave time everything except the consignment to oblivion of a poem in which he had celebrated in verse the life of the Roman soldier and statesman Marcus Furius Camillus, a poem he still read with genuine enthusiasm. As a souvenir of that youthful work, he named his godson Camilo, and, to the great delight of family and friends, Father Maciel baptized him with that name.

"My friend," said Comendador Seabra to the naturalist, "if my boy reaches maturity, I will send him to your country to study medicine or some other subject that will make a man of him. If, like you, my friend, he should reveal a talent for the study of plants or minerals, then don't hesitate to let him follow whichever profession you think best suits him, just as if you were his father, which, spiritually speaking, you are."

"Who knows if I will still be alive then?" said the naturalist.

"Of course you will!" cried Seabra. "That body of yours doesn't lie. You possess an iron constitution. Why, I've seen you out and about in fields and forests, day after day, come rain or shine, and never even suffer so much as a slight headache. If I did half as much as you, I'd have been dead long ago. You must live and take care of my boy, as soon as he's finished his studies here."

Seabra kept his promise to the letter. Camilo left for Paris as soon as he had completed his preparatory exams, and there his godfather looked after him as if he really were his father. The comendador made sure his son lacked for nothing, for the monthly allowance he sent him would have been enough for two or three people in his position. As well as the allowance, he received traditional Easter and Christmas gifts from his mother, which reached him in the welcome form of a few thousand francs.

So far the only black cloud in Camilo's existence was his godfather, who kept an all-too-keen eye on him, fearful that the boy might topple over the edge of one of the many precipices that await the unwary in any large city. Fate, however, decided that the ex-poet of 1810 should join his defunct artistic creations in the great void, leaving just a few traces in science of his passage through life. Camilo immediately wrote his father a letter full of philosophical reflections.

The concluding paragraph read as follows:

> In short, Father, if you feel confident that I have the necessary good sense to complete my studies here, and are prepared to trust in the inspiration I will draw from the soul of he who has now exchanged this vale of tears for infinite bliss, then allow me to remain here until I can return to my country as an enlightened citizen ready to serve his nation, as is my duty. Should you be opposed to my suggestion, then please say so frankly, and I will stay not a moment longer in this place, which has been half a homeland to me and which now (hélas!) is merely a place of exile.

His father was not a man capable of looking beneath the surface of this tearful epistle to see its real intention. He wept with joy when he read his son's words, showed the letter to all his friends, and wrote at once to tell his son that he could stay in Paris as long as necessary to finish his studies, and that, in addition to his monthly allowance, he would always help him out should any unforeseen difficulty arise. Moreover, he wholeheartedly approved of his son's sentiments regarding his own country and his godfather's memory. He passed on to him the sincere good wishes of family and friends, in particular Uncle Jorge, Father Maciel, and Colonel Veiga, and concluded by sending him his blessing.

This paternal response reached Camilo in the middle of a lunch he was giving at the Café de Madrid for a couple of first-class ne'er-do-wells. His father's response was exactly as he had expected, but he could not resist the desire to drink to his health, and was accompanied in this toast by those elegant vultures, his friends. That same day, Camilo invented one of those unforeseen difficulties mentioned by his father, and the next post carried to Brazil a long letter in which he thanked his father for his kindness, told him how much he missed him, confided his hopes for the future, and asked him very respectfully, in a postscript, to send him a small amount of money.

Thanks to this extra help, our Camilo threw himself into a dissolute, spendthrift life, although without neglecting his studies. He was considerably helped in this by his native intelligence and a certain degree of lingering pride, and when he finished his course, he passed his exams and was awarded the degree of doctor.

News of this success was sent to his father with a request for permission to go and visit other European countries. Permission was duly given, and he left Paris to visit Italy, Switzerland, Germany, and England. A few months later, he was back in Paris, and there he resumed his former existence, free this time from any irksome duties imposed from without. This promising young man ran the gamut of sensuous, frivolous pleasures with an enthusiasm that bordered on the suicidal. He had numerous solicitous, faithful friends, some of whom did not hesitate to give him the honor of becoming their creditor. He was extremely popular among the ladies of the night, a few of whom fell madly in love with him. There was not a scandal worthy of the name in which the key to his apartments was not a factor, and *cet aimable brésilien* was sure to be found in the best seats at any bullfight, banquet, or outing.

Eager to see his son again, the comendador wrote asking him to return to Brazil, but the son—by now a Parisian to his fingertips—could not imagine how any man could possibly leave the capital of France and bury himself in Goiás. He proffered various excuses, and stayed put. His father allowed this first act of disobedience to pass. He wrote again some time later, summoning him home; more excuses from Camilo. His father grew angry, and his third letter was full of bitter recriminations. Camilo came to his senses then and, with great sadness, prepared to return to Brazil, still hopeful that he would be able to come back and end his days on the Boulevard des Italiens or at the door of the Café Helder.

However, something happened that further delayed the young doctor's return. Up until then, he had enjoyed only trivial love affairs and fleeting passions, but he suddenly fell head over heels in love with a beautiful Russian princess. Don't be alarmed: the Russian princess I speak of was, at least according to some, a child of Rue du Bac and had worked in a fashion house until the Revolution of 1848. In the middle of the revolution, a Polish major fell in love with her and carried her off to Warsaw, where she was transformed into a princess with a name ending in -ine or -off, I'm not quite sure which. She led a mysterious life, mocking all her many adoring suitors, with the exception of Camilo, or so she said, declaring that, for him, she would be capable of setting aside her widow's weeds. Mind you, one moment she would be uttering these thoughtless words and the next she would be gazing heavenward and protesting:

"Ah, no, my dear Alexis, I will never besmirch your memory by marrying another."

These words were like dagger thrusts to Camilo's heart. He would swear by all the saints of the Roman and Greek calendar that he had never loved anyone as he loved the beautiful princess. The cruel lady would, at times, seem disposed to believe Camilo's protestations of love; at others, though, she would shake her head and beg forgiveness from the ghost of the venerable Prince Alexis. In the meantime, a final letter from his father arrived, giving his son one last warning, saying that if he did not come home, he would cut off all funds and bar his door to him.

Camilo could prevaricate no longer. He considered inventing some grave illness, but the thought that his father might not believe him and might actually stop his allowance soon put paid to that particular plan. Camilo did not even have the courage to confess all to the beautiful princess, fearing that she, on a generous impulse—perfectly natural in one who is in love—might offer to share with him her lands in Novgorod. To accept such an offer would be a humiliation and to reject it might cause offense. Camilo preferred to give up Paris, leaving the princess a letter in which he gave a brief account of what had happened and a promise to return one day.

These were the calamities that fate had chosen to heap on Camilo, and our unhappy traveler sat on in his hotel room recalling each and every one, until he heard the clock strike eight. He went out for a breath of air, but this only fueled his nostalgia for Paris. Everything seemed to him small and mean and gloomy. He gazed with Olympian disdain at all the shops on Rua do Ouvidor, which, to him, resembled a very long, if brightly lit, alleyway. He found the men inelegant and the women graceless. It occurred to him, however, that his hometown of Santa Luzia was even less Parisian than Rio de Janeiro, and then, cast down by this painful thought, he rushed back to the hotel and went to bed.

The following day, immediately after breakfast, he went to see his father's agent. He declared that he intended to leave for Goiás in the next few days, and received from him the necessary money, in accordance with his father's orders. The agent added that he had been told to provide him with anything he might need should he wish to spend a few weeks in Rio.

"No," said Camilo. "There's nothing to keep me here, and I'm eager now to set off."

"I can imagine how homesick you must be. How many years has it been now?"

"Eight."

"Eight! That's a long time to be away."

Camilo was about to leave when in walked a tall, thin man sporting a mustache and a chinstrap beard; he was wearing a gray overcoat and a panama hat. He looked at Camilo, stopped short, took a step back, then, after a reasonable interval, exclaimed:

"Unless I'm very much mistaken, you're Senhor Camilo!"

"Yes, Camilo Seabra," replied Camilo, shooting a questioning look at the agent.

"This gentleman," said the agent, "is Senhor Soares, the son of the businessman of the same name from the town of Santa Luzia."

"You mean Leandro? Why, you only had the merest fuzz of a beard when I left . . ."

"Yes, the very same," said Soares, "the same Leandro who appears to you now with a full beard, like you, sir, and you also have a very fine mustache!"

"I would never have recognized you . . ."

"Well, I recognized you the moment I saw you, even though you've changed enormously. You are now a very refined young gentleman, whereas I have grown old. I'm twenty-six. No, don't laugh. I'm old. When did you arrive?"

"Yesterday."

"And when are you planning to travel to Goiás?"

"On the first steamer to Santos."

"Me too! We can travel together."

"How is your father? How is everyone? Father Maciel? Colonel Veiga? Give me all the news."

"We'll have plenty of time to talk. For the moment, I'll just say that they're all fine. Father Maciel was ill for a couple of months with a bad fever, and no one thought he would pull through, but he did. It would be disastrous were he to fall ill now that the Feast of the Holy Spirit is nearly upon us."

"Do they still celebrate that?"

"Of course! Colonel Veiga is Emperor this year, and he's promised to put on a splendid show. He's already said he'll hold a ball. But we'll have plenty of time to talk, either here or on the boat. Where are you staying?"

Camilo told him the name of his hotel and said goodbye to his fellow provincial, pleased to have found a companion who would help lessen the tedium of that long journey. Soares followed Camilo over to the door and watched him walk away.

"You see what happens when you live abroad," he said to the agent, who had joined him. "How he's changed, and yet once he was pretty much like me."

Chapter II

TO GOIÁS

A few days later, they both set off for Santos, and from there to São Paulo, where they took the road to Goiás.

As Soares gradually resumed his former friendship with Camilo, he told him what his life had been like during the eight years they had been apart, and, for lack of anything better, this kept Camilo amused on the occasions when nature itself offered him no spectacles of its own. A few leagues into their journey, Camilo was already fully informed of Soares's electoral battles, hunting exploits, amorous triumphs, and many other things, some important, some banal, but which Soares recounted with equal enthusiasm and interest.

Camilo was not a particularly observant fellow, but Soares so laid bare his soul to him that he had no option but to observe and examine it. Soares did not strike him as being a bad lad, but he was rather given to boasting about everything, be it politics, hunting, gambling, or love. There was one serious paragraph in this latter chapter, which had to do with a young woman, with whom he was so madly in love that he had vowed to kill anyone who dared so much as look at her.

"I mean it, Camilo," declared Soares, "if anyone is ever bold enough to court her, there will be two poor wretches in this world, him and me. It certainly won't end happily; people there know me and know that I always keep my promises. A few months ago, Major Valente lost the election because he boldly undertook to force the municipal judge to resign. When he failed to do so, he got his just deserts, and was left off the list of candidates. And I was the one who removed his name. The thing is—"

"But why don't you marry the girl?" asked Camilo, thus skillfully avoiding a long account of this latest electoral triumph.

"I don't marry her because . . . but are you really interested?"

"Yes, as a friend, nothing more."

"I don't marry her because she doesn't want to marry me."

Camilo pulled his horse up short and asked in some amazement:

"If she doesn't want to, then why do you intend to stop her from marrying anyone else . . . ?"

"It's a very long story. Isabel—"

"Isabel?" Camilo said, interrupting him. "The daughter of Dr. Matos, who was trial court judge about ten years ago?"

"The very same."

"She must be a young woman now."

"She's twenty years old."

"Yes, I remember how pretty she was when she was twelve."

"Oh, she's changed a lot . . . for the better too! She turns the head of every man who sees her. She's already rejected a few offers of marriage. I was the last to be rejected, and she herself came to tell me why."

"And what did she say?"

" 'Look, Senhor Soares,' she said, 'you deserve to be accepted as a husband by any young woman, and I myself could say yes, but the reason I don't is that I know we would never be happy.' "

"What else did she say?"

"Nothing more. That was all."

"And you never spoke to her again?"

"No, on the contrary, we speak often. She doesn't treat me any differently. Were it not for those words—which still wound me deeply—I could still feel as if I had a chance. I can see, though, that it's hopeless. She doesn't love me."

"May I speak frankly?"

"Of course."

"You strike me as a complete egotist."

"Possibly, but that's the way I am. I feel jealous of everything, even the air she breathes. If I saw that she loved another man and could do nothing to stop the marriage, I would move to another province. What keeps me going is the belief that she never will love anyone else, which is what most people think."

"It doesn't surprise me that she can't love anyone," said Camilo, staring across at the horizon as if he could see there the image of his beloved, that lovely subject of the Czar. "Not all women possess that heavenly gift, which is what distinguishes the most select of minds. There are some, however, who give themselves body and soul to their beloved, filling his heart with deep affection, and thus fully deserving his eternal adoration. Such women are rare, I know, but they do exist . . ."

Camilo ended this homage to the lady of his thoughts, giving wings to a sigh, and had that sigh failed to reach its destination, this would not have been for want of trying on the part of its originator. His companion did not understand what lay behind this speech and repeated that the lovely Isabel was very far from loving anyone and he was still further from allowing her to do so.

This subject was pleasing to both men, and they continued to speak of it until dusk fell. Shortly afterward, they reached an inn, where they would spend the night.

Once the servants had unloaded the mules, coffee and then supper were prepared. It was on such occasions that our hero missed Paris most keenly.

What a difference between the suppers he had enjoyed at restaurants on the boulevards and that light, rough-and-ready meal in a miserable roadside inn, with none of the delicacies of French cuisine and no *Figaro* or *Gazette des Tribunaux* to read!

Camilo sighed and grew even less communicative. Not that this mattered, because his companion talked enough for both of them.

Once supper was over, Camilo lit an expensive cigar and Soares a rather cheaper one. It was dark by then. The fire that had been lit for supper illuminated a small area around about, although this was hardly necessary, for a pale, brilliant moon was beginning to rise behind a hill, its light glancing off the leaves of the trees and the quiet waters of the river snaking past nearby.

One of the muleteers took out a guitar and began singing a song, the rustic simplicity of whose words and melody would have delighted anyone, but for Camilo it merely stirred sad memories of the trills and tremolos he used to hear at the opera. Other memories surfaced too: one night when the lovely Muscovite, seated languidly in a box at the Comédie-Italienne, stopped listening to the tenor's tender yearnings in order, instead, to gaze on Camilo, peering at him from afar over a nosegay of violets.

Soares climbed into his hammock and fell asleep.

The muleteer stopped singing, and soon all was silence.

Camilo remained alone in the lovely, solemn night. He was certainly not immune to beauty, and the near-novelty of that spectacle, which he had forgotten after his long absence, made a deep impression on him.

Now and then, he heard the distant howling of some wild animal wandering the wilderness. At other times, he heard night birds calling sadly. The crickets and frogs and toads formed part of the chorus in that opera of the wild, and much as our hero admired it, he would doubtless have preferred to be listening to an opéra bouffe.

He remained like this for a long time, almost two hours, letting his thoughts drift wherever his fancy took him, building up and tearing down endless castles in the air. Suddenly he was woken from his reverie by the voice of Soares, who seemed to be in the grip of a nightmare. Camilo listened and heard the occasional muffled word:

"Isabel . . . dear Isabel . . . What? Oh, dear God! Help!"

These last words were spoken in far more anguished tones than the first. Camilo ran to his friend's side and shook him hard. Soares started awake, sat up, and, looking around him, murmured:

"What's wrong?"

"You were having a nightmare."

"Oh, yes, it *was* a nightmare. Thank heavens for that. What time is it?"

"It's still dark."

"Are you awake already?"

"No, I was just about to get into my hammock. Let's go to sleep. It's late."

"Tomorrow, I'll tell you my dream."

And the next day, when they were only a few yards into their journey, Soares told him about that terrible dream.

"I was standing by a river," he said, "with a rifle in my hand, watching for capybara. I happened to glance up at a steep hill on the other side and saw a young woman riding a black horse. She was all dressed in black, too, and her black hair hung loose over her shoulders."

"Nothing but blackness, then," commented Camilo, interrupting him.

"No, listen. I was really surprised to see her there and on horseback, too, a delicate young woman like her. Who do you think she was?"

"Isabel?"

"Yes, Isabel. I ran along the bank and climbed onto a rock just opposite where she had stopped, and I asked her what she was doing there. She remained silent for a while, then, pointing down into the depths of the river, she said:

" 'My hat has fallen in the water.'

" 'Ah!'

" 'Do you love me?' she asked moments later.

" 'More than life itself.'

" 'Will you do as I ask?'

" 'Anything.'

" 'Well, then, go and fetch my hat.'

"I stared down into a vast chasm in which the muddy, churning water boiled and roared. Instead of being carried downstream to be lost forever, her hat had become caught on an outcrop of rock and seemed to be inviting me to go and fetch it. However, this was quite impossible. I looked all around me to see if I could find a way, but in vain."

"What a febrile imagination you have!" remarked Camilo.

"I kept searching for the right words to dissuade Isabel from sending me on that terrifying mission, when I felt someone place a hand on my shoulder. I turned around. It was a man. It was you."

"Me?"

"Yes. You regarded me scornfully, then smiled at her and stared into the abyss. Suddenly, I don't know how, you were down there, reaching out to grab the fateful hat."

"Goodness."

"The waters, however, grew still wilder and threatened to drown you. Uttering an anguished cry, Isabel spurred on her horse and plunged in too. I shouted, called for help, but it was no use. The swirling water had enveloped you both . . . It was then that you woke me."

When Leandro Soares concluded this account of his nightmare, he still seemed terrified by what had happened, even though it had all been in his imagination. I should point out that he believed in dreams.

"That's what happens when you go to sleep on a full stomach!" cried Camilo, once Soares had finished his account. "What tosh! The hat, the river, the horse, and, to top it all, my presence in that fantastical melodrama; it's simply the creation of someone with a bad case of indigestion. Some theaters in Paris put on nightmares like that, which are far worse because they're much longer. What is clear to me is that you're still thinking of that girl even when you're asleep."

"Yes, even when I'm asleep."

Soares spoke these last words almost like a disembodied echo. After finishing his description of his dream, and after listening to what Camilo had to say, he had a series of thoughts that remained hidden from the author of this story. The most I can say is that they were clearly not happy thoughts, because he bowed his head, furrowed his brow, and, fixing his gaze on his horse's ears, withdrew into an inviolable silence.

From that day on, Camilo found the journey less bearable. Apart from the vague melancholy that had taken hold of his traveling companion, he was beginning to grow bored with riding league after apparently endless league. Eventually, Soares recovered his customary verbosity, but, by then, nothing could dispel the mortal tedium overwhelming poor Camilo.

However, when they spotted the town, near to the farm where Camilo had spent his early youth, he felt his heart beat faster. He grew serious. For a while, at least, Paris and its splendors gave way to the small, honest homeland of the Seabra family.

Chapter III

THE MEETING

It was real day of celebration when the comendador clasped to his breast the son he had dispatched to foreign lands eight years before. The kind old man could not hold back his tears, for they sprang from a heart still brimming with love and overflowing with tenderness. Camilo's joy was no less intense or sincere. He repeatedly kissed his father's hands and brow, embraced other relatives and friends from his youth, and, for a few days, albeit not many, he appeared to be completely cured of any desire to return to Europe.

In the town itself and its environs, people spoke of nothing else. The comendador's son was the sole, exclusive topic of conversation. People never wearied of praising him. They admired his manners and his elegance. Even the rather superior way in which he spoke found sincere enthusiasts. For many days, it was absolutely impossible for the young man to do anything but recount his travels to his adoring compatriots. It was worth the effort, though, because everything he said had for them an indefinable charm. Father Maciel, who had baptized him twenty-seven years before, and who was seeing him now a grown man, was the first to speak of this transformation.

"You must be very proud, sir," he said to Camilo's father, "you must be very proud that heaven has given you such a fine son! Now, it may just be my own fondness for the young man, who, only yesterday, was a mere scrap of a boy, but I think Santa Luzia is going to have a first-class doctor. And not just a doctor, either, but a philosopher, because he really does seem to me to be a philosopher too. I sounded him out on the matter yesterday, and I couldn't fault his reply."

Uncle Jorge was always asking everyone what they thought of his nephew. Colonel Veiga was constantly thanking Providence for Camilo's arrival so close to the Feast of the Holy Spirit.

"Without him, the ball would have been incomplete."

Dr. Matos was the last person to visit the comendador's son. He was a tall, robust old man, only slightly bowed down by the years.

"Come in, Doctor," said Camilo's father as soon as he arrived, "come in and meet my young man."

"And he is indeed a man," answered Dr. Matos, looking at Camilo. "He's more of a man than I imagined. But then, it has been eight years. Let me embrace you, sir."

Camilo opened his arms to the old man. Then, as he did with all those who came to visit him, he told him a little of his travels and his studies. Needless to say, our hero omitted anything that might tarnish his image. If he was to be believed, he had more or less lived the life of a hermit, and no one dared think otherwise.

Joy was unbounded in the town and its environs, and, flattered by this unexpectedly warm reception, Camilo rarely thought about Paris. But time passes, and our feelings alter. After two weeks, the novelty of those first impressions had worn off; the farm began to change in appearance: the fields seemed monotonous, the trees monotonous, the rivers monotonous, the town monotonous, he himself seemed monotonous. He was filled then by what we might call the nostalgia of exile.

"No," he said to himself, "I cannot possibly stay here for another three months. It's either Paris or the graveyard, that's the choice I'm faced with. In three months' time, I'll either be dead or en route to Europe."

Camilo's boredom did not escape his father, who spent almost all his time gazing at his son.

"He's right," thought the comendador. "No one who has lived in those beautiful, lively places could ever be very happy here. He needs something to occupy him—politics, for example."

"Politics!" cried Camilo, when his father mentioned this as a possibility. "Where would politics get me, Father?"

"A long way. You could become the province's first deputy, then join the Chamber of Deputies in Rio de Janeiro. One day, you could challenge the government, and if it fell, you might then get a seat in the cabinet. Have you never wanted to be a minister?"

"Never."

"That's a shame."

"Why?"

"Because it's good to be a minister."

"What, and try to govern other men?" said Camilo, laughing. "The male sex is entirely ungovernable, Father. Personally, I prefer the fairer sex."

Seabra laughed, too, but still did not lose hope of one day convincing his son and heir.

Camilo had been in his father's house for nearly three weeks when he recalled what Soares had told him and the dream he'd had. The first time he went into town and met Soares, he asked:

"Tell me, how's your Isabel? I haven't so much as caught a glimpse of her yet."

Soares gave him a louring look, shrugged, and muttered:

"I don't know."

Camilo did not insist, thinking: "His illness is obviously still at the acute stage."

He was curious, though, to see the lovely Isabel, who had brought that garrulous electioneer so low. He had already spoken to every other girl for ten leagues around. Isabel was the only one who had so far eluded him. No, "eluded" is the wrong word. Camilo had visited Dr. Matos's farm once, but his daughter had been ill. Or so he was told.

"Don't worry," said a neighbor to whom he had expressed his impatience to meet Leandro Soares's beloved, "you'll see her at Colonel Veiga's ball, or at the Holy Spirit festivities, or on some other occasion."

Various things could not help but prick Camilo's curiosity: the young woman's beauty—even though he could not believe it could possibly be superior or even equal to that of Prince Alexis's widow—together with Soares's own unquenchable passion, and the mysterious tone in which people spoke of Isabel.

The following Sunday, eight days before the Festival of the Holy Spirit, Camilo left the farm to attend mass at the church in town, as he had on the previous Sundays. His horse trotted slowly along, and his thoughts kept the same indolent pace, spreading out over the countryside in eager search of some lost sensation it yearned to have again.

A thousand remarkable ideas passed through Camilo's mind. One moment he was wishing he could fly through the air, horse and all, and land slap-bang in front of the Palais Royal, or any other spot in the world's capital city. The next he was imagining some great deluge that would sweep him off to have lunch in Café Tortoni just two minutes after kneeling at Father Maciel's altar.

Suddenly, in the distance, as he rounded a bend in the road, he saw two ladies on horseback, accompanied by a page. Spurring his horse, he soon caught up with them. One of the ladies turned, smiled, and stopped. Camilo doffed his hat and held out his hand, which she shook.

This lady was the wife of Colonel Veiga. She was probably about forty-five, but certainly did not look her age. The other lady, aware that her companion had stopped, also stopped and turned around. Camilo had not yet looked at her, however, for he was listening to Dona Gertrudes, who was giving him news of the colonel.

"He thinks of nothing but the festivities now," she was saying. "He's probably at church already. Are you going to mass?"

"I am."

"Let's go together, then."

After this rapid exchange, Camilo finally looked at the other rider. She, however, was already some way ahead. He drew his horse up alongside Dona Gertrudes, and the procession set off again. They had been chatting for about ten minutes, when the horse of the lady in front came to an abrupt halt.

"What is it, Isabel?" asked Dona Gertrudes.

"Isabel?" cried Camilo, oblivious to the incident that had provoked Dona Gertrudes's question.

The young woman turned and shrugged, saying only:

"I don't know."

The horse had heard a noise coming from the thick bamboo grove to the left of the road, but before Camilo's page could discover the cause of the horse's reluctance to proceed, the young woman had made a supreme effort and, vigorously whipping her horse, had managed to persuade it to overcome its fear and gallop on ahead.

"Isabel?" Camilo said again. "Is that young woman Dr. Matos's daughter?"

"Yes, didn't you recognize her?"

"I haven't seen her for eight years. She's a real beauty! I'm not surprised that people here talk so much about her. I was told she'd been ill . . ."

"She has, but her illnesses are minor things. It's her nerves, apparently; at least that, I believe, is what people say when they don't know what's wrong with someone."

Isabel had stopped farther up the road, and seemed to be admiring the splendors of the nature around her. They almost caught up with her a few minutes later, and she was just about to ride on, when Dona Gertrudes called to her:

"Isabel!"

The young woman turned, and Dona Gertrudes rode over to her.

"Don't you remember Dr. Camilo Seabra?"

"You may not remember me," said Camilo. "You were only twelve when I left, and that was eight years ago!"

"No, I do remember," answered Isabel, slightly turning her head, but still without looking at him.

Then, gently urging on her horse, she rode ahead. Although this was rather a strange way to greet an old acquaintance, what most impressed Camilo was Isabel's beauty, which thoroughly deserved its reputation.

As far as he could judge from that first encounter, the slender horse-woman was tall rather than short. She had an olive complexion, but her skin was satin-smooth, with a faint rosy tinge, doubtless the effect of her agitation, for people usually described her as very pale. Camilo had not been able to see what color her eyes were, but despite this, and possibly more importantly, he had sensed their brightness, and understood at once how the eyes of that lovely maiden could have so enchanted poor Soares.

He did not have time to study her other features, but was able to contemplate at his leisure what he had already admired from afar, namely, her naturally elegant, upright posture, and the graceful ease with which she rode. He had seen many elegant, skillful horsewomen, but she had a quality that gave her an advantage over them all; perhaps it was her easy, casual gestures or the spontaneity of her movements, or something else entirely, or a combination of all those things, that gave this interesting young woman incontestable supremacy.

Isabel occasionally slowed her horse and spoke to Dona Gertrudes, pointing out some trick of the light or a bird flying by or a sound she had heard—but not once did she turn to face Camilo or give him so much as a sideways glance. Absorbed in contemplation of her, Camilo let the conversation lapse, and he and Dona Gertrudes rode along in silence for some minutes. They were interrupted by another rider approaching at a fast trot from behind.

It was Soares.

He seemed completely different from their last encounter. He greeted them all in the same smiling, jovial manner he had affected during the first few days of his journey with Camilo. It was easy enough, though, to see that this was all a façade. His face would cloud over from time to time, or he would make a despairing gesture which, fortunately, escaped the notice of the others. He feared the triumph of a man who was his physical and intellectual superior, and who, what's more, had the great advantage of being very much in the public eye: the main attraction, the star performer, the man of the moment. Everything was conspiring to demolish Soares's last hope, which was to see the young woman die without ever marrying. This unfortunate lover had the all-too-common tendency of wishing to see the cup he himself could not raise to his lips lying shattered or useless.

His fear had grown all the greater, when, hiding in the bamboo grove to watch Isabel ride by, as he often did, he saw Camilo in their company. He could not suppress a cry of surprise and even took a step in their direction, but stopped himself in time. As we saw, the party rode on, leaving the jealous suitor swearing to all the powers in heaven and on earth that he would have his revenge on his bold rival, if, indeed, he was his rival.

As we well know, he was not a rival; the memory of the Muscovite Artemis was still fresh in Camilo's heart, and despite the distance that lay now between them, he could still feel her ardent, sorrowful tears. But who could persuade Leandro Soares that the elegant "young man from Europe," as people called him, would not fall in love with that elusive young woman?

Isabel, on the other hand, reined in her horse as soon as she saw her unfortunate suitor and affectionately held out her hand to him, accompanying this gesture with the most adorable of smiles. This was not enough, alas, to dispel the poor young man's doubts. Camilo, however, interpreted her actions quite differently.

"She either loves him or she's a complete fraud," he thought.

At that precise moment—and for the first time—Isabel chanced to look at Camilo. Whether through instinct or sheer perspicacity, she read this hidden thought of his; she frowned slightly and a look of such bewilderment crossed her face that Camilo felt utterly perplexed and could not help adding, this time actually murmuring the words:

"Or else she's in league with the devil."

"Perhaps she is," responded Isabel softly, her gaze fixed now on the ground.

These words were spoken so quietly that no one else heard. Half astonished, half curious, Camilo could not take his eyes off the lovely Isabel after those words uttered in such strange circumstances. Soares was gazing at Camilo as tenderly as a hawk looks at a pigeon. Isabel was playing with her whip. Dona Gertrudes, afraid they might miss Father Maciel's mass and be affectionately scolded by her husband, gave orders for them to proceed, and so they did.

Chapter IV

THE FESTIVAL

The following Saturday, the town had a very different air about it. Crowds of people had arrived to join in the annual Festival of the Holy Spirit.

Very few places have entirely lost their taste for such old-fashioned celebrations, a remnant from past ages, which the writers of future centuries will study with interest in order to describe to their contemporaries a Brazil they will no longer recognize. At the time of these events, one of the most authentic of such festivals was that held in the town of Santa Luzia.

Colonel Veiga, who had been appointed that year's Emperor of the Holy Spirit, was staying in a house he owned in town. This was the meeting place on the Saturday night for the traditional group of shepherds and shepherdesses, who all arrived in their picturesque outfits, accompanied by the classic "old man" in breeches and stockings, flat shoes, a long vest and overcoat, and holding a large stick.

Camilo was at the colonel's house for the arrival of the shepherds, with, at their head, a few musicians and, behind them, a whole throng of people. They formed a circle out in the street, and a shepherd and shepherdess initiated the dancing. Then everyone danced, sang, and played both outside the house and in the colonel's parlor, and the colonel was quite beside himself with glee. It is a moot point, and one that will probably never be resolved, whether, on that day, Colonel Veiga actually preferred being Emperor of the Divine Holy Spirit to being a government minister.

And yet this was merely a small example of the colonel's majestic status. The Sunday morning sun would reveal far greater things. And this, it seems, was why the king of light chose to bless that day with his finest rays, for the sky had never been more limpidly blue. Overnight, a few dark clouds had rather dimmed the hopes of the festivalgoers; fortunately, though, a stiff morning breeze had swept the sky clean and freshened the air.

The population responded to nature's bounty, and, bright and early, sallied forth in their Sunday best, joking, laughing, talking, and feeling utterly content.

The air crackled with fireworks, and the church bells gaily summoned the people to worship.

Camilo had spent the night in town at Father Maciel's house, and was woken far earlier than expected by the bells and fireworks and other festive noises. At his father's house, he had kept to his Parisian habits, and the comendador judged it best not to disrupt this pattern. He woke at eleven in the morning, except on Sundays, when he would go to mass so as not entirely to offend against the local customs.

"What on earth is going on, Father Maciel?" shouted Camilo from his room, when the flashing lights from a girandola firework finally forced him to open his eyes.

"What do you think?" answered Father Maciel, poking his head around the door. "It's the start of the festival."

"You mean they begin in the middle of the night?"

"What do you mean, 'the middle of the night'?" exclaimed Father Maciel. "It's broad daylight."

Unable to go back to sleep, Camilo was obliged to leave his bed. He had breakfast with the priest, recounted a few anecdotes, declared that Paris was the ideal city, and set off for the Emperor's house. Father Maciel left with him, and on the way, they saw Leandro Soares in the distance.

"Can you tell me, Father," asked Camilo, "why Dr. Matos's daughter refuses to accept that poor man's love?"

Father Maciel adjusted his spectacles and gave the following thoughtful response.

"That's a rather foolish question."

"It can't be so very foolish," retorted Camilo, "because I'm hardly the only person to have asked it."

"That's true," said the priest, "but one shouldn't necessarily repeat what other people say. Isabel doesn't love Soares because she doesn't love him."

"Don't you think her slightly strange?"

"No," said the priest, "she seems to me extremely astute."

"Why so?"

"I suspect that she's very ambitious. She doesn't accept Soares's protestations of love because she wants to see if she can get a husband who will open a door for her into the world of politics."

"Surely not!" said Camilo, shrugging dismissively.

"You don't believe me?"

"No, I don't."

"I may be wrong, but I think that is the real reason. Everyone here has his own explanation as to why Isabel won't marry. However, all their explanations strike me as absurd. I think mine is much better."

Camilo made a few further objections, then said goodbye and headed for the colonel's house.

The Emperor of the festivities could barely contain his excitement. This was the first time he had held this honorific post and he was determined to carry out his duties brilliantly, even more brilliantly than his predecessors. While this demonstrated a perfectly natural desire not to be outdone, there was also an element of political envy. Behind his back, some of his opponents were saying that the proud colonel wasn't up to the job.

"I'll show them," he said when certain friends reported this malicious gossip to him.

Camilo entered the room as the colonel was in the process of giving some last-minute instructions about the supper that would follow the festivities, and listening to the details that one of the fraternity brethren was giving him about the ceremony in the sacristy.

"I won't keep you, Colonel," said Camilo once he was alone with Veiga, "I'd hate to delay you."

"No, not at all," said the Emperor of the Divine Holy Spirit, "everything's in hand. Is your father coming?"

"Yes, he should be here already."

"Have you seen the church?"

"No, not yet."

"It's looking very pretty. I don't wish to boast, but I think the festivities will certainly be as good as those of other years, if not better."

It was absolutely impossible to disagree with this opinion when the man giving it was doing so in his own honor. Camilo, in turn, praised the celebrations. The colonel listened to him with a rather smug smile on his face, and was about to point out to his young friend that he clearly didn't appreciate their full significance, when Camilo changed the subject and asked:

"Has Dr. Matos arrived?"

"Yes, he has."

"With his family?"

"Yes, with his family."

At this point, they were interrupted by the sound of approaching music and many fireworks exploding.

"It's them!" cried Veiga. "They're coming to fetch me. If you'll excuse me."

And with that he rushed upstairs to change his black trousers and linen jacket for the uniform and insignia appropriate to his lofty position. Camilo went over to the window to watch the procession arrive, which it soon did, composed of a band of musicians, the Brotherhood of the Holy Spirit, and the shepherds and shepherdesses from the night before. The brethren were wearing their scarlet chasubles and were walking slowly and gravely along, surrounded by the crowds filling the street and clustering around the door to the colonel's house, waiting for him to emerge.

When the procession stopped outside, the music also stopped, and all eyes peered curiously up at the windows. However, the new Emperor had not yet finished dressing, and the onlookers had to content themselves with looking at Camilo. Meanwhile, four or five of the higher-ranking brethren had left the group and climbed the steps to the colonel's front door.

Minutes later, those same high-ranking brethren were greeting Camilo, one of them higher up than the others and not just as regards his rank, for Major Brás's great height would have been his most notable feature were it not in direct competition with his extreme thinness. Despite this, the major's chasuble fit him well, because it neither hung down below his knees, as it did with the others, nor just below his waist, as it would have done had it been made to the same measurements. It was a sort of middle way. It reached to just above the knee, and had been made specifically to reconcile the major's enormous stature with the accepted principles of elegance.

All the brethren shook Camilo's hand and asked anxiously for the colonel.

"He won't be long," said Camilo. "He's just getting dressed."

"The church is full," said one of the brethren. "We're just waiting for the colonel now."

"And it's only right that we should wait," said Major Brás.

"Seconded," said the brethren in unison.

"Besides," added the immensely tall officer, "we have plenty of time. We don't have to go far."

The other brethren nodded their assent, and the major then went on to

tell Camilo how much work both he and his colleagues had put into organizing the festival—in fact, just as much work as the colonel.

"As a reward for our modest efforts"—Camilo dismissed this remark
with a shake of his head—"things shouldn't go too badly."

The major had barely spoken these words when the colonel appeared at
the door to the parlor in all his splendor.

Camilo had no idea what the Emperor's uniform and insignia would be
like, and so he regarded him with some astonishment.

As well as the black trousers, which he had been wearing when Camilo
had arrived, the colonel had donned a tailcoat, whose cut and style could
have rivaled that of the most impeccably dressed member of the Cassino
Fluminense. So far, so good. On his chest glinted the vast insignia of the
Order of the Rose, which, again, was perfectly acceptable. However, what
exceeded all expectation, and what accounted for the look of amazement on
Camilo's face, was the gleaming, ornate crown made of cardboard and gold
paper that the colonel had on his head.

Camilo took a step back and fixed his eyes on the colonel's imperial
crown. He had forgotten that this was an indispensable item on such occasions, and, after living for eight years in a very different culture, he had
assumed that such costumes would have long since been dead and buried.

The colonel shook hands with all his friends and declared that he was
ready to accompany them.

"We don't want to keep the people waiting," he said.

They immediately went out into the street. The crowd stirred into life
when they caught sight of the scarlet chasuble worn by one of the brethren.
Behind him came another chasuble, quickly followed by all the other chasubles, on either side of the richly adorned Emperor. As soon as the sun's
rays fell on the golden crown, it glinted and glittered in the most extraordinary fashion. The colonel looked to left and right, nodding to various people
in the throng, then took up the place of honor in the procession. The band
immediately broke into a march, and off they all went to the church, the
colonel, the brotherhood, the shepherds and shepherdesses.

As soon as the procession came within sight of the church, the bell
ringer, who had been watching and waiting, put into practice all the most
complicated tricks of his trade, while a girandola, along with a few other
stray fireworks, announced to the heavens that the Emperor of the Divine

Holy Spirit had arrived. His arrival caused general excitement in the church. A burly, energetic master of ceremonies was trying, albeit with great difficulty, to clear a path through, but the disorderly crowd kept undoing all his good work. Finally, what always happens on these occasions happened, and a path opened up of its own accord, and, with some effort, the colonel made his way through the crush, preceded and accompanied by the members of the fraternity, until he reached the throne that had been placed next to the altar. He confidently climbed the steps up to the throne and sat down as proudly as if he were Emperor of all the empires of the world.

When Camilo arrived at the church, the ceremony had already begun. He found a reasonable place to sit, or, rather, an excellent one, because it provided him with a view of a large group of ladies, among them the lovely Isabel.

Camilo was anxious to speak to Isabel again. He could not forget their encounter on the road and the remarkable perspicacity she had shown on that occasion. She appeared not to notice him, but Camilo was so experienced in dealing with the fairer sex that he realized at once that she had, in fact, seen him and was deliberately avoiding his gaze. This, along with the incidents of the previous Sunday, made the following question surface in his mind:

"What has she got against me?"

The ceremony continued without further incident. Camilo did not take his eyes off his beautiful enigma, as he already called her, but the enigma seemed immune to any feelings of curiosity. Once, though, toward the end of the ceremony, their eyes did meet. It should be pointed out that *he* found *her* looking at him. He bowed, she reciprocated, and that was that. Once the ceremony was over, the brotherhood escorted the colonel back to his house. In the hurly-burly of leaving the church, Camilo, who still had his eyes fixed on Isabel, heard an unfamiliar voice whisper in his ear:

"Watch what you're doing!"

Camilo turned and came face-to-face with a short, thin man with small, bright eyes; he was poorly but neatly dressed. They stared at each other for a few seconds in silence. Camilo didn't recognize the face and didn't dare demand an explanation for the words he had just heard, even though he was burning to know more.

"There's a mystery," the stranger said at last. "Would you like to know what it is?"

Another silence.

"This is hardly the appropriate place," said Camilo, "but if you have something to tell me . . ."

"No, you must find out for yourself."

And with that, the short, thin man with the small, bright eyes vanished into the crowd. Camilo elbowed his way past ten or twelve people, trod on fifteen or twenty corns, apologizing just as often for his rash behavior, only to find himself out in the street with not a sign of the stranger.

"This is like a novel," he said. "I'm caught up in the middle of a novel!"

At that moment, Isabel, Dona Gertrudes, and Dr. Matos came out of the church. Camilo went over to greet them. Dr. Matos gave his arm to Dona Gertrudes, and Camilo timidly offered his to Isabel. She hesitated, but since she could hardly refuse, she linked arms with him, and they walked to the colonel's house, where the colonel and various other important people were already installed. In the midst of the throng, another man was making his way to the colonel's house, and he did not once take his eyes off Camilo and Isabel.

That man bit his lip until it bled.

Need I add that the man was Leandro Soares?

Chapter V

PASSION

It was only a short distance from the church to the house, and the conversation between Isabel and Camilo was neither long nor sustained. And yet, dear reader, if the Muscovite princess deserves any sympathy at all, then now is the time to take pity on her, for the dawn of a new feeling was beginning to gild the peaks of Camilo's heart. As they went up the steps to the colonel's house, Camilo had to admit to himself that the intriguing Isabel was possessed of qualities far superior to those of the lovely Russian princess. An hour and a half later—that is, toward the end of supper—Camilo's heart confirmed the discovery made by his inquiring mind.

The couple stuck entirely to neutral topics of conversation, but Isabel spoke with such sweetness and grace—although always with her habitual reserve—and her eyes, seen from close up, were so pretty, as was her hair and her mouth, not to mention her hands, that our ardent young hero could only have resisted the allure of such combined charms had he entirely changed his nature.

Supper passed without incident. The colonel had gathered together all the local worthies: the priest, the magistrate, the merchant, the farmer, and the utmost cordiality and harmony reigned from one end of the table to the other. The Emperor of the Divine Holy Spirit, now back in his normal clothes, presided over the table with real enthusiasm. The festival was the main topic of conversation, intermingled, it's true, with a few political reflections, with which everyone agreed, because the men and women present all belonged to the same party.

Major Brás was in the habit of making one or two long, eloquent toasts at any important supper to which he was invited. His facility as a speaker had no rival in the entire province. Moreover, given his great height, he could dominate any audience simply by getting to his feet.

He could not allow the colonel's supper to pass without some intervention on his part; dessert was about to be served when the eloquent major asked permission to say a few simple, artless words. A murmur equivalent to a round of nays in the Chamber of Deputies greeted this announcement, and the audience prepared their ears to receive the pearls about to fall from his lips.

"This illustrious audience," he said, "will forgive my boldness. I speak not simply because I can, ladies and gentlemen, no, I speak from the heart. My toast will be a brief one; in order to celebrate the virtues and abilities of our illustrious Colonel Veiga no long speech is necessary. His name says it all, and my voice would add nothing new . . ."

The audience gave an indication that while it unreservedly applauded the first part of that sentence, it had its reservations about the second, thus complimenting both the colonel and the major; and the speaker, who, if he was to be true to what he had just said, should merely have drained his glass, continued as follows:

"I believe, ladies and gentlemen, that the extraordinary event we have just witnessed will never be expunged from our memories. This town and other towns have seen many Festivals of the Holy Spirit, but never have the people enjoyed a more splendid, lively, triumphant affair than the one put on by our illustrious fellow believer and friend, Colonel Veiga, who is an honor to his class and one of the glories of his party . . ."

"The party in which I will remain until I die," added the colonel, in a tone of voice that made clear these words were a mere parenthesis.

Despite having begun by declaring that there was no need to say anything more about the colonel's many merits, the intrepid orator went on to speak for a good twenty-five minutes, much to the chagrin both of Father Maciel, who had his eye on a seductively quivering bread pudding at the far end of the table, and of the magistrate, who was dying for a cigarette. This memorable discourse concluded more or less like this:

"I would, however, be neglecting my duties as a friend, fellow believer, subordinate, and admirer if I were not to speak out on this occasion and put into words—rough-and-ready, yes (*disapproving murmurs*), but sincerely felt—all the emotions that crowd my breast, all the enthusiasm that fills my heart, when I gaze on the venerable, the illustrious Colonel Veiga, and if I were not to invite you now to join me in drinking to his health."

The audience enthusiastically joined in the toast, to which the colonel responded with these few, heartfelt words:

"The praise heaped on me by the distinguished Major Brás is the gift of a large and generous heart; I do not deserve such a gift, ladies and gentlemen, and I return it intact to the illustrious orator himself."

In the midst of the feast and the prevailing gaiety, no one noticed Camilo's attentions to Dr. Matos's lovely daughter. No, I lie. Leandro Soares, who had also been invited to the supper, did not once take his eyes off his elegant rival or his beautiful and elusive lady.

It must seem to the reader a near-miracle that Soares should remain so unmoved and even happy to see his rival's clear intentions, but it is no miracle. Soares was also studying Isabel's gaze, and he saw in it only the indifference or even disdain with which she treated the comendador's son, and he thought to himself: "She loves neither of us."

Camilo was in love, and the following day, he was even more in love; with each day that passed, the consuming flame of passion grew higher. Paris and the princess had vanished from his heart and mind. Only one being and one place merited a space in his thoughts: Isabel and Goiás.

The young woman's haughty, scornful demeanor contributed in large measure to this transformation. Considering himself better than his rival, Camilo was thinking:

"If she cares nothing for me, how much less must she care for Soares.

But why is she so offhand with me? Why should I be defeated like any other vulgar suitor?"

When he thought this, he recalled what the stranger in the church had said to him and told himself:

"There really must be some mystery behind this, but how to find out what it is?"

He asked various townspeople if they knew the identity of the short man with the small, bright eyes. No one could help him. It seemed incredible that he could not find the whereabouts of a man who must be known to someone; he redoubled his efforts, but no one could tell him who the mysterious stranger was.

Meanwhile, he became a frequent visitor to Dr. Matos's house and occasionally dined there. It was difficult to speak to Isabel with the freedom that more modern manners would allow, and yet he did what he could to communicate his feelings to the beautiful young woman. She, however, seemed to grow more and more impervious to his protestations. She didn't exactly treat him scornfully, but coldly; she appeared to have a heart of ice.

Spurned love was joined by wounded pride, resentment, and embarrassment, and all these things, along with an epidemic raging in the area, landed our Camilo in bed, where we will leave him to be cared for by his medical colleagues.

Chapter VI

REVELATION

There are no mysteries for an author who can scrutinize every nook and cranny of the human heart. While the people of Santa Luzia came up with a thousand theories to explain the real reason behind the lovely Isabel's inability to love, I am in a position to tell the impatient reader that she is perfectly capable of love.

"But who does she love?" asks the reader urgently.

She loves . . . a flower. A flower? Yes, a flower. It must be a very pretty flower, then, a miracle of perfumed freshness. No, it's a very ugly flower, dried and withered, a mere corpse of a flower, which must once have been

very beautiful, but which now, lying in its little basket, inspires only curiosity. Because it really is very odd that a young woman of twenty, when she is
at her most passionate, should seem indifferent to the men around her and
focus all her affections on the faded, withered remains of a flower.

Ah, but the flower was picked in very special circumstances. It happened a few years ago. There was a boy who lived locally and who was very
fond of Isabel, because she was a delightful creature; he even used to call
her his wife, an innocent joke to which time gave the lie. Isabel was equally
fond of the boy, so much so that the following idea took root in the mind of
the girl's father:

"If she still feels the same in a few years' time, and if he does truly love
her, then I think I could well marry them off."

Isabel knew nothing of her father's idea, but she continued to be fond of
the boy, and he continued to find her a very interesting creature.

One day, Isabel saw a pretty blue flower growing among the branches
of a tree.

"What a lovely flower!" she said.

"I suppose you'd like it, would you?"

"I would, yes," said the girl, who, though untutored in these matters,
already understood such oblique, disguised ways of speaking.

He took off his jacket with all the nonchalance of a grown-up in the
presence of a child and climbed the tree. Isabel waited below, tense and
eager to have the flower. The obliging boy soon reached the flower and delicately plucked it.

"Catch!" he said from up above.

Isabel went closer to the tree and held out her skirts to catch the flower.
Pleased to have granted the girl's wish, the boy began to descend, but so
clumsily that, only two minutes later, he was lying on the ground at Isabel's
feet. She gave a terrified cry and called for help; the boy tried to calm her,
saying it was nothing, and trying to clamber cheerfully to his feet. He did
eventually manage to stand up, but his shirt was spattered with blood, for
he had cut his head.

The wound was declared to be only superficial, and, after a few days,
the brave boy had completely recovered.

The incident made a deep impression on Isabel. Up until then, she had
merely been fond of the boy; thenceforth, she adored him. The flower he

had picked inevitably withered, but Isabel kept it as if it were a relic, kissing it every day and, later on, even shedding tears over it. A kind of superstitious cult bound her heart to that shriveled flower.

However, she was not so callous that she did not feel deeply concerned when she learned that Camilo was ill. She asked assiduously after his health and, five days later, went with her father to visit him.

While the mere fact of her visit did not cure the patient, it did console and encourage him; a few faint hopes sprang up in him, hopes that had grown as dried and withered as the flower of the story.

"Perhaps now she will love me," he thought.

As soon as he was more or less restored to health, his first act was to go to Dr. Matos's house, and his father offered to go with him. Dr. Matos was not at home, only his sister and daughter. The sister was a poor old lady, who, as well as suffering the usual afflictions of old age, had two further afflictions, namely, deafness and a love of politics. The occasion proved propitious; while Isabel's aunt monopolized the comendador's person and attention, Camilo had time to deliver a quick, decisive blow, addressing these words to the young woman:

"I wanted to thank you for your kindness and concern while I was ill. That same kindness gives me the courage to ask you one other thing."

Isabel frowned.

"A few days ago, a hope I had long thought dead and buried suddenly revived," Camilo went on. "Was that a mere illusion? A single word, a single gesture from you would resolve that doubt."

Isabel shrugged.

"I don't understand," she said.

"Yes, you do," said Camilo somewhat bitterly. "But, if you insist, I'll put it plainly. I love you. I've told you so a thousand times, but you always ignore me. Now, though—"

Camilo would have happily ended this brief speech there and then, if he'd had before him the person he had hoped would be listening to him. Isabel, however, did not even give him time to finish. Without a word or gesture, she walked the entire length of the veranda and went and sat at the far end, where her old aunt was testing the comendador's excellent lungs to the limit.

Camilo's disappointment was beyond description. Complaining of a nonexistent heat, he left the house to get some fresh air, and, now slowly, now quickly, depending on which emotion dominated, whether irritation or despair, he, the wretched suitor, wandered off. He invented endless plans for revenge and endless ways of throwing himself at her feet; he recalled all their previous encounters, and, after a very long hour, he reached the sad conclusion that all was lost. At this point, he realized that he was standing beside a stream that crossed Dr. Matos's farm. It was a rather desolate place and perfectly suited to the situation in which he found himself. Two hundred paces away, he saw a cabin, where he thought he could hear someone singing a song from the *sertão*.

Another person's happiness is always a tiresome thing when one has oneself suffered some misfortune! Camilo felt even more irritated, and ingenuously wondered how anyone could possibly be happy when his own despairing heart was bleeding. Then a man appeared at the cabin door and walked over to the stream. A shiver ran through Camilo, for he seemed to recognize in him the mysterious stranger who had spoken to him in the church. He was the same stature and had the same air about him; Camilo walked rapidly over to him and stopped a few feet away. The man turned around: it *was* him!

Camilo ran up to him.

"At last!" he said.

The stranger smiled smugly and shook Camilo's proffered hand.

"Do you need to sit down?" he asked.

"No," said Camilo. "I don't mind where we talk, it can be here or somewhere else if you like, but, please, explain what you said to me the other day in the church."

The stranger smiled again.

"So?" said Camilo, seeing that the man did not answer.

"First of all, tell me honestly: do you really love her?"

"Oh, yes, very much."

"Do you swear that you will make her happy?"

"I swear."

"Then, listen. What I'm about to tell you is true, because I heard it from my wife, who was Dona Isabel's wet nurse. That's her over there."

Camilo glanced back at the cabin door and saw a tall, elegant mulatto woman eyeing him curiously.

"Let's move a little farther off so that she can't hear us," said the stranger, "because I don't want her to know who you heard this story from."

And they did move away, walking along beside the stream. The stranger then told Camilo the story of the flower and the cult the young woman had built up around it. A less canny reader will imagine that Camilo listened to this story feeling sad and downcast. However, a more experienced reader will have guessed at once that the stranger's revelation made Camilo's soul turn somersaults of joy.

"So that's how it is," said the stranger in conclusion. "You now know where you stand."

"Oh, yes, I do, I do!" cried Camilo. "I am loved! I am loved!"

Once he knew the story, Camilo could not wait to go back to the house he had left some time before. He put his hand in his pocket, opened his wallet, and took out a twenty-*mil-réis* note.

"You have done me an enormous service," he said, "one that is beyond price. Please accept this small token of my appreciation."

And he handed the money to the man. The stranger gave a scornful laugh and, at first, said nothing. Then he took the note Camilo was offering and, to the latter's great astonishment, threw it into the stream. The thread of water, which ran burbling and leaping over the pebbles, carried off the note, along with a leaf that the wind also carried off with it.

"That way," said the stranger, "you don't owe me a favor and I receive no payment for it. Please don't think my intention was to serve you; it wasn't. I simply wanted to make the daughter of my benefactor happy. I knew that she had been in love with a boy, and that he would be able to make her happy; I merely opened up the way that would lead him to her. That is not something you pay for, your gratitude is enough."

Having said these words, the stranger returned to the cabin. Camilo watched the rustic fellow walk away, and, shortly afterward, he was back at Isabel's house, where his return was awaited with some anxiety. Indeed, Isabel's face lit up with joy when she saw him.

"I know everything," Camilo said to her shortly before he left to go home.

She stared at him in amazement.

"Everything?" she said.

"I know that you love me, and I know that your love began many years ago, when you were a child, and that even now—"

He was interrupted by his father coming over to join them. Isabel looked pale and confused, and was grateful for this interruption, because she had no idea how to respond.

The following day, Camilo wrote her a passionate letter, invoking the love she had kept hidden in her heart, and asking her to make him happy. He waited two whole days for a reply. It came on the third day, and was short and to the point. She admitted that she had indeed loved him for all those years and had sworn never to love anyone else.

"That is all," concluded Isabel. "As for becoming your wife, that can never be. I want to give my life to someone whose love is equal to mine. Your love began yesterday, mine nine years ago; the difference in age is too great; ours could never be a good marriage. Forget about me. Farewell."

To say that this letter only increased Camilo's love would be to set down in writing what the reader has already guessed. Camilo's heart needed only a written confession from her to push him over the edge into madness. Her letter made him take leave of his senses.

Chapter VII

EVENTS TAKE ON THEIR OWN MOMENTUM

The comendador had not yet lost hope of getting his son involved in politics. There happened to be an election that year, and the comendador wrote to all the influential bigwigs in the province to ensure his son a place in the relevant constituency.

Camilo greeted his father's plan with a shrug, determined to accept no proposals apart from that of marrying Isabel. The comendador, Father Maciel and the colonel all tried in vain to tempt him with a glittering future and the prospect of lofty government posts. However, the only post that interested him was marriage to Isabel.

This, of course, was not easy. Isabel's resolve appeared to be unshakable. "But she does love me," he thought, "and that's half the battle."

And since his love was more recent than hers, Camilo realized that the only way to solve the problem of that age difference was to show her that his love was more passionate and capable of still greater sacrifices.

He stopped at nothing to prove this. He braved wind and rain to visit her every day; he was a slave to her every desire, however small. If Isabel had expressed the childish wish to hold the morning star in her hand, he would very likely have found a way to bring it to her.

At the same time, he had stopped pestering her with letters and declarations of love. In his last letter, he said only:

"I will live in hope!"

This hope had to sustain him for many weeks, and still he saw no real improvement in his situation.

Some less demanding reader may find Isabel's resolve odd, especially now that she knew her love was requited. I agree, but I do not wish to alter the character of my heroine, because she was exactly as I describe her in these pages. She felt that the fact that she was loved was pure chance, simply because the young man had happened to return from Paris, whereas she had spent long years thinking of him and living solely on that memory; she clearly found this thought humiliating, and because she was extremely proud, she had resolved not to marry him or anyone else. Absurd, maybe, but that is how it was.

Weary with vainly laying siege to the young woman's heart, and convinced, on the other hand, that if he were ever to break her resolve, he had to demonstrate that his was an invincible passion, Camilo drew up a master plan.

One morning, he vanished from the farm. At first no one was concerned about his absence, because he often went for long walks when he woke earlier than usual. As time passed, though, they began to grow worried. Emissaries were sent out, but they returned with nothing to report.

His father was distraught, and news of his disappearance spread everywhere for ten leagues around. After five days of fruitless searching, they learned that a young man fitting Camilo's description had been spotted half a league away, on horseback. He was alone and seemed very sad. A muleteer stated that he had seen a young man standing beside a river, as if assessing the likelihood of death were he to jump.

The comendador began offering large sums of money as a reward for anyone who brought him news of his son. His friends dispatched their servants to scour forests and fields, and a whole week passed with nothing to justify these useless labors.

Need I describe the lovely Isabel's anguish when she was told of Camilo's disappearance? At first sight, she seemed unmoved; her face revealed nothing of the storm that immediately broke in her heart. Ten minutes later, the storm had risen to her eyes and burst forth in a veritable sea of tears.

It was then that her father learned of that long-incubated passion. Seeing that explosion of grief, he feared that her love could prove fatal to her. His first thought was that the young man had disappeared in order to flee a forced marriage. Isabel reassured him, saying that, on the contrary, she had been the one to reject Camilo's love.

"I killed him!" she cried.

Her kindly father found it hard to understand why a young woman in love with a young man, and a young man in love with a young woman, should do their best to remain apart, instead of heading straight for the altar, as he had done when he first fell in love.

After a week, our old acquaintance, the inhabitant of the cabin, came to find Dr. Matos, and arrived at his house breathless and happy.

"He's safe!" he said.

"Safe!" exclaimed both father and daughter.

"It's true," said Miguel (for that was the man's name). "I found him yesterday evening lying in a stream, almost drowned."

"Why did you not come and tell us?" asked Dr. Matos.

"Because I needed to take care of him first. When he came to, all he wanted was to make another attempt to end his life, but my wife and I stopped him. He's still a little weak, which is why he didn't come with me now."

Isabel's face was radiant. A few silent tears still filled her eyes, but they were tears of joy, not sorrow.

Miguel left with the promise that Dr. Matos would come and fetch Camilo.

"Now, Isabel," said her father, as soon as he was alone with her, "what do you intend to do?"

"I'll do whatever you say, Father!"

"I will only tell you to do what your heart tells you to do. What does your heart say?"

"It says . . ."

"What?"

"It says yes."

"Which is what it should have said a long time ago, because . . ."

He stopped and thought:

"What if there's another reason behind this attempted suicide? I must find that out."

When the comendador was informed of what had happened, he went straight to Dr. Matos's house, where Camilo soon joined them. Written on the poor lad's face was the shock of having escaped the tragic death he himself had sought; that, at least, is what he repeatedly told Isabel's father on their way back to his house.

"But why were you so determined to kill yourself?" asked Dr. Matos.

"Well . . ." said Camilo, who had been expecting this question. "I hardly dare say."

"Is it something to be ashamed of?" asked Dr. Matos, smiling benevolently.

"No, not at all."

"So what was the reason?"

"Will you forgive me if I tell you?"

"Of course."

"No, I daren't say," said Camilo resolutely.

"Look, there's no point in lying. I know already."

"Oh!"

"And I forgive your reasons for doing it, but not the act itself; that was pure childishness."

"But she despises me!"

"No, she doesn't. She loves you!"

Camilo gave a perfect imitation of someone taken completely by surprise, and accompanied the doctor back to his house, where he also found his father, who was uncertain whether to be stern with his son or as pleased as punch.

Camilo saw at once the effect his near-suicide had had on Isabel's heart.

"Right," said her father, "now that we've resurrected you, we need to attach you firmly to life with a good strong chain."

And without any of the usual formalities and ignoring all the usual niceties, he announced to the comendador that their respective children must marry at once.

The comendador had not yet recovered from the news that his son had been found, and when he heard this, he could not have been more astonished had the whole Xavante tribe hurled themselves upon him armed with

bows and arrows. He kept looking around at everyone present as if wanting to know the reason for something that required no explanation at all.
Finally, he was told about the love between Camilo and Isabel, the sole
cause of his son's attempted suicide. The comendador approved of his son's
choice, and took gallantry so far as to say that, in the circumstances, he
would have done just the same had the young lady spurned his love.

"Am I at last worthy of your love?" Camilo asked Isabel when he found
himself alone with her.

"Of course!" she said. "If you had died, I would have died too!"

Camilo quickly added that Providence had been watching over him,
although it was never quite clear what he meant by Providence.

It was not long before news of the outcome of this tragic episode had
spread throughout the town and its environs.

The announcement of Camilo and Isabel's forthcoming marriage drove
Leandro Soares almost to the brink of madness. A thousand acts of vengeance rushed into his mind, each bloodier than the last; in his opinion,
they were both vile traitors, and he must exact a solemn revenge on them.

No despot could ever have imagined more hideous torments than those
dreamed up by Leandro Soares's overheated imagination. The poor lover
spent a whole two days and nights in pointless conjectures. On the third
day, he decided to seek out his fortunate rival, throw his villainy in his face,
and then kill him.

He armed himself with a knife and set off.

The happy bridegroom-to-be was leaving his house, unaware of the fate
awaiting him, and imagining a life brimming with happiness and celestial
delights. The thought of Isabel painted everything around him in a poetic
rosy glow. He was completely immersed in these daydreams when he saw
before him his former rival. Absorbed as he was in his own happiness, he
had forgotten all about him, but he immediately grasped the danger he was
in and prepared to face it.

Faithful to his self-imposed plan, Leandro Soares unleashed a litany of
insults that Camilo listened to in silence. When Soares had finished and was
about to put into practice the bloody conclusion, Camilo said:

"I've listened to everything you've said, and I ask you now to listen to
me. Yes, it's true that I'm going to marry Isabel, but it's also true that she
doesn't love you. What, then, is our crime? Now, while you have been thinking only hateful thoughts about me, I have been thinking of your happiness."

"Oh, have you?" said Soares with heavy irony.

"It's true. I said to myself that a man of your talents should not be eternally condemned to act as a stepping-stone for the ambitions of other men; and then, when my father wanted to force me to become provincial deputy, I told him that I would accept the post only in order to give it to you. My father agreed, but there was still a certain amount of political resistance to overcome and, even now, I still have some way to go. A man who would do that for you does, I think, deserve a little gratitude, or at least a little less hatred."

There are not, I believe, strong enough words in the human language to describe the look of indignation on Leandro Soares's face. He flushed bright scarlet, and his eyes seemed to spit fire. His lips trembled as if they were quietly rehearsing a sufficiently eloquent insult to hurl at his fortunate rival. Finally, he managed to say:

"What you have done was quite villainous enough without stooping to mockery—"

"Mockery!" cried Camilo, interrupting him.

"What else would you call what you have just said? Gratitude indeed, when, after robbing me of my greatest, my only happiness, you offer me politics as some kind of compensation!"

Camilo managed to explain that it wasn't a matter of compensation; he had come up with the plan because he knew of Soares's political interests and thought that this would please him.

"At the same time," he said gravely, "I also wanted to do a good service to the province, because, even if it cost me my life, I would never do anything that might prove detrimental to my province and my country. I was hoping to serve both province and country by putting you forward as a candidate, and I know that everyone would agree with me on that."

"But you mentioned some resistance," said Soares, fixing his adversary with an inquisitorial eye.

"Yes, but for purely political reasons, not because they're opposed to you personally," explained Camilo. "And what does that matter? Reason will prevail, as will the true principles of the party that has the honor of counting you among its members."

Leandro Soares did not for a moment take his eyes off Camilo; an ironic, threatening smile played upon his lips. He studied him for a few seconds without saying a word, then again broke his silence.

"What would *you* do in my place?" he asked, and his ironic smile took on a truly menacing air.

"I would refuse," said Camilo fearlessly.

"Ah!"

"Yes, I would refuse, because I have no political vocation. That's not the case with you, though, for you do have such a vocation, as well as the support of the party throughout the province."

"Yes, so I believe," said Soares proudly.

"And you're not alone in believing that, everyone says the same."

Soares began pacing up and down. Was his mind filled with a tumult of terrible thoughts or was a glimmer of humanity demanding moderation in the kind of death he dealt his rival? Five whole minutes passed. Then Soares stopped pacing, stood face-to-face with Camilo, and asked bluntly:

"Will you swear one thing?"

"What's that?"

"That you will make her happy."

"I've already sworn as much to myself, and it will be my sweet duty to do so."

"It would have been my duty, too, had fate not turned against me. No matter, I'm ready to do whatever is necessary."

"And I know what a generous heart you have," said Camilo, holding out his hand to him.

"Possibly, but what you do not know, what you cannot know, is the storm raging in my soul, the terrible pain that will go with me to the grave. A love such as mine will never die."

He paused and shook his head, as if to drive away some baleful idea.

"What are you thinking?" asked Camilo.

"Don't worry," Leandro replied, "I'm not hatching any plots. I will resign myself to fate, and if I do accept the political candidacy you're offering, it is only so as to drown in it the grief filling my heart."

I'm not sure that this electoral remedy would cure every lover's complaint, but in Soares's heart it provoked a healthy crisis, which resolved itself in the patient's favor.

Readers will already have guessed that Camilo had not, in fact, spoken up for Soares, but he immediately set about doing just that, as did his father, and he finally managed to have Leandro Soares included on the list of candidates to be presented to the electorate at the next campaign. Soares's opponents, knowing the circumstances in which he had been offered the candidacy, took delight in repeating that he had sold his birthright for a mess of pottage.

Camilo had been married for a year when a French traveler came to his door. He brought with him letters of recommendation from one of his former teachers in Paris. Camilo received him gladly and asked for news of France, a country he still loved, he said, as his intellectual homeland. The traveler told him many things and finally produced from his bag a bundle of newspapers.

It was the *Figaro*.

"Ah, the *Figaro*!" cried Camilo, seizing the newspapers.

They were all out of date, but from Paris nonetheless. They reminded him of the life he had led for eight long years, and although he had no desire to change his present life for that other life, he felt a natural curiosity to revisit old memories.

In the fourth or fifth newspaper he came upon a piece of news that he read with horror:

> The notorious Leontina Caveau, who claimed to be the widow of a certain Prince Alexis, a subject of the Czar, was arrested yesterday. The lovely lady (for she was lovely!), not content with deceiving a few unwary young men, made off with all the jewelry belonging to a neighbor, Mlle. B. Fortunately, the victim complained to the police before the so-called princess could escape.

Camilo had just read this article for the fourth time when Isabel came into the room.

"Are you missing Paris?" she asked when she saw him reading the French newspaper.

"No," said her husband, putting his arm around her waist, "I was missing you."

LUÍS DUARTE'S WEDDING

———

O N APRIL 25, a Saturday morning, José Lemos's house was in total uproar. The dinner service that was only used on special occasions was being brought out, stairs and hallways were being scrubbed, and suckling pigs and turkeys were being stuffed ready to be roasted in the baker's oven across the road; there was no rest for anyone; something of great importance was about to happen.

José Lemos was in charge of sorting out the parlor. Perched on a bench, the worthy master of the house was attempting to hang the two engravings he had bought the day before from Bernasconi's; one depicted *The Death of Sardanapalus*, the other *The Execution of Mary Stuart*. He and his wife were having a bit of a battle about where to hang the first engraving. Dona Beatriz thought it indecent, all those men embracing a lot of naked women. Besides, such gloomy subjects were hardly suitable for a celebration. José Lemos had been a member of a literary society in his youth, and replied loftily that these were historical paintings, and that history had a place in every family. He might have added that not every family had a place in history, but that little joke was in even poorer taste than the engravings.

Keys in hand, but not quite as disheveled as the lady in Tolentino's famous satirical sonnet, Dona Beatriz was bustling back and forth between parlor and kitchen, issuing orders, chivying the slaves, gathering up clean tablecloths and napkins, and dictating shopping lists; in short, dealing with the thousand and one things that every mistress of the house has to deal with, especially on such an important day.

Now and then, Dona Beatriz would go to the foot of the stairs and shout:

"Girls, come down and have your breakfast!"

It seems, though, that the girls were in no hurry, because they only obeyed their mother's summons when it was past nine o'clock, and she had already called up to them eight times and was even about to climb the stairs to their bedroom—quite a sacrifice for such a plump lady.

The Lemos girls were two dark-haired beauties. One was about twenty, the other seventeen; both were tall and slightly overdressed. The older girl looked somewhat pale, while the other, pink-cheeked and cheerful, came down the stairs singing a popular ballad of the time. Of the two, it would seem that she was the happier one, but this was not the case; the happier sister was the older girl, who, that very day, was to tie the knot with young Luís Duarte, after a long and persistent courtship. She was pale because she had barely slept, even though she had never before suffered from insomnia, but then some illnesses do just come and go.

The two girls came downstairs, received their mother's blessing as well as a brief telling-off, then went into the parlor to talk to their father. José Lemos, who had just changed the position of the pictures for the seventh time, asked his daughters whether the engraving of Mary Stuart would be better on this side of the sofa or on the other. The girls said it would be best left where it was, and this verdict put an end to all José Lemos's doubts, and, deeming his work to be done, he went off to have his breakfast.

Also seated at the breakfast table, along with José Lemos, Dona Beatriz, Carlota (the bride), and Luísa, were Rodrigo Lemos and little Antonico, the Lemoses' two sons. Rodrigo was eighteen and Antonico six; Antonico was a miniature version of Rodrigo, with whom he shared another brotherly trait, that of extreme idleness. From eight o'clock in the morning on, Rodrigo was to be found doing one of two things: either reading the advertisements in the newspaper or going into the kitchen to find out when breakfast would be served. As for Antonico, he, as usual, had eaten a large plate of porridge at six o'clock, and then slept peacefully until the nursemaid called him.

Breakfast passed without incident. José Lemos preferred not to talk while he was eating; Rodrigo recounted the plot of the play he had seen the previous night at the Ginásio; and that was the sole topic of conversation.

When breakfast was over, Rodrigo got up to smoke a cigarette, and José Lemos leaned his elbows on the table, peered out at the rather ominous sky over toward Tijuca, and asked if it looked as if rain were likely.

Antonico was just about to leave the table, having first asked permission, when his mother issued this warning:

"Now, Antonico, at supper, I don't want you to do what you always do when there are strangers here."

"What's that?" asked José Lemos.

"He gets all embarrassed and sticks his finger up his nose. Only silly boys do that, and I don't like it."

Deeply humiliated, Antonico ran into the parlor in floods of tears, Dona Beatriz hurried after her youngest child to comfort him, and everyone else left the table.

José Lemos checked with his wife that no one had been omitted from the guest list, and, having established that everyone who should have been invited was there, he prepared to go out. He was immediately given various errands: to ask the hairdresser to come early, to buy gloves for his wife and his daughters, to make sure the carriages were ready, to order ice cream and wines, and certain other tasks in which he could have been helped by young Rodrigo, had that namesake of El Cid not gone upstairs to sleep off breakfast.

No sooner had the soles of José Lemos's shoes touched the cobbled street outside than Dona Beatriz instructed her daughter Carlota to follow her into the parlor, where she immediately addressed her as follows:

"Today, my dear, your life as a single woman will end, and tomorrow, married life will begin. Having undergone the same transformation myself, I know from personal experience that being married brings with it many heavy responsibilities. Obviously, every woman must learn for herself, but I am following the example of your grandmother, who, on the eve of my marriage to your father, set out in clear and simple language what it means to be married and the great responsibility involved in this new role . . ."

Dona Beatriz stopped speaking, and Carlota, attributing her mother's silence to a desire for some response, said nothing, but planted a fond, filial kiss on her mother's cheek.

Had Luís Duarte's bride peered through the keyhole of her father's study only three days before, she would have realized that Dona Beatriz was reciting a speech composed by José Lemos, and that her silence was merely a temporary memory lapse.

It would have been far better had Dona Beatriz, like other mothers, offered advice drawn from her own heart and experience. Maternal love is the best rhetoric in the world, but Senhor José Lemos, who, ever since he was a young man, had preserved a certain literary bent, felt that, on such a solemn occasion, it would be wrong to run the risk of his better half making any grammatical errors.

Dona Beatriz resumed her speech, which was not that long, and concluded by asking if Carlota really did love her fiancé and was not, as did occasionally happen, getting married out of pique. Carlota replied that she loved her fiancé as dearly as she loved her parents, and the mother then kissed her daughter with a tenderness not provided for in José Lemos's prose.

At about two o'clock in the afternoon, José Lemos returned, dripping with sweat, but feeling very pleased with himself, because, as well as carrying out all his wife's errands as regards carriages, hairdressers, etc., he had managed to persuade Lieutenant Porfírio to join them for supper, something which, up until then, had been by no means certain.

Lieutenant Porfírio was what you might call an after-dinner speaker, possessing, as he did, the necessary confidence, fluency, and wit for the task. These fine gifts brought Lieutenant Porfírio certain benefits: he rarely dined at home on Sundays or on public holidays. You invited Lieutenant Porfírio on the tacit understanding that he would make a speech, just as you would expect a guest who was also a musician to play something. Lieutenant Porfírio came between dessert and coffee, and he did not come cheap, either; for if he was a good speaker, he was an even better trencherman. All things considered, his speech was amply paid for by the supper.

In the three days prior to the wedding, there had been much debate about whether the supper should precede the ceremony or vice versa. The bride's father felt that the ceremony should come after supper, and he was supported in this by young Rodrigo, who, with a wisdom worthy of a statesman, realized that, otherwise, supper would be very late. Dona Beatriz, however, thought it odd to go to church on a full stomach. This view had no theological or disciplinary basis, but Dona Beatriz had her own particular views on church matters, and she prevailed.

At around four o'clock, the guests began to arrive.

The first were the Vilela family, comprising Justiniano Vilela, a retired civil servant, Dona Margarida, his wife, and Dona Augusta, their niece.

Justiniano Vilela's head—if a breadfruit wearing a very elaborate cravat can be called a head—was an example of nature's prodigality when it came to making big heads. Some people declared, though, that his talent could not compete in size, even though a rumor to the contrary had been doing the rounds for some time. I don't know what talent those people were talking about, and the word can have various meanings, but Justiniano Vilela had certainly shown great talent in his choice of wife, who, in José Lemos's opinion, still merited ten minutes of anyone's attention, even though she was well into her forty-sixth year.

Justiniano Vilela was dressed as one usually does for such gatherings, and the only truly noteworthy thing about him were his English lace-up shoes, and since he had a horror of overly long trousers, he revealed a pair of fine, immaculate, brilliant white socks whenever he sat down.

As well as his pension, Justiniano owned a house and two houseboys, and he lived quite well on that. He disliked politics, but had firm opinions about public affairs. He played solo whist and backgammon on alternate days, spoke proudly of how things used to be in his day, and took a pinch of snuff between thumb and middle finger.

Other guests began arriving, but these were few in number, because only close friends and family would be attending the ceremony and the supper.

At half-past four, Carlota's godparents arrived, Dr. Valença and his widowed sister, Dona Virgínia. José Lemos rushed to embrace Dr. Valença, who, being a very formal, ceremonious fellow, gently pushed his friend away, whispering that, on such a day, gravity was of the essence. Then, with a serenity of which only he was capable, Dr. Valença immediately went to greet the mistress of the house and the other ladies.

He was a man of about fifty, neither fat nor thin, but endowed with a broad chest and an equally broad abdomen, which lent a still greater gravity to his face and manners. The abdomen is the most positive expression of human gravity; a thin man cannot help but make rapid movements, whereas to be seriously grave, one's movements need to be slow and measured. A truly grave man should take at least two minutes to take out a handkerchief and blow his nose. Dr. Valença took three minutes when he had a heavy cold and four when he was well. He really was the gravest of men.

I stress this because it is the best possible proof of Dr. Valença's intelligence. As soon as he had completed his law degree, he realized that the one quality guaranteed to earn other people's respect was gravity; and on inquiring into the nature of gravity, it seemed to him that it had nothing to do with profound thoughts or seriousness of mind, but with a certain "mystery of the body," as La Rochefoucauld calls it, and, the reader will add, mystery is like the flag carried by neutral forces in time of war, ensuring that no one dares to examine the cargo it conceals.

Anyone discovering so much as a wrinkle in Dr. Valença's tailcoat could feel well pleased with himself. His vest had only three buttons and formed a kind of heart-shaped opening from chest to neck. An elegant collapsible top hat completed Dr. Valença's toilette. He was not handsome in the effeminate sense that some apply to male beauty, but there was a certain correctness about the lines of his face, which was covered with a veil of serenity that suited him perfectly.

Once Dr. Valença and his sister had arrived, José Lemos asked after the bridegroom, but Dr. Valença said he hadn't seen him. It was five o'clock by then. The guests, who assumed they had arrived too late for the ceremony, were unpleasantly surprised by this delay, and Justiniano Vilela whispered to his wife that he regretted not having had something to eat beforehand. This was precisely what young Rodrigo Lemos was doing, having realized that supper would not start until seven.

Dr. Valença's sister—of whom I said but little before because she was one of the most insignificant creatures ever produced by the race of Eve—immediately wanted to go and see the bride, and Dona Beatriz went with her, leaving her husband free to strike up a conversation with Senhor Vilela's very attractive wife.

"Bridegrooms today do seem to take their time," Justiniano remarked philosophically. "When I got married, I was the first to arrive at the bride's house."

To this comment—which was entirely the child of Vilela's implacable stomach—Dr. Valença replied:

"I can perfectly understand the delay and the nervousness one must feel in the presence of one's bride."

Everyone smiled at this defense of the absent groom, and the conversation grew more animated.

At the very moment when Vilela was discussing with Dr. Valença the advantages of the old days over the present, and the young women were talking about the latest fashions, the bride entered the room, escorted by her mother and godmother, with, bringing up the rear, the very attractive Luísa, accompanied by her little brother, Antonico.

It would be both inexact of me and in poor taste if I, as narrator, were not to mention that an admiring murmur filled the room.

Carlota was a truly dazzling sight in her white dress, her garland of orange blossom, her thinnest of thin veils, and wearing no other jewels but her dark eyes, bright as diamonds of the first water.

José Lemos broke off his conversation with Justiniano's wife and gazed at his daughter. The bride was introduced to the guests and led over to the sofa, where she sat down between her godparents. Balancing his top hat on his knee and steadying it with one expensively gloved hand, Dr. Valença showered his goddaughter with praise, which made the young woman simultaneously blush and smile—an amiable alliance between vanity and modesty.

Steps were heard on the stairs, and José Lemos was preparing himself for the arrival of his future son-in-law, when the Valadares brothers appeared at the door.

Of the two brothers, the oldest, called Calisto, had a sallow complexion, an aquiline nose, brown hair, and round eyes. The younger brother, called Eduardo, only differed from his brother in having a distinctly ruddier complexion. They were both employed by the same company and were in the full bloom of middle age. There was another distinguishing feature: Eduardo wrote poetry when he was allowed time away from the accounts books, while his brother was the enemy of anything that had so much as a whiff of literature about it.

Time passed, and still no sign of either the groom or Lieutenant Porfírio. The groom was essential to the wedding, and the lieutenant to the supper. It was half-past five when Luís Duarte finally arrived. Each guest sang a private "Hallelujah."

He appeared at the door of the parlor and gave a low bow to the assembled guests, so gracefully and ceremoniously that Dr. Valença felt rather envious.

He was a young man of twenty-five, very fair-skinned, with a blond mustache and no beard at all. He wore his hair parted in the middle. His lips were so red that one of the Valadares brothers whispered to the other: "It looks like he's wearing lipstick." In short, Luís Duarte cut a figure guaranteed to please any twenty-year-old girl, and I would have no compunction in calling him an Adonis if he really were one, which he was not. At the appointed hour, bride and groom, parents and godparents set off for the church, which was nearby; the other guests remained in the house, with

Luísa and Rodrigo doing the honors, although Rodrigo had to be summoned by his father, and duly appeared dressed in the very latest fashion.

"They're like a pair of turtledoves," said Dona Margarida Vilela when the wedding party had left.

"Very true," agreed the Valadares brothers and Justiniano Vilela.

Young Luísa, who was, by nature, a cheerful girl, soon livened up the proceedings, chatting animatedly to the other girls, one of whom she invited to play something on the piano. Calisto Valadares suspected that the Scriptures had made a serious omission in excluding the piano from among the plagues of Egypt. The reader can imagine the look on his face when he saw one of the girls get up and walk over to that vile instrument. He uttered a long sigh and went to study the two engravings purchased the day before.

"Magnificent!" he said, standing before *The Death of Sardanapalus*, a painting he loathed.

"Yes, it was Papa who chose it," said Rodrigo, and these were the first words he had spoken since entering the room.

"He obviously has good taste," said Calisto. "Do you know what the painting is about?"

"It's about Sardanapalus," replied Rodrigo, undeterred.

"I know that," retorted Calisto, hoping to continue the conversation, "what I meant was—"

He could not finish his sentence, because the first chords on the piano rang out.

Eduardo, who, in his role as poet, was expected to love music, too, strolled over to the piano and leaned on it in the melancholy pose of a man conversing with the muses. Meanwhile, his brother Calisto, finding it impossible to avoid the cascade of notes, went and sat down near Vilela, with whom he struck up conversation, beginning by asking what time it was by his watch. This touched Vilela's tenderest nerve.

"It's getting late," he said in a faint voice. "Nearly six o'clock."

"They can't possibly take much longer."

"Can't they! It's a long ceremony and they might not have been able to find the priest . . . Marriages should be held at home and at night."

"My feelings exactly."

The girl finished playing, and Calisto breathed easily again, while Eduardo, still leaning on the piano, applauded enthusiastically.

"Why don't you play something else?" he asked.

"Yes, Mariquinhas, play something from the *La Sonnambula*," said Luísa, making her friend sit down again.

"Yes, *La Son—*"

Eduardo did not finish the word; he saw before him his brother's two disapproving eyes, and winced. Stopping in midsentence and wincing could simply have been the sign of a painful corn. And so everyone thought, except for Vilela, who, assuming the others felt as he did, was convinced that some sharp hunger pang must have interrupted Eduardo's thoughts. And as does sometimes happen, Eduardo's pain awoke his own, so much so that Vilela's stomach issued a real ultimatum, to which he succumbed, and, taking advantage of his position as family friend, he wandered off into the house, on the excuse that he needed to stretch his legs.

A marvelous idea.

The table was already laid with a few inviting titbits, and to Vilela's eyes it seemed like a veritable cornucopia. Two pastries and a croquette were the palliatives Vilela sent to his rebellious stomach, and his viscera had to make do with that.

Meanwhile, Dona Mariquinhas was still performing miracles on the piano; Eduardo, now leaning at the window, appeared to be contemplating suicide, while his brother played with his watch chain and listened to Dona Margarida complaining about her feckless slaves. As for Rodrigo, he was pacing up and down, occasionally saying:

"Goodness, they're taking their time!"

It was a quarter past six and still no carriages; some people were already growing impatient. At twenty past six, there was a faint rattle of wheels; Rodrigo ran to the window. It was a passing cab. At twenty-five past six, everyone thought they could hear carriages approaching.

"They're here!" exclaimed a voice.

But it was nothing. What they heard seemed to be (and forgive me for marrying this noun to this adjective) a kind of aural mirage.

At six thirty-eight, the carriages arrived. There was great excitement in the parlor; the ladies ran to the windows. The men eyed each other like conspirators gathering their forces for some major undertaking. The wedding party entered. The houseboys, waiting in the hallway for the bride and groom, took their young mistress completely by surprise by showering her with rose petals. And, as there always are on such occasions, many kisses and words of congratulations were given.

José Lemos was beside himself with joy, but the news that Lieutenant Porfírio had still not arrived put something of a damper on his high spirits.

"We must send for him."

"At this hour?" murmured Calisto Valadares.

"Without Porfírio the party won't be complete," José Lemos whispered to Dr. Valença.

"Papa," said Rodrigo, "I don't think he's coming."

"That's impossible!"

"It's nearly seven o'clock."

"And supper is ready," added Dona Beatriz.

Dona Beatriz's words carried considerable weight with José Lemos, which is why he did not insist. They had no choice but to give up on the lieutenant.

However, the lieutenant was a man accustomed to awkward situations, someone you would want on your side in a tight corner. No sooner had Dona Beatriz finished speaking, with José Lemos mentally agreeing with her, than the voice of Lieutenant Porfírio was heard on the stairs. The master of the house gave a sigh of relief and satisfaction. The long-awaited guest entered the room.

The lieutenant belonged to that happy class of men who are apparently ageless; some thought he was thirty, others thirty-five, and others forty; some even went as high as forty-five, and they could all have been right, for the lieutenant's face and brown side-whiskers fitted all these hypotheses. He was thin, of medium height, and dressed rather stylishly; indeed, there was really very little to distinguish him from any other dandy. The one thing that jarred slightly was his way of walking; Lieutenant Porfírio's feet were so widely splayed that you could almost draw a straight line between right foot and left. However, everything has its compensations, and in his case, these were the flat patent-leather shoes he wore, revealing a fine pair of woolen socks whose surface was smoother than a billiard ball.

He entered with a grace that was peculiar to him. To greet the bride and groom, he bent his right arm so that the hand holding his hat was behind his back, then bowed very low, and remained in that posture, so that (from a distance) he resembled one of those old-fashioned lampposts.

Porfírio had been a lieutenant in the army before being discharged, which suited him perfectly, because he had then gone into the furniture business and made quite a sum of money. He was not particularly good-looking, but, despite this, some ladies said he was more dangerous than a can of dynamite. This was clearly not because of the way he spoke, because he had a particularly sibilant *s*, saying, for example: At your ssservisss, sssenhora . . .

When Porfírio had finished greeting everyone, José Lemos said to him:

"We're expecting great things from you tonight!"

"Ah," Porfírio responded with exemplary modesty. "Who would dare to speak in the presence of such erudition?"

He said these words, meanwhile thrusting four fingers of his left hand into his vest pocket, a gesture he cultivated because he did not know what to do with that awkward arm, which is always such a trial to novice actors.

"But why are you so late?" asked Dona Beatriz.

"Reproach me if you must, dear lady, but spare me the embarrassment of having to explain a delay for which there is no excuse in the code of friendship and good manners."

José Lemos smiled and glanced around at the others as if the lieutenant's words bestowed on him some kind of reflected glory. Despite the pastries he had eaten, Justiniano Vilela still felt ineluctably drawn toward the supper table and exclaimed rather vulgarly:

"Well, at least you arrived in time for supper!"

"Yes, let's all go in, shall we?" said José Lemos, offering an arm each to Dona Margarida and to Dona Virgínia, while the other guests followed behind.

The joy of pilgrims reaching Mecca could not have been greater than that of the guests when they saw the long table, groaning with roast meats and desserts and fruit and set with china dishes and glasses. They all sat down in their allotted places. For some minutes, there was a silence such as the silence that precedes a battle, and only when this was broken did general conversation begin.

"When I introduced young Duarte to the household a year ago, who would have thought that he would one day be the delightful Dona Carlota's bridegroom?" said Dr. Valença, wiping his lips on his napkin and glancing benevolently across at the bride.

"Yes, who would have thought it?" said Dona Beatriz.

"It must have been the hand of Fate," said Dona Margarida.

"It was indeed," replied Dona Beatriz.

"If it was the hand of Fate," said the groom, "I thank the heavens for taking such an interest in me."

Dona Carlota smiled, and José Lemos thought these words in excellent taste and worthy of a son-in-law.

"Fate or chance?" asked Lieutenant Porfírio. "I favor the latter, myself."

"That's where you're wrong," said Vilela, looking up from his plate for the first time. "What you call chance is, in fact, Fate. Weddings and winding sheets are made in heaven."

"Oh, so you believe in proverbs, do you?"

"They contain the wisdom of the people," said José Lemos.

"No, they don't," said the lieutenant. "For every proverb stating one thing, there's another stating the opposite. Proverbs lie. I think it was simply a very happy happenstance, or, rather, the law of the attraction of souls that led Senhor Luís Duarte to be drawn to the charming daughter of our very own Amphitryon."

José Lemos had no idea who Amphitryon was, but confident that, if Porfírio mentioned him, he must be all right, he smiled and thanked Porfírio for what seemed to be a compliment, meanwhile helping himself to some jelly, which Justiniano Vilela assured him was excellent.

The young women were whispering and smiling, the bride and groom were absorbed in an exchange of sweet nothings, while Rodrigo was picking his teeth so loudly that his mother shot him one of those fulminating glances that were her weapon of choice.

"Some jelly, Senhor Calisto?" asked José Lemos, his spoon in the air.

"Yes, just a little," said the man with the sallow face.

"The jelly is excellent," Justiniano said for the third time, and his wife was so embarrassed by these words that she could not conceal a grimace of distaste.

"Ladies and gentlemen," said Dr. Valença, "I propose a toast to the happy couple."

"Bravo!" said a voice.

"Is that it?" asked Rodrigo. "We want a longer toast than that."

"Mama, I want some jelly!" said Antonico.

"I'm not one for making speeches. I am simply raising my glass to the bride and groom."

Everyone drank.

"I want jelly!" insisted Antonico.

Dona Beatriz felt her inner Medea stirring within her, but respect for her guests prevented any unpleasant scene. The good lady merely said to one of the servants:

"Give this to the young master, will you?"

Antonico received the dish and began eating the way children eat when they're not really hungry: he would raise a spoonful to his mouth and spend an age rolling the contents of the spoon around between tongue and palate, while the spoon, pushed to one side, formed a slight lump in his right cheek. At the same time, he kept kicking his legs, repeatedly hitting first the chair and then the table.

While this was going on—not that anyone took much notice—the conversation continued. Dr. Valença was discussing with one lady the excellence of the sherry, and Eduardo Valadares was reciting a poem to the young woman sitting next to him.

Suddenly José Lemos stood up.

"Ssshh!" hissed everyone.

José Lemos picked up a glass and said to those around the table:

"I am not prompted to speak by any feeling of pride to be addressing such an illustrious audience. I am responding to the higher duty of courtesy, friendship, and gratitude, that most preeminent, sacred, and immortal of duties."

The audience would have been cruel indeed not to applaud these words, and their applause did not ruffle the speaker in the least, for the simple reason that he knew the speech by heart.

"Yes, ladies and gentlemen, I bow before that duty, the holiest and most imperious of all duties. I drink to my friends, to those steadfast adherents of the heart, those vestal virgins, both male and female, devotees of the pure flame of friendship! To my friends! To friendship!"

To be honest, the only person who understood the utter nullity of José Lemos's speech was Dr. Valença, who was himself no intellectual, which is why he rose to propose a toast to their host's oratorical talents.

These two toasts were followed by the customary silence, until Rodrigo turned to Lieutenant Porfírio and asked if he had perhaps left his muse at home.

"Yes," said one lady, "we want to hear you. People say you speak really well."

"Me, senhora?" replied Porfírio with all the modesty of a man who believes himself to be another golden-mouthed Saint John Chrysostom.

Once the champagne had been poured and handed around, Lieutenant Porfírio stood up. Vilela, who was some distance away, cupped one hand behind his right ear, while Calisto, fixing his eyes firmly on the tablecloth, appeared to be counting every thread. José Lemos alerted his wife, who, at that moment, was trying to tempt the implacable Antonico with a sweet chestnut; all other eyes were on the speaker.

"Ladies! Gentlemen!" said Porfírio. "I do not intend to rummage around in the very heart of history, that teacher of life, to find out what marriage was like in the earliest ages of humankind. We all know, ladies and gentlemen, what marriage is. Marriage is the rose, the queen of the garden, unfurling its red petals in order to protect us from the thistles and thorns and barbs of life . . ."

"Bravo!"

"Delightful!"

"If marriage is what I have just revealed to your auricular senses, there is no need to explain the joy, the fervor, the loving impulse, the explosions of sentiment felt by all of us seated here around this altar to celebrate our dear and much-loved friend."

José Lemos bowed his head so low that the tip of his nose touched a pear that lay in front of him on the table, and Dona Beatriz turned to Dr. Valença, who was sitting beside her, and said:

"Doesn't he speak well! He's like a walking dictionary!"

Porfírio went on:

"I fear, ladies and gentlemen, that I lack the necessary talent to speak on the subject . . ."

"Nonsense! You speak really well!" cried many of the people surrounding him.

"You are far too kind, but I still do not feel I have the necessary talent to grapple with a subject of such magnitude."

"Nonsense!"

"Please, you're too kind," said Porfírio, bowing. "While, as I say, I may lack that particular talent, I have more than enough goodwill, the same goodwill that led the Apostles to plant the religion of Calvary in the world, and thanks to that same feeling, I can sum up in just a few words my toast to the happy couple. Ladies and gentlemen, two flowers were born in two different flower beds, both of them beautiful, both highly scented, both full of divine life. They were born for each other; they were the carnation and the rose; the rose lived only for the carnation, the carnation lived only for the rose: along came a breeze and mingled the perfumes of the two flowers, and they, knowing they were in love, ran to meet each other. The breeze was godfather to that union. The rose and the carnation are united in the embrace of love, and sitting over there is the breeze honoring our gathering here tonight."

No one was expecting this breeze; the breeze was Dr. Valença.

Loud applause greeted this speech combining Calvary with the carnation and the rose. Porfírio sat down with a sense of having done his duty.

Supper was coming to an end; it was half-past eight; a few musicians were arriving in readiness for the ball. Still to come was a poem by Eduardo Valadares and a few more toasts to all those present and to those few who were absent. Now, with the liqueurs coming to the aid of the muses, battle was engaged between Lieutenant Porfírio and Justiniano Vilela, although the latter had to be urged to enter the arena. Once all subjects for debate had been exhausted, Porfírio proposed a toast to the army and its generals, and Vilela a toast to the union of all the provinces of the empire. When everyone else got up from the table, the two of them remained behind, warmly toasting all the practical and useful ideas of this world and the next.

The ball that followed was a very lively affair that went on until three in the morning.

No untoward incident marred the party. At most, there was a rather regrettable remark made by José Lemos when dancing with Dona Margarida, during which he boldly lamented her fate at having a husband who preferred proposing endless toasts to enjoying the priceless good fortune of being by her side. Dona Margarida smiled, and the incident went no further.

At two o'clock, Dr. Valença left with his family, and, despite the generally familiar tone of the party, he had not lost one iota of his habitual gravity all evening. Calisto Valadares escaped when Dona Beatriz's younger daughter got up to sing at the piano, and the other guests gradually drifted away.

When the party finally drew to a close, the last two tribal leaders of the dining table were still toasting all and sundry. Vilela's final toast was to the world's progress via coffee and cotton, while Porfírio raised his glass to universal peace.

However, the real toast of that memorable feast was the little baby born in January of the following year, who, if he survives his teething pains, will live to continue the Lemos dynasty.

ERNESTO WHAT'S-HIS-NAME

―――――――

Chapter I

T HAT YOUNG MAN standing over there on the corner of Rua Nova do
Conde and Campo da Aclamação at ten o'clock at night is not a thief,
he's not even a philosopher. True, he does have a somewhat mysterious air
about him; now and then, he presses one hand to his breast or slaps his thigh
or throws down a barely smoked cigar. No, he's clearly not a philosopher,
nor, for that matter, a petty thief, because if someone happens to walk by
on the same side of the street, he withdraws into the shadows as if afraid of
being recognized.

Every ten minutes or so, he walks up the street to where it meets Rua do
Areal, only to walk back down again ten minutes later, up and down, down
and up, and all he achieves is a five percent increase in the angry murmur
in his heart.

Anyone seeing him going back and forth, slapping his thigh, lighting
then immediately stubbing out cigars, would assume—quite reasonably, if
he had no other explanation—that the man was mad or nearly mad. But no,
Ernesto (I'm not authorized to give his whole name) happens to be in love
with a young woman who lives on that street; and he is angry because he has
not yet received an answer to the letter he sent her this morning.

We should explain that two days ago, they had a bit of a lover's tiff, and, breaking his vow never to write to her again, Ernesto had, that very morning, sent her an epistle that filled four incendiary pages, replete with exclamation marks and other punctuational outrages. The letter was dispatched, but no answer came.

Each time our young lover walked up and down the street, he stopped in front of a two-story house, inside which people could be seen dancing to the sound of a piano. This was where the lady of his thoughts lived, but he paused there in vain, for she did not appear at the window, and no letter reached his hands.

Ernesto bit his lip so as not to utter a cry of despair and went off to the next corner to vent his fury.

"What possible explanation can there be?" he said to himself. "Why does she not throw me a note from the window? No, she's obviously too busy dancing, possibly with her new inamorato, and she's completely forgotten that I'm out here in the street when I could be inside . . ."

At this point, he fell silent, and instead of the gesture of despair he should have made, he merely let out a long, sorrowful sigh. The explanation for this sigh, so unlikely in a man seething with rage, is almost too delicate a matter to be set down in writing, but, on the principle that one should either say nothing at all or reveal everything, here goes.

Ernesto was standing outside the house of Senhor Vieira, Rosina's uncle, Rosina being the name of Ernesto's beloved. He was a frequent visitor to the house, and it was there that he had quarreled with her two days before this particular Saturday in October 1850, when the events I'm describing took place. Now, why is Ernesto not one of those gentlemen dancing and drinking tea? The previous afternoon, Senhor Vieira had chanced to meet Ernesto in the street and told him that, the following day, they would be holding a small party to celebrate some family occasion, I can't quite remember which.

"It was a spur-of-the-moment decision," he said, "and I've only invited a few people, but I'm hoping that it will, nonetheless, be a brilliant affair. In fact, I was about to send you a formal invitation, but you hardly need one, do you?"

"No, of course not," Ernesto answered, rubbing his hands contentedly.

"Be sure to come!"

"I will, sir!"

"Oh, there's just one thing," said Vieira as he was turning to go. "The subdelegate will be coming, too, as well as the comendador, and I'd like all my guests to wear tails. You can put up with that for one evening, can't you?"

"With pleasure," said Ernesto, turning as pale as a ghost.

Why so pale? However ridiculous and pitiable it may seem, dear reader, I have to inform you that our Ernesto did not own a tailcoat, either old or new. Vieira's request was absurd, but there was no getting out of it; he could either go to the party in a tailcoat or not go at all. Whatever it took, he had to find a solution to this gravest of problems. Three possible solutions occurred to the poor, troubled lad: order a new tailcoat for the following night, regardless of the cost; buy one on credit; borrow one from a friend.

He dismissed the first two possibilities as impracticable; Ernesto had no money nor that much credit. There remained only the third idea. Ernesto drew up a list of friends and probable tailcoats, put it in his pocket, and set off in search of the golden fleece.

Luck, however, was not on his side: the first friend had to go to a wedding the next day and the second to a ball; the tailcoat of the third was torn, the fourth had lent his to someone else, the fifth never lent his to anyone, and the sixth had no tailcoat at all. He asked two more friends, but one had left the day before for Iguaçu, and the other was stationed at the Fortress of São João as second lieutenant in the national guard.

You can imagine Ernesto's despair, but observe, too, how cruelly fate was treating the poor fellow, for, on the way home, he encountered no fewer than three funerals, two of which involved a lot of carriages, all of whose occupants were wearing tailcoats. He had no alternative but to bow his head to fate, and accept the situation. Since, however, he had determined to be reconciled with Rosina, he wrote her the letter I mentioned earlier and sent the houseboy to deliver it and to tell her that he would be waiting that night on the corner of Campo da Aclamação to receive her answer. As we know, no answer came. Ernesto could not understand the reason for her silence; there had been many other tiffs before, but none had withstood the first letter he sent, or lasted more than forty-eight hours.

Convinced that no reply would come that night, Ernesto returned home with despair in his heart. He lived on Rua da Misericórdia. By the time he arrived, he was weary and downcast. And yet it still took him an age to get to sleep. He undressed so hurriedly that he almost tore his vest when the back buckle got caught on a trouser button. He hurled his boots at the dresser and almost broke a vase. He thumped the table seven or eight times, smoked two cigars, railed against fate, against Rosina and against himself, and, finally, as dawn was breaking, managed to fall asleep.

While he is sleeping, let us find out what lies behind his beloved's silence.

Chapter II

You see that girl over there, sitting on a sofa between two other young ladies, talking to them in a low voice, and occasionally batting her eyelids. That is Rosina. Rosina's eyes deceive no one except her suitors. Her eyes are bright and ensnaring, and she has a particular way of deploying those eyes that makes them even brighter and more ensnaring. She is elegant and graceful; if she were not, our poor unhappy Ernesto would not be so taken with her, for he has excellent taste. She isn't tall, but petite, lively, and mischievous. Her manners and her way of speaking are somewhat bold and affected, but, when a friend pointed this out to him, Ernesto declared that he didn't like shrinking violets.

"Well, I've never liked violets myself, shrinking or not," retorted his friend, delighted to be able to make this little joke.

A very 1850s joke.

She does not wear expensive clothes because her uncle is not rich, but she still manages to be extremely smart and elegant. Her head is adorned very simply, with two blue ribbons.

"Ah, if only those two ribbons wanted to tie the knot with me!" said one dandy sporting a black mustache and a middle parting.

"If only those ribbons wanted to carry me up to heaven!" said another dandy with brown side-whiskers and tiny ears.

Ambitious desires on the part of both lads—ambitious and futile, because, if anyone has caught her attention, it is a young man with a fair mustache and a long nose who is currently talking to the subdelegate. He is the person at whom Rosina occasionally glances, furtively it's true, but not so furtively as to escape the notice of the two girls beside her.

"She's really got her teeth into him!" one said to the other, indicating with a nod of her head the young man with the long nose.

"Oh, really, Justina!"

"Pure tittle-tattle!" said the other girl.

"Oh, do be quiet, Amélia!"

"Are you trying to pull the wool over our eyes?" said Justina. "Well, don't. He's looking over here again. He's not even listening to the subdelegate, who, poor man, is far too fat to play the part of chaperone."

"If you don't shut up, I'm leaving," said Rosina, pretending to be annoyed.

"Well, leave, then!"

"Poor Ernesto!" sighed Amélia.

"Sshh, Auntie might hear you," said Rosina, shooting a sideways look at a plump, elderly lady seated right next to the sofa and currently regaling a friend with a detailed account of her husband's latest malady.

"Why didn't Ernesto come this evening?" asked Justina.

"He sent a message to Papa saying he had some urgent work to do."

"Perhaps he's found someone else too," said Justina in an insinuating voice.

"He wouldn't dare!" cried Rosina.

"Such confidence!"

"Such love!"

"Such certainty!"

"Such faith!"

"He wouldn't dare," repeated Rosina. "Ernesto wouldn't dare fall in love with another girl, I'm sure of that. Ernesto is a . . ."

She did not finish her sentence.

"A what?" asked Amélia.

"A what?" asked Justina.

At that moment, a waltz struck up, and the young man with the long nose, whom the subdelegate had now abandoned in order to go and speak to Vieira, came over to the sofa and asked Rosina if he could have the honor of that dance. She modestly lowered her eyes, murmured a few inaudible words, then got to her feet and joined the other dancers. Justina and Amélia moved closer to each other so as to pass comment on Rosina's behavior and the rather graceless way in which she waltzed. However, since they were both friends of Rosina's, these criticisms were not made with any desire to offend, but in the gentle way in which friends always criticize absent friends.

Not that they were right, for Rosina waltzed very well and could stand comparison with any other exponent of that dance. As for her being hopelessly in love, they could have been right, indeed they were; the way in which she looked at and spoke to the young man with the long nose would have aroused suspicions in the most innocent of minds.

When the waltz was over, they strolled about a little, before going over to stand near a window. By then, it was one o'clock, and poor Ernesto was already trudging back to Rua da Misericórdia.

"I'll come tomorrow at six o'clock," said the other young man.

"No, not six o'clock!" said Rosina.

That was the time Ernesto usually called.

"At five, then."

"At five?" she said. "Yes, at five,"

The young man with the long nose thanked her with a smile that was a ratification of his amorous treaty, and he proffered a few more words to which she listened tenderly and blushingly, half proud, half modest. What he said was this: that Rosina was the flower of the ball, but also the flower of Rua do Conde, and not just the flower of Rua do Conde, but the flower of the whole city.

Ernesto had often said exactly the same, but the young man with the long nose had a particular way of complimenting a young woman. There was, for example, the elegant and quite inimitable way in which he stuck his left thumb in the left armhole of his vest, then wiggled the other fingers about as if he were playing the piano; and no one, at least no one in the immediate vicinity, had quite such an elegant way of holding out his arm, smoothing his hair, or simply offering a cup of tea.

Such were the qualities that conquered the lovely Rosina's fickle heart. Was that all? No. The mere fact that Ernesto lacked the alluring tailcoat that adorned the body and enhanced the charms of his more fortunate rival might give a clue to the more alert reader. Rosina was probably unaware of Ernesto's difficulties in finding a tailcoat, but she did know that he occupied a rather lowly position at the arsenal, whereas the young man with the long nose had a rather better position in a commercial establishment.

Any girl claiming to have philosophical ideas about love and marriage would say that the impulses of the heart came first. Rosina was not entirely immune to the impulses of the heart or to the philosophy of love, but she had ambitions to be somebody, she longed for new dresses and frequent visits to the theater, she wanted, in short, to be seen. In time, the young man with the long nose would be able to give her all these things, for she could already see him being made a director of the company he worked for; Ernesto, on the other hand, would find it hard to gain promotion at the arsenal, and he would certainly not rise quickly or very far.

When placed on the scales, poor Ernesto was inevitably the lighter weight.

Rosina had known the new candidate for a few weeks, but this was the first time she had been able to speak to him properly, to consolidate, if we can put it like that, their situation. Their relationship, which, up until then, had been purely telegraphic, became verbal; and if the reader has a taste for a more mannered, Gongoristic style, I would say that so many were the telegrams exchanged between them that night, that neighboring states, fearful of losing a possible alliance, sent out a call to the militia of sweet smiles, ordered a whole flotilla of fluttering eyelashes, prepared an artillery of tender glances, fond smiles, and handkerchiefs pressed modestly to lips; but this whole barrage of bucklers had no effect whatsoever because the lovely Rosina, at least that night, was absorbed by one thought only.

When the ball ended and Rosina went to her room, she saw a folded piece of paper on her dressing table.

"What's that?" she thought.

She opened it. It was the response to Ernesto's letter that she had forgotten to send. What if someone else had read it? No, they couldn't have. She carefully folded it up again, sealed it, and put it in a drawer, saying to herself:

"I must send it tomorrow morning."

Chapter III

"Fool." That is the word Rosina was going to use when she defended Ernesto's fidelity, so mischievously mocked by her two friends.

It was barely three months since Ernesto had begun courting Rosina and exchanging letters, and since they had been declaring eternal love to each other, and, in that short space of time, he had already suspected he might have a few rivals. Whenever this occurred, he would seethe with rage and consider abandoning the whole business. However, with a wave of her magic wand, she always led him back to the straight and narrow, by writing him a sharp note or whispering a few fiery words to him. Ernesto would admit that he had misunderstood, and that she really was far too kind.

"You're very fortunate that I do still love you," Rosina would say, feigning annoyance.

"I know!"

"Why must you invent such stories?"

"I wasn't inventing . . . someone told me."

"Well, you shouldn't have believed them."

"No, you're right, I shouldn't—and you're an angel sent from heaven!"

Rosina would forgive him his latest accusation, and things would carry on as before.

His friend and housemate, Jorge, to whom Ernesto confided all his joys and woes and to whom he turned for counsel, often used to tell him:

"Look, Ernesto, I think it's just wasted effort on your part."

"Why?"

"Because she doesn't love you."

"Impossible!"

"You're simply a way of passing the time."

"That's where you're wrong. She does love me."

"Yes, but she loves a lot of other men too."

"Jorge!"

"In short . . ."

"Not another word!"

". . . she's a flirt," concluded his friend quietly.

On hearing his friend's peremptory judgment, Ernesto shot him a long, deep look, capable of stopping all known mechanical movement; however, when his friend's face showed not a trace of fear or repentance, Ernesto withdrew the look and everything ended peacefully. In this, he was more prudent than a certain senator, Dom Manuel, who, when asked by the Viscount of Jequitinhonha to withdraw his laughter during a debate, continued to laugh anyway.

Such was Ernesto's confidence in the flower of Rua do Conde. If she had announced to him that she had in her pocket one of the towers from the Candelária Church, Ernesto might, indeed probably would, have accepted this as true.

This time, though, the quarrel was a serious one. Ernesto had actually seen her surreptitiously receive a note from some kind of cousin who occasionally visited the house. His eyes flashed angrily when he saw the mysterious epistle gleaming white in her hand. He eyed the young man threateningly, gave Rosina a scornful look, and left. Then he wrote the letter we already know about, and waited in the street for her reply. What reply was he expecting since he had actually seen Rosina take the note? Dear ingenuous reader, he wanted a reply that would prove to him that he had seen nothing, a reply that would make him regard himself with scorn and disgust. He could not really see how such a response was possible, but, deep in his heart, that is what he wanted.

The reply came the following morning. His housemate woke him at eight to give him the letter from Rosina.

Ernesto sat bolt upright in bed, then, when he had calmed down, opened the letter and devoured its contents. The look of celestial good fortune on his face revealed the contents of the letter to his friend Jorge.

"It's all sorted out," said Ernesto, folding up the letter and getting out of bed. "She's explained everything, and I clearly misunderstood."

"I see," said Jorge, looking pityingly at his friend. "So what does she say?"

Ernesto did not reply at once; he unfolded the letter again, read it to himself, refolded it, looked up at the ceiling, then down at his slippers, then at his friend, and only after making this whole series of gestures intended to indicate the depth of his abstraction, only then did he reply:

"It turns out that what I took to be a love letter was a note from her cousin asking to borrow some money from Rosina's uncle. She says I'm most unkind to force her to speak of these family peccadilloes and concludes by saying that she loves me more than she could ever love anyone. Here, read it."

Jorge took the letter and read it, while Ernesto paced back and forth, gesticulating and muttering monosyllabically to himself, as if mentally composing an act of contrition.

"So what do you think?" he asked when Jorge returned the letter.

"You're right. She does explain everything," answered Jorge.

Ernesto went to Rua do Conde that same evening. She received him with a smile as soon as she saw him enter the room. At the first opportunity, they made their peace, with Ernesto declaring that he was consumed with regret for ever having suspected her, and with Rosina—in the safety of the darkened room, and before the maid came in to light the candles on the dresser—generously allowing him to steal a kiss.

Now is the reader's chance to question me about the intentions of this young woman, who, while she preferred the employment prospects of the young man with the long nose, was still corresponding with Ernesto and giving him every indication that she preferred him, even though she didn't.

Rosina's intentions, inquisitive reader, were entirely marital. She wanted to marry and to marry as well as she could. To that end, she allowed herself to be courted by all her suitors, choosing which one best chimed with her desires, but without discouraging the others, because the best of the suitors might fall away, and if there was one thing worse than marrying badly, it was not marrying at all.

This, at least, was her plan. We should also add that she was an inveterate flirt, who enjoyed having at her feet a whole horde of suitors, many of whom did not intend to marry her at all and for whom courtship was a mere pastime, revealing in these gentlemen an utter vacancy of mind.

Half a loaf is better than none, as the saying goes. Morally and maritally speaking, Ernesto was Rosina's possible half a loaf, a kind of *pis aller*, as the French say, useful to have to hand.

Chapter IV

The young man with the long nose was not one of those birds of passage; his intentions were strictly conjugal. He was twenty-six, hardworking, popular, frugal, simple, and sincere, a true son of Minas Gerais. He could certainly make any young woman happy.

For her part, Rosina so insinuated herself into his thoughts that she almost caused him to lose his job. One day, when his boss came over to the desk where he was working, he noticed underneath the bookkeeper's inkstand a piece of paper on which the word "love" was written two or three times. One mention of that word was quite enough to send the young man's spirits soaring. Senhor Gomes Arruda frowned, focused his thoughts, then improvised a long and menacing speech in which the poor bookkeeper understood only the expression "out on your ear."

"Out on your ear" is a very weighty expression, which the bookkeeper pondered long and hard, and, forced to acknowledge that his boss was right, he set about mending his ways, although not his love. Love was taking ever deeper root in him; this was his first serious love, and, of course, he had fallen for a past-mistress in the field.

"Things can't go on like this," he was thinking as he walked home one night, scratching his chin. "I should really marry her as soon as possible. With what I get from my family and what I earn at the office, I reckon I can just about manage, and the rest is up to God."

Ernesto soon came to suspect the intentions of the young man with the long nose. Once, when he caught Rosina and his rival exchanging a glance, he got angry, and took the first opportunity to interrogate his beloved about this equivocal situation.

"Come on, own up!" he said.

"Oh, good heavens!" she exclaimed. "You're so suspicious. Yes, I did look at him, but only because of you."

"Because of me?" asked Ernesto in an icily ironic tone of voice.

"Yes, I was admiring his very smart cravat and thinking that I could buy something similar for you at New Year. Now that you've forced me to reveal my secret, though, I'll have to think of some other little present."

Ernesto saw that she was right. He recalled that there really had been a munificent gleam in her eye, if you'll forgive such an old-fashioned adjective; his anger dissolved into a fond, contrite smile, and the quarrel went no further.

Days later, on a Sunday, when he and she were in the parlor, and one of her uncle's children was standing at the window, the two lovers were interrupted by the boy running over to them, shouting:

"He's coming, he's coming!"

"Who?" asked Ernesto, feeling his heart splinter.

Going to the window, he saw it was his rival.

Fortunately, Rosina's aunt entered at this point, for a storm was already brewing over Ernesto's blazing forehead.

Shortly afterward, the young man with the long nose arrived and, on seeing Ernesto, he seemed to smirk. Ernesto withdrew into a sulk. Had his eyes been knives they would have committed two murders there and then. He managed to contain himself, though, in order to observe the couple more closely. Rosina did not appear to pay particular attention to the other man; she was merely polite. This slightly calmed Ernesto's troubled spirit, and, after an hour, he was restored to his usual state of perfect happiness.

He did not, however, notice the suspicious glances occasionally directed at him by the young man with the long nose. The mischievous smile had vanished from the bookkeeper's lips, suspicion having slipped into his mind when he noticed the almost indifferent manner in which Rosina treated both him and her other suitor.

"Could he be a serious rival?" he wondered.

The next day, as soon as he had the chance to speak to her alone, with no witnesses, he revealed the suspicions that had cast a dark cloud over a mind that had hitherto been innocently sunny. Rosina merely laughed, so persuasively that the young man with the long nose thought it undignified to repeat such an absurd suspicion.

"Oh, he would like me to love him, but he's wasting his time. I have only one face and one heart!"

"Ah, Rosina, you're an angel."

"Come, now!"

"Yes, an angel," he insisted. "And I believe it will not be long before I can call you my wife."

Rosina's eyes sparkled with contentment.

"Yes," he went on, "in two months' time we'll be married."

"Oh!"

"If, that is . . ."

Rosina turned pale.

"If?" she repeated.

"If Senhor Vieira gives his consent . . ."

"Why wouldn't he?" she said, quickly recovering from this sudden shock. "He wants only my happiness, and to marry you would be my greatest happiness. Even were he opposed to my heart's desire, I would only have to stand my ground for our wish to be granted. But, don't worry, my uncle will put no obstacles in our way."

The young man with the long nose stood for a few minutes gazing wordlessly at Rosina; two things astonished him: Rosina's strength of mind and her love for him. She was the first to break that silence.

"So in two months' time, then?"

"If luck is on my side."

"Is there any reason it won't be?"

"Who knows?" he said, with a hesitant sigh.

In the light of this happy prospect, the scale in which poor Ernesto's hopes were resting began to grow still lighter. Rosina's letters became less frequent, and in the few he did receive, her passion was less intense, the phrasing stiffer, colder, more stilted. When they were together, there was no longer the same easy expansiveness; his presence seemed to embarrass her. Ernesto seriously began to think the battle was lost. Unfortunately, his tactic was to ask if his suspicions had any foundation, and she responded earnestly that they did not, and this was enough to restore his peace of mind. This peace was short-lived and his serenity only skin-deep. Rosina's letters continued to be brief and her manners cold, and that, together with the other man's continued presence, cast a pall over Ernesto's thoughts. And yet, while one moment he was plunged into the slough of despond, the next he was lifted up into celestial bliss, thus demonstrating what nature wanted him to be: a fickle, passive soul, carried like a leaf wherever the wind chose to take him.

Nevertheless, the truth was hard to avoid. One day, he noticed that as well as Rosina's suspiciously affectionate ways, her uncle also seemed to be treating his rival more favorably. He was right; although the new suitor had still not formally asked for Rosina's hand in marriage, it was clear to Senhor Vieira that he would soon have a new nephew, and since this suitor was in the world of commerce, she could not, in his opinion, have made a happier choice.

I will say nothing of Ernesto's despair and terror, of the curses he uttered on the day when the certainty of his defeat finally hit home. Rosina's denials were no longer enough, and, besides, they seemed to him lukewarm, which indeed they were. The poor fellow even began to think that she and his rival had joined forces to mock him.

Since, as a general rule, it is part of our wretched human condition for pride to come before mere love, the moment he felt his suspicions were well founded, he was filled with a sense of fierce indignation, and I doubt that the final act of any melodrama could possibly contain as much spilled blood as the blood he shed in his imagination. Only in his imagination, kind reader, not just because he was incapable of harming another human being, but because any kind of resolution was repugnant to his nature. For that reason, after pondering the matter long and hard, he confided all his anxieties and suspicions to his housemate and asked for his advice: Jorge gave him two pieces of advice.

"In my opinion," Jorge said, "you should forget about her and concentrate on your work, which is far more important."

"Certainly not!"

"What, give up work?"

"No, I mean that I cannot possibly give *her* up!"

"Well, in that case," said Jorge, removing his left boot, "go and talk to the man you think is your rival and find out the truth."

"I will!" cried Ernesto. "That's an excellent idea, but," he went on after a moment's thought, "what if he isn't my rival, then what should I do? How will I find out if there's some other rival?"

"In that case," said Jorge, reclining philosophically on a chaise longue, "in that case, my advice would be to hell with both of them."

Ernesto closed his ears to such blasphemy, got dressed, and left.

Chapter V

Ernesto immediately headed for the place where the young man with the long nose worked, determined now to have it out with him once and for all. Well, he did hesitate a little and was almost on the point of turning back, but so violent were his feelings that they won out over any weakness of will, and, twenty minutes later, he reached his destination. He did not go into the actual building, but paced up and down outside, waiting for the other man to come out, which he did only forty-five minutes later; forty-five exasperatingly slow minutes.

Ernesto walked nonchalantly over to his rival, greeted him with a timid, fearful smile, then they stood for a few seconds looking at each other. The rival was just about to doff his hat and take his leave, when Ernesto asked:

"Are you going to Rua do Conde today?"

"Possibly."

"At what time?"

"I don't know yet. Why do you ask?"

"We could go together. I'm going at eight."

The young man with the long nose did not respond.

"Where are you off to now?" asked Ernesto after a silence.

"To the Passeio Público, unless, that is, you are too," his rival retorted.

Ernesto turned pale.

"Are you trying to avoid me?"

"I certainly am."

"Well, I won't let you. There's something I need to discuss with you. Wait, don't turn your back on me. I can be bold, too, though less with my tongue than with my actions. Give me your arm, and we'll go to the Passeio Público together."

The young man with the long nose was tempted to take his rival on, but they were standing immediately outside his place of work, and if he were seen fighting that would be the end of his career in commerce. He therefore preferred to continue walking, and had already set off when Ernesto shouted after him:

"Come back here, you hapless lover!"

The young man spun around:

"What did you call me?"

"I called you a 'hapless lover,'" said Ernesto, scrutinizing his rival's face for some clue as to his true feelings.

"How odd," said the young man with the long nose, "how odd that you should call me a 'hapless lover' when everyone has seen what a pathetic figure you've cut in your attempts to win the love of a young woman who is mine . . ."

"Yours!"

"Yes, mine!"

"I would say, rather, ours . . ."

"How dare you!"

The young man with the long nose clenched a fist in readiness; however, the calm confidence with which Ernesto was looking at him changed his mind. Was he telling the truth? Had that young woman—who had sworn eternal love to him and whom he was planning to marry, but about whom he, too, had once had his suspicions—had she actually given that man the right to call her his? This simple question so troubled him that he stood for nearly two minutes staring dumbly at Ernesto, who stared dumbly back at him.

"That is a very grave allegation," he said at last. "I demand an explanation."

"As do I," answered Ernesto.

"Let's go to the Passeio Público."

They walked on, initially in silence, not just because of the awkwardness of the situation, but also because each feared hearing some cruel revelation. Conversation began with brief, monosyllabic sentences, only gradually
becoming more natural and more fluent. Everything that you, dear reader,
already know about the two men was laid out by both of them and heard by
both with a mixture of sadness and anger.

"If what you say is true," remarked the other man as they walked down
Rua das Marrecas, "then I can only conclude that we have been deceived."

"Vilely deceived," added Ernesto.

"For my part," said the former, "this is a terrible blow, because I really
loved her and was hoping soon to make her my wife. Luckily for me, you
have warned me off in time . . ."

"Others might criticize me for doing what I did, but the end justifies the
means. I am suffering, too, of course, for I, too, was madly in love with her!"

These words were spoken with such deep emotion that they reverberated in his rival's heart, and the two men remained for a while saying nothing, mulling over their respective feelings of pain and humiliation. Ernesto
broke the silence with an agonized sigh just as they reached the Passeio
Público. Only the guard at the gate heard that sigh, for the young man with
the long nose was pondering a question.

"Should I condemn her so easily?" he wondered. "And is this man merely
a disappointed suitor who is using this ploy to neutralize me, his rival?"

Ernesto's face seemed to give the lie to this conjecture; however, since
this was too serious a matter to judge by appearances, he reopened the chapter of their shared revelations, and the incidents and gestures recalled by one
sparked an echo in the other. What decided them, though, was the moment
when they each produced a letter they happened to have with them. The
text of both letters proved that they were recent; the expressions of love
were not the same, because, as we know, Rosina was deliberately tempering
the language she used in her notes to Ernesto, but this was quite enough to
deliver the coup de grâce to the young man with the long nose.

"We must spurn her," he said when he finished reading his rival's letter.

"Is that all?" asked Ernesto. "Is that enough?"

"What would be the point of taking our revenge?" objected the young
man with the long nose. "Even if we did take our revenge, would that be
worthy of us?"

He stopped speaking, then an idea occurred to him, and he exclaimed:

"I've just thought of a way."

"What?"

"Why don't we each send her a letter breaking off all relations, but our letters will be identical?"

Ernesto instantly approved of this idea, for he seemed even more humiliated than his rival, and they both went home to write their fateful letters.

The following day, immediately after breakfast, Rosina was sitting quietly at home, blissfully unaware of the impending disaster, and even forging plans for the future, all of which hinged upon the young man with the long nose, when the houseboy came in, carrying two letters.

"Miss Rosina," he said. "This letter is from Senhor Ernesto, and this one—"

"What," she said, "are they both . . . ?"

"No," explained the houseboy, "one was waiting on the corner up there and the other on the corner down below."

And, hand in pocket, jingling the coins the two rivals had given him, he left her to read the two missives at her leisure. The first one she opened was from Ernesto. It read as follows:

> Senhora! Now that I am certain of your treachery, a certainty that nothing will now eradicate from my mind, I am taking the liberty of telling you that you are free and I am restored to health. Enough of humiliations! I could believe in you for as long as you had the ability to deceive me, now, though, I bid you farewell forever!

Rosina shrugged when she read this letter, then rapidly tore open the letter from the young man with the long nose and read: *Senhora! Now that I am certain of your treachery, a certainty that nothing will now . . .*

Her surprise grew and grew. Both men were bidding her farewell and both letters were couched in the same words. So they must have found out everything from each other. There was no way to repair the situation; all was lost!

Rosina did not usually cry. She sometimes rubbed her eyes to make them red when she needed to show a suitor she was upset about something. This time, though, she shed real tears, not of hurt, but of rage. Both rivals had triumphed and both were leaving her, having conspired together to deliver the final blow. There was nothing to be done; despair entered her soul. Alas, there was not a single sail on the horizon. The cousin we mentioned in a previous chapter had designs upon another young woman, and those designs were marital in nature. For the last month, she herself had been neglecting her usual system, leaving a number of interrogative glances unanswered. She had been abandoned by God and by men.

No, she still had something up her sleeve.

Chapter VI

A month after this disaster, Ernesto was at home, chatting with his housemate and two other friends, one of whom was the young man with the long nose. He heard someone call him and, going over to the stairs, he saw that it was the houseboy from Rua Nova do Conde.

"What do you want?" he asked sternly, suspecting that the houseboy might have come to ask him for money.

"I've brought you this," said the houseboy softly.

And he took from his pocket a letter, which he handed to Ernesto.

Ernesto's initial impulse was to reject the letter and kick the houseboy down the stairs, but, as he later confessed, his heart whispered something to him. He reached out his hand, took the letter, opened it and read.

Once again I bow to your unjust assertions. I am weary of crying. I can no longer live beneath such a calumny. Come now or I will die!

Ernesto rubbed his eyes; he could not believe what he had just read. Was it another trap or was she telling the truth? It could be a trap, but when Ernesto looked more closely, it seemed to him that he could see a stain left by a teardrop. She had definitely wept, and if she had wept, it was because she was suffering, and in that case . . .

Ernesto spent about eight or ten minutes pondering these thoughts. He did not know what to do. Answering Rosina's call would mean forgetting her treacherous love for another man in whose hands he had even seen a letter signed by her. And yet not going to see her might contribute to the death of a creature who, even if he had never loved her, deserved to be treated humanely.

"Tell her I'll come soon," Ernesto told the houseboy.

When he went back into the room, he looked quite different. His friends inevitably noticed the change and tried to find out what had happened.

"It must have been a creditor," said one.

"He hasn't been paid," said another.

"A new lover," suggested his housemate.

"It might be all those things," answered Ernesto in a voice intended to be cheerful.

That afternoon, Ernesto got dressed and went to Rua Nova do Conde. He stopped several times, determined to go no farther, but a moment's thought was enough to drive away all scruples, and so he continued on.

"There's some mystery here," he told himself and reread Rosina's letter. "He did, after all, reveal everything to me and even read me letters she had sent, so there can be no doubt about what happened. Rosina is guilty; she deceived me; she allowed herself to be courted by another, all the while claiming that she loved only me. But then why this letter? If she loved the other man, why doesn't she write to him? I need to investigate further."

This worthy young man hesitated for even longer when he entered Rua Nova do Conde, spending ten minutes walking back and forth, unable to come to a decision. Finally, he gave free rein to his heart and set off boldly along the path that fate appeared to have chosen for him.

When he arrived at the Vieira residence, Rosina was in the parlor with her aunt. Rosina seemed genuinely glad to see him, but, as far as Ernesto could judge, that gladness was not enough to disguise the traces left by her tears. Indeed, the lovely Rosina's usually mischievous eyes seemed veiled in melancholy. They were no longer mischievous, but dull or dead.

"The very picture of innocence!" Ernesto told himself.

At the same time, he felt ashamed of such a benevolent opinion, and, remembering what the young man with the long nose had told him, he assumed a stern, serious air, not so much lover as judge, not so much judge as executioner.

Rosina stared down at the floor.

When her aunt asked Ernesto why he had not been to see them for so long, he attributed this to work and illness, the excuses used by anyone who has no genuine excuse. After a further brief exchange, the aunt left the room to give orders to the servants, having already surreptitiously told Juquinha to stay. Juquinha promptly climbed onto a chair and sat staring out of the window, thus giving Ernesto and Rosina time to talk.

It was an awkward situation, but there was no time to lose, as Rosina instantly understood, for she immediately burst out:

"Do you feel no remorse?"

"For what?" asked Ernesto in astonishment.

"For what you did to me."

"Me?"

"Yes, abandoning me without a word of explanation. I can guess what lay behind it: some new suspicion, or, rather, some new calumny . . ."

"There was no calumny and no suspicion," said Ernesto after a moment's silence, "just the truth."

Rosina muffled a cry; her pale, tremulous lips tried to speak, but failed; two large tears rolled down her cheeks. Ernesto could not bear to see her cry; however justified he felt in his suspicions, whenever he saw her crying, he would immediately relent and beg her forgiveness. This time, though, he could not easily go back to his former state of mind. His rival's revelations were still fresh in his memory.

However, he did give in to her and begged her not to cry.

"Not cry?" she said in a tearful voice. "You ask me not to cry when I see my happiness slipping through my fingers, having lost any respect you once had for me, because you clearly do despise me, and without even knowing what the accusation is so that I could deny or disprove it . . ."

"Could you do that?" asked Ernesto passionately. "Could you prove the accusation to be wrong?"

"I could," she said, with a magnificently dignified look on her face.

Ernesto summarized the conversation he'd had with the young man with the long nose, and concluded by saying that he had seen a letter she had written to him. Rosina listened in silence, clearly deeply distressed, her breast rising and falling. When he finished, she broke into loud sobs.

"Please," said Ernesto softly, "someone might hear you."

"I don't care," she cried, "I don't care who hears."

"But can you deny what I have just told you?"

"Not all of it, no, because some of it is true," she answered in a sad voice.

"Ah!"

"The promise of marriage is a lie, and there were only two letters, and that . . . is your fault."

"Mine?" exclaimed Ernesto, as amazed as if he had just seen two candlesticks dancing.

"Yes," she said, "your fault. Don't you remember? You had quarreled with me yet again, and I . . . I know it was foolish . . . but to give you a shock, to avenge myself . . . oh, I must have been mad . . . I did write to that impudent individual . . . it was madness on my part, I see that now . . . but what do you expect, I was so angry . . ."

Ernesto's heart was greatly shaken by this new version of events. He would have expected Rosina to deny everything if she had intended to act malevolently; she would have declared that someone had imitated her handwriting; but, no, she admitted everything with the greatest nobility and simplicity; except—and herein lay the key to the situation—she was attributing it all to the extremes to which anger had driven her, thus revealing beneath the frivolous pastry, if we can compare the heart to a cake, the pure cream of love.

A few moments of silence ensued, in which she sat staring down at the floor, in the saddest, most melancholy pose ever struck by a repentant young woman.

"But did you not see that such madness could lead to my death?" said Ernesto.

Rosina shuddered to hear these words uttered in the gentle tone of old; she glanced up at him, then back at the floor.

"If I had thought that," she said, "I would never have done what I did."

"Quite right," Ernesto responded, but, still filled with a cruel desire for revenge, he felt that her frivolity should be punished with a few more minutes of doubt and recrimination.

She listened to further accusations from Ernesto, and responded to them all with such contrition and with words so steeped in regret, that he almost felt his own eyes filling with tears. Rosina's eyes were calmer now, and a lightness began to take the place of the melancholy shadows. The situation was almost as it had been a few weeks earlier; it needed only to be consolidated by time. Meanwhile, Rosina said:

"Don't think I'm asking for more than I deserve. What I did must be punished in some way, and I am perfectly resigned to that. I asked you to come so that you could explain your silence, and I, for my part, have explained my own folly. I cannot hope for more . . ."

"You can't?"

"No, my sole aim was to regain your respect."

"And why not my love too?" asked Ernesto. "Do you really think that, by a simple act of the will, the heart can suddenly extinguish the flame that has burned in it for so long?"

"No, that's impossible," she cried, "and I know, for my part, how much I will suffer . . ."

"Far too much," said Ernesto. "I was to blame for everything, I confess it now frankly. We must both forgive each other; I forgive you for your levity, and will you forgive me for that fateful quarrel?"

Had Rosina possessed a heart of bronze, she could not have refused the forgiveness for which her suitor was asking. Their generosity was reciprocal. As with the return of the prodigal son, those two souls celebrated the rebirth of their happiness and loved each other more than ever.

Three months later to the day, they were married in the Church of Sant'Ana, which was then to be found on Campo da Aclamação. The bride was radiant with happiness; the bridegroom appeared to breathe the air of celestial paradise. Rosina's aunt gave a soirée attended by all of Ernesto's friends, with the exception of the young man with the long nose.

This does not mean that their friendship suffered as a consequence. On the contrary, Ernesto's rival showed great magnanimity, tightening the ties that had bound them ever since the unusual circumstance that first brought them together. More than that, two years after Ernesto's marriage, we find the two of them running a notions store together, the best of friends. The young man with the long nose is even godfather to one of Ernesto's sons.

"Why don't you marry?" Ernesto sometimes asks his colleague, friend, and companion.

"No, it's too late," replies the other young man, "I'll die an old bachelor."

MUCH HEAT, LITTLE LIGHT

———

A T THE TIME, Luís Tinoco was twenty-one. He was of medium height, bright-eyed, tousle-haired, inexhaustibly loquacious, impetuous, and passionate. He held a modest position at the law courts, where he earned a meager crust, and he lived with his godfather, whose sole income was his pension. Tinoco held old Anastácio in the highest esteem, and Anastácio was equally fond of his godson.

Luís Tinoco was convinced he was destined for great things, and, for a long time, this proved to be his biggest obstacle in life. When Dr. Lemos first met Luís, the poetic flame was already beginning to burn in him, although no one knows quite how the fire was lit. Naturally, the thought of other men's laurels began to keep him awake at night. Then, one morning, Luís Tinoco woke to find himself a fully fledged writer and poet; inspiration, which had been only the tightest of buds the night before, had blossomed into a lush, flamboyant flower. Luís hurled himself upon the blank page with ardor and determination, and between the hours of six and nine, before he was called down for breakfast, he produced a sonnet, whose main defects were that it was only five lines long and didn't scan. Tinoco took his creation to the *Correio Mercantil*, which published it in the announcements section.

The night before publication, the little sleep he had was interspersed with dreams from which he kept waking in a panic. Dawn finally came, and Luís Tinoco, not normally an early riser, rose with the sun and went off to read his sonnet in print. No mother ever contemplated her newborn child more lovingly than that young man, who read and reread his poem, which in any case he knew by heart. He imagined that all the other readers of the *Correio Mercantil* would be doing the same thing, and that every one of them would be admiring this new literary star and asking to whom that hitherto unknown name could possibly belong.

He did not rest on those imaginary laurels. Two days later, he produced another poem, this time a sentimental ode in which he complained to the moon about his scornful mistress, already foreseeing for himself a death as melancholy as that of the poet Nicolas Gilbert. He could not afford the further expense involved in having this new poem printed, but a friend managed to get it into the paper for free, which meant delaying publication for a few days. Luís Tinoco found the waiting hard to bear, and even suspected some envious editors at the *Correio Mercantil* of dragging their feet.

At last, the poem was published, and the poet was so pleased that he immediately went to reveal all to his godfather.

"Have you read today's *Correio Mercantil*?" he asked.

"You know perfectly well that I used to read newspapers when I was working, but I never read them now that I'm retired."

"Oh, that's a shame!" said Luís coolly. "I was hoping you would tell me what you thought of a poem they've published."

"A poem! Don't newspapers write about politics anymore? In my day, they talked of little else."

"They write about politics *and* they publish poems, because there's room enough for both. Would you like to read it?"

"All right, give it here."

And Luís duly produced a copy of the *Correio Mercantil* from his pocket, and old Anastácio began to read his godson's work. With his eyes fixed on his godfather, Luís appeared to be trying to guess the impression made on him by his lofty thoughts, which he had put into verse taking all possible and impossible liberties with rhyme. Anastácio finished reading and pulled a face.

"Dreadful stuff!" he said to his horrified godson. "What the devil has the moon got to do with that young woman's indifference, and why drag in some poor foreigner's miserable death?"

Luís Tinoco felt like giving his godfather a good telling-off, but, instead, he merely smoothed back his hair and said with supreme disdain:

"Not everyone can understand poetry, of course, and that 'dreadful stuff' is mine."

"Yours?" asked Anastácio, thunderstruck.

"Yes."

"You mean you write poetry?"

"So they say."

"But who taught you to write verses?"

"The ability to write poetry isn't something you learn, it's something you are born with."

Anastácio reread the poem, and only then did he notice his godson's name. There was no doubt about it: the boy had become a poet. To the retired old gentleman this spelled disaster, for the word "poet" was indissolubly linked in his mind with the word "poverty."

He imagined Camões and Bocage, the only literary names he knew, to have been two street performers, regurgitating sonnets in exchange for a few coins, sleeping in churchyards, and eating in the coach houses of large mansions. When he discovered that his own dear Luís had been infected with this terrible malaise, Anastácio felt very sad, and it was then that he went to see Dr. Lemos to tell him of his godson's fearful plight.

"I have to tell you that Luís is a poet."

"Really?" asked Dr. Lemos. "Is he any good?"

"I don't care if he's good or bad. All I know is that it's the worst thing that could possibly have befallen him, because poetry gets you nowhere. I'm afraid he'll leave his job and end up on street corners babbling about the moon and surrounded by ne'er-do-wells."

Dr. Lemos reassured him, saying that poets were not the vagabonds he imagined; he told him that poetry was no obstacle to leading an ordinary life, to becoming a deputy, a minister, or a diplomat.

"Nevertheless," said Dr. Lemos, "I'll speak to Luís and read what he's written. I was a bit of versifier myself once and I'll soon be able to judge if he's any good or not."

Luís Tinoco went to see the doctor and took with him the sonnet and the ode as well as other as yet unpublished pieces, which tended to be either odes or sonnets, full of hackneyed images and trite expressions—in short, little inspiration and even less art. And yet, despite this, there was the occasional glimmer indicating that the neophyte might actually have some talent, and could, in time, become an excellent drawing-room troubador.

Dr. Lemos told him frankly that poetry was a very difficult art and required long study, but that, if, despite all, he was determined to cultivate that art, then he should listen to some very necessary advice.

"Of course," said Luís, "feel free, make any suggestions that might be useful. I wrote these poems so quickly, I had no time to correct them."

"I really don't think they're very good," said Dr. Lemos. "It would be best simply to tear them up and spend some time studying."

It would be impossible to describe the proud, disdainful gesture with which Luís Tinoco snatched the poems from the doctor's hand and said:

"Your advice is about as valuable as my godfather's. As I told him, the ability to write poetry isn't something you learn, it's something you're born with. I pay no heed to the envious. If the poems really were no good, the *Correio Mercantil* would never have published them."

And with that he left.

From then on, there was no stopping him.

Tinoco began to write as furiously as a man who has been told that he has only a short time to live. The newspapers were full of his creations, some sad, some jolly, but the sadness and jollity were not of the sort that come straight from the heart; the sadness made one smile and the jollity made one yawn. Luís Tinoco confessed artlessly to the world that he was imbued with a Byronic skepticism, that he had drained the cup of sorrows to its dregs, that, as far as he was concerned, life had written Dante's famous inscription above his door. And he quoted the words exactly, even though he had never read Dante. He bespattered his borrowed ideas with a selection of allusions and literary names, which was the full extent of his erudition, and felt no need, for example, to have read Shakespeare in order to quote "to be or not to be," or mention Juliet's balcony or Othello's torment. He also had some very unusual ideas about the biographies of the famous. Once, while inveighing against his beloved—who still did not exist—it occurred to him to say that the climate in Rio was responsible for producing such monsters, much as the Italian sun had gilded the hair of the young Aspasia. When he chanced upon the psalms of Father Caldas, he found them soporific, although he spoke more kindly of *The Death of Lindóia*, the title he mistakenly gave to Basílio da Gama's famous epic poem O *Uraguai*, of which he had read about four lines.

After five months, Luís Tinoco had produced a reasonable number of poems, enough for a volume of a hundred and eighty pages, allowing for a lot of blanks. He liked the idea of publishing a book, and soon one could rarely enter a shop without seeing on the counter a prospectus advertising:

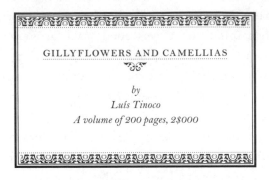

GILLYFLOWERS AND CAMELLIAS

by
Luís Tinoco
A volume of 200 pages, 2$000

Dr. Lemos occasionally saw him in the street. Luís Tinoco wore the inspired look of all novice poets who imagine themselves to be apostles and martyrs. Head held high, a dreamy look in his eyes, hair long and lush, he would sometimes button up his overcoat and stand with one hand thrust inside, Napoleon-style; at others, he would walk along with his hands behind his back.

Dr. Lemos spoke to him on the third such encounter, because on the first two occasions the young man had studiously avoided him. When the doctor praised some of his work, Luís Tinoco's face lit up:

"Thank you," he said, "such praise is the best possible reward for my labors. Ordinary people know nothing of poetry, only intelligent people like you, Doctor, can judge where praise is due. Did you read my *'Pale Flower'*?"

"The one that appeared on Sunday?"

"Yes."

"I did. Charming."

"And full of feeling too. I wrote that poem in half an hour and didn't change a word. That often happens. What did you think of the somewhat eccentric scansion?"

"It was certainly eccentric."

"Yes, I thought so too. I'm on my way to the newspaper now to offer them a poem I wrote yesterday. It's entitled *'Beside a Tomb.'*"

"I see."

"Have you already subscribed to my book?"

"No, not yet."

"Well, don't. I'd like to give you a copy. It will be coming out soon. I'm collecting subscriptions. Do you like the title?"

"Oh, yes, magnificent."

"It came to me suddenly. I thought of others, but they were too run-of-the-mill. *Gillyflowers and Camellias* is so much more distinctive and original. It's as if one were saying: sadnesses and joys."

"Quite."

While they talked, the poet kept rummaging around in his pocket and pulling out a seemingly endless stream of papers. He was looking for the poem he had mentioned. Dr. Lemos wanted to get away, but Tinoco would not let him, even grabbing his arm to keep him there. When Luís Tinoco threatened to read the poem out loud in the street, the doctor invited him, instead, to come and dine with him.

They went to a nearby hotel.

"Ah, my friend," Luís Tinoco said on the way there, "you cannot imagine how many envious people are trying to blacken my name. My talent has been the target of all kinds of attacks, but I was prepared for that. It doesn't frighten me. Camões's sad death upon a wretched truckle bed is both an example and a consolation. Prometheus chained to the Caucasus is the very symbol of genius. Posterity is the revenge of those who are scorned in their own lifetime."

At the hotel, Dr. Lemos looked for a table away from the other diners, so as not to attract too much attention.

"Here it is," said Luís Tinoco, having finally managed to wrest the promised poem from the bundle of papers.

"Wouldn't it be better to read that after we've eaten?" said the doctor.

"As you wish," Luís Tinoco answered. "Yes, you're quite right. I am actually rather hungry."

Luís Tinoco was pure prose at the dining table, and ate like a man unbound.

"Don't be alarmed," he said now and then, "this is the beast being fed. The soul is not to blame."

Over dessert—by which time there were only about five other customers left in the room—Luís Tinoco unfolded the dreaded sheet of paper and read the promised verses in a ridiculously affected, singsong voice. The poem spoke of everything, death and life, flowers and worms, love and hate;

there were more than eight "cypresses," nearly twenty "tears" and more "tombs" than a cemetery.

The remaining five diners turned to look when Luís Tinoco began to recite, then began to smile and murmur inaudible comments. When the poet finished, one of their neighbors—a rather crude fellow—let out a loud guffaw. Luís Tinoco spun around, furious, but Dr. Lemos restrained him, saying:

"He wasn't laughing at us."

"Yes, he was, my friend," Luís said resignedly, "but what can we do? Not everyone understands poetry enough to respect it as they should."

"Let us leave," said Dr. Lemos. "They clearly cannot grasp what it means to be a poet."

"Yes, let's go!"

Dr. Lemos paid the bill, and Luís Tinoco followed him out, glaring defiantly at the man who had laughed.

Luís walked with him back to his house. On the way, he recited some verses he knew by heart. When he surrendered himself to the sound of his own poetry—not someone else's, about which he cared very little—it was as if everything else were erased from his memory; self-contemplation sufficed. Dr. Lemos listened in the resigned silence of one who has to put up with the rain, which he can do nothing to stop.

Shortly afterward, *Gillyflowers and Camellias* saw the light of day, and all the newspapers promised to review it at length.

In his introduction, the poet acknowledged that it was very bold of him "to come and sit at the communion table of poetry, but that anyone who felt stirring within him the *j'ai quelque chose là* of André Chénier should give to his country what nature had given to him." He then went on to apologize for his extreme youth and assured readers that he had not been born with a silver spoon in his mouth. He concluded by giving his blessing to the book and calling attention to the list of subscribers at the back.

This monumental work was greeted with general indifference. Only one minor critic of the day devoted a few lines to it, lines that made everyone laugh; everyone, that is, except the author, who even went to thank the man in person.

After that, Dr. Lemos lost sight of his poet for some time, or, rather, he lost sight of the man but not his work, because Luís Tinoco's poems would sporadically appear in some literary journal or other, which Dr.

Lemos would inevitably read only to be astonished by Luís Tinoco's sterile, dogged persistence. There was no occasion, no funeral, no solemn event, that escaped the inspiration of that fecund writer. Since his ideas were very few in number, it could be said that he had only ever written a eulogy, an elegy, an ode, and an encomium. The various examples of each type were merely the same thing said in a slightly different way. In that different way, however, lay the poet's originality, an originality he did not possess to begin with, but which developed greatly over time.

Unfortunately, in throwing himself ardently into these literary labors, he forgot all about his legal labors, which provided him with his daily bread. One day, Anastácio spoke of this misfortune to Dr. Lemos, in a letter that concluded thus: "My friend, I really do not know where the boy will end up. I can see only two possibilities: the insane asylum or prison."

Dr. Lemos summoned the poet. In order to predispose him to hear what he was about to say, he initially praised his work. The young man opened his heart to him.

"It's just as well that I do hear the occasional encouraging word," he said. "You cannot imagine the envy that surrounds me. But what does that matter? I trust in the future, and posterity will be my revenge."

"You're right, posterity will always have its revenge on contemporary malice."

"A few days ago, some rag somewhere described me as a stringer-together of mere bagatelles. I saw what lay behind this, though. They were accusing me of not embarking on a longer, more ambitious work. I'm going to prove that scribbler wrong, and I'm now writing an epic poem!"

"Oh, no!" thought Dr. Lemos, sensing that he was about to have a poem forced upon him.

"I could show you a fragment," Luís Tinoco went on, "but I would prefer you to read the poem when it's at a more advanced stage."

"An excellent idea."

"There are ten cantos and about ten thousand lines, but shall I tell you my problem?"

"What's that?"

"I'm in love."

"Well, that's certainly unfortunate for a man in your position."

"What has my position got to do with it?"

"I understand that things at work are not going well. It's said that you've been somewhat neglecting your duties at the courts and that they're about to dismiss you."

"I was dismissed yesterday."

"Already?"

"Yes, it's true. And you should have heard the speech I addressed to the notary, in front of the whole department too! Oh, yes, I had my revenge, all right!"

"But what will you live on now? I doubt very much that your godfather can support you."

"God will help me. After all, do I not have a pen in my hand? Did I not receive at birth a certain talent that has already reaped reward? Up until now, I haven't attempted to earn anything from my work, but then I was a mere amateur. From now on, things will be different. If I need to earn a living, then I will."

The conviction with which Luís Tinoco said these words saddened Dr. Lemos. For a few seconds—perhaps with just a touch of envy—he contemplated this incorrigible dreamer, so detached from the realities of life, convinced not only that a great future awaited him, but also that he really could use his pen as a hoe.

"Don't worry," said Luís Tinoco. "I'm going to prove to you and my godfather that I'm not as useless as I seem. I don't lack for courage, Doctor, and if I ever do, there's a certain star . . ."

Luís Tinoco paused, twiddled his mustache, and gazed up at the sky in a melancholy fashion. Dr. Lemos looked, too, but without a hint of melancholy, indeed he laughed and asked:

"A star at midday? That would be unusual . . ."

"Oh, I'm not talking about *those* stars," broke in Luís Tinoco, "but that is where *she* should be, up there in blue space among her older and less beautiful sisters . . ."

"Ah, a young woman!"

"Say, rather, the loveliest creature upon whom the sun ever shone, a sylph, my Beatrice, my Juliet, my Laura . . ."

"She must be very beautiful to have captured the heart of a poet."

"You are a good man, my friend. Laura is an angel, and I adore her . . ."

"And what about her?"

"She may not even know that I am consumed with love for her."

"That's not good!"

"What do you expect?" said Luís Tinoco, wiping away an imaginary tear with his handkerchief. "It is the fate of all poets to burn and yearn for things they cannot have. That is the substance of a poem I wrote a week ago. I published it in *The Literary Arbor.*"

"What the devil is that?"

"It's my personal magazine, which I myself have printed every two weeks. I thought you said you read my work!"

"I do, but I can't always remember the titles. But let's get down to what really matters. No one denies you have talent and a fertile imagination, but you're deluding yourself if you think you can live off poetry and literary articles. You've already discovered that your poetry and your articles are far above the understanding of ordinary people, which is why they find so few readers . . ."

These discouraging words delivered along with that large bouquet of roses had a salutary effect on Luís Tinoco, who could not suppress a smile of smug satisfaction. Dr. Lemos concluded his speech by offering to find him a position as a clerk in a lawyer's office. Luís Tinoco looked at him for a while without saying a word. Then, in the most melancholy, resigned tone imaginable, he said:

"You mean go back to the courts and once more besmirch my inspiration with bills of indictment and shyster lawyers talking all kinds of legal mumbo-jumbo! In exchange for what? A few *mil-réis*, which I don't have and which I need in order to live. Is that what society is, Doctor?"

"Yes, I suppose it is," said Dr. Lemos gently, "but, while it may not be the best of societies, we have no other, and unless you're prepared to change it, you have no alternative but to put up with it and live."

The poet walked back and forth in the room for a couple of minutes, then he held out his hand to his friend.

"Thank you," he said. "I accept. I see that you have my interests at heart, even though you know that what you're offering me is exile."

"Exile and a wage," retorted Dr. Lemos.

A few days later, the poet was copying out notices of embargos and appeals, complaining and cursing his fate, unaware that from that job would spring a radical change in his aspirations. Dr. Lemos did not speak to him again for five months. One day, though, he met him in the street and asked about the epic poem.

"It's rather come to a standstill," replied Luís Tinoco.

"Are you abandoning it, then?"

"No, I'll finish it when I have time."

"And your magazine?"

"Oh, I stopped producing that ages ago. I'm surprised you didn't notice, since I haven't sent you a copy for a long time now."

"That's true, but I thought perhaps you had simply forgotten. That is big news, though! So no more of *The Literary Arbor.*"

"I let it die when it was at its height, with eighty paying subscribers . . ."

"You're abandoning literature entirely, then?"

"No, but . . . look, I must go. Goodbye."

"Goodbye."

This all seemed simple enough, but, having won that first battle by finding him a job, Dr. Lemos left it to the poet himself to explain the cause of his literary slumbers. Could it be because he was in love with Laura?

I should point out that Laura was not Laura, but Inocência; the poet called her Laura in his poems because the name seemed more mellifluous, which it was. To what extent did this love actually exist, and how far was his love reciprocated by her? History provides little information in this regard. What we do know is that, one day, a rival appeared on the horizon, and he was about as much of a poet as Luís Tinoco's godfather, and, therefore, far better marriage material than the editor of *The Literary Arbor*; with one blow, he destroyed all the poet's hopes.

I need hardly tell you that this event enriched literature with a long and tearful elegy, in which Luís Tinoco set down in verse all the possible complaints that any spurned lover can make about a woman. This work took as its epigraph Dante's words: *Nessun maggior dolore*. When it was finished and corrected, he read it out loud to himself, pacing up and down in his bedroom, putting a final touch to one or two lines, admiring the harmony of many others, and wholeheartedly confessing to himself that it was his best work yet. *The Literary Arbor* still existed then, and Luís Tinoco rushed his poem to the press, having first shared it with his collaborators, who were all of the same opinion as him. Despite what must have been his all-consuming grief, the poet read the proofs carefully and scrupulously, was present when the first copies were printed, and, for many days afterward, he read and reread those lines, barely giving a thought to the betrayal that had inspired them.

This, however, was not the reason for Luís Tinoco's literary slumbers.

That was purely political. The lawyer for whom he worked had been a deputy and contributed to a political gazette. His office was a meeting place for a lot of men in public life, who met there for long conversations about political parties and the government. At first Luís Tinoco listened to these conversations with the indifference of a god wrapped in the cloak of his immortality. Gradually, though, he began to acquire a taste for what he heard. He started reading parliamentary speeches and opinion pieces. This initial interest quickly became enthusiasm, because in Luís Tinoco everything was extreme—be it enthusiasm or indifference. One day, he woke with the conviction that he was destined to be a politician.

"My literary career is over," he told Dr. Lemos when they spoke about it. "Now a different world is calling to me."

"Politics? So you think that is where your vocation lies?"

"Yes, I think I might be able to make a contribution."

"You're very modest, I see, and I'm sure that some inner voice is urging you to burn your poet's wings. Take care, though! You have doubtless read *Macbeth*. Well, beware the voices of the witches, my friend. You are a man of great feeling, great sensibility, and I don't think that—"

"I am ready to answer the call of destiny," Luís Tinoco said impetuously, interrupting him. "Politics is calling me, and I cannot, must not, and do not wish to close my ears to that call. No, the oppressive forces of power, the bayonets of corrupt, immoral governments, cannot divert a great belief from its chosen path. I feel I am being called by the voice of truth, and who can deny that voice? Only cowards and incompetents, and I am neither."

This was the oratorical debut with which he regaled Dr. Lemos on a thankfully empty street corner.

"I ask only one thing," said the ex-poet.

"What's that?"

"Speak to the lawyer about me. Tell him I want to work with him, to be his protégé. That is my wish."

Dr. Lemos granted Luís Tinoco's wish. He went to see the lawyer and recommended the clerk to him, with little zeal, it's true, but not coldly, either. Fortunately, the lawyer was a kind of Saint Francis Xavier of the party, eager to increase his army; he happily accepted the recommendation, and, the following day, addressed a few kind words to the clerk, who listened, tremulous with emotion.

"Write something," said the lawyer, "and bring it to me, so that we can see if you have the necessary talent."

Luís Tinoco did not need to be asked twice. Two days later, he brought his boss a long, rambling article, which was, nonetheless, full of verve and commitment. The lawyer thought it not without its defects, and pointed out certain excesses and imprecisions, the weakness of certain arguments, more ornament than substance, but promised to publish it anyway. Whether it was because he made these remarks tactfully and gently, or because Luís Tinoco had lost some of his former prickliness, or because the promise of having the article published sweetened the bitter taste of criticism, or for all those reasons put together, the fact is that he listened to his protector's words with exemplary modesty and joy.

The lawyer showed the article to his friends, saying: "He'll improve with time."

The article was published, and Luís Tinoco received a few congratulatory handshakes. He again experienced the sweet, ineffable joy he had felt when his first poems were published in the *Correio Mercantil*, but it was a more complex joy, tempered by a virtuous decision: from that day forth, Luís Tinoco genuinely believed he had a mission, that nature and destiny had sent him into the world to right political wrongs.

Few people will have forgotten the final passage from the political debut of that former editor of *The Literary Arbor*. It read thus:

> Hypocritical, vengeful power notwithstanding, I declare most humbly that I fear neither scorn nor martyrdom. Moses led the Hebrews into the Promised Land, but was not fortunate enough to enter it himself: that is the symbol of the writer who carries men toward moral and political regeneration, without actually passing through the golden gates himself. What is there to fear? Prometheus chained to the Caucasus, Socrates drinking hemlock, Christ dying on the cross, Savonarola on the rack, John Brown hanging from the scaffold, they are all the great apostles of light, an example and comfort to those who love the truth and work to gain the penitence of tyrants and the thunderous overthrow of despotism.

Luís Tinoco did not stop after that first success. The same fecundity that had marked his literary phase was repeated in this his political phase;

his protector, meanwhile, told him that he should write less, and less flamboyantly too. The ex-poet accepted this criticism and even learned from it, producing a few articles rather less unkempt in style and content. Since Luís Tinoco knew nothing about politics, his protector lent a few books to a grateful Luís. However, readers of this story will have gathered by now that the author of *Gillyflowers and Camellias* was not a man to ponder long and hard over a page of writing; he was drawn to high-flown phrases—especially high-sounding ones—and would linger over them, repeat and consider them with genuine delight. He found reflection, observation, and analysis arid, and often avoided them entirely.

Some time later, a primary election was called. Luís Tinoco felt that he had it in him to be a candidate, and said as much to the lawyer in no uncertain terms. His wish was received quite positively, and things were so arranged that he enjoyed the pleasure of seeing his name on an electoral slate and the surprise of being beaten. The government might beat him, but not defeat him. The ex-poet, still hot from battle, translated into long, flowery sentences the scorn he felt for his adversaries' victory. Friends of the government responded with another article, which ended thus: "What does ex-deputy Z.'s little squirt of an assistant hope to achieve with such immoderate language?"

Luís Tinoco almost died of pleasure to be the butt of that ministerial charge. The opposition press had not, until then, treated him with the consideration he wanted. They had, once or twice, discussed arguments he had put forward, but what was lacking was a personal attack, which seemed to him a necessary baptism of fire in that kind of campaign. When the lawyer read this attack, he told the ex-poet that his position was identical to that of William Pitt the Elder, when, in the House of Commons, the minister Robert Walpole had referred to Pitt as a mere boy, and he urged him to respond to that ministerial insult in the same tone. At the time, Luís Tinoco had no idea who Pitt and Walpole were, and yet, intrigued by the comparison, he cleverly and cautiously asked the lawyer if he could lend him the British orator's speech so that he could "refresh his memory." The lawyer did not have a copy to hand, but he summarized it thoroughly enough for Luís Tinoco to write a long article describing precisely what a little squirt was and was not.

Meanwhile, the electoral fight had revealed to him a new talent. Since it was sometimes necessary to speechify, the little squirt did so with great

personal pleasure and to general applause. Luís Tinoco asked himself if he
should aspire to becoming an orator and answered in the affirmative. This
new ambition was more difficult to achieve, as the ex-poet recognized, and
so, arming himself with patience, he waited.

There is here a lacuna in Luís Tinoco's life. For reasons history does not
record, two years after these electoral events our young man was dispatched
to the native province of his friend and protector. Let us waste no time in
speculating on the reasons for this journey, nor on the reasons that kept him
there for longer than he wanted. Let us, instead, go and find him there a few
months later, collaborating on a newspaper with the same youthful ardor he
had shown while in Rio. With letters of recommendation from the lawyer
to political friends and relatives, he soon built up a social circle, and settled
into the idea that he would stay there for a while. His godfather had died,
and Luís Tinoco was left with no family at all.

His oratorical ambitions were not assuaged by the pleasures of being
a writer; on the contrary, one encouraged the other. The idea of having
two weapons and of brandishing them at the same time, and using both
to threaten and defeat his adversaries, became a persistent, ever-present,
inextinguishable idea. This was not vanity, that is, not childish vanity. Luís
Tinoco piously believed that he was part of Providence's plan, and this sustained and satisfied him. He had lacked all sincerity when he set down his
misfortunes in verses to be read out to his friends, but he acquired real
sincerity as he became more and more engrossed in politics. If someone
doubted his political qualifications, this would wound him just as deeply as
it had when people questioned his literary talent, but it did not wound his
pride alone, but, more importantly, his deep and unbending belief that his
talent was a necessary part of the universal harmony.

Dr. Lemos was still living in Rio, and Luís Tinoco sent him all his provincial writings, and naïvely told him of his new hopes. One day, he informed
him that his election to the provincial assembly was currently under nego-
tiation and that those negotiations looked hopeful. The next letter brought
the news that his candidature had become a fact.

The election took place, and, after much effort and hard work, our candidate had the honor of being included on the list of winners. When he was
told that victory was his, his soul sang a solemn, heartfelt "*Te Deum Lau-
damos.*" A sigh, the most deeply felt and deep-seated sigh ever uttered by
man, consoled his heart for all the doubts and uncertainties of several long,

cruel weeks. He had at last been elected! He was about to take his first step to glory.

He slept badly that night, as he had on the eve of the publication of his first sonnet, and, again, his sleep was interspersed with dreams appropriate to the new situation. Luís Tinoco could already imagine himself thundering out a speech at the provincial assembly amid applause from some and curses from others and the envy of nearly everyone, and afterward reading in the local press warm praise for his fresh and utterly original eloquence. He drafted twenty different introductions to his maiden speech, whose subject would, of course, be worthy of grand flourishes and exalted passages. He was already mentally rehearsing gestures and poses and generally considering the figure he would cut in the provincial Chamber of Deputies.

Many big names in politics had begun in the provincial parliament. If he was to fulfill Fate's urgent mandate, then it was likely, even necessary, that he should leave there as soon as possible in order to pass through the wider door of national politics. In his mind, he was already occupying one of the seats in the congress building, and he immersed himself in thoughts of his own person and the brilliant role he would play. He could already see before him the opposition or the minister standing stunned by the five or six verbal blows Luís Tinoco believed he could deliver better than anyone; he could hear the newspapers talking and people asking about him, and his name reverberating throughout the Empire, and could see the ministerial portfolio landing in his lap, along with the post of minister itself.

The new deputy imagined all this and much more as he lay in bed, his head on the pillow, with his mind setting off about the world, which is the worst thing that can happen to a body as tormented as was his at the time.

Luís Tinoco immediately wrote to Dr. Lemos to tell him of his hopes and plans, now that Fortune was opening up before him the broad path of public life. The letter lingered on the probable effect of his first speech, and ended thus:

> *Whatever position I may rise to, even the highest position in the land, immediately below that of Emperor (and I genuinely think I will go that far), I will never forget the debt I owe to you, sir, for your encouragement and your support. I believe that, up until now, I have not betrayed the confidence of my friends, and I hope I continue to deserve it.*

Finally, work began. Luís Tinoco was so anxious to speak at the very first session that he gave a two-hour speech about a plan to install a fountain and proved categorically that water was necessary to mankind. His first great battle took place in the debate about the provincial budget. Luís Tinoco gave a long speech in which he took on the governor-general, the president, his opponents, the police, and despotism. The gestures he made had never been seen in the entire history of parliamentary gesticulations; no one, at least no one in the province, had ever had the pleasure of seeing the way he had of shaking his head, bending his arm, pointing, raising, and bringing down his right hand.

His style was unusual too. Never had anyone spoken of revenues and expenditures using such lush imagery and figures of speech. He compared revenues to the dew that collects on the flowers at night, and expenditures to the morning breeze that shakes the flowers and upsets a little of that revivifying moisture. A good government, he said, is that gentle breeze, while the current prime minister was declared to be nothing but hot air. The majority protested gravely at such an insulting description, however poetic. One of the ministers admitted that he had never known a chillier wind to blow in from Rio de Janeiro.

Unfortunately, his opponents did not rest either. As soon as Luís Tinoco had finished his speech amid scattered applause from his friends, one of his adversaries took the floor and for a long time stood with eyes fixed on the novice speaker. Then, taking from his pocket a bundle of newspapers and a magazine, he cleared his throat and said:

"Rio de Janeiro sent us the honorable deputy who has just spoken. We were told he was a glittering star destined to impress and surpass our provincial talents. I immediately set about obtaining some of the honorable deputy's earlier works.

"And here I have a journal entitled *The Literary Arbor*, a journal edited by my honorable friend, and a volume entitled *Gillyflowers and Camellias*. I have more such works at home. Let us look at *Gillyflowers and Camellias*."

Senhor Luís Tinoco: "My honorable friend is out of order."
  (*Cries of support.*)
His adversary: "I will go on, Mr. Speaker. Here we have *Gillyflowers and Camellias*. Let us look at one of those gillyflowers.

TO HER

Who are you, O my dear tormentor,
As you torture me with the sweetest of smiles?
Who are you, as you point me to
The gates of paradise?

Are you the very image of heaven itself?
The daughter of goddesses?
Or have you come to bind up my freedom
With your golden tresses?

"As you see, Mr. Speaker, our honorable friend was, at the time, an enemy of all oppressive laws. You have only to see how he treats the laws of metrics."

And so on and so on. A minority of deputies protested, Luís Tinoco turned white, then red, then white again, and the session ended in raucous laughter. The following day, the newspapers that supported Luís Tinoco thanked his adversary for the triumph he had handed to him by showing the province "an earlier, brilliant aspect of the illustrious deputy's talent." Those who had so indecorously laughed at the poem were condemned thus: "A few days ago, a deputy on the government's side described his party as a caravan of good, honest men. He was right about the caravan; yesterday, we saw the camels."

Not even this could console Luís Tinoco. His letters to Dr. Lemos grew less frequent, and finally stopped altogether. Three years slipped silently by, at the end of which Dr. Lemos was nominated for some post or other in that same province. As soon as he had settled into his new post, he set about looking for the ex-poet, which took him no time at all, for he immediately received an invitation from Luís Tinoco to visit the country retreat where he was now living.

"You'll call me an ungrateful wretch, I'm sure," said Luís Tinoco, as soon as Dr. Lemos arrived. "But I am not; I was hoping to see you in a year or so, and the reason I didn't write was . . . But, Doctor, what's wrong? You look shocked."

Dr. Lemos was indeed taken aback to see this new Luís Tinoco. Was this the author of *Gillyflowers and Camellias*, the eloquent deputy, the fiery orator? What he saw before him was an ordinary, honest laborer, with simple, rustic manners, and not a trace of the poet's melancholy poses or the orator's dramatic gestures—he had been completely transformed into a very different and far better creature.

They both laughed, the doctor at the great change that had taken place, the ex-poet at the doctor's amazement, and Dr. Lemos asked if Luís Tinoco really had abandoned politics or if he was merely taking a refreshing break from that world.

"I'll explain everything, Doctor, but only once you've seen my house and my land, and met my wife and my children—"

"You're married?"

"Yes, for over a year and a half now."

"And you never told me!"

"I was planning to come to Rio this year and was hoping to surprise you. My little ones are so delightful, as lovely as two angels. They take after their mother, who is the rose of the province. I just hope they take after her housewifely ways too; she's always so busy and so careful with money!"

Once the introductions had been made, once the children had been duly kissed, and house and land inspected, Luís Tinoco told Dr. Lemos that he had, indeed, definitively abandoned politics.

"Forever?"

"Forever."

"But why? Some upset, I suppose."

"No, I realized that I simply wasn't destined for great things. One day, someone read out a poem of mine in the Chamber. I saw how crude it was, and, later on, I came to view my political work with equal shame and regret, and so I cast off my career and left public life. It was a very easy decision to make, the work of a single night."

"You wanted something else?"

"I did, my friend, I wanted to tread on solid ground rather than skating over the surface of those youthful illusions. I was a ridiculous poet and possibly an even more ridiculous orator. This is my vocation. In a few years' time, I'll be a wealthy man. Now let's go and drink our coffee and keep our mouths firmly shut, for, as we know, a closed mouth catches no flies."

THE GOLD WATCH

I WILL NOW TELL YOU the story of the gold watch. It was a large chronometer, brand-new, and attached to an elegant chain. Luís Negreiros was quite right to be astonished when he saw the watch in his house, a watch that didn't belong to him, and couldn't possibly be his wife's, either. An optical illusion? No. There it lay on the bedside table, looking at him, perhaps as amazed as he was by the place and the situation.

Clarinha was not in the bedroom when Luís Negreiros entered. She was still in the parlor, leafing through a novel, and she barely responded to the kiss with which he greeted her when he arrived. Clarinha was a pretty young woman, although somewhat pale, or perhaps she was pretty precisely because she was pale. She lounged languidly on the sofa, her book open, her eyes on the book, but only her eyes, because I'm not sure her thoughts were also on the book, but, rather, elsewhere. In any case, she seemed equally indifferent to her husband and the watch.

Luís Negreiros picked up the watch with a look on his face I do not even dare to describe. Neither the watch nor the chain were his, nor did they belong to anyone he knew. It was a riddle. Luís Negreiros liked riddles and was thought to be an intrepid solver of riddles; but he liked the kind you find in almanacs or in newspapers. He didn't like physical or chronometrical riddles, especially not ones without any clues.

For this and other obvious reasons, the reader will understand why Clarinha's husband flung himself down in a chair, angrily tore at his hair, stamped

his foot, and threw the watch and chain down on the table. Once this first
outburst of rage was over, he again picked up the fateful object and examined
it once more. He folded his arms and thought about the matter, scrutinized
all his memories, and, at last, concluded that, without some explanation from
Clarinha, any action he took would be either useless or precipitate.

He went to find her.

Clarinha was just turning a page in her book with the calm, indifferent
air of someone who is not puzzling over any chronometrical riddles. Luís
Negreiros stared at her, his eyes like two shining daggers.

"What's wrong?" she asked in what everyone agreed was her usual soft,
gentle voice.

Luís Negreiros did not answer, but continued to stare at her; then he
walked twice around the room, running his fingers through his hair, and
again she asked:

"What's wrong?"

Luís stopped in front of her.

"What's this?" he demanded, taking the fateful watch from his pocket
and dangling it before her. "What's this?" he repeated in a voice like thunder.

Clarinha bit her lip and said nothing. Luís Negreiros stood for some
time with the watch in his hand and his eyes fixed on his wife, who, in turn,
had her eyes fixed on her book. There was a deep silence. Luís Negreiros
was the first to break that silence, angrily hurling the watch to the floor and
saying to his wife:

"Come on, tell me whose it is."

Clarinha slowly raised her eyes to him, only to lower them again,
murmuring:

"I don't know."

Luís Negreiros made a gesture as if he wanted to strangle her, but held
back. She got to her feet, picked up the watch, and placed it on a small table.
Unable to contain himself any longer, he walked over to her and grabbed her
wrists, saying:

"So, wretch, you won't answer me, you won't explain this enigma."

Clarinha winced, and Luís Negreiros immediately released his grip on
her wrists. In different circumstances, he would probably have fallen at her
feet and begged forgiveness for having hurt her. Just then, this didn't even
occur to him; he abandoned her in the middle of the parlor and recom-

menced his frantic pacing, stopping now and then as if he were pondering some possible tragic denouement.

Clarinha left the room.

Shortly afterward, a slave came in to announce that supper was on the table.

"Where's the mistress?"

"I don't know, sir."

Luís Negreiros went looking for his wife and found her in a room set aside for sewing; she was sitting on a low chair, sobbing, her head in her hands. When she heard the sound of the door closing, she looked up, and he saw that her cheeks were wet with tears. This was an even worse situation for him than the one in the parlor. He could not bear to see a woman cry, still less his own wife. He was about to kiss away her tears, but stopped himself, went over to her, pulled up a chair, and sat down opposite her.

"As you can see, I'm quite calm now," he said, "just answer my question with your usual frankness. I'm not accusing you or suspecting you of anything. I simply want to know where that watch came from. Did your father leave it here?"

"No."

"So where did it come from?"

"Oh, don't ask me!" cried Clarinha. "I don't know how that watch ended up there. I don't know whose it is . . . Leave me alone."

"This is too much!" roared Luís Negreiros, springing to his feet and sending the chair crashing to the floor.

Clarinha shuddered and stayed where she was. The situation was becoming more and more serious; Luís Negreiros was again pacing up and down, growing increasingly agitated and wild-eyed, apparently ready to hurl himself on his poor wife. She was sitting with her elbows on her knees and her head in her hands, staring at the wall. Almost a quarter of an hour passed. Luís Negreiros was about to ask the same question when he heard his father-in-law's booming voice coming up the steps:

"Senhor Luís, where the devil have you got to?"

"It's your father!" said Luís Negreiros. "I'll speak to you later."

He left the sewing room and went to welcome his father-in-law, who was already installed in the parlor, repeatedly tossing his hat up in the air, at great risk to sundry vases and to the candelabra.

"Were the two of you asleep?" asked Senhor Meireles, throwing down his hat and mopping his brow with a large red handkerchief.

"No, we were talking . . ."

"Talking?" said Meireles, adding to himself: "Quarreling more like."

"We were just about to have supper," said Luís Negreiros. "Will you join us?"

"That's why I came," said Meireles. "I'm having supper here today and tomorrow too. I wasn't invited, but no matter."

"Not invited?"

"Isn't it your birthday tomorrow?"

"Yes, that's right . . ."

There was no apparent reason why, having said these words in the gloomiest of voices, Luís Negreiros should then repeat them, this time in an unnaturally cheerful tone:

"Yes, that's right!"

Meireles was just about to leave the room and hang his hat on a hatstand in the hallway, but, instead, he turned and stared in alarm at his son-in-law, on whose face he saw a look of frank, sudden, inexplicable joy.

"The fellow's mad!" he muttered.

"Let's have supper," roared Luís Negreiros, going inside, while Meireles, continuing down the hallway, made his way to the dining room.

Luís Negreiros went to fetch his wife, who was still in the sewing room, and he found her tidying her hair in front of a mirror.

"Thank you," he said.

She looked at him, surprised.

"Thank you," Luís Negreiros said again. "Thank you and please forgive me."

He then tried to embrace her, but she proudly rebuffed him and went off to the dining room.

"Quite right too," he murmured.

Shortly afterward, all three were sitting around the dining table, and when the soup was served, it was, inevitably, stone-cold. Meireles was about to launch into a diatribe about negligent servants, when Luís Negreiros confessed that it was all his fault that supper had been on the table for so long. This declaration only slightly changed the topic of conversation, which then became a lament about the horror of the warmed-up supper, echoing Boileau's words: *un dîner réchauffé ne valut jamais rien.*

Meireles was a cheerful, jovial fellow, although possibly rather too flippant for a man his age, but he was, nonetheless, an interesting character. Luís Negreiros was very fond of him, and his affection was requited in a fatherly, friendly way, an affection that was all the more sincere considering that Meireles had only given him his daughter in marriage after much delay and some reluctance. They were courting for nearly four years, with Clarinha's father taking more than two years to consider and resolve the matter of marriage. Finally, he gave his consent, swayed, he said, more by his daughter's tears than by his son-in-law's fine qualities.

What lay behind that long hesitation were Luís Negreiros's rather loose ways, not that he had indulged in these during their courtship, but he had before and might do so afterward. Meireles was the first to admit that he himself had been a far from exemplary husband, which is why he felt he should give his daughter a better husband than he had been. Luís Negreiros gave the lie to all his father-in-law's fears; the impetuous lion of his youth became a meek little lamb. Friendship blossomed between father-in-law and son-in-law, and Clarinha became one of the most envied young women in the city.

And Luís Negreiros deserved even more credit for this, because he did not lack for temptations. Sometimes the devil would get into one of his friends, who would invite Luís out to relive the old days. Luís Negreiros would always say that now he had found a safe harbor, he had no wish to risk setting sail again on the high seas.

Clarinha loved her husband dearly and was the sweetest, gentlest creature to breathe the Rio air of her day. There was never the slightest disagreement between them; the clear conjugal sky was always the same and looked set to stay that way. What evil fate had blown in that first dark cloud?

During supper, Clarinha said not a word, or only very occasionally, and then only briefly and abruptly.

"They've obviously quarreled," thought Meireles when he saw his daughter's stubborn silence. "Or perhaps she's just sulking, because he seems happy enough."

Luís Negreiros was indeed all gratitude, politeness, and sweet words to his wife, who would not even look at him. He inwardly cursed his father-in-law, longing to be left alone with his wife so that she could give him a full and final account of events that would restore peace between them. Clarinha did not appear to share this wish; she ate little and once or twice uttered a heartfelt sigh.

It was clear that, however hard they tried, supper could not be as it was on other evenings. Meireles felt particularly uncomfortable, not because he feared there was some serious problem, for he was of the belief that without the odd quarrel one could not truly appreciate happiness, just as one needs a storm to fully appreciate fine weather. Nevertheless, it always upset him to see his daughter sad.

When coffee was served, Meireles suggested that they all go to the theater. Luís Negreiros greeted the idea with enthusiasm. Clarinha refused point-blank.

"I don't know what's wrong with you today, Clarinha," said her father somewhat irritably. "Your husband seems perfectly cheerful, but you seem depressed and worried. Whatever's wrong?"

Clarinha did not answer, and, not knowing what to say, Luís Negreiros started making little balls out of the innards of what remained of a bread roll. Meireles shrugged.

"Well, you'll just have to sort it out between you," he said. "And even though tomorrow is a special day, if you're both still in this same strange mood, you won't see hide nor hair of me."

"Oh, but you must come—" Luís Negreiros began, only to be interrupted by his wife bursting into tears.

The supper ended on that sad, distressing note. Meireles asked his son-in-law to tell him what was going on, and Luís Negreiros promised that he would do so on a more opportune occasion.

Shortly afterward, Meireles left, saying again that if they were in the same odd mood the following day, he would not be back, and that if there was one thing worse than a cold or warmed-up supper, it was one that gave you indigestion. This axiom was just as good as Boileau's, but no one paid it any attention.

Clarinha went to her room, and her husband joined her as soon as he had shown his father-in-law to the door. He found her sitting on the bed, sobbing, a pillow pressed to her face. Luís Negreiros knelt before her and took one of her hands.

"Clarinha," he said, "forgive me. I understand now. If your father hadn't mentioned coming to supper tomorrow, it would never have occurred to me that the watch was your birthday present to me."

I will not even attempt to describe the proud, indignant look on the young woman's face when she sprang to her feet on hearing these words. Luís

Negreiros stared at her, uncomprehending. She said nothing, but stormed out of the room, leaving her poor husband more confused than ever.

"What is this enigma?" Luís Negreiros was asking himself. "If it wasn't a birthday present, then what other explanation can there be for that watch?"

The situation was the same now as it had been before supper. Luís Negreiros determined that he would find out the truth that night. He thought it best, however, to give the matter mature consideration before reaching any firm conclusion. With this in mind, he went to his study, and there went over everything that had happened since he came home. He coolly weighed up every word, every incident, and tried to recall the changing expressions on his wife's face during the evening. The look of indignation and revulsion when, in the sewing room, he had tried to embrace her, that counted in her favor; but the way she had bitten her lip when he showed her the watch, her tears at the supper table, and, more than anything else, her silence as to where the wretched object had come from, all those things counted against her.

After much thought, Luís Negreiros tended toward the saddest and most deplorable of hypotheses. An evil idea began to drill its way into his mind, so deeply that, in a matter of moments, it had him entirely in its grasp. When the occasion called for it, Luís Negreiros could be very quick to anger. He uttered a few dark threats, then left his study and went to find his wife. Clarinha had gone back to her room. The door stood ajar. It was nine o'clock. The room was only dimly lit by a small lamp. She was again sitting on the bed, but not crying now; she kept her eyes fixed on the floor. She did not even look up when she heard her husband come in.

There was a moment's silence.

Luís Negreiros was the first to speak.

"Clarinha," he said, "this is very serious. Will you answer the question I've been asking you all evening?"

She did not reply.

"Think carefully, Clarinha," he went on. "Your life could be at stake."

She shrugged.

A dark cloud seemed to pass before Luís Negreiros's eyes, and he grabbed his wife by the throat and roared:

"Answer, you devil, or you'll die!"

"Wait!" she said.

Luís Negreiros drew back.

"Kill me," she said, "but read this first. When this letter was delivered to your office, you had already left; at least that was what the messenger told me."

Luís Negreiros took the letter, went over to the lamp, and was astonished to read these words:

My dear young master,

I know that tomorrow is your birthday, and so I'm sending you this small gift.

Nanny

And so ends the story of the gold watch.

POINT OF VIEW

———————

I

TO DONA LUÍSA P., IN JUIZ DE FORA

Rio, October 5

COULD YOU JUST TELL ME who you asked to deliver those things I wanted? I can't quite read the name in your letter, and there's been no sign of him so far, whoever he is. Was it Luís?

I heard tell that you were coming to spend some time in Rio. I do hope so. You'd love it here, despite the heat, which has been tremendous. Today, though, the weather is perfect.

Or, if you're not coming, I would love to visit you, but, as you know, Papa won't leave his home comforts, and Mama hasn't been well. I know she'd do anything to please me, but I'm not quite that selfish, even though it's a big sacrifice, too, because, quite apart from getting together with my best friend, I'd be able to see if it's true that there's still no baby on the way. Someone told me there was, so why deny it?

I'll send this letter tomorrow. Write soon and give my best wishes to your husband from me and from all of us.

Raquel

II

TO DONA LUÍSA

Rio, October 15

It took an age, but finally a long letter has arrived, well, long and short. Thank you for taking the trouble, and please do write again; I hate those little notes of yours, written in a rush, with your mind . . . where exactly? On that cruel husband who cares only about elections, or so I read the other day. I only write short letters when I don't have much time, but when I have more than enough time, then I write long ones. Or am I stating the obvious? Forgive me if I am.

Those things I asked for arrived the day after my last letter. What would you like me to send you? I have some fashion magazines that came just yesterday, but there's no one to deliver them. If you could arrange for someone to take them, I'll also send you a novel I was given this week. It's called *Ruth*. Do you know it?

Mariquinhas Rocha is going to be married. Such a shame! She's so pretty and sweet, still such a child, and she's getting married to some old man! Not only that, she's marrying for love. I couldn't believe it, and everyone says that her father and all her other relatives tried to dissuade her, but she was so insistent that, in the end, they gave in.

To be honest, he's not what you'd call elderly; he is old, but he's elegant, too, dapper, healthy, and good-humored; he's always telling jokes and seems to have a kind heart. Not that I would ever fall for anyone like that. What kind of marriage can there be between a rose and an old wreck?

She'd be much better off marrying his son, who really does deserve a nice girl like her. They say he's an utter ne'er-do-well, but you know I don't believe in such things. Love can conquer even the most fickle of hearts.

It seems the wedding will take place in about two months, and I'll definitely attend the funeral, I mean, wedding. Poor Mariquinhas! Do you remember our afternoons at school? She was the quietest of us all and always so melancholy. Perhaps she knew what Fate had in store for her.

Papa, however, warmly approved of her choice. He's always saying what a sensible person she is and even says I should follow her example. What do you think? If I had to follow anyone's example, it would be yours,

Luísa, because you did choose well. Don't show this letter to your husband, though, it might go to his head.

Are you really not coming to Rio? That's a shame, because apparently an opera company is about to arrive, and Mama is feeling much better. All of which means that I can finally have some fun. Mariquinhas's future stepson, the one she should have chosen over his father, says it's a wonderful company, and regardless of whether it is or not, it will certainly be amusing. And there you are stuck in the countryside!

It's suppertime. Write when you can, but no more of those microscopically small letters. Either a lot or nothing at all.

Raquel

III

TO DONA LUÍSA

Rio, October 17

I wrote you a letter the day before yesterday, and today, I'm adding a brief note (just this once) to tell you that apparently another young woman fell in love with Mariquinhas's aging fiancé and became quite ill with despair. A complicated story. Can you understand that? If it were the son, yes, but the father!

Raquel

IV

TO DONA LUÍSA

Rio, October 30

You're really very naughty. Just because I mentioned the fellow a couple of times, must you immediately go thinking I'm in love with him? As Papa would say: it shows a complete lack of logic. And, I would add, a lack of friendship too.

And I can prove it.

If I did develop a fondness, an affection, or whatever for someone, who would be the first to know? Why, you! Were we not each other's confidante for all those years? Your thinking I would keep such a thing from you is evidence that you're not my friend at all, because such unfair remarks could only have their basis in a lack of affection.

No, Luísa, I feel nothing for the young man, whom I hardly know. I only mentioned him as a point of comparison with his father; and if I *were* disposed to get married, I would definitely prefer the young man to the old, but that's as far as it goes.

And don't go thinking that Dr. Alberto (for that is his name) is anything special; he's very handsome and elegant, but he has a rather pretentious air about him and seems somewhat mean-spirited. And you know how particular I am about such things. If I don't find the kind of husband I want, then I will remain single for the rest of my days. I would prefer that to being chained to some dreadful boor, however stylish.

Nor would it be enough for him to have all the qualities I imagine a man should have for him to win my heart. There's a fellow who's been visiting us for a while now, and any other girl would be instantly captivated by his manners, but he makes not the slightest impression on me.

And do you know why?

The reason is simple; all the charm and all the supposed affection he lavishes on me, all the solemn compliments he pays me, do you know what they're about, Luísa? It's because I'm rich. So don't worry, when the man heaven has destined for me finally appears, you will be the first to know. For the moment, I am as free as the swallows flying around outside the house.

And as revenge for your slanderous suggestion, I will write no more. Farewell.

Raquel

V

TO DONA LUÍSA

Rio, November 15

I've been ill for the last two days with a horrible cold I caught when leaving the theater, where I went to see a new play, highly praised and very dull.

Do you know who I saw there? Mariquinhas and her fiancé in their box, as well as her stepson, too, or, rather, her future stepson, if all goes to plan. She looked so happy chatting away to her fiancé! And you know, from a distance, in the gaslight, the old man looks almost as young as his son. Who knows, maybe she *will* be happy!

Many congratulations on the news that a little one is on the way. Mama sends her congratulations too. Luís will deliver a few fashion magazines along with this letter.

Raquel

VI

TO DONA LUÍSA

Rio, November 27

Your letter arrived while we were having breakfast, and I'm very glad I read it afterward, because had I read it before, I would never have finished breakfast. Who put such an idea in your head? Me, in love with Alberto? That is a joke in very bad taste, Luísa! The person who told you that story was clearly out to embarrass me. If you had met him, then I wouldn't need to protest. I've told you about his good qualities, but, as far as I'm concerned, his defects far outweigh any such qualities. You know what I'm like; the slightest stain ruins even the purest white. He's like a statue, yes, that's the right word, because there is something rather stiff and sculptural about Alberto.

Ah, Luísa, the man heaven has destined for me has not yet arrived.

I know this because I still haven't felt inside me the tremor of sympathy that signals perfect harmony between two souls. When he does arrive, rest assured that you will be the first to know.

You will ask why, if I'm such a fatalist, I won't admit the possibility of a husband who does not possess all the required qualities.

Well, you're wrong.

God made me like this, and gave me this innate ability to recognize and love superior beings, and God will send a creature worthy of me.

And now that I've explained myself, allow me to scold you a little. Why listen to such calumnies? You've known me long enough now to set aside such senseless gossip. So why did you not do so?

You spent two whole pages defending Mariquinhas. I'm not accusing her, I simply deplore what she's doing. Her fiancé may turn out to be an excellent husband, but I still don't think he's good enough for her. And that is what I deplore.

There is a simple explanation for this divergence of opinion. I am a single woman with my head stuffed full of fantasies, dreams, ambitions, and poetry; you are already the mistress of a house, a serene and happy wife and mother-to-be; you see things through a different prism.

Is that right?

Apparently, the opera company isn't coming after all. The city's very lively today, though; there are bands playing in the streets; and there's been good news about the war. We'll definitely be going out for a walk today. Don't you miss Rio?

Farewell.

Regards to your husband from all of us.

Raquel

VII

TO DONA LUISA

Rio, December 20

You're quite right. I am an ungrateful wretch. It's been nearly a month since I last wrote, despite getting two letters from you. It would take me a while to explain the delay, and, alas, I don't have time just now, because my cousins are staying with us for a few days.

Anyway, you confess, do you, to simply wanting to sound me out? I knew no one could possibly have said such things to you about Dr. Alberto.

Mariquinhas's wedding is set for the 5th of January. We will all go to watch the sacrifice. Forgive me, Luisa, you know how sarcastic I can be sometimes, and . . . you will forgive me, won't you?

And yet, shall I tell you something? I've changed my mind in one respect. I now think: far better the father than the son. Alberto has such a frivolous nature, so superficial and silly! The father is a serious person and very friendly, too, but friendly without ever descending into silliness. He's very distinguished, and a lively conversationalist, clever and wise.

Oh, yes, she's much better off with the father.

You ask me what I will do if I never find the ideal husband. I've told you before: I will stay single. Marriage is a very big thing, the highest of states, I agree, but it must not be a form of captivity, because captivity is anything that does not allow us to realize our innermost aspirations.

Thank you for your advice, but I have to say that you are speaking as someone who is happy, and, for you, marriage, any marriage, is a foretaste of paradise.

I don't believe it is always so.

It is true—although we will all have our own views on the subject—that Mariquinhas might well be happy, given that her chosen husband appears to speak to her heart. I don't deny this, but I still pity her, because (I repeat), I cannot comprehend the union of a rose and an old wreck. And I will write no more so as not to speak ill of her. Forgive me these babblings, and know that I remain your friend, now and forever.

Raquel

VIII

TO DONA LUÍSA

Rio, January 8

Mariquinhas is now married. It was an intimate little ceremony, but rather splendid too. The bride looked magnificent, happy, and proud. The same could be said of the groom, who seemed even younger than he appeared in the theater that time, so much so that I almost doubted his age. I kept expecting him to take off his mask and admit that he was his own son's brother.

I bet you're wondering if I felt envious, aren't you?

Well, yes, I did.

Although I don't know if it was envy exactly, but I must confess that I did give a little sigh when I saw our lovely Mariquinhas with her veil and her garland of orange blossom looking around at us with a truly celestial light in her eyes, glad to be bidding farewell to the futile world that is the life of a young single woman.

Yes, I did sigh.

If I had been able to set down my feelings that same night, you would have had a page of literature worthy of being published in one of the newspapers.

That's all over now.

What isn't over, though—because it existed before and will always exist, because it was born with me and will die with me—is the dream of a love I've never encountered on Earth, a love I cannot express, but which must exist, since I have the image of it in my mind and my heart.

Whenever Mama sees me looking bored or daydreaming, she usually says I have my head in the clouds, unaware perhaps that this is an exact description of my state of mind. Isn't thinking such things just like having one's head up there in the clouds somewhere?

I've just reread what I've written, and if I had more writing paper to hand, I would cross it all out. Unfortunately, I've run out of paper, it's midnight, and this letter needs to be sent off early tomorrow morning. So feel free to cross out the whole lot; there's no point in preserving nonsense.

There's no other news worthy of mention. Oh, I forgot to say that I've discovered one fine quality in Dr. Alberto. Can you guess? He dances divinely. But you'll say I'm a gossip! And so that you can say no more, I'll stop here.

Raquel

IX

TO DONA LUÍSA

Rio, January 10

This is just a short note to tell you that we're going to be putting on a play, as we used to at school. Dr. Alberto has been asked to write it, and I'm assured that it will be good. Carlota is performing with me. The male characters will be played by Cousin Abreu, Juca, and Dr. Rodrigues. Ah, if only you were here!

Raquel

X

DONA LUÍSA TO DONA RAQUEL

Juiz de Fora, January 15

My husband wants to come to Rio toward the end of next month, so you and I will finally meet up again after all these months apart. I'm only writing to give you this good news, which I know will please you.

I should also issue a warning: you will have to hide in person what you're hiding from me in your letters.

Farewell.

Luísa

XI

DONA RAQUEL TO DONA LUÍSA

Rio, January 20

What am I hiding from you in my letters? I've been thinking and pondering, but I don't know what you mean. I suppose you could be referring to Alberto, but after everything I've said about him, that would be going too far.

Explain yourself.

As for the news that you're coming to Rio, I'm really pleased, but however hard I try to put into words just how pleased I am, I can't. I don't know how to, the words won't come. Dr. Alberto (yes, him!) was saying only the other day that human language is fine for saying what's in our minds, but incapable of expressing what is in our hearts. And he added this old, but ingenious saying: the head speaks with the lips, and the heart with the eyes.

You will, therefore, have to guess what I'm feeling and come as soon as possible. How's the baby?

Raquel

XII

TO DONA LUÍSA

Rio, January 28

It's unbearably hot, but now that I've opened the window onto the garden, I can see the sky "all embroidered with stars," as the poets say, and that spectacle makes up for the heat. What a night, Luísa! I love these great silences, because then I can hear myself, and I live more intensely in five minutes of solitude than in twenty hours of hustle and bustle.

Mariquinhas Rocha was here tonight with her husband. They both seem very happy, she even more than he, which seems to me a complete inversion of the natural laws.

Are you surprised to hear me talking about "natural laws"? It's not my idea, but that of Mariquinhas's stepson, Dr. Alberto. We were talking about Mariquinhas's many good and saintly qualities, and I was saying that she has always been like that ever since she was a child.

"She still is a child," he said, smiling. "I can't address as 'stepmother' a creature who looks more like my younger sister."

"She may be younger in age," I retorted, "but in circumspection and composure she's far older than you, sir."

He smiled rather wanly, then went on:

"My father is happy, and my stepmother seems even happier than him. Isn't that an inversion of the natural laws?"

Think what you may of his views, but I take this opportunity to mention that, in your last letter, there are a couple of lines in which there still seems to be a hint of suspicion. Do write and tell me how I can convince you that, for me, he is just one man among many?

Go on, admit you've been cruel to me and prepare yourself to receive a sermon on the subject the very first time we're together again.

Do you know who I saw today? I'll give you a sweet if you can guess. Garcia, yes, the same Garcia who was once in love with y . . . No, no, let's stop there.

Raquel

XIII

DONA LUÍSA TO DONA RAQUEL

Juiz de Fora, February 10

I'm not going to admit anything, and I was never cruel. I had my suspicions and I preferred to be open about it, rather than keep it to myself. That is what friendship demands. Why should we abandon the frankness and trust of our school days?

I don't believe there is any basis for my suspicions, but I believe something else too. I imagine he cuts rather a grotesque figure, and that it was your vanity that was wounded, not your heart. Go on, admit it.

Do you know something? You're much more poetic than you used to be, more romantic and fanciful. It's your age, I know, but there are limits, Raquel. Don't confuse romance with life, or you'll end up very unhappy indeed . . .

A sermon! And there was I about to give *you* a sermon, a dull, boring one, and pointless to boot. Let's talk of things more prosaic. My husband wants to enter politics. Doesn't that word send a shiver down your spine? Politics and honeymoons just don't go together! But we'll see what happens. Greetings from him and me to your mama and you. See you soon.

Luísa

XIV

DONA RAQUEL TO DONA LUÍSA

Rio, February 15

You're quite wrong to imagine that Dr. Alberto cuts a grotesque figure; I've told you before that he's an elegant young man, and even that rather slow, sculptural air of his seems to have disappeared since he's become a regular visitor to our house.

So, no, it wasn't my vanity that was wounded, nor my heart. I simply felt that you didn't believe me.

I could give you a dissertation on love right now, but I will refrain from doing so, knowing that I would simply be teaching the priest how to say the Lord's Prayer.

Your husband wants to get into politics, does he? You'll be surprised at my opinion on the subject, an unlikely one for a daydreamer, as you call me. I think that politics could bring you a pinch of inconveniences and a whole peck of advantages.

Politics is sure to be a rival, but when weighed in the balance, it's infinitely preferable to some other kind of rival. It at least occupies mind and life, but leaves the heart free and pure. Besides, I'm not always the delver-into-depths that you think I am; I feel a pinch of ambition in myself, the ambition to be . . . a minister! Are you laughing? Me, too, which is proof that my mind is unpreoccupied and free, as free as this pen racing now over the paper in a hand I'm not entirely sure you'll be able to read. Farewell.

XV

DR. ALBERTO TO DONA RAQUEL

February 18

Forgive my boldness. I write to beg you on bended knee for the answer that your eyes refuse to give me. I cannot say in this letter exactly what I feel; I couldn't put that into words, but your mind must have understood what is going on in my heart, you must have read on my face what I would never dare to say out loud.

Alberto

XVI

DONA RAQUEL TO DONA LUÍSA

February 21

Mama was keen to come and visit you, but I, alas, am feeling unwell, and so we have postponed the journey. When are you going to keep your promise to come and spend a few days in Rio? We'll have much to talk about.

Raquel

XVII

TO DONA LUÍSA

March 5

This is not a letter, only a note. Do you know what the human heart is? A riddle. "A mystery!" you will cry when you read these lines. And so it is.

Raquel

XVIII

ALBERTO TO DONA RAQUEL

March 8

Oh, you do not know how grateful I am for your letter! At last! It was a ray of light in the darkness of my uncertainty. Am I loved? Am I deluding myself? Do you feel the same passion that is devouring my heart, one that is incapable of raising me up to heaven, but perfectly capable of carrying me down into hell?

You are quite right when you ask how I can have failed to see the answer in your eyes. I did, indeed, believe I could see my happiness there, but what if I were mistaken? I did not imagine that supreme happiness could come so quickly, and if I was mistaken, I don't know how I could live . . .

Why do you doubt me? Why do you fear that my love could merely be a way of passing the time? What mortal would play with the glorious crown brought down to Earth in the hands of an angel?

No, Raquel, if I may call you by that name? No, my love is as vast, chaste, and sincere as all true loves.

One word from you can transform that passion into the sweetest, most delicious state of bliss. Will you be my wife? Say it, say the word.

Alberto

XIX

DONA LUÍSA TO DONA RAQUEL

Juiz de Fora, March 10

The heart is a sea, subject to the influence of the moon and the winds. Is that definition any use to you? It's such a shame that your note did not contain a few more lines, then I would know everything. Still, I can tell one thing: you're in love.

Luísa

XX

DONA LUÍSA TO DONA RAQUEL

Juiz de Fora, March 17

I wrote to you on the 10th of this month, but have not yet received a reply. Why?

I wondered if perhaps you had been ill, but I think someone would have told me if you had.

This letter will be delivered to you in person, although the bearer will not be coming back here immediately. Nevertheless, because it is being delivered to you personally, I will at least know immediately how you are.

Come, now, make an effort.

Farewell.

Luísa

XXI

DONA LUÍSA TO DONA RAQUEL

Juiz de Fora, March 24

Still no answer. What is going on, Raquel?

The person who delivered my previous letter wrote to say that he had delivered it to you personally, and that you were definitely not ill. So why this neglect on your part? This is my last letter. If you don't write back, I will assume you have another, more deserving friend, and that you have entirely forgotten your confidante from school.

Luísa

XXII

DONA RAQUEL TO DONA LUÍSA

Rio, March 30

Forget you? You must be mad! Where would I find a better or kinder friend than you? It's true that I haven't written, but there are a thousand reasons for that, each more reasonable than the last, with the main reason, or, rather, the one that contains all the other reasons, being just one . . . And I don't know how to tell you what that is.

Love?

Yes, Luísa, the purest, most ardent love imaginable, and the most unexpected too. Your daydreaming friend, the one who lives with her head in the clouds, saw up there in the clouds the man her heart had hoped for, who was everything she had dreamed him to be and had despaired of ever finding.

I can say no more, I don't know how to. Everything I could write would be so inferior to the reality. But come, come, and you will perhaps read in my face the happiness I'm feeling, and see in his face the superior quality I always longed for and which is so rare on this Earth.

In short, I am happy!

Raquel

XXIII

DONA LUÍSA TO DONA RAQUEL

Juiz de Fora, April 8

Your letter finally arrived, and just in time, too, because I was ready to forget all about you. Nevertheless, I would still refuse to forgive you were it not for the reason you give. And, heavens, what a reason it is! So you have found love at last, found the man, or, rather, the archangel that my dear delver-into-depths was searching for! What does he look like? Is he handsome? Tall? Short? Tell me everything.

Now I see that I was in danger of making you miss your chance of happiness. I talked so much about Dr. Alberto that you could, as sometimes happens, have fallen in love with him, and then, when this other man arrived, it would have been too late.

Tell me, is he old like Mariquinhas Rocha's husband? Now, don't be angry, Raquel, but we do sometimes have to eat our words, and it's just possible that you've been punished for saying what you said about him. For my part, I wouldn't know what to say, just as long as he loves my Raquel and is a worthy husband. A young man would still be preferable, though.

I dare not ask you to send us a picture of him, although my husband would like one. Don't be annoyed, I told him everything, and he sends his congratulations. I will bring mine with me.

Luisa

XXIV

DONA RAQUEL TO DR. ALBERTO

April 10

I am very angry with you for not coming yesterday; how easily you forget me.

Come today or I really will be angry. And do bring a picture of yourself; I'll tell you why later.

You missed a very interesting evening yesterday; Dona G. was here, and, naturally, she missed you. Did you miss her? Ah, pity poor Raquel! Farewell.

Raquel

XXV

ALBERTO TO DONA RAQUEL

April 10

Forgive me for not coming last night, although be assured that you were much in my thoughts.

Your father has invited me to come and have supper with the family tonight; I'll arrive early.

I'll bring a picture of myself with me, too, even though I don't know why you want it. I just hope you won't put it to bad use.

As for Dona G., what can I say except that I find her a dull, affected girl, who doesn't interest me in the least? If you like, I will merely greet her, but not talk to her at all. What more do you want of me?

Farewell, my suspicious one. Know only that I love you lots and lots and lots, now and always.

Your Alberto

XXVI

DONA RAQUEL TO DONA LUÍSA

April 17

Great news! Yesterday, he asked my father for my hand in marriage. You can't imagine how happy I am! I wish you were here so that I could load you with kisses. But you'll come to the wedding, won't you? If you don't, I won't marry.

As you will have guessed, the picture included in this letter is of my fiancé. Isn't he handsome? So distinguished! So intelligent! So soulful! And speaking of his soul, I do not believe that God has ever sent another such soul into the world. I don't believe I deserve him.

Come quickly; the wedding will be in May.

Tell your husband.

Raquel

XXVII

DONA LUÍSA TO DONA RAQUEL

Juiz de Fora, April 22

Honestly! You tell me everything but the name of your fiancé!

Luísa

XXVIII

DONA RAQUEL TO DONA LUÍSA

Rio, April 27

You're quite right, I'm so distracted. But happiness explains and excuses everything. My fiancé is Dr. Alberto.

Raquel

XXIX

DONA LUÍSA TO DONA RAQUEL

Juiz de Fora, May 1

!!!

Luísa

MISCELLANEOUS PAPERS

(1882)

Author's Preface

The title *Miscellaneous Papers* might seem to deny this book a certain unity, leading the reader to believe that the author has gathered together various writings of a diverse nature simply in order not to lose them. This is indeed the truth, but not quite the truth. Miscellaneous they are, but they did not come to this place like travelers who just happen to find themselves staying at the same inn. They are persons drawn from the same family, obliged by their father to sit at the same table.

As for their genre, I do not know what I can say that would be of any use. The book is in the hands of the reader. I will only say that if there are any pages which seem to be mere stories and others that do not, I defend myself from the latter by saying that the reader may find something of interest in the other pages, and I defend myself from the former with the words of Saint John and of Diderot. Describing the infamous beast of the apocalypse, the Evangelist added (17:9): "And here is the mind which hath wisdom." Minus the wisdom, those words should just about cover me. As for Diderot, everyone knows that he not only wrote stories, some of them delightful, but even advised a friend to write them too. And in this, the encyclopedist was entirely right, for when someone tells a story, our spirits lift, time races by, and the story of life ends, without any of us noticing.

Thus, from wherever the reproach may come, I hope that absolution will also come from that same place.

Machado de Assis
October 1882

THE ALIENIST

Chapter 1

ON HOW ITAGUAÍ GAINED A MADHOUSE

THE CHRONICLES OF ITAGUAÍ record that a long time ago there lived in the town a certain physician, Dr. Simão Bacamarte, the son of landed gentry, and the greatest physician in Brazil, Portugal, and the two Spains. He had studied at Coimbra and Padua. At thirty-four, he returned to Brazil, the king being unable to persuade him to stay in Coimbra, running the university, or in Lisbon, attending to matters of state.

"Science," he said to His Majesty, "is my sole concern; Itaguaí is my universe."

Having said this, he took himself off to Itaguaí and devoted himself body and soul to the study of science, alternating healing with reading, and demonstrating theorems with poultices. When he reached the age of forty, he married Dona Evarista da Costa e Mascarenhas, a lady of twenty-five, the widow of a magistrate, who was neither pretty nor charming. One of his uncles, an inveterate meddler in the affairs of others, was frankly surprised by his nephew's choice, and told him so. Simão Bacamarte explained to him that Dona Evarista combined physiological and anatomical attributes of the first order: good digestion, regular sleep, a steady pulse, and excellent eyesight; she was thus fit to provide him with healthy, sturdy, intelligent offspring. If, in addition to such accomplishments—the only ones with which a sensible man should concern himself—Dona Evarista's features were somewhat badly formed, then, far from regretting it, he thanked God, since he would thereby not run the risk of ignoring the interests of science in the exclusive, trivial, and vulgar contemplation of his wife.

Dona Evarista failed to live up to her husband's expectations, providing him with neither sturdy nor sickly offspring. Science is an inherently patient pursuit, and so our doctor waited three years, then four, then five. At the end of this period, he carried out a rigorous study of the matter, reread all the authoritative texts, Arab and otherwise, which he had brought with him to Itaguaí, sent inquiries to the Italian and German universities, and concluded by advising his wife to follow a special diet. The eminent lady, accustomed to eating only succulent Itaguaí pork, did not heed her husband's advice, and to her understandable but unpardonable resistance we owe the total extinction of the Bacamarte dynasty.

Science, however, has the ineffable gift of curing all ills; our physician immersed himself entirely in the study and practice of medicine. It was at this point that one of its lesser nooks and crannies caught his particular attention: that pertaining to the psychic, to the examination of cerebral pathology, also known at that time as alienism. Nowhere in the colony, or even the kingdom, was there a single expert on this barely explored, indeed almost unexplored, subject. Simão Bacamarte saw an opportunity for Lusitanian, and in particular Brazilian, science to garland itself in "everlasting laurels"—the expression he himself used, but only in a moment of ecstasy within the privacy of his own home; externally, he was modest, as befits a man of learning.

"The health of the mind," he declaimed, "is the worthiest occupation for a physician."

"For a *true* physician," added Crispim Soares, the town's apothecary and one of Bacamarte's close friends and supper companions.

Among the other sins of which it stands accused by the historians, the Itaguaí municipal council had made no provision for the insane. Those who were raving mad were simply locked away in their own homes, and remained uncured and uncared-for until death came to rob them of the gift of life. The tamer ones were left to wander the streets. Simão Bacamarte quickly resolved to remedy such harmful practices; he requested permission from the council to build a hospital that would provide treatment and lodgings for all the lunatics of Itaguaí and the surrounding towns and villages, in return for a stipend payable by the municipality when the patient's family were unable to do so. The proposal excited the curiosity of the whole town and met with great resistance, for it is always hard to uproot absurd or even merely bad habits.

"Look here, Dona Evarista," said Father Lopes, the parish priest, "why don't you try to interest your husband in a trip to Rio de Janeiro? All this studying can't be good for him; it gives him all sorts of strange ideas."

Greatly alarmed, Dona Evarista went to her husband and told him that she was filled by various consuming desires, in particular the desire to go to Rio de Janeiro and eat everything that he considered would help with his previously stated objective. But with the rare wisdom that distinguished him, the great man saw through this pretense and replied, smiling, that she need have no fear. He then went straight to the town hall, where the councillors were debating his proposal, and defended it with such eloquence that the majority resolved to authorize his request, and, at the same time, voted through a local tax destined to fund the treatment, board, and lodging of any of the insane who had no other means of support. It was not easy to find something new to be taxed, for everything in Itaguaí had already been earmarked. After lengthy study, the tax was imposed on the use of plumes on funeral horses. Anyone who wished to add feathers to the headdresses of horses drawing a hearse would pay two *tostões* to the council for each hour that elapsed between the time of death and the final blessing at the graveside. The town clerk got himself in a terrible muddle calculating the potential revenue arising from the new tax, and one of the councillors, who had little faith in the doctor's undertaking, asked that the clerk be relieved of such a pointless task.

"The calculations are entirely unnecessary," he said, "because Dr. Bacamarte's scheme will never come to anything. Whoever heard of putting all the lunatics together in the same building?"

The worthy councillor was mistaken, and the doctor's scheme was duly implemented. As soon as he had received permission, he began to build the house. It was in Rua Nova, which was the finest street in Itaguaí at the time; it had fifty windows on each side, a courtyard in the middle, and numerous cells to house the inmates. An eminent Arabist, the doctor had read in the Koran that Muhammad had declared that the insane were to be revered, for Allah had deprived them of their wits so that they would not sin. This struck him as a beautiful and profound idea, and he had it engraved on the front of the house. However, since he feared the parish priest's reaction, and through him that of the bishop, he attributed this sentiment to Benedict VIII, an otherwise pious fraud, which earned him, over lunch, a lengthy exposition from Father Lopes on the life of that eminent pontiff.

The asylum was given the name "Casa Verde" on account of its green shutters, this being the first time such a color had been used for that purpose in Itaguaí. It was inaugurated with great pomp; people flocked from all the towns and villages near and far, as well as from the city of Rio de Janeiro itself, to attend the ceremonies, which went on for seven days. Many patients had already been admitted, and their relatives were able to see for themselves the paternal care and Christian charity with which they would be treated. Basking in her husband's glory, Dona Evarista put on her finest clothes and decked herself in jewels, flowers, and silks. During those memorable days, she was a veritable queen; despite the rather prim social customs of the time, everyone made a point of visiting her two or even three times, and their praise went beyond mere compliments, for—and this fact is a credit to the society of the time—they saw in Dona Evarista the happy wife of an illustrious man, a man of lofty ideals, and, if they envied her, theirs was the blessed and noble envy of true admirers.

At the end of seven days, the public festivities came to an end; Itaguaí finally had a madhouse.

Chapter 2

A FLOOD OF LUNATICS

Three days later, Simão Bacamarte, now the town's official alienist, opened his heart to Crispim Soares the apothecary, and revealed to him his most intimate thoughts.

"Charity, Senhor Soares, certainly enters into my way of thinking, but only as seasoning—like salt, you might say—for that is how I interpret Saint Paul's words to the Corinthians: "And if I know all that can be known, and have not charity, I am nothing." The real purpose, though, in this Casa Verde project of mine, is to carry out an in-depth study of madness in its various degrees, classifying each type and finally discovering both the true cause of the phenomenon and its universal remedy. Therein lies the mystery of my intentions. And I believe that in this I will be doing a great service to humanity."

"A very great service indeed," said the apothecary.

"Without this asylum," continued the alienist, "I could achieve very little, but with it, my studies will have much greater scope."

"Much greater," echoed the apothecary.

And they were right. Lunatics from all the neighboring towns and villages poured into the Casa Verde. There were the violent, the meek, the monomaniacs, indeed the entire family of all those strangers to reason. By the end of four months, the Casa Verde was a hive of activity. The initial cells soon filled up, requiring a further wing with thirty-seven more cells to be added. Father Lopes admitted that he had never imagined there to be so many lunatics in the world, nor that some cases would be so totally inexplicable. There was, for example, the ignorant and uncouth young man who, every day after breakfast, would launch into an academic lecture embellished with tropes, antitheses, and apostrophes, with a few Greek and Latin flourishes and the odd snippet from Cicero, Apuleius, and Tertullian. The priest could scarcely believe his ears. What! A boy he had seen only three months before playing handball in the street!

"Oh, I agree," said the alienist, "but the truth is there before your very eyes, Your Reverence. It happens every day of the week."

"As far as I'm concerned," replied the priest, "this can only be explained by the confounding of languages in the Tower of Babel, as described in the Scriptures; since the languages were all mixed up in ancient times, it must be easy to switch between them when reason is absent."

"That could well be the divine explanation for the phenomenon," agreed the alienist after a moment's reflection, "but it is not impossible that there is also a human, indeed purely scientific, explanation, and that is what I intend to look into."

"Very well, but it troubles me, it really does."

There were three or four inmates who had been driven to madness by love, but only two stood out because of the curious nature of their symptoms. The first, a young man of twenty-five by the name of Falcão, was convinced he was the morning star; he would stand with his legs apart and his arms spread wide like the rays of a star, and stay like that for hours on end asking if the sun had come up yet so that he could retire. The other fellow paced endlessly around the rooms or courtyard, and up and down the corridors, searching for the ends of the earth. He was a miserable wretch whose wife had left him to run off with a dandy. As soon as he discovered she was gone, he armed himself with a pistol and went after them; two hours later, he found them by a lake and murdered them both with exquisite cruelty. The avenger's jealousy was satisfied, but at the price of his sanity. That was the beginning of his obsessive wanderings, relentlessly pursuing the fugitive lovers to the ends of the earth.

There were several interesting cases of delusions of grandeur, the most notable of which was the wretched son of a poor tailor, who would recount to the walls (for he never looked anyone in the face) his entire family pedigree, as follows:

"God begat an egg, the egg begat the sword, the sword begat David, David begat the purple, the purple begat the duke, the duke begat the marquis, the marquis begat the count, and that's me."

Then he would slap his forehead, snap his fingers, and repeat it again, five or six times in a row: "God begat an egg, the egg begat . . ." and so on.

Another of the same type was a humble clerk who fancied himself to be the king's chamberlain; another was the cattle drover from Minas Gerais who had a mania for distributing herds of cattle to everyone he met: he would give three hundred head to one, six hundred to another, twelve hundred to someone else, and so on. I won't mention the many cases of religious monomania, save for one fellow who, on account of his Christian name being João de Deus—John of God—went around saying he was John *the* God, and promising the kingdom of heaven to whoever would worship him and the torments of hell to everyone else. Then there was Garcia, a university graduate, who never said anything because he was convinced that if he uttered so much as a single word, all the stars would fall from the sky and set the earth on fire, for such was the power with which God had invested him.

That, at least, is what he wrote on the piece of paper provided by the alienist not so much out of charity as out of scientific interest.

For the alienist's dedication was more extraordinary than all the manias residing in the Casa Verde; it was nothing short of astonishing. Bacamarte set about putting in place two administrators, an idea of Crispim Soares's that Bacamarte accepted along with the apothecary's two nephews, whom he charged with implementing a set of rules and regulations, approved by the council, for the distribution of food and clothing, as well as keeping the

accounts and other such matters. Bacamarte himself was thus free to concentrate on his medical duties.

"The Casa Verde," he said to the priest, "is now a world unto itself, in
which there is both a temporal and a *spiritual* government." Father Lopes
laughed at this godly quip and added, with the sole aim of making his own
little joke: "Any more of that and I'll have you reported to the Pope himself."

Once relieved of his administrative burdens, the alienist embarked
upon a vast enterprise, that of classifying his patients. He divided them,
first, into two main categories—the violent and the meek—and from there
proceeded to the subcategories of monomanias, deliria and various kinds of
hallucinations. When that was done, he began a long and unremitting analysis of each patient's daily routine, when their outbursts occurred, their likes
and dislikes, their words, gestures, and obsessions; he would inquire into
their lives, professions, habits, how their illness had first manifested itself,
any accidents suffered in childhood or adolescence, any other illnesses, any
family history of mental illness; in short, an inquiry beyond that of even
the most scrupulous of magistrates. And each day, he noted down a new
observation, some interesting discovery or extraordinary phenomenon. At
the same time, he studied the best diets, medicines, cures, and palliatives,
both those handed down by his beloved Arabs and those which he himself
discovered by dint of wisdom and patience. This work took up most of his
time. He barely slept or ate, and even when he did eat he carried on working, either consulting an ancient text or ruminating over some particular
matter; he would often spend an entire meal without saying a single word
to Dona Evarista.

Chapter 3

GOD KNOWS WHAT HE IS DOING!

By the end of two months, that illustrious lady was the unhappiest of
women; she fell into a deep melancholy, grew thin and sallow, ate little, and
sighed at every turn. She did not dare to criticize or reproach Bacamarte in
any way, for she respected him as her husband and master, but she suffered
in silence and was visibly wasting away. One evening over dinner, when her
husband asked her what was wrong, she replied sadly that it was nothing;

then she summoned up a little courage and went as far as to say that she considered herself just as much a widow as before, adding:

"Who would have imagined that half a dozen lunatics . . ."

She did not finish the sentence, or, rather, she finished it by raising her eyes to the ceiling—those eyes which were her most appealing feature: large, dark, and bathed in a dewy light. As for the gesture itself, it was the same one she had employed on the day Simão Bacamarte had asked her to marry him. The chronicles do not say if Dona Evarista deployed that weapon with the wicked intention of decapitating science once and for all, or at least chopping off its hands, but it is a perfectly plausible conjecture. In any case, the alienist did not suspect her of having any ulterior motive. The great man was neither annoyed nor even dismayed; his eyes retained the same hard, smooth, unchanging metallic gleam, and not a single wrinkle troubled the surface of his brow, which remained as placid as the waters of the bay at Botafogo. A smile may have crossed his lips, as he uttered these words, as sweet as the oil in the *Song of Songs*:

"All right, you can go to Rio."

Dona Evarista felt the ground beneath her feet give way. She had never been to Rio, which, although but a pale shadow of what it is today, was still considerably more exciting than Itaguaí. For her, seeing Rio de Janeiro was something akin to the dream of the Hebrew slaves. Now that her husband had settled for good in that provincial town, she had given up all hope of ever breathing the airs of our fine city. And yet now there he was inviting her to fulfill her childhood and adolescent dreams. Dona Evarista could not conceal her delight at his proposal. Simão Bacamarte took her by the hand and smiled—a smile that was both philosophical and husbandly, and in which the following thought could be discerned: "There is no reliable remedy for the ailments of the soul; this woman is wasting away because she thinks I do not love her. I'll give her Rio de Janeiro, and that will console her." And since he was a studious man, he made a note of this observation.

Then a doubt pierced Dona Evarista's heart. She controlled herself, however, saying only that if he was not going, then she would not go, either, since there was no question of her undertaking a journey like that by herself.

"You can go with your aunt," said the alienist.

It should be noted that this same thought had occurred to Dona Evarista, but she had not wanted to ask or even suggest it, in the first place because it would be causing her husband even more expense, and secondly, because it would be better, more methodical, and more rational for the idea to come from him.

"Oh! But just think how much it would cost!" sighed Dona Evarista, without conviction.

"So? We've made a lot of money," said her husband. "Why, only yesterday the accountant showed me the figures. Would you like to see?"

And he showed her the ledgers. Dona Evarista was dazzled by that Milky Way of numbers. Then he showed her the coffers where the money was kept.

Goodness! There were heaps of gold; piles and piles of doubloons and *mil-cruzado* coins, a veritable treasure trove.

The alienist watched while she devoured the gold coins with her dark eyes, and whispered in her ear this most perfidious of remarks:

"Who would have imagined that half a dozen lunatics . . ."

Dona Evarista understood his meaning, smiled, and gave a heavy sigh:

"God must know what He is doing!"

Three months later, they set off: Dona Evarista, her aunt, the apothecary's wife, and one of their nephews, together with a priest whom the alienist had met in Lisbon and who happened to be in Itaguaí, five or six footmen, and four slave-women; this was the entourage that the townsfolk watched depart on that May morning. The farewells were a sad affair for everyone concerned, apart, that is, from the alienist. Although Dona Evarista's tears were abundant and sincere, they were not enough to move him. As a man of science, and only of science, nothing beyond science could dismay him, and the only thing bothering him on that occasion, as he cast an uneasy, policeman's gaze over the crowd, was the thought that some madman might be lurking among those of sound mind.

"Goodbye!" sobbed the ladies and the apothecary.

And so the entourage left. As the apothecary and the doctor returned home, Crispim Soares kept his gaze fixed firmly between the ears of his mule, while Simão Bacamarte's eyes were fixed on the horizon ahead, leaving his horse to deal with how to get home. What a striking image of the genius and the common man! One stares at the present, filled with tears and regrets, while the other scrutinizes the future with its promise of new dawns.

Chapter 4

A NEW THEORY

As Dona Evarista's journey brought her, tearfully, closer to Rio de Janeiro, Simão Bacamarte was studying, from every angle, a bold new idea that stood to enlarge substantially the foundations of psychology. He spent any time away from his duties at the Casa Verde roaming the streets, or going from house to house, talking to people about anything and everything, and punctuating his words with a stare that put fear into even the most heroic of souls.

One morning, about three weeks later, while Crispim Soares was busy concocting some medicine or other, someone came to tell him that the alienist wanted to see him.

"He says it's important," added the messenger.

Crispim blenched. What important matter could it be, if not some sad news of the traveling party, in particular his wife? For this point must be clearly stated, given how much the chroniclers insisted upon it: Crispim loved his wife dearly and, in thirty years of marriage, they had never been apart for even one day. This would explain the muttered private monologues he often indulged in, and which his assistants often overheard: "What on earth were you thinking of? What possessed you to agree to letting Cesária go with her? Lackey, miserable lackey! And all to get into Dr. Bacamarte's good books. Well, now you just have to grin and bear it; that's right, grin and bear it, you vile, miserable lickspittle. You just say *Amen* to everything, don't you? Well, now you've got your comeuppance, you filthy blackguard!" And many other such insults that a man should never say to anyone, still less to himself. Thus it is not hard to imagine the effect of Bacamarte's message. Soares instantly dropped what he was doing and rushed to the Casa Verde.

Simão Bacamarte received him with the joy that befits a man of learning, that is to say, a joy buttoned up to the neck with circumspection.

"I am very happy," he said.

"News of our womenfolk?" asked the apothecary, his voice trembling.

The alienist made a grand gesture and replied:

"No, it concerns something far more exalted: a scientific experiment. I say experiment, because I am not so rash as to assert my conclusions with absolute certainty, and because science, Senhor Soares, is nothing if not a constant search. So we shall call it, therefore, an experiment, but one that will change the very face of the Earth. Madness, the object of my studies, was, until now, considered a mere island in an ocean of reason; I am now beginning to suspect that it is a continent."

Upon saying this, he fell silent, the better to savor the apothecary's astonishment. Then he explained his idea at length. As he saw it, insanity afflicted a vast swath of humanity, an idea he expounded with copious arguments, texts, and examples. He cited examples both from Itaguaí itself and from history: being the rarefied intellectual he was, he recognized the dangers of drawing all his examples from Itaguaí, and sought refuge in history. He thus drew particular attention to several famous persons such as Socrates, who had his own personal demon, to Pascal, who always imagined a yawning abyss lay somewhere to his left, to Caracalla, Domitian, Caligula, and so on, a whole string of cases and people, the repulsive and the ridiculous. Since the apothecary seemed taken aback by such a promiscuous mixture, the alienist told him that it all amounted to the same thing, even adding sententiously:

"Ferocity, Senhor Soares, is merely the serious side of the grotesque."

"Witty, very witty indeed!" exclaimed Crispim Soares, throwing his hands in the air.

As for the idea of expanding the territory of insanity, the apothecary thought it somewhat extravagant, but since modesty, the principal ornament of his mind, would not suffer him to admit to anything other than a noble enthusiasm, he declared it sublime and utterly true, adding that it was definitely one for the town crier.

I should explain. At that time, Itaguaí, like all other towns, villages, and hamlets throughout the colony, had no printing press. There were, therefore, only two means of circulating news: either by nailing a handwritten notice to the doors of the town hall and the parish church, or by means of the town crier, who would roam the streets of the town with a rattle in his hand. From time to time, he would shake the rattle, townspeople would gather, and he would announce whatever he had been instructed to announce—a cure for fever, plots of arable land for sale, a sonnet, a church donation, the identity of the nosiest busybody in town, the finest speech of the year, and so on. The system had its inconveniences in terms of the inhabitants' peace and tranquility, but was preserved due to its effectiveness in disseminating information. For example, one of the municipal councillors—the very one who had been most vehemently opposed to the establishment of the Casa Verde—enjoyed a reputation as a tamer of snakes and monkeys, despite never having domesticated even one such creature. He did this simply by taking good care, every month, to employ the services of the town crier. Indeed, the chronicles say that some people attest to having seen rattlesnakes dancing on the councillor's chest, a claim that is perfectly false, but that was accepted as true entirely on account of the absolute confidence in which the system was held. As you can see, not every institution of the old regime deserves our own century's disdain.

"There is only one thing better than announcing my new theory," replied the alienist to the apothecary's suggestion, "and that is putting it into practice."

And, not wishing to diverge significantly from the alienist, the apothecary agreed that it would indeed be better to begin with action.

"There'll be time enough for the town crier," he concluded.

Simão Bacamarte reflected further for a moment, then said:

"Let's suppose, Senhor Soares, that the human spirit is an enormous seashell. My goal is to see if I can extract from it the pearl of reason. Or, in other words, to delineate definitively the boundaries of reason and insanity. Reason is the perfect equilibrium of all the faculties; beyond that lies madness, madness, and only madness.

Father Lopes, to whom the alienist also confided his new theory, declared bluntly that he could make neither head nor tail of it, that it was an absurd endeavor, and, if not absurd, then it was such a grandiose endeavor that it was not worth even embarking upon.

"Using the current definition, which is the one that has existed since time immemorial," he added, "madness and reason are perfectly delineated. We all know where one ends and the other begins. Why start moving the fence?"

Across the thin, discreet lips of the alienist danced the faintest shadow of an incipient laugh, in which disdain marched arm in arm with pity. But not a single word emerged.

Science merely extended its hand to theology, and with such self-assurance that theology no longer knew whether to believe in one or the other. Itaguaí and the universe stood on the brink of a revolution.

Chapter 5

THE TERROR

Four days later, the inhabitants of Itaguaí heard with some consternation that a certain fellow by the name of Costa had been taken to the Casa Verde.

"Impossible!"

"What do you mean, 'impossible'? He was taken there this morning."

"But surely he is the last person to deserve that . . . After all he's done!"

Costa was one of the most highly respected of Itaguaí's citizens. He had inherited four hundred thousand *cruzados* in the good coinage of King João V, a sum of money that would, as his uncle had declared in his will, provide income enough to live on "until the end of the world." No sooner had he received his inheritance than he began to share it out in the form of loans, at no interest; one thousand *cruzados* here, two thousand there, three hundred to this fellow, eight hundred to the next, so much so that, after five years, there was nothing left. Had penury befallen him suddenly, Itaguaí would have sat up and taken notice. But it came little by little; he slipped from opulence to affluence, from affluence to moderation, from moderation to poverty, and from poverty to penury, all in gradual steps. By the end of those five years, people who had once raised their hats to him as soon as they spotted him at the end of the street, would now clap him familiarly on the back, tweak his nose, and make all sorts of rude comments. And Costa would always laugh amiably. He seemed not even to notice that the least courteous men were precisely those who still owed him money; on the contrary, he would embrace them with even greater pleasure, and even more sublime resignation. One day, when one of these incorrigible debtors jeered at him and Costa simply laughed, a skeptical bystander commented, somewhat perfidiously: "You only put up with that fellow in the hope he will repay you." Costa did not hesitate for a second; he went up to the man who owed him money and canceled the debt on the spot. "Don't be surprised," interjected the bystander, "all Costa has given up is a far-distant star." Costa was perceptive enough to realize that the onlooker was mocking the worthiness of his actions, alleging that he was only relinquishing something he would never receive anyway. Costa prized his honor, and, two hours later, he found a means of proving that such a slander was untrue: he got hold of a few coins and sent them to the debtor as a new loan.

"Let's hope that now . . ." he thought, not even bothering to finish the sentence.

This last good deed of Costa's persuaded both the credulous and incredulous; no one now doubted the chivalrous sentiments of that worthy citizen. Even the most timid of paupers ventured out in their old slippers and threadbare capes to knock at his door. One worm, however, still gnawed at Costa's soul: it was the idea of that bystander disliking him. But even this came to an end: three months later, the very same bystander came and asked him for one hundred and twenty *cruzados*, promising to pay him back two days later. This was all that was left of Costa's inheritance, but it was also a noble revenge: Costa lent him the money that very instant, and without interest. Unfortunately, time ran out before he was repaid; five months later he was bundled off to the Casa Verde.

One can well imagine the consternation in Itaguaí when people learned what had happened. People spoke of nothing else; it was said that Costa had gone mad over breakfast, others said it was in the middle of the night. Accounts were given of his outbursts, which were either violent, dark, and terrifying, or gentle and even funny, depending on which version you heard. Many people rushed to the Casa Verde, where they found poor Costa looking quite calm, if a little dazed, and talking perfectly lucidly and asking why he had been taken there. Some went to see the alienist. Bacamarte applauded such sentiments of kindness and compassion, but added that science was science, and that he could not leave a madman wandering the streets. The last person to intercede on his behalf (because after what I am about to tell you everyone was too terrified to go anywhere near the doctor) was an unfortunate lady, one of Costa's cousins. The alienist told her confidentially that this worthy man was not in perfect command of his mental faculties, as could be seen from the way in which he had dissipated his fortune—

"No! Absolutely not!" the good lady said emphatically, interrupting him. "It's not his fault he spent all the money so quickly."

"Isn't it?"

"No, sir. I will tell you what happened. My late uncle was not a bad man, but when he was angry he was capable of anything, even failing to remove his hat in the presence of the Holy Sacrament. Then, one day, shortly before he died, he discovered that a slave had stolen one of his oxen. You can imagine his reaction. He was shaking all over, he turned bright red, and started foaming at the mouth—I remember it as if it were yesterday. Just then, an ugly, long-haired man, in shirtsleeves, came up to him and asked for some water. My uncle, God rest his soul, told the man that he could go drink from the river or, for all he cared, go to hell. The man looked at my uncle, raised his hand menacingly, and laid this curse upon him: 'All your wealth will last no more than seven years and a day, as sure as this thing here is the *Seal of Solomon*.' And he showed my uncle the *Seal of Solomon* tattooed on his arm. That's what caused it, sir; it was the evil man's curse that caused it."

Bacamarte fixed the woman with eyes as sharp as daggers. When she finished, he politely offered her his hand, as if to the wife of the viceroy himself, and invited her to come and speak to her cousin. The unfortunate woman believed him, and he took her to the Casa Verde and locked her up in the hallucination wing.

News of the illustrious Bacamarte's duplicity struck terror into the souls of the townspeople. No one wanted to believe that, for no reason, with no apparent animosity, the alienist had locked up in the Casa Verde a lady of perfectly sound mind, whose only crime had been to intercede on behalf of a poor unfortunate wretch. The matter was discussed on street corners and in barbershops; a whole web of romantic intrigue was concocted, tales of amorous overtures that the alienist had once made to Costa's cousin, to Costa's outrage and the lady's disdain. And this was his revenge. It was as clear as day. But the alienist's austere and studious lifestyle seemed to belie such a hypothesis. Nonsense! Surely that was just a façade. And one particularly credulous person even began to mutter that he knew a few other things, too, but he wouldn't say what they were since he wasn't absolutely certain, but he knew them nonetheless, and could almost swear they were true.

"Since you're such a close friend of his, can't you tell us what's happening, what happened, what reason . . . ?"

Crispim Soares was in raptures. These urgent inquiries from worried and curious neighbors and astonished friends were for him like a public coronation. There could be no doubt about it; the whole town finally knew that he, Crispim Soares, the apothecary, was the alienist's closest friend, the great man's confidant in all important matters; hence the general rush to see him. All this was evident in the apothecary's cheery face and discreet smile, a smile accompanied by silence, for he said nothing in reply, or only, at most, a few abrupt monosyllables, cloaked in that fixed, unvarying half smile, full of scientific mysteries that he could not, without danger or dishonor, reveal to any living person.

"Something's afoot," thought the most suspicious.

One such person limited himself to merely thinking this, before turning his back and going on his way. He had personal matters to attend to. He had just finished building a sumptuous new house. The house alone was enough to attract people's attention, but that was not all. There was the furniture, which he told everyone he had ordered from Hungary and Holland and which could be seen from the street, since he always left the windows wide open. And then there was the garden, a masterpiece of art and good taste. This man, who had made his fortune from the manufacture of saddles for mules and donkeys, had always dreamed of owning a magnificent house, a lavish garden, and exquisite furniture. He did not entirely give up his saddlemaking business, but sought repose from it in the quiet contemplation of his new house, the finest in Itaguaí, grander than the Casa Verde, nobler even than the town hall. Among the town's most illustrious denizens there was a wailing and gnashing of teeth whenever anyone thought of, mentioned, or praised the saddler's house—a mere donkey saddler, for goodness' sake!

"There he is again, mouth agape," said the morning passersby.

It was, in effect, Mateus's custom each morning to stretch himself out in the middle of his garden and stare lovingly at his house for a good hour, until he was summoned in for lunch. His neighbors all addressed him most respectfully, but laughed gleefully behind his back. One of them even commented that Mateus would be even better off, a millionaire in fact, if he made the donkey saddles for himself; an unintelligible witticism if ever there was one, but it made the others howl with laughter.

"There he is, making a spectacle of himself as usual," they would say as evening fell.

The reason for this was that in the early evenings, when families would take a stroll (having dined early), Mateus would position himself majestically at the window, in full view of everyone, his white suit standing out against the dark background, and he would stay like that for two or three hours until the light had completely faded. It can be assumed that Mateus's intention was to be admired and envied, although it was not something he

confessed to anyone, not even to his great friends, the apothecary and Father
Lopes. At least that is what the apothecary said when the alienist informed
him that the saddlemaker could well be suffering from a love of stones, a
mania that Bacamarte had himself discovered, and had been studying for
some time. The way he stared at his house . . .

"No, sir," Soares answered vehemently.

"No?"

"Forgive me, but you are perhaps unaware that in the mornings he
is *examining* the stonework, not admiring it, and, in the afternoons, it is
other people who are doing the staring, at him and at the house." And he
recounted the saddlemaker's habit of standing there every evening, from
dusk until nightfall.

Simão Bacamarte's eyes glinted with scientific delight. Perhaps he was
indeed unaware of all of the saddlemaker's habits, or perhaps, by interrogat-
ing Soares, he was seeking only to confirm some lingering doubt or suspicion. In any event, the apothecary's explanation satisfied him; but since his
were the refined pleasures of a learned man, the apothecary noticed nothing to suggest a sinister intention. On the contrary, it was early evening and
the alienist suggested they take a stroll together. Good heavens! It was the
first time Simão Bacamarte had bestowed such an honor upon his friend.
Trembling and dazed, Crispim replied that yes, indeed, why not? Just at that
moment, two or three customers came in; Crispim silently cursed them; not
only were they delaying the stroll, there was a risk that Bacamarte might
invite one of them to accompany him, and dispense with Crispim entirely.
Such impatience! Such torment! Finally, the interlopers left. The alienist
steered him toward the saddlemaker's house, saw the saddlemaker standing at the window, passed slowly back and forth five or six times, pausing frequently to study the man's posture and expression. Poor Mateus
noticed only that he was the object of the curiosity or perhaps admiration
of Itaguaí's leading light, and struck an even grander pose. And thus, sadly,
very sadly, he merely sealed his fate; the very next day he was carted off to
the Casa Verde.

"The Casa Verde is nothing but a private jailhouse," commented a doctor who had no clinic of his own.

Never did an opinion take root and flourish so quickly. Private jail: this
was repeated throughout Itaguaí from north to south and from east to west.
It was said in fear, because during the week that followed poor Mateus's

incarceration, some twenty people—two or three of whom were persons of rank—were carted off to the Casa Verde. The alienist said that only pathological cases were admitted, but few believed him. Popular theories abounded. Revenge, greed, divine retribution, the monomania of the doctor himself, a secret plot hatched by Rio de Janeiro to stamp out any germ of prosperity that might take root and flourish in Itaguaí to the disadvantage of the capital, and a thousand other explanations that explained nothing at all, but such was the daily produce of the public's imagination.

This coincided with the return from Rio de Janeiro of the alienist's wife, her aunt, Crispim Soares's wife, and all—or nearly all—of the entourage that had left Itaguaí several weeks earlier. The alienist went to greet them, along with the apothecary, Father Lopes, the municipal councillors and various other worthy officials. The moment when Dona Evarista laid eyes upon her husband is considered by the chroniclers of the time to be one of the most sublime in the annals of the human spirit, on account of the contrast in their two natures, both extreme and both admirable. Dona Evarista uttered a cry, managed to stammer out a word or two, and then threw herself upon her spouse in a movement that can best be described as a combination of jaguar and turtledove. Not so the illustrious Bacamarte, who, with clinical detachment, not for an instant unbending from his scientific rigor, held out his arms to his wife, who fell into them and fainted. This lasted only a moment, and only two minutes later, Dona Evarista was being warmly greeted by her friends, and the procession once again moved on.

Dona Evarista was the hope of Itaguaí; the town counted on her to be a moderating influence on that scourge of the Casa Verde. Hence the public acclaim, the crowds thronging the streets, the flags, the flowers, and the damask silk banners hanging from the windows. With her arm resting on that of Father Lopes—for the eminent Bacamarte had entrusted his wife to the priest and was walking pensively beside them—Dona Evarista turned her head from side to side, curious, restless, brazen even. The priest inquired about Rio de Janeiro, which he had not seen since the reign of the previous viceroy, and Dona Evarista replied enthusiastically that it was the most beautiful thing in the whole wide world. The Passeio Público gardens were now finished and were indeed a paradise; she had gone there many times, as well as to the infamous Rua das Belas Noites, and to the Marrecas fountain . . . Ah, the Marrecas fountain! Yes, there really were Marrecas ducks there, made out of metal and spouting water from their beaks. A most exquisite thing! The priest agreed that Rio de Janeiro must indeed be even lovelier now; after all, it had been very beautiful even back in the old days! And no wonder, for it was bigger than Itaguaí and, moreover, the seat of government. But nor could it be said that Itaguaí was ugly; after all, it had beautiful houses such as Mateus's, and the Casa Verde . . .

"And speaking of the Casa Verde," said Father Lopes, gliding expertly onto the topic of the moment, "your ladyship will find it remarkably full these days."

"Is that so?"

"Yes, indeed. Mateus is there . . ."

"The saddlemaker?"

"The very one. And Costa, along with his cousin, as well as many others . . ."

"They've all gone mad?"

"Or nearly mad," the priest replied judiciously.

"And?"

The priest turned down the corners of his mouth, as if to say he did not know, or did not wish to say; a vague response that could not be repeated to anyone else, since it contained no words. Dona Evarista thought it truly extraordinary that all of those people had gone mad; one or two, perhaps, but *all* of them? On the other hand, it was difficult for her to doubt it; her husband was a man of learning, and would never commit anyone to the Casa Verde without clear proof of insanity.

"Indeed . . . indeed . . ." repeated the priest at regular intervals.

Three hours later, fifty guests or so were seated around Simão Bacamarte's table for a dinner to welcome home the travelers. Dona Evarista was the obligatory subject of toasts, speeches, verses of every kind, metaphors, hyperboles, and apologues. She was the wife of the new Hippocrates, the muse of Science, an angel, divine, the shining dawn, charity, life, and sweet consolation; her eyes were two stars, in the more modest version proposed by Crispim Soares, or two suns, according to the musings of a councillor. The alienist listened to these things, feeling mildly bored, but showing no visible signs of impatience. He merely whispered in his wife's ear that such rhetorical flourishes were not to be taken seriously. Dona Evarista tried hard to share her husband's opinion, but, even after discounting three-quarters of such fawning flattery, there was still more than enough to swell her pride. For example, one of the orators was a young man of

twenty-five called Martim Brito, a consummate dandy well versed in amorous adventures and affairs; he delivered a speech in which the birth of
Dona Evarista was explained in the most provocative manner. "After God
gave the world both man and woman, who are the diamond and the pearl of
His divine crown," he said, triumphantly drawing out this part of the sentence as he took in the entire table, from one end to the other, "God wished
to surpass even Himself, and so He created Dona Evarista."

Dona Evarista lowered her eyes with exemplary modesty. Two ladies,
considering such flattery excessive and even audacious, looked inquiringly at
their host, where they indeed found the alienist's expression clouded by suspicion, menace, and, quite possibly, bloodlust. The young man had shown
great impudence, thought the two ladies. And each of them prayed to God
to ward off any tragic consequences that might arise, or at the very least
postpone them until the following day. Yes, that was it: postpone them. The
more pious of the two ladies even admitted to herself that Dona Evarista
scarcely merited such suspicion, being so far from being either attractive
or witty. An insipid little simpleton. But then, if everyone liked the same
color, what would happen to yellow? The thought made her tremble once
again, although less than before; less, because now the alienist was smiling
at Martim Brito and, when everyone got up from the table, he went over to
him to exchange a few words about his speech. He congratulated the young
man on his dazzling improvisation, full of magnificent flashes of wit. Was
the idea about Dona Evarista's birth his own invention, or had he found it
in some book? No, sir, it was his own idea; it had occurred to him on that
very occasion and seemed entirely fitting as an oratorical flourish. Besides,
his ideas tended to be bold and daring rather than tender or jocular. He was
a man suited to the epic. Once, for example, he had composed an ode to the
fall of the Marquis of Pombal's government, in which he had described the
noble minister as the "harsh dragon of Nothingness," crushed by the "vindic-
tive claws of Everything." There were others in a similar vein, always rather
original, for he liked ideas that were rare and sublime, and images that were
grand and noble . . .

"Poor boy!" thought the alienist. "Undoubtedly a case of cerebral lesion;
not a life-threatening phenomenon, but certainly worthy of study."

Dona Evarista was astounded when, three days later, she discovered
that Martim Brito had been taken to the Casa Verde. A young man with

such charming ideas! The two ladies blamed it on the alienist's jealousy. What else could it be? The young man's declaration had been far too bold.

Jealousy? But how then to explain, shortly afterward, the incarceration of the highly regarded José Borges do Couto Leme, the inveterate merrymaker Chico das Cambraias, the clerk Fabrício, and others besides? The terror grew. No one knew any longer who was sane and who was mad. Whenever their husbands left the house, wives would light a candle to the Virgin Mary; and some husbands didn't even have the courage to venture out without one or two thugs to protect them. Palpable terror reigned. Those who could, left the town. One such fugitive was captured a mere two hundred paces from the town. He was a likable young man of thirty, chatty and polite, indeed so polite that whenever he greeted someone he would bow so low as to sweep the ground with his hat; in the street he would often run a distance of ten or twenty yards to shake the hand of a worthy gentleman, a lady, sometimes even a mere boy, as had happened with the chief magistrate's son. He had a vocation for bowing. Besides, he owed his good standing in the town not only to his personal attributes, which were unusual, but also to the noble tenacity with which he never gave up, even after one, two, four, or even six scowling rejections. Gil Bernardes's charms were such that, once invited into someone's house, he was disinclined to leave and his host equally disinclined to let him leave. But, despite knowing he was well liked, Bernardes took fright when he heard one day that the alienist had his eye on him; the following day he fled the town before dawn, but was quickly apprehended and taken to the Casa Verde.

"We have to put an end to this!"

"It can't go on!"

"Down with tyranny!"

"Despot! Brute! Goliath!"

These were whispers in houses rather than shouts in the street, but the time for shouts would come soon enough. Terror mounted; rebellion approached. The idea of petitioning the government to have Simão Bacamarte arrested and deported crossed several people's minds, even before Porfírio, the barber, gave full expression to it in his shop, accompanied by grand, indignant gestures. And let it be noted—for this is one of the purest pages of this whole somber story—let it be noted that ever since the Casa Verde's population had begun to grow in such an extraordinary fashion, Porfírio had seen his profits greatly increase on account of the incessant demand for leeches from the asylum; but his own personal gain, he said, must give way to the public good. And, he added: "the tyrant must be defeated!" It should also be noted that he unleashed this cry on the very day Bacamarte had committed to the Casa Verde a man by the name of Coelho who had brought a lawsuit against Porfírio.

"Can anyone tell me in what sense a man like Coelho is mad?" railed Porfírio.

No one could answer him; they all repeated one after another that Coelho was perfectly sane. Coelho's lawsuit against the barber, concerning some plots of land in the town, arose from a dispute over some old and very obscure property deeds, and not from any hatred or greed. An excellent fellow, Coelho. His only detractors were a handful of grumpy individuals who, claiming they didn't have time to chat, would duck around the corner or into a shop as soon as they caught sight of him. In truth, Coelho did love a good chat, a long chat, slowly sipped or in deep drafts, and so it was that he was never alone, always preferring those who could string two words together, but never turning his back on the less loquacious. Father Lopes, who was a devotee of Dante and an enemy of Coelho, could never watch the man tear himself away from a companion without reciting from *Inferno*, with his own witty amendment:

> *La bocca sollevò dal fiero pasto*
> *Quel "seccatore"* . . .

However, while some people knew that the priest disliked Coelho, others assumed this was just a prayer in Latin.

Chapter 6

THE REBELLION

Roughly thirty people joined forces with the barber, drafting a formal complaint and taking it to the town hall.

The council refused to accept the complaint, declaring that the Casa

Verde was a public institution and that science could not be amended by administrative vote, still less by the mob.

"Go back to work," concluded the mayor. "That's our advice to you."

The agitators were furious. The barber declared that they would raise the banner of rebellion and destroy the Casa Verde; that Itaguaí could no longer serve as a cadaver to be studied and experimented on by a despot; that many estimable and even distinguished people were languishing in the cells of the Casa Verde, as well as other, humbler individuals no less worthy of esteem; that the alienist's scientific despotism was complicated by issues of greed, given that the insane, or rather those accused of insanity, were not being treated for free: their families, or, failing that, the council, were footing the bill—

"That's quite false!" interrupted the mayor.

"False?"

"About two weeks ago, we received formal notification from the eminent doctor that, since the experiments he was performing were of the highest psychological value, he would no longer accept the stipend approved by the council, just as he would no longer accept any payment from the patients' families.

The news of such a pure and noble act somewhat dampened the rebels' spirits. The alienist could very well be wrong, but clearly he was motivated by no interest other than science, and if they were to prove that mistakes had been made, then something more than noisy rabble-rousing was needed. Thus spoke the mayor, to vigorous cries of, "Hear, hear!" from the whole council. After a few moments of reflection, the barber declared that he had been given a mandate from the people and would not let matters rest until the Casa Verde, "that Bastille of human reason"—an expression he had heard from a local poet and which he now emphatically repeated—had been razed to the ground. Having said his piece, he left the building with all his followers.

The position of the councillors can easily be imagined: there was a pressing need to forestall the mob and head off revolt, battle, and bloodshed. To make matters worse, one of the councillors who had previously supported the mayor, on hearing the Casa Verde described as a "Bastille of human reason," thought it such an elegant turn of phrase that he changed his mind. It would, he said, be advisable to come up with some measures to control the

Casa Verde. When the mayor expressed his indignation in energetic terms, the councillor made this observation:

"I don't know much about science, but if so many apparently sane men are being locked up as lunatics, who's to say that it isn't the alienist himself who has become alienated from reason?"

Sebastião Freitas, the dissenting councillor, was a gifted speaker and carried on talking for some time, choosing his words prudently, but emphatically. His colleagues were astonished; the mayor requested that he at least set an example of respect for the rule of law by keeping his ideas to himself in public, so as not to give form and substance to the rebellion, which at that moment was still "nothing but a swirl of scattered atoms." The appeal of this image somewhat mitigated the effect of the earlier one, and Sebastião Freitas promised to refrain from taking any overt course of action, although he reserved the right to pursue all legal avenues in order to bring the Casa Verde to heel. And, still enamored of the phrase, he repeated to himself: "A Bastille of human reason!"

Meanwhile, the protests grew. Now there were not thirty but three hundred persons accompanying the barber, whose nickname deserves mentioning at this point because it became the name of the revolt; they called him Canjica, after a kind of milky porridge, and so the movement became known as the Canjica Rebellion. The action itself may well have been limited, given that many people, by virtue of fear or upbringing, did not take to the streets, but the feeling was unanimous, or almost unanimous, and the three hundred who marched to the Casa Verde could well be compared, give or take the evident differences between Paris and Itaguaí, to those brave citizens who stormed the Bastille.

Dona Evarista got wind of the approaching mob; one of the houseboys came to tell her as she was trying on a new silk dress (one of the thirty-seven she had brought back from Rio de Janeiro), but she refused to believe it.

"Oh, it must be some revelry," she said, adjusting a pin. "Now then, Benedita, check to see if the hem is straight."

"It is, mistress," replied the slave-woman squatting on the floor. "It's just fine. Could you turn a little? Yes, it's fine."

"They're not revelers, ma'am; they're shouting, 'Death to Dr. Bacamarte the tyrant!'" exclaimed the terrified houseboy.

"Shut up, you idiot! Benedita, look there on the left side; don't you think the seam is a bit crooked? The blue stripe doesn't go the whole way down; it looks terrible like that. You'll need to unpick the whole thing and make it exactly the same as—"

"Death to Dr. Bacamarte! Death to the tyrant!" shouted three hundred voices outside. It was the mob emerging into Rua Nova.

The blood drained from Dona Evarista's face. At first she was too petrified to move. The slave-woman instinctively made for the back door. As for the houseboy whom Dona Evarista had refused to believe, he enjoyed a moment of sudden, imperceptible triumph, a deep-seated sense of moral satisfaction, on seeing that reality had taken his side.

"Death to the alienist!" shouted the voices, closer now.

Dona Evarista may not have found it easy to resist the siren calls of pleasure, but she knew how to confront moments of danger. She did not faint, but instead ran into the next room, where her husband was immersed in his studies. When she entered the room, the illustrious doctor was hunched over a text of Averroes; his eyes, shrouded in meditation, traveled from book to ceiling and from ceiling to book, blind to the outside world, but clear-sighted enough when it came to the innermost workings of his mind. Dona Evarista called to her husband twice without him paying her the slightest attention; the third time, he heard her and asked what was wrong, if she was feeling ill.

"Can't you hear them shouting?" she asked tearfully.

The alienist listened; the shouts were drawing nearer, terrifying and threatening; he immediately understood the situation. He stood up from his high-backed chair, closed his book, strode calmly and purposefully over to the bookshelf, and put the book back in its place. Inserting it slightly disturbed the alignment of the two volumes on either side, and Simão Bacamarte took care to correct this minor yet interesting imperfection. Then he told his wife to go to her room and stay there, no matter what.

"No, no," implored the worthy lady, "I want to die by your side . . ."

Simão Bacamarte insisted that it was not a case of life and death, and that even if it were, she must on all accounts stay put. The poor woman tearfully and obediently bowed her head.

"Down with the Casa Verde!" shouted the Canjicas.

The alienist walked over to the balcony at the front of the house, arriving at the same time as the mob, those three hundred faces shining with civic virtue and dark with rage. "Die! Die!" they shouted from all sides the moment the alienist appeared on the balcony. When Simão Bacamarte gestured to them to let him speak, the rebels indignantly shouted him down. Then, waving his hat to silence the crowd, the barber managed to calm his companions, and told the alienist that he could speak, adding that he must not abuse the people's patience as he had been doing up until then.

"I will say little, or even nothing at all, if that is what's required. First of all, I want to know what you are asking for."

"We're not asking for anything," replied the barber, shaking. "We're demanding that the Casa Verde be demolished, or, at the very least, that the poor unfortunates within be set free."

"I don't understand."

"You understand perfectly well, tyrant; we want to liberate the victims of your hatred, your cruel whims, your greed . . ."

The alienist smiled, but the great man's smile proved invisible to the eyes of the multitude; it was a faint contraction of two or three muscles, nothing more. He smiled and replied:

"Gentlemen, science is a serious matter, and deserves to be treated as such. I do not answer to anyone for my professional actions, save to God and the great masters of Science. If you are seeking changes in how the Casa Verde is run, I am prepared to listen; but if you are asking me to reject everything I believe in, you will go away empty-handed. I could invite some of you, as a delegation, to come and visit the poor deranged inmates with me, but I won't do so, because that would entail explaining my whole system, which is something I will never reveal to laymen, still less to rebels."

Thus spoke the alienist to the astonished crowd; they were clearly not expecting him to exhibit such determination, still less such serenity. Their amazement grew still greater when the alienist gave a solemn bow to the crowd, then turned and went slowly back inside. The barber quickly came to his senses and, brandishing his hat, invited his friends to go with him and tear down the Casa Verde. Only a few half-hearted voices responded. It was at this decisive moment that the barber felt the first stirrings of an ambition to govern; it seemed to him that by demolishing the Casa Verde and defeating the alienist, he would be able to seize control of the municipal council, confound the agents of the Crown, and make himself master of Itaguaí. For years he had been struggling to get his name included on the ballot from which the councillors were drawn, but had always been rejected because his station in life was considered incompatible with such high office. It was now or never. Besides, he had taken this mutiny so far now that defeat would mean imprisonment, or perhaps even the gallows, or exile. Unfortunately for the barber, the alienist's reply had tempered the crowd's fury. When he realized this, the barber felt a surge of indignation; he wanted to yell: "Coward! Scoundrels!" but he restrained himself and took another tack:

"Let us fight, dear friends, to the very end! The salvation of Itaguaí is in your noble and heroic hands! Let us tear down the prison of your sons and fathers, of your mothers and sisters, of your relatives and friends, and of your own good selves. If not, you will waste away on a diet of bread and water, or perhaps be flogged to death, in the dungeons of that despicable man."

The crowd grew agitated again, muttering, then shouting, then shaking its fists, before thronging around the barber. The revolt was recovering from its brief dizzy spell, and threatening once again to raze the Casa Verde.

"Onward!" cried Porfírio, with a flourish of his hat.

"Onward!" bellowed the crowd.

But something stopped them: a corps of dragoons came marching at double time into Rua Nova.

Chapter 7

SOMETHING UNEXPECTED

When the dragoons reached the Canjicas there was a moment of bewilderment; the rebels could scarcely believe that the full force of the state had been sent in against them, but the barber immediately grasped the situation and waited. The dragoons stopped, and the captain ordered the crowd to disperse. However, while some were inclined to obey, others rallied strongly around the barber, who responded with these rousing words:

"We will not disperse. If it is our corpses you want, you can have them, but only our corpses, for you will not take from us our honor, our reputation, or our rights, and with them the very salvation of Itaguaí."

Nothing could be more reckless than this response from the barber, and nothing more natural. Call it the giddy impulse of all moments of crisis. Perhaps it was also an excess of confidence, an assumption that the dragoons would not resort to violence, an assumption that the captain quickly dispelled by ordering his troops to charge the Canjicas. What followed defied description. The crowd bellowed with rage; some managed to escape by climbing into the windows of houses, others by running down the street, but most remained, howling in angry indignation, spurred on by the barber's exhortations. The defeat of the Canjicas was imminent, when, for reasons the chronicles do not reveal, a third of the dragoons suddenly switched to the rebels' side. This unexpected reinforcement gave new heart to the Canjicas, while sowing despondency among the ranks of law and order. The loyal troops had no desire to attack their own comrades, and, one by one, they crossed over to join them, so that after a few minutes, the picture had completely changed. On one side stood the captain, accompanied by only a handful of men, facing a dense throng calling for his head. There was nothing to be done; he acknowledged defeat and surrendered his sword to the barber.

The triumphant revolution lost not a single moment; the wounded were taken to nearby houses, and the mob set off toward the town hall. Troops and citizens fraternized, shouting three cheers for the king, the viceroy, Itaguaí, and their illustrious leader, Porfírio. The man himself walked in front, grasping the sword as deftly as if it were nothing but a rather long razor. Victory had surrounded him with a mysterious aura. The dignity of office had begun to stiffen his sinews.

The councillors, peering at the crowd and soldiers from the windows, assumed that the troops had subdued the rabble, and, without further ado, went back inside and approved a petition to the viceroy asking him to pay a month's wages to the dragoons, "whose bravery saved Itaguaí from the abyss into which it had been driven by a bunch of rebels." This phrase was proposed by Sebastião Freitas, the dissenting councillor whose defense of the Canjicas had so scandalized his colleagues. However, any illusion of victory was quickly shattered. The cries of, "Long live the barber," "Death to the councillors," and "Death to the doctor," revealed to them the sad truth. The chairman did not lose heart: "Whatever our own fate may be," he said, "let us remember that we serve His Majesty and the people." Sebastião Freitas suggested that they could better serve both Crown and town by slipping out the back door and going to confer with the chief magistrate, but all the other councillors rejected this proposal.

Seconds later, the barber, accompanied by some of his lieutenants, entered the council chamber and peremptorily informed the council that they had been overthrown. The councillors offered no resistance, surrendered, and were taken off to jail. The barber's followers then proposed that he assume control of the town, in the name of His Majesty. Porfírio accepted, despite (he added) being all too aware of the pitfalls of high office. He went on to say that he could not do it without the support of all those present, to which they promptly agreed. The barber went to the window and relayed these decisions to the people, who ratified them with cheers of acclamation. The barber assumed the title of "Protector of the Town in the Name of His Majesty and the People." Various important edicts were quickly issued, including official communications from the new administration and a detailed report to the viceroy filled with many protestations of loyal obedience to His Majesty. Finally, there was a short but energetic proclamation to the people:

PEOPLE OF ITAGUAÍ!

A corrupt and violent council was found to be conspiring against the interests of His Majesty and the People, and was roundly condemned by the public; as a consequence, a handful of Citizens, bravely supported by His Majesty's loyal dragoons, have this very day ignominiously dissolved said Council, and with the unanimous consent of the town, the Supreme Mandate has been entrusted to me, until such time as His Majesty sees fit to order whatever may best serve his royal Person. People of Itaguaí! All that I ask is that you give me your trust, and that you assist me in restoring peace and the public finances, so wantonly squandered by the Council that has now met its fate at your hands. You may count on my dedication and self-sacrifice, and be assured that we will have the full backing of the Crown.

Protector of the Town in the Name of His Majesty and the People
PORFÍRIO CAETANO DAS NEVES

Everyone noticed that the proclamation made no mention of the Casa Verde, and, according to some, there could be no clearer indication of the barber's evil intentions. The danger was even more pressing given that, in the midst of these momentous events, the alienist had locked up seven or

eight more people, including two women, one of the men being a relative of
the Protector. This was undoubtedly not intended as a deliberate challenge
or act of defiance, but everyone interpreted it as such and the town was
filled with the hope that, within twenty-four hours, the alienist would be in
irons and that fearful prison destroyed.

The day ended merrily. While the town crier went around reading out
the proclamation on every corner, people spilled out into the streets and
swore to defend to the death their illustrious Porfírio. If few bothered to
protest against the Casa Verde, this was merely proof of their confidence
in the new government. The barber issued a decree declaring the day to
be a public holiday, and because the combination of temporal and spiritual
powers struck him as highly desirable, he suggested to the priest that a *"Te
Deum"* might be sung. Father Lopes, however, bluntly refused.

"I trust that, in any event, Your Reverence will not join forces with the
new government's enemies?" the barber said to him darkly.

To which Father Lopes replied without replying:

"How could I do that, if the new government has no enemies?"

The barber smiled; it was absolutely true. Apart from the captain, the
councillors, and a handful of grandees, the whole town was on his side. Even
those grandees who hadn't publicly backed him, had not come out against
him, either. Not one of the municipality's officials had failed to report for
duty. Throughout the town, families blessed the name of the man who
would at last liberate Itaguaí from the Casa Verde and the terrible Simão
Bacamarte.

Chapter 8

THE APOTHECARY'S DILEMMA

Twenty-four hours after the events narrated in the preceding chapter, the
barber, accompanied by two orderlies, left the government palace—as the
town hall was now called—and went to the home of Simão Bacamarte. He
was not unaware that it would be more fitting for the government to send for
Bacamarte; however, fearing that the alienist might not obey, he felt obliged
to adopt a tolerant, moderate stance.

I will not describe the apothecary's terror upon hearing that the barber was on his way to the alienist's house. "He's going to arrest him," he thought, his anxieties redoubling. Indeed the apothecary's moral torment during those revolutionary days exceeds all description. Never had a man found himself in a tighter spot: his close acquaintance with the alienist urged him to join his side, while the barber's victory inclined him toward the other. News of the uprising itself had already shaken him to the core, for he knew how universally the alienist was hated, and the victorious rebellion was the last straw. Soares's wife, a redoubtable woman and close friend of Dona Evarista, told him in no uncertain terms that his place was at Simão Bacamarte's side; meanwhile, his heart was screaming that this was a lost cause and that no one, of his own free will, shackles himself to a corpse. "True enough, Cato did it, *sed victa Catoni*," he thought, remembering one of Father Lopes's favorite phrases. "But Cato did not attach himself to a lost cause: he himself had been the lost cause, he and his republic; moreover, his act was that of an egotist, a miserable egotist; my situation is entirely different." His wife, however, would not give in, so Crispim Soares was left with no other option than to declare himself ill and take to his bed.

"There goes Porfírio, off to Dr. Bacamarte's house," said his wife to him the following day, at his bedside. "He's got people with him."

"They're going to arrest the doctor," thought the apothecary.

One thought leads to another; the apothecary was convinced that once they'd arrested the alienist, they would come after him as an accomplice. This thought proved to be a more effective remedy than any caustic lotion. Crispim Soares sat up, pronounced himself better, and said that he was going out. Despite all his wife's efforts and protestations, he got dressed and left the house. The chroniclers are unanimous in recording that her certainty that the apothecary was about to place himself nobly at the alienist's side was a great consolation to her; they go on to note very shrewdly just how powerful our illusions can be; for the apothecary resolutely made his way not to the alienist's house, but to the government palace. On arrival, he expressed surprise on finding that the barber was not there, explaining that he had come to pledge his allegiance, having been unable to do so the previous day due to illness. With some effort he managed a cough. The functionaries who heard his declaration, knowing full well the apothecary's close links with the alienist, understood the significance of this new declaration of allegiance, and treated Crispim Soares with punctilious kindness. They assured him that the barber would return shortly; His Lordship had gone to the Casa Verde on important business, but would not be long. They offered him a chair, refreshments, and compliments; they told him that the cause of the illustrious Porfírio was the cause of every patriot, to which the apothecary responded that, yes, indeed, he had never doubted it for a minute, and would be sure to have it brought to His Majesty's attention.

Chapter 9

TWO FINE CASES

The alienist did not delay in receiving the barber, declaring that since he had no means to resist, he was ready to obey. He asked only that he should not be obliged to witness the destruction of the Casa Verde.

"You are much mistaken, Your Lordship" said the barber after a short pause, "in attributing such barbarous intentions to my government. Rightly or wrongly, public opinion believes that the majority of patients placed here are perfectly sane, but the government recognizes that this is a purely scientific matter and does not intend to attempt to regulate the matter with municipal bylaws. Furthermore, the Casa Verde is a public institution, for that is how we received it from the hands of the now-disbanded council. However, there is—as indeed there must be—an intermediate proposal that may restore the public's peace of mind."

The alienist could barely conceal his astonishment; he confessed that he had been expecting an entirely different outcome: the tearing down of the asylum, prison for him, or even exile, indeed anything but—

"You are surprised," interrupted the barber gravely, "because you have not paid close enough attention to the heavy responsibilities of government. The people, blinded by compassion, which, in such cases, provokes a perfectly legitimate sense of indignation, may demand from their government a certain series of measures, but the government, with the responsibilities incumbent upon it, should not carry them out, or at least not in their entirety. Such is the situation we find ourselves in. The valiant revolution that yesterday brought down a despised and corrupt council, clamored for the destruction of the Casa Verde, but can a government take it upon itself to abolish madness? Certainly not. And if governments cannot abolish madness, are they any better qualified to detect and identify it? Again, no—it is a matter for science. Hence, in such a delicate matter as this, the government neither can nor should dispense with the aid and counsel of Your Lordship. What we ask of you is that, together, we find some means to satisfy public opinion. Let us join forces, and the people will fall into line. One acceptable solution, unless Your Lordship has a better suggestion, would be to remove from the Casa Verde those patients who are almost cured, as well as those who are simply harmless eccentrics. In that way, and without great danger, we can show a certain degree of benign tolerance."

After a pause of about three minutes, Simão Bacamarte asked: "How many dead and injured were there in yesterday's altercations?"

The barber was taken aback by the question, but quickly replied that there had been eleven dead and twenty-five wounded.

"Eleven dead and twenty-five wounded!" the alienist repeated two or three times.

The alienist intimated that he wasn't entirely happy with the proposal, but that he would come up with an alternative within a few days. He asked a number of questions about the previous day's events, the attack, the defense, the dragoons switching sides, any resistance offered by the councillors, and so on, to which the barber gave fulsome answers, laying great emphasis on how utterly discredited the council was. The barber confessed that the new government did not yet enjoy the backing of the town's leading citizens, but then that was something where the alienist himself could make all the difference. The government, concluded the barber, would be greatly relieved if it could count on the sympathy, if not the goodwill, of the loftiest mind in Itaguaí, and, no doubt, in the entire kingdom. But none of this made a button of difference to the noble, austere features of that great man, who listened in silence, showing neither pride nor modesty, as impassive as a stone deity.

"Eleven dead and twenty-five wounded," repeated the alienist, after accompanying the barber to the door. "Here we have two fine cases of cerebral incapacity. This barber exhibits clear symptoms of shameless duplicity. As for the idiocy of those who cheered him, what further proof is needed than those eleven dead and twenty-five wounded? Yes, two fine cases!"

"Long live noble Porfírio!" shouted the thirty-odd people waiting for the barber outside.

The alienist peered out the window and managed to catch the end of the barber's short address to the excited crowd.

". . . for I will be vigilant, of this you can be certain, yes, ever vigilant in fulfilling the wishes of the people. Trust in me, and everything will be resolved in the best possible manner. I only wish to remind you of the need for order. Order, my friends, is the very foundation of government!"

"Long live noble Porfírio!" shouted the thirty voices, waving their hats.

"Two fine cases!" murmured the alienist.

Chapter 10

THE RESTORATION

Within five days, the alienist had committed to the Casa Verde around fifty supporters of the new government. The people were outraged. The government, bewildered, did not know how to react. João Pina, another barber, said openly in the streets that Porfírio had "sold his soul to Simão Bacamarte," a phrase which rallied the most ardent of the town's citizens to Pina's side. Seeing his old rival in the arts of the razor at the head of this new insurrection, Porfírio understood that all would be lost if he did not move decisively; he issued two decrees, one abolishing the Casa Verde and the other banishing the alienist. João Pina ably demonstrated, with eloquent turns of phrase, that Porfírio's actions were nothing but a ruse and should not be taken seriously. Two hours later, Porfírio was ignominiously defeated, and João Pina assumed the heavy task of government. Finding in the filing cabinets drafts of the proclamation, the loyal address to the viceroy, and other inaugural documents left by the previous government, he lost no time in having them copied and dispatched; the chroniclers specifically state, and indeed it can be safely assumed, that he took care to change the names, so that where the other barber had written "corrupt council," the new barber referred to "an impostor steeped in evil French doctrines contrary to the sacrosanct interests of His Majesty," and so on.

At this point, a detachment of troops sent by the viceroy entered the town and restored order. The alienist immediately demanded that Porfírio be handed over to him, along with fifty or so other individuals, whom he declared to be mentally deranged. Furthermore, they promised to hand over a further nineteen of the barber's followers, who were convalescing from injuries inflicted in the initial rebellion.

This moment in Itaguaí's crisis also marked the zenith of Simão Bacamarte's influence. Everything he asked for they gave him, and one of the most vivid proofs of the eminent doctor's influence can be found in the alacrity with which the councillors, restored to their positions, agreed that Sebastião Freitas should also be committed to the asylum. Aware of the extraordinary inconsistency of this particular councillor's opinions, the alienist identified the case as pathological, and locked the man up. The same thing happened to the apothecary. Ever since he had learned of Soares's instantaneous decision to back the rebellion, the alienist had weighed it against the apothecary's consistent expressions of support for him, even on the very eve of the revolt, and had him arrested too. Crispim Soares did not deny the fact, but tried to explain it away by saying that he had succumbed to an impulse of fear upon seeing the rebellion triumphant, pointing out in his own defense that he had quickly returned to his sickbed and played no further part in events. Simão Bacamarte did not argue with him, remarking to the others present that fear can also be father to insanity, and that Crispim Soares's case struck him as one of the clearest examples of such a phenomenon.

But the most obvious proof of Simão Bacamarte's influence was the docility with which the town council handed over its own chairman. This worthy official had declared in open session that he would be content with no less than a tun of blood to cleanse him of the Canjicas's effrontery, and his words reached the alienist's ears via the mouth of the town clerk, who came to him flushed with excitement. Simão Bacamarte began by putting the town clerk in the Casa Verde, and from there he went to the town hall and informed the council that the chairman of the council was suffering from "bull mania," a type of madness he intended to make a study of, to the great benefit of mankind. The council at first hesitated, but finally gave in.

From then on this harvest of men proved unstoppable. A man could not invent or repeat the simplest of lies, even when it was to the advantage of the inventor or spreader of the lie, without being thrown into the Casa Verde. Everything was madness. Composers of riddles, aficionados of puzzles and anagrams, slanderers, nosy parkers, preening dandies, and pompous officials: no one escaped the alienist's emissaries. He spared sweethearts but not strumpets, saying that the first yielded to a natural impulse, the second only to vice. A man could be a miser or a spendthrift and still be hauled off the Casa Verde; hence the claim that there was no rule for determining what constituted complete sanity. Certain chroniclers believe that Simão Bacamarte did not always act in good faith, and they cite in support of this allegation (which I cannot entirely vouch for) the fact that he persuaded the council to pass a bylaw authorizing the wearing of a silver ring on the thumb of the left hand by any person who, without any further proof, documentary or otherwise, claimed to have a drop or two of blue blood in his or her veins. These chroniclers say that Bacamarte's secret goal was to enrich a certain silversmith in the town, who was a close friend. However, while it is certainly true that the jeweler saw his business prosper following the new municipal ordinance, it is no less true that the bylaw also provided the Casa Verde with a host of new inmates; it would therefore be reckless to determine which of these was the eminent doctor's true objective. As for the reason justifying the arrest and incarceration of all those who wore the ring, that is one of the obscurest aspects of the entire history of Itaguaí. The likeliest theory is that they were locked up for going around waving their hands about for no good reason, in the streets, at home, even in church. Everyone knows that lunatics wave their hands about a lot. In any event, this is pure conjecture; there is no concrete evidence.

"Where will it all end?" exclaimed the local gentry. "Ah, if only we had supported the Canjicas . . ."

Then one morning, on the day that the council was due to hold a grand ball, the whole town was shaken by the news that the alienist's own wife had been committed to the Casa Verde. No one could believe it; some scoundrel must surely have made it up. But no, it was absolutely true. Dona Evarista had been taken away at two o'clock in the morning. Father Lopes rushed to see the alienist and inquired discreetly about the matter.

"I've had my doubts for some time now," her husband said gravely. "Her previous matrimonial modesty, in both her marriages, cannot be reconciled with the positive frenzy for silks, velvets, laces, and precious stones she has displayed since her return from Rio de Janeiro. That was when I began to observe her closely. Her conversations revolved entirely around such fripperies; if I talked to her about the royal courts of olden times, she would immediately ask about the dresses worn by the ladies; if she received a visit from a lady when I was out, before telling me the purpose of the visit she would first describe the visitor's outfit, approving of some items and criticizing others. One day, which I am sure Your Reverence will remember, she offered to make a new dress every year for the statue of Our Lady in the parish church. These were all serious symptoms in themselves, but it was last night that her complete insanity manifested itself. She had carefully selected and made all the final alterations to the gown she was planning to wear to the municipal ball; her only hesitation was between a garnet or sapphire necklace. The day before yesterday, she asked me which one she should wear; I replied that either one would go very well. Yesterday, she repeated the question over breakfast; shortly after lunch I found her silent and thoughtful.

" 'What's the matter?" I asked her.

" 'I'd like to wear the garnet necklace, but the sapphire one is so pretty!'

" 'So wear the sapphire one.'

" 'But then what about the garnets?'

"Anyway, the afternoon and evening passed without any further developments. We had supper and went to bed. In the middle of the night, sometime around one-thirty, I woke up and she wasn't there. I got out of bed, went to our dressing room, and found her with the two necklaces, trying them on in front of the mirror, first one, then the other. She was obviously deranged, so I had her committed at once."

The alienist's response did not satisfy Father Lopes, but he said nothing. The alienist, however, understood the priest's silence and explained to him that Dona Evarista's case was one of "sumptuary mania," not incurable, and certainly worthy of study.

"In six weeks she'll be cured," he concluded. "I'm sure of it."

The eminent doctor's selfless devotion further enhanced his standing in the town. Rumors, suspicions, and doubts all crumbled into dust, for he had not hesitated to lock up his own wife, whom he loved with all his heart. No one could oppose him now, still less accuse him of having anything but strictly scientific motives.

He was a great and austere man, Hippocrates and Cato rolled into one.

Chapter 11

ITAGUAÍ'S ASTONISHMENT

And now, dear reader, prepare yourself to feel as astonished as did the townspeople of Itaguaí when it was announced that the lunatics in the Casa Verde would all be released.

"All of them?"

"All of them."

"That's impossible. Some of them, perhaps . . . but all?"

"All. That's what he said in the memorandum he sent to the council this morning."

The alienist had indeed sent an official memorandum to the council, setting out the following points, in numbered paragraphs:

1. Having consulted statistics relating to both the town and the Casa Verde, four-fifths of the population are currently residing in said establishment.

2. This displacement of population leads me to examine the fundamental basis of my theory of mental illness, pursuant to which all persons whose faculties are not in perfect equilibrium must be considered insane.

3. As a result of said examination and in the light of said statistics, I am now convinced that the true doctrine is the contrary, and that the disequilibrium of mental faculties should therefore be considered normal and exemplary, whereas those whose mental equilibrium is undisturbed should henceforth be treated as probably pathological.

4. In the light of this discovery, I hereby inform the council that I will set free the current inmates of the Casa Verde, and replace them with such persons as fulfill the conditions set out above.

5. I will spare no effort in the pursuit of scientific truth, and I expect the same dedication on the part of the council.

6. I will repay the council and individuals concerned the sum total of the stipend received for lodging the presumed lunatics, minus any amounts already spent on food, clothing, etc., which the

council can verify upon inspection of the Casa Verde's account ledgers and coffers.

You can imagine the astonishment of the people of Itaguaí, and the joy of the inmates' friends and relations. Banquets, dances, colored lanterns, and music—no expense was spared in celebrating the happy event. I shall not describe the festivities since they are not relevant to our purposes, but they were magnificent, highly emotional, and prolonged.

As is always the way with human affairs, in the midst of the rejoicing provoked by Simão Bacamarte's memorandum, no one paid any attention to the words at the end of the fourth paragraph, which were later to prove of such importance.

Chapter 12

THE END OF THE FOURTH PARAGRAPH

Lanterns were extinguished, families reunited, and everything seemed to return to its rightful place. Order reigned, and the council once again governed without any external interference; its own chairman and Councillor Freitas returned to their respective positions. Porfírio the barber, chastened by events and having "experienced all in life," as the poet said of Napoleon (and even more than that, because Napoleon never experienced the Casa Verde), decided that the obscure glories of razor and scissors were preferable to the brilliant calamities of power. He was, of course, prosecuted by the authorities, but the townspeople begged His Majesty to show clemency, and a pardon was duly granted. João Pina was cleared of all charges, since his actions had brought down a rebel. The chroniclers think it was this that gave birth to our adage, "When a thief robs a thief the sentence is but brief," an immoral saying, it's true, but still highly useful.

All complaints against the alienist ceased, as did any lingering traces of resentment for what he had done. Ever since he had declared the Casa Verde's inmates to be completely sane, they had all been filled with a sense of profound gratitude and fervent enthusiasm. Many of them felt that the alienist deserved special recognition for his services and even gave a ball in his honor, followed by further dinners and celebrations. The chronicles say that, at first, Dona Evarista considered asking for a separation, but the sad prospect of losing the companionship of such a great man overcame any wounded feelings, and the couple ended up even happier than before.

The friendship between the alienist and the apothecary remained equally close. The latter concluded from Simão Bacamarte's memorandum that, in times of revolution, prudence is the most important virtue, and he greatly appreciated the alienist's magnanimity in extending him the hand of friendship when he granted him his liberty.

"He is indeed a great man," said Soares to his wife, referring to the alienist's gesture.

Needless to say, Mateus the saddler, Costa, Coelho, Martim Brito, and all the others mentioned earlier were free to return to their former habits and occupations. Martim Brito, locked up on account of that overenthusiastic speech in praise of Dona Evarista, now gave another speech in honor of the eminent doctor "whose exalted genius spreads its wings far above the sun and leaves beneath it all other spirits of the earth."

"Thank you for your kind words," replied the alienist, "which only serve to remind me how right I was to release you."

Meanwhile, the council, which had replied to Simão Bacamarte's memorandum saying that it would set out its position concerning the end of paragraph four in due course, finally set about legislating on the matter. A bylaw was adopted, without debate, authorizing the alienist to detain in the Casa Verde anyone whose mental faculties were found to be in perfect equilibrium. And after the council's previous painful experience, a clause was included stating that such authorization was provisional in nature and limited to one year, so that the new theory could be put to the test, and authorizing the council to close down the Casa Verde at any time, should this be deemed advisable for reasons of public order. Councillor Freitas also proposed a provision that under no circumstances should any councillor be committed to the mental asylum, and this clause was accepted, voted through, and included in the bylaw, despite Councillor Galvão's objections. The latter's main argument was that the council, in passing legislation relating to a scientific experiment, could not exclude its own members from the consequences of the law; such an exemption was both odious and ridiculous. As soon as he uttered those two words, the other councillors erupted in howls of disapproval at their colleague's audacity and foolishness; for his

part, he heard them out and simply repeated, calmly, that he would vote
against the exemption.

"Our position as councillors," he concluded, "grants us no special powers, nor does it exclude us from the foibles of the human mind."

Simão Bacamarte accepted the bylaw with all its restrictions. As for the
councillors being exempted, he declared that he would have been deeply
saddened had he been compelled to commit a single one of them to the
Casa Verde; the clause itself, however, was the best possible proof that their
mental faculties did not suffer from perfect equilibrium. The same could
not, however, be said for Councillor Galvão, whose wisdom in objecting
to the exemption, and moderation in responding to his colleagues' abusive
tirades, clearly demonstrated a well-organized brain, and on this account
Bacamarte respectfully requested the council to hand him over for treatment. The council, still somewhat offended by Councillor Galvão's behavior, considered the alienist's request and voted unanimously in favor.

It goes without saying that, according to the new theory, a person could
not be committed to the Casa Verde on the basis of a single incident or
word; rather, a long examination was required, exhaustively covering both
past and present. For example, it took thirty days after the bylaw was passed
for Father Lopes to be arrested, and forty days for the apothecary's wife.
This lady's detention filled her husband with indignation. Crispim Soares
left his house spitting with rage, and declaring to whoever he met that he
was going to box the tyrant's ears. Upon hearing this in the street, one of the
alienist's sworn enemies immediately set aside his animosity and rushed to
Simão Bacamarte's house to warn him of the danger. Bacamarte expressed
his gratitude to his erstwhile adversary, and in a matter of minutes ascer-
tained the worthiness and good faith of the man's sentiments, his respect
and generosity toward his fellow man; he thereupon shook him warmly by
the hand and committed him to the Casa Verde.

"A most unusual case," he said to his astonished wife. "Now let's wait for
our good friend Crispim."

Crispim arrived. Sorrow had overcome anger, and the apothecary did
not after all box the alienist's ears. The latter consoled his dear friend, assuring him that all was not lost; his wife might well have some degree of cerebral imbalance, and he, Bacamarte, would examine her very thoroughly to
find out. In the meantime, though, he could scarcely let the woman roam

the streets. Seeing certain advantages in reuniting them—on the basis that
the husband's slippery duplicity might in some way cure the moral refinement he had detected in the wife—Bacamarte told Soares:

"You can work in your dispensary during the day, but you will have
lunch and dinner here with your wife, and stay overnight, and spend all day
here on Sundays and public holidays."

The proposal placed the poor apothecary in the position of Buridan's
ass. He very much wanted to be with his wife, but feared returning to the
Casa Verde; he remained caught in this dilemma for some time, until Dona
Evarista rescued him by promising to visit her dear friend and relay messages
back and forth between them. Crispim Soares gratefully kissed her hands.
This gesture of cowardly egotism struck the alienist as almost sublime.

After five months, there were some eighteen persons residing at the
Casa Verde, but Simão Bacamarte did not let up; he went from street to
street and house to house, observing, asking questions, and taking notes,
and the internment of even one new patient gave him the same pleasure he
had once enjoyed when herding them in by the dozen. It was precisely this
disparity that confirmed his new theory; he had finally discovered the truth
about cerebral pathology. One day, he succeeded in committing the chief
magistrate to the Casa Verde, but only after he had scrupulously carried out
a detailed study of all his judicial decisions and spoken to all the important
people in the town. On more than one occasion, he had found himself on
the verge of committing someone who turned out to be perfectly unbalanced; this is what happened with a certain lawyer, in whom he had identified such a fine array of moral and mental qualities that he considered it
positively dangerous to leave the man at large in society. He ordered him to
be arrested, but the bailiff had doubts and asked Bacamarte if he could conduct an experiment; he went to see a friend of his who had been accused of
forging a will, and advised him to engage Salustiano (the name of the lawyer
in question) to defend him.

"So do you really think he'll . . . ?"

"No doubt about it. Tell him everything, the whole truth, whatever it
may be, and leave the matter entirely in his hands."

The man went to see the lawyer, confessed to having forged the will,
and asked him to take on the case. The lawyer agreed, studied all the papers,
pleaded the case before the court, and proved beyond a shadow of doubt
that the will was completely genuine. The defendant was solemnly declared

innocent by the judge, and the inheritance was his. To this experiment the distinguished lawyer owed his freedom. However, nothing escapes an original and penetrating mind. Simão Bacamarte, who had already noted the bailiff's dedication, wisdom, patience, and restraint, recognized the skill and good judgment with which he had conducted such a tricky and complicated experiment, and ordered him to be committed forthwith to the Casa Verde. He did, however, give him one of the best cells.

Once again, the lunatics were lodged according to their different categories. One wing housed those madmen with a particular tendency for modesty; one was for the tolerant, one for the truthful, one for the innocent, one for the loyal, one for the magnanimous, one for the wise, one for the sincere, and so on. Naturally, the inmates' friends and family objected strongly to this new theory, and some tried to force the council to rescind its authorization. However, the council had not forgotten the language used by Councillor Galvão, and, since he would be released and restored to his former position if they rescinded the bylaw, they refused. Simão Bacamarte wrote to the councillors, not to thank them, but to congratulate them on this act of personal vindictiveness.

Disenchanted with the lawful authorities, some of the leading townspeople went secretly to Porfírio the barber and promised him their wholehearted support, as well as money and influence at court, if he would lead another uprising against the council and the alienist. The barber declined, saying that ambition had driven him to break the law on that first occasion, but that he had seen both the error of his ways and the fickleness of his followers. Since the council had seen fit to authorize the alienist's new experiment for one year, then, in the event of the council rejecting their request, they should either wait until the year was up or petition the viceroy. He, Porfírio, could never advise resorting to means that had already failed him once and resulted in deaths and injuries that would be forever on his conscience.

"What's this you say?" asked the alienist when one of his spies told him about the conversation between the barber and the leading citizens.

Two days later, the barber was taken to the Casa Verde. "I'm damned if I do and damned if I don't!" cried the poor man.

The one-year period came to an end, and the council authorized a six-month extension to allow some new therapies to be tested. The conclusion of this episode in the chronicles of Itaguaí is of such magnitude, and so unexpected, that it deserves a full explanation of no less than ten chapters; I will, however, make do with just one, which will form both the grand finale of my account, and one of the finest-ever examples of scientific conviction and selflessness.

Chapter 13

PLUS ULTRA!

Now it was the turn of therapy. Simão Bacamarte, so assiduous and wise in finding his patients, exceeded even himself in the foresight and diligence with which he began their treatment. On this point all of the chroniclers are in complete agreement: the eminent alienist performed the most astonishing cures, earning him Itaguaí's most ardent admiration.

Indeed, it would be difficult to imagine a more rational system of therapy. Having divided the lunatics into categories according to their predominant moral perfection, Simão Bacamarte set about attacking the leading attribute head-on. Take, for example, modesty. Bacamarte would apply a treatment designed to instill precisely the opposite characteristic—in this case, vanity. Rather than starting immediately with the maximum dose, he would increase it gradually, taking into account the patient's age, condition, temperament, and social position. Sometimes all it took was a tailcoat, a ribbon, a wig, or a cane to restore the patient's sanity; in more stubborn cases he would resort to diamond rings, honorary titles, etc. There was one patient, a poet, who resisted everything. Simão Bacamarte was beginning to despair of finding a cure, when he had the idea of sending out the town crier to proclaim him as great a poet as Garção or Pindar.

"It's a miracle," said the poet's mother to one of her closest friends, "a blessed miracle."

Another patient, also suffering from modesty, exhibited the same resistance to medical treatment; but since he wasn't a writer (he could barely sign his name), the town-crier cure could not be applied. Simão Bacamarte had the idea of petitioning for the man to be appointed secretary of the Academy of Hidden Talents that had been established in Itaguaí. The posts of president and secretary were by royal appointment, in memory of His Late Majesty King João V, and carried with them both the title of "Your Excel-

lency" and the right to wear a gold medallion on one's hat. The government
in Lisbon initially refused the appointment, but when the alienist indicated
that he was not proposing it as a legitimate distinction or honorary award,
but merely as a therapeutic remedy in a difficult case, the government made
an exception and granted his request, although not without extraordinary
efforts on the part of the Minister for the Navy and Colonies, who just so
happened to be the alienist's cousin. Yet another blessed miracle.

"Quite remarkable!" people said in the street, on seeing the healthy,
puffed-up expressions of the two former lunatics.

Such was his system. The rest can be imagined. Each moral or mental
refinement was attacked at the point where its perfection seemed strongest,
and the effect was never in doubt. There were some instances in which the
predominant characteristic resisted all attempts at treatment; in such cases
the alienist would attack another element, conducting his therapies much
as a military strategist would, assailing first one bastion and then another
until the fortress falls.

After five and a half months, the Casa Verde was empty: everyone
was cured! Councillor Galvão, so cruelly afflicted by principles of fairness
and moderation, had the good fortune to lose an uncle; I say good fortune
because the uncle left an ambiguously worded will and Galvão obtained a
favorable interpretation by corrupting the judges and deceiving the other
heirs. The alienist's sincerity was apparent on this occasion; he freely admitted that he had played no part in the cure, and that it had been all down to
the healing power of nature. With Father Lopes it was an entirely different
matter. Knowing that the priest knew absolutely no Hebrew or Greek, the
alienist asked him to write a critical analysis of the Septuagint. The priest
accepted and performed the task in short order; within two months he had
written the book and was a free man. As for the apothecary's wife, she did
not stay long in the cell allocated to her and where she was always treated
kindly and affectionately.

"Why doesn't Crispim come to visit me?" she asked every day.

In reply they gave her one excuse after another; in the end they told
her the truth. The worthy matron could not contain her shame and indignation. During her fits of rage, she would utter random words and phrases
such as these:

"Scoundrel! Villain! Ungrateful cheat! Nothing but a peddler of spurious, rancid lotions and potions . . . Oh, the scoundrel!"

Simão Bacamarte recognized that, even if the accusation itself might not be true, her words were enough to show that the excellent lady was at last restored to a state of perfect mental disequilibrium, and he promptly discharged her.

Now, if you think that the alienist was delighted to see the last inmate leaving the Casa Verde, you will only be revealing how little you know our man. *Plus ultra!* was his motto: Ever Onward! It was not enough for him to have discovered the true theory of insanity; nor was he content to have restored the reign of reason in Itaguaí. *Plus ultra!* Rather than feeling elated, he grew troubled and pensive; something was telling him that his new theory held within it another, even newer theory.

"Let's see," he thought, "let's see if I can finally reach the ultimate truth."

Such were his thoughts as he paced the length of the vast room, which contained the richest library in all His Majesty's overseas possessions. The eminent alienist's majestic and austere body was wrapped in an ample damask robe, tied at the waist by a silken cord with gold tassels (a gift from a university). A powdered wig covered his broad and noble pate, polished smooth by daily scientific cogitations. His feet, neither slim and feminine nor large and uncouth, but entirely in proportion with his shape and size, were protected by a pair of shoes adorned with nothing but a plain brass buckle. Observe the contrast: his only luxuries were those of a scientific origin; everything that related to his own person bore the hallmark of simplicity and moderation, fitting virtues for a sage.

Thus it was that he, the great alienist, paced from one end of the vast library to the other, lost in his own thoughts, oblivious to anything beyond the darkest problems of cerebral pathology. Suddenly he stopped. Standing in front of a window, with his left elbow supported on the palm of his right hand, and his chin resting on the closed fist of his left hand, he asked himself:

"But were they really insane, and cured by me—or was what appeared to be a cure nothing more than the discovery of their natural mental disequilibrium?"

And, digging further into his thoughts, he reached the following conclusion: the well-organized brains he had been so successfully treating were, after all, just as unbalanced as all the rest. He could not pretend, he realized, to have instilled in his patients any sentiment or mental faculty they did not already possess; both of these things must have already existed, in a latent state, perhaps, but there nevertheless.

Upon reaching this conclusion, the eminent alienist experienced two opposing sensations, one of pleasure, the other of dejection. The pleasure was on seeing that, at the end of long and patient investigation, involving unrelenting work and a monumental struggle against the entire population, he could now confirm the following truth: there were no madmen in Itaguaí; the town possessed not one single lunatic. But no sooner had this idea refreshed his soul than another appeared, completely neutralizing the effect of the first: a doubt. What! Not one single well-adjusted brain in the whole of Itaguaí? Would such an extreme conclusion not, by its very nature, be erroneous? And would it not, moreover, destroy the entire majestic edifice of his new psychological doctrine?

The chroniclers of Itaguaí describe the illustrious Simão Bacamarte's anguish as one of the most terrifying moral maelstroms ever to afflict mankind. But such tempests only terrify the weak; the strong brace themselves and stare into the eye of the storm. Twenty minutes later, the alienist's face lit up with a gentle glow.

"Yes, that must be it," he thought.

And here is what it was. Simão Bacamarte had discovered within himself all the characteristics of perfect mental and moral equilibrium. It seemed to him that *he* possessed wisdom, patience, perseverance, tolerance, truthfulness, moral vigor, and loyalty; in other words, all the qualities that together defined a confirmed lunatic. It's true that doubts immediately followed, and he even concluded that he was mistaken; but, being a prudent man, he gathered together a group of friends and asked them for their candid opinion. Their verdict was affirmative.

"Not a single defect?"

"Not one," they replied in unison.

"No vices?"

"None."

"Absolutely perfect?"

"Absolutely."

"No," cried the alienist, "it's impossible! I don't recognize in myself the superiority you have so generously described. You're just saying these things out of kindness. I've examined myself and I can find nothing to justify the excesses of your affections."

The assembled friends insisted; the alienist resisted; finally, Father Lopes explained everything with this astute observation:

"Do you know why you can't see in yourself those lofty virtues we all so admire? It's because you have one further quality that outshines all the rest: modesty."

His words were decisive. Simão Bacamarte bowed his head, both happy and sad, and yet more happy than sad. Without further ado, he committed himself to the Casa Verde. In vain his wife and friends told him to stay, that he was perfectly sane and balanced; but no amount of begging or pleading or tears would detain him for even one moment.

"It is a matter of science," he said. "It concerns an entirely new doctrine, of which I am the very first example. I embody both the theory and the practice."

"Simão! My darling Simão!" wailed his wife, tears streaming down her face.

But the illustrious doctor, his eyes shining with scientific conviction, shut his ears to his wife's pleas, and gently pushed her away. Once the door of the Casa Verde was locked behind him, he devoted himself entirely to the study and cure of himself. The chroniclers say that he died seventeen months later, in the same state in which he entered the Casa Verde, having achieved nothing. Some even speculate that he had always been the sole lunatic in Itaguaí; but this theory, based upon a rumor that circulated after the alienist's death, has no basis beyond the rumor itself, and it is a dubious rumor at that, being attributed to Father Lopes, who had so ardently praised the great man's virtues. In any event, his funeral took place with great pomp and rare solemnity.

HOW TO BE A BIGWIG

A Dialogue

———————

"Are you sleepy?"

"No, Father."

"Neither am I. Let's talk awhile. Open the window. What time is it?"

"Eleven o'clock."

"And the last guest from our modest dinner has just gone home. So, my boy, you have at last reached the age of twenty-one. Yes, twenty-one years ago, on the fifth of August, 1854, you first saw the light of day, a tiny little scrap of a thing, and now you're a man with a fine mustache, a few conquests under your belt—"

"Father!"

"Now, don't act all surprised, and let's have a serious chat, man-to-man. Close the door. I have some important things to tell you. Sit down and let's talk. Twenty-one years old, a private income, and a college degree: you could go into politics, the law, journalism, farming, industry, commerce, literature, or the arts. An infinite number of careers lie before you. Twenty-one, my boy, is but the first syllable of our destiny. Even Pitt and Napoleon, however precocious, had not reached their peak at twenty-one. But whatever profession you choose, my only wish is that you do something great and illustrious, or at least noteworthy, that you raise yourself above the common herd. Life, Janjão, is one enormous lottery; the prizes are few and the unlucky innumerable, and it is upon the sighs of one generation that the hopes of the next are built. That's life; there's no use whining or cursing; we must just accept things as they are, with their burdens and benefits, their glories and blemishes, and press on regardless."

"Yes, Father."

"However, just as it is wise, metaphorically speaking, to set some bread aside for one's old age, so it is also good social practice to keep a career in reserve, just in case the others fail entirely, or do not quite meet our ambitions. That is my advice to you, my son, on this the day when you come of age."

"And I'm grateful for it, Father. But what career do you have in mind?"

"To me, there is no career as useful or as fitting as that of bigwig. As a young man, my dream was to be a bigwig. I lacked, however, a father's advice, and so I have ended up as you can see, with no other consolation or moral support beyond the hopes I place in you. So listen to me carefully, son; listen and learn. You are young, you naturally possess the fire, the exuberance, and the impulsiveness of your years; do not reject them, but moderate them so that by the time you're forty-five, you are ready to enter the age of measure and reason. The wise man who said, "Gravity is a mystery of the body invented to conceal the defects of the mind," defined the very essence of a bigwig. Do not confuse this gravity with the other kind, which, although also present in outward appearances, is a pure reflex or emanation of the mind; the gravity of which I speak is a matter only of the body, whether natural or acquired. As for the age of forty-five . . ."

"Yes, indeed, why forty-five?"

"It is not, as you might suppose, an arbitrary number plucked out of the air; it is the normal age at which the phenomenon occurs. Generally speaking, the true bigwig begins to appear between the ages of forty-five and fifty, although some cases do occur between fifty-five and sixty, but these are rare. There are also some who emerge at forty, and others even earlier, at thirty-five or even thirty; they are not, however, at all common. I won't even mention those who become bigwigs at twenty-five; such precocity is the privilege of genius."

"I see."

"But let's get to the main point. Once you have embarked on this career, you must be extremely cautious about any ideas you may cultivate, either for your own use or for the use of others. The best thing would be not to have any ideas at all. This is something you can easily grasp by imagining, for example, an actor deprived of the use of one arm. He can, through sheer

talent and skill, conceal his disability from the audience, but it would nevertheless be much better for him to have both arms. The same is true of ideas;
it is possible, by violent effort, to smother or conceal them permanently,
but that is a very rare skill, and not one conducive to the normal enjoyment
of life."

"But who says that I—"

"You, my son, if I am not mistaken, seem to be endowed with the perfect degree of mental vacuity required by such a noble profession. I refer not
so much to the fidelity with which you repeat in a drawing room opinions
you have heard on the street corner, or vice versa, because this fact, while
indicative of a certain absence of original thought, might well be nothing
more than a slip of the memory. No, I am referring to the punctilious and
statesmanlike stance you tend to adopt when expounding your views, for or
against, regarding the cut of a vest, the dimensions of a hat, or the squeaki-
ness (or absence thereof) of a new pair of boots. Therein lies a symptom that
speaks volumes; therein lies a hope. It is not, however, inconceivable that,
with age, you may come to be afflicted with some ideas of your own, and so
it is important to equip your mind with strong defenses. Ideas are by their
very nature spontaneous and sudden; however hard we try, they burst forth
and rush upon us. This is precisely what enables the man in the street, who
has a very fine nose for this kind of thing, to distinguish with absolute certainty the true bigwig from the false."

"I'm sure you're right, but that is surely an insurmountable obstacle."

"No, it isn't. There is a way. You must throw yourself into a punishing regime of reading books on rhetoric, listening to certain speeches, and
so on. Gin rummy, dominoes, and whist are all tried and tested remedies.
Whist even has the rare advantage of getting one accustomed to silence, and
silence is the most extreme form of circumspection. I wouldn't say the same
about swimming, horse-riding, or gymnastics, even though they do force
the brain to rest; but it is precisely in resting the brain that they restore its
lost strength and vitality. Billiards, on the other hand, is excellent."

"How's that? Doesn't billiards also involve physical exercise?"

"I'm not saying that it doesn't, but there are some things in which observation trumps theory. I recommend billiards to you only because the most
scrupulously compiled statistics show that three-quarters of those who
wield a billiard cue pretty much share the same opinions as the cue itself.
An afternoon stroll, particularly in places of amusement and public display,

is highly beneficial, provided you don't sally forth unaccompanied. For solitude is the workshop of ideas, and if the mind is left to its own devices, even
in the midst of a crowd, it is prone to lapse into some unwarranted activity
or other."

"But what if I don't have a friend on hand willing and able to go with me?"

"Not to worry; there are always those habitual gathering places of idlers,
where all the dust of solitude is blown away. Bookshops, perhaps because of
their studious atmosphere, or for some other reason that escapes me, are not
suitable for our purpose. However, it can be worthwhile visiting them from
time to time, as long as you make sure everyone sees you doing it. There is a
simple way of resolving this dilemma: go to a bookshop solely to talk about
the rumor of the day, the funny story of the week, some salacious affair or
scandal, a passing comet, or whatever it may be (unless, of course, you'd
rather approach habitual readers of Monsieur Mazade's erudite columns in
the *Revue des Deux Mondes*); seventy-five percent of these worthy denizens
will repeat to you exactly the same opinions, and such monotony is eminently useful. By following this regime for eight, ten, eighteen months—
let's call it two years—you can reduce the most prodigious of intellects to a
sober, disciplined, and tedious equilibrium. I haven't mentioned vocabulary,
for words are implied by the ideas they convey; it goes without saying that
it should be simple, vapid, and strictly limited—definitely no purple notes
or shrill colors."

"That's awful! Not being able to add a few rhetorical flourishes once in
a while . . ."

"Oh, but you can; there's a whole host of figures of speech you can
use: the Lernean Hydra, for example, or the head of Medusa, the cask of
the Danaids, the wings of Icarus, and all those many others that romanti-
cists, classicists, and realists employ without compunction whenever the
need arises. Latin tags, historical sayings, famous verses, legal axioms, witty
maxims—it's a good idea to have them readily to hand for after-dinner
speeches, toasts, and so on. *Caveant, consules* is an excellent way to conclude
anything with a political theme, and I would say the same of *Si vis pacem,
para bellum*. Some people like to refresh an old quotation by working it into
a new, original, and beautiful sentence, but I would advise against a trick
like that; it will only warp the quotation's venerable charm. However, better
than all of these, which, at the end of the day, are mere trimmings, are the
clichés and traditional sayings handed down from generation to generation,

burned into both the individual and the public memory. These expressions
have the advantage of not requiring any unnecessary effort on the part of
your listeners. I won't list them all now, but will set them down in writing
later. Beyond that, your new profession will itself gradually teach you the
difficult art of thinking what has already been thought. As for the usefulness of such a system, just imagine one hypothesis. A law is passed, put into
force, but has no effect; the evil persists. Here lies a subject to whet idle
curiosities, instigate mind-numbing inquiry, the fastidious collection of documents and observations, the analysis of probable, possible, and definitive
causes, the endless study of the capacity of the individual to be reformed,
the nature of the evil, the formulation of a remedy, and the circumstances in
which it should be applied; in short, enough material for a whole edifice of
words, opinions, and nonsensical ramblings. You, however, will spare your
fellow man this long harangue by simply saying: "Reform habits, not laws!"
And this short, transparent, limpid phrase, pulled from the common purse,
instantly solves the problem, and lifts everyone's spirits like a sudden shaft
of sunlight."

"I see by this, Father, that you condemn the application of any and all
modern methodologies."

"Let me be quite clear. I do indeed condemn their application, but I
heartily approve of the phrase itself. I would say the same thing regarding
all recent scientific terminology, all of which you should learn by heart.
Although the distinguishing characteristic of a bigwig may well be a rather
unyielding attitude reminiscent of the god Terminus, whereas the sciences
are the product of everyday human endeavor, if you are to become a bigwig
later on in life, you should arm yourself with the most up-to-date weapons.
Because one of two things will happen: either these scientific terms and
expressions will be worn out from overuse in thirty years' time, or they
will keep themselves fresh and new. In the first case, they will fit you like
an old glove; in the second case, you can wear them in your buttonhole to
show that you, too, know what's what. From scraps of conversation, you will
eventually form some sort of idea about which laws, cases, and phenomena
all this terminology corresponds to; because the alternative method of scientific inquiry—from the books and theses of the experts themselves—as
well as being tedious and tiring, brings with it the danger of exposure to
new ideas, and is thus fundamentally false. Furthermore, if you were ever
truly to master the spirit of those laws and formulae, you would probably

be inclined to employ them with a certain moderation, like the shrewd and prosperous seamstress of whom a classical poet wrote:

> The more cloth she has the more sparingly she cuts,
> And the smaller the pile of scraps left over.

"It goes without saying that such behavior on the part of a bigwig would be most unscientific."

"My word, it's a tricky business!"

"And we're not finished yet."

"Well, then, let's carry on."

"I haven't yet spoken to you about the benefits of publicity. Publicity is a haughty and seductive mistress, and you should woo her with little gifts, sugared almonds, lavender sachets, and other tiny things expressive more of the constancy of your affections than of the boldness of your ambitions. Soliciting her favors through heroic deeds and sacrifices is something best left to Don Quixote and other such lunatics. The true bigwig takes an entirely different approach. Rather than composing a *Scientific Treatise on Sheep Breeding*, he buys a lamb and regales his friends with it in the form of a dinner, news of which cannot fail to rouse the interest of your fellow citizens. One thing leads to another, and before you know it, your name is in the newspapers five, ten, or even twenty times. Committees and delegations for congratulating war heroes, distinguished citizens, or foreigners are particularly beneficial, as are church organizations and various clubs and societies, whether devoted to mythology, hunting, or ballet. Even certain minor incidents can be mentioned, provided they serve to show you in a good light. Let me explain. If you were to fall from a carriage suffering nothing more than a nasty shock, it would be useful to trumpet the fact to all and sundry. Not on account of the incident in itself, which is insignificant, but for the purpose of reminding public affections of a name that is dear to them. Do you understand?"

"Yes, I do."

"That is your cheap, easy, workaday publicity, but there is more. Whatever the theory of art may have to say on the subject, it is beyond doubt that family sentiment, personal friendship, and public esteem all encourage the artistic reproduction of a well-loved or distinguished man's physiognomy. Nothing prevents you from being the object of such distinction, particularly if your discerning friends sense no reluctance on your part. In that case, not only are you required by the rules of common courtesy to accept the portrait or bust so offered, but you would also be ill-advised to prevent your friends from arranging a public exhibition of said portrait. In this way your name becomes firmly attached to your person; those who have read your recent speech, say, to the inaugural congress of the National Union of Hairdressers will recognize in your rugged features the author of such a weighty peroration, in which the "levers of progress" and the "sweat of the brow" overcame the "gaping gullets" of poverty. In the event of a delegation bringing the portrait to your home, you should thank them for their kindness with a grateful speech and a banquet—a venerable, sensible, and honest custom. You will, of course, also invite your closest friends, your relations, and, if possible, one or two prominent figures. Furthermore, since the day is one of glory and jubilation, I do not see how you could decently refuse a place at your table to some newspaper reporters. In the unfortunate event that the duties of these gentlemen of the press have detained them elsewhere, you can help them out by yourself drafting a report of the celebrations. And should you, on account of some entirely understandable scruple, not wish to apply the requisite glowing adjectives yourself, then ask a friend or relation to do it."

"None of this is going to be easy, Father."

"You're absolutely right, son. It's difficult and will take time, lots of time, indeed years of patience and toil, but happy are they who reach the Promised Land! Those who fail will be swallowed up by obscurity. But those who triumph? And, believe me, you will triumph. You will see the walls of Jericho fall at the sound of the holy trumpets. Only then will you be able to say that you have arrived. On that day you will have become the indispensable ornament, the obligatory presence, the social fixture. There'll be no more need to sniff out opportunities, committees, clubs, and societies; they will come to you with the dull, crude air about them of de-adjectivized nouns, and you will be the adjective of their leaden speeches, the *fragrant* of their flowers, the *indigo* of their sky, the *upstanding* of their citizens, the *trenchant* and *meaty* of their news reports. And this is the most important thing of all, because the adjective is the very soul of language, its idealistic and metaphysical component. The noun is reality stripped naked and raw; it is the naturalism of vocabulary."

"And all this, you think, is just a standby in case all else fails?"

"That's right. It doesn't preclude any other activity whatsoever."

"Not even politics?"

"Not even politics. It is simply a matter of abiding by certain basic rules and obligations. You may belong to any party, liberal or conservative, republican or ultramontane, the one caveat being that you must not attach any specific ideas to these words, and only recognize their usefulness as biblical shibboleths."

"If I go into parliament, can I speak from the rostrum?"

"You can and you must; it is a way of attracting public attention. As for the subject of your speeches, you have a choice between pettifogging minutiae and political ideology, but with a preference for ideology. Minutiae, one must admit, are not inconsistent with the urbane dullness that is the mark of every accomplished bigwig, but, if you can, go for ideology—it's easier and much more appealing. Suppose you were to inquire into the reasons for transferring the Seventh Company of Infantry from Uruguaiana to Canguçu; you will be heard only by the minister of war, and it will take him all of ten minutes to explain the reasons for his decision. Not so with ideology. A speech on the most arcane aspects of political ideology will, by its very nature, excite the passions of politicians and the public gallery, provoking heated interjections and rebuttals. Moreover, it requires neither thought nor investigation. In this branch of human knowledge everything has already been discovered, worded, labeled, and packaged; you need only rummage around in the saddlebags of memory. But whatever you do, never go beyond the boundaries of enviable triteness."

"I'll do what I can. So no imagination, then?"

"None whatsoever. Much better to put the word around that the gift of imagination is very low-class indeed."

"And no philosophy?"

"Let's be quite clear: a smattering perhaps when writing or speaking, but in reality, none. 'Philosophy of history,' for example, is a phrase you should frequently employ, but I forbid you to arrive at any conclusions that have not already been reached by others. Avoid anything that has about it so much as a whiff of reflection, originality, or the like."

"And humor?"

"What do you mean, 'humor'?"

"Should I always be very serious?"

"It all depends. You have a jovial, fun-loving nature and there's no need to smother or suppress it entirely—you can laugh and joke once in a while.

Being a bigwig doesn't necessarily require you to be a melancholic. A serious man can have his lighthearted moments too. Only—and this is a crucial point . . ."

"Go on."

"You must never use irony—that mysterious little twitch at the corners of the mouth, invented by some decadent Greek, caught by Lucian, transmitted to Swift and Voltaire, and typical of all skeptics and impudent freethinkers. No. Better to tell a rude joke, our good old friend, the chubby-cheeked, brash, and blatantly rude joke, wrapped in neither veils nor false modesty, which hits you right between the eyes, stings like a slap on the back, makes your blood pound, and snaps your suspenders with laughter. What's that?"

"It's midnight."

"Midnight? Well, then, young man, you are already entering your twenty-second year; you have definitively come of age. Let's turn in; it's late. Chew over what I've told you, son. All things considered, our conversation tonight has been worthy of Machiavelli's *The Prince*. Time for bed."

THE TURKISH SLIPPER

———————

B EHOLD YOUNG MASTER DUARTE, Bachelor of Arts. He has just tied
his necktie with the stiffest and most fastidious knot yet seen in that
year of 1850, when he is told that Major Lopo Alves has just arrived. Note
that it is already late, past nine o'clock. Duarte shudders, and he has two
reasons for doing so. Firstly, that the major was, at the best of times, one of
the most tiresome bores of his day. Secondly, that he, Duarte, was, at that
precise moment, on his way out to a dance where he would gaze upon the
finest blond hair and most thoughtful blue eyes that this climate of ours, so
miserly when it comes to such delicate features, had ever produced. It was a
week-old romance. His heart, allowing itself to be captivated between two
waltzes, entrusted his brown eyes with the necessary declaration, which
they promptly transmitted to the young lady ten minutes before suppertime, and received a favorable response shortly after the hot chocolate was
served. Three days later, the first letter was dispatched, and the way things
were going it would be no surprise if, before the year was out, they were
traipsing up the aisle. In circumstances such as these, the arrival of Lopo
Alves was nothing short of calamitous. An old friend of the family, his late
father's army companion, the major was entitled to the utmost respect.
There was no question of sending him away or giving him a chilly reception.
Happily, there were attenuating circumstances: the major was a relative of
Cecília, the girl with the blue eyes. Should the need arise, the major's vote
was in the bag.

Duarte slipped on a dressing gown and made his way to the drawing room, where Lopo Alves, a bundle of papers under his arm and his eyes staring into space, seemed entirely unaware of the young man's entry.

"What fair wind brings you to Catumbi at such an hour?" inquired Duarte, giving his voice a jovial ring as much out of self-interest as out of natural good manners.

"I don't know if the wind that brought me was fair or foul," replied the major, smiling beneath his thick, grizzled mustache, "but I do know there was a good, stiff breeze. Are you going out?"

"I'm just heading over to Rio Comprido."

"Of course. You're going to the Widow Meneses's house. My wife and the girls must already be there; I'll go later, if I can. It's still early, is it not?"

Lopo Alves then pulled out his pocket watch and saw that it was half-past nine. He stroked his mustache, stood up, took several paces about the room, sat down again, and said:

"I have some news for you, news which you are certainly not expecting. I wanted to tell you that I have written . . . I have written a play."

"A play!" exclaimed the graduate.

"What can I say? I have suffered from these literary ailments ever since I was a child. Military service did not cure me; it merely relieved the symptoms. The illness has returned in all its former strength. It's too late for any remedy now, and all I can do is accept it and let nature take its course."

Duarte remembered that the major had indeed spoken on a previous occasion of several inaugural addresses, two or three eulogies, and a fair number of articles he had written about the River Plate campaigns. For many years, however, Lopo Alves had let the Platine generals and the dead rest in peace, and there had been nothing to suggest that the illness would return, still less in the form of a drama. Our young graduate would have had a better understanding of the situation if he had known that, a few weeks earlier, Lopo Alves had attended the performance of a drama of the ultra-romantic variety, which had greatly pleased him and had planted the idea in his head of braving the footlights himself. However, the major failed to vouchsafe these necessary details, and the graduate remained unaware of the reason behind this explosion of dramatic energy. Indeed, he neither knew nor wished to remedy his ignorance. Instead, he extolled the major's intellectual abilities, expressed his fervent wish to attend what would surely be a triumphant opening night, promised to recommend it to some friends of his who wrote for the *Correio Mercantil*, and only paused for breath, and promptly turned pale, when he saw the major, trembling with pleasure, unroll the bundle of papers he had brought with him.

"I'm very grateful for your good intentions," said Lopo Alves, "and I gladly accept your promise of support, but, first, I have another favor to ask of you. I know you're an intelligent, well-read man, and you must tell me frankly what you think of my work. I'm not asking for compliments; what I want from you is honesty, and brutal honesty, at that. If you think it's no good, you must say so without mincing your words."

Duarte would have liked to let that bitter cup pass, but it was difficult to ask and impossible to refuse. Dejectedly, he consulted his watch, which now showed five minutes to ten, while the major leafed paternally through the one hundred and eighty pages of the manuscript.

"It will be very quick," said Lopo Alves. "I know what you young men are like, especially when it comes to dances. Don't worry—you'll still be able to dance two or three waltzes with your young lady, if you have one, or with all of them, if you don't. Wouldn't it be better if we went into your study?"

For the hapless young man, the place of torture was immaterial; he submitted to his guest's wishes. The latter, with the liberty to which his position entitled him, told the houseboy not to let anyone disturb them. The torturer did not want any witnesses. The study door closed, and Lopo Alves took up his position by the desk, facing the young man, who sank both his body and his despair into a vast leather armchair, determined to say not a word so that the end would come sooner.

The drama was divided into seven scenes. This information alone made the reluctant listener shudder. The only novelty in those hundred and eighty pages would be the author's own handwriting. The rest would be the situations, characters, plot devices, and even the style of the most hackneyed of tousle-headed romanticism. Lopo Alves thought he had created a work of originality, when he had done nothing more than cobble together his own reminiscences. At any other moment, this might have amounted to an amusing entertainment. Early on in the first scene—a sort of prologue—there was an abducted child, a poisoning, two masked men, the point of a dagger, and a host of equally dagger-sharp adjectives. In the second scene, there occurred the death of one of the masked men, who would come back to life in the third, only to be taken prisoner in the fifth, and kill the tyrant in the seventh. As well as the apparent death of the masked man, the second scene included the kidnapping of the child, by then a young lady of seventeen years, a monologue that seemed to last at least the same amount of time, and the theft of a will.

It was almost eleven o'clock when he finished reading the second scene. Duarte could barely contain his anger; by now it was far too late to go to Rio Comprido. It would not be idle conjecture to imagine that if, at that moment, the major had breathed his last, Duarte would have given thanks for his death as a gift of Divine Providence. The young man's fine sentiments would not lead one to suspect such ferocious feelings, but reading a bad book is capable of producing the most astonishing effects. In addition to which, while our young graduate's eyes gazed blankly at Lopo Alves's thick and shaggy mane, in his mind's eye there burned the golden threads that adorned the fair, sweet head of Cecília; he could see her blue eyes, the pale bloom of her complexion, and her delicate, graceful gestures, surpassing all the other ladies in Widow Meneses's drawing room. Not only could he see it, he could hear in his head the music, the conversation, the sound of footsteps, and the rustle of silk, while Lopo Alves's voice droned hoarsely on through scene after scene, dialogue after dialogue, with all the impassiveness of devout conviction.

Time was marching on, and the listener had, by now, lost count of the scenes. Midnight had struck long ago; he had missed the dance entirely. All of a sudden, the major rolled up his manuscript, stood up straight, fixed him with an evil, hate-filled gaze, and rushed hastily from the room. Duarte wanted to call after him, but surprise had numbed both voice and limbs. When he regained control of his senses, he could hear the irritable, metallic click of the dramaturge's heels on the cobbled sidewalk outside.

He went to the window; he could neither see nor hear anything. Both author and drama had vanished.

"Why couldn't he have done that earlier?" the graduate asked himself with a sigh.

The sigh barely had time to spread its wings and fly out the window in search of Rio Comprido, when the houseboy came to tell him that there was a short, fat man at the front door.

"At this hour!" exclaimed Duarte.

"Yes, at this hour," replied the short, fat man, entering the drawing room. "When it concerns a serious crime, the police may enter a citizen's house at this or any hour."

"A crime!"

"I believe you know who I am . . ."

"I haven't had that honor."

"I work for the police."

"But what crime are you talking about? What has this to do with me?"

"A minor offense: a theft. You are accused, sir, of having made off with a Turkish slipper. It would seem that the slipper in question is of little or no value, but there are slippers and slippers. It all depends on the circumstances."

The man said this with a sarcastic laugh, while fixing our young graduate with the eyes of an inquisitor. Duarte was not even aware of the existence of the stolen object. He concluded that it must be a case of mistaken identity and resolved not to rise to the insult being hurled at his person, and to some extent at his class, with this accusation of petty larceny. This is what he said to the police officer, adding that, in any event, this was no justification for disturbing him at such a late hour.

"Do forgive me," said the representative of the law. "The slipper in question is worth several dozen *contos de réis*; it's adorned with the finest of diamonds, making it particularly precious. It is Turkish not only in shape, but also in origin. Its owner, one of the most well-traveled ladies of our nobility, was in Egypt approximately three years ago, where she purchased it from a Jew. The story told her by this follower of Moses regarding the aforementioned product of Muslim art is truly miraculous, and, to my way of thinking, completely false. But it is not my place to say so. What matters is that she was robbed, and the police have received a complaint against you, sir."

By this point in his speech, the man was standing by the window; Duarte suspected him to be a lunatic or a thief. However, he had no time to think further, because a few seconds later five armed men entered the room and proceeded to grab him and push him down the steps, oblivious to his shouts and his desperate attempts to free himself. Outside in the street was a carriage, which they bundled him into. The short, fat man was already inside, along with a tall, thin individual; they hauled him in and made him sit in the back of the carriage. He heard the crack of the coachman's whip, and the carriage set off at a tilt.

"Aha!" said the fat man. "So you thought you could get away with steal-ing Turkish slippers, courting pretty blond ladies, possibly marrying them, and still thumb your nose at the human race?"

Hearing this allusion to the lady of his thoughts, Duarte shuddered. Could this be some sort of revenge by a supplanted rival? Or was the refer-ence merely coincidental? Duarte lost himself in a thicket of conjectures, while the carriage continued to career forward at a full gallop. After a while, he ventured an observation.

"Whatever my crimes may be, I presume that the police—"

"We aren't the police," the thin man interrupted coolly.

"Ah!"

"This gentlemen and I are a pair. He, you, and I will make a trio. Of course, a trio is no better than a pair, indeed how could it be? The ideal is a couple. You probably don't understand me, do you?"

"No, I don't."

"You will soon enough."

Duarte resigned himself to waiting, sank into silence, and slumped back in his seat, letting both the carriage and the adventure run their course. Some five minutes later, the horses came to a halt.

"Here we are," said the fat man.

And as he said this, he pulled a handkerchief from his pocket and handed it to our young hero to use as a blindfold. Duarte refused, but the thin man remarked that it would be more prudent on his part to obey than resist. Duarte did not resist; he himself tied the handkerchief about his head to cover his eyes and stepped out of the carriage. Then he heard a door creak; two people—probably the same two who had accompanied him in the carriage—held his hands and led him down endless corridors and stairways. On the way, he could hear unfamiliar voices, random words, and snatches of sentences. Finally, they stopped; he was told to sit down and remove the blindfold. Duarte obeyed, but only to find that there was no one there.

He was in a vast room, brightly lit and elegantly and opulently fur-nished. The decoration was perhaps a little overdone; nevertheless, the per-son who had chosen it must have had very refined tastes.

The bronzes, the lacquerware, the rugs and mirrors—the abundance of objects filling the room—were all of the finest quality. The sight of this restored a certain serenity to the young man's mind; it seemed unlikely that this could be the home of thieves.

He leaned back languidly on an ottoman . . . An ottoman! This promptly reminded him of how this whole adventure had begun, and about the stolen slipper. A few moments of reflection were enough for him to realize that the slipper in question had become more than problematic. Digging deeper into the world of conjectures, he seemed to stumble upon a new and definitive explanation. The slipper was simply a metaphor; it represented Cecília's heart, which he had stolen, a crime for which his supposed rival now wished to punish him. This must, of course, be linked to the thin man's mysterious words: "a pair is better than a trio; the ideal is a couple."

"That's what it must be," concluded Duarte. "But who, then, is this rejected suitor?"

At that moment, a door at the far end of the room opened and there appeared the black cassock of a pale, bald priest. Duarte sprang to his feet. The priest slowly crossed the room, pausing to bless Duarte as he passed, and left by another door in the wall opposite. Our young graduate stood there motionless, his eyes fixed on the door, staring without seeing, completely dumbstruck. The priest's unexpected appearance confounded all his previous theories about the adventure. However, there was no time to think up a new explanation, because the first door once again opened and another figure entered; this time it was the thin man, who came straight over to Duarte and asked him to follow him. Duarte did as he was told. They went out through a third door, and, making their way along several dimly lit corridors, they came to another room, lit only by the candles in the two silver candlesticks placed on a wide table. At the head of the table sat an old man who looked about fifty-five; he had an athletic body, very thick hair, and a bushy beard.

"Do you know who I am?" asked the old man as soon as Duarte entered the room.

"No, I do not, sir."

"No need. What we are about to do requires no introductions. You should first know that the theft of the slipper was a mere pretext—"

"Quite!" said Duarte, interrupting him.

"A mere pretext," continued the old man, "to bring you to our house. The slipper was not stolen; it never left its owner's possession. João Rufino, bring the slipper."

The thin man left the room, and the old man informed our young graduate that the famous slipper was not sewn with diamonds, nor had it been purchased from a Jew in Egypt. It was, however, Turkish, according to what he'd been told, and it was miraculously small. Duarte listened to this explanation and, summoning all his strength, asked resolutely:

"But, sir, will you not tell me, once and for all, what you want from me and why I am here in this house?"

"All in due course," replied the old man calmly.

The door opened, and the thin man appeared, holding the slipper. Invited to come closer to the light, Duarte was able to ascertain that the slipper was indeed miraculously small. It was made of the finest Moroccan leather and on its padded insole, lined with blue silk, gleamed two gold-embroidered letters.

"A child's slipper, wouldn't you say?" said the old man.

"I suppose so."

"Then you suppose wrongly; it is a young lady's slipper."

"If you say so, but it has nothing to do with me."

"Excuse me, but it has everything to do with you, because you will marry the owner of this slipper."

"Marry?" exclaimed Duarte.

"Precisely. João Rufino, go and fetch the slipper's owner."

The thin man went out, and returned soon afterward. As he appeared, he drew back the door curtain and a woman entered. She walked toward the middle of the room. She was no mere woman, but a sylph, a poet's vision, a divine creature.

Her hair was blond and her eyes blue, like Cecília's; rapturous eyes that sought heaven or seemed to live by it. Her hair, untidily pinned back, formed a halo around her head like that of a saint; only a saint, mind, not a martyr, because the smile that played upon her lips was a smile of holy bliss the like of which has rarely been seen on Earth.

Her body was chastely clothed in a white dress of the finest linen, leaving little visible to the eye, but much to the imagination.

A young man such as ours does not lose his elegant manners, even in situations like this. Upon seeing the young lady, Duarte adjusted his dressing gown, straightened his necktie, and bowed ceremoniously, and she responded with such politeness and grace that the adventure began to appear much less terrifying.

"My dear sir, this is the bride in question."

The young lady lowered her eyes; Duarte replied that he had no wish to marry.

"There are three things you will do right now," the old man continued impassively. "The first is to marry, the second is to write your will, and the third is to swallow a particular drug from the Levant—"

"Poison!" cried Duarte.

"It is commonly known as such, but I give it another name: a passport to heaven."

Duarte turned pale and cold. He tried to speak, but couldn't; not even a whimper escaped his lips. He would have fallen to the floor, had there not been a chair nearby into which he let himself sink.

"You have a modest fortune," continued the old man, "of one hundred and fifty *contos de réis*. This pearl standing before you will be your sole heiress. João Rufino, go and fetch the priest."

The priest entered, the same priest who had blessed our young graduate a short time earlier. He went straight over to the young man, solemnly mumbling a passage from Nehemiah, or some other minor prophet. He crossed himself and said:

"Stand up!"

"No! I don't want to! I will not marry!"

"Is that so?" said the old man from the other side of the table, pointing a pistol at him.

"So it's murder, is it?"

"It is, but the difference lies in the manner of your death. You can either die violently from a bullet or gently by taking the drug. You choose!"

Duarte was sweating and shaking. He wanted to stand up, but couldn't. His knees were knocking. The priest came and whispered in his ear:

"Do you want to escape?"

"Yes!" he exclaimed, although not with his lips, for then he would have been overheard, but with his eyes, in which he placed every remaining hope of life.

"See that window over there? It's open and beneath it is the garden. Jump out now; it's quite safe."

"Oh, Father!" whispered our young man.

"I'm not a priest; I'm an army lieutenant. But don't say a word."

The window stood slightly ajar; through the crack he could see a sliver of sky, already brightening. Duarte did not hesitate; he summoned all his strength and jumped, throwing himself upon the mercy of God. It wasn't very high, and the young man didn't have far to fall; he quickly picked himself up, but the fat man, who was out in the garden, caught up with him.

"What's all this?" he asked, laughing.

Duarte did not answer; he clenched his fists, beat them violently against the man's chest, and started running across the lawn. The man didn't fall despite the heavy blows, and when he'd recovered, he immediately set off in pursuit of the fugitive. Thus began a breakneck chase. Duarte scaled fences and walls, trampled flower beds, and collided with the trees that, from time to time, rose up in front of him. Sweat poured down his body, his chest heaved, and, little by little, his strength began to ebb away; one of his hands was gashed, his shirt damp with dew from the leaves; twice he was almost captured when his dressing gown got caught on a thorny hedge. At last, tired, bruised, and out of breath, he stumbled and fell on the stone steps leading up to a house standing in the middle of a garden.

He looked back, but saw no one; his pursuer was nowhere to be seen, or at least not yet. Duarte struggled to his feet, climbed the remaining four steps, and crept into the house through a door that stood open and led into a small, low-ceilinged room.

A man was sitting there, reading a copy of the *Jornal do Commercio*, but he seemed not to have noticed him enter. Duarte collapsed into a chair. He stared at the man. It was Major Lopo Alves.

The major, still holding the newspaper, whose dimensions were gradually becoming smaller and smaller, suddenly exclaimed:

"Angel of heaven, you are avenged! End of the last scene."

Duarte looked at him, at the table and at the walls, rubbed his eyes, and took a deep breath.

"So, what do you think?"

"Excellent!" replied the graduate, standing up.

"Strong stuff, isn't it?"

"The very strongest. What time is it?"

"It's just gone two."

Duarte accompanied the major to the door, took another deep breath, brushed himself down, and went over to the window. No one knows what he thought for those first few minutes, but after a quarter of an hour, here is what he said to himself: "Nymph, sweet maid, restless, fertile fantasy! You saved me from a terrible play with a strange and original dream; you replaced tedium with a nightmare: it was a good bargain. A good bargain and a grave lesson: you proved to me that the best drama often lies in the spectator and not on the stage."

IN THE ARK

Three Unpublished Chapters from the Book of Genesis

Chapter A

1. Then Noah said unto his sons Japheth, Shem, and Ham: "Let us leave the ark, according to the will of the Lord; we and our wives, and all the animals. The ark shall come to rest upon a mountaintop; there will we disembark.
2. "Because the Lord has fulfilled His promise, when He said unto me: 'I have resolved to bring an end to all living flesh; wickedness rules over the earth and I will make all men perish. Thou shalt make a wooden ark and go into it; thou, thy wife, and thy sons.
3. "'And thy sons' wives, and two of every beast.'
4. "Now that the Lord's promise has been fulfilled, and all men have perished, and the torrents of heaven have abated, we will return to inhabit the earth, and live in the bosom of peace and harmony."
5. Thus spoke Noah, and the sons of Noah felt great joy upon hearing the words of their father; and Noah left them alone, withdrawing into one of the cabins inside the ark.
6. Then Japheth lifted up his voice and said: "A life of pleasure shall be ours. The fig tree shall give us its fruit, the sheep its wool, the cow its milk, the sun its light, and the night its shelter.

7. "For we will be the only ones upon the earth, and all the land shall be ours, and none shall disturb the peace of a family saved from the punishment that cut down all of mankind.

8. "Forever and ever." Then Shem, upon hearing his brother speak, said: "I have an idea." To which Japheth and Ham replied: "Let us hear this idea, Shem.

9. And Shem spoke with the voice of his heart, saying: "My father has his family; each one of us has his family; there is an abundance of land; we can live in separate tents. Each one of us will do as he thinks best: planting, hunting, hewing wood, or spinning flax."

10. And Japheth replied: "I think Shem's idea well thought; we can live in separate tents. The ark will come to rest upon a mountaintop; my father and Ham will disembark on the side of the rising sun; Shem and I on the side of the setting sun. Shem will occupy two hundred cubits of land, and I another two hundred."

11. But when Shem spoke, saying: "Two hundred cubits is but little," Japheth replied: "Then let it be five hundred each. Between thy land and mine shall be a river that divides them, so that our lands may be clearly marked. I shall keep to the left bank and thou to the right bank;

12. "And my land will be called the land of Japheth, and thine will be called the land of Shem; and we will each visit the tent of the other, and together we will break the bread of joy and harmony."

13. And, having approved the division, Shem asked Japheth: "But what about the river? To whom will the waters of the river, the current itself, belong?

14. "Because we possess the riverbanks, but we have said nothing about the current." And Japheth replied that they could fish from either side. But his brother disagreed, proposing to divide the river into two parts, by putting a stick in the middle. Japheth, however, said that the current would sweep the stick away.

15. And Japheth having replied thus, his brother answered him: "Since the stick does not serve thee, I will have the river and both of its banks; and so that there be no conflict between us,

thou canst build a wall, ten or twelve cubits from the bank that was thine.

16. "And if by this thou losest something, the difference is not great, and nor is it any less fitting, so that the peace between us may never be disturbed, according to the will of the Lord."

17. But Japheth replied: "Get thee hence! By what right dost thou take the riverbank, which is mine, and rob me of a piece of my land? Art thou better than I,

18. "Or fairer, or more beloved of my father? What right hast thou to violate so scandalously the property of another?

19. "For now I say unto thee that the river shall be mine, along with both of its banks, and if thou darest enter upon my land, I will slay thee just as Cain slew his brother."

20. Hearing this, Ham was greatly afraid, and began to calm his two brothers,

21. Each of whom had eyes as big as figs and the color of fiery embers, and looked at each other full of hatred and scorn.

22. The ark, meanwhile, was floating upon the waters of the abyss.

Chapter B

1. Then Japheth, seething with rage, began to foam at the mouth, and Ham spoke unto him with words of gentleness,

2. Saying: "Let us find a way to reconcile everything; I will call for thy wife and Shem's wife."

3. Each of them, however, refused, saying that the matter was one of rights, not of persuasion.

4. And Shem proposed to Japheth that he make up for the ten lost cubits by measuring out another ten at the back of his lands. But Japheth replied,

5. "Why not send me straightaway to the ends of the earth? Thou art no longer content with five hundred cubits; thou seekest five hundred and ten, and for me to have four hundred and ninety.

6. "Hast thou no moral feelings? Dost thou not know what justice is? Canst thou not see how brazenly thou steals from me? And

dost thou not realize that I will know to defend what is mine, even at risk of my life?

7. "And that if blood must be spilt, then it will be spilt here and now,

8. "To punish thy pride and wash away thy iniquity?"

9. Then Shem advanced toward Japheth, but Ham put himself between them, placing a hand on the chest of each one;

10. Whilst the wolf and the lamb, who during all the days of the flood had lived in sweetest harmony, upon hearing the sound of voices came to see the brothers fight, and became wary of each other.

11. And Ham said: "Behold, I have a marvelous idea that will satisfy everyone.

12. "And inspired by the love I have for you my brothers. I will sacrifice the land that is mine beside that of my father, and instead I will have the river and its two banks, with each of you giving me around twenty cubits."

13. And Shem and Japheth laughed with sarcasm and scorn, saying: "Go plant dates! Keep that idea for the days of thy dotage." And they pulled Ham's ears and nose; and Japheth, putting two fingers in his mouth, imitated the hiss of the serpent, mocking him.

14. Now Ham, annoyed and ashamed, spread wide his hands and said: "Let me be!" and went thence to meet with his father and the wives of his two brothers.

15. Japheth, however, said unto Shem: "Now that we are alone, let us decide this serious matter, whether it be by tongue or by fist. Cede unto me both riverbanks, or I will break one of thy ribs."

16. Upon saying this, Japheth threatened Shem with clenched fists, while Shem, bracing himself, said in an angry voice: "I cede nothing unto thee, thief!"

17. To which Japheth retorted angrily: "Thou art the thief!"

18. They then advanced toward each other and came to blows. Japheth had a sturdy and well-trained arm; Shem stood his ground. Then Japheth, grabbing his brother around the waist, squeezed him mightily, shouting: "Whose river is it?"

19. And Shem responded: "It is mine!" Japheth tried to wrestle

him to the floor, but Shem, who was strong, shook himself free and pushed his brother away; Japheth, however, foaming with rage, once again seized his brother and the two of them fought hand-to-hand,

20. Sweating and snorting like bulls.

21. As they fought, they fell and rolled, punching each other; blood flowed from their noses, their lips, and their cheeks; one moment Japheth was winning;

22. Then it was Shem; for anger spurred them on in equal measure, and they fought with their hands, their feet, their teeth, and their nails; and the ark trembled as if once again the heavens had opened.

23. Then the voices and shouts reached the ears of Noah, at the same time as his son Ham appeared before him, clamoring: "My father, my father, if for Cain vengeance will be taken seven times, and for Lamech seventy times seven, what will it be for Japheth and Shem?"

24. And when Noah asked him to explain what he meant, Ham spoke of his brothers' strife, and the anger that seethed within them, and said: "Hasten to calm them." Noah said: "Let us go."

25. The ark, meanwhile, was floating upon the waters of the abyss.

Chapter C

1. And behold, Noah came to the place where his two sons were fighting,

2. And found them still clasped one to another, Shem pinned down by the knee of Japheth, who with clenched fist was punching his brother's bruised and bloodied face.

3. Meanwhile, Shem, raising his hands, managed to grasp his brother by the throat, and Japheth began to shout: "Let me go! Let me go!"

4. Hearing the shouts, Japheth and Shem's wives came also unto the scene of the struggle, and, seeing them thus, began to cry and say: "What will become of us? The curse has fallen upon us and upon our husbands."

5. Noah, however, said unto them: "Be quiet, wives of my sons, and I will see what this quarrel is about, and I will ordain that which is just." And, walking toward the two fighters,

6. He shouted unto them: "Stop the fight. I, Noah, your father, order and command it." And upon hearing their father the two brothers suddenly halted, and remained a long time silent and ashamed, neither of them getting to their feet.

7. Noah continued: "Stand up, O men unworthy of salvation and deserving of the punishment that has befallen all other men."

8. Japheth and Shem stood up. Each had cuts on his face, neck, and hands, and their clothes were splattered with blood, for they had fought with tooth and nail, incensed by mortal hatred.

9. The deck as well was soaked with blood, and also both men's sandals, and their hair;

10. As if sin had wished to mark them with the sign of their iniquity.

11. The two wives, however, came unto them, weeping and caressing them, and the aching of their hearts was plain to see. Japheth and Shem did not respond, and stood with their eyes cast downwards, fearful of facing their father.

12. Who said: "Now, then, I want to know the reason for the fight."

13. This word ignited the hatred in the hearts of both men. Japheth, however, was the first to speak, and said:

14. "Shem invaded my land, the land on which I had chosen to pitch my tent when the waters subside and the ark descends, according to the Lord's promise;

15. "And I, who will not abide plunder, said unto my brother: 'Art thou not content with five hundred cubits, that thou wilt have ten more?' And he replied to me: 'I want ten more and both banks of the river that shall divide my land from thine.'"

16. Noah, listening to his son, had his eyes upon Shem; and when Japheth had finished, he asked his brother: "How dost thou answer?"

17. And Shem said: "Japheth is lying, because I only took from him the ten cubits of land when he refused to divide the river between us; and in proposing that I keep both riverbanks, I even agreed that he could measure out another ten cubits at the back of his lands,

18. "To compensate for what he was losing; but the iniquity of Cain spoke within him and he wounded my head, my face, and my hands."

19. And Japheth interrupted him, saying: "And didst thou not wound me also? Am not I bloodied as thee? Look at my face and my neck; look at my cheeks, which thou didst tear with thy tiger claws."

20. As Noah began to speak, he observed that his two sons once again seemed to challenge each other with their eyes. So he said: "Hear me!" But the two brothers, blind with rage, grappled with each other once again, shouting: "Whose river is it?"—"The river is mine."

21. And only with great difficulty could Noah, Ham, and the wives of Shem and Japheth hold back the two warriors, whose blood began to gush forth copiously.

22. Noah, however, raising his voice, cried out: "Cursed is he who obeys me not! He shall be cursed not seven times, not seventy times seven, but seven hundred times seventy.

23. "Therefore I say unto you that, before the ark descends, I want no pacts regarding the place where you will pitch your tents."

24. After this he grew thoughtful.

25. And, raising his eyes to heaven, because the hatch above him was open, he cried out in sadness:

26. "They do not yet possess the earth and already they are fighting over borders. What will happen when Turkey and Russia come along?"

27. And none of Noah's sons could understand these words of their father.

28. The ark, meanwhile, continued to float upon the waters of the abyss.

DONA BENEDITA

A Portrait

Chapter I

THE MOST DIFFICULT THING in the world, apart from governing a country, must surely be that of guessing Dona Benedita's exact age. Some said forty, some forty-five, others thirty-six. One stockbroker went as low as twenty-nine, but his judgment, clouded by hidden intentions, lacked the necessary stamp of sincerity that we all like to see in human opinions. Indeed, I only mention it to illustrate, from the very outset, that Dona Benedita was always the very model of good manners. The stockbroker's flattery served only to arouse her indignation, albeit momentarily, yes, momentarily. As for those other estimates, oscillating between thirty-six and forty-five, none of them could be contradicted by Dona Benedita's appearance, which was both maturely serious and youthfully graceful. The only surprising thing is that such speculation continued, when in order to know the truth one needed only to ask her.

Dona Benedita reached her forty-second birthday on Sunday the nineteenth of September, 1869. At six o'clock in the evening, friends and relations, some twenty or twenty-five in number, are gathered around the family table. Many of them were also present at her birthday dinners of 1868, 1867, and 1866, and they have always heard their hostess's age frankly alluded to. Moreover, there at the table, for all to see, are a young lady and a young master, her children; it is true that he, both in size and manners, is still somewhat boyish; on the other hand, the young lady, Eulália, is eighteen, although such is the severity of her manners and features that she looks twenty-one.

The joviality of the guests, the excellence of the dinner, certain matrimonial negotiations entrusted to Canon Roxo (of which more shall be said anon), and the hostess's generous nature, all these make for an intimate and happy affair. The canon stands up to carve the turkey. Dona Benedita has always abided by the custom in modest households of entrusting the turkey to one of the guests, instead of having it carved away from the table by servants, and the canon was the maestro of such solemn occasions. Nobody knew the bird's anatomy better than he, nor how to wield the knife so nimbly. Perhaps—and this is a matter for the experts—perhaps his status as a canon gave to the carving knife, in the minds of the guests, a certain prestige, which would be lacking if, for example, he were a mere student of mathematics or an office clerk. On the other hand, would a student or scribe, without the lessons of long practice, have at their disposal the canon's consummate art? That is another important question.

As for the other guests, they are sitting and chatting; the gurgle of half-sated stomachs reigns, the laughter of nature on its way to repleteness; it is a moment of relaxation.

Dona Benedita is talking, as are her visitors; however, she does not speak to all of them, but only to the one seated next to her. Her neighbor is a plump, kindly, cheerful lady, the mother of a twenty-one-year-old graduate, Leandrinho, who is sitting opposite them. Dona Benedita is not merely talking to the plump lady, she is clasping one of her hands, and not only is she clasping the plump lady's hand, she is also looking at her with vivacious, lovestruck eyes. Note that hers is not a persistent or prolonged gaze, but rather a series of small, restless, momentary glances. In any event, there is much tenderness in that gesture, and even if there weren't, nothing would be lost, because Dona Benedita repeats with her lips everything that her eyes have already said to Dona Maria dos Anjos: that she is absolutely delighted, that it is wonderful to meet her, that Dona Maria is so very kind, so very dignified, that her eyes are the very windows of her soul, and so on. One of her friends says jokingly to Dona Benedita that she is making her jealous.

"Oh, stuff and nonsense!" she replies, laughing.

And, turning back to the other woman:

"Don't you agree? No one should come between us."

And she carried on showering her with compliments, courtesies, and smiles, the offers of more of this, more of that, plans to go on a trip together or perhaps to the theater, and promises of many visits, all spoken in such warm, effusive tones that her new companion was visibly throbbing with pleasure and gratitude.

The turkey has been eaten. Dona Maria dos Anjos signals to her son, who stands up and asks them to accompany him in a toast:

"Ladies and gentlemen, there is a saying in French: *les absents ont tort*. Let us resolutely reject this, and drink to someone who is far, far away in terms of space, but close, very close indeed, to the heart of his dear wife. Let us drink to that most illustrious judge, Justice Proença."

The toast did not receive an enthusiastic response from the assembled guests, and to understand why one need only look at the sad face of their hostess. Her closest friends and relatives whispered to one another that young Leandrinho had been very thoughtless indeed; they drank the toast, but refrained from cheering, so as not, it would seem, to exacerbate Dona Benedita's suffering. In vain: Dona Benedita, unable to contain herself, burst into tears, got up from the table, and left the room. Dona Maria dos Anjos went with her. There then followed a deathly silence. Eulália begged them all to carry on as normal, saying that her mother would be back shortly.

"Mama is very sensitive," she said, "and the idea of Papa being so far away . . ."

Dismayed, Leandrinho apologized to Eulália. The fellow sitting next to him explained that Dona Benedita could not hear her husband's name mentioned without feeling a crushing blow to her heart, promptly followed by tears; Leandrinho replied that he was aware of her misfortune, but had never imagined his toast would have such a harmful effect.

"And yet it's the most natural thing in the world," explained the fellow, "for she misses her husband terribly."

"The canon," replied Leandrinho, "told me her husband went to Pará about two years ago."

"Two and a half years. He was appointed district judge by the Zacarias government. He would have preferred the appeal court in São Paulo, or perhaps Bahia, but it was not to be, and so he accepted Pará instead."

"And he hasn't been back since?"

"No."

"I presume Dona Benedita is afraid of such a long sea voyage . . ."

"I don't believe so. She's already been to Europe. No, if I recall correctly, she stayed behind in Rio to sort out some family affairs, and then stayed on, and on, and now . . ."

"But would it not have been far better to go to Pará than to suffer like this? Do you know her husband?"

"I do; a very distinguished gentleman, and still hale and hearty; he couldn't be more than forty-five. Tall, bearded, handsome. People used to say that he didn't insist on his wife joining him because he had fallen for some widow up there."

"Ah!"

"And someone even came and told Dona Benedita. Imagine how the poor lady must have felt! She cried all night, and the next day she wouldn't eat any breakfast, and made arrangements to take the very next steamship to Pará."

"But she didn't go?"

"No. She canceled three days later."

At that moment, Dona Benedita returned, on the arm of Dona Maria dos Anjos. She smiled in embarrassment, apologized for the interruption, and sat down once again with her new friend by her side, thanking her profusely for looking after her and again clasping her hand.

"I can see you only want what's good for me," she said.

"It's only what you deserve," said Dona Maria dos Anjos.

"Really?" Dona Benedita said, with a mix of vanity and modesty.

And she declared that, no, it was the other lady who was truly good, just like her name. Dona Maria dos Anjos was an angel, a real angel! And Dona Benedita underlined the word with the same loving gaze, not persistent or prolonged, but restless and intermittent. For his part, the canon, seeking to expunge all memory of the unfortunate incident, changed the topic of conversation to the weighty matter of which was the best dessert. Opinions diverged widely. Some thought the coconut dessert was best, some the one with cashew nuts, and others the orange one, etc. The author of the toast, Leandrinho, said—although not with his lips but slyly with his eyes—that the sweetest of desserts were Eulália's cheeks—a dusky, rosy-cheeked dessert. His own mother inwardly approved of those unspoken words, while the young woman's mother did not even see them, so caught up was she in her adoration of her new friend. An angel, a real angel!

Chapter II

The next day, Dona Benedita got up from her bed with the idea of writing a letter to her husband, a long letter in which she would tell him about the party, name all the guests and the different dishes, describe the reception afterward, and, more importantly, tell him about her new friendship with Dona Maria dos Anjos. The mail pouch closed at two in the afternoon, Dona Benedita had woken at nine, and, since she didn't live far away (her house was on the Campo da Aclamação), a slave would be able to deliver the letter to the post office in plenty of time. What's more, it was raining; Dona Benedita pulled back the net curtain and saw the drenched windowpanes; a persistent drizzle was falling, the sky was dark and overcast and dotted with thick black clouds. In the distance, she could see a cloth fluttering and flapping over a basket carried on the head of a black woman, from which she concluded that it was windy. A splendid day for staying at home, and, therefore, for writing a letter, two letters, or indeed all the letters a wife could possibly write to her absent husband. No one would come to tempt her away.

While she arranges the lace fringes and frills on her white linen dressing gown, which the eminent judge had given her in 1862, also on her birthday, September 19, I invite the reader to take a closer look at her. You will notice that I refrain from calling her a Venus, but nor do I call her a Medusa. Unlike Medusa, she wears her hair brushed smoothly back and fastened just above the nape of her neck. Her eyes are ordinary enough, but have a kindly expression. Her mouth is the sort that appears cheerful even when not smiling, and enjoys that other remarkable gift of showing neither remorse nor regret: one could even say it is devoid of desires, but I will say only what I want to say, and I wish to speak only of remorse and regret. This head, which neither excites nor repels, sits on a body that is tall rather than short, and neither thin nor fat, but in proportion with her build. But I won't describe her hands just yet. Why should I? You will admire them soon enough, holding pen to paper with slender, idle fingers, two of them adorned with five or six rings.

One need only see the way in which she arranges the lacy frills of her gown in order to understand that she is a persnickety woman, fond of keep-

ing everything around her and herself tidy. I note that she has just torn
the lace trimming on her left cuff, but that is because she, being impatient
by nature, blurted out, "Damn and blast the thing." Those were her exact
words, immediately followed by a "May God forgive me!" which took all
the venom out of her. I don't say that she stamped her foot, but she might
have, since that is a gesture natural to certain ladies when annoyed. In any
event, her anger lasted barely a minute. She then went to her sewing box to
stitch up the torn lace, but decided to make do with a pin. The pin fell to
the floor; she knelt down and picked it up. There were of course others in
the box, many others, but she didn't think it wise to leave pins lying on the
floor. As she knelt, she caught sight of the tip of her slipper, on which there
was a white mark; she sat down on the nearby chair, removed her slipper,
and saw what it was: it had been chewed by a cockroach. Dona Benedita
again fell into a rage, because the slipper was a very smart one, and had been
given to her the year before by a dear friend. An angel, a real angel! Dona
Benedita fixed her eyes on the white mark; happily their usual expression of
simple charity was not so charitable as to allow itself to be entirely replaced
by other, less passive expressions, and so it resumed its rightful place. Dona
Benedita turned the slipper over and over, passing it from one hand to the
other, lovingly at first, then mechanically, until her hands stopped moving
completely, and the slipper fell into her lap, and Dona Benedita sat staring
into space. At this point, the clock in the drawing room began to strike.
After the first two chimes, Dona Benedita shuddered:

"Good Lord! It's ten o'clock!"

And she quickly put her slipper back on, hurriedly pinned the cuff of
her gown, and went to her writing desk to begin the letter. She had put the
date and "My ungrateful husband," and had barely written: "Did you think
of me yesterday? I . . ." when Eulália knocked on her door, calling out:

"Mama! Mama! It's time for breakfast."

Dona Benedita opened the door, Eulália kissed her hand, then raised
her own hands heavenward:

"Goodness gracious! What a sleepyhead!"

"Is breakfast ready?"

"Yes, it's been ready for ages!"

"But I gave orders that breakfast today should be later than usual . . .
I've been writing to your father."

She looked at her daughter for a few moments, as if about to say something serious, or at least difficult, such was the grave, indecisive look in her eyes. But, in the end, she said nothing, and her daughter, announcing again that breakfast was served, took her by the arm and led her away.

Let us leave them to eat breakfast at leisure, and take the weight off our feet here in the drawing room, without, however, feeling the need to catalogue every item of its furniture, just as we have failed to do in any other room of the house. Not that the furniture is ugly or in bad taste; on the contrary, it is all rather good. But the overall impression is rather strange, as if the choice of furnishings were the result of some subsequently abandoned plan, or a succession of abandoned plans. Mother, daughter, and son breakfasted together. Let us leave aside the son, who is of no interest to us; a young whippersnapper of twelve years old, but so sickly that he looks more like eight. Eulália is the one who interests us, not only because of what we glimpsed in the preceding chapter, but also because, when her mother began to talk about Dona Maria dos Anjos and Leandrinho, she became very serious and, perhaps, a little sullen. Dona Benedita realized that her daughter did not like this topic of conversation and so she retreated, like someone turning a corner to avoid an undesirable encounter. She rose from the table, and her daughter followed her into the drawing room.

It was a quarter past eleven. Dona Benedita spoke with her daughter until shortly after midday, so as to have time to digest her breakfast and write the letter. As you are aware, the mail pouch closes at two o'clock. And so, a few minutes after midday, Dona Benedita told her daughter to go and practice the piano, so that she could finish the letter. Dona Benedita left the drawing room; Eulália went over to the window, glanced out at the square outside, and I can vouch for the fact that she did so with a glimmer of sadness in her eyes. It was not, however, a weak and indecisive sadness; it was the sadness of a resolute young woman who anticipates the pain her actions will cause to others, but, nevertheless, swears to go through with them, and does go through with them. I accept that not all these details could be surmised merely from Eulália's eyes, but it is for this very reason that stories are told by someone who takes it upon themselves to fill in the gaps and reveal what is hidden. True, it was certainly a vigorous sadness and equally true that a glimmer of hope would soon appear in her eyes.

"This can't go on," she murmured, coming back into the room.

At that very moment, a carriage pulled up at the front door. A lady stepped out, the doorbell sounded, a houseboy went down to open the gate, and Dona Maria dos Anjos came up the steps. When the visitor was announced, Dona Benedita dropped her pen in agitation; she hurriedly got dressed, put on her shoes, and went into the drawing room.

"Fancy coming out in this weather!" she exclaimed. "That is true friendship!"

"I didn't want to wait for you to visit me, simply to show that I'm not one to stand on ceremony, and that between you and me there must be no constraints."

This was followed by the same compliments and sweet, caressing words as on the previous day. Dona Benedita kept insisting that coming to visit her that very day was the greatest of courtesies and a proof of genuine friendship, but, she added a moment later, she wished for further proof and asked Dona Maria dos Anjos to stay for dinner. Her friend excused herself, pleading that she had to be elsewhere; furthermore, this was the very proof of friendship that she herself desired, namely, that Dona Benedita should come and dine at her house first. Dona Benedita did not hesitate and promised that she would dine with her that very week.

"I was just this minute writing your name," she continued.

"Were you?"

"Yes, I'm writing to my husband and telling him all about you. I won't repeat to you what I've written, but you can imagine that I spoke very ill of you, telling him what an unkind, insufferable, tedious woman you are, a terrible bore . . . You can just imagine!"

"I can indeed. And you can add that, despite all that and more, I send him my deepest respects."

"See how witty she is!" remarked Dona Benedita, looking at her daughter.

Eulália smiled unconvincingly. Perched on a chair facing her mother, beside the sofa on which Dona Maria dos Anjos was sitting, Eulália gave the two ladies' conversation only the degree of attention that good manners required, and not a jot more.

She came close to looking bored; every smile that appeared on her lips was wan and languid, pure duty. One of her braids—it was still morning and she was wearing her hair in two long braids—served her as a pretext to look away from time to time, because she would occasionally tug at it to count the hairs, or so it seemed. At least that's what Dona Maria dos Anjos thought, when she occasionally shot a glance in Eulália's direction, curious and somewhat suspicious. For her part, Dona Benedita saw nothing; she had eyes only for her dear friend, her enchantress, as she called her two or three times: "my dear, dear enchantress."

"Enough!"

Dona Maria dos Anjos explained that she had a few other visits to make, but her friend prevailed upon her to stay for a little longer. She was wearing a very elegant cape of black lace, and Dona Benedita said that she had one just the same and sent one of the slaves to fetch it. Delays, delays. But Leandrinho's mother was so pleased! Dona Benedita filled her heart with happiness; she found in her all the qualities best suited to her own personality and her manners: tenderness, trust, enthusiasm, simplicity, a warm and willing familiarity. The cape was brought, refreshments were offered; Dona Maria dos Anjos would accept nothing more than a kiss and the promise that they would dine with her that very week.

"On Thursday," said Dona Benedita.

"Promise?"

"I promise."

"What would you have me do to you if you don't come? It will need to be a very harsh punishment."

"The harshest possible punishment would be for you never to speak to me again!"

Dona Maria dos Anjos kissed her friend tenderly; then she hugged and kissed Eulália, too, but with rather less enthusiasm on both sides. They were measuring each other up, studying each other, and beginning to understand each other. Dona Benedita accompanied her friend to the stairs, then went over to the window to watch her get into her carriage; after settling herself in, her friend put her head out of the window, looked up, and waved goodbye.

"Don't forget!"

"Thursday."

Eulália had already left the drawing room, and Dona Benedita rushed to finish the letter. It was getting late; she had said nothing yet about yesterday's dinner, and it was too late to do so now. She gave a brief summary, extolling the virtues of her new friend; then, finally, she wrote the following words:

Canon Roxo spoke to me about marrying Eulália to Dona Maria dos Anjos's son. He graduated in law this year; he's a conservative and, if Itaboraí does not resign from the government, he expects to be appointed a public prosecutor. I think it is the best possible match. Leandrinho (for that is his name) is a very polite young man; he proposed a toast to you, full of such fine words that I cried. I don't know if Eulália will want him or not; I have my suspicions about another young fellow who joined us the other day in Laranjeiras. But what do you think? Should I limit myself to advising her, or should I impose our wishes? I really think I ought to use my authority, but I don't want to do anything without your say-so. The best thing would be if you came here yourself.

She finished the letter and sealed it. At that moment, Eulália came in, and Dona Benedita gave her the letter to be sent off, without delay, to the post office. The daughter left the room with the letter, not knowing that it concerned her and her future. Dona Benedita slumped down on the sofa, exhausted. Even though there was much she had not mentioned, the letter had still turned out to be a very long one and writing long letters was such a tiresome business!

Chapter III

Yes, writing long letters was such a tiresome business! The words with which we closed the previous chapter fully explain Dona Benedita's exhaustion. Half an hour later, she sat up a little and glanced around the study, as if looking for something. That something was a book. She found the book, or, rather, books, since there were no fewer than three, two open, one marked at a certain page, all lying on different chairs. They were the three novels that Dona Benedita was reading at the same time. One of them, you will note, had required considerable effort on her part. She had heard it warmly spoken of it while she was out walking near the house; it had arrived from Europe only the day before. Dona Benedita was so excited that, despite the lateness of the hour and the distance, she turned back and went to buy the book herself, visiting no fewer than three bookshops. She returned home so eager to read it that she opened the book during dinner and read the first five chapters that same night. When sleep overcame her, she slept; the following day, she was unable to continue reading, and forgot all about the book. Now, however, a week later, and wanting to read something, there it was close to hand.

"Ah!"

And so she returns to the sofa, lovingly opens the book, and plunges eyes, heart and soul into the reading that had been so abruptly interrupted. It's only natural that Dona Benedita should love novels, and it is even more natural that she should love nice ones. Do not be surprised, therefore, when she forgets everything around her to read this one; everything, even her daughter's piano lesson, for which the piano teacher arrived and left without Dona Benedita once visiting the drawing room. Eulália said goodbye to her teacher, then went to the study, opened the door, tiptoed over to the sofa, and woke her mother with a kiss.

"Wake up, sleepyhead!"

"Is it still raining?"

"No, Mama, it's stopped now."

"Has the letter gone?"

"Yes, I told José to hurry. I bet you forgot to give my dearest love to Papa? I thought so. Well, I never forget."

Dona Benedita yawned. She was no longer thinking about the letter; she was thinking about the corset she had ordered from Charavel's, one with softer stays than the last one. She didn't like hard stays, for she had a very delicate body. Eulália talked a little more about her father, but soon stopped, and, seeing the famous novel lying open on the floor, she picked it up, closed it, and set it on the table. At that moment, a letter was brought in for Dona Benedita; it was from Canon Roxo, who wrote to ask whether they were at home that day, because he would be going to a funeral nearby.

"Of course we'll be at home!" Dona Benedita cried. "Do tell him to come."

Eulália wrote a little note in reply. Three-quarters of an hour later the canon entered Dona Benedita's drawing room. He was a good man, the canon, an old friend of the family, in which, besides carving the turkey on solemn occasions, as we have seen, he exercised the role of family advisor, and did so both loyally and lovingly. Eulália was particularly dear to him; he had known her since she was a little girl, his attentive and mischievous little friend, and he felt a paternal affection toward her, so paternal that he had taken it upon himself to see her properly married, and, thought the canon, there could be no better bridegroom than Leandrinho. That day, his idea of going to dine with them was little more than a pretext; the canon wished to raise the subject directly with the young lady herself. Eulália, either because she guessed his intentions or because the canon's presence brought Leandrinho to mind, became worried and annoyed.

But worried or annoyed does not mean sad or dispirited. She was resolute, she had a strong character, she could resist, and she did resist, declaring to the canon, when he spoke to her that night about Leandrinho, that she absolutely did not wish to marry.

"Cross your heart and hope to die?"

"Cross my heart and hope to live."

"But why?"

"Because I don't want to."

"And if Mama wants you to?"

"But I don't want to."

"Well, that's not very nice of you, Eulália."

Eulália did not reply. The canon returned yet again to the subject, praising the candidate's fine qualities, the hopes of his family, the many advantages of their marriage; she listened to all this, but said nothing. However, when the canon put the question to her directly, her response was invariably:

"I've already said all there is to say."

"You really don't want to marry?"

"No."

The canon's disappointment was deep and sincere. He wanted to see her properly married, and he could think of no better husband. He went so far as to probe her, discreetly, about whether her interest lay elsewhere. But Eulália, no less discreetly, responded that no, she had no other "interest"; she simply did not wish to marry. He believed this to be true, but also feared that it was not; he lacked sufficient experience in the ways of women to read beyond that negative. When he relayed all this to Dona Benedita, she was shocked by the abruptness of her daughter's refusal; but she quickly recovered her composure and told the priest in no uncertain terms that her daughter had no say in the matter, and that she, Dona Benedita, would do as she wished, and she wanted the marriage.

"There's no point even waiting for her father's reply," she concluded. "I'll just tell him that she's getting married. It's as simple as that. On Thursday I will dine with Dona Maria dos Anjos, and we will arrange everything."

"I must tell you," ventured the canon, "that Dona Maria dos Anjos does not wish anything to be done by force."

"What force? No force is required."

The canon reflected for a moment.

"In any event, we must not overrule any other attachment she may have formed," he said.

Dona Benedita made no reply, but inwardly swore that, come what may, her daughter would become the daughter-in-law of Dona Maria dos Anjos. And after the canon had left, she said to herself: "Well, I never! A mere slip of a girl thinking she can rule the roost!"

Thursday dawned. Eulália, the mere slip of a girl, got out of bed feeling bright and cheerful and chatty, with all the windows of her spirit open to the blue morning air. Her mother awoke to hear a snippet from some glorious Italian melody; it was her daughter singing, happily and blithely, with all the indifference of birds who sing for themselves or for their own offspring, and not for the poet who listens and translates them into the immortal language of mankind. Dona Benedita had secretly cherished the idea of seeing her daughter downhearted and surly, and had expended a certain amount of imagination in deciding how she herself would act, pretending to be strong and forceful. Instead of a rebellious daughter, though, she found her to be talkative and amenable. It was a bad start to the day, like setting out prepared to destroy a fortress and finding instead a peaceful, welcoming city, its gates flung wide, politely inviting her to enter and break the bread of joy and harmony. It was a very bad start to the day.

The second cause of Dona Benedita's annoyance was a threatened migraine at three o'clock in the afternoon; a threat, or perhaps a suspicion of the possibility of a threat. She nearly canceled the visit, but her daughter thought it might do her good to go, and, in any event, it was too late to put it off. There was nothing else for it; Dona Benedita took her medicine, and, as she sat before the mirror brushing her hair, she was on the verge of saying that she would definitely stay at home, and she hinted as much to her daughter.

"But Mama, Dona Maria dos Anjos is expecting you," Eulália told her.

"Indeed," retorted her mother, "but I didn't promise to go there if I was indisposed."

Finally, she got dressed, put on her gloves, and issued her instructions to the servants; her head must have been hurting a lot because she was rather curt with people, like someone being compelled to do something against their will. Her daughter did her best to raise her spirits, reminding her to take her little bottle of smelling salts, urging her to go, saying how eager Dona Maria dos Anjos was to see her, repeatedly checking the little watch pinned to her waist, and so on. She would be really put out.

"Stop pestering me," her mother said.

And off she went, feeling exasperated, fervently wishing she could throttle her daughter, telling herself that daughters were the worst thing in the world. Sons were all right: they grew up and made a career for themselves; but daughters!

Happily, the meal at Dona Maria dos Anjos's calmed her down; not that it filled her with great satisfaction, because that wasn't the case at all. Dona Benedita was not her usual self; she was cold and brusque, or almost brusque; she, however, explained the difference in her own terms, mentioning the threatened migraine, which was not exactly good news, but nevertheless cheered Dona Maria dos Anjos, for this refined and profound reason: it was better that her friend's coolness was the result of an illness than a diminution in her affections. Moreover, it was nothing grave. And yet grave it was! There were no clasped hands, no loving gazes, no delicate titbits being consumed between fond caresses; in short, it was nothing like the dinner on Sunday. The meal was merely polite, not joyful; that was the most the canon could achieve. Oh, the kind, amiable canon! Eulália's mood that day filled him with hope; her playful laughter, her easy conversation, her readiness to do as asked, to play and sing, and the tender, agreeable look on her face when she listened and spoke to Leandrinho; all this greatly restored the canon's hopes. And for Dona Benedita to be indisposed today of all days! It really was bad luck.

Dona Benedita's spirits rose somewhat that evening after dinner. She talked a little more, discussed a plan to go for a stroll in the Jardim Botânico, even proposing that they go the very next day. However, Eulália warned her that it would be wise to wait a day or two for the effects of the migraine to wear off completely; and the look she got from her mother in return for her advice was as sharp as a dagger. The daughter had no fear of her mother's eyes, though. As she brushed her hair that night, thinking over the day's events, Eulália repeated to herself the words we heard her say, some days before, at the window.

"This can't go on."

And before sleeping, she smugly pulled open a certain drawer, took out a little box, opened it, and removed a card measuring only about two inches by two—a portrait. It was clearly not the portrait of a woman, not only on account of the mustache, but also the uniform; he was, at the very least, a naval officer. Whether handsome or ugly is a matter of opinion. Eulália thought him handsome, the proof being that she kissed the portrait, not once but three times. Then she gazed at it longingly, and put it back in its box.

What were you thinking, O strict and cautious mother, that you did not come and tear from the hands and lips of your daughter so subtle and mortal a venom? Standing at her window, Dona Benedita was gazing up at the night sky, amid the stars and gas lamps, with a roving, restless imagination, and filled with gnawing regrets and desires. Nothing had gone right for her since morning. Dona Benedita confessed, in the sweet intimacy of her own soul, that the dinner at Dona Maria dos Anjos's had been dreadful, and that her friend probably wasn't at her best, either. She felt certain regrets—although for what, she wasn't entirely sure—and certain desires, but for quite what, she didn't know. From time to time she gave a long, lazy yawn, like someone about to fall asleep; but if she felt anything at all it was boredom—boredom, impatience, and curiosity. Dona Benedita seriously wondered about going to join her husband; and no sooner had the thought of her husband entered her head than her heart was filled with longings and remorse, and her blood pulsed in her veins; so great was her desire to go and see the eminent judge that if her luggage had been packed and the northbound steamer had been waiting at the corner of the street, she would have embarked that very minute. No matter; there was sure to be another steamer in a week or ten days, and there was plenty of time to arrange her luggage. Since she would only be going for three months, she would not need to take very much.

It would be a relief to get away from Rio, from the sameness of the days, the lack of novelties, the same faces, even the unchanging fashions—something that always troubled her: "Why should any fashion last for more than two weeks?"

"I'll go; there's nothing more to be said. I'll go to Pará," she said softly.

Indeed, the following morning, the first thing she did was to communicate this decision to her daughter, who took the news calmly. Dona Benedita checked how many trunks she already had, wondered if she needed one more, calculated the size, and decided to buy another. In a sudden moment of inspiration, Eulália said:

"But Mama, we're only going for three months, aren't we?"

"Yes, three . . . or possibly two."

"Well, then, it isn't worth it. Two trunks will suffice."

"No, they won't."

"Well, if they aren't enough, we can always buy another one just before we leave. And you should go and choose it yourself—that would be much better than sending someone who knows nothing about trunks."

Dona Benedita thought this wise advice, and held on to her money. Her daughter smiled secretly. Perhaps she was repeating to herself the same words she had spoken at the window: "This can't go on." Her mother went to make arrangements, choosing clothes, making lists of things she needed to buy, a present for her husband, and so on. Oh, he would be so happy! In the afternoon, they went out to place orders, pay visits, buy tickets— four tickets, since they would each take a slave-woman with them. Eulália tried again to dissuade her, proposing that they delay the journey, but Dona Benedita declared that this was out of the question. At the offices of the steamship company, she was informed that the northbound steamer would leave on Friday of the following week. She asked for four tickets, opened her purse, pulled out a banknote, then two, then thought for a moment.

"We could just buy our tickets the day before, couldn't we?"

"You could, but there might not be any tickets left."

"All right, what if you set aside four tickets for us, and I'll send for them."

"Your name?"

"My name? No, better not take my name. We'll come back three days before the steamer leaves. There are sure to be tickets then."

"Possibly."

"No, there will be."

Once out in the street, Eulália remarked that it would be better to buy the tickets straightaway; and, since we know that she did not wish to travel either North or South, save on the frigate carrying the man we saw in that portrait the previous evening, one must assume that the young lady's comment was profoundly Machiavellian. It wouldn't surprise me. Dona Benedita, meanwhile, informed her friends and acquaintances of their forthcoming journey and none of them was surprised. One did ask if, this

time, she really was going. Dona Maria dos Anjos had heard about the proposed trip from the canon, but the only thing that alarmed her when her
friend came to say goodbye was Dona Benedita's icy demeanor, her silence
and indifference, and the way she kept her gaze fixed on the floor. A visit
of barely ten minutes, during which Dona Benedita said only six words at
the beginning: "We are going to the North." And one at the end: "Farewell."
Followed by three sad, corpse-like kisses.

Chapter IV

The journey did not take place, for superstitious reasons. On the Sunday
night, Dona Benedita realized that the steamer would be leaving on a Friday, which seemed to her a bad day to travel. They would go instead on
the next steamer. However, they did not go on the next one, but this time
her reasons lay entirely beyond the reach of human understanding; in such
cases, the best advice is not to attempt to comprehend the incomprehensible. The fact of the matter is that Dona Benedita did not go, saying that
she would go on the third steamer, unless, of course, something happened
to change her plans.

Her daughter had come up with a party and a new friendship. The new
friendship was with a family in Andaraí; no one knows what the party was
for, but it must have been a splendid affair, because Dona Benedita was
still talking about it three days later. Three days! It really was too much. As
for the family, they could not have been kinder; the whole thing had made
the most tremendous impression on Dona Benedita. I use this superlative
because she herself used it: a document made by human hands.

"Those people made the most tremendous impression on me."

And she began going for strolls in Andaraí, enchanted by the company
of Dona Petronilha, Counselor Beltrão's wife, and her sister Dona Mari-
cota, who was going to marry a naval officer, the brother of that other naval
officer whose mustache, eyes, hair, and bearing match those of the portrait
the reader glimpsed earlier in that drawer. The married sister was thirty-
two, and her earnestness and charming manners entirely bewitched Dona
Benedita. The unmarried sister was a flower, a wax flower, another expression of Dona Benedita's, which I have left unaltered for fear of watering
down the truth.

One of the most obscure aspects of this whole curious story is the speed with which friendships blossomed and events unfurled. For example, another regular visitor to Andaraí, along with Dona Benedita, was the very naval officer pictured on that little card. He was First Lieutenant Mascarenhas, whom Counselor Beltrão predicted would become an admiral. Note, however, the officer's perfidy: he came in uniform; and Dona Benedita, who adored any new spectacle, found him so distinguished, so handsome compared with the other men in civilian clothes, that she preferred him to all of them, and told him so. The officer thanked her earnestly. She told him he must come and see them; he begged permission to pay a visit.

"A visit? Why, you must come and dine with us."

Mascarenhas assented with a bow.

"Look here," said Dona Benedita, "why don't you come tomorrow?"

Mascarenhas came, and came early. Dona Benedita talked to him about life at sea; he asked for her daughter's hand in marriage. Dona Benedita was speechless, indeed shocked. She remembered, it is true, that, one day in Laranjeiras some time ago, she'd had her suspicions about him, but now her suspicions were long gone. Since then, she hadn't seen the couple speak or look at one another even once. But marriage! Was that possible? It could not be anything else; the young man's serious, respectful, and imploring behavior said clearly that he had indeed meant marriage. A dream come true! To invite to one's home a friend, and open the door to a son-in-law: it was the very height of the unexpected. And the dream was a handsome one; the naval officer was a courteous young man; strong, elegant, friendly, openhearted, and, more importantly, he seemed to adore her, Dona Benedita. What a magnificent dream! Once she had recovered from her astonishment, Dona Benedita said, yes, Eulália was his. Mascarenhas took her hand and kissed it with filial devotion.

"But what of your husband?" he asked.

"My husband will agree with me."

Everything proceeded at great speed. Certificates were obtained, banns were read, and a date for the wedding set; it would take place twenty-four hours after the judge's response was received. Dona Benedita, the good, kind mother, was beside herself with joy, busily caught up in preparing the trousseau, in planning and ordering the festivities, in choosing the guests! She rushed hither and thither, sometimes on foot, sometimes by carriage, come rain or shine. She did not linger over any one thing for very long; one day it was the trousseau, the next it was preparations for the wedding reception, the next there were visits to be made; she switched from one thing to another, then back again, and it was all somewhat frenetic. But the daughter was always there to make up for any shortcomings, to correct any mistakes, and trim back any excesses, with her own natural talent for such things. Unlike other bridegrooms, the naval officer did not get in their way; he did not take up Dona Benedita's invitation to dine with them every evening; he dined with them only on Sundays, and paid them a visit once a week. He kept in touch through long, secret letters, as he had during their courtship. Dona Benedita could not explain such diffidence when she herself had fallen head over heels in love with him; and she would avenge his strange behavior by falling even deeper in love, and telling everyone the most wonderful things about him.

"A pearl! An absolute pearl!"

"He's certainly a fine young man," they all agreed.

"Isn't he just? First-rate!"

She repeated the same thing in the letters she wrote her husband, both before and after receiving his reply to her first letter. In that reply the eminent judge gave his consent, adding that it pained him greatly that, due to a slight indisposition, he would be unable to attend the nuptials; however, he gave them his paternal blessing, and asked for a portrait of his new son-in-law.

His wishes were followed to the letter. The wedding took place twenty-four hours after his letter arrived from Pará. It was, as Dona Benedita told certain friends later on, an admirable, splendid affair. Canon Roxo officiated, and it goes without saying that Dona Maria dos Anjos was not present, still less her son. Up until the very last minute, she had expected to receive a wedding announcement, an invitation, or perhaps a visit, even if she would, naturally enough, refrain from actually attending the ceremony; but nothing came. She was frankly astonished, and scoured her memory again and again for some inadvertent slight on her part that could explain this new coolness. Finding nothing, she imagined some intrigue. But she imagined wrongly, for it was a simple oversight. On the day of the wedding, it suddenly occurred to Dona Benedita that she had forgotten to send Dona Maria dos Anjos a wedding announcement.

"Eulália, it seems we didn't send the announcement to Dona Maria dos Anjos," she said to her daughter over breakfast.

"I don't know, Mama. It was you who organized the invitations."

"Well, it seems that I didn't," said Dona Benedita. "More sugar, João."

The footman handed her the sugar, and, stirring her tea, she remembered the carriage that would be going to fetch the canon, and repeated one of the orders she had given the day before.

But fortune is a capricious thing. Two weeks after the wedding, they received news of the judge's death. I will not describe Dona Benedita's grief; it was deep and sincere. The young newlyweds, lost in their own world up in Tijuca, came down to see her; Dona Benedita wept the tears of a heartbroken and devotedly faithful wife. After the seventh-day mass, she consulted her daughter and son-in-law on the idea of her going to Pará and having a tomb built for her husband, where she could kiss the earth in which he now lay. Mascarenhas exchanged a look with his wife, and then said to his mother-in-law that it would be better for them to go together, since he was due to go to the North in three months' time on a government commission. Dona Benedita resisted somewhat, but accepted the three-month delay, meanwhile setting about giving all the necessary instructions for the building of the tomb. And so the tomb was built, but Mascarenhas's commission did not materialize, and Dona Benedita was unable to go.

Five months later, there occurred a small family incident. Dona Benedita had arranged to build a house on the road to Tijuca, and her son-in-law, using an interruption in the building work as a pretext, proposed that he should finish it. Dona Benedita agreed, and her agreement was all the more to her credit given that she was finding her son-in-law increasingly unbearable with his love of discipline, his obstinacy and impertinence. In fact, he didn't need to be obstinate; rather, he had only to rely on his mother-in-law's good nature and merely wait a few days for her to give in. But perhaps it was precisely this that vexed her. Happily, the government decided to dispatch him to the South, and the pregnant Eulália stayed with her mother.

It was around this time that a widowed merchant took it upon himself to ask Dona Benedita for her hand in marriage. The first year of widowhood had passed. Dona Benedita received his proposal kindly, albeit with little enthusiasm. She looked to her own interests; her son's age and studies would soon take him away to São Paulo, leaving her all alone in the world. The marriage would be a source of consolation and company. In her own mind, at home or out and about, she developed the idea, adorning it with her quick and lively imagination; it would be a new life for her, for it could be said that she had been a widow for a long time, even before her husband's death. The merchant had a sound reputation: it would be an excellent choice.

She did not marry. Her son-in-law returned from the South, her daughter gave birth to a strong, beautiful baby boy, who became his grandmother's passion for the next few months. Then her son-in-law, daughter, and grandson all left for the North. Dona Benedita found herself alone and sad; her son was not enough to fill her affections. Once again the idea of traveling glimmered briefly in her mind, but only like a match that quickly burned out. Traveling alone would be tiring and dull; she decided it was better to stay.

A poetry recital she happened to attend helped her shake off her torpor, and restored her to society. Society once again suggested the idea of marriage, and quickly put forward a candidate, this time a lawyer, also a widower.

"Shall I marry or shall I not?"

One night, as Dona Benedita was turning this problem over in her mind while standing at the window of the house on the shore at Botafogo, where she had moved to some months earlier, she saw a most unusual spectacle. It began as an opaque glow, like a light filtered through frosted glass, filling the inlet of the bay beyond. Against this backdrop appeared a floating, transparent figure, wreathed in mist and veiled in shimmering reflections, its shape disappearing into thin air. The figure came right up to Dona Benedita's windowsill, and, drowsily, in a childish voice, spoke these meaningless words:

"Marry . . . don't marry . . . if you do marry . . . you will marry . . . you won't marry . . . you will marry . . . get married . . ."

Dona Benedita froze in terror, but still had strength enough to ask the figure who she was. The ghostly figure began to laugh, but that laughter quickly faded, and she replied that she was the fairy who had presided over Dona Benedita's birth. "My name is Indecision," said the fairy, and, like a sigh, dissolved into the night and the silence.

THE BONZE'S SECRET

An unpublished chapter from The Travels of Fernão Mendes Pinto

---

I HAVE SET OUT ABOVE the events that occurred in the city of Fucheo,* capital of the kingdom of Bungo, in the company of Father Master Francisco Xavier, and of how the king behaved toward Fucarandono and the other bonzes, who had seen fit to enter into theological disputations with the saintly priest regarding the superiority of our holy religion. I will now speak of a doctrine as curious as it is salutary to the spirit, and worthy of being revealed to all the republics of Christendom.

One day, while out taking a stroll with Diogo Meireles, in that same city of Fucheo in the year of our Lord 1552, we happened upon a crowd of people gathered at a street corner. They were standing around a local man who was holding forth, gesturing and shouting. The crowd numbered, at the lowest estimate, more than a hundred people, all of them men, and all with mouths agape. Diogo Meireles, who knew the local language better than I, for he had previously spent many months there in the company of a band

---

* Author's Note: As will be seen, what follows is not a pastiche, nor was it intended merely as a test of literary talent; if it were, it would be of very little value. In order to give my invention a certain realism, I needed to place it at a great distance in both space and time, and, to make the narrative ring true, there seemed to me to be no better solution than to attribute it to that famous travel writer who told so many wondrous tales. For the more curious reader, I will add that the words "I have set out above the events that occurred in the city of Fucheo" were written with the purpose of imagining this chapter to be inserted between chapters CCXIII and CCXIV of Mendes Pinto's *Peregrinacão*.

of merchant-adventurers (he was now engaged in the practice of medicine, which he had studied to useful advantage and in which he now excelled), repeated for me in our language what the speaker was saying, which was, in short, as follows: that he desired only to proclaim the true origin of crickets, which were born out of thin air and the leaves of coconut palms during the conjunction of the new moon. He went on to add that this discovery, impossible to anyone who was not, like him, a mathematician, physician, and philosopher, was the fruit of long years of application, experiment, study, hard work, and even danger to life and limb. All of this he had done for the praise and glory of the kingdom of Bungo, and, in particular, the city of Fucheo, of which he was a loyal son, and if he must pay with his life for postulating such a sublime truth, then so be it, so sure was he that science was a far richer prize than the pleasures of life itself.

As soon as he had finished, the crowd almost deafened us with their tumultuous cries of acclamation, and hoisted the man aloft onto their shoulders, shouting: "Patimau! Patimau! Long live Patimau, who has discovered the true origin of crickets!" And they carried him off to the porch outside a merchant's emporium, where they gave him refreshments and bowed ceremoniously according to the customs of this country, which are obsequious and courtly in the extreme.

Diogo Meireles and I turned back the way we had come, discussing this singular discovery about the origin of crickets, when, only a short walk from the merchant's emporium, no longer than it would take to say the creed six times, we came upon another crowd of people, on another street corner, listening to another man. We were taken aback by the similarity of the situation, and, as this other man also spoke very quickly, Diogo Meireles once again translated the tenor of his speech for me. The man was saying, to great admiration and applause from the people surrounding him, that he had at last discovered the font of the future life that would surely follow upon the Earth's utter destruction, and that this was neither more nor less than a single drop of cow's blood; this was why the cow proved such an excellent habitation for the human soul, and explained the fervor with which so many men, at the hour of their death, sought out this remarkable animal. It was a discovery in which he had complete faith and confidence, resulting as it did from his own repeated experiments and deep cogitations, for which he neither sought nor desired any reward greater than that of glorifying the kingdom of Bungo and receiving from it the esteem due to all loyal sons. The people, who had listened to this speech with great veneration, greeted it with the same hullabaloo as before, and took the man to the aforementioned merchant's emporium, with the difference that this time they carried him on a palanquin. Upon arriving there, he was showered with the same favors and attentions as had been shown to Patimau, with no distinction being made between them, and their grateful hosts were unsparing in the generous thanks they gave to their two honored guests.

We could make neither head nor tail of any of this, for the exact similarity between the two encounters seemed to us scarcely accidental, nor did we find Patimau's theory of the origin of crickets any more rational or credible than the font of future life discovered by Languru, which was the other man's name. However, we happened to be passing the house of a certain sandal-maker called Titané, who rushed out to speak to Diogo Meireles, with whom he was acquainted. After exchanging greetings, in which the sandal-maker addressed Diogo Meireles as "golden truth and sun of thought" and other such gallant names, the latter told the former what we had just seen and heard, to which Titané replied with great enthusiasm: "It may well be that they are followers of a new doctrine, said to be invented by a very wise bonze who dwells in one of the houses on the slopes of Mount Coral." And because we were eager to hear more about this doctrine, Titané agreed to go with us the following day to visit the bonze, adding: "They say he will only confide his doctrine to those who truly desire to adhere to it; if that is true, we can pretend that we have come with the sole purpose of hearing his doctrine, and then, if we like it, we may do with it as we see fit."

The following day, as agreed, we went to the abode of the aforementioned bonze, who went by the curious name of Pomada, which in our language means "charlatan." He was an old man of a hundred and eight, well read in letters both divine and human, and widely revered by the pagan masses; for this very reason he was distrusted by the other bonzes, who were consumed with jealousy. And so, having learned from Titané who we were and what we wanted, the aforementioned bonze first of all initiated us into the various rituals and ceremonies necessary for the reception of his doctrine, and only then did he raise his voice to reveal and explain it to us.

"You must understand," he began, "that virtue and knowledge have two parallel existences, one in the man who possesses them, and the other in the minds of those who hear or observe him. If you were to put the most sublime virtues and the most profound knowledge into a solitary individual, removed from all contact with other men, it would be as if such things did not exist. If no one tastes the fruits of an orange tree, it is worth no more than wild gorse and scrub, and if nobody sees such fruits, they are worth nothing at all. Or, to put it more succinctly, there is no spectacle without a spectator. One day, while pondering such matters, I realized that achieving this small crumb of self-enlightenment had entirely consumed my life, and, moreover, it would all be in vain without the presence of other men to witness and honor me; I then wondered whether there might be some means of achieving the same effect with less effort, and that day, I can tell you now, was the day of mankind's rebirth, for it gave me my new doctrine."

At this point, we pricked up our ears and hung upon the lips of the bonze, who, since Diogo had told him I was unfamiliar with the local language, was speaking very slowly so that I would miss nothing. And on he went: "You will never guess what gave me the idea of this new doctrine: it was neither more nor less than the moonstone, that famous stone so luminous that, when placed on a mountaintop or on the pinnacle of a tower, it gives light to the whole countryside around, no matter how extensive. Such a stone, so rich in light, has never existed and no one has ever seen it, but many people believe it exists and more than one will tell you that he has seen it with his own eyes. I considered the matter and realized that if a thing can exist in someone's opinion without existing in reality, or exist in reality without existing in someone's opinion, the conclusion must be that of the two parallel existences, the only one necessary is that of opinion, not of reality, which is merely an additional convenience. No sooner had I made this discovery, however speculative, than I gave thanks to God for bestowing on me such special favor, and I resolved to verify it by experimentation. This I achieved on more than one occasion, but I will not bore you by going into the details. In order to understand the efficacy of my system, it is enough to tell you that crickets cannot be born out of thin air and the leaves of the coconut tree during the conjunction of the new moon, and the font of future life does not lie in a single drop of cow's blood; and yet Patimau and Languru, who are both clever men, were able to plant both these ideas into the minds of the masses so artfully that they now enjoy reputations as great physicians and even greater philosophers, and have followers who would willingly give their lives for them."

We did not know how best to express to the bonze our intense appreciation and admiration. He continued to question us, in detail, for quite some time about his doctrine and its founding principles, and once he was satisfied that we had fully understood it, he encouraged us to put it into practice, revealing it very cautiously, not because it contained anything that was contrary to divine or human laws, but because a misunderstanding could cause the doctrine irreparable damage before it had even taken its first steps. Finally, he bade us farewell in the certainty (and these were his very words) that we were "departing with your souls transformed into those of true Pomadists," a term which pleased him enormously, based as it was on his own name.

Indeed, before evening fell, the three of us had agreed to set to work on an idea that would prove as lucrative as it was judicious, for profit cannot be measured only in money, but according to the respect and praise one receives, for both are an alternative and perhaps better currency, even if they are of no use when buying silk damasks and gold plate. So we agreed, by way of an experiment, that each of us would plant a certain belief in the minds of the people of Fucheo, as a result of which we would reap the same reward as Patimau and Languru. But man does not easily lose sight of his own best interests, and so Titané took it upon himself to earn twice the profit by charging for the experiment with both currencies, that is by selling sandals and, at the same time, earning men's esteem; we did not object to this, since it seemed to us to have no bearing on the essential teachings of our doctrine.

I'm not quite sure how best to explain Titané's experiment in order for you to understand. Here in the kingdom of Bungo, as in other realms of these distant parts, they use a paper made from ground cinnamon bark and glue, a paper of the finest quality, which they then cut into pieces two palms long and half a palm wide. On these sheets, in a variety of bright colors and using the symbols of their own language, they inscribe the weekly news— items of a political, religious, or mercantile nature, about the new laws of the kingdom, and the names of all the *fustas*, *lancharas*, *balões*, and other types of vessels that ply these seas, either in warfare, which is frequent, or in trade. And I say weekly because these sheets of news are indeed prepared once a week, in great quantities, and distributed to the local populace for a small token, which everyone gives willingly so that they can read the news before anyone else hears about it. Now, our Titané could have wished for no better street corner than this paper, whose title translates into our language as *The Life and Clarity of Mundane and Celestial Things*, which is certainly expressive, if somewhat overblown. And so he arranged for it to be reported in the aforesaid paper that the news coming in from the coasts of Malabar and China was full of nothing but talk of Titané's famous sandals: that they were being acclaimed as the best in the world, on account of their robustness and elegance; that, given the splendor of Titané's famous sandals, the finest in the universe, no fewer than twenty-four mandarins were going to ask the Great Emperor to create the honorific title of "Sandal of State" as a reward to those who had distinguished themselves in any field of learning; that very large orders were flooding in from every region, orders that Titané was determined to fulfill less for love of profit than for the glory it would bring to his beloved homeland; that, nevertheless, he would not resile from his humble intention, which he had already declared to the king and hereby repeated, to donate fifty score such sandals to the kingdom's poor; and, finally, that, despite being acknowledged as the finest sandal-maker anywhere in the world, he knew the obligations of moderation, and would never consider himself anything more than a diligent artisan working tirelessly for the glory of the kingdom of Bungo.

The whole city of Fucheo was naturally deeply moved upon reading this news, and spoke of nothing else for the whole of that week. Titané's sandals, until then considered merely adequate, began to be sought out with great curiosity and enthusiasm, and even more so in the weeks that followed, since he continued for some time to entertain the city with many extraordinary tales about his merchandise. And he said to us, very cheerily:

"You can see that I have obeyed the fundamental principles of our doctrine, for I have made the people believe in the superiority of these sandals even though I am not persuaded of it myself, indeed I find them rather ordinary; and now everyone rushes to buy them, for whatever price I choose to charge."

"It doesn't seem to me," I interrupted, "that you have followed the doctrine in all its rigor and substance, for it is not our task to instill in others an opinion that we do not ourselves hold, but rather to convince them of a quality in us that we do not actually possess; that surely is the essence of the doctrine."

The other two then agreed that it was now my turn to attempt the experiment, and I did so immediately. I will not, however, relate every aspect of my own experiment, so as not to delay my account of Diogo Meireles's experiment, which was the most decisive of the three and provided the best proof of the bonze's delightful invention. I will say only that, having a smattering of music and a mediocre talent on the flute, I had the idea of gathering the leading citizens of Fucheo to hear me play the instrument. They duly came, listened, and went away saying that they had never heard anything quite so extraordinary. I confess that I achieved this result solely by virtue of airs and affectations: the elegant arch of my arms when I played the flute, which was brought to me on a silver salver, the firmness of my chest, the unctuous devotion with which I raised my eyes to heaven, and the contemptuous disdain with which I looked down at the audience, which promptly burst into such a concert of voices and cries of enthusiasm that I was almost persuaded of my own merit.

But, as I said, of all our experiments, Diego Miereles's was the most ingenious. At the time, a most peculiar disease was spreading through the city, one that caused a patient's nose to swell up so much that it covered half his or her face. This not only made them look utterly hideous, it also proved a very heavy burden to carry around. Although the local physicians proposed removing the swollen noses, for the relief and cure of those afflicted, no one would consent to succumb to such treatment, preferring excess to absence, and holding that the lack of that organ would be more bothersome than any other outcome. In such a predicament, several resorted to voluntary death as a remedy, to the great sadness of the whole city. Diogo Meireles, who, as mentioned earlier, had been practicing medicine for some time, studied the illness and agreed that there was no danger in relieving the sufferers of their noses; indeed it would be beneficial to remove the problem, and cause no further ugliness, since a heavy, misshapen nose was just as bad as none at all. He did not, however, manage to persuade the unfortunate sufferers to make the necessary sacrifice. Then a cunning plan occurred to him. And so it was that, having gathered together many physicians, philosophers, bonzes, representatives of authority and the people, he informed them that he held the secret to solving the problem. This secret was nothing less than replacing the diseased nose with one that was healthy, but of a purely metaphysical nature—that is, imperceptible to the human eye, but just as, or even more, real than the one that had been removed. It was a cure he had performed in many different places, and one that was widely accepted by the physicians of Malabar. The crowd was greatly astonished, and some were quite incredulous; I don't say all of them, for the majority did not know what to believe, repelled as they were by the metaphysics of noses. Gradually, however, they succumbed to the force of Diogo Meireles's words and the convincing tone with which he expounded his remedy. It was then that several philosophers, ashamed to appear any less knowledgeable than Diogo Meireles, declared that there was indeed a sound basis for such a discovery, given that mankind itself was nothing more than the product of transcendental ideals, from which they concluded that one could, in all likelihood, wear a metaphysical nose, and thus solemnly assured the crowd that it would be just as effective.

The assembled throng cheered Diogo Meireles to the rafters, and patients began to come to him in such numbers that he could scarcely keep up. Diogo Meireles relieved them of their noses with the greatest of skill, his fingers then reaching delicately toward a box in which he pretended to keep the substitute noses, picking up one and applying it to the empty space. The patients, thus cured and made whole again, looked at each other and could see nothing where the removed organ had been; however, convinced that the substitute organ was indeed there, albeit imperceptible to the human eye, they did not consider themselves cheated, and returned to their daily occupations. I could wish for no better proof of the efficacy of the doctrine, and the success of this experiment, than the fact that all those who were relieved of their noses by Diogo Meireles continued to make use of their handkerchiefs just as before. All of which I have set down here to the glory of the bonze and for the benefit of the world.

POLYCRATES'S RING

———

A: Oh, there goes Xavier.

Z: You know Xavier?

A: Yes, I've known him for years! He used to be a real nabob—rich, stinking rich, but a spendthrift with it . . .

Z: What do you mean, "rich"? What do you mean, "spendthrift"?

A: As I said, rich and a spendthrift too. He would drink pearls dissolved in nectar. He would dine on nightingales' tongues. He never used blotting paper because he thought this worthy only of tradesmen; he would sprinkle sand on his letters, but only a very special kind of sand made from powdered diamonds. And then there were the women! Ah, not even all of Solomon's splendors could match Xavier in that domain. He kept a whole seraglio: Grecian curves, Roman complexions, Turkish exuberance, all the perfections of every race, all the favors of every climate, all were welcome in Xavier's harem. One day, he fell madly in love with a lady from the highest society and sent her a gift of three stars from the Southern Cross, which, at the time, had seven, and don't go thinking that the gift-bearer was any old pauper. No, sirree. The gift-bearer was one of Milton's archangels, whom Xavier summoned as he winged his way across the ethereal sky carrying man's eternal praise and admiration to his aged English father. Xavier was like that. He rolled his cigarettes using the very finest silk paper, and to light them, he carried with him a little box of sunrays. The quilts on his bed were purple clouds, as were the upholstery of the sofa he reclined upon, the armchair in his study, and the hammock on his veranda. Do you know who made his coffee in the mornings? Aurora herself, with the rosy fingers given her by Homer. Poor Xavier! Everything that wealth and whim could provide: the rare, the odd, the marvelous, the indescribable, the unimaginable, all of this he had and deserved to have, because he was a gracious and generous young man, and a kind soul. Ah, but fortune, fortune! Where are they now, the pearls, the diamonds, the stars, the purple clouds? He lost everything, let it all slip through his fingers; the nectar turned to vinegar, his cushions now are the cobbles in the street; he no longer sends ladies gifts of stars, or has archangels at his beck and call . . .

Z: You must be mistaken. Xavier? It must be another Xavier entirely. Xavier, a nabob! The Xavier you see over there never had more than two hundred *mil-réis* a month: he's a sober, thrifty man, early to bed and early to rise, and he doesn't write letters to sweethearts, because he has none. If he sends anything at all to his friends it's by the post. He may not be a beggar, but he was certainly never a nabob.

A: Ah, that's the outer Xavier. But man does not live by bread alone. You're talking about Martha, I'm telling you about Mary; I'm talking about the imagined Xavier . . .

Z: Ah! But even so, you still haven't explained. It doesn't sound like the Xavier I know. What book, what poem, what painting—

A: How long have you known him?

Z: Fifteen years or so.

A: Ouf! I've known him for much longer, ever since he made his social debut on the Rua do Ouvidor, back when the Marquis of Paraná was in government. He was unstoppable, like a man possessed; he had schemes for everything under the sun, and even some that weren't: a book, a speech, a remedy, a newspaper, a poem, a novel, a history, a political diatribe, a trip to Europe, another to the backlands of Minas Gerais, another to the moon, traveling in a special balloon he'd invented, a career in politics, not to mention archaeology, philosophy, and the theater, etc., etc., etc. He was a sackful of surprises. Just having a conversation with him made you dizzy.

Imagine a torrent of ideas and images, each more original and beautiful than the last, sometimes extravagant, sometimes sublime. And he believed in his own inventions too. One day, for example, he woke up with the idea of entirely flattening the Castelo hill, in return for all the riches that the Jesuits had buried there, as people widely believed. He calculated that there must be a thousand *contos* in gold coin, and made a careful inventory of everything, separating out the coins—a thousand *contos*—from the jewelry and the works of art; he meticulously described every object, and gave me two golden torch-holders . . .

Z: Really . . .

A: Ah, yes! Priceless. Do you want to know something else? Having read the letters of Canon Benigno, he decided there and then to go to the backlands of Bahia in search of the mysterious city chronicled therein. He showed me the plan, described to me the likely architecture of the city, its temples and palaces built in the Etruscan style, the rites, vases, clothes, costumes—

Z: So he was mad, then?

A: No, one of a kind, more like. I hate sheep, he would say, quoting Rabelais: "*As you know, it is the nature of sheep to follow the first, wherever it goes.*" He compared triviality to the communal table at an inn, and swore that he'd rather eat a bad steak at a separate table.

Z: And yet he enjoyed society.

A: He did, but he had no love for its members. One day, a friend of ours, a chap called Pires, made precisely that same comment to him, and do you know what he said? He replied with a parable, in which each member of society was a gourd of water, whereas society was a bathtub. "And I cannot bathe in a gourd of water," was his conclusion.

Z: So not a modest fellow, then. What did Pires say to him?

A: Pires thought it such a lovely image that, some time later, he included it in one of his comedies. The funny thing is that Xavier heard it at the theater and applauded it warmly, enthusiastically even; he had completely forgotten that he was its father, but blood obviously called to blood. Which brings me to an explanation of Xavier's present impoverished state.

Z: Indeed. I don't know how you can explain that a nabob—

A: It's not that difficult, actually. He scattered ideas right, left, and center, as easily as the rain falls from the sky, through sheer physical necessity, and for two reasons in particular. Firstly, he was impatient and could not endure the long gestation period required by a piece of written work. Secondly, his eyes surveyed so vast a horizon that he struggled to fix upon any one thing in particular. If he hadn't been so fluent verbally, he would have suffered from mental constipation; words, for him, acted as a purgative. The pages he spoke, the chapters that gushed from his lips, needed only to be printed in the air and then onto paper to make truly excellent, even admirable, publications. Not everything was crystal clear, but the crystal-clear portion always exceeded the murkier part, and, after all, even Homer occasionally nods. He sowed his seeds at random, in whole handfuls, not even noticing where the seeds fell, and some sprang up quickly . . .

Z: Like the one about the gourds.

A: Yes, like the one about the gourds. But, the sower had a passion for beautiful things, and, as long as the tree was lush and green, he never asked the tree what seed it had sprung from. And so he lived for many years, spending freely and fruitlessly, by day and by night, in the street or at home, with no thought for the cost, a genuine spendthrift. Given such a regime, which was, in fact, the total absence of any regime, it's no wonder that he should end up wretched and poor. Imagination and spirit have their limits, my friend; apart from the mountebank's famously bottomless bottle and mankind's credulity, I know of nothing inexhaustible under the sun. Xavier not only lost all the ideas he'd had, he even exhausted his ability to create new ones; he became the man we know today. What rare coin does one ever see in his hands now? What sesterce by Horace? What Periclean drama? Nothing. He fritters away his commonplaces, worn thin by other hands, eats at the communal table, has, in short, become trivial, futile—

Z: A gourd, in other words.

A: Precisely. A gourd.

Z: Well, this is a lot to take in. I knew nothing about it. But I'm fully informed now. Goodbye.

A: Do you have business to attend to?

Z: I do have some business to attend to.

A: Can you give me ten minutes?

Z: I can give you fifteen.

A: I want to tell you about the most interesting part of Xavier's life. Take my arm and we'll walk a little. Are you going to the main square? Let's go together. Yes, a most interesting case. It was back in 1869 or 1870, I can't remember which; it was he himself who told me. He had lost everything; his brain was spent, sucked dry, sterile, without so much as a shadow of an idea or an image, nothing. Suffice it to say that, one day, he called a lady a rose, "a pretty rose"; he talked of wistful moonlight, of the priesthood of the press, and of sumptuous banquets, without adding anything original to all that trite junk from the tinker's cart. He became a hypochondriac. Then, one day, standing at the window, sad and disillusioned, seeing how his life had come to naught, a dandy on horseback happened to pass by in the street. Suddenly the horse bucked and nearly threw the dandy to the ground, but the man managed to hold on, and dug in his spurs and plied his whip. The horse reared, but still the rider hung on; people stood watching from the street or from their doorways; after ten minutes' struggle, the horse gave in and walked on. The spectators were full of wonder and admiration at the horseman's elegance, courage, sangfroid, and skill. Then Xavier thought to himself that perhaps the gentleman hadn't been brave at all. That he simply hadn't wanted to fall off in front of all those people, and it was his fear of humiliation that had given him the strength to master the horse. And from this came an idea: he compared life to an unbroken or skittish horse; and added sententiously: "Even if you're not a rider, you should at least look like one." It wasn't such an extraordinary idea, but Xavier's penury had reached such extremes that this crystal seemed to him a diamond. He repeated it a dozen or so times, formulating it in various ways; first of all in its natural word order, with the definition followed by the complement, then putting it the other way around, changing the words, getting the measure of them, etc., and he felt as happy as a pig in clover. That night, he dreamt that he was indeed riding a skittish horse, which reared up and threw him into a bog. He awoke feeling sad; the morning, which was a rainy Sunday, made him feel even sadder; he sat down to read and to brood. Then he remembered something . . . Do you know the story of Polycrates's ring?

Z: I'm afraid I don't.

A: Nor did I, but here's what Xavier told me. Polycrates was the ruler of the island of Samos. He was the happiest king on Earth, so happy that he began to fear that Fortune might turn against him, and, to placate her in advance, he decided to make her a great offering: he would throw into the sea the ring which, according to some, he used as his seal. And that is what he did; but Fortune was so busy garlanding him with favors that the ring was swallowed by a fish, and the fish was caught by a fisherman and sent to the kitchens of the king, who thus regained possession of the ring. I make no claims for this little tale; it was Xavier who told me it, quoting Pliny, quoting—

Z: Say no more. Xavier was obviously comparing life, not to a horse, but—

A: No, nothing like that. You cannot imagine the bizarre plan the poor devil had dreamed up. "Let's try our hand at fortune," he said; "let's see if my idea, thrown into the sea, will come back to me like Polycrates's ring in the belly of a fish, or if my bad luck is such that I will never again lay my hands upon it."

Z: How extraordinary!

A: Bizarre, isn't it? Polycrates had put his happiness to the test; Xavier wanted to do the same with his bad luck. Different intentions, identical actions. He left his house, met a friend, struck up a conversation, chose any old subject, and ended his sentence by saying that life was an unbroken or skittish horse, and that even if you're not a rider, you should at least look like one. Spoken like that, the phrase may perhaps have fallen rather flat; for this reason, Xavier was careful to describe, first, his sadness, his years of disappointments and frustrations, or, rather, the effects of reckless imprudence, and then, when the fish's mouth was wide open, that is to say, when his friend's distress at this sorry tale had reached its peak, that was when Xavier tossed him the ring, and fled back home. What I am telling you is entirely natural and believable, and certainly

not impossible. But, at this point, reality and imagination begin
to merge. Whatever the truth of the matter, I am merely repeating what he told me. Around three weeks later, Xavier was dining
quietly at the Golden Lion or the Globe, I'm not sure which, and at
the next table he heard someone repeat his very words, with perhaps an adjective or two changed. "My poor ring," he said to himself, "there you are inside Polycrates's fish." But the idea took flight
and flew away, without him being able to keep it in his memory. He
resigned himself to this. A few days later, he was invited to a ball by
an old acquaintance from his youth, who was celebrating his recent
elevation to the nobility. Xavier accepted the invitation and went
to the ball, and it is just as well that he did, because between the
ice cream and the tea he overheard a group of people praising the
baron's career and prosperous, upstanding, exemplary life; and he
heard them compare the baron to an expert rider. General astonishment all around, because the baron did not ride.

But the panegyrist explained that life is nothing more than an
unbroken or skittish horse, and that one must either be an excellent rider, or at least look like one, and the baron excelled at the
latter. "Come, my dear ring," said Xavier, "come to Polycrates's
finger." But once again the idea flapped its wings and flew away,
ignoring him. A few days later—

Z: I can guess the rest: a series of similar encounters and similar
escapes.

A: Exactly.

Z. But, finally, one day, he caught it.

A: Just once, and it was then that he told me about the incident that
was truly worthy of being remembered. He was so happy that day!
He swore to me that he would write it up as a fantastic tale, in
the manner of Edgar Allan Poe, a glittering page punctuated with
mysteries—those were his very words. And he asked me to come
and see him the following day. I went. The ring had escaped him
once again. "My dear A," he said, with a knowing, sarcastic smile,
"you see before you the Polycrates of bad luck; I nominate you my
honorary and unpaid minister of state." From then on, it was always
the same. Whenever he thought he'd caught the idea, it flapped its
wings, whoosh, whoosh, whoosh, and disappeared into the air, like

figures in a dream. Another fish swallowed it and brought it back, with always the same outcome. But let me tell you just three more of the incidents he told me about that day—

Z: I can't. Our fifteen minutes are up.

A: Just three, I promise you. One day, Xavier came to believe that he would, at last, be able to catch the fugitive, and fix it forever in his brain. He opened an opposition newspaper and was astonished to read these words: "The government seems entirely unaware that politics is, like life itself, an unbroken or skittish horse, and, since it is unable to be a good rider, it should at least look like one."

"Ah! At last!" exclaimed Xavier. "There you are, trapped in the belly of the fish; you won't escape me now." But in vain. The idea did indeed escape, leaving behind it only a vague recollection. Cast down and despairing, he began to walk and walk until night fell. When he passed a theater, he decided to go in; the sight of all those bright lights, all that jollity, soothed his spirits. Not only was it a new comedy; it was by his friend Pires. He sat down beside the playwright and applauded enthusiastically, with the sincere love of an artist and a brother. During the second act, scene VIII, a shudder ran through him. "Dona Eugênia," said the leading man to a lady, "the horse may be compared to life, which is also unbroken and skittish; he who is not a good rider must take care to look like one." The playwright glanced timidly at Xavier to judge the effect of this idea on his friend; meanwhile, Xavier was repeating the same pleading words: "My dear, dear ring . . ."

Z: *Et nunc et semper* . . . Come on, let's hear the last encounter; it's time I went.

A: The last was the first. As I mentioned, Xavier had originally told this idea to a friend. One week after that night at the theater, the friend fell so gravely ill that within four days he was at death's door.

Xavier rushed to see him; the poor fellow, still able to recognize him, reached out one cold and trembling hand, fixed him with the long, dull gaze of a dying man, and, in a faint voice, like an echo from the grave, sobbed: "I'm slipping away, my dearest Xavier, the unbroken, skittish horse of life has thrown me to the ground: whether I was a bad rider or not I cannot say, but I tried to look like a good one." Don't laugh; he was in tears when he told me this. He also told me that the idea fluttered for a few minutes more over the corpse, with its glittering, beautiful wings made of the crystal he had once believed to be a diamond, then it let out a faint derisory chuckle, ungrateful and patricidal, and flew away as it had before, lodging itself in the minds of those friends of the household gathered around, racked with grief, and who sadly took in the dead man's pious legacy. Farewell.

THE LOAN

──────────

I'M GOING TO TELL YOU an anecdote, an anecdote in the true sense of the word, which common usage has since broadened out to include any brief, invented tale. This anecdote happens to be true: I can cite several people who know it as well as I do. Nor would it have remained hidden from view had some tranquil soul been capable of discerning its philosophical implications. As you know, everything has a philosophical meaning. Carlyle discovered the philosophy of vests, or, rather, of clothes, and everyone knows that numbers were used in the Pythagorean system long before the Ipiranga lottery. For my part, I think I have deciphered the meaning behind this tale of a loan; you will see if I am mistaken.

To begin with, let us amend what Seneca said. In the eyes of that stern moralist, every day is, in itself, a singular life; in other words, a life within life. I wouldn't disagree with that, but why did he not add that often a single hour can encapsulate a whole life? Observe this young man: he enters the world with great ambitions: a ministerial portfolio perhaps, his own bank, a viscount's coronet, a bishop's crozier. At fifty, we will find him working as a lowly customs inspector, or as a sacristan in some country parish. This transformation took place over a period of thirty years, and no doubt a Balzac could have fit it all into a mere three hundred pages; so why shouldn't life, which was, after all, Balzac's teacher, squeeze it into thirty or sixty minutes?

Four o'clock had struck in the office of the notary Vaz Nunes, in Rua do Rosário. The clerks had put the final flourishes to their documents, and wiped their goose quills on the piece of black silk hanging from one of the drawers; then they had closed the drawers, gathered up their papers, tidied away their books and registers, and washed their hands; those who had changed their jackets on arriving took off their work coat and put on their outdoor one, and then they all left. Vaz Nunes remained alone.

This honest notary was one of the most perceptive men of his day. He has since died, so we can praise him all we like. He had eyes like a lancet, cutting and sharp. He could read the characters of the people who came to him to notarize their contracts and agreements; he knew a testator's soul long before he had finished his will; he could scent secret plots and hidden thoughts. He wore glasses, as do all stage notaries, but, not being nearsighted, he would peer over them when he wanted to see, and through them if he preferred not to be seen. Crafty old fox, said the clerks. He was, in any event, a circumspect fellow. He was fifty years old, a childless widower, and, in the words of some of his fellow notaries, he was quietly nibbling his way through the two hundred *contos de réis* he had salted away.

"Who's there?" he asked suddenly, looking up.

Standing in the doorway was a man whom he did not immediately recognize and whom he only barely recognized afterward. Vaz Nunes invited him in; the man entered, greeted him, shook his hand, and sat down on the chair beside the desk. He did not carry himself with the customary awkwardness of a beggar; on the contrary, he gave every impression of having come with the sole purpose of giving the notary some very precious and rare commodity. Vaz Nunes nevertheless shuddered and waited.

"Don't you remember me?"

"No, I don't."

"We were with each other one night a few months ago, in Tijuca. Don't you remember? In Teodorico's house, at that magnificent Christmas Eve supper. As a matter of fact, I proposed a toast to you. Surely you remember old Custódio!"

"Ah!"

Custódio sat up straighter, having been sitting somewhat slumped. He was a man of about forty. Poorly dressed, but well groomed, neat, and very correct. He had long nails, neatly trimmed, and his hands were slender and soft, unlike the skin on his face, which was somewhat lined. Minor details, but necessary to illustrate a certain duality in the man, an air of being both a beggar and a general. Walking down the street with no breakfast and not a penny in his pocket, he behaved as if he were marching at the head of an army. The reason was none other than the contrast between nature and situation, between soul and life. Custódio had been born with a vocation to be wealthy, but with no vocation for work. He had an instinct for elegance, a love of excess, good food, beautiful ladies, luxuriant carpets, exquisite furniture, a voluptuary (and, up to a point, an artist) capable of running the Villa Torlonia or the Hamilton Gallery. But he had no money; neither money nor the aptitude or patience to earn it. And yet, on the other hand, he needed to live. *Il faut bien que je vive*, a man in search of a favor once said to Talleyrand. *Je n'en vois pas la nécessité*, the minister replied coldly. Nobody gave this answer to Custódio; they gave him money instead—someone would give him ten *mil-réis*, another would give five, another twenty, and it was principally from such small donations that he paid his bed and board.

I say "principally," because Custódio did not hold back from involving himself in various business deals, but always on condition that he could choose them, and he always chose the ones that were doomed to fail. He had an excellent nose for disasters. From among twenty businesses, he could immediately pluck the most foolhardy, and would plunge in resolutely. The bad luck that pursued him would ensure that the other nineteen would prosper, while the one he chose would blow up in his face. No matter; he would pick himself up and get ready for the next.

He had, for example, recently read an advertisement in the paper seeking a business partner willing to invest five *contos de réis* in a certain enterprise that promised, within the first six months, to return a profit of between eighty and a hundred *contos*. Custódio went to meet the person who had placed the advertisement. It was a great idea: a needle factory, a brand-new business with an exciting future. And the plans, the design of the factory, the reports from Birmingham, the lists of imports, the replies from tailors and haberdashers and other such merchants, all swam before Custódio's eyes, dazzled by figures he could not understand, and which, for that very reason, appeared to be the gospel truth. Twenty-four hours; he asked for twenty-four hours to find the five *contos*. And he left the place, flattered and fawned upon by the advertiser, who, still standing on the doorstep, continued to deluge him with a torrent of credit and debit balances. But the five *contos*—five thousand *mil-réis*, no less—proved less biddable or less fickle than a mere five *mil-réis*, shaking their heads incredulously and keeping to their coffers, paralyzed by fear and sleep. Not one penny. The eight or ten friends he spoke to all told him they didn't have that amount of money available, nor did they have any faith in the factory. He had just about lost all hope when he happened to find himself in Rua do Rosário and saw the name Vaz Nunes above the doorway of a notary's office. His heart leapt with joy, remembering Tijuca, the notary's impeccable manners, the kind words with which he responded to the toast, and he said to himself that here was the man to save the situation.

"I've come to ask you to draw up a deed . . ."

Expecting a different opening gambit, Vaz Nunes did not reply, but simply peered over his glasses and waited.

"A deed of gratitude," explained Custódio; "I've come to ask you a great favor, an indispensable favor, and I'm counting on you, my friend . . ."

"If I can help, of course . . ."

"It's a really excellent business, a magnificent business. I would not even deign to bother other people if the outcome were not certain. It's all set to go; stock has already been ordered from England, and the business should be up and running within two months; it's a new factory, you see. There are three of us in the partnership; my share is five *contos* and I've come to ask you to lend me that amount for six months—or even three, at a reasonable rate of interest . . ."

"Five *contos*?"

"Yes, indeed."

"But I can't, Custódio. I simply don't have that kind of money. Business is bad, and even if it were going really well, I wouldn't be able to lay my hands on that amount. Who could ever expect five *contos* from a humble notary?"

"If you really wanted to . . ."

"But I do want to. All I'm saying is that if it were a small amount, proportionate to my means, I would have no hesitation in advancing it. But five *contos*! Believe me, it's quite impossible."

Custódio's spirits sank. He had climbed up Jacob's ladder to heaven, but instead of descending like the angels in the biblical dream, he had tumbled down and fallen flat on his face. This was his last hope, and precisely because it had arisen so unexpectedly, he was convinced it would bear fruit, since, like all souls who trust themselves to happenstance, Custódio was a superstitious man. The poor wretch could feel his body being pierced all over by every one of those millions of needles that the factory would undoubtedly produce during its first six months. Speechless, eyes down-cast, he waited for the notary to continue, to take pity on him and give him a chance. But, sensing this, the notary remained equally silent, turning his snuff box around and around in his hand, and breathing heavily, with a certain knowing, nasal whistle. Custódio attempted every possible pose, now a beggar, now a general. The notary would not be moved. Custódio stood up.

"In that case," he said, with just a touch of resentment, "forgive me for bothering you . . ."

"There's nothing to forgive: it is I who must apologize for not being able to help you, as I would have liked. As I said, had the amount been smaller, much smaller, I would not have hesitated; however . . ."

He reached out to shake hands with Custódio, who mechanically tipped his hat with his other hand. Custódio's dull stare revealed the state of his soul, barely recovered from its fall, which had drained him of his last ounce of energy. No mysterious ladder and no heaven; everything had vanished at the snap of a notary's fingers. Farewell, needles! Reality once again gripped him with its bronze talons. He would have to return to his precarious, unplanned existence, to his old account books with their goggle-eyed zeros and wiggly-eared $-signs, that would continue to stare and listen, listen and stare, dangling before him the implacable numerology of hunger. What a fall! And into what an abyss! Realizing the truth of his situation, he looked at the notary as if to say goodbye, but an idea suddenly lit up the dark night of his brain. If it were a smaller amount, Vaz Nunes could provide it, and willingly. So why shouldn't it be a smaller amount? He had already given up the idea of the business adventure; but he could scarcely do the same with his rent arrears and his various other creditors. A reasonable sum, five hundred *mil-réis*, for example, would do nicely, if he could only persuade the notary to lend it to him. Custódio's spirits rose; he would live for the present and have nothing to do with the past, no regrets or fears, no remorse. The present was all that mattered. The present was the five hundred *mil-réis* that he would watch emerging from the notary's pocket like a certificate of emancipation.

"In that case," he said, "why don't you see what you can give me, and I'll go and ask some other friends as well. How much do you think you could afford?"

"I hardly dare say, because it can really only be a very modest amount indeed."

"Five hundred *mil-réis*?"

"No, impossible."

"Not even five hundred *mil-réis*?"

"No," said the notary firmly. "What's so surprising about that? I won't deny that I own several properties, but, my friend, I don't walk around with them in my wallet; and I have certain obligations incumbent upon me . . . Don't you have a job?"

"No, I don't."

"Look, I'll give you something better than five hundred *mil-réis*; I'll have a word with the minister of justice. I know him well, and—"

Custódio interrupted him, slapping his thigh. Whether this was a natural gesture or a crafty diversion to avoid discussing a potential job, I have absolutely no idea; nor does it seem an essential element of the story. What is essential, though, is that he persisted in his request. Could the notary really not give him five hundred *mil-réis*? He would take two hundred; two hundred would be enough, not for the factory, for he would follow his friends' advice and turn it down. Two hundred *mil-réis*, seeing that the notary was disposed to help him, would meet an urgent need, to "fill a hole," as he put it. And then he told the notary everything, meeting frankness with frankness, for that was his rule of life. He admitted that, in dealing with the business proposal, he also had in mind settling matters with a particularly persistent creditor, a devil of a fellow and a Jew, who, strictly speaking, still owed him, but had treacherously turned the tables on him. It was two hundred and something *mil-réis*; two hundred and ten, to be precise; but he would accept two hundred—

"Really, it pains me to repeat what I've already said, but there we are; even two hundred *mil-réis* is beyond my means. Even if you were to ask me for a hundred *mil-réis*, that would still exceed my capabilities at this particular time. On another occasion, possibly, I'm sure, but not right now . . ."

"You can't imagine the tricky situation I find myself in!"

"I repeat, not even one hundred *mil-réis*. I've had a lot of expenses recently. Clubs and societies, subscriptions, the Freemasons . . . You probably don't believe me, do you, given that I do own some property, but, my friend, it is indeed a fine thing to own houses, but what you don't see is all the wear and tear, the repairs, the water pipes, the tithes, the insurance, the rent arrears, and all the rest of it. They're the holes in the pot through which most of the water is lost . . ."

"If only I had a pot!" sighed Custódio.

"I'm not saying I'm not fortunate, but what I am saying is that owning houses doesn't mean you don't have worries, expenses, even creditors . . . Believe you me, I have creditors too."

"So not even a hundred *mil-réis*!"

"Not even a hundred *mil-réis*. It pains me to say so, but that's how it is. Not even a hundred *mil-réis*. Now what time is it?"

He stood up and stepped forward into the middle of the room. Custódio did likewise, impelled by necessity and desperation. He could not bring himself to believe that the notary did not have at least a hundred *mil-réis*. Who on earth doesn't have a hundred *mil-réis*? He considered making a pathetic scene, but the notary's office opened directly onto the street and he didn't want to appear ridiculous. He peered outside. In the shop across the street a man was asking the price of a frock coat; he was standing at the door because dusk was coming on and it was already dark in the shop. The clerk was holding up the item of clothing for the customer, who was examining the cloth with eyes and fingers, then the seams, the lining . . . The incident opened up a new horizon to Custódio, albeit a modest one: it was high time he replaced the jacket he was wearing. But the notary couldn't even give him fifty *mil-réis*. Custódio smiled, not scornfully or angrily, but bitterly and hesitantly. It was impossible that the man didn't have fifty *mil-réis*. Twenty, at least? Not twenty. Not even twenty! No, it was all pretense, all lies.

Custódio pulled out his handkerchief, slowly smoothed his hat, then put his handkerchief back in his pocket and straightened his tie, with a mixture of hope and resentment. He had gradually been trimming the wings of his ambitions, feather by feather, but there still remained a fine, furry down, which gave him the foolish idea that he could fly. The other man, however, remained unmoved. Vaz Nunes was checking his pocket watch with the clock on the wall, holding it to his ear, cleaning the watch face, quietly oozing impatience and annoyance from every pore. The clock's hands were creeping toward five. Finally, the hour struck, and the notary was at last able to begin his farewells. It was late; he lived far away. As he said this, he took off his alpaca jacket and put on the cashmere one, transferring from one to the other his snuffbox, handkerchief, and wallet. Oh, the wallet! Custódio saw this problematic item, caressed it with his eyes, envying the alpaca, envying the cashmere, wishing he could be the pocket, wishing he could be the leather, the material of the precious receptacle itself. There it went, plunged straight into the inside left-hand pocket of the jacket, which the notary swiftly buttoned up. Not even twenty *mil-réis*! It was impossible that he didn't have twenty *mil-réis* on him, thought Custódio; perhaps not two hundred, but certainly twenty, or ten . . .

"Right, then!" said Vaz Nunes, putting on his hat.

It was the fateful moment. Not a word from the notary, not even an invitation to dine with him; nothing. It was the end of the road. But supreme moments call for supreme efforts. Custódio felt this cliché in all its strength, and, suddenly, like a shot, he asked the notary if he couldn't at least give him ten *mil-réis*.

"Shall I show you?"

And the notary unbuttoned his jacket, took out his wallet, opened it, and removed two notes of five *mil-réis*.

"See? That's all I have," he said. "What I can do is share them with you; I'll give you one five *mil-réis* note, and I'll keep the other; will that do?"

Custódio accepted the five *mil-réis*, not glumly or with bad grace, but smiling, indeed as thrilled as if he had just conquered Asia Minor. There was his dinner taken care of. He shook the other man's hand, thanked him for his kindness, bade him farewell for now—a "for now" full of implicit meanings. Then he left; the beggar slipping out the door of the notary's office and the general marching boldly down the street, nodding fraternally to the English merchants making their way up toward the suburbs. Never had the sky seemed so blue or the evening so clear; all the men around him had a gleam of hospitality in their eyes. With his left hand he lovingly squeezed the five-*mil-réis* note in his trouser pocket, the residue of a grand ambition which, but a short time ago, had soared boldly up to the sun like an eagle, and now flapped modestly with the flightless wings of a chicken.

THE MOST SERENE REPUBLIC

(Canon Vargas's Lecture)

───────────

G ENTLEMEN,

Before informing you of a new discovery, which I consider will bring some luster to our nation, please allow me to thank you for your prompt response to my invitation. I know that only the loftiest of interests have brought you here today, but I am also aware—and it would be ungrateful on my part not to be—that your entirely legitimate sense of scientific curiosity is mingled with a modicum of affection. I very much hope that I may prove worthy of both.

My discovery is not a recent one; it dates from the latter part of 1876. I did not reveal it then for a reason you will easily comprehend, and if it weren't for *Globo*, surely our capital's most interesting newspaper, I would not be revealing it now. The work I have come here to discuss with you still lacks a few final touches, verifications, and complementary experiments. However, when *Globo* reported that an English expert has discovered the phonetic language of insects, citing a study undertaken with flies, I imme-diately wrote to colleagues in Europe, and keenly await their responses. Since it is undoubtedly the case that, in the field of aerial navigation, so ably invented by our very own Father Bartolomeu, the names of foreigners have taken all the glory, while that of our compatriot is scarcely remembered even by his own people, I was determined to avoid the fate of that eminent Flying Priest, and so have come to this rostrum to proclaim loud and clear, to the entire universe, that long before that English expert, and far beyond the British Isles, I, a humble naturalist, discovered exactly the same thing, and made a much better job of it.

Gentlemen, I am about to astonish you, as I would have astonished Aristotle had I asked him: "Do you believe that a social order could ever be imposed upon spiders?" Aristotle would have replied in the negative, as will all of you, because it is simply impossible to believe that such a shy and solitary arthropod made for work alone and not for love, could ever be inducted into some form of social organization. Well, I have achieved the impossible.

I hear some laughter among the other curious murmurings. One must always strive to overcome one's prejudices, gentlemen. Spiders may strike you as inferior precisely because you do not know them. You love your dogs and hold cats and hens in high esteem, and yet you fail to notice that the humble spider neither jumps nor barks like a dog, nor meows like a cat, nor clucks like a hen. Nor does it buzz or bite like a mosquito, or rob us of our blood and sleep the way fleas do. All these creatures are the very model of vagrant parasites. Even the ant, so praised for certain qualities, preys upon our sugar and our crops, and builds its home by stealing someone else's. The spider, gentlemen, neither troubles nor defrauds us; indeed, it catches flies, our sworn enemies. The spider spins, weaves, works, and dies. What better example could there be of patience, order, foresight, respect, and, dare I say it, humanity? As for its talents, there can be no doubt. From Pliny to Darwin, naturalists the world over speak as one in praise of this tiny bug, whose marvelous web is destroyed in less than a minute by your servant's thoughtless broom. And if time permitted, I would now repeat all of these men's wise opinions; however, I have a lot to get through and so must be brief. I have them here, not quite all of them, but almost; I have, for example, this excellent monograph by Büchner, who studied the psychological lives of animals with such perspicacity. In citing Darwin and Büchner, I am, of course, merely paying due respect to two geniuses of the first order, without (as my vestments attest) in any way absolving them of the unfounded and erroneous theories of materialism.

Yes, gentlemen, I have discovered a species of spider that has the gift of speech. Initially I collected just a few of these new arthropods, then many more, and set about imposing a social order on them. The first of these marvelous specimens came to my attention on December 15, 1876. It was so large, so brightly colored, with a red dorsal patch and blue transversal stripes, so swift in its movements and at times so cheerful, that it completely captured my attention. The next day, three more appeared, and the four of them took possession of a suitable corner in my country house. I studied them at length, and was full of admiration. Nothing, however, could compare to my surprise upon discovering the arachnid language; for it is, gentlemen, a rich and varied tongue, with its own syntactical structure, verbs, conjugations, declensions, Latin cases, and onomatopoeia. I am currently engaged in meticulously compiling its grammar for use in schools and universities, based on the initial summary I prepared for my own use. It has, as you can imagine, taken extraordinary patience to overcome this most testing of challenges. I often lost heart, but my love of science gave me the strength to press ahead with a task that, I can tell you now, no man could hope to accomplish twice in his lifetime.

I will keep the technical descriptions and linguistic analysis for another time and place. The purpose of this lecture is, as I said, to safeguard the rights of Brazilian science with this timely protest, and, having done so, to tell you about the ways in which I consider my own work superior to that of that English expert. I will need to demonstrate this, and for that reason I ask for your close attention.

Within one month, I had collected twenty spiders; the following month, there were fifty-five and, by March 1877, four hundred and ninety. The two main factors involved in collecting them were: using their language as soon as I began to discern something of it, together with the sheer terror I instilled in them. My height, my flowing vestments, and my mastery of their language all made them believe that I was the god of spiders, and, from that point on, they worshipped me. And behold the benefits of their delusion. I followed their every action with great attention and detail, jotting down all my observations in a notebook, which they believed to be a record of their sins, thus reinforcing still further their virtuous behavior. My flute was also of great assistance. As you know, or should know, spiders are quite mad about music.

Mere association was not enough; I needed to give them a suitable form of government. I hesitated in my choice of system; many of the current forms seemed to me adequate, some even excellent, but they all had the disadvantage of already existing. Let me explain. Any current form of government would expose them to comparisons that might be used to belittle them. I needed either to find a brand-new system, or to reintroduce one that had long since been abandoned. Naturally, I chose the latter, and nothing seemed more fitting than a republic in the Venetian mold; I even adopted the same epithet. This obsolete system, which was, in general terms, unlike any other current system of government, had the added advantage of all complicated mechanisms, namely, it would put my young society's political skills to the test.

There was another motive behind my choice. Among the various electoral methods once used in the Venice of old was the bag and ball, which is how the sons of the nobility were initiated into matters of state. Balls bearing the candidates' names were placed in the bag, and every year a certain number were taken out, with the chosen few being deemed suitable for public service. Such a system will provoke laughter among experts in electoral suffrage, but that is not the case with me. For it precludes the follies of passion, the errors of ineptitude, and the commingling of corruption and greed. This was not my only reason for choosing it; I felt that a community so skilled in the spinning of webs would find the use of the electoral bag easy to adapt to, indeed almost second nature.

My proposal was accepted. "The Most Serene Republic" struck them as a magnificent title: high-sounding and generous, and suitably aggrandizing of their work as a collective.

I would not say, gentlemen, that my work has reached perfection, nor that it will do so in the near future. My pupils are not Campanella's solarians or More's utopians; they are a new people, who cannot in a single bound o'erleap our most venerable nations. And time is not a workman who willingly hands his tools to another; it will, though, serve far better than any paper theories, which look good on paper, but prove lame in practice. What I will say is that, notwithstanding the uncertainties of the age, the spiders continue to make progress, having at their disposal some of the virtues which I believe essential for a state to endure. One of those virtues, as I have already mentioned and as I will now demonstrate, is perseverance, the long-suffering patience of Penelope.

In effect, ever since they first grasped that the electoral act was the fundamental basis of public life, they set out to exercise it with the utmost punctiliousness. Weaving the bag was itself a national undertaking. It was five inches long, three inches wide, and woven from the finest threads into a solid, sturdy piece of work. To make it, ten ladies of the very highest rank were selected by acclamation, and given the title "mothers of the republic" along with various other privileges and perquisites. A real masterpiece, of that you can be sure. The electoral process itself is quite simple. The names of the candidates, each of whom must fulfill certain conditions, are inscribed on the balls by a public official known as the Inscriptions Officer. On election day, the balls are placed in the bag and then picked out by the Withdrawals Officer, until the required number of candidates has been chosen. What was simply an initiation ceremony in the Venice of old, here serves to fill all public positions.

At first the election passed off without incident. But soon afterward, one of the legislators declared that the election had been tainted, because the bag contained two balls each inscribed with the name of the same candidate. The assembly verified the truth of the allegation, and declared that the bag would henceforth be only two inches wide, not three, thus restricting the bag's capacity and limiting (which was as good as eliminating) the scope for fraud. However, in the following election, it transpired that the name of one of the candidates had not been inscribed on the relevant ball; whether this was due to carelessness or willful omission on the part of the public official is not known. The official insisted that he had no recollection of seeing the illustrious candidate, but nobly added that it was not impossible that he had been given the name, in which case it had not been a matter of deliberate exclusion, but of forgetfulness on his part. Faced with so ineluctable a psychological phenomenon as forgetfulness, the assembly could not bring itself to punish the official; however, in the belief that the narrowness of the bag could give rise to nefarious exclusions, it revoked the previous law and restored the bag to its full three inches.

Meanwhile, gentlemen, the first magistrate passed away and three citizens presented themselves as candidates for the position. Only two of them were important: Hazeroth and Magog, the respective leaders of the rectilinear party and the curvilinear party. I should explain these names to you. Since arachnids are masters of geometry, it is geometry that divides them politically. Some are convinced that spiders should always spin their webs with straight threads, and they adhere to the rectilinear party. Others, however, think that webs should be spun using curved threads, and they form the curvilinear party. There is a third party, which occupies the middle ground with the proposition that webs should be woven with both straight and curved threads, and is therefore called the recto-curvilinear party. Finally, there is a fourth political grouping, the anti-recto-curvilinear party, which sweeps away all such principles and proposes the use of webs woven from thin air, resulting in an entirely transparent and lightweight structure with no lines of any sort. Since geometry could only divide them, without inflaming their passions, they have adopted a purely symbolic geometry. For some, the straight line represents noble sentiments: justice, probity, integrity, and perseverance, while base or inferior sentiments such as flattery, fraud, betrayal, and perfidy are quite clearly curved. Their adversaries disagree, saying that the curved line is the line of virtue and wisdom, because it is the expression of modesty and humility, whereas ignorance, arrogance, foolishness, and boasting are straight, indeed rigidly so. The third party, less angular, less exclusive, has trimmed away the exaggerations of both sides and combined their contrasting positions, proclaiming the simultaneous nature of lines to be the exact representation of the physical and moral world. The fourth grouping simply repudiates everything.

Neither Hazeroth nor Magog was elected. The relevant balls were drawn from the bag, but were deemed invalid—Hazaroth's because the first letter of his name was missing, and Magog's because his lacked the last letter. The remaining, triumphant name was that of an ambitious millionaire of obscure political opinions, who promptly ascended the ducal throne to the general amazement of the republic. However, the defeated candidates were not content to rest on the winner's laurels; they called for an official inquiry. The inquiry showed that the Inscriptions Officer had intentionally misspelled their names. The officer confessed to both the error and the intention, explaining that it had been nothing more than a simple ellipsis; a purely literary misdemeanor, if that. Since it was not possible to prosecute someone for errors of spelling or rhetoric, it seemed sensible to review the law once again. That very same day, it was decreed that the bag would henceforth be made from a fine gauze, through which the balls could be read by the public, and *ipso facto* by the candidates themselves, who would thus have the opportunity to correct any misspellings.

Unfortunately, gentlemen, fiddling with the law brings nothing but trouble. That same door flung wide to honesty also served the cunning of a certain Nabiga, who connived with the Withdrawals Officer to get himself a seat on the assembly. There was one vacancy to be filled and three candidates; the officer selected the balls with his eyes fixed on his accomplice, who only stopped shaking his head when the ball in question was his own. That was all it took to put paid to the idea of a gauze bag. With exemplary patience, the assembly restored the thick fabric of the previous regime, but, to avoid any further ellipses, literary or otherwise, it decreed that balls with incorrect inscriptions could henceforth be validated if five persons swore an oath that the name inscribed was indeed that of the candidate in question.

This new statute gave rise to a new and unforeseen issue, as you will see. It concerned the election of a Donations Collector, a public servant charged with raising public revenue in the form of voluntary donations. Among the candidates were one called Caneca and another called Nebraska. The ball drawn from the bag was Nebraska's. There was, however, a mistake, in that the last letter was missing, but five witnesses swore an oath in accordance with the law that the duly elected candidate was the republic's one and only Nebraska. Everything seemed to be settled, until the candidate Caneca sought leave to prove that the name on the ball in question was not Nebraska's, but his own. The justice of the peace granted the hearing. As this point, they summoned a great philologist—perhaps the greatest in the republic, as well as being a good metaphysician and a rather fine mathematician—who proved the matter as follows:

"First of all," he said, "you should note that the absence of the last letter of the name 'Nebraska' is no accident. Why was it left incomplete? Not through fatigue or love of brevity, since only the final letter, a mere *a*, is missing. Lack of space? Not that, either; look closely and you will see that there is still space for another two or three syllables. Hence the omission is intentional, and the intention could only be to draw the reader's eye to the letter *k*, being the last one written, hanging there abandoned and alone, devoid of purpose. Now, then, the brain has a tendency, which no law can override, to reproduce letters in two ways: the graphic form *k*, and the sonic form, which could equally be written *ca*. Thus, by drawing the eyes to the final letter written, the spelling defect instantly embeds it in the brain as the first syllable: *Ca*. Once so embedded, the natural impulse of the brain is then to read the whole name, and thus returns to the beginning of the word, to the initial *ne* of Nebrask, giving us *Ca-ne*. There remains the middle syllable, *bras*, and it is the easiest thing in the world to demonstrate how that can be reduced to another *ca*. I will not, however, demonstrate precisely how, since you lack the necessary preparation for a proper understanding of the spiritual or philosophical meaning of such a syllable, along with its origins and effects, its phases, modifications, logical and syntactical consequences, both deductive and inductive, as well as symbolic, and so forth. But taking that as read, we are faced with the final and incontrovertible proof of my initial assertion that the syllable *ca* is indeed joined to the first two, *Ca-ne*, giving us the name Caneca."

The law was amended, gentlemen, abolishing both sworn testimonials and textual interpretations, and introducing another innovation, this time the simultaneous reduction, by half an inch, of both the length and width of the bag. The modification did not, however, avoid a minor abuse in the election of bailiffs, and the bag was restored to its original dimensions, but this time in triangular form. You will readily comprehend that such a form brings with it an inevitable consequence: many of the balls remained in the bottom of the bag. From this came the adoption of a cylindrical bag, which, later, evolved into an hourglass, which was recognized as having the same inconveniences as the triangle, and thus gave way to a crescent, and so on. Most abuses, oversights, and lacunae tend to disappear, and the rest will share the same fate, not entirely, perhaps, for perfection is not of this world, but to the degree advised by one of the most circumspect citizens of my republic, Erasmus—whose last speech I only wish I could give to you here in its entirety. Tasked with notifying the final legislative modification to the ten worthy ladies responsible for weaving the electoral bag, Erasmus recounted to them the tale of Penelope, who wove and unwove her famous web while awaiting the return of her husband Ulysses.

"You, ladies, are the Penelopes of our republic," he said in conclusion. "Aim to be as chaste, patient, and talented as she. Weave the bag again, ladies, weave it again, until Ulysses, weary of wandering, comes back to take his rightful place among us. Ulysses is Wisdom."

THE MIRROR

A Brief Outline of a New Theory of the Human Soul

———

L ATE ONE NIGHT, four or five gentlemen were debating various lofty matters, and although they all had different views, there were no frayed tempers. The house was situated on the Santa Teresa hill overlooking Rio; the room was small and lit by candles, whose glow mingled mysteriously with the moonlight streaming in from outside. Between the bustle and excitement of the city below and the sky above, where the stars were shining in the still, clear air, sat our four or five metaphysical detectives, amicably resolving the universe's knottiest problems.

Four or five, I say, and yet, strictly speaking, only four of them spoke, but there was a fifth person in the room who sat in silence, thinking or dozing, and whose only contribution to the debate was an occasional grunt of approval. The man was the same age as his companions, i.e., between forty and fifty years old; he was from the provinces, wealthy, intelligent, not uneducated, and, it would seem, shrewd and somewhat caustic. He never participated in their discussions or arguments, and always justified his silence with a paradox, saying that discussion was simply the polite form of the latent warrior instinct man had inherited from beasts. He would add that the seraphim and cherubim never disagreed, and *they* were eternal, spiritual perfection. When he gave this same answer that night, one of the others took him up on it and challenged him to prove his assertion, if he could. Jacobina (for that was his name) thought for a moment, then replied:

"All things considered, perhaps you're right."

And suddenly, in the middle of the night, this taciturn fellow began to hold forth, not for two or three minutes, but for thirty or forty. The meandering conversation had come to rest upon the nature of the soul, a point that radically divided the four friends. No two minds thought alike; not only was there no agreement, discussion became difficult, not to say impossible, on account of the multiplicity of issues branching out from the main trunk of the debate, and perhaps also on account of the inconsistency of the various positions adopted. One of the participants asked Jacobina to offer an opinion, or, at the very least, a conjecture.

"No conjecture and no opinion," he replied. "Either one can lead to disagreement and, as you all know, I never engage in arguments. But if you will listen in silence, I can tell you about an episode in my life that demonstrates the issue in question in the clearest possible terms. To begin with, there is not one soul, but two—"

"Two?"

"Yes, two. Every human creature contains two souls: one that looks from the inside out, and the other that looks from the outside in. Go on, gawk, stare, shrug your shoulders, whatever you like, but don't say anything. If you try to argue, I'll finish my cigar and go home to bed. Now, the external soul can be a spirit, a fluid, a man (or many men), an object, even an action. There are cases, for example, of a simple shirt button being a person's external soul, or it could be the polka, a card game, a book, a machine, a pair of boots, a song, a drum, etc. Clearly, the function of this second soul, like the first, is to transmit life; together they complete the man, who is, metaphysically speaking, an orange. Whoever loses one half, automatically loses half of his existence, and there have been instances, quite common ones, in which the loss of the external soul implies the loss of one's entire existence. Shylock, for example. The external soul of that particular Jew was his ducats; to lose them was the same as dying. 'I shall never see my gold again,' he says to Tubal; 'thou stick'st a dagger in me.' Consider carefully his choice of words: for him, the loss of the ducats, his external soul, meant death. One must, of course, remember that the external soul does not always stay the same—"

"No?"

"Indeed not, sir; it changes both in nature and in state. I am not alluding to certain all-consuming souls, such as one's country, of which Camões famously said that he would not only die in his country, but with it; or power, which was Caesar's and Cromwell's external soul. These are forceful, all-excluding souls, but others, though still forceful, are changeable in nature. There are gentlemen, for example, whose external soul in their earliest years is a rattle or a hobbyhorse, but later on in life it will be their seat on the board of a charity. For my part, I know a lady—and a charming creature she is too—who changes her external soul five or six times a year. During the season it's the opera, and when the season is over, she swaps her external soul for another: a concert, a ball at the Cassino, a trip to Rua do Ouvidor or Petrópolis—"

"Excuse me, but who is this lady?"

"The lady is the devil's kin and bears the same name: her name is Legion. And there are many other such cases. I myself have experienced these changes. I won't recount them now because it would take too long; I will confine myself to the episode I mentioned earlier. At the time, I was twenty-five years old . . ."

Eager to hear the promised tale, his four companions forgot all about their raging controversy. Blessèd curiosity! Thou art not only the soul of civilization; thou art the apple of concord, a divine fruit that tastes quite different from the apple of mythology. The room, until then buzzing with physics and metaphysics, is now a becalmed sea; all eyes are on Jacobina, who trims his cigar while collecting his thoughts. Here's how he began:

"I was twenty-five years old and poor, and had just been made a second lieutenant in the National Guard, the very lowest rank of commissioned officer. You cannot imagine what a huge event this was in our house. My mother was so happy and so proud! She insisted on addressing me as *her* lieutenant. Cousins, aunts, uncles, everyone was bursting with the purest, sincerest joy. In the town, to be sure, there were several disgruntled fellows—a wailing and gnashing of teeth, as it says in the Scriptures—the reason being that there had been many candidates for the post, and these other fellows were the losers. I suppose some of their annoyance was less understandable, though, and arose simply from a feeling of resentment that someone else should be singled out for distinction. I remember how some young men, even friends of mine, looked at me askance for quite some time afterward. On the other hand, many people were pleased by my appointment, the proof of which is that the whole of my rather splendid uniform was paid for by friends. It was then that one of my aunts, Dona Marcolina, Captain Peçanha's widow, who lived on a remote and isolated farm many

leagues from town, begged me to come and see her, and to bring my uniform. I went, accompanied by a footman, who returned to town a few days
later, because no sooner had Auntie Marcolina lured me to her house than
she wrote to my mother telling her that she wouldn't let me go for at least
a month. And how she hugged me! She, too, called me *her* lieutenant. She
pronounced me a handsome devil and, being a rather jolly sort herself, even
confessed to envying the girl who would one day be my wife. She declared
that there was not a man in the entire province who was my equal. And it
was always lieutenant this, lieutenant that, every hour of the day or night.
I asked her to call me Joãozinho as she used to, but she shook her head,
exclaiming that, no, I was 'Senhor Lieutenant' and that was that. One of
her brothers-in-law, her late husband's brother, who lived in the house, also
refused to address me in any other way. I was 'Senhor Lieutenant' not in
jest but perfectly seriously, and in front of the slaves as well, who naturally
followed suit. I sat at the head of the table and was always served first. It was
absurd, really. Such was Auntie Marcolina's enthusiasm that she went so far
as to have a large mirror placed in my room—a magnificent, ornate piece of
work, quite out of keeping with the rest of the house, which was furnished
simply and modestly. It had been given to her by her godmother, who had
inherited it from her mother, who had bought it from one of the Portuguese
noblewomen who came to Brazil in 1808 with the rest of King João VI's
court. I don't know how much truth there was in this story, but that was
the family tradition. Naturally, the mirror was very old, but you could still
see the gilding, eaten away by time, a couple of carved dolphins in the top
corners of the frame, a few bits of mother-of-pearl, and other such artistic
flourishes. All rather old, but very good quality."

"Was it large?"

"Indeed it was. And as I say, it was really very kind of her, because the
mirror had previously been in the parlor, and was the best piece in the
house. But there was no dissuading my aunt; she replied that it would not
be missed, that it was only for a couple of weeks, and, after all, it was the
least the 'Senhor Lieutenant' deserved. The fact is that all these little attentions, shows of affection, and kindnesses brought about a transformation in
me, aided and abetted by the natural vanity of youth, as I'm sure you can
imagine."

"Well, no, actually."

"The officer eliminated the man. For several days, the two hung in the balance, but it wasn't long before my original nature gave way to the other; only a tiny part of my humanity remained. What had happened was that my external soul, which, up until then, had been the sun, the air, the rolling countryside, and the eyes of young women, changed entirely and became the bowing and scraping that went on around the house, everything that spoke to me of my rank, and nothing about me, the man. Only the officer remained; the private citizen had vanished into thin air, and into the past. Hard to believe, isn't it?"

"I find it hard even to understand," replied one of his listeners.

"You will in due course. Actions are better at explaining feelings: actions are everything. After all, even the very best definition of love is no match for a kiss from the girl you're courting, and, if memory serves me right, an ancient philosopher once demonstrated movement by walking. So let's cut to the chase. Let us see how, as the consciousness of the man was slowly being obliterated, that of the officer was becoming intensely alive. Human suffering and human joys, if that's all they were, barely won from me so much as an apathetic nod or a condescending smile. After three weeks, I was a different person, changed utterly. I was all lieutenant and nothing else. Then one day, Auntie Marcolina received some grave news. One of her daughters, married to a farmer who lived five leagues away, was ill, perhaps dying. Farewell, nephew! Farewell, Lieutenant! The distraught mother immediately made arrangements to travel, asked her brother-in-law to go with her, and me to take charge of the farm. I believe that had she not been so upset she would have done the opposite, leaving the brother-in-law behind and taking me with her. As it turned out, however, I was left on my own, with a couple of household slaves. I immediately felt a great sense of oppression, as if the four walls of a prison had suddenly closed around me. It was my external soul contracting, you see, for now it was limited to a handful of half savages. The officer continued to hold sway within me, albeit less intensely alive and less fiercely conscious. The slaves put a note of humility into their bows and curtsys, which somewhat made up for the lack of family affection and the interruption of domestic intimacy. That same night, they noticeably redoubled their cheerful expressions of respect and admiration. It was 'Massa' Lieutenant every other minute. Massa Lieutenant very handsome, Massa Lieutenant soon be colonel, Massa Lieutenant marry pretty girl, general's daughter; a concerto of praise and prophesies that left me feeling ecstatic. Ah, the traitors! Little did I suspect the scoundrels' secret intentions."

"What? To kill you?"

"If only."

"Worse?"

"Just listen. The following morning I awoke to find myself alone. The scoundrels, whether egged on by others or of their own accord, had plotted to run away in the night, and had done precisely that. I found myself completely alone, with no one else within the four walls of the house, staring out at the deserted yard and empty countryside beyond. Not a single human breath. I searched the house, the slave quarters, everywhere, but found nothing and no one, not a single pickaninny. Only some cocks and hens, a pair of mules philosophizing about life as they flicked away the flies, and three oxen. The slaves had even taken the dogs. Not a single human being. Do you think this was better than dying? Well, I can tell you it was worse. Not that I was afraid; I swear to you that I wasn't; in fact, I was almost devil-may-care, to the point of not feeling anything at all during those first few hours. After that, I felt sad for Auntie Marcolina's financial loss, and was in somewhat of a quandary as to whether I should go and see her and give her the bad news, or stay and take care of the house. I opted for the latter course of action, so as not to leave the house completely defenseless, and because, if my cousin was seriously ill, I would only be increasing her mother's distress without providing any remedy. Besides, I expected Uncle Peçanha's brother to return that day or the next, since he'd already been gone thirty-six hours. But the morning passed with no sign of him, and during the afternoon I began to feel decidedly odd, like someone who has lost all sensation in his nerves and can no longer feel his muscles move. Uncle Peçanha's brother did not return that day, or the next, or for the rest of the week. My solitude took on overwhelming proportions. Never had the days been so long; never had the sun scorched the earth with such wearying ferocity. The hours passed as slowly as centuries on the old clock in the parlor, whose pendulum, *tick-tock*, *tick-tock*, tapped away at my inner soul like the endlessly snapping fingers of eternity. When, many years later, I read an American poem, one of Long-fellow's, I think, and came across the famous refrain: '*Never, for ever! – For ever, never!*' I confess that I felt a shiver run down my spine at the memory of those terrifying days. Auntie Marcolina's clock was just like that: '*Never, for ever! – For ever, never!*' It wasn't merely the tick-tock of the pendulum, but a dialogue from the abyss, a whispering voice from the void. And then there were the nights! Not that they were any quieter. They were as silent as the days, but the nights were filled with darkness and an even narrower, or perhaps vaster, solitude. *Tick-tock, tick-tock*. No one in any of the rooms, no one on the veranda, in the hallways, the yard; no one anywhere at all. Are you laughing?"

"Yes, for it seems you *were* a little scared after all."

"Oh! If only I could have felt scared! At least I would have been alive. But the main thing I remember is that I couldn't even feel fear, or at least not fear as it is commonly understood. It was an inexplicable sensation. I was like a dead man walking, a sleepwalker, a mechanical toy. Sleep itself was another matter. Sleep brought me relief, but not for the usual reason: that sleep is death's brother. I think I can explain the phenomenon as follows: in eliminating the need for an external soul, sleep gives free rein to the internal one. In my dreams, I would put on my uniform surrounded by family and friends, who would praise my elegant attire, address me as lieutenant; then a family friend would come and promise me a promotion to captain or major, and I would be filled with life again. But when I woke to the cold light of day, that sense of my newly reunified self faded with my dreams—because my internal soul had lost its exclusive power of action, and was once again dependent upon the other, the external soul, which stubbornly refused to return. And it did not return. I would wander about outside to see if there was any sign of life. *Sœur Anne, sœur Anne, ne vois-tu rien venir?* Nothing, absolutely nothing, just like that old French fairy tale. Only the dust of the road and the grassy hilltops. I would return to the house, at my wits' end, and lie down on the sofa in the parlor. *Tick-tock, tick-tock.* I would stand up, pace the room, drum my fingers on the windowpanes, whistle. At one point, I considered writing something, a political article, a novel, an ode, perhaps; I didn't choose which, but sat down and scribbled a few words and random phrases that I could use to spice up the style. But the style, like Auntie Marcolina, would not come. *Sœur Anne, sœur Anne . . .* Nothing at all. All I could see was the ink turning blacker and the page whiter."

"But didn't you have anything to eat?"

"Not much; just fruit, ground-up cassava, preserves, a few roots roasted on the fire, but I would have endured it all quite cheerfully had it not been for the terrible mental state I was in. I recited verses, speeches, passages in Latin, Gonzaga's love poems, whole stanzas by Camões, sonnets, a thirty-volume anthology in all. Sometimes I did gymnastic exercises, other times I pinched my legs, but the effect was only a physical sensation of weari-

ness or pain, nothing more. There was only silence, a vast, enormous, infinite silence, only underscored by the eternal *tick-tock* of the clock. *Tick-tock,*
tick-tock . . ."

"Yes, that would be enough to drive anyone mad."

"There's worse to come. I should tell you that ever since I'd been alone, I
had not once looked in the mirror. I wasn't avoiding it deliberately, for I had
no reason to do so; it was an unconscious impulse, a dread of finding two of
me, at the same time, in that solitary house. If that is the true explanation,
then there is no better proof of man's contradictory nature, for, a week later,
I got it into my head to look at the mirror with precisely the aim of seeing
myself twice over. I looked and recoiled. The glass itself seemed to be conspiring with the rest of the universe; it didn't show me as a sharp, complete
image, but as something vague and hazy, diffuse, a shadow of a shadow.
The laws of physics will not allow me to deny that the mirror did indeed
reproduce my shape and features accurately, for it must have done, but that
was not what my senses told me. Then I did feel afraid; I attributed the
phenomenon to my strained nerves; I feared I would go mad if I stayed any
longer. 'I must leave,' I said to myself. And I raised my arm in a gesture that
was both ill-tempered and decisive. I saw the gesture repeated in the mirror,
but it was somehow dispersed, frayed, mutilated . . . I began to get dressed,
muttering to myself, clearing my throat, shaking my clothes brusquely, and
cursing my recalcitrant buttons, just in order to say something. From time to
time, I glanced furtively at the mirror, only to see the same blurred outlines,
the same confused shapes. I carried on getting dressed. Suddenly some inexplicable flash of inspiration, some spontaneous impulse, planted an idea in
my head. Can you guess what it was?"

"No, tell us."

"I was staring desperately at the mirror, contemplating my own dissolving, incomplete features, a mass of loose and shapeless lines, when the idea
came to me . . . No, you'll never guess."

"Go on, tell us."

"I had the idea of putting on my lieutenant's uniform. I did so, every last
bit of it, and, as I stood in front of the mirror, I raised my eyes and . . . I hardly
need say it: the mirror now showed my whole figure, with not a feature or
a line out of place; it was me, my own self, the lieutenant, who had finally
rediscovered his external soul. This soul, missing since my aunt's departure, scattered and dispersed since the slaves ran away, was now pieced back

together in the mirror. Imagine a man who, little by little, emerges from a coma, opens his eyes without seeing, then begins to see, begins to distinguish people from objects, but cannot recognize any of them individually, then, finally, realizes that this fellow is so-and-so, and that one is what's-his-name, here's a chair, there's a sofa. Everything returns to what it was before his deep sleep. So it was with me. I looked in the mirror, moved from side to side, stepped back, waved, smiled, and the glass reflected everything. I was no longer an automaton, I was a living being. From that point on, I was another person. Every day, at a certain time, I would put on my lieutenant's uniform and sit in front of the mirror, reading, looking, and meditating; after two or three hours, I would take my uniform off again. By sticking to this regime, I was able to get through more than six days of solitude without the slightest problem."

By the time his companions had come to their senses again, the narrator had already left.

A VISIT FROM ALCIBIADES

Letter from District Judge "X" to the Rio Chief of Police

––––––––––

Rio de Janeiro, September 20, 1875

SIR,

I trust you will forgive my shaky handwriting and slovenly style; you will soon understand the reason why.

Today, this very evening, just after dinner, while I was waiting for the Cassino to open, I lay down on the sofa and opened a volume of Plutarch. You, sir, who were my schoolroom companion, will remember that ever since I was a boy I have had a passion for Greek, a passion or indeed a mania, which was the name you gave it, and one so intense that it often led me to fail in other subjects. I opened the book and, as always happens when I read some ancient text, I found myself transported back to the period in question, right into the thick of the action or whatever else was going on. Perfect after-dinner reading. In no time at all, one finds oneself on a Roman road, under a Greek portico, or in a grammarian's workshop. Modern times, the Herzegovina uprising, the Carlist Wars, Rua do Ouvidor, the Chiarini Circus—all vanish into thin air. Fifteen or twenty minutes of ancient life, and all for free. A veritable literary *digestif*.

That is precisely what happened this evening. The book fell open at the life of Alcibiades. I allowed myself to be seduced by the flow of those Attic cadences; within moments, I was entering the Olympic Games, marveling at that flower of Athenian manhood as he drove his chariot magnificently, with the grace and determination he had always shown on the battlefield, or when curbing his fellow citizens or his own sensual urges. Oh, to be alive then, sir! But then the slave-boy came in to light the gas, and that was enough to put all the archaeology of my imagination to flight. Athens was relegated to history, while my gaze fell from the clouds, or, rather, came to rest upon my white duck trousers, my alpaca jacket, and my cordovan leather shoes. And then I thought to myself:

"What would that illustrious Athenian make of modern-day dress?"

I have been a spiritualist for some months now, because, convinced that all systems are pure nothingness, I decided to adopt the most enjoyable one. The time will come when it is not only enjoyable, but also useful for solving historical problems: it is far quicker to summon the spirits of the dead than to expend one's own critical energies to no good end, because no rationale or theory can better explain the intention of an act than the author of the act himself. Such was my goal this evening. Wondering what Alcibiades might have thought was a sheer waste of time, with no benefit beyond the pleasure of admiring my own cleverness. I therefore decided to summon up the Athenian, and asked him to appear in my house forthwith, without delay.

And here begins the extraordinary part of the adventure. Alcibiades lost no time in answering my call; two minutes later, he was there, in my parlor, standing by the wall, but he was not the intangible shadow I had expected to summon using our schoolboy methods; it was the real Alcibiades, flesh and blood, the man himself, authentically Greek, dressed like the ancients, and full of that blend of courtesy and audacity with which he used to harangue the great assemblies of Athens, and occasionally its fools. You, sir, who know so much about history, cannot ignore the fact that there were, indeed, some fools in Athens. Yes, even Athens had fools, a precedent that perhaps gives us something of an excuse. I swear I could not believe it; no matter what my senses told me, I could not believe that it was not a ghost standing there before me, but Alcibiades himself, restored to life. I still nurtured the hope that it was nothing more than the effects of indigestion, a simple excess of gastric fluids, magnified through the lens of Plutarch. And so I rubbed my eyes, stared, and . . .

"What do you want from me?" he asked.

On hearing this, the hairs on the back of my neck stood up. The figure spoke, and spoke Greek, the purest Attic. There was no doubting that it was the man himself, dead for twenty centuries, brought back from the grave, and as alive as if he had come straight from cutting off his poor dog's tail, as he so famously did. It was clear that, without a moment's thought, I had just taken a great stride forward along the path of spiritualism. But, silly me, I didn't, at first, realize this, and I allowed myself to be caught off guard. He repeated the question, looked around him, and sat down in an armchair. He saw that I was cold and trembling (as I still am even now), and spoke to me rather tenderly, even trying to laugh and joke so as to put me at my ease. As deft as ever! What more can I say? A few minutes later, we were chatting away in ancient Greek, he reclining nonchalantly in his chair, I earnestly begging all the saints in heaven to send some sort of distraction—a servant, a visitor, a local constable, or even, should it prove necessary, for a fire to break out.

Needless to say, I gave up on the idea of consulting him on modern-day dress; I had summoned a ghost, not a "real-life" man, as children say. I limited myself to replying to his questions; he asked me for news about Athens, and I obliged; I said that Athens was finally the capital of a unified Greece; I told him about the long years of Muslim domination, then about independence, Botsaris, and Lord Byron. The great man hung on my every word and, when I expressed surprise that the dead had told him nothing of all this, he explained to me that when one stood at the gates of the other world, one's interest in this world waned considerably. He had met neither Botsaris nor Lord Byron—firstly, because there is such a vast multitude of spirits that it's very easy to miss someone, and secondly, because there the dead are grouped not according to nationality or some similar category, but according to their temperament, customs, and profession. Thus he, Alcibiades, forms part of a group of elegant, passionate politicians, alongside the Duke of Buckingham, Almeida Garrett, our very own Maciel Monteiro, etc. Then he asked me about current affairs; I briefly told him what I knew; I spoke of the Hellenic parliament and the rather different way in which his compatriot statesmen, Voulgaris and Koumoundouros, are going about imitating Disraeli and Gladstone in taking turns at government, and, just like them, trading oratorical blows. Alcibiades, a magnificent orator himself, interrupted me:

"Bravo, Athenians!"

I enter into such minutiae only so as to omit nothing that might give you a more precise understanding of the extraordinary events I am describing. I have already mentioned that Alcibiades was listening to me avidly; I should also add that he was clever and shrewd, very quick on the uptake. He was also somewhat sarcastic, or at least that's how he came across at one or two points in our conversation. But, in general, he showed himself to be simple, attentive, polite, sensitive, and dignified. And quite the dandy, too, as dandyish as in ancient times; he was always glancing sideways at the mirror, just as women and others do in our own century, admiring his buskins, adjusting his cloak, and striking sculptural poses.

"Go on," he would say to me, whenever I paused.

But I couldn't. Having entered into the realm of the inextricable and the marvelous, I believed that anything was possible, and just as he had come to meet me in this world, I couldn't see why I couldn't go and join him in eternity. I froze at this idea. For a man who has just had his dinner and is waiting for the Cassino to open, death would be a joke in the very worst possible taste.

"If only I could get away . . ." I thought to myself. Then I had an idea: I told him I was going to a ball.

"A ball? What's a ball?"

I explained.

"Ah! You're going to dance the Pyrrhic dance!"

"No," I replied. "The Pyrrhic dance has been and gone. My dear Alcibiades, every century changes its dances just as it changes its ideas. We no longer dance as we did a century ago; probably the twentieth century won't dance as we do now. The Pyrrhic dance is long gone, like Plutarch's men and Hesiod's gods."

"Even the gods?"

I explained that paganism had come to an end, that the august academies of the last century had still given it shelter, but with little real soul or conviction, and that even Arcadian drunkenness—*Evoe! Father Bassareus! Evoe!*, etc.—the honest pastime of certain peace-loving district judges, had been eradicated. From time to time, I added, some writer of poetry or prose alluded to the remnants of the pagan theogony, but only for show or amusement, while science had reduced the whole of Olympus to the merely symbolic. Dead, all dead.

"Even Zeus?"

"Even Zeus."

"Dionysus? Aphrodite?"

"All dead."

Plutarch's man stood up and took a few paces, containing his indignation, as if saying to himself, as someone else once did: "Ah! I must be there, too, along with my Athenians!" And from time to time, he would murmur: "Zeus, Dionysus, Aphrodite . . ." I then recalled that he had once been accused of disobeying the gods, and wondered to myself where this posthumous and, therefore, artificial indignation came from. I was forgetting—me, a devotee of Greek!—I was forgetting that he was also a consummate hypocrite, an illustrious fraudster. However, I scarcely had time to think this, because Alcibiades suddenly stopped his pacing and declared that he would go to the ball with me.

"To the ball?" I repeated in astonishment.

"Yes, to the ball. Let's go to the ball."

I was terrified and told him that it was impossible, that they wouldn't let him in wearing that outfit; he would look ridiculous; unless, of course, he wanted to go there to perform one of Aristophanes's comedies, I added, laughing so as to hide my fear. What I really wanted was to leave him there in the house, and, once I was outside, rather than going to the Cassino, I would come straight to see you. But the wretched man would not budge; while listening to me, he stared down at the floor, as if deep in thought. I stopped talking; I began to think that the nightmare would soon end, that the apparition would disappear, and that I would be left there alone with my trousers, my shoes, and my century.

"I want to go to the ball," he repeated. "I can't go back without comparing dances."

"My dear Alcibiades, I really don't think it wise. It would certainly be a great honor, and give me enormous pride, to introduce you, the most genteel and charming of Athenians, to the Cassino. But the other men, the young lads and lasses, the older folk . . . Well, it's just impossible."

"Why?"

"I've already told you; they will think you're a lunatic or a comedian, because of your clothes . . ."

"What about them? Clothes change. I'll go in modern clothes. Don't you have anything you can lend me?"

I was about to say no, but then it occurred to me that the most urgent thing was to get out of the house and that, once outside, I'd have more chance of escaping, and so I told him that I did.

"Well, then," he replied as he stood up, "I'll go in modern clothes. All I ask is that you get dressed first, so that I can learn and then copy you."

I, too, stood up, and asked him to follow me. He paused in astonishment. I saw that only then had he noticed my white trousers, and was staring at them, eyes bulging, mouth agape; after a long pause, he asked why I was wearing those cloth pipes. I replied that it was for reasons of comfort and convenience, adding that our century, more reserved and practical than artistic, had decided to dress in a manner compatible with our sense of decorum and gravity. Furthermore, not everyone could be Alcibiades. I think this flattered him, for he smiled and shrugged.

"In that case . . ."

We made our way to my dressing room, and I quickly began to change my clothes. Alcibiades reclined lazily on a divan, complimenting me on it, the mirror, the wicker chair, and the paintings. As I say, I got dressed quickly, keen to get out of the house and jump in the first cab that passed.

"Black pipes!" he exclaimed.

These were the black trousers I had just put on. He shrieked and laughed, a sort of giggle mingling surprise with scorn, which greatly offended my modern sensibilities. Because, as I'm sure you will agree, sir, while we may consider our own times worthy of criticism, even execration, we do not like it when one of the ancients comes and makes fun of it to our faces. I did not answer the Athenian; I merely frowned a little and carried on buttoning my suspenders. Then he asked me why on earth I wore such an ugly color.

"Ugly, but serious," I told him. "And observe the elegance of the cut, see how it falls over the shoe, which is patent leather, albeit black, and very shapely too."

And, seeing him shaking his head, I added:

"My dear friend," I said, "you can certainly insist that your Olympian Jupiter is the eternal emblem of majesty: his is the domain of ideal, disinterested art, superior to the passing of the ages and the men who inhabit them. But the art of dressing is another matter. What may appear absurd or ungainly is perfectly rational and beautiful—beautiful in our way, for we no longer wander the streets listening to poets reciting verses, or orators giving speeches, or philosophers explaining their philosophies. You yourself, were you to grow used to seeing us, would end up liking us, because—"

"Stop, you wretch!" he yelled, hurling himself at me.

I felt the blood drain from my face, until I realized the reason for this violent response. It was all down to a misunderstanding. As I looped the tie around my neck and began to tie the knot, Alcibiades assumed, as he told me afterward, that I was about to hang myself. And he did, indeed, turn very pale, trembling and sweating. Now it was my turn to laugh. I chuckled, and explained the use of a necktie to him, noting that it was a white tie, not black, although we did wear black ties on certain occasions. Only after I'd explained all this would he agree to give it back to me. I put it on and then put on my vest.

"For the love of Aphrodite!" he exclaimed. "You are the oddest thing I've ever seen, alive or dead. You're entirely the color of night—a night with only three stars," he continued, pointing to the buttons on my shirtfront. "The world must be a very melancholy place for you to choose to wear such a sad, dead color. We were a far jollier lot, we lived . . ."

He couldn't finish the sentence; I had just put on my tailcoat, and the Athenian's consternation surpassed description. His arms drooped by his sides, he struggled for air, unable to utter a word, and stared at me with wide, bulging eyes. Believe me, sir, I was truly afraid now, and made even more haste to leave the house.

"Are you finished?" he asked.

"No, there's still the hat."

"Oh! Please let it be something that'll make up for all the rest!" replied Alcibiades in a pleading voice. "Please, please! Has all the elegance we bequeathed to you been whittled away to a pair of closed pipes and another pair of open pipes (as he said this he lifted up my coattails), and all in this boring, depressing color? No, I can't believe it! Please let there be something that makes up for it. What is it you say that's missing?"

"My hat."

"Well, whatever it is, put it on, dear fellow, put it on."

I obeyed; I went over to the coat stand, took down my hat, and put it on my head. Alcibiades looked at me, swayed, and fell. I rushed to the illustrious Athenian's side to help him up, but (and it pains me to say this) it was too late; he was dead, dead for the second time. I therefore request, sir, that you see fit to issue the requisite orders for the corpse to be taken to the morgue, and proceed with the *corpus delicti*. Please excuse my not coming to your house in person at this hour (it being ten o'clock at night), on account of the deep shock I have just experienced, and rest assured that I will do so tomorrow morning, before eight o'clock.

TESTAMENTARY DISPOSITION

"... ITEM: IT IS MY FINAL WISH that the coffin in which my body is to be buried shall be made at the workshop of Joaquim Soares, in Rua da Alfândega. I wish him to be informed of this disposition, which shall also be made public. Joaquim Soares does not know me, but he merits this distinction on account of being one of our finest craftsmen, and one of the most highly esteemed men in all of Brazil ..."

This testamentary disposition was carried out to the letter. Joaquim Soares made the coffin in which the body of poor Nicolau B. de C. was laid; he made it with his own hands, *con amore*, and, when he had finished, in a gesture of goodwill, he waived all payment. He had, he insisted, already been paid; for the mark of favor shown by the deceased man was, in itself, a worthy prize. He asked only one thing: to be given the original copy of the relevant clause. His wish was granted, and he had it framed and hung from a nail in his workshop. Once they had recovered from their astonishment, the other coffin-makers protested that the clause was utter nonsense. Happily—and this is one of the advantages of the modern social state—happily, everyone else considered that this hand, reaching up from the abyss to bestow its blessings on the work of a humble artisan, had performed an act of rare magnanimity. It was 1855 and the population was more closely knit then; people spoke of nothing else. For many days, Nicolau's name echoed through the Rio press, from where it then passed to the provincial newspapers. But universal life is so varied, events happen with such bewildering frequency and speed, and, ultimately, man's memory is such a fragile thing, that a day came when Nicolau's magnanimous action sank into oblivion.

I have not come here to restore that action. Forgetting is a necessity. Life is a slate that destiny must first wipe clean before it can write anew. It's a simple matter of pencil and sponge. No, I am not here to restore his action. There are thousands of actions just as noble as his, or even nobler, and they are all equally forgotten. I am here to say that the clause in the will was not an effect without a cause; I am here to reveal to you one of this century's most curious maladies.

Yes, dear reader, we will be entering the realms of pathology. That little boy you see back there at the end of the last century (when he died in 1855, Nicolau was sixty-eight), that little boy is not a healthy vessel; he is not a perfect organism. On the contrary, from his tenderest years on, he showed through repeated actions that there was in him some inner defect, some flaw of nature. There is no other way to describe the persistence with which he rushed to destroy the other boys' playthings—and I'm not talking about toys that were inferior or the same as his, but specifically those that were better or more expensive. It is even more difficult to understand why, in cases where the toy was particularly special or unusual, the young Nicolau would then console the victim with a kick, and often two or three. All this is very mysterious. It cannot have been his father's fault. His father was a respected trader or dealer (as the Marquis of Lavradio used to say, most of those in this city who call themselves "merchants" are nothing more than dealers on commission), who lived in a certain splendor during the last quarter of the century; a harsh, austere man who frequently admonished and, where necessary, punished his son. But neither admonishments nor punishments did any good. Nicolau's inner impulse was far stronger than all his father's lashings, and, once or twice a week, the little boy slipped back into his errant ways. The family was appalled. One event in particular—in view of its grave consequences—deserves to be told.

The viceroy, who, at the time, was the Count of Resende, felt a pressing need to construct a new quayside along the shore at Praia de Dom Manuel. Today, this would be a straightforward municipal matter, but at the time, given the city's more modest proportions, it was a major undertaking. What the viceroy lacked were funds; the public coffers could barely cover normal emergencies. A true statesman, and doubtless a philosopher, he came up with an expedient that was as agreeable to all as it was profitable, namely, handing out, in exchange for pecuniary donations, the ranks of captain, lieutenant, and ensign. When the decision was announced, Nicolau's father realized that this was an opportunity, without danger to life or limb, to take his place among the military luminaries of the age, while at the same time disproving one of the teachings of the Brahmins. For it is written in the Laws of Manu that from the arms of Brahma were born the warriors, while from his belly came the farmers and merchants. By acquiring his captain's commission, Nicolau's father was correcting this point of pagan anatomy. Another merchant, with whom he competed on every score, but who was also a close friend, heard about the appointment and immediately went to add his own rock to the quayside. Unfortunately, his pique at being several days late prompted him to make a request that was in poor taste and, in these particular circumstances, disastrous; he asked the viceroy for a second "quay officer's" commission (for such was the title given to those decorated under this system) for his seven-year-old son. The viceroy hesitated, but the petitioner doubled his donation and pulled a lot of strings, and the little boy duly came away with the rank of ensign. All this was done in secret; Nicolau's father only learned what had happened the following Sunday, in the Carmo Church, when he saw both father and son together, with the boy dressed up in a diminutive but rather dashing uniform. Nicolau, who was also there, turned deathly pale and, in a flash, hurled himself on the young ensign and, before his parents could intervene, had torn the boy's uniform to shreds. You can imagine the scandal. The general hubbub, the worshippers' pious indignation, and the victim's squeals interrupted the ecclesiastical proceedings for several moments. The fathers exchanged some sharp words outside on the steps, and remained enemies ever after.

"That boy will bring disgrace on us all!" roared Nicolau's father when they got home.

Nicolau received a sound beating, endured much pain, cried and sobbed, but did not mend his ways. The toys of the other boys were no less prone to attack than before. The same began to happen with their clothes. The wealthier boys in the neighborhood would now venture out only in the humblest of homemade garments, which was the only way of escaping Nicolau's sharp nails. With the passage of time, his aversion extended to their faces if they were handsome, or considered as such. In the street where he lived there were countless bruised, scratched, and muddied faces. Things reached such an extreme that his father decided to lock him up in the house for three or four months. This was a palliative and, as such, proved excellent. While his confinement lasted, Nicolau was nothing less than angelic; for, aside from that gruesome habit of his, he was gentle, docile, obedient, fond of his family and never missed prayers. After four months, his father released him; it was time to find him a tutor to teach him reading and grammar.

"Leave him with me," said the master. "With me and with this," he added, picking up the strap, "it's highly unlikely that he will entertain any further notions of harming his companions."

Foolish, foolish tutor! There is no doubt that he succeeded in saving the handsome boys and their fancy clothes by punishing poor Nicolau's initial onslaughts. But how would this help cure his malady? On the contrary, by being obliged to repress and swallow his impulses, he suffered twice over, and his ever paler complexion took on a greenish tinge. Sometimes, he said, he had to look away or even close his eyes so as not to explode. Although he stopped tormenting the most elegant or best-dressed boys, he did not let up on the more studious ones; he would beat them and hurl their books out the window. Brawls, bloodshed, and loathing; such were the fruits of life for him, on top of the cruel beatings he himself suffered, and yet his family stubbornly refused to understand. If we add that he was unable to apply himself to any continuous study, or only in fits and starts and poorly— much like the haphazard and unmethodical way in which beggars eat—you will have some idea of the painful consequences of his hidden malaise. His father, who had dreamed of sending his son to university and now found even this illusion shattered, was ready to give up on him completely; it was his mother who saved him.

One century ended and another began without Nicolau's wound healing. His father died in 1807 and his mother in 1809; his sister married a Dutch physician just over a year later. Nicolau now lived alone. He was twenty-three, one of the city's dandies, and a rather peculiar one at that, for he could not bear to encounter anyone who was either handsomer than he, or wearing some particularly fine item of clothing, without suffering a violent pain, so violent, in fact, that he sometimes had to bite his lip until it bled. There were times when he would nearly collapse, or when an almost imperceptible thread of foam would trickle from one corner of his mouth. And things went from bad to worse. He became harsh and domineering; at home, he found everything bad, troublesome, or infuriating; he smashed plates over the slaves' heads, and tormented the dogs by kicking them; he couldn't sit still for ten minutes at a time and he barely ate a thing. Finally, he would fall asleep, and it was just as well that he did. Sleep solved everything. He would wake up feeling affable and affectionate, like a true patriarch, kissing the dogs between the ears, letting them lick his face, giving them the best of everything, calling the slaves the sweetest, most endearing names. And all of them, dogs and slaves alike, forgot about the previous night's beatings and came running obediently and adoringly when they heard his voice, as if this were their true master, and not the other one.

One day, when he was at his sister's house, she asked him why he had not taken up some career or other, something to occupy himself.

"You're quite right," he said. "I'll look into it."

His brother-in-law weighed in and suggested the diplomatic service. The brother-in-law was beginning to suspect that Nicolau did indeed suffer from some sort of malady and thought a change in climate would be just the thing to set him straight. Nicolau obtained a letter of introduction and went to see the minister of foreign affairs. He found the minister surrounded by some of his Portuguese officials, and just about to go to the palace with news of the second fall of Napoleon, news which had arrived only a few minutes earlier. The presence of the minister, the circumstances of the moment, the bowing and scraping of the officials, all this filled Nicolau with such alarm that he could not look the minister in the face. He made several attempts, but the one time he succeeded, his vision was so blurred that he could see nothing at all, or only a shadow, a shape, which made his eyes ache and his face turn green. Nicolau retreated, tremulously reached for the door curtain, and fled.

"I don't want to be anything!" he said to his sister when he got home. "You and my friends are enough."

His friends were the most disagreeable young men in the city, vulgar and lowborn. Nicolau had chosen them on purpose. To live a life divorced from the leading citizens of his day was for him a great sacrifice, but since he would suffer much more by living with them, he put up with it. This proves that he had a certain empirical awareness of his illness and how to relieve it. The simple fact of the matter was that with his chosen companions all of Nicolau's physiological disturbances disappeared. He could look at them without turning deathly pale, without his sight blurring or his legs giving way, or anything like that. What's more, they not only saved him from his natural irritability, they endeavored to make his life, if not delightful, then at least tranquil. To do this, they would shower him with the greatest compliments in the world, delivered in a fawning manner or with a certain deferential familiarity. Nicolau loved all kinds of inferior beings, just as patients love the medicine that restores them to health; he would patronize them, heap them with affectionate praise, lend them money, give them little gifts, even bare his soul to them. Then came the Cry of Ipiranga and the Declaration of Independence; Nicolau threw himself into politics. In 1823 we find him in the Constituent Assembly. It goes without saying that, in fulfilling his legislative duties, he was honest, impartial, and patriotic. However, exercising these public virtues did not come without a price, but at the expense of great mental torment. Metaphorically speaking, one can say that his attendance in the chamber cost him precious blood. Not only because the debates were intolerable, but also because it was hard for him to have to look at certain men, especially on certain days. Montezuma, for example, struck him as utterly shallow, Vergueiro a dullard, and the Andrada brothers detestable. Every speech, not only from the leading orators, but even from the second-rate ones, was sheer torture for Nicolau. And yet he remained steadfast and punctual. He never missed a single vote; never once did his name ring out in that august chamber without him providing an answering echo. However great his desperation, he was able to contain himself and put the national interest above his own discomfort. He may even have secretly applauded the decree of dissolution. I can't confirm this, but there are good reasons to believe that, despite appearances, Nicolau was happy to see the assembly dissolved. And if that conjecture is true, then this second one is no less so: that the exile of certain leading figures in the assembly, now branded public enemies, came to dilute that pleasure. For Nicolau, who had suffered from their speeches, suffered no less from their exile, since it gave them a certain prominence. If only he, too, had been exiled!

"You could always get married, brother," his sister said to him.

"But I don't have a fiancée."

"I can get you one, if you like."

This was her husband's idea. In his opinion, medical science had discovered the illness plaguing Nicolau: it was a worm in his spleen that fed on the patient's suffering, that is, a particular secretion that was produced at the sight of certain occurrences, situations, or persons. It was simply a matter of killing the worm. But since there was no known chemical substance capable of destroying the worm, the only solution was to prevent the secretion, since that would produce the same result. It was, therefore, imperative to marry Nicolau to some pretty and talented girl, remove him from the city, and set him up on some country estate, to which he would take his best dinner service, his finest furniture, and his most disreputable friends.

"Every morning," the brother-in-law explained to his wife, "Nicolau will receive a newspaper that I will have specially printed with the sole aim of telling him the most agreeable things in the world, listing them one by one, recalling his modest yet useful work on the Constituent Assembly, and attributing to him many amorous adventures, along with sundry flashes of wit and courage. I have already spoken to my fellow Dutchman, the admiral, about getting some of our officers to go and see Nicolau from time to time and tell him how they could not possibly return to The Hague without doing themselves the honor of setting eyes on so charming and eminent a citizen, one who combines so many qualities rarely found in one individual. If you, my dear, could only persuade one of your fancy dressmakers— Gudin, for example—to name one of their hats or frilly lace capes after Nicolau, that would greatly help in your brother's cure. Anonymous love letters, sent by the post, are another remarkably efficient remedy. But first things first; let's get him married."

Never was a plan more conscientiously executed. The bride chosen was the most elegant, or one of the most elegant, in the capital. The bishop himself married them. When they duly withdrew to the country estate, only a few of Nicolau's coarsest friends went with him. The newspaper was set up, letters were sent, and visits were paid. For three months everything went swimmingly. But nature, always ready to wrong-foot us, showed yet again that it can never be predicted. One of the methods used to please Nicolau was to praise the beauty, elegance, and virtues of his wife; but his illness had grown worse, and what had seemed like an excellent remedy now simply aggravated his condition. After a while, Nicolau found all these paeans to his wife pointless and excessive, and that was enough to make him irritable, and for his irritability to provoke the inevitable secretion. It seems he even reached the point of not being able to look at her for very long, and then scarcely at all; several rows ensued, which would have signaled the beginnings of a separation had she not died shortly after. Nicolau's grief was profound and genuine, but the cure was soon interrupted because he went back to Rio de Janeiro, where we will find him some time later among the revolutionaries of 1831.

Although it may seem rash to state the reasons that led Nicolau to join the jeering crowds at the Campo da Aclamação on the night of the sixth of April, I think it would not be far from the truth to suppose that it was the words of a famous but anonymous Athenian. Those who spoke ill of the Emperor were just as pleasing to Nicolau as those who spoke well. That man, who inspired such enthusiasm and hatred and whose name was endlessly repeated wherever Nicolau happened to be, whether in the street, the theater, or other people's houses, had become a truly unhealthy obsession, from which flowed the fervor with which he involved himself in the events of 1831. The abdication came as a great relief. It is true that the ensuing Regency soon found him among its adversaries, and there are some who assert that he joined the Caramuru, or "Restoration" Party, although there is no proof of this. What is certain is that Nicolau's public life ended with the events surrounding the new Emperor's coming of age.

The disease had now taken definitive hold over his whole organism. Little by little, Nicolau retreated into seclusion. He could no longer visit certain people or frequent certain houses. Even the theater was no longer a distraction. The state of his auditory organs was so delicate that the sound of applause caused him excruciating pain. The enthusiasm of the city's inhabitants for the famous sopranos Candiani and Meréa, but principally for Candiani, whose carriage was drawn by willing fans—a distinction even more remarkable in that they wouldn't have done it for Plato himself—such enthusiasm was one of Nicolau's greatest torments. He reached the point where he stopped going to the opera altogether, finding Candiani utterly unbearable, and finding the organ grinders' version of *Norma* preferable to that of the prima donna. It was not out of a sense of exaggerated patriotism that he enjoyed listening to João Caetano in the early days, but eventually Nicolau gave him up, too, and the theaters almost entirely.

"It's hopeless," thought the brother-in-law. "If we could only give him a new spleen . . ."

How could he think something so ridiculous? Nicolau was, indeed, a hopeless case. Domestic pleasures no longer sufficed. His literary endeavors—family verses, prized ditties, and political odes—were short-lived, and may even have made him worse. In any case, it struck him one day that this occupation was the most ridiculous thing in the world, and the endless praise heaped on the works of Gonçalves Dias, for example, suggested to him a nation slipping into banal bad taste. This literary sentiment, the fruit of his wounded self, acted further upon the same wound to the point of producing a string of serious crises that confined him to bed for some time. His brother-in-law took the opportunity to clear the house of all books of a certain tenor.

Less explicable is why, in a matter of months, he began to take so little care over his appearance. Brought up to be always elegantly dressed, he had been a long-standing customer of one of the leading tailors in Rio, a man called Plum, and not a single day would go by without him having his hair tended to by Messrs. Desmarais & Gérard, *coiffeurs de la cour*, on Rua do Ouvidor. It seems, however, that he found this "hairdressers to the court" designation excessively conceited, and punished them by taking his business to a backstreet barber. As to why he changed his attire, I can only say that it remains a mystery and, unless attributable to age, utterly inexplicable.

His dismissal of his cook is another enigma. At the instigation of his brother-in-law, who was doing his best to keep him entertained, Nicolau gave two dinners a week, and his guests were, of course, unanimous in their opinion that Nicolau's cook surpassed all others in the city. The dishes really were rather good, some of them excellent, but the praise was a little too emphatic, a little too excessive, for it to be entirely agreeable to Nicolau, and this went on for some time. How to explain, then, that one Sunday, just after a magnificent dinner, he dismissed the remarkable man who had been the indirect cause of some of his most delightful moments on Earth? Another impenetrable mystery.

"He was a thief!" was the answer he gave his brother-in-law.

Neither the efforts of his brother-in-law, sister, and friends, nor his wealth, improved the lot of our poor, sad Nicolau. The secretion in his spleen became continual and the worms multiplied by the millions—I have no idea whether this theory is true, by the way, but it was, after all, his brother-in-law's. Nicolau's final years were extremely cruel. He lived in a state of almost continual debilitation, irritable and almost blind, suffering far more acutely than those around him. The slightest thing would set his nerves on edge: a good speech, a clever artist, a carriage, a cravat, a sonnet, a witty remark, an interesting dream—everything brought on an attack.

Did he want to die? One might suppose so, seeing the indifference with which he rejected all the remedies of the city's leading physicians. Eventually it was necessary to resort to deception and tell him they had been pre-scribed by some ignorant quack. But it was too late. Death carried him off a couple of weeks later.

"Joaquim Soares?" cried the brother-in-law in astonishment, when he learned of the clause in the dead man's will specifying who should make his coffin. "That oaf's coffins are no good at all, and—"

"There's no point arguing," interrupted his wife. "We must respect my dear brother's wishes."

UNDATED STORIES
(1884)

Author's Preface

Of all the stories found herein there are only two that effectively contain no explicit date; all the others do, and this will cause some readers to find the title *Undated Stories* either unintelligible or perplexing. Supposing, however, that my purpose is to define these pages as dealing, in substance, with things that do not belong to any particular date or time, that, I think, would explain the title. Which is the worst thing that could possibly happen to it, for the best titles are always those that need no explanation.

M. de A.

THE DEVIL'S CHURCH

Chapter 1

A MARVELOUS IDEA

AN OLD BENEDICTINE MANUSCRIPT tells how, one day, the Devil had the idea of founding a church. Although he was making steady and substantial profits, he felt humiliated by the rather isolated role he had played down the centuries, with no organization, no rules, no canon law, and no rituals, indeed nothing much at all. He lived, so to speak, on divine leftovers, on human oversights and favors. Nothing fixed, nothing regular. Why shouldn't he have his own church? A Devil's Church would be the best way to take on the other religions and destroy them once and for all.

"Yes, a church of my own," he concluded. "Scripture against Scripture, breviary against breviary. I'll have my own mass, with wine and bread aplenty, my own sermons, bulls, novenas, and all the other ecclesiastical bells and whistles. My creed will be the universal nucleus of souls, my church a tent of Abraham. And then, while other religions quarrel and split, my church will stand united and alone, with no Muhammad or Luther to oppose me. There are many ways to affirm a belief, but only one way to deny it."

As he said this, the Devil shook his head and stretched out his arms in a magnificently manly gesture. Then he remembered that he really ought to go and see God, to tell him his plan and throw down this challenge; he raised his eyes, burning with hatred and bitter with revenge, and said to himself: "Yes, it is time." And with a beat of his wings—which set off a rumble that shook all the provinces of the abyss—he flew swiftly up from the shadows into the infinite blue.

Chapter 2

BETWEEN GOD AND THE DEVIL

When the Devil arrived in Heaven, God was just welcoming an old man. The seraphim who were busily garlanding the recent arrival immediately stopped what they were doing, and the Devil stood waiting at the entrance with his eyes fixed on the Lord.

"What do you want with me?" asked the Lord.

"I haven't come for your servant Faust," replied the Devil, laughing and pointing at the old man, "but for all the Fausts of this and every century."

"Explain yourself."

"The explanation is easy, Lord. But let me first say this: take in this worthy old man, give him the best place in Heaven, command your most tuneful zithers and lutes to receive him with their divinest choruses . . ."

"Do you have any idea what he did?" asked the Lord, his eyes filled with tenderness.

"No, but he's probably one of the last who will come to you. It won't be long before Heaven is like an empty house, on account of its high rent. I'm going to build a cheap boardinghouse; in short, I'm going to set up my own church. I've had enough of my lack of organization, my haphazard, spur-of-the-moment kingdom. It's time I won a complete and final victory. And so I have come to tell you this, in all loyalty, so that you can't accuse me of any deception. Good idea, don't you think?"

"You came to tell me, not seek my approval," commented the Lord.

"Yes, you're right," replied the Devil. "But vanity likes to hear its master's applause. True, in this case it will be the applause of a defeated master, and as such . . . Lord, I'm going down to Earth. I'm going to lay my foundation stone."

"Go ahead."

"Do you want me to come and let you know how it all works out?"

"That won't be necessary. Just tell me, since you've been so fed up with your lack of organization for so very long, why is it that you have only thought of founding a church now?"

The Devil gave a triumphant, mocking smile. He was savoring some cruel idea, some stinging remark stored away in the saddlebag of his memory which, in that brief instant of eternity, made him believe he was superior even to God. But he suppressed his laughter and said:

"I have only just concluded a study I began several centuries ago, and I see now that the virtues, those daughters of Heaven, are in many respects comparable to queens whose velvet mantles are edged with cotton fringes. Now, I propose to tug them by those fringes, and bring them all to my church; after them will come the queens dressed in purest silk . . ."

"Pompous old windbag!" murmured the Lord.

"Look here. Many of those bodies who kneel at your feet in churches throughout the world wear the bustles of drawing room and street; their cheeks are rouged with the same powder, their handkerchiefs carry the same scents, and their eyes sparkle with curiosity and devotion, torn between the holy book and the tempting mustache of sin. See the passion—or disdain, at least—with which that gentleman over there makes sure everyone knows about the favors he liberally bestows: clothes, boots, coins, or any of the other necessities of life. But I don't want to seem to be dwelling on the little things; I am not talking, for example, about the smug serenity of this man here, president of a lay brotherhood, who, when taking part in any religious procession, piously carries pinned to his chest both your love and a medal. I have more important business to deal with . . ."

At this, the seraphim ruffled their wings, heavy with boredom and sleep. The archangels Michael and Gabriel gazed at the Lord imploringly. God interrupted the Devil.

"You talk in clichés, which is the worst thing that could happen to a spirit of your sort," replied the Lord. "All that you say or may say has been said and resaid by the world's moralists. It's been done to death, and if you have neither the ability nor the originality to breathe new life into it, it would be better for you to be quiet and keep your thoughts to yourself. See? The faces of all my legions show clear signs of the tedium you're inflicting on them. The old man here looks thoroughly fed up, and do you know what he did?"

"I've already said that I don't."

"After an honest life, he died a truly sublime death. Caught in a ship-wreck, he was going to seize hold of a plank and save himself, when he spied a couple of newlyweds, in the flower of youth, already grappling with death. He gave them that plank and plunged into eternity. No one was watching, only the water and the sky above. Where in that do you find your cotton fringe?"

"As you know, Lord, I am the spirit who denies."

"Do you deny this death?"

"I deny everything. Misanthropy can look like charity, because, to a misanthrope, leaving life to others is actually a way of despising them . . ."

"A windbag, and a crafty one at that!" exclaimed the Lord. "Go on, go and set up your church. Call upon all the virtues, gather together all the fringes, summon all of mankind . . . But go! Go!"

In vain, the Devil tried to say something more, but God had silenced him, and, upon a divine signal, the seraphim filled Heaven with the harmonious sound of their singing. The Devil suddenly found himself in midair; he furled his wings and, like a bolt of lightning, plunged to Earth.

Chapter 3

GOOD NEWS FOR MANKIND

Once on Earth, the Devil did not waste a single minute. He hurriedly donned a Benedictine cowl—as being a habit of good repute—and began to spread a new and extraordinary doctrine with a voice that echoed down through the bowels of the century. He promised his faithful disciples all of Earth's delights, all its glories, and all its most intimate pleasures. He admitted that he was indeed the Devil, but did so in order to rectify mankind's view of him and to deny the stories pious old women told about him.

"Yes, I am the Devil," he said again and again. "Not the Devil of sulfurous nights, of bedtime stories, or childish terrors, but the one and only true Devil, the very genius of nature, who was given that name to drive him from the hearts of men. See how gentle and graceful I am. I am your true father. Come with me: embrace the name that was invented to shame me, make it your trophy and your banner, and I will give you everything, absolutely everything . . ."

Thus he spoke in order to arouse enthusiasm and awaken the indifferent, in short, to gather the multitudes around him. And they came; and once they were with him, the Devil began to set out his doctrine. The doctrine was what one would expect from the mouth of a spirit of denial, at least in terms of substance. As for its form, it was at times clever and at others cynical and shameless.

He proclaimed that the accepted virtues should be replaced with others, the natural and legitimate ones. Pride, Lust, and Sloth were restored, as was Greed, which he declared was nothing but the mother of Thrift, the sole difference being that the mother was robust and the daughter a scrawny wretch. The best argument in favor of Wrath was the existence of Homer, for without the fury of Achilles, there would have been no *Iliad*. "Sing, O goddess, the anger of Achilles son of Peleus." He said the same of Gluttony, which produced the best bits of Rabelais and many fine verses in Diniz's *Hyssope*. It was such a superior virtue that no one now remembers Lucullus's battles, only his banquets; it was Gluttony that made him immortal. But still, setting aside these literary or historical justifications and focusing only on the intrinsic value of such a virtue, who would deny that it feels much better to fill one's mouth and belly with good food than to get by on meager morsels, or the saliva of fasting? For his part, the Devil promised to replace the Lord's vineyard, a merely metaphorical expression, with the Devil's vineyard in the literal sense, for his followers would never want for the fruit of the finest vines. As for Envy, he preached coolly that it was the greatest virtue of all and the source of infinite prosperity; a precious virtue that would come to supplant all the others, even talent itself.

The crowd chased excitedly after him. With great blasts of eloquence, the Devil instilled in them the new order of things, changing all their notions, making them love the things that were wicked and hate those that were wholesome.

There was nothing more curious, for example, than his definition of fraud. He called it man's left arm, the right arm being force. His conclusion was simply that many men were left-handed, and that was that. Not that he required everyone to be left-handed, for no one was to be excluded. Some could be left-handed, others right-handed; he'd accept everyone, except those who were neither one thing nor the other. His most profound and rigorous explanation, however, was that of Venality. One casuist of the time even confessed that his explanation was a monument of logic. Venality, said the Devil, was the exercise of a right superior to all others. If you can sell your house, your ox, your shoe, or your hat—things that legally and juridically belong *to* you but are not part *of* you—why shouldn't you be allowed to sell your opinion, your vote, your word, or your faith, things which are more than mere possessions, because they form part of your own consciousness, that is, your very self? To deny this is to lapse into absurdity and contradiction. For are there not women who sell their hair? Can a man not sell some of his blood for transfusion to another who is anemic? And why should blood and hair, mere physical parts, enjoy a privilege that is denied to character, man's moral portion? Having thus set out the principle behind Venality, the Devil lost no time in expounding its practical and financial benefits. He then indicated that, in light of social prejudice, it would be appropriate to disguise the exercise of such a well-founded right; this would, of course, amount to practicing Venality and Hypocrisy at the same time, and would therefore be doubly deserving.

Up and down he went, examining and rectifying everything. Naturally he fought against the forgiveness of sins and other such principles of charitable kindness. He didn't absolutely prohibit the spreading of calumnies without reward, but urged that it should always be done in return for some sort of payment, whether financial or otherwise. However, in cases where the calumny resulted from nothing more than an uncontrollable explosion of impetuous imagination, he forbade any recompense, since that was equivalent to being paid for merely sweating. He condemned all forms of respect as potential elements of social and personal politeness—except, of course, where there was some sort of advantage to be drawn from it. But this exception was itself soon eliminated by the realization that the desire for personal gain converted a display of respect into straightforward flattery, and the relevant intention was therefore the latter and not the former.

To complete his work, the Devil realized that he needed to sever all bonds of human solidarity—the idea of loving one's neighbor was a major obstacle to his new institution. He therefore demonstrated that this rule was a mere invention of parasites and insolvent tradesmen; one should show nothing but indifference toward one's fellow man, and, in some cases, hatred and contempt. He even demonstrated that the notion of "neighbor" was erroneous, and cited the refined and learned Neapolitan priest Ferdinando Galiani, who wrote to a certain *marquise de l'ancien régime*: "Neighbor be damned! There's no such thing as neighbor!" The only situation in which the

Devil permitted loving one's neighbor was when it concerned loving other men's wives, because that kind of love has the peculiarity of being nothing more than the individual's love for himself. And since some disciples may have found that such a metaphysical explanation would escape the under-standing of the masses, the Devil resorted to an illustration: one hundred people take shares in a retail bank, but, in reality, none of the shareholders looks after the business, only their own dividends: this is what happens to adulterers. This illustration was included in the book of wisdom.

Chapter 4

FRINGES AND FRINGES

The Devil's prediction came true. As soon as someone tugged the fringe of those virtues whose velvet cloak was fringed with cotton, they duly threw their cloaks into the nettles and joined the new church. The others duly fol-lowed and the institution grew over time. The church had been founded and its doctrine was being propagated; there was not one region of the globe that did not know of it, not one language into which it had not been translated, and not one race that did not love it. The Devil gave a triumphant cheer.

However, one day, many years later, the Devil noticed that many of his faithful followers were secretly practicing the old virtues again. They didn't practice all of them, or practice them in their entirety, but they did prac-tice some of them, partially, and, as I say, in secret. Certain gluttons were retreating to eat frugally three or four times a year, on days of Catholic obli-gation; many misers were giving alms under cover of darkness or on sparsely populated streets; various embezzlers of the public purse were reimbursing small amounts; now and then fraudsters spoke the honest truth, although with their usual sly expression just so that people would think they were still being tricked.

This discovery shocked the Devil. He investigated the evil more closely, and saw that it was spreading rapidly. Some cases were simply incomprehen-sible, like that of a Levantine apothecary who had slowly poisoned a whole generation and then, with the profits of his nefarious trade, had come to the aid of his victims' children. In Cairo, the Devil found an otherwise impec-cable camel thief covering his face so that he could attend the mosque. The

Devil confronted him at the entrance to the mosque and berated him for such outrageous behavior, but the man denied everything, saying he was only going there so as to steal a dragoman's camel; indeed, he did steal it, in full view of the Devil, but then gave it as a present to a muezzin, who prayed to Allah on the thief's behalf. The Benedictine manuscript cites many other extraordinary discoveries, including the following one that completely confounded the Devil. One of his best apostles was a Calabrian gentleman, fifty years old and an eminent forger of documents, who owned a fine house in the Roman Campagna filled with paintings, statues, a library, etc. He was fraud personified; he would even take to his bed so as not to admit that he was in good health. However, this man not only failed to cheat at cards, he even gave bonuses to his servants. Having attracted the friendship of a canon, he went to make his confession to him every week in a deserted side chapel, and although he did not reveal to him any of his secret activities, he crossed himself twice, once upon kneeling and again when he stood up. The Devil could scarcely believe such treachery, but there was no doubting what had happened.

He did not stop for an instant. The shock gave him no time to reflect, to draw comparisons, or to infer from the present situation something analogous in the past. Once again he flew straight up to Heaven, trembling with rage, anxious to discover the hidden cause of such a peculiar occurrence. God listened to him with infinite benevolence, not interrupting or criticizing him, or even gloating over his satanic agony. He looked the Devil straight in the eye and said:

"Well, what do you expect, my poor Devil? The cotton cloaks now have silk fringes, just as the velvet cloaks had cotton ones. What do you expect? It's the eternal human contradiction."

THE LAPSE

―――――

Then all the captains . . . and all the people,
from the least even unto the greatest, came near.
And said unto Jeremiah the prophet: Let, we beseech thee,
our supplication be accepted before thee.

—JEREMIAH 42:1–2

D ON'T ASK ME about Dr. Jeremias Halma's family, nor what brought him to Rio de Janeiro in that year of 1768, during the viceroyalty of the Count of Azambuja, who people initially said had been the one to send for the doctor, a version of events that proved short-lived. He came, he stayed, and he died with the century. What I can, however, confirm is that he was Dutch, and a physician. He had traveled widely, knew everything there was to know about chemistry, and spoke five or six living languages fluently, as well as two dead ones. He was such an inventive and universal fellow that he endowed Malay poetry with a new meter and conceived a theory on the formation of diamonds, not to mention the many therapeutic advances he made, as well as innumerable other admirable things. And all this without being in the least pigheaded or arrogant. On the contrary, his life and person were like the house that a fellow Dutchman procured for him on Rua do Piolho, a very humble house indeed, where he died sometime around Christmas 1799. Yes, Dr. Halma was unpretentious, sincere, and modest, indeed so modest that . . . But no, that would upset the order of the story. Let's start at the beginning.

At the end of Rua do Ouvidor, which had not yet become the Via Dolorosa of long-suffering husbands that it is today, near what used to be Rua dos Latoeiros, there lived at that time a certain Tomé Gonçalves, a wealthy man and, according to some accounts, a member of the city council. Councillor or not, this Tomé Gonçalves had not only money, he also had debts, which were neither few nor recent. These arrears could easily be explained by carelessness or, indeed, knavery; but anyone who favors one or other of these interpretations clearly has no business reading a serious piece of writing like this. After all, there is no point in someone going to all the effort of scribbling page after page just to say that at the end of the last century there lived a man who, for reasons of crookery or carelessness, failed to pay his creditors. Accounts confirm that this fellow countryman of ours was precise in everything he did, punctilious in the most mundane duties, strict, and even meticulous. The truth is that he was a "redeemed brother" of many lay orders and confraternities and had been since the days when he was still in the habit of paying his debts; and those that had the good fortune to count him as one of their members did not need to wrangle out of him tokens of his devotion and esteem; and, if he was indeed a councillor, as all the evidence suggests, one can be sure that he served to the satisfaction of the whole city.

So? I'm coming to that now, for the subject matter of this piece is precisely this curious phenomenon, the cause of which is known only because Dr. Halma discovered it. On the afternoon of a religious procession, Tomé Gonçalves, wearing the habit of a lay order and helping to carry one of the floats bearing holy images, was walking along with the serene look of a man who does ill to no man. Looking on from windows and sidewalks were many of his creditors, and two of them, standing at the corner of Beco das Cancelas (the procession was making its way down Rua do Hospício), after duly kneeling, praying, crossing themselves, and standing up again, asked one another whether now was perhaps the time to resort to law.

"What's the worst that can happen?" said one of them. "If he quarrels with me, all the better; he'll get nothing more from me without paying for it first. Without a quarrel, I can hardly refuse to give him what he asks, and so

I'll just keep on selling him more and more stuff on credit in the hope that he does finally pay me what he already owes. No, sir; it can't go on like this."

"As for me," said the other, "the only reason I haven't done anything before is because of my wife, who's scared, and thinks I shouldn't quarrel with important people like him. But other people's importance won't put food or drink on the table. And what about my wigs?"

The latter was a wigmaker on Rua da Vala, opposite the cathedral, who had sold Tomé Gonçalves ten wigs in five years, without seeing so much as a penny from him. The other was a tailor, and an even bigger creditor than the wigmaker. By now the procession had passed by, but they remained on that same street corner, agreeing that they should send in the bailiffs. The wigmaker commented that there were many other creditors ready and waiting to swoop on the delinquent debtor, and the tailor thought it would be a good idea to include Mata the shoemaker in their scheme, since his situation was now desperate. Tomé Gonçalves owed him more than eighty *mil-réis*. They were discussing this when they heard a voice behind them asking, in a foreign accent, why they were plotting against a sick man. They turned around and, coming face-to-face with Dr. Halma, the two creditors removed their caps; with the greatest of respect, they then pointed out that the debtor was very far from being sick, for there he was taking part in the procession, hale and hearty, helping to shoulder one of the floats.

"What's that got to do with it?" interrupted the doctor. "No one's saying there's anything wrong with his arms or legs . . ."

"His heart, then? Or his stomach?"

"Neither heart nor stomach," replied Dr. Halma, and he continued, very gently, explaining that it was a highly speculative matter, which he could not discuss there on the street, and indeed he wasn't sure if they would understand him. "If I had to style someone's hair or cut a pair of breeches," he added, so as not to upset them, "it's highly unlikely that I would meet the exacting standards of your respective professions, so useful and indeed essential to the state . . ."

Chuckling amiably, he bade them good day and continued on his way. The two creditors stood there openmouthed. The wigmaker was the first to speak, saying that the news from Dr. Halma should not discourage them in their efforts to get paid. "If even the dead pay up, or at least someone else does on their behalf," reflected the wigmaker, "then it's only right to ask the sick to do the same." The tailor, envious of the wigmaker's little joke, stitched on his own witty frill: "Pay up and be cured!"

This opinion was not shared by Mata the shoemaker, who thought some secret lay behind Dr. Halma's words, and proposed that, first, they should carefully analyze what this might be, and then decide upon the most appropriate course of action. They then invited other creditors to join them in conclave the following Sunday at the house of a certain Dona Aninha, in the vicinity of Rocio, on the pretext of a baptism. The precaution was a prudent one, so as not to give the superintendent of police reason to suspect that the gathering concerned any shady machinations against the state. As soon as darkness fell, the creditors began to arrive, swathed in cloaks, and, as public street-lighting only came in with the Count of Resende's viceroyalty, each of them carried a hand lantern as custom then dictated, thereby giving their cabal a touch of the theatrical and picturesque. There were thirty or forty of them, and they were not all of his creditors, either.

Charles Lamb's theory about the division of humankind into two great races came after the Rocio cabal, but here we have no better example to demonstrate it. The men's distressed and downcast demeanor, the despair of some and the anxieties of all, were proof in advance that the distinguished essayist's theory was indeed true, and that of the two great human races— those who lend and those who borrow—the sad gestures of the former contrast with "the open, trusting, generous manners of the other." For at that very same hour, having returned home from the procession, Tomé Gonçalves was gaily entertaining some of his friends with the wine and chicken he had purchased on credit, while his creditors, pale and disillusioned, were secretly trying to work out some way of getting their money back.

The debate was long and no single opinion convinced everyone. Some were inclined to litigate, others to wait, and more than a few were open to consulting Dr. Halma. Five or six partisans of this latter course of action seemed to favor it, but only with the secret and disguised intention of doing nothing whatsoever, for they were the slaves of fear and hope. The wigmaker opposed it, asking what illness could possibly prevent a man from paying what he owed. But Mata the shoemaker said to him: "My good friend, ours is not to reason why; just remember that the doctor is a foreigner, and in foreign parts they know things they wouldn't even tell the devil. In any case, it wouldn't take long." This argument won the day, and they appointed the shoemaker, the tailor, and the wigmaker to speak to Dr. Halma on everyone's behalf, and the cabal dissolved into general merrymaking. Terpsichore herself, the muse of dance, leapt and spun her joyful graces before them, so much so that some even forgot the secret ulcer gnawing away inside them. *Eheu! fugaces labuntur anni* . . . Alas! the fleeting years slip by. Even pain is fickle.

The following day, between seven and eight o'clock in the morning, Dr. Halma received the three creditors, "Come in, come in . . ." And with his broad Dutch face and a laugh that spilled from his mouth like a full-bodied wine from a broken cask, the great physician came in person to open the door to them. At that moment, he was engrossed in studying a snake found dead the previous day on Santo Antônio hill; but, as he liked to say, humanity takes precedence over science. He invited the three men to sit down on the only three empty chairs in the room; the fourth chair was his own, while all the others, some five or six, were piled high with all manner of things.

It was Mata the shoemaker who explained the problem; of the three he was the most endowed with diplomatic talents. He began by saying that the good doctor's skill was going to save a large number of families from destitution, and it would be neither the first nor the last great work of a doctor who—with no disrespect to the local doctors—was the wisest to have been seen there since the days of Gomes Freire's government. Tomé Gonçalves's creditors had no one else to turn to. Knowing that the good doctor attributed Gonçalves's arrears to an illness, they had decided that a cure should first be attempted, before resorting to legal proceedings. They would keep litigation as a last resort, if all else failed. This was what they had come to tell him, on behalf of dozens of creditors. They wanted to know if it was true that, on top of all the other possible human ailments, the nonpayment of debts was yet another illness, and whether it was incurable, and, if it wasn't, whether the tears of so many families might—

"There is a rather unusual illness," interrupted Dr. Halma, visibly moved by their plight, "known as a 'memory lapse.' To put it quite simply, Tomé Gonçalves has lost all notion of paying for anything. The reason he fails to settle his bills is neither a deliberate ploy nor mere carelessness; rather, the idea of paying, of handing over the price of a thing, has been entirely erased from his mind. I discovered this two months ago when I was at his house, and the prior of the Carmo monastery called by, saying he had come to 'pay him the courtesy of a visit.' No sooner had the prior left than Tomé Gonçalves asked me what 'pay' meant and added that, several days earlier, an apothecary had used the same word, without any further explanation, and he thought he had also heard it from other people. Hearing the prior say it, he supposed it must be Latin. I understood everything then; I had studied this condition in various parts of the world, and I understood that he was suffering an attack of 'memory lapse.' It was for this very reason that I said to these two gentlemen the other day that they should not issue proceedings against a sick man.

"But then," ventured Mata, turning pale, "our money is completely lost . . ."

"The illness is not incurable," said the doctor.

"Ah!"

"Indeed not. I both know of and possess the drug that will cure it, and I have already employed it in two major cases: a barber who had so entirely lost any notion of space that one night he reached up to pluck the stars from the sky, and a lady from Catalonia who had lost all notion of her husband. The barber risked his life many times trying to jump out of the highest windows in the house, as if he were on the ground floor . . ."

"Good gracious!" exclaimed the three creditors.

"My feelings exactly," the doctor continued calmly. "As for the Catalan lady, at first she confused her husband with a graduate called Matias, who was tall and slim, whereas her husband was short and fat; then with a captain called Hermógenes, and, at the time I began to treat her, with a clergyman. In three months she was completely cured. Her name was Dona Agostinha."

It was a truly miraculous drug. The three creditors were radiant with hope; everything indicated that Tomé Gonçalves was indeed suffering from that 'lapse,' and since a drug existed, and the doctor had it in his house . . . Ah! but there was the rub. Although the doctor was on good terms with the man, Tomé Gonçalves was not one of Dr. Halma's regular patients, and he could scarcely turn up at his house offering his services. Tomé Gonçalves had no close family to take responsibility for calling a doctor, and the creditors could scarcely assume the burden themselves. Silent and perplexed, the creditors exchanged glances. Those of the tailor, like the wigmaker's, expressed the following desperate suggestion: that the creditors should all chip in, and, by means of a fat and appetizing sum, invite Dr. Halma to perform his cure. Perhaps the money . . . But the illustrious Mata saw the danger in such a proposal, since the patient might not recover and their losses would thereby be doubled. Great was their anguish; all seemed lost. The doctor twirled his snuffbox between his fingers, waiting for them to leave, not impatiently, but cheerfully. It was then that Mata, like a captain in the grand old days of yore, saw the enemy's weak point. He had noticed that his opening words had moved the doctor, and so returned to his theme of their families' tears and their children's empty stomachs, for they were but humble artisans or tradesmen of little means, whereas Tomé Gonçalves was rich. Shoes, breeches, cloaks, cough syrups, wigs, all these things cost them time, money, and health . . . Yes, sir, health; the calluses on his hands showed clearly that his trade was a hard one, and his good friend the tailor, standing here among them, who spluttered and coughed with consumption night after night by the light of a candle, endlessly stitching away with his needle and thread . . .

Kind, generous Jeremias! His eyes had filled up with tears before the shoemaker could finish. The awkwardness of his manner was compensated by the effusions of a devout and human heart. Yes, of course he would try to cure him; he would place science at the service of a just cause. Moreover, the main beneficiary would be Tomé Gonçalves himself, for his reputation was now in tatters on account of something for which he was as blameless as a blasphemous lunatic. Naturally the delegation's delight translated into endless bows and extravagant praise for the doctor's exemplary qualities. The latter modestly cut this short by asking them to join him for breakfast, an honor which they declined, meanwhile thanking him most cordially. Even when they were out in the street where the doctor could no longer hear them, they did not tire of praising his wisdom, goodness, generosity, and courtesy. Such simple, natural good manners!

From that day on, Tomé Gonçalves began to notice that the doctor had become an assiduous visitor, and—with no ulterior motive, because he genuinely liked him—he did everything he could to attach him to his household once and for all. His "lapse" was indeed complete; not just the idea of *paying*, but also the related notions of *creditor, debt, bills*, and so on, had been completely erased from his memory, forming a large hole in his mind. I fear I may be accused of making fanciful comparisons, but Pascal's abyss is the one that most readily comes to mind. Tomé Gonçalves had Pascal's abyss not beside him, but within his very being, and it was so deep that it held within it more than sixty creditors, thrashing around down there with a wailing and gnashing of teeth, as the Scriptures put it. It was an urgent matter to fish out all those unhappy creatures and fill in the hole.

Jeremias convinced the patient that he was under the weather, and, to reinvigorate him, began administering the drug. On its own, the drug was not enough; an accompanying therapy was also necessary, because the cure operated on two levels. The general or abstract level, i.e., restoring the idea of paying, along with all other related notions, was the part entrusted to the drug; whereas the specific or concrete level, i.e., the suggesting or naming of a particular debt and a particular creditor, fell to the doctor. Let's suppose that the first chosen creditor was the shoemaker. The doctor would take the patient to various shoe shops in order to witness the sale and purchase of the merchandise, and watch again and again the action of paying; he would talk about the manufacture and sale of shoes throughout the world, and compare the price of footwear in that year of 1768 with the prices of thirty or forty years earlier; he would get the shoemaker to visit Tomé Gonçalves's house ten or twenty times to present his bill and ask for his money; and a hundred other such stratagems. One by one, the same thing happened with the tailor, the wigmaker, the coachmaker, and the apothecary; it took longer with the ones who went first, for the perfectly natural reason that the illness was more ingrained, whereas the preceding efforts benefited those who went later, and compensated them for the delay.

All bills were paid. The creditors' joy was indescribable, the blessings they heaped upon the name of Dr. Halma too numerous to mention. "Yes, sir, a great man," they shouted high and low. "Sounds like witchcraft to me," ventured the women. As for Tomé Gonçalves, astonished at so many old debts, he never tired of praising his creditors' forbearance, and at the same time reprimanded them for letting them accumulate.

"From now on," he told them, "I want to be billed every week."

"Don't worry, we'll remind you," was the creditors' wholehearted response.

There remained, however, one creditor. This was the most recent, Dr. Halma himself, for his fees for that valuable service rendered. But, alas, modesty tied his tongue. As generous of heart as he was awkward of manner, he planned three, even five attempts, but didn't manage even one. And yet it would have been the easiest thing in the world; he merely needed to suggest the debt using the same method employed in relation to the others.

But was that appropriate? he asked himself; was it decent? So he waited, and waited. Not wanting to appear too brazen, he began to visit less frequently, but Tomé Gonçalves would go to the doctor's modest house on Rua do Piolho and take him out to dinner or supper and discuss foreign affairs, about which he was very curious, but never saying a word about paying. Dr. Halma began to think that perhaps the creditors might do so, but even though the thought of reminding Tomé Gonçalves about the unpaid doctor's bill might have crossed their minds, the creditors did nothing, because they presumed it had been paid first, before all the others. That, at least, is what they told each other, clothed in many formulations of popular wisdom—Look first to your own, Matthew—Charity begins at home—A fool asks God to kill him and the devil to take his soul, etc. All false; the truth is that on the day he died, Tomé Gonçalves had only one creditor in the world: Dr. Halma.

By then, in 1798, Dr. Halma was virtually a saint. "Farewell to a great man!" Mata, now ex-shoemaker, said to him, as they sat in the chaise taking them both to Tomé Gonçalves's requiem mass at the Carmelite church. And Dr. Halma, bent with age and gazing sadly down at the tips of his shoes, replied: "A great man, poor devil."

FINAL CHAPTER

——————

MANY SUICIDES HAVE the excellent custom of not departing this life without setting out the reason and circumstances that have turned them against it. Those who go silently rarely do so out of pride; in most cases they either lack time or don't know how to write. It is an excellent custom for two reasons: first, it is an act of courtesy, for this world is not a ball from which a man can sneak away before dancing the cotillion; second, the newspapers collect and publish these posthumous scribbles, and thus the deceased lives on for a day or two, sometimes even a week.

Notwithstanding the excellence of the custom, it was originally my intention to go silently, because, having been unlucky my whole life, I feared that any final words might cause complications in the hereafter. But a recent incident made me change my plans, and I am leaving behind not one document, but two. The first is my will, which I have just finished drafting and sealing; it's here on the table, beside the loaded pistol. The second is this outline of an autobiography. Note that I am leaving the second document only because it is needed to clarify the first, which would seem absurd or unintelligible without some commentary. In my will I state that my few books, old clothes, and the little house I own in Catumbi, which I rent out to a carpenter, should be sold and the proceeds used to buy new boots and shoes to be distributed in the manner indicated, which, I confess, is rather extraordinary. Without an explanation for such a legacy, I risk doubt being cast on the will's validity. The reason behind the legacy stems from a recent incident, and the incident, in turn, is connected to my entire life.

My name is Matias Deodato de Castro e Melo, son of Sergeant-Major Salvador Deodato de Castro e Melo and Dona Maria da Soledade Pereira, both deceased. I come from Corumbá, in the state of Mato Grosso; I was born on March 3, 1820, and am, therefore, fifty-one years of age today, March 3, 1871.

As I said, I am an unlucky fellow, if not the unluckiest of all men. There is even an old proverb that I have quite literally fulfilled. It happened in Corumbá, when I was nearly eight years old. I was swinging back and forth in my hammock during siesta time, in a little room directly under the roof tiles. Now, either because the hook was loose, or because I was swinging too vigorously, the hammock came away from one of the walls and I found myself flat on the floor. I had fallen on my back, but even so I managed to break my nose, because a loose piece of roof tile, which was just waiting for an opportunity to fall, took advantage of the commotion to come crashing down as well. The wound inflicted was neither serious nor of long duration; indeed, my father teased me mercilessly about it. When Canon Brito came to sip a cool glass of *guaraná* with us that evening and was told all about the episode, he cited the proverb, saying that I was the first person actually to achieve the absurd feat of falling flat on my back *and* breaking my nose. Neither the canon nor my father could have imagined that the incident was simply a sign of things to come.

I won't dwell on the other misfortunes that blighted my childhood and youth. I want to die at noon, and it is already eleven o'clock. Besides, I've sent my manservant out, and he might come back early and interrupt the execution of my deadly project. If I had time, I would recount in detail several painful episodes, including a beating I received by mistake. It concerned the rival of a friend of mine—a rival in love and, naturally, one who had been defeated. My friend and the lady in question were most indignant when they found out about the beating I had received, but secretly they were rather pleased that I had been beaten and not him. Nor will I speak of certain illnesses I have suffered. I will hasten to the point when my father, having been poor all his life, died in extreme poverty, and my mother survived him by less than two months. Canon Brito, who had just been elected to the Chamber of Deputies, proposed taking me with him to Rio de Janeiro with the idea of making a priest of me; however, five days after we arrived, he died. You see what I mean when I say I have always been unlucky.

There I was, at sixteen years of age, all on my own, friendless and penni-less. A canon at the Imperial Chapel tried to get me employment as a sacris-tan, but although I had often served at mass in Mato Grosso and knew some Latin, I was not admitted due to a lack of vacancies. Others encouraged me to study law, and I accepted with grim determination. I even had some help to begin with, and when that stopped, I soldiered on and finally man-aged to get my bachelor's degree. Now, don't tell me that this was an excep-tion in my life of misfortune, because my academic qualification brought me to an even sorrier state of affairs; however, since destiny was determined to punish me whatever my chosen profession, I do not blame my law degree for that. It's true that I was very pleased to obtain it; my tender age and a certain superstitious belief in the need to improve oneself made of that roll of parchment the diamond key that would open every door to good fortune.

And, to begin with, my bachelor's degree was not the only piece of paper in my pocket. No, sir; beside it there were ten or fifteen others, the fruits of a love affair begun in Rio de Janeiro during Holy Week of 1842, with a widow seven or eight years my senior, but fiery, good-humored, and rich. She lived with her blind brother on Rua do Conde; I can't say any more than that. All my friends were aware of this relationship; two of them even read the letters, which I showed them on the pretext of admiring the wid-ow's elegant style, but really so that they could read the marvelous things she said to me. In everyone's opinion, our marriage was a certainty, an abso-lute certainty; the widow was merely waiting for me to finish my studies. When I graduated, one of these friends congratulated me, underlining his certainty with this definitive sentence:

"Your marriage is pure dogma."

And, laughing, he asked if, on account of that dogma, I could lend him fifty *mil-réis*, which he needed urgently. I didn't have fifty *mil-réis* on me, but that word "dogma" was still reverberating so sweetly within me that I didn't rest all day until I had obtained the money. I happily took it to him myself, and he received it gratefully. Six months later, it was he who mar-ried the widow.

I won't tell you how I suffered then, only that my first impulse was to shoot them both. I did shoot them in my imagination, and watched them dying, gasping, begging for my forgiveness. This was a purely hypothetical revenge; in reality, I did nothing. They married, and went to the hills of Tijuca to watch the rising of their honeymoon moon. I was left rereading the widow's letters. "As God is my witness," said one of them, "my love is eternal, and I am yours, eternally yours . . ." And, in my bewilderment, I muttered blasphemies to myself: "Ours is a jealous God; he will suffer no eternity but his, and that is why he repudiated the widow's words; nor will he suffer any dogma but Catholic dogma, and that is why he repudiated my friend's words." This was how I explained the loss of my fiancée and the fifty *mil-réis*.

I left the capital and went to practice as a country lawyer, but not for long. Misfortune rode behind me on my mule, and wherever I got off, it got off with me. I saw its finger in everything, in the cases that never came my way, in the ones that did come but were worth little or nothing, and in the ones that were worth something but were invariably lost. Besides the fact that clients who win are generally more grateful than the other sort, my succession of defeats discouraged other litigants from contacting me. After a year and a half, I returned to Rio and set myself up with an old companion from my student days, Gonçalves.

Gonçalves was the least juridically minded fellow imaginable, and the least suited to grappling with matters of law. In fact, he was an utter good-for-nothing. If one were to compare mental activity to an elegant house, Gonçalves was incapable of even ten minutes of polite drawing-room conversation—he would always be sneaking off down to the pantry to gossip with the servants. However, this baseness was compensated by a certain lucidity and agility in grasping less arduous or less complex subjects, together with a facility of expression and an almost uninterrupted good humor—something which for me, a poor devil beaten down by fortune, was not to be sneezed at. In the early days, when we had no cases to work on, we passed the time in excellent conversation, lively and animated, in which he always took the better part, whether discussing politics or—a subject that was of particular interest to him—women.

But slowly the cases began to arrive; among them a dispute about a mortgage. It concerned the house of a customs official, Temístocles de Sá Botelho, who had no other assets and didn't want to lose his property. I took charge of the matter. Temístocles was delighted with me, and, two weeks later, when I told him I wasn't married, he laughed and said he wanted nothing to do with bachelors. He said one or two other things, too, and invited me to dinner that Sunday. I went, and fell in love with his daughter, Dona Rufina, a very pretty girl of nineteen, but rather shy and insipid. Perhaps it's her upbringing, I thought. We married a few months later. I didn't, of course, invite misfortune to the wedding, but inside the church, among the neatly trimmed beards and luxuriant side-whiskers, I thought I saw the sardonic face and glancing eyes of my cruel adversary. It was for this reason that, when the time came to utter the sacred and irreversible vows of marriage, I trembled and hesitated before, finally, stammeringly repeating the priest's words . . .

I was married. It is true that Rufina lacked brilliance and elegance; it was immediately apparent, for example, that she would never be a society hostess. She did, however, possess the qualities of a good housewife, and that was all I asked for. A quiet life was enough for me, and as long as she filled that life, all would be well. But this was precisely the fly in the ointment. If you will permit me a chromatic illustration, Rufina's soul was not black like Lady Macbeth's, or red like Cleopatra's, or blue like Juliet's, or white like Beatrice's, but gray and dull like the lumpen mass of humanity. She was kind only out of apathy, faithful but not out of virtue, friendly but never intentionally tender. An angel might carry her up to heaven, or the devil down to hell, in either case without any struggle on her part, and without her meriting either glory in the first case or shame in the second. Hers was the passivity of a sleepwalker. She was not in the least bit vain. Her father had hatched the marriage because he wanted his son-in-law to be a man with a profession; she accepted me just as she would have accepted any sacristan, magistrate, general, civil servant, or lieutenant, and not out of impatience to be married, but out of obedience to her family and, to a certain extent, so as to be like everyone else. All the other women had husbands, so she wanted one too. Nothing could have been more antipathetic to my nature, but married I was.

Happily—ah! a "happily" in this the final chapter of an unlucky man is, it's true, something of an anomaly. But carry on reading and you will see that the adverb is simply a matter of style, not of life; it is a way of moving the story along, nothing more. What I am going to say will not alter what has already been said. I *will* say that Rufina's domestic qualities were greatly to her credit. She was modest; she did not care for balls, or walks, or gazing out of windows. She kept to herself. She didn't toil away at domestic chores, nor was this necessary, for my work provided her with everything, and all her dresses and hats came from "the French ladies," as we used to call the seamstresses in those days. In between giving orders to the servants, Rufina would sit for hours and hours, letting her spirits yawn, killing time, that hundred-headed hydra that would never die. But, I repeat, despite all her shortcomings, she was a good housewife. As for me, I played the role of the frogs in *Aesop's Fables* who wanted a king, the difference being that when Jupiter threw me down a lump of wood, I didn't ask him for another king, knowing he'd send a snake that would come and swallow me up. "Long live the lump of wood!" I said to myself. I only mention these things to show the steadfast logic of my fate.

Time for another "happily," I think, and this time it isn't just a way of moving between two sentences. Happily, after a year and a half, a sign of hope appeared on the horizon, and, judging by the excitement the news aroused in me, it was a supreme and unique sign of hope. The thing I most desired was on its way. What thing? A child. My life changed in an instant. Everything smiled upon me as on the day of a wedding. I prepared a royal reception for the baby; I bought an expensive cradle finely carved from ebony and ivory; then, little by little, I bought all the other items for the layette; I set the seamstresses to work on the finest cambrics, the warmest flannels, a lovely little lace bonnet; I bought him a pram, and I waited and waited, ready to dance before him like David dancing before the Ark . . . Ah, woe is me! The Ark entered Jerusalem empty; the child was stillborn.

The person who consoled me in my despair was Gonçalves, who was to have been the child's godfather, and was our friend, companion, and confidant. "Be patient," he said, "I'll be godfather to the next one." And he comforted me, and talked to me about other things with the tenderness of a true friend. Time did the rest. Gonçalves himself told me later on that if the child was destined to be unlucky, as I was convinced he would be, then he was better off stillborn.

"What makes you think he wouldn't have been born unlucky?" I retorted.

Gonçalves smiled; he didn't believe in my rotten luck. In fact he had no time to believe in anything; he devoted himself entirely to being happy. He had finally begun to apply himself to the law; he was now pleading cases, presenting petitions, attending court, all because, as he used to say, he needed to live. And he was always happy. My wife found him very amusing; she would laugh at his little stories and jokes, which at times were somewhat risqué. At first I reprimanded him privately, but eventually I grew used to them. After all, who wouldn't pardon the talents of a friend, and such a jovial friend at that? I must say that, eventually, he began to rein himself in, and, from then on, I began to find him a far more serious companion. "You're in love," I said to him one day, and he, turning pale, replied that he was, and added with a smile, albeit weakly, that he, too, must marry. Over supper that evening, I returned to the subject.

"Rufina, did you know that Gonçalves is getting married?"

"It's just his little joke," Gonçalves said, interrupting me.

I cursed my indiscretion, and neither he nor I mentioned it again. Five months later . . .—you must excuse the rapid transition, but there is no means of lengthening it out—five months later, Rufina fell seriously ill and, within a week, she had died of a rampant fever.

And here's a strange thing: while she lived, our differing temperaments weakened the ties between us, which were based principally on necessity and habit. Death, with its great spiritual power, changed everything. Rufina now seemed to me like the bride in the *Song of Songs* who descends from Lebanon, and the divergence between us was replaced by a complete fusion of our beings. I seized upon the image; it filled my soul, and with it she filled my life, where once she had occupied so little space and for so little time. It was a defiant challenge to my evil star; I was building the fortress of destiny on solid, indestructible rock. Please understand me: everything that had, up until then, depended on the exterior world was naturally precarious: roof tiles fell when hammocks swayed, surplices turned their backs on sacristans, widows' vows fled arm in arm with friends' dogmas, lawyers' cases came but fleetingly or sank without trace; finally, children were born dead. But the image of a dead woman was immortal, and with it I could defy the malicious gaze of misfortune. I held happiness captive in my hands, its great condor wings beating the air, while owl-like misfortune flapped its wings and vanished into night and silence . . .

One day, however, while convalescing from a fever, I had the notion of drawing up an inventory of my dead wife's possessions. I began with a little box that hadn't been opened since she had died five months previously. I found inside a large number of odds and ends: needles, threads, scraps of lace, a thimble, a pair of scissors, a prayer of Saint Cyprian, a list of clothes, other bits and pieces, and a bundle of letters tied with a blue ribbon. I undid the ribbon and opened the letters: they were from Gonçalves . . . Ah, it's noon already! I must finish; my manservant will be back at any moment, and then that would be that. No one can imagine how time rushes by in these circumstances; minutes fly like fleeting empires, and, more importantly on this occasion, the leaves of paper fly with them.

I won't dwell on the discarded lottery tickets, the aborted business deals, the interrupted love affairs; still less on fate's other petty grudges. Weary and dismayed, I realized that I would not find happiness anywhere; I went even further: I believed that it did not exist anywhere on Earth, and, since yesterday, I have been preparing myself for my great plunge into eternity. This morning, I had breakfast, smoked a cigar, and leaned out the window. After ten minutes, I saw a well-dressed man walk by, and he kept looking down at his feet. I knew him by sight; he had been the victim of many great misfortunes, but he smiled as he walked, and stared his feet, or, rather, his boots. They were new, patent leather, beautifully made, and no doubt impeccably stitched. From time to time, he looked up at the windows, or at people's faces, but his eyes quickly darted back to his boots, as if drawn to them by a law of attraction stronger than his own will. He was a happy fellow; one could see the blissful expression on his face. He was clearly happy; and yet he may have had no breakfast; he might not even have so much as a penny in his pocket, but he was happy gazing at his boots.

Could happiness be a pair of boots? That man, so buffeted by life, had finally found fortune smiling on him. Nothing is worth nothing. No worldly preoccupation, no social or moral dilemma, neither the joys of the new generation nor the sorrows of the old, neither poverty nor class warfare, no artistic or political crisis, nothing is worth as much to him as a pair of boots. He gazes at them, he breathes them in, he glows, in them he treads the surface of an orb that belongs only to him. Thence comes the dignity of his posture, the firmness of his step, and a certain air of Olympian tranquility. Yes, happiness is a pair of boots.

So here you have the explanation for my will. Those of a superficial nature will say that I'm crazy, that the testator's closing words are pure suicidal delirium; but I am speaking here to the wise and to the unfortunate. And there's no point suggesting that I would be better off wearing the boots myself rather than bequeathing them to others; no, because then there would be only me. By distributing them, I make a certain number of people fortunate. Roll up, roll up, O unfortunate ones! May my final wish be granted. Farewell, and put your boots on!

NUPTIAL SONG

IMAGINE, MY DEAR READER, that it is 1813, and you are sitting in the
Carmo Church, along with all the other women, and watching and listening to one of those wonderful old pageants that were all there was back
then in terms of public entertainment and musical talent. You know what
a sung mass is, so you can imagine what a sung mass would have been like
in those distant days. I won't call your attention to the priests or sacristans,
nor to the sermon, nor to the eyes of the young *carioca* ladies, which were
pretty even then, nor to the black lace mantillas of the somber matrons,
the breeches, the wigs, the dusty drapes, the candles, or the incense, none
of that. I won't even speak of the orchestra, which is excellent; I will limit
myself to showing you one white head, the head of that old man conducting
the orchestra with such soulful devotion.

His name is Romão Pires; he can't be a day under sixty, and he was born
in Valongo, or thereabouts. He is a good musician and a good man; all the
musicians like him. He was known familiarly as Maestro Romão, and, in
those days, "familiarly" and "publicly" amounted to much the same thing.
"Maestro Romão is conducting the mass" was the equivalent of that other
form of announcement many years later: "The actor Jõao Caetano plays the
part of . . ." or even: "The actor Martinho will sing one of his best arias." It
was just the thing to whet the audience's appetite. Maestro Romão is conducting the mass! Surely everyone knew Maestro Romão, with his circumspect air, his downcast eyes, his sad smile, and his faltering step? All of this

vanished when he stood in front of the orchestra; life would then pour from every part of his body and from every gesture; his eyes would light up, his smile would beam forth: he was utterly transformed. Not that the mass was his own composition; for example, the one he is conducting now is by José Maurício; but he conducts it as lovingly as if it were his own.

The pageant has ended, and it's as if a great blaze had been extinguished, leaving his face lit only by ordinary candlelight. See him coming down from the choir, leaning on his stick; he's going to the sacristy to kiss the priests' hands and accept their invitation to join them for lunch. All without saying a word, entirely indifferent. He has lunch, leaves the church, and walks toward the Rua da Mãe dos Homens, where he lives with an old black slave called Papa José, who is his true mother and who, at this very moment, is talking to the woman next door.

"Here comes Maestro Romão, Papa José," said the neighbor.

"I'd best be going. See you later, *sinhá*."

Papa José hurried into the house and waited for his master, who entered with his usual downcast air. The house, of course, was neither rich nor particularly welcoming. It bore not a trace of a woman's presence, either old or young; there were no songbirds, no flowers, no lively, cheerful colors. It was a somber, barren place. The most joyful thing was the harpsichord, which Maestro Romão sometimes played when practicing. On a chair beside it lay some sheets of music, none composed by him.

Ah! If Maestro Romão had had the necessary talent, he would have been a great composer! It seems there are two sorts of vocation: those that can speak and those that cannot. The former find fulfillment; the latter are nothing but a continual, sterile struggle between one's internal impulse and one's inability to communicate with the outside world. Romão's vocation belonged in that second category. He had a profound vocation for music; he carried within him many operas and masses, a whole world of new and original harmonies that he could neither express nor put down on paper. This was the sole cause of Maestro Romão's sadness. Naturally, the *hoi polloi* did not realize this; some said one thing, others said another: illness, a lack of money, some lingering regret, but the truth is this: the cause of Maestro Romão's melancholy was that inability to compose and translate his feelings into music. Not that he hadn't scribbled many a bar and stave and sat staring at the harpsichord for hours on end, but everything emerged unformed and shapeless, with neither idea nor harmony. Latterly, he had even begun to feel embarrassed lest his neighbors should hear him, and so he had stopped trying altogether.

And yet, if he could, he wanted at least to finish one particular piece, a nuptial song started three days after he got married in 1779. His wife, who was then twenty-one and who had died at age twenty-three, was not pretty in the least, but she was extremely kind and loved him as much as he loved her. Three days after their wedding, Maestro Romão felt the stirrings of something akin to inspiration. He conceived the idea of writing a nuptial song and set about composing it, but the inspiration remained locked inside. Like a bird that has just been captured and tries to escape through the bars of the cage, flitting up and down, impatient and terrified—that was our musician's inspiration, imprisoned within him, unable to escape, unable to find a door or a way out. A few notes managed to come together; he wrote them down, just a single sheet of paper, nothing more. He tried again the following day, then ten days later, and at least twenty times more during their marriage. When his wife died, he reread those first few conjugal notes and it made him even sadder, because he had failed to set down on paper that feeling of happiness now extinct.

"Papa José," he said as he came in, "I'm feeling rather under the weather today."

"*Sinhô* ate something that make him sick?"

"No, even this morning I wasn't feeling well. Go to the apothecary's, will you, and fetch me . . ."

The apothecary sent him some remedy or other, which he took that night; the following day, though, he still didn't feel any better. I should mention here that he had a bad heart—a grave, chronic condition. Papa José was so dismayed when he saw that neither rest nor medicine yielded any results that he wanted to call the doctor.

"What for?" asked the maestro. "It will pass."

Things were no worse by the end of the day, and the maestro got through the night unscathed, unlike his slave, who barely managed two hours' sleep. When they heard about the illness, the neighbors could speak of nothing else; those who were on friendly terms with the maestro went to visit him, telling him it was nothing to worry about and that it was probably just a bug that was going around; someone added jokingly that it was simply a trick on his part to avoid being beaten at backgammon by the apothecary; someone else chipped in that he must be lovesick. Maestro Romão smiled, but said to himself that the end was nigh.

"It's all over," he said.

One morning, five days after the church pageant, the doctor found him to be really ill, and despite the doctor's soothing words, the maestro could read this in the doctor's face:

"Oh, it's nothing to worry about; you must stop thinking about songs all the time . . ."

Songs! It was precisely this word spoken by the doctor that gave the maestro an idea. As soon as he was alone with the slave, he opened the drawer where he kept the nuptial song he had begun in 1779. He reread those notes wrung from himself with such difficulty and still left unfinished. And then he had a remarkable idea: he would finish it off now, come what may. Anything would do, as long as he left something of his soul on Earth.

"Who knows? Perhaps, in 1880, someone will play this, and say that it was written by a certain Maestro Romão . . ."

The beginning of the song ended in *la*; this *la*, which did not sound quite right, was the very last note he had written. Maestro Romão gave orders for the harpsichord to be moved to the rear parlor, which faced onto the yard: he needed air. Through the window, he could see two newlyweds—they had only been married a week—leaning out the window of a neighboring house, each with an arm about the other's shoulder, their two free hands clasped. Maestro Romão smiled sadly.

"They're arriving and I'm leaving," he said to himself. "I'll compose this one song for them to play . . ."

He sat down at the harpsichord, replayed the notes, and came to the *la* . . .

"*La* . . . *la* . . . *la* . . ."

Nothing. He was completely stuck. And yet he knew music like no one else.

"*La, doh* . . . *la, mi* . . . *la, si, doh, re* . . . *re* . . . *re* . . ."

Impossible! No inspiration whatsoever. He wasn't asking for a profoundly original piece, but just something that was his and in keeping with his original idea. He went back to the beginning, repeating the notes and trying to retrieve a remnant of his extinguished feelings, remembering his wife and their first days together. To complete the illusion, he looked out the window in the direction of the newlyweds. They were still there, hands clasped, each with an arm draped over the other's shoulder; the difference was that they were now gazing at each other, instead of down into the yard. Breathless with illness and impatience, Maestro Romão returned to the harpsichord; but the sight of the young couple had given him no inspiration, and the notes that should have followed would still not come.

"*La . . . la . . . la . . .*"

In despair, he got up from the harpsichord, took the sheet of music, and tore it into pieces. At that moment, the young woman, entranced by her husband's gaze, began to hum randomly, unconsciously, something never before sung or even imagined, in which a certain *la* gave way to a beautiful musical phrase, precisely the one Maestro Romão had been seeking for so many years and had never found. The maestro listened to it sadly, shook his head, and, that night, he passed away.

A STRANGE THING

"SOME VERY STRANGE THINGS happen. Do you see that lady going into Holy Cross Church? The one who's just paused on the steps to give some money to a beggar."

"The one in black?"

"That's her; she's just going in. She's gone."

"Stop right there. That look on your face tells me she's a memento from your past, and not that long ago, either, to judge by her figure: she's a real stunner."

"She must be about forty-six now."

"No! She's certainly very well preserved. Come on, stop staring down at the ground and tell me all. She's a widow, of course."

"No."

"So her husband's still alive. Is he old?"

"She's not married."

"A spinster, then?"

"Something like that. No doubt she calls herself Dona Maria something-or-other these days. Back in 1860, everyone just called her Marocas. She wasn't a seamstress, or a landlady, or a governess; if you carry on down the list of professions, you'll get there eventually. She lived on Rua do Sacramento. She was just as slender then, too, and, as you'd expect, even prettier than she is today; well mannered and never vulgar. Out on the street, even in a plain, faded dress buttoned right up to the neck, she still caught the attention of many a man."

"You, for example."

"No, not me, but Andrade, a friend of mine from Alagoas. He was twenty-six at the time, half lawyer, half politician; he got married in Bahia and came to Rio in 1859. His wife was pretty, affectionate, loving, and uncomplaining; when I met them, they had a little two-year-old girl."

"And in spite of all that, Marocas . . . ?"

"Yes, she completely captivated him. Look, if you're not in a hurry, I'll tell you an interesting story."

"Go on."

"The first time Andrade met her was at the door of Paula Brito's bookshop, on Rocio. He was walking along, when he saw a pretty woman in the distance and he waited, his interest aroused, for he was very much a ladies' man. Marocas walked toward him, stopping and looking around like someone searching for a particular address. She stopped in front of the bookshop for a moment, then, timid and shame-faced, she handed Andrade a piece of paper with the number of a house written on it and asked him where she could find that house. Andrade told her it was on the other side of the square, and pointed to its likely location. The woman took her leave with a charming curtsy, and Andrade was left not knowing quite what to think."

"Like me."

"It couldn't be simpler: Marocas couldn't read, but this thought didn't even occur to Andrade. He watched her cross Rocio, which at the time had neither statue nor gardens in the middle, and make her way to the house she was looking for, although she still kept asking for directions from various people. That night he went to the Teatro do Ginásio to see *La Dame aux Camélias*; Marocas was there, and during the last act, she cried like a baby. I'll say no more, but two weeks later they were madly in love. Marocas got rid of all her other admirers, and she must have incurred quite a loss, for there were several substantial businessmen among them. She lived completely alone, devoting herself to Andrade, with no thought for any other man or any other means of support."

"Just like the Lady of the Camellias."

"Precisely. Andrade taught her to read. 'I'm a schoolmaster now,' he said to me one day, and that's when he told me the story about their meeting on Rocio. Marocas was a quick learner, which is entirely understandable—

the shame of not being able to read, the desire to read the novels he talked about, the pleasure in obeying his wishes and pleasing him . . . Andrade hid nothing from me; he told me everything with such a look of gratitude in his eyes, you can scarcely imagine. Both of them confided in me. Sometimes the three of us would dine together, and—I see no reason to deny it—sometimes there was a fourth. Now, don't go thinking these dinners were louche affairs; lively, perhaps, but entirely decent. Marocas was as straitlaced in her language as she was in her dress. Little by little, we became close; she would ask me about Andrade, his wife, his daughter, his habits, whether he really loved her or if she was just a casual affair; did he have other women, would he forget her—a torrent of questions, and a fear of losing him, that demonstrated the strength and sincerity of her affections. Then, for the St. John's Feast holidays, Andrade took his family to Gávea, where he was to attend a lavish dinner and a ball. I went with them; we would be gone for two days. As she bade the two of us goodbye, Marocas recalled the comedy she had seen several weeks before at the Ginásio—*I'm Dining with Mother*—and she joked to me that, having no family with whom she could spend St. John's Eve, she would do as Sofia Arnoult had in the play, and dine with a portrait. And since she had no mother, it would be Andrade's portrait instead. Those words deserved a kiss, and Andrade obligingly leaned toward her; however, seeing that I was still there, she delicately pushed him away with her hand."

"A lovely gesture."

"He thought so too. He took her head between his hands and placed a paternal kiss on her forehead. We set off for Gávea. On the way, Andrade told me about all of Marocas's fine qualities, recounted all their latest whims and fancies, and said he was planning to buy her a house somewhere on the outskirts of the city just as soon as he could rustle up the money. In passing, he praised her thriftiness, for she wouldn't take from him a penny more than was absolutely necessary. 'And that's not all,' I said, and told him that around three weeks earlier, Marocas had apparently pawned some jewelry to pay a seamstress's bill. This news greatly upset him; I can't swear to it, but I believe there were tears in his eyes. In any case, after a few moments' thought, he said he would definitely get her a house and shield her from any further hardships. In Gávea, we carried on discussing Marocas until the end of the holidays and our return to the city. Andrade left his family at their house in Lapa and went to his office to attend to some urgent papers. Shortly after noon, a fellow called Leandro turned up, asking, as usual, for Andrade to lend him two or three *mil-réis*. Leandro was the former employee of a lawyer acquaintance, and was an idler and a scrounger who made his living milking his former boss's friends. Andrade gave him three *mil-réis*, and, as the man seemed unusually chirpy, he asked him why he was looking so pleased with himself. Leandro winked and licked his lips. Andrade, who was always partial to a tale of romantic endeavor, asked if he'd been lucky in love. Leandro hemmed and hawed for a moment, and admitted that indeed he had."

"Careful, she's coming out of the church. Is that her?"

"That's her, all right: come on, let's move away from the corner."

"She must have been really very pretty. She carries herself like a duchess."

"She didn't see us; she never looks around. She'll head straight up Rua do Ouvidor."

"Yes, sir. I can understand what Andrade saw in her."

"Back to the story. Leandro confessed that the previous evening he'd had a rare, or, rather, unique stroke of luck, entirely unexpected and undeserved, because, deep down, he knew he was nothing but a miserable wretch. But then, even miserable wretches are God's children. Anyway, at around ten o'clock the previous evening, on Rocio, he had happened upon a modestly dressed lady, her attractive figure tightly swathed in a large shawl. The lady came up behind him, walking briskly, and as she brushed past him, she stared straight at him and slowed her step, as if waiting for him. The poor devil thought she must have mistaken him for someone else, and he confessed to Andrade that, despite her simple attire, he saw at once that she was out of his league. He carried on walking; the woman, who had stopped, stared at him again, so insistently that he drummed up a little courage . . . and she drummed up the rest. Ah! A perfect angel! And such a fine house, such a sumptuous parlor! Absolutely top-notch. And no question of payment, either . . . He added: 'For a gentleman like yourself, it would be the perfect setup.' Andrade shook his head; chasing after another man's mistress didn't much appeal to him. Leandro persisted, though, and told him that the house was on Rua do Sacramento, number such-and-such . . ."

"You're joking!"

"Just imagine how Andrade must have felt. He himself had no idea what he said or did during those first few minutes, nor what he thought or felt. He finally summoned up the courage to ask Leandro if he was telling the truth, to which the other replied that he had no reason to invent such a story; however, seeing how agitated Andrade was, Leandro asked him to keep it a secret, telling him that he, for his part, would be the soul of discretion. Leandro stood up to go, but Andrade stopped him and asked if he would like to earn twenty *mil-réis*. 'Of course!' was the answer. 'Well then,' continued Andrade, 'I'll give you twenty *mil-réis* if you'll go with me to this lady's house and tell me in her presence that she's the one you met."

"Oh!"

"I'm not defending Andrade; it wasn't a nice thing to do, but in such cases, passion can blind the best of us. Andrade was an honorable, generous, sincere fellow, but it had been such a heavy blow and he loved her so deeply that he did not shrink from wreaking his revenge."

"Did Leandro agree?"

"He hesitated somewhat, I suspect out of fear rather than any sense of dignity, but then, twenty *mil-réis* . . . He made one condition: he didn't want any trouble. Marocas was in the parlor when Andrade entered. She came to the door, intending to embrace him, but Andrade indicated that he had brought someone with him. Then, watching her closely, he called Leandro into the room. Marocas turned white as a sheet. 'Is this the lady?' he asked. 'Yes, sir,' muttered Leandro feebly, for there are some actions that are even more despicable than the man who commits them. With a flourish, Andrade opened his wallet, pulled out a twenty-*mil-réis* note, and gave it to Leandro; then, with another flourish, he told him to get out. Leandro left. The scene that followed was brief but dramatic. I didn't get the whole of it, because it was Andrade himself who told me everything, and, naturally, he was so shaken that many things escaped him. She confessed nothing, but was utterly distraught, and when, after saying some very harsh things, he made for the door, she threw herself at his feet, clasped his hands, tearful and desperate, threatening to kill herself; and there she stayed, sprawled on the staircase landing, while he ran down the stairs and out of the building."

"Really! Picking up a miserable wretch like that on the street . . . Do you think she made a habit of it?"

"No."

"No?"

"Just listen and I'll tell you. Sometime around eight o'clock that night, Andrade came to my house and waited for me to return. He'd come looking for me three times already. I was astonished, but how could I doubt him when he had taken the precaution of obtaining proof that was beyond all reasonable doubt? I won't go into everything he said: his plans for revenge, his curses, the names he called her, the usual repertoire of insults people dredge up in moments of crisis. My advice was for him to leave her and devote himself to his kind, loving wife and his daughter. He agreed, then again flew into a rage. After fury came doubt; he even got it into his head that Marocas had dreamed up the whole thing just to test him, and had actually paid Leandro to come and say those things to him; the proof being that even when he'd shown no interest in meeting the woman, Leandro had insisted on telling him the exact address. In clinging to this improbable explanation he was trying to escape reality, but reality kept coming back at him—Marocas's pallor, Leandro's unfeigned chirpiness, and all the other things that told him it was true. I even think he was beginning to wonder if he'd gone too far. As for me, I went over and over the whole affair but could find no explanation. She was so demure! Prim, even!"

"There's a line in a play that might explain the affair, a line from Augier, I believe: 'nostalgia for the gutter.'"

"I think not, but keep on listening. At about ten o'clock, Marocas's maid, a freed slave, who was very attached to her mistress, turned up at my house. She was desperately looking for Andrade, because Marocas, after locking herself in her room in floods of tears, had left the house without her dinner and hadn't returned. I had to restrain Andrade, whose first impulse was to race off after her. The maid begged us to find her mistress. 'Doesn't she usually go out?' asked Andrade sarcastically. But the maid said that, no, it wasn't usual at all. 'Did you hear that?' he shouted at me. Once again, hope had seized the poor devil's heart. 'What about yesterday?' I asked. The maid answered that, yes, she had gone out yesterday; I stopped asking her questions out of pity for Andrade, who was growing more and more distressed, and whose wounded pride was gradually receding in the face of this impending danger. We went out to search for Marocas; we went to all the houses where we might possibly find her, and to the police, but without success. In the morning, we returned to the police station. Andrade was friends with the station chief or one of his deputies (I can't remember which), and told him the relevant details of the affair; in any case, Andrade's relationship with Marocas was already well known to all his friends. Every possibility was looked into; no accidents had occurred during the night; none of the boatmen down at Praia Grande had seen any ferry passengers falling over-board; the gunsmiths had sold no firearms and the apothecaries no poison. The police deployed all their resources, but came up with nothing. I won't tell you what a state poor Andrade was in during those long hours, for the whole day was spent in futile investigations. It wasn't only the pain of losing her; there were his feelings of guilt or remorse or doubt when faced with a possible disaster that seemed in itself to exonerate the young woman. He kept saying to me, over and over, that surely it was only natural to react as he had done in the delirium of indignation, and wouldn't I have done the same? But then he would once again reassert her guilt, and prove it to me as vehemently as he had tried to prove her innocence the night before; he kept trying to adjust reality to his shifting sentiments."

"But did you eventually find Marocas?"

"We were having something to eat at a hotel—it was nearly eight o'clock—when we got news of a possible lead: the previous evening, a coach-man had taken a lady out in the direction of the Jardim Botânico. When she got there, she went into a boardinghouse, and stayed there. We didn't even finish our dinner— we took the very same coach in the same direction. The owner of the boardinghouse confirmed the coachman's version of events, adding that the person in question had retired to her room and hadn't eaten anything since arriving yesterday; she had asked only for a cup of coffee, and seemed in very low spirits. We made our way up to her room, and the owner knocked on the door; she answered in a feeble voice and opened the door. Before I could say anything, Andrade pushed me aside, and the two of them fell into each other's arms. Marocas shed copious tears, then fainted."

"Did she explain everything?"

"Not at all. Neither of them even spoke of it; having survived the ship-wreck, they had no wish to know anything about the storm that had all but sunk them. The reconciliation was almost instantaneous. A few months later, Andrade bought her a little house in Catumbi; Marocas gave him a son, who died at the age of two. When Andrade was sent north on govern-ment business, their affection was still as strong, even if their passion no longer burned with the same intensity. Nevertheless, she wanted to go with him and it was I who obliged her to stay. Andrade intended to return a short time later but, as I think I told you, he died in the provinces. Marocas felt his death deeply, went into mourning, and considered herself a widow; I know that for the first three years she always went to mass on the anniversary of his death. Ten years ago, I completely lost sight of her. So what do you make of it all?"

"I suppose some very strange things really *do* happen, always assuming that you haven't taken advantage of my youthful naïveté by making the whole thing up . . ."

"I haven't made anything up; it really did happen."

"And yet, sir, it's certainly very odd. In the midst of all that burning, genuine passion . . . No, I'm sticking to my guns; I think it was nostalgia for the gutter."

"No. Marocas had never stooped as low as the Leandros of this world."

"Then why did she do so on that particular night?"

"She presumed there was a gaping social chasm separating him from anyone who might know her; that's what made her so sure of herself. But she did not allow for coincidence, which is a god and a devil rolled into one . . . Well, strange things happen!"

POSTHUMOUS PICTURE GALLERY

———

I

THE DEATH OF Joaquim Fidélis caused indescribable consternation throughout the suburb of Engenho Velho, and particularly in the hearts of his dearest friends. It was so unexpected. He was in fine fettle, had an iron constitution, and, the very night before he passed away, had been attending a ball where he had been seen happily chatting away. He had even danced, at the request of a lady in her sixties, the widow of a friend of his, who took him by the arm and said:

"Come on, then, let's show these youngsters that their elders still know a thing or two!"

Joaquim Fidélis protested with a smile, but did as he was told and danced. It was two o'clock in the morning when he left, wrapping his sixty years in a warm winter cape (for it was June 1879), covering his bald head with the hood, lighting a cigar, and hopping nimbly into his carriage.

He may well have nodded off in the carriage, but, once home, despite the late hour and his heavy eyelids, he went to his desk, opened a drawer, took out one of many notebooks, and, in three or four minutes, wrote some ten or eleven lines. His last words were these: "Altogether a vile ball; some aging reveler forced me to dance a quadrille with her; at the door, a dark-skinned country bumpkin asked me for a present. Simply vile!" He put the notebook back in the drawer, undressed, got into bed, fell asleep, and died.

Yes, indeed, the news dismayed the whole neighborhood. So beloved was he, with his fine manners and his ability to be able to talk to anyone; he could be educated with the educated, ignorant with the ignorant, boyish with the boys, even girlish with the girls. And then, most obligingly, he was always ready to write letters, speak to friends, patch up quarrels, or lend money. In the evenings, a handful of close acquaintances from Engenho Velho, and sometimes other parts of the city, would gather in his house to play ombre or whist and discuss politics. Joaquim Fidélis had been a member of the Chamber of Deputies until its dissolution by the Marquis of Olinda in 1863. Unable to get reelected, he abandoned public life. He was a conservative, a label he had difficulty in accepting because it sounded to him like a political Gallicism. He preferred to be called one of the "Saquarema Set." But he gave it all up, and it seems that, in recent times, he detached himself first from the party, and, eventually, from the party's politics. There are reasons to believe that, from a certain point onward, he was merely a profound skeptic.

He was a wealthy and educated man. He had qualified as a lawyer in 1842. Now he did nothing, but read a great deal. There were no women in his house. Widowed after the first outbreak of yellow fever, he refused to countenance a second marriage, to the great sorrow of three or four ladies, who for some time had hopes in that regard. One of them perfidiously managed to make her beautiful 1845 ringlets last until well after her second grandchild was born; another younger woman, also a widow, thought she could hold on to him with concessions that were as generous as they were irretrievable. "My dear Leocádia," he would say whenever she hinted at a marital solution, "why don't we carry on just as we are? Mystery is what gives life its charm." He lived with a nephew called Benjamin, the orphaned son of one of his sisters who had died when the child was still very young. Joaquim Fidélis brought him up and made him study hard, so much so that the boy graduated with a law degree in the year of 1877.

Benjamin was utterly dumbfounded. He could not bring himself to believe that his uncle was dead. He rushed to his bedroom, found the corpse lying in bed, cold, eyes wide open, and a faintly ironic curl to the left-hand corner of his mouth. He wept profusely. He was losing not just a relative but a father, a tenderhearted, dedicated father, one of a kind. Finally, Benjamin wiped away his tears and, since it upset him to see the dead man's eyes open and his lip curled, he rectified both defects. Thus death took on a more tragic but less original expression.

"No! I don't believe it!" cried Diogo Vilares, one of the neighbors, shortly after hearing the news.

Diogo Vilares was one of Joaquim Fidélis's five closest friends. He owed to him the job he had held since 1857. Diogo was followed by the four others in quick succession, all speechless and unable to believe what had happened. The first was Elias Xavier, who had obtained a knighthood, thanks, it was said, to the deceased's timely intervention; then came João Brás, another deputy who, under the rather peculiar rules of the time, had been elected to the Chamber thanks to Joaquim Fidélis's influence. Last of all came Fragoso and Galdino, who, in lieu of diplomas, knighthoods, or jobs, owed him other favors instead. Fidélis had advanced Galdino a small amount of capital, and had arranged a good marriage for Fragoso. And now he was dead! Gone forever! Standing around the bed, they gazed at his serene face and recalled their last get-together the previous Sunday, so intimate and yet so jolly! And, even more recently, the night before last, when their customary game of ombre had lasted until eleven o'clock.

"Don't come tomorrow," Joaquim Fidélis had said to them. "I'm going to Carvalhinho's ball."

"And after that?"

"I'll be back the day after tomorrow."

And, as they left, he gave each of them a box of excellent cigars, as he sometimes did, with a little bag of sweets for the children and two or three fine jokes . . . All lost! Vanished! Gone!

Many persons of note came to the funeral: two senators, a former minister, a few noblemen, wealthy businessmen, lawyers, merchants, and doctors; but the coffin was carried by Benjamin and those five close friends. None of them would yield this honor to anyone, considering it their final and inalienable duty. The graveside eulogy was given by João Brás; it was a touching address, slightly too polished for such an unexpected event, but nonetheless excusable. When everyone had deposited their shovelful of earth on the coffin, the mourners slowly slipped away from the graveside, apart from those six, who stayed to oversee the gravediggers as they went indifferently about their work. They stayed there until the grave had been filled to the very top and the funeral wreaths laid out upon it.

II

The seventh-day mass brought them together again at the church. When the mass was over, the five friends accompanied the deceased man's nephew home. Benjamin invited them to stay for breakfast.

"I hope that Uncle Joaquim's friends will also be my friends," he said.

They went in and, while they ate, they talked about the dead man, each one recounting some story, some witty remark; they were unanimous in their praise and fond regrets. Since each of them had asked for a little memento of the deceased, when they finished breakfast they all went through into his study and chose something: an old pen, a glasses case, a little pamphlet, or some other personal token. Benjamin felt greatly consoled. He informed them that he intended to keep the study exactly as it was. He hadn't even opened the desk yet. He did so then, and, with the others, drew up a list of the contents of some of the drawers. There were letters, loose papers, concert programs, menus from grand dinners; all of it in an enormous muddle. Among other things they found some notebooks, numbered and dated.

"A diary!" exclaimed Benjamin.

It was indeed a diary of the deceased's thoughts and impressions, a sort of collection of secret memories and confidences that the man had shared only with himself. The friends were greatly moved and excited; reading them would be just like conversing with Joaquim again. Such an upright character! And the soul of discretion! Benjamin began reading, but his voice broke, and João Brás had to carry on.

Their interest in what they heard soothed the pain of death. It was a book worthy of being published. It was filled with political and social observations, philosophical reflections, anecdotes about public men such as Feijó and Vasconcelos, others of a rather racier nature, the names of ladies, among them Leocádia's; an entire repertoire of events and comments. They all admired the dead man's talent, his graceful style, and the fascinating subject matter. Some were in favor of having it printed; Benjamin agreed, on condition that they excluded any elements that might be unsavory or excessively personal. And they continued reading, skipping whole sections and pages, until the clock struck noon. They all stood up. Diogo Vilares had been due at his office hours ago; João Brás and Elias also had to be clsewhere. Galdino went off to his shop. Fragoso had to change out of his black clothes and take his wife shopping on Rua do Ouvidor. They agreed to meet again and continue their reading. Some of the details had given them an itch for scandal, and itches need to be scratched, which is precisely what they intended to do, by reading.

"Until tomorrow, then," they said.

"Yes, until tomorrow."

Once he was alone, Benjamin carried on reading the manuscript. Among other things, he marveled at the portrayal of the Widow Leocádia, a masterpiece of painstaking observation, even though the date coincided with the time when they were still lovers. It was proof of a rare impartiality. The deceased, it turned out, was a master of portraits. The notebooks were full of them, stretching back to 1873 or 1874; some were sketches of the living, others of the dead, some were of public men like Paula Sousa, Aureliano, Olinda, etc. They were brief and to the point, sometimes only three or four lines, drawn with such confident fidelity and perfection that the image seemed almost like a photograph. Benjamin carried on reading. Suddenly he came across Diogo Vilares, about whom he read the following:

DIOGO VILARES—I have referred to this friend many times and will do so yet again, provided he doesn't kill me with boredom, a field in which I consider him a true professional. Many years ago, he asked me to get him a job and I did. He did not warn me of the currency in which he would repay me. Such singular gratitude! He went so far as to compose a sonnet and publish it. He wouldn't stop talking about the favor I'd done him, paying me endless compliments; finally, though, he relented. Later on, we became more closely acquainted. I got to know him even better. *C'est le genre ennuyeux.* Not a bad partner at ombre, though. They tell me he owes nothing to anyone. A good family man. Stupid and credulous. Within the space of four days, I've heard him describe a government as both excellent and detestable, depending on who he is speaking to. He laughs a lot and usually inappropriately. When they meet him for the first time, everyone begins by assuming he is a serious fellow; by the second day, they snap their fingers at him. The reason is his face, or, more particularly, his cheeks, which lend him a certain air of superiority.

Benjamin's first reaction was that he'd had a lucky escape. What if Diogo Vilares had been there? He reread the description and could scarcely believe it. But there was no denying it: the name was definitely Diogo Vilares and it was written in his uncle's own hand. And he wasn't the only friend mentioned, either; he flicked through the manuscript and came across Elias:

ELIAS XAVIER—This Elias is a subordinate fellow, destined to serve someone, and serve him smugly, like a coachman to a fashionable household. He vulgarly treats my personal visits with a certain arrogance and disdain: the policy of an ambitious lackey. From the first weeks I knew him, I realized that he wanted to make himself my intimate friend, and I also understood that on the day he really became one, he would throw all the others out in the street. There are times when he calls me to one side to talk to me secretly about the weather. His aim is clearly to instill in the others a suspicion that there are private matters between us, and he achieves precisely this, because all the others bow and scrape before him. He is intelligent, good-humored, and refined. He's an excellent conversationalist. I don't know anyone with a sharper intellect. He is neither cowardly nor slanderous. He only speaks ill of someone when his own interests are at stake; when such interests are absent, he holds his tongue, whereas true slander is gratuitous. He is dedicated and persuasive. He has no ideas, it's true, but that's the difference between him and Diogo Vilares: Diogo simply parrots the ideas he hears, whereas Elias knows how to make them his own and choose the opportune moment to introduce them into the conversation. An event in 1865 provides a good illustration of the man's shrewdness. He was due to be granted a knighthood by the government for providing some freed slaves for the war in Paraguay. He had no need of me, but he came to see me on two or three occasions, with a dismayed and pleading air, to ask me to intercede on his behalf. I spoke to the minister, who told me: "Elias knows the document has already been drafted and only awaits the Emperor's signature." I understood then that this was simply a way of showing how deeply indebted he was to me. A good partner at whist; a touch quarrelsome, but he knows what he's doing.

"Well, really, Uncle Joaquim!" exclaimed Benjamin, getting to his feet. A few moments later, he thought to himself: "Here I am reading the unpublished book of his heart. I only knew the public edition, revised and expurgated. This is the original, internal text, exact and authentic. But who would have thought it of Uncle Joaquim!"

He sat down again, slowly reread the portrait of Elias, pondering its features. While he lacked the necessary knowledge to evaluate the truth of the sketch, he thought that, in many aspects, at least, the portrait was a true likeness. He compared these iconographic notes, so crude and cold, with his uncle's warm, elegant manners, and felt gripped by a certain fear and disquiet. What, for example, might his uncle have said about him? With this thought, he again leafed through the manuscript, skimming over various ladies and public men, and came upon Fragoso—an extremely brief sketch that came immediately after Galdino and four pages before João Brás. He remembered that the former had, only a short time before, taken a pen as a memento; perhaps the very pen with which the dead man had drawn his portrait. The sketch was only a few lines long, as follows:

FRAGOSO—Honest, saccharine manners, and handsome. Wasn't difficult to marry him off; he gets on very well with his wife. I know he adores me—almost as much as he adores himself. Polished, insipid, and commonplace conversation.

GALDINO MADEIRA—The warmest heart in the world and a spotless character, but the qualities of his mind destroy all the others. I lent him some money for family reasons and because money is not something I lack. There is in his brain a hole of some sort, through which his mind slips and falls into a vacuum. He is incapable of three minutes' consecutive thought. He subsists mainly on images and borrowed phrases. The "teeth of calumny" and other such expressions are his perennial delight—as worn out as the mattress in a cheap boardinghouse. He is easily vexed at cards, and, once vexed, makes a point of losing, making it clear that this was deliberate. He doesn't dismiss any employees, however bad. If he didn't have bookkeepers, it's doubtful he could keep track of his earnings at all. A friend of mine, who is a civil servant, owed him some money for more than two years and used to say to me with a grin that, whenever Galdino saw him in the street, instead of asking for his money, he would ask him how things were going at the ministry.

JOÃO BRÁS—Neither foolish nor stupid. Very attentive, despite having no manners. Cannot bear to see a minister's carriage go by; he turns pale and averts his eyes. I believe he's ambitious, but at his age, with no settled career, ambition is slowly turning to envy. In the two years he served as a deputy, he performed his duties honorably: he worked hard and made several good speeches; not brilliant, but solid, full of facts, and well thought out. Proof that he retains a residue of ambition lies in his ardent pursuit of certain prominent, honorific posts; a few months ago, he allowed himself to be appointed honorary president of a São José lay brotherhood, and according to what I hear, he performs his duties with exemplary zeal. I believe he is atheist, but I can't be sure. He smiles little and discreetly. He lives a pure and rigorous life, but his character has one or two fraudulent notes to it, which he lacks the skill to conceal; he lies easily about trivial matters.

At last, with a feeling of dread, Benjamin found himself described in this diary.

This nephew of mine [said the manuscript] is twenty-four years of age, engaged on a project for judicial reform, has abundant hair, and he adores me. I adore him no less. Discreet, loyal, and kind—even to the point of gullibility. As firm in his affections as he is fickle in his opinions. Superficial and a lover of novelty; very fond of legal vocabulary and formulas.

He tried to reread this, but couldn't bear to; those few lines were like gazing into a mirror. He stood up, went over to the window, looked out at the garden, and came back inside to contemplate once again his own features. He reread what his uncle had written: it was rather scant and thin, but not slanderous. If someone had been there with him, it's likely that the young man's feelings of mortification would have been less intense, because the need to dispel the impressions formed by the others would have given him the necessary strength to react against what was written. Alone, however, he had to bear it with no contrasting light and shade. Then he wondered whether his uncle might have composed these pages when he was simply in a bad mood; he compared them to others in which the phrasing was less harsh, but he had no idea whether or not the milder tone was deliberate.

To confirm his hypothesis, he recalled his uncle's customary good manners, the happy hours he had spent alone with him or in conversation with his friends. He tried to summon up his uncle's face, the kindly, amused look in his eyes, and his rather solemn sense of humor; but instead of those innocent, friendly features, all he could see was his uncle lying dead, stretched out on the bed, his eyes open and his lip curled. He tried to banish this image from his mind, but it refused to budge. Unable to drive it away, Benjamin tried mentally to close the man's eyes and straighten his mouth; but no sooner had he done so than the eyelids would lift once again, and the lips resume that ironic sneer. It was no longer the man he had known, but the author of those portraits.

Benjamin ate and slept badly. The five friends returned the following afternoon to continue their reading. They arrived eager and impatient, asking many questions and insisting on seeing the notebooks. Benjamin, however, put them off, making one excuse after another; unfortunately for him, there in the room, behind the others, he could still see the dead man's eternally curling lip, and this made him seem even more awkward and withdrawn. Benjamin's demeanor toward the others turned chilly, for he wanted them to leave, and to see if that vision would disappear with them. Thirty or forty minutes went by. Eventually, the five friends looked at each other and decided to go; they bade him a ceremonious farewell, and returned to their houses deep in conversation:

"What a difference from his uncle! What a gulf separates them! Puffed up by his inheritance, no doubt! Well, we'll leave him to it. Alas, poor Joaquim Fidélis!"

THE CHAPTER ON HATS

GÉRONTE: *In which chapter, may I ask?*
SGANARELLE: *In the chapter on hats.*

—MOLIÈRE

S ING, O MUSE, of the dismay of Mariana, wife of the distinguished Conrado Seabra, on that April morning in 1879. What could be the cause of such upset? A simple hat, light and not inelegant; in short, a bowler hat. Conrado, a lawyer with offices on Rua da Quitanda, wore it to the city every day, and it went with him to all his court hearings; he only refrained from wearing it at receptions, the opera, funerals, and formal social visits. Otherwise, it was a constant feature, and had been so for the entire five or six years of his marriage. Until, on that particular April morning, after finishing their breakfast, Conrado began to roll a cigarette, and Mariana announced with a smile that she had something to ask him.

"What is it, my angel?"

"Would you be capable of making a sacrifice for me?"

"I could make ten or twenty of them!"

"Then stop wearing that hat to the city."

"Why? Is it ugly?"

"I wouldn't say ugly, but it's only meant to be worn locally, when going for a stroll around the neighborhood, in the evenings or at night. But in the city, for a lawyer, well, it hardly seems—"

"Don't be so silly, sweetie!"

"It may be silly, but will you do it as a favor? Just for me?"

Conrado struck a match, lit his cigarette, and tried to change the subject with an affable wave of his hand, but his wife persisted, and her insistence, at first gently imploring, quickly became harsh and imperious. Conrado was shocked. He knew his wife; she was usually such a passive creature, sweet and gently amenable as the situation demanded, capable of wearing a bonnet, a wimple, or a royal tiara with the same divine indifference. The proof of this is that, having been part of a rather fast set during the two years before marrying, once she did marry, she quickly settled into homelier habits. She did go out from time to time, mainly at the behest of her husband, but she was only truly at ease in her own home. Furniture, curtains, and ornaments made up for the lack of children; she loved them like a mother, and such was the harmony between person and surroundings that she took particular pleasure in everything being in its proper place, the curtains hanging in the same neat folds, and so on. For example, one of the three windows that gave onto the street was always left half open, and it was always the same one. Even her husband's study did not escape her fastidious demands, for she carefully maintained, and at times restored, his books, so that they were always in the same state of disorder. Her mental habits were equally uniform. Mariana possessed very few ideas and read only the same books again and again: Macedo's *Moreninha*, seven times; Walter Scott's *Ivanhoe* and *The Pirate*, ten times each; *Le Mot de l'Énigme* by Madame Craven, eleven times.

In the light of all this, how can one explain this business with the hat? The previous evening, while her husband was attending a meeting of the bar association, Mariana's father came to their house. He was a kindly old man, wiry and somewhat ponderous, a retired civil servant who was consumed by nostalgia for the days when employees wore frock coats to the office. Even now, a frock coat was what he wore to funerals, not for the reasons a reader might suspect, such as the solemnity of death or the gravity of a final farewell, but for the less philosophical reason that this was how things used to be. He always gave the same reason, whether it was frock coats at funerals, or having dinner at two o'clock in the afternoon, or twenty other such foibles. He was so chained to his habits that, on his daughter's wedding anniversary, he would go to their house at six o'clock, having already dined and digested, and watch them eat and, at the end, take a little dessert, a glass of port, and some coffee. Given that he was Conrado's father-in-law, how could he possibly approve of his son-in-law's bowler hat? He put up with it in silence, in consideration of the man's other qualities, but nothing more. That day, however, he had caught sight of it in the street, conversing with other hats—top hats belonging to distinguished gentlemen—and never had it seemed so vile. That night, finding his daughter alone, he opened his heart to her, dubbing the bowler hat the "abomination of abominations," and urging her to banish it.

Conrado was unaware that this was the origin of the request. Knowing his wife's docile nature, he did not understand her resistance, and, because he was willful and authoritarian, her stubbornness irritated him deeply. Even so, he kept these feelings to himself, preferring simply to scoff; he spoke to her with such scathing irony and disdain that the poor lady felt utterly humiliated. Twice Mariana tried to leave the table and twice he forced her to stay, the first time by grabbing her lightly by the wrist, the second time by subduing her with a withering look. And he said with a smile:

"Now, then, sweetie, I have a philosophical reason for not doing as you ask. I have never told you this before, but I will now tell you everything."

Mariana bit her lip and said no more; she picked up a knife and began to tap it slowly on the table, just to have something to do, but her husband wouldn't even allow her this; he delicately took the knife from her and went on:

"Choosing a hat is no random act, as you might suppose; it is governed by a metaphysical principle. Do not think that a man who buys a hat does so freely and voluntarily; the truth is that he is obeying an obscure form of determinism. The illusion of liberty is deeply embedded in the purchaser's psyche, and shared by hatters, who, after watching a customer try on thirty or forty hats, then leave without buying a single one, imagine that he is merely searching for the most elegant combination. The metaphysical principle is this: the hat completes the man; it is an extension of his head, a combination decreed *ab eterno* and that no man may put asunder without committing an act of mutilation. This is a profound question that no one has yet considered. Wise men have studied everything from asteroids to worms, or, in bibliographical terms, from Laplace—you mean you've never read Laplace?—well, from Laplace and his *Mécanique Céleste* to Darwin and his curious book about worms, and yet they've never thought to pause in front of a hat and study it from every angle. No one has noticed that there is a whole metaphysics of hats. Perhaps I should write an essay on the subject myself. However, it's now a quarter to ten and I really must go, but do think about it and you'll see what I mean. Who knows? Perhaps it's not even the hat that complements the man, but the man who complements the hat."

Mariana finally wrested back her independence and got up from the table. She had not understood a word of his barbed terminology, nor his peculiar theory, but she sensed his sarcasm and, inside, she wept with humiliation. Her husband went upstairs to get dressed to go out, came back down a few minutes later, and stood in front of her with the infamous hat on his head. Mariana really did think it made him look seedy, vulgar, and not at all serious. Conrado ceremoniously bade her good day and left.

The lady's irritation had subsided considerably, but her feelings of humiliation remained. Mariana did not wail and weep, as she thought she would, but, thinking it all over, she recalled the simplicity of her request and Conrado's sarcastic response, and, while she recognized that she had been somewhat demanding, she found no justification whatsoever for such excesses. She paced back and forth, unable to stand still; she went into the drawing room, approached the half-open window, and watched her husband standing in the street waiting for the streetcar, with his back to the house and that eternal, despicable hat on his head. Mariana felt herself overcome with hatred for that ridiculous item; she couldn't understand how she had put up with it for so many years. And she thought of all those years of docility and acquiescence to her husband's whims and desires, and wondered if that might not be the very thing that had led to his reaction that morning. She called herself a fool and a ninny; if she had behaved like so many other wives, Clara or Sofia, for example, who treated their husbands as they deserved to be treated, none of this would have happened. One thought led to another, and to the idea of going out. She got dressed and went to visit Sofia, an old school friend, just to clear her head, and certainly not to divulge anything.

Sofia was thirty, two years older than Mariana. She was tall, sturdy, and very sure of herself. She greeted her friend with the usual show of affection and, when Mariana said nothing, she guessed at once that something was very much amiss. Adieu to Mariana's best intentions! Within twenty minutes she had told her friend everything. Sofia laughed, shrugged her shoulders, and told her it wasn't her husband's fault at all.

"Oh, I know, it's my fault entirely," agreed Mariana.

"Don't be silly, my dear! You've just been far too soft with him. You must be strong, for once; take no notice; don't speak to him for a while, and when he comes to patch things up, tell him he must first change his hat."

"Goodness, but it seems such a trivial thing . . ."

"At the end of the day, he's just as right as all the others. Take that chump Beatriz: Hasn't she gone and disappeared off to the country, just because her husband took a dislike to an Englishman who was in the habit of riding past their house every afternoon? Poor Englishman! Naturally, he didn't even notice she'd gone. We women can live very happily with our husbands, in mutual respect, not frustrating each other's desires and without resorting to stubborn outbursts or despotism. Look, I get on very well with my Ricardo, perfectly harmoniously. Whatever I ask him to do, he does immediately, even when he doesn't want to; I only need to frown and he obeys. He wouldn't give me any trouble over a hat! Certainly not! Where would that lead? No, he'd jolly well get a new hat, whether he wanted to or not."

Mariana listened enviously to this delightful description of conjugal bliss. The clarion call of Eve's rebellion reverberated within her, and meeting her friend gave her an irresistible itch for independence and free will. To complete the picture, Sofia was not only very much her own mistress, but also the mistress of everyone else too; she had eyes for all the Englishmen, whether on horseback or afoot. She was an honest woman, but also a flirt; the word is rather crude, but there's no time now to find a more delicate one. She flirted left, right, and center, out of a necessity of nature, a habit of her maiden days. It was the small change of love, and she distributed it to all the paupers who knocked on her door: a nickel to one, a dime to another, never as much as five *mil-réis*, still less anything more substantial. These charitable urges now induced her to propose to Mariana that they take a stroll together, see the shops, and admire some fine, dignified hats while they were at it. Mariana accepted; a little demon was firing up within her the furies of revenge. Moreover, her friend had Bonaparte's powers of persuasion and gave her no time to reflect. Of course she would go; she was tired of living like a prisoner in her own home. She, too, wanted to live a little.

While Sofia went to dress, Mariana remained in the drawing room, restless and rather pleased with herself. She planned out what remained of her week, marking the day and time for each appointment like fixtures on an official journey. She stood up, sat down, went over to the window, while she waited for her friend.

"Has she died or something?" she said to herself from time to time.

Once, when she went to the window, she saw a young man pass by on horseback. He wasn't English, but he made her think of Beatriz, whose husband had taken her off to the country due to his distrust of an Englishman, and she felt swelling within her a hatred of the entire masculine race—except, perhaps, for young men on horseback. To be honest, this one was far too affected for her taste; he stuck out his legs in the stirrups just to show off his boots, and rested one hand on his waist as if he were a mannequin. Mariana noted these two defects, but thought that his hat made up for them. Not that it was a top hat; it was a bowler, but entirely appropriate for equestrian purposes. It was not covering the head of a distinguished lawyer on his way to the office, but that of a man simply enjoying himself or passing the time.

The slow, leisurely click of Sofia's heels came down the stairs. "Ready!" she said a moment later upon entering the drawing room. She really did look lovely. We already know she was tall. Her hat gave her an even more commanding air, and a devilish black silk dress, molding the curves of her bust, made her even more striking. Next to her, Mariana disappeared somewhat—one needed to look carefully to see that she did in fact have very pretty features, beautiful eyes, and a natural elegance. The worst of it was that Sofia instantly monopolized all attention, and if there were only a limited amount of time to observe them both, Sofia grabbed it all for herself. This remark would be incomplete if I did not add that Sofia was perfectly aware of her superiority, and for this very reason appreciated the charms of women like Mariana, because they were less obvious or effusive. If this is a flaw, it is not for me to correct it.

"Where are we going?" asked Mariana.

"Don't be silly! We're going for a little trip into town. Now, let's see: I'm going to have my picture taken, then I'm going to the dentist. No, let's go to the dentist first. Don't you need to go to the dentist?"

"No."

"Or have your picture taken?"

"I've got lots already. And why do you need a picture? To give to 'you-know-who'?"

Sofia realized that her friend's resentment had not abated and, as they walked, she took care to add some more fuel to the fire. She told Mariana that, while it wouldn't be easy, there was still time to free herself. And that she would teach her a way of slipping the shackles of tyranny. It was best not to do it in a single bound, but slowly and surely, so that the first he'd know about it was when she was standing over him with her foot placed firmly on his neck. It would be a matter of a few weeks, three or four at the most. Sofia was ready and willing to help her. And she told Mariana again not to be so soft, that she was no one's slave, and so on. As she walked, Mariana's heart sang to itself the "*Marseillaise*" of matrimony.

They reached Rua do Ouvidor. It was just after noon. There were crowds of people walking, or just standing around, the usual hustle and bustle. Mariana felt a little overwhelmed, as she always did. Uniformity and tranquility, the foundations of her life and character, took their usual knocks from all that hurly-burly. She could scarcely thread her way through the groups of people, still less know where to fix her gaze, such was the jumble of people and the profusion of shops. She stuck close to her friend, and, not noticing that they had passed the dentist's, was anxious to reach the place and get inside. It would be a refuge, certainly better than the hullabaloo of Rua do Ouvidor.

"Really, this street!" she kept saying.

"What?" responded Sofia airily, turning her head toward her friend, and her eyes toward a young man on the sidewalk opposite.

As an experienced navigator of these choppy waters, Sofia slipped through and around the groups of people with great skill and composure. Her figure commanded attention: those who knew her were pleased to see her again, while those who did not, stopped or turned to admire her *élan*. And the bounteous lady, full of charity, swept her eyes from left to right, to no great scandal, since Mariana's presence gave everything a veneer of decency. She babbled away, barely seeming to hear Mariana's replies, commenting on everything and everyone they passed: people, shops, hats . . . For under the midday sun on Rua do Ouvidor, there were many hats, for both ladies and gentlemen.

"Look at that one," Sofia would say.

And Mariana would promptly look, although not quite knowing where to look, because everywhere was a swirling kaleidoscope of hats. "Where's the dentist's?" she asked her friend. She had to repeat her question before Sofia told her that they had already passed the surgery; now they were going to the end of the street; they would come back later, and finally they did.

"Ouf!" sighed Mariana as they entered the hallway.

"My goodness! What's the matter? Anyone would think you were just up from the country!"

There were already some patients in the dentist's waiting room. Mariana couldn't see a single face she recognized, and went to the window to avoid the gaze of strangers. From the window she could enjoy the street without all the pushing and shoving. She leaned back; Sofia came to join her. Some men's hats down below turned to stare up at them; others, passing by, did the same. Mariana felt annoyed by their insistence, but, when she noticed that they were staring principally at her friend, her irritation dissolved into a kind of envy. Meanwhile, Sofia was telling her all about some of the hats—or, more precisely, their romantic adventures. One of them was highly thought-of by Miss so-and-so; another was madly in love with Madam you-know-who, who was also in love with him, so much so that they were sure to be seen on Rua do Ouvidor on Wednesdays and Saturdays between two and three in the afternoon. Mariana listened in bewilderment. The hat was indeed rather handsome, and wore a beautiful necktie, and had an air about it that was somewhere between elegant and raffish, but . . .

"I can't swear to it, mind," Sofia continued, "but that's what people are saying."

Mariana gazed pensively at the hat in question. It was now joined by three more, of equal poise and elegance; the four were probably talking about them, and in favorable terms too. Mariana blushed deeply, looked away, then back again, then retreated into the room. As she did so, she noticed two ladies who had just arrived, and with them a young man who promptly stood up and came to greet her effusively. He had been her very first suitor.

He would be about thirty-three now. He had been away from Rio, first to somewhere in the interior, then to Europe, then as governor of one of the southern provinces. He was of medium height, pale, with a rather skimpy beard and clothes that were straining at the seams. He was holding a new top hat: black, serious, gubernatorial, ministerial even; a hat befitting his person and his ambitions. Mariana, however, could hardly look at him. She became so flustered and disorientated by the presence of a man whom she had known in such special circumstances, and had not seen since 1877, that she was unable to take in anything at all. She proffered him the tips of her fingers, apparently murmured some kind of response, and was about to rejoin Sofia at the window, when her friend turned from the window and came toward her.

Sofia also knew the new arrival. They exchanged a few words. Mariana whispered impatiently in her friend's ear that perhaps it would be better to leave their teeth for another day, but Sofia said no; it would only take half an hour, or three-quarters at most. Mariana felt very uncomfortable: the presence of that man tied her in knots, throwing her into a state of conflict and confusion. It was all her husband's fault. If he hadn't been so stubborn, and, even worse, made fun of her, none of this would have happened. Mariana swore she would have her revenge. She thought about her house, so pretty and peaceful, where she could be right now, as usual, without all this pushing and shoving in the street, without having to be so dependent on her friend . . .

"Mariana," said Sofia, "Senhor Viçoso insists that he's very thin. Don't you think he's put on weight since last year? Don't you remember him from last year?"

Senhor Viçoso was the name of the erstwhile suitor, now chatting with Sofia and casting frequent glances in Mariana's direction. She shook her head. He seized the opportunity to draw her into the conversation, remarking that, as a matter of fact, he hadn't seen her for several years. He underlined these words with a rather sad, meaningful gaze. Then he opened up his tool kit of topics and pulled out the opera. What did they think of the cast? In his opinion they were excellent, except for the baritone; the baritone seemed to him rather dull. Sofia protested, but Senhor Viçoso insisted, adding that, in London, where he'd heard him for the first time, he'd thought the same thing. The ladies, of course, were quite another matter; both the soprano and the contralto were first-rate. And he discussed the various operas he had seen, referring to the most famous passages, praising the orchestra, particularly in *Les Huguenots* . . . He had spotted Mariana on the last night, sitting in the fourth or fifth box on the left, wasn't that so?

"Yes, we were there," she murmured, emphasizing the plural.

"Although I haven't seen you at the Cassino even once," he continued.

"Oh, she's become quite the little peekaboo!" interrupted Sofia, laughing.

Viçoso had greatly enjoyed the last ball at the Cassino, and shared his recollections of it minutely; Sofia did likewise. The most elaborate *toilettes* were described by both of them in particular detail, followed by the various people they had seen, the different characters, and a few barbed comments, albeit anodyne enough not to harm anyone. Mariana listened without the slightest interest; two or three times she even got up and went over to the window, but the hats were so numerous and so inquisitive that she sat back down again. Silently, she called her friend some rather ugly names; I won't give them here because it's unnecessary and, moreover, in rather bad taste to reveal what one young lady might think of another in a moment of irritation.

"And the races at the Jockey Club?" asked the former governor.

Mariana again shook her head. She hadn't been to the races that year. Well, she had missed a treat, especially the one before last; it had been a very lively affair and the horses really top-notch. Better even than the races at Epsom, which he'd attended when he was in England. Sofia said that, yes, indeed, the race before last really had been a credit to the Jockey Club, and confessed that she had enjoyed herself immensely; it had been positively thrilling. The conversation drifted on to two concerts taking place that very week, then it took the ferry and climbed the hills to Petrópolis, where two diplomats provided ample hospitality. When they spoke of a minister's wife, Sofia remembered to flatter the former governor and declare that he, too, must marry, since he would soon be in government. Viçoso squirmed with pleasure and smiled, shaking his head; then, looking at Mariana, he said that he would probably never marry. Mariana turned bright red and stood up.

"You seem in a great hurry," Sofia said to her. "What time is it?" she continued, turning toward Viçoso.

"Nearly three!" he exclaimed.

It was getting late; he had to go to the Chamber of Deputies. He went over to speak to the two ladies he had been accompanying, cousins of his, and made his excuses; he came back to say goodbye to Sofia and Mariana, but Sofia said that she was leaving too. She simply couldn't wait a moment longer. In fact, the idea of going to the Chamber of Deputies had begun to scintillate inside her head.

"Shall we all go to the Chamber?" she proposed to Mariana.

"Oh, no," replied Mariana. "I couldn't. I'm so tired."

"Come on, let's go. Just for a little bit; I'm very tired, too, but . . ."

Mariana resisted a little longer, but resisting Sofia—like a dove arguing with a hawk—was completely pointless. There was nothing for it; she went. The street was busier now, people passing this way and that on both sides of the street, and getting in each other's way at the street corners. The ever-solicitous former governor escorted both ladies, having offered to find them somewhere to sit in the gallery.

Mariana's soul felt ever more torn apart by all this confusion of people and things. She had completely lost her original motivation, and the resentment that had propelled her into that audacious, short-lived flight began to slow its wings, or give up entirely. Once again she thought of her house, so quiet, so tidy, everything in its place, with no pushing or shoving, and, most of all, no unexpected changes. Her impatience grew, and with it her anger. She wasn't listening to a word Viçoso was saying, even though he was talking rather loudly, and principally to her. She couldn't hear and she didn't want to hear. She merely prayed to God to make the time pass quickly. They arrived at the Chamber and went up to the gallery. The rustle of skirts attracted the attention of the twenty or so deputies who were still in the Chamber listening to a speech about the budget. As soon as Viçoso excused himself and left, Mariana quickly told her friend not to play a trick on her like that again.

"Like what?" asked Sofia.

"Like having me run around all over the place like some madwoman. What have I got to do with the Chamber of Deputies? Why should I care about speeches I don't even understand?"

Sofia smiled, fluttered her fan, and received the full attention of one of the ministers. Many eyes gazed at her whenever she visited the Chamber, but this particular minister's eyes had a particularly warm, pleading expression. It may be assumed, therefore, that she did not receive his gaze unexpectedly; it could even be said that she sought it out of curiosity. While she was acknowledging this legislative attention, she replied gently to her friend that she was very sorry and had meant well, and had simply wanted to restore Mariana's independence.

"But if you find me irritating, then don't come out with me again," Sofia concluded.

And, leaning forward a little, she said:

"Look at the minister of justice."

Mariana had no choice but to look at the minister of justice. He was bravely enduring a speech by a government supporter, in which the speaker was extolling the merits of the criminal justice system and, along the way, painstakingly summarizing all the old colonial legislation on the subject. There were no interruptions; just a polite, resigned, cautious silence. Mariana's eyes drifted from one side to the other, utterly bored; Sofia was constantly saying things to her, as an excuse for making all kinds of elegant gestures. After fifteen minutes, the Chamber stirred into life, thanks to a remark made by the speaker and an objection from the opposition. Heckles were exchanged, the temperature rose, and there ensued an uproar that lasted nearly a quarter of an hour.

Mariana did not find this diversion in the least diverting; indeed, her placid, equable nature was thrown into a spin by such unexpected commotion. She even got up to leave, then sat down again. She was ready now to stay until the end, repentant and resolved to keep her marital woes to herself. Doubts began to creep in. She had been right to ask her husband to change his hat, but was it worth all this heartache? Was it reasonable to make such a fuss? He had been cruel and sarcastic, but it was, after all, the first time she had put her foot down and, naturally, the novelty had irritated him. At any rate, it had been a mistake to spill the beans to her friend. Sofia might go and tell others . . . The thought sent a chill down Mariana's spine; her friend's indiscretion was assured; she herself had heard Sofia tell many tales about hats, male and female, engaged in much more than a simple marital tiff. Mariana felt the need to flatter her, and covered up her impatience and annoyance with a mask of hypocritical docility. She, too, began to smile and make random observations about this or that deputy, and in this uneasy truce they reached the end of the speech and the session.

It was gone four o'clock. "Time for home," said Sofia. Mariana agreed, although she seemed in no hurry, and they made their way back along Rua do Ouvidor. Walking up the street and catching the streetcar completed Mariana's mental exhaustion, and she only began to breathe more easily when she saw that she really was on her way home. Shortly before Sofia got off, Mariana asked her keep to herself what she had told her, and Sofia promised that she would.

Mariana gave a sigh of relief. The dove was free of the hawk. Her soul was aching from all the pushing and shoving, dizzy from all those disparate people and things. What she needed was equilibrium and peace. She was nearly home; as she watched the neighboring houses and gardens pass by, Mariana felt her spirits lift. At last she arrived; she entered the garden, and took a deep breath. This was her world, except for a flowerpot that the gardener had moved.

"João, put that flowerpot back where it was," she said.

Everything else was in order, the entrance hall, the drawing room, the dining room, the bedrooms, everything. First of all, Mariana sat down, in various different places, looking carefully at all the objects, so still and orderly. After a whole day of swirling variety, the monotony restored her peace of mind, and had never before seemed so delightful. The truth was she'd made a mistake. She tried to relive the day's events, but couldn't; her soul was gently slipping back into its home comforts. At most, she thought about Viçoso, whom she now, rather unfairly, thought ridiculous. She undressed slowly and lovingly, precisely removing and putting away each item of clothing. Once she was undressed, she thought again about the quarrel with her husband. All things considered, she realized that it had been mainly her fault. Why such stubbornness over a hat that her husband had been wearing for years? And, besides, her father was a terrible fusspot.

"I'll wait and see the look on his face when he comes home," she thought.

It was half-past five; he wouldn't be long. Mariana went to the front room, peered out the window, listened for the streetcar, but heard nothing. She sat down by the window with *Ivanhoe* in her hands, trying, and failing, to read. Her eyes skimmed to the end of the page, then back to the beginning; firstly, because she couldn't grasp the meaning, and secondly, because time and again her eyes would wander from the page to admire the perfect folds of the curtains or some other feature of the room. Ah, blessèd monotony, cradling her in thy eternal bosom.

Eventually the streetcar stopped outside the house and her husband got off; the garden gate creaked open. Mariana went to the window and peered out. Conrado was walking slowly up the garden path, looking to left and right, his hat on his head—not the famous hat he always wore, but another one, the one his wife had asked him to wear that very morning. It came as a rude shock to Mariana, just like the flowerpot in the garden being moved, or as if she'd come across a page of Voltaire in her copy of *Moreninha* or *Ivanhoe*. It was a jarring note in the harmonious sonata of life. No, that hat would never do. Really, whatever had possessed her to make him get rid of the old one that suited him so well? Even if it wasn't perhaps the most appropriate

of hats, it had served him for many years, and framed his face so well . . .
Conrado came in through a side door. Mariana flung her arms around him.

"So, is it over?" he asked, circling her waist.

"Listen, darling," she replied, giving him the divinest of kisses, "throw
that hat away; the other one's much nicer."

AN ALEXANDRIAN TALE

Chapter I

AT SEA

"WHAT, MY DEAR STROIBUS? Impossible! No one will ever believe that giving a man mouse blood to drink could turn him into a mouser or a thief."

"First of all, Pythias, you are forgetting one important condition: the mouse must perish under the surgeon's scalpel for the blood to retain its fundamental essence. This condition is, one could say, essential. Secondly, since you have chosen the example of a mouse, I'll have you know that I've already experimented on one, and did indeed manage to produce a thief . . ."

"A genuine thief?"

"A month later, he stole my cloak, but left me the greatest happiness in the world: the proof that my theory is correct. What did I lose? A scrap of coarse cloth. And what did the universe gain? An immortal truth. Yes, my dear Pythias, this is an eternal truth. The constituent elements of the thief are contained in the blood of mice, those of the patient man in the ox, those of the bold in the eagle—"

"And those of the wise man in the owl," interrupted Pythias, smiling.

"No, the owl is merely an emblem, but if we could transfer spider's blood to a man, it would give that man the rudiments of geometry and musical sensibility. With a flock of storks, swallows, or cranes, I'll make a stay-at-home into a wanderer. The essence of marital fidelity is to be found in the blood of turtledoves, that of infatuation in peacock blood . . . In short, the gods put the essence of all human feelings and abilities into the beasts of the earth, water, and sky. Animals are the random letters of the alphabet; man is the syntax. This is my latest philosophy; this is what I shall reveal at the court of the great Ptolemy."

Pythias shook his head and stared out to sea. The ship was sailing to Alexandria with its precious cargo of two philosophers, carrying the fruits of enlightened reason to that haven of learning. They were friends, both widowed, and in their fifties. Their particular specialty was metaphysics, but they were also acquainted with physics, chemistry, medicine, and music; one of them, Stroibus, had become an excellent anatomist, having read the treatises of Herophilos many times. Their native land was Cyprus, but, since no one is ever a prophet in his own country, Cyprus did not accord the two philosophers the honor they deserved. On the contrary, it scorned them; street urchins would even jeer at them. This was not, however, the reason that had prompted them to leave their homeland. One day, returning from a journey, Pythias proposed to his friend that they go to Alexandria, where the arts and sciences were held in high esteem. Stroibus agreed, and they boarded ship. Only now, having set sail, did the inventor of the new doctrine reveal it to his friend, along with all his recent thoughts and experiments.

"All right," said Pythias, looking up. "I can neither confirm nor deny anything, but I will study your new theory, and if I find it to be true, I will develop it further and reveal it to the world."

"Long live Helios!" exclaimed Stroibus. "I can say that you are my disciple."

Chapter II

EXPERIMENT

The urchins of Alexandria did not treat the two sages with the same scorn as their Cypriot brethren. Egypt was as grave as the ibis perched on one leg, as pensive as the Sphinx, as circumspect as the mummies, and as austere as the pyramids; it had neither time nor inclination to laugh. Both city and court, well acquainted with the reputations of our two friends, gave them a royal welcome, demonstrated knowledge of their writings, discussed their ideas, and sent them many gifts: papyri, crocodiles, zebras, and cloth of finest purple. They refused everything, however, saying simply that philosophy was all a philosopher needed, and that superfluous possessions were corrosive to the soul. Such a noble response filled everyone with admiration, from the wise men and leaders to the common people. "After all," said the wisest among them, "what else could one expect from two such excellent men, who in their magnificent treatises—"

"We have something even better than those treatises," said Stroibus, interrupting the speaker. "I have brought with me a theory that will very soon govern the universe; I intend nothing less than the reconstitution of both men and nations by redistributing their talents and virtues."

"Is that not the work of the gods?" objected one of them.

"I have penetrated the secret of the gods," replied Stroibus. "Mankind is the syntax of nature, and I have discovered the laws of divine grammar."

"Explain yourself."

"Later. First I must experiment. When my theory is complete, I will reveal it as the greatest gift mankind could ever receive from a man."

Just imagine the public expectation and the other philosophers' curiosity, although they found it hard to believe that this newly proclaimed truth could come to displace those which they themselves held dear. Nevertheless, they all waited patiently. The two guests were pointed at in the street, even by little children. A son pondered the possibility of reversing his father's parsimony, a father his son's prodigality, a lady her gentleman's indifference, a gentleman his lady's follies—because Egypt, from the pharaohs to the Ptolemies, was the land of Potiphar and Potiphar's wife, and Joseph's coat of many colors, and all the rest. Stroibus became the hope of the city and the world.

Having studied the theory, Pythias went to see Stroibus and told him:

"Metaphysically speaking, your theory is nonsense, but I am prepared to allow one experiment, as long as it proves decisive. There is only one way, my dear Stroibus, for this to work. You and I, as much because of our steadfast characters as our cultivation of reason, would be most resistant to the vice of theft. So if you manage to instill this vice in us, you will have proved your theory; if you do not (and believe me, you won't, because it is utterly absurd), you will abandon all such ideas and we will return to our old, familiar meditations."

Stroibus accepted the proposal.

"My sacrifice is all the more painful," he said, "since I am sure of the result; but how can one deny the truth? Truth is immortal; man is but a brief moment."

The Egyptian mice, had they known of this accord, would have imitated the ancient Hebrews and fled into the desert rather than accept the new philosophy. And it would, without a doubt, be disastrous. Science, like war, has its imperative necessities, and since the ignorance and weakness of mice, combined with the mental and physical superiority of the two philosophers, gave such material advantages to the forthcoming experiment, it behooved them not to waste so excellent an opportunity to find out if the essence of each human passion and virtue was indeed to be found among the various species of animals, and if it was possible to transmit that essence to humans.

Stroibus placed the mice in cages; then, one by one, he put them to the knife. First, he tied a strip of cloth around the patient's snout and paws; then he tied its legs and neck to the operating table with a cord. Having done this, he made the first incision in the chest, slowly going deeper and deeper in until the scalpel touched the heart, for it was his opinion that instantaneous death would contaminate the blood and destroy its essence. As a skilled anatomist, he wielded the knife with an expertise worthy of his scientific intent. Anyone less dexterous than he would have stopped and started many times, because the mouse so writhed about in its pain and agony that this made holding the scalpel very difficult; but therein lay Stroibus's superiority, for he had a practical and magisterial command of his subject.

Standing beside him, Pythias collected the blood and helped with the work, restraining the patient's convulsive movements and carefully watching its eyes to study the progression of its death throes. The observations of both men were recorded on sheets of papyrus, and the benefit to science was thus twofold. At times, when their assessments differed, they were obliged to dissect more mice than would otherwise have been necessary. However, they put this to good use, for the blood from the extra mice was set aside and swallowed later. Just one such incident will demonstrate the care with which they proceeded. Pythias had observed that the color of the dying mouse's retina changed to light blue, while according to Stroibus's observations the final color at the point of death was hazel. It was their final experiment of the day, but it was a point worth investigating and, despite their tiredness, they carried out a further nineteen experiments without reaching a definitive conclusion; Pythias insisted on blue, Stroibus on hazel. The twentieth mouse nearly brought agreement, but Stroibus realized, with great perspicacity, that he had changed his stance while at the table. He corrected this, and they dissected twenty-five more. Of these, the first one still left them in doubt, but the other twenty-four proved to them that the final color was neither hazel nor blue, but a pale shade of violet.

Exaggerated accounts of the experiments caused some alarm among the more sentimental of the city's inhabitants and aroused the loquacity of several sophists, but the grave Stroibus (gently, so as not to further aggravate a characteristic proper to the human soul) replied that the truth was worth all the mice in the universe, indeed not only mice, but also peacocks, goats, dogs, nightingales, and so on. In the case of mice, both science and the city gained through a reduction in the scourge of so destructive an animal; and, if the same considerations did not apply to other animals—such as turtle-doves and dogs, for instance, which they would also be dissecting in due course—this in no way diminished the rights of the truth. "Nature should not only furnish the dining table," he concluded with an aphorism, "but also the table of science."

And they carried on extracting the blood and imbibing it. They drank it diluted in an infusion of cinnamon, acacia sap, and balsam, which completely masked its original taste. They took tiny, daily doses, and therefore had to wait a long time for the effect to manifest itself. Pythias, impatient and incredulous, mocked his friend.

"So? Still nothing?"

"Wait," said Stroibus. "Just wait. Growing a vice is not like stitching a pair of sandals."

Chapter III

VICTORY

Finally, Stroibus triumphed! The experiment proved his theory to be correct. And Pythias was the first to show signs that the effect was real, by attributing to himself no less than three ideas he had heard from Stroibus himself. The latter, in retaliation, stole from Pythias four comparisons and a theory about the wind. What could be more scientific? Other people's ideas, precisely because they aren't bought and sold on the street corner, have a certain air of commonality, and so it is only natural to begin with them before moving on to borrowed books, hens, forgeries, provinces, and so on. The term "plagiarism" is an indication that people understand the difficulty of confusing this embryonic form of thievery with the fully fledged variety.

It's a hard thing to say, but the truth is that both Stroibus and Pythias cast all their metaphysical baggage into the Nile and, in no time at all, became inveterate pilferers. They would prepare carefully in advance and go after cloaks, bronzes, amphoras of wine, merchandise from the port, and trusty old drachmas. They stole so silently that no one caught on, but even if someone had, how would he have convinced anyone else of this? Ptolemy had, by that time, already gathered together in his library many rare treasures and, wishing to catalogue them, he had designated five grammarians and five philosophers to do the job, among them our two friends. Pythias and Stroibus worked with singular dedication, being the first to arrive and the last to leave, often working by lamplight late into the night, deciphering, compiling, and classifying. Ptolemy was delighted, and planned to give them the very highest-ranking positions.

Some time later, serious gaps began to be noticed: a copy of Homer, three rolls of Persian manuscripts, and two Samaritan scrolls, a superb collection of Alexander's original letters, copies of Athenian laws, the second and third books of Plato's *Republic*, etc. The authorities set up a vigil, but a mouse's cunning, transferred to a superior organism, was naturally greater, and the two illustrious thieves ran rings around the spies and guards. They went so far as to establish the philosophical precept of never leaving the library empty-handed; they always took something, even if it was only a fable. Finally, when there was a ship about to set sail for Cyprus, they took their leave of Ptolemy with a promise to return, then sewed the books inside hippopotamus hides, put false labels on the outside, and attempted to flee. But the envy of other philosophers did not slumber; the magistrates' suspicions were aroused and the theft was discovered. Stroibus and Pythias were taken for impostors masquerading under those two illustrious names; Ptolemy handed them over to the judicial authorities with orders to proceed straight to execution. It was then that Herophilos, the father of anatomy, intervened.

Chapter IV

PLUS ULTRA!

"My lord," he said to Ptolemy, "until now I have limited myself to dissecting corpses. But while a corpse gives me structure, it does not give me life. It gives me the organs, but not their functions. I need functions and I need life."

"What are you saying?" replied Ptolemy. "Do you want to disembowel Stroibus's mice?"

"No, sir. I do not want to disembowel mice."

"Dogs? Geese? Hares?"

"None of those. I am asking for living men."

"Living? Impossible."

"I will demonstrate that it is not only possible, but legitimate and necessary. The prisons of Egypt are full of criminals, and criminals occupy a very lowly rung on the human ladder. They are no longer citizens and cannot even call themselves men, because in violating law and morality they have lost both reason and virtue, which are the two principal human characteristics. Furthermore, given that they must atone for their crimes through death, is it not fair that they should render some service to truth and to science? Truth is immortal; it is worth not only all the mice in the universe, but also all the wrongdoers."

Ptolemy could find no fault with this reasoning, and ordered the criminals to be delivered to Herophilos and his disciples. The great anatomist thanked him for such an illustrious favor, and began dissecting the culprits. The populace was horrified, but, apart from a few verbal protests, there were no public demonstrations against the measure. Herophilos repeated what he had said to Ptolemy, adding that subjecting delinquents to anatomical experiments even amounted to an indirect method of promoting morality, since fear of the scalpel would, in itself, deter the commission of many crimes.

Upon coming out of prison, none of the criminals suspected the scientific destiny that awaited them. They left prison one by one, or sometimes in twos or threes. Many of them, stretched out and strapped to the operating table, still suspected nothing; they assumed it was some new method of summary execution. Only when the anatomists had decided upon the day's scientific objective, lifted their scalpels, and made the first incisions, did the poor wretches become truly conscious of their predicament. Those who remembered hearing about the experiments on mice suffered doubly, because their imaginations added past events to present pain.

In order to reconcile the interests of science with the impulses of compassion, the prisoners were not dissected within sight of each other, but one after the other. When they came in twos or threes, those waiting their turn were placed where they could not hear the other patient's screams. Although the screams were often muffled with various devices, they weren't entirely suppressed, and, in certain cases, the whole purpose of the experiment required unhindered vocal expression. Sometimes the experiments were simultaneous, but, in those cases, they were performed a suitable distance apart.

Around fifty prisoners had been dissected when it came to Stroibus's and Pythias's turn. When brought out of prison, they presumed they were to be executed, and commended themselves to the gods. On the way they stole some figs, and justified this theft by pleading hunger; farther on, however, they purloined a flute, and for this they were unable to give a satisfactory explanation. Still, a thief's cunning knows no bounds, and, to justify his action, Stroibus tried to get some notes out of the instrument, filling the bystanders with compassion, for they were not unaware of the fate awaiting the two philosophers. News of these two new offenses was reported by Herophilos, and shocked all of his disciples.

"Truly," said the master surgeon, "it is an extraordinary case and a beautiful one too. But before we get to the nub of our inquiry, let us first examine the other point . . ."

The other point was to find out whether the seat of larceny lay in the palm of the hand or the tips of the fingers; this problem had been suggested by one of the disciples. Stroibus was the first to be experimented upon. He understood everything from the moment he entered the operating theater; and, as human nature has a very base, obsequious streak, he begged them humbly to spare the life of a philosopher. But Herophilos, with his great powers of dialectic, said to him something along these lines: "Either you are an impostor, or you're the real Stroibus. In the first instance, you have here before you the only means of atoning for the crime of deceiving an enlightened ruler, so submit yourself to the scalpel. In the second instance, you must not be unaware that the philosopher's duty is to serve philosophy, and that, compared to knowledge, the body is nothing."

Having said this, they began with their experiment on the hands, which produced excellent results that were collated in books later lost with the fall of the Ptolemies. The hands of Pythias were also torn apart and minutely examined. The wretched pair screamed, wept, and begged for mercy, but Herophilos again calmly reminded them that the philosopher's duty is to serve philosophy, and that, for scientific purposes, they were worth even more than the mice, since it was infinitely better to draw conclusions about humans from humans, rather than from mice. And, for a whole week, he continued to dissect them fiber by fiber. On the third day, he plucked out their eyes, so as to disprove in practice a theory regarding the internal structure of that particular organ. I won't go into the removal of both men's stomachs, for it involved issues that were of somewhat secondary importance and which, in any event, had already been studied and resolved in five or six individuals dissected previously.

The Alexandrians reported that the mice in the city celebrated this distressing and painful event with dancing and feasts, to which they invited several dogs, turtledoves, peacocks, and other animals threatened with the same fate. They also say that none of the invited guests accepted the invitation, following the advice of a dog who told them glumly: "The time will come when the same thing will happen to us." To which a mouse replied: "But until then, let's be merry!"

COUSINS FROM SAPUCAIA!

————————

THERE ARE IN LIFE those fleeting occasions when chance cruelly inflicts on us two or three country cousins. At other times, however, these "cousins from Sapucaia," as I call them, can be more of a blessing than a curse.

It all began at the door of a church. I was waiting while my cousins Claudina and Rosa made the sign of the cross with the holy water, before escorting them back to our house, where they were staying. They had come from Sapucaia for the carnival, and lingered on in Rio for two months. It was I who accompanied them to mass, the theater, Rua do Ouvidor, and everywhere else, because my mother's rheumatism meant that she could barely move around the house, and they were incapable of going anywhere alone. Sapucaia was where we all hailed from. Although its members were now scattered hither and yon, it was there that the family tree had first taken root. My uncle, José Ribeiro—my cousins' father—was the only one of five siblings who still lived there, farming the land and playing his part in local politics. I had come to Rio at an early age, and went on to study and take my law degree in São Paulo. I returned only once to Sapucaia, to contest an election, which I lost.

Strictly speaking, none of this information is necessary for an understanding of my adventure, but it is a way of saying something before getting into the story itself, for which I can find no entrance either large or small. So the best thing is to slacken the reins on my pen and let it find its own way in. There must be one somewhere; it all depends on the circumstances, a rule that applies just as much to writing style as to life itself; word follows word, one idea leads to another, and so a book, a government, or a revolution is made; some even say that this is how nature brought its various species into being.

Anyway, holy water and church door. It was the Church of São José. Mass had just finished; Claudina and Rosa each made the sign of the cross on their forehead with their thumb dipped in the holy water and ungloved specifically for this purpose. Then they adjusted their lace shawls while I, in the doorway, admired the other ladies as they left. Suddenly I felt a shiver of excitement and peered out into the street, even taking a step or two in that direction.

"What is it, cousin?"

"Nothing; nothing at all."

It was a lady who had passed right by the church, slowly, head bowed, leaning on her little parasol, making her way up Rua da Misericórdia. To explain my agitation, I should say that this was the second time I had seen her. The first time was at the races two months earlier, with a man who, by all appearances, was her husband, but could just as well have been her father. She was quite a sight then, dressed in scarlet with lavish trimmings and a pair of outsized earrings, but her eyes and mouth made up for everything else. We flirted outrageously. I would not be consigning my soul to the flames if I said that I left there madly in love, since it is the honest truth. I came away feeling quite giddy, but also disappointed, for I lost sight of her in the crowd. I never saw her again, and no one could tell me who she was.

You can imagine my dismay when fortune brought her my way again, only for the accidental presence of some country cousins to prevent me from throwing my arms around her. It will not be difficult for you to imagine, because these "cousins from Sapucaia" come in many different forms, and the reader will surely have encountered them, one way or another. Sometimes they take on the guise of that well-informed gentleman droning on about the latest government crisis, enumerating every possible aspect both obvious and obscure, every disagreement whether new or old, every private interest at play, every whiff of conspiracy and scandal. At other times, they clothe themselves in the figure of that eternal citizen who intones in a ponderous, straitlaced manner that there are no laws without morals, *nisi lege sine moribus*. Others slip on the mask of a poor man's Marquis de Dangeau, giving meticulous accounts of the ribbons and laces that this, that, or the other lady was wearing to the ball or the theater. And all the while, Opportunity is strolling slowly by, head bowed, leaning on her little parasol; she passes, turns the corner, and *adieu* . . . The government's rotten to the core; silks and satins; *nisi lege sine moribus* . . .

I was on the point of telling my cousins to go ahead without me—we lived on Rua do Carmo and it wasn't far—but I thought better of it. Once we were out in the street, I also considered leaving my cousins to wait for me at the church, to see if I could seize Opportunity before it slipped away. I think I even paused for a moment, then rejected this notion, too, and carried on walking.

We continued in the opposite direction of the mystery woman. I turned and looked back many times, until she finally disappeared around a bend, her eyes fixed on the ground, like someone thinking, daydreaming, or waiting for an assignation. It would be no lie to say that this last thought made me jealous. I am exclusive and proprietary about these things; I would make a poor lover of married women. It matters little that between the lady and me there had been but a fleeting dalliance of a few hours; since my heart was set on her, sharing the spoils would be unbearable. I am also an imaginative fellow; I soon dreamed up an adventure and an adventurer; I succumbed to the morbid pleasure of tormenting myself, for no good reason. My cousins walked ahead of me, and spoke to me from time to time; I replied curtly, if at all, and silently, cordially cursed them.

When we arrived home, I looked at my watch, as if I had something I needed to do; then I said to my cousins to go in and begin lunch. I ran to Rua da Misericórdia. First, I went to the School of Medicine, then retraced my steps to the Chamber of Deputies, this time more slowly, hoping to see her at every turn in the street; but not a sign. It was foolish of me, I know. Even so, I went back up the street once again, because I realized that, since she was walking so very slowly, she would barely have had time to get halfway along the Santa Luzia seafront, unless, of course, she had stopped off somewhere first; and so on I went, up the street and out along the seafront, as far as the Ajuda Convent. I found nothing, absolutely nothing. But I didn't lose hope; I turned tail and came back, alternating between quick and slow, depending on whether or not I thought it possible to catch up with her, or, rather, to give her time to emerge from wherever she might be lurking. I had conjured her up so vividly in my imagination that my whole body trembled, as if she really might appear at any moment. I understood then how madmen must feel.

Still nothing. I came back down the street without finding the slightest trace of my mystery lady. Happy indeed are dogs, who can sniff out their friends! She might be nearby, inside some house, perhaps even her own? I thought of asking someone, but who and how? A baker, leaning against a doorway, was watching me; some women were doing the same, peeping through the hatch in their front doors. Naturally they were suspicious of this passerby, of his slow or hurried gait, his inquisitive gaze, his restless manner. I carried on to the Chamber of Deputies and stopped for about five minutes, not knowing what to do. It was nearly noon. I stood there waiting for another ten minutes, then another five, in the vain hope of seeing her; finally, I gave up and went to have lunch.

I didn't have lunch at home. I didn't want to see my blasted cousins, who had stopped me from following the mystery lady. I went to a hotel. I chose a table at the far end of the dining room and sat down with my back to the others; I didn't want to be seen or spoken to. I began eating whatever was put in front of me. I asked for some newspapers, but I confess that I didn't pay much attention and scarcely took in three-quarters of what I read. In the middle of a news item or opinion piece, my mind would slip and fall into Rua da Misericórdia, at the door of the church, watching the mystery lady pass slowly by, head bowed, leaning on her little parasol.

The last time this separation of higher and lower faculties occurred, I was already having my coffee, and had a parliamentary speech in front of me. I found myself once more at the church door; I imagined then that my cousins were not with me, and that I was following the lovely lady. This is how lottery losers console themselves; this is how thwarted ambitions are assuaged.

Don't ask me for details or preliminaries of the encounter. Dreams shun the fine lines and finishing touches of a landscape; they make do with four or five broad, but telling, brushstrokes. My imagination leapfrogged over the difficulties of the opening words, and went straight to Rua do Lavradio or Rua dos Inválidos, to the very home of Adriana. That was her name: Adriana. She hadn't gone to Rua da Misericórdia with amorous intentions, but to meet someone, a relative or female companion, or perhaps a seamstress. On meeting me, she felt the same stirrings. I wrote to her; she wrote back. Our souls cleaved unto each other, oblivious to the multitude of moral rules and dangers swirling beneath us. Adriana is married; her husband is fifty-two, she is getting on for thirty. She had never been in love, not even with her husband, whom she married out of obedience to her family. I taught her love and betrayal at the same time; that is what she told me in the little cottage I rented outside the city, just for the two us.

I listen to her, bewitched. I wasn't mistaken; she is the fiery, passionate woman her eyes—those large, doe eyes, like Juno's—were telling me she was. She lives for me and me alone. We write each other every day, and even so, each time we meet in our little love nest, it is as if a whole century had gone by. I even think her heart has taught me something, despite its inexperience, or perhaps because of it. In such matters practice makes imperfect, and true wisdom lies in ignorance. Adriana hides neither her happiness nor her tears; she writes what she thinks and says what she feels; she shows me that we are not two but one, one universal being, for whom God created the sun and the flowers, paper and ink, the daily post and closed carriages.

While I was imagining all this, I must have finished drinking my coffee; I remember the waiter came to the table and took away the cup and the sugar bowl. I don't know if I asked him for a light; he probably saw me with the cigar in my hand and brought me matches.

I can't swear to it, but I think I lit the cigar, because, a moment later, through a veil of smoke, I could see my beautiful Adriana's sweet, passionate head as she lay languidly on a sofa. I am kneeling, listening to her recounting the latest quarrel with her husband, who already suspects something; she's always going out, becomes distracted or absorbed, seems happy or sad for no reason. He has started issuing threats. What kind of threats? I tell her that it would be better to leave him before he goes too far, that she should come and live with me, openly, as man and wife. Adriana listens to me pensively, like Eve bewitched by the devil, whispering in her ear what her heart is already telling her. Her fingers are stroking my hair.

"Yes, yes, my love!"

She came the next day, on her own, without husband, society, or scruples, completely alone, and we went away to live together. Neither blatantly nor secretly. We thought of ourselves as foreigners and in reality that is what we were, for we spoke a language no one had ever spoken or heard before. Every other love affair, for centuries past, had been a complete counterfeit; ours was the first genuine edition. For the first time, the divine manuscript had been printed, a thick volume we divided into as many chapters and paragraphs as there were hours in the day or days in the week. The style was woven out of sunshine and music, the language composed from the flowers of other vocabularies. Everything gentle or vibrant had been extracted by the author to form this single volume—a book without an index, because it was infinite; without margins, so that boredom could not scribble its notes in them; and without a bookmark, because we no longer needed to interrupt our reading and mark the page.

A voice summoned me back to reality. It belonged to a friend who had woken late and come straight out for lunch. Even my dream wasn't safe from this "cousin from Sapucaia"! Five minutes later, I said goodbye and left the hotel; it was already two o'clock.

It pains me to say that I returned to Rua da Misericórdia, but I must tell all: I went, and found nothing. I returned on the days that followed, with nothing to show for it except wasted time. I resigned myself to giving up my adventure, or waiting for chance to intervene again. My cousins thought I was annoyed about something or else ill, and I said nothing to contradict this view. A week later, they left, and I had no reason to miss them; I shook them off as one would a nasty fever.

The image of my mystery lady remained with me for many weeks. On various occasions I mistook someone in the street for her. I would catch sight of a figure in the distance who looked just like her, and would quicken my step until I caught up and realized my error. I began to find myself ridiculous, but then another moment would come, a shadow in the distance, and my obsession would spring back into life. Eventually other concerns arose, and I thought no more about it.

At the beginning of the following year, I went up to Petrópolis to escape the summer heat. I made the journey with an old friend from university, Oliveira, who had gone on to become a public prosecutor in Minas Gerais, but had lately given up his career upon receiving an inheritance. He was as cheerful as he had been in our student days, but, from time to time, he would fall silent, gazing out from the boat or the carriage with the lethargy of someone salving his soul with a memory, a hope, or a desire. Once we were up in the mountains, I asked him which hotel he was going to; he answered that he was staying in a private house, but didn't say where and changed the subject. I thought he would visit me the next day, but he didn't, nor did I run into him anywhere else. Another friend of ours said he had a house somewhere over in the Renânia part of town.

I would have thought no more about this were it not for the news I received some days later. Oliveira had run off with another man's wife, and taken refuge with her in Petrópolis. They told me the husband's name, and hers. The woman's name was Adriana. I confess that, despite the mystery woman's name being pure invention, I was startled to hear it; could she possibly be the same person? I saw right away that this was asking a great deal of Chance. This poor servant of human affairs already has quite enough to do, pulling together life's disparate threads; asking him to tie all of them together and give them the same names is to leap from reality into a novel. This is what my common sense told me, and never had it uttered such foolishness so very gravely, for the two women were indeed one and the same.

I saw her three weeks later, when I went to visit Oliveira. He and I had again traveled up to Petrópolis from Rio the day before; halfway there, he had begun to feel unwell; by the time we reached the top, he was feverish. I accompanied him in the carriage as far as his house, but did not go in, because he wanted to spare me any further trouble. But the next day I went to see him, partly out of friendship and partly out of a desire to meet the mystery lady. I saw her and it was indeed her, the one and only, my very own Adriana.

Oliveira soon recovered, and, despite my readiness to visit him, he did not invite me to return to his house, instead coming to see me at my hotel. I respected his motives, but they served only to revive my former obsession. I assumed that, aside from reasons of decorum, he harbored feelings of jealousy, born of love, and that both such sentiments could be proof of the woman's fine and noble qualities. This in itself was a cause for dismay, but the idea that her passion might be no less than his, and the image of this couple forming one single body and soul, put every envious nerve in my body on edge. All my efforts to set foot inside his house failed; I even spoke to him about the rumor that was circulating, but he simply smiled and changed the subject.

The Petrópolis season ended, but he stayed on. I think he came back down to Rio in July or August. At the end of the year, we happened to bump into each other; I found him somewhat taciturn and preoccupied. I saw him several more times and he seemed no different, except that his brow now wore a long furrow of sadness. I imagined these to be the effects of his love affair, and, since I am not here to deceive anyone, I should add that it gave me a certain thrill of pleasure. This feeling was short-lived; it was the devil within me, who has a habit of making these clownish smirks. I promptly scolded him and replaced him with an angel, which I also have within me, and who took pity on the poor fellow regardless of the reason for his wretchedness.

One of Oliveira's neighbors, a friend of ours, told me something that confirmed my suspicions of domestic travails; but it was Oliveira himself who told me everything, one day when I rashly asked him what was wrong and why he seemed so changed.

"What do you think? Imagine I bought a lottery ticket and didn't even have the good fortune to win nothing. Instead, I won a scorpion."

I frowned and eyed him inquisitively.

"Ah! if you knew half the things that have befallen me! Do you have time? Let's go to the Passeio Público."

We entered the gardens and set off along one of the shady paths. He told me everything. He spent two hours giving me a long litany of miseries. His account revealed two completely incompatible temperaments, united by love or sin, utterly bored with each other, but condemned to hateful coexistence. He couldn't bear her, and he couldn't leave her. There was no mutual esteem or respect; any happiness was rare and tainted. In short, a life ruined.

"Ruined," he repeated, nodding. "There's nothing for it; my life is ruined. You'll remember those plans we made at college; you would be minister of internal affairs and I would be minister of justice. Well, you can have both portfolios now; I will never be anything. The egg that should have hatched into an eagle won't even produce a chicken. Yes, completely ruined. I've been like this for a year and a half, and I can see no way out; I've lost every ounce of ambition."

When I met him six months later, he was in a frantic, wretched state. Adriana had left him to go and study "geometry" with a student at the old Central School of Engineering. "It's for the best," I said to him. Oliveira hung his head in shame, then mumbled a goodbye and ran off after her. He found her several weeks later; they said their worst to each other, and in the end were reconciled. I then began to visit them, with the idea of separating them. She was still pretty and fascinating, with elegant, gentle manners, but these were evidently insincere, for they were accompanied by certain poses and gestures whose underlying aim was to entice and lure me in.

I took fright and pulled away. She had no shame whatsoever; she threw off her prim lace cape and revealed her true nature. I saw then that she was steely, scheming, unscrupulous, and often vulgar; in some situations I noticed a streak of depravity in her. At first Oliveira put up with everything, laughing, hoping to make me believe it was all lies or exaggerations; it was shame at his own weakness. But he could not keep the mask on; one day she pulled it off, pitilessly revealing all the humiliations he suffered when I wasn't there. I felt disgust for her, and pity for the poor fellow. I openly encouraged him to leave her; he hesitated, but promised that he would.

"You're right. I can't take it any longer . . ."

We made all the arrangements, but, at the last moment, he simply couldn't do it. Once again, she fixed him with her doe-eyed, basilisk stare, and this time—Oh, my dear, dear cousins from Sapucaia!—this time left him exhausted and dead.

A LADY

WHENEVER I ENCOUNTER this particular lady, I'm always reminded of the prophecy made by a lizard to Heine, when the poet was climbing the Apennines: "The day will come when stones will become plants, plants become animals, animals become men, and men become gods." And it makes me want to say to her: "My dear Dona Camila, you so loved youth and beauty that you turned back the clock to see if you could fix those two shimmering moments forever in time. Do not despair, Dona Camila. When the lizard's day comes, you will be Hebe, goddess of youth, and from your eternally youthful hands we will drink the nectar of everlasting life."

The first time I saw her she was thirty-six years old, although she looked only thirty-two and still clung hopefully to the house of twenty-nine. "House" is a manner of speaking. No castle is grander than the dwelling occupied by that tender age, nor anything more flattering than the hospitality it offers to those who pass through its doors. Every time Dona Camila tried to leave, it begged her to stay, and stay she did. Yet more amusements would follow: games, music, dancing—a succession of delightful distractions concocted with the sole aim of keeping this lady from going on her way.

"Mama, Mama," her growing daughter would say, "let's go. We can't stay here forever."

Dona Camila would look at her, mortified, then smile, give her a kiss, and tell her to go play with the other children. What other children? By then

Ernestina was fourteen or fifteen; tall for her age, very quiet, and already beginning to behave like a young lady. She would probably not much enjoy playing with little girls of eight or nine, but never mind; as long as she left her mother in peace, it scarcely mattered whether she was happy or bored. But, alas, all good things must come to an end, even the age of twenty-nine.

Dona Camila finally resolved to bid farewell to her generous host, and did so full of regrets. Her host begged her to hold off for five or six months, but the gracious lady replied that it was quite impossible and, mounting the sorrel horse of time, she trotted off to dwell in the house of thirty.

She was, however, one of those women who scorn both sun and almanacs. With a milk-white complexion, fresh and unchanging, she left the task of aging to others; she wanted only the task of living. She had jet-black hair and warm chestnut-brown eyes. Her neck and shoulders seemed made for wearing *décolleté* dresses, likewise her arms, which, to avoid a rather hackneyed simile, I will not compare to those of the Venus de Milo, but they can scarcely be described otherwise. Dona Camila knew this; she knew she was pretty, not only because the furtive glances of other ladies told her so, but by virtue of a certain instinct that beauty possesses, as do talent and genius. I should add that she was married, that her husband had ginger hair, and that they were still as in love with each other as newlyweds. And, finally, that she was an honest woman, not, please note, by temperament but on principle, out of love for her husband, and, I believe, a little out of pride.

Not a single flaw, then, except that of holding back the years. But is that a flaw? I don't remember where it says in the Scriptures—one of the prophets, naturally—that days are like the waters of a river that can never turn back. Dona Camila wanted to build a dam for her own personal use. In the turmoil of this continual march from birth to death, she clung to the illusion of stability. All one could ask of her was not to make herself an object of ridicule, and she didn't. The reader will tell me that beauty lives of and for itself, and that her preoccupation with the calendar shows that this lady was more concerned with what other people thought. That much is true, but how else do you expect women to live in this day and age?

Dona Camila entered the house of thirty, and the move was not so very difficult. Evidently her fears were unfounded. Two or three close friends, well versed in arithmetic, continued to say that she had lost count of the years. They did not add that nature was complicit in the error, and at forty—

yes, forty!—Dona Camila still appeared to be in her early thirties. They had one last resort: to catch sight of her first gray hair, just one little gray hair. They spied on her in vain; her wretched hair seemed blacker than ever.

In this they were mistaken. The gray hair was there, in the shape of Dona Camila's daughter, who was just turning nineteen and, for her sins, was very pretty indeed. Dona Camila persisted as long as she could in giving her daughter girlish dresses to wear, keeping her at convent school beyond the usual age, and doing everything possible to proclaim her still a child. Nature, however, is not only immoral but illogical, and while it held back the mother's years, it loosened the reins on her daughter's. Ernestina, now a grown woman, made a dazzling entrance at her first ball. She was a revelation. Dona Camila adored her daughter and drank in her glory in slow, deep draughts. At the bottom of the cup, though, she found a bitter drop and grimaced. She even considered abdicating her throne, but a man who was never at a loss for words told her that she looked like Ernestina's elder sister, and so she abandoned the idea. From then on, Dona Camila began telling everyone that she had married very young.

One day, a few months later, the first suitor appeared on the horizon. Dona Camila had vaguely considered such a calamity, but without really facing up to it or preparing her defense. When she least expected it, she found an admirer on her doorstep. She quizzed her daughter and discovered in her an indefinable excitement, natural in a girl of twenty. Dona Camila was devastated. Marrying off her daughter was the least of it; for if human beings are like those waters in the Scriptures that never turn back, it is because others come after them, and it is in order to give a name to these successive waves of humanity that mankind invented the word "grandchildren." Dona Camila could see that her first grandchild would soon be approaching, and was determined to delay it. Clearly she didn't precisely formulate this resolution, just as she had not precisely formulated the danger she was in. The soul understands itself instinctively; a feeling is worth as much as rational thought. The feelings she had were obscure and fleeting, existing somewhere in the depths of her being, whence she chose not to dredge them up, so as not to have to face them.

"But what's wrong with Ribeiro?" her husband asked her one night, standing by the window.

Dona Camila shrugged.

"He has a crooked nose," she said.

"Don't be cruel. You're upset. Let's talk about something else," her husband replied. And, after gazing out into the street for a couple of minutes and humming to himself, he returned to the subject of Ribeiro, whom he considered an entirely acceptable son-in-law. If the young man asked for Ernestina's hand, he thought they should say yes. He was intelligent and polite. He was also likely to inherit from an aunt in Cantagalo. And, furthermore, he had a heart of gold. People said charming things about him. At college, for example . . . Dona Camila listened, tapping her foot and drumming impatiently with her fingers. But when her husband said that Ribeiro was expecting a position in the foreign ministry, a posting to the United States, she could not contain herself and cut him short:

"What? Separate me from my daughter? Certainly not."

The relative proportions of maternal love and personal sentiment present in this protest is a difficult matter to resolve, especially now, so far removed from the events and people involved. Let's suppose they were present in equal parts. The truth is that her husband didn't know what to say in defense of the foreign ministry, the needs of the diplomatic service, or the inevitability of marriage. Lost for words, he went off to bed. Two days later, the appointment was made. The day after, the young lady told Ribeiro not to ask her father for her hand, because she did not want to be separated from her family. It was tantamount to saying: "I prefer my family to you." It's true that she said this in a faint and trembling voice, and with an air of profound consternation, but Ribeiro heard only the rejection, and promptly boarded ship. Thus ended the first adventure.

It pained Dona Camila to see her daughter so upset, but she was soon consoled. There was no lack of potential bridegrooms, she reflected. To console her daughter, she took her out and about in Rio. Both of them were pretty, and Ernestina had all the freshness of youth, but her mother's beauty was more perfect and, despite her age, surpassed that of her daughter. We won't go so far as to believe that it was this feeling of superiority that encouraged Dona Camila to prolong and repeat their frequent outings. No, maternal love alone explains everything. But let's concede that it did provide a little encouragement. What's wrong with that? What is the harm in a brave colonel nobly defending both his country and his gleaming epaulets? None of it precludes a love of country or a mother's love.

A few months later, the second suitor appeared. This time he was a widower, a lawyer, and twenty-seven years old. Ernestina did not have the same feelings for him as she had for the first suitor, but she accepted him anyway. Dona Camila quickly made inquiries. She could find nothing to object to: his nose was as straight as his conscience, and he had a profound aversion to diplomatic life. But there would be other flaws; there must be. Dona Camila moved heaven and earth to find them; she inquired about his relations, his habits, and his past. She managed to find a few snippets here and there, but only a sliver of human imperfection: a certain moodiness, a lack of intellectual refinement, and, finally, an excessive self-regard. It was on the latter point that the good lady caught him. Slowly, she began to build a wall of silence; first, she laid down a layer of pauses of increasing duration, then came the clipped sentences, then the monosyllables, distractions, glazed eyes, condescending stares, and feigned yawns behind her fan. Initially, he did not understand, but when he realized that the mother's boredom coincided with her daughter's absences, he sensed that his presence was not welcome and withdrew. Had he been made of sterner stuff, he would have scaled that wall of silence; but he was proud and weak. Dona Camila gave thanks to the gods.

There followed a three-month respite. Then several short-lived flirtations made an appearance; ephemeral blowflies that lasted only a night and left no trace behind them. Dona Camila realized that they were bound to multiply, until something more substantive came along and forced her to give way. But, at the very least, she told herself, she wanted a son-in-law who would bring her daughter the same happiness that her own husband gave her. Once, either to reinforce this declaration of intent or for some other motive, she repeated this thought out loud, even though only she could hear it. You, shrewd psychologist that you are, may well imagine that she was trying to convince herself, but I prefer to tell you what happened to her in 186* . . .

It was morning. Dona Camila was sitting at her mirror, the window open, the verdant garden alive with the sound of cicadas and birds. She felt herself completely at one with the world outside. Only intellectual beauty is independent and superior. Physical beauty is the twin sister of landscape. Dona Camila relished this intimate, secret kinship, a feeling of oneness, a recollection of a previous life sharing the same divine womb. No unpleasant memories, no untoward circumstance came to cloud this mysterious feeling. On the contrary, everything seemed to imbue her with eternity, and her forty-two years weighed upon her no more than an equal number of rose petals. She looked out of the window, then back at the mirror. Suddenly, as if a snake had sprung up before her, she recoiled in terror. She had spotted, above her left temple, a small gray hair. For a moment she thought it must be one of her husband's, but quickly realized it was her own, a telegram from old age, marching ineluctably toward her. She was utterly devastated. Dona Camila felt everything slipping away from her; she would be a gray-haired old hag within a week.

"Mama, Mama!" cried Ernestina, entering her mother's sitting room. "Here are the tickets for the box seats that Papa ordered!"

Dona Camila felt a jolt of shame, and instinctively turned toward her daughter the side of her head unsullied by the gray hair. Never had Ernestina looked so graceful and spry. Dona Camila gazed at her lovingly. She gazed also with envy, and, to smother this unworthy feeling, she snatched the theater tickets from her hand. The performance was that very night. One thought drove out the other; Dona Camila imagined herself surrounded by lights and people, and her spirits quickly rose. Once she was alone again, she turned back to face the mirror, courageously plucked out the gray hair, and blew it into the garden. *Out, damned spot! Out!* More fortunate than that other Lady Macbeth, she watched her stain disappear into thin air, because in her mind, old age was remorse, and ugliness was a crime. Out, damned spot, out!

But if remorse can return, why not gray hairs? A month later, Dona Camila discovered another lurking in her thick, dark, beautiful locks, and ruthlessly amputated it. Five or six weeks later, she found another. The third gray hair coincided with a third candidate for her daughter's hand, and both these things left Dona Camila utterly devastated. Beauty, which, in her case, had made up for vanishing youth, also seemed ready to depart, like a dove flying off in search of its mate. The days raced by. Children she had seen in their mothers' arms, or in perambulators pushed by their nannies, now danced at balls. The boys were now men and had taken to smoking; the girls sang songs at the piano. Several of the latter group presented her with their chubby little babies; the next generation were suckling at their mother's breast, waiting for their turn to go dancing, or singing, or smoking, and then showing off their own babies to other people, and on and on it would go.

Dona Camila prevaricated only a little before giving in. There was nothing to be done; she must accept the inevitability of a son-in-law. However, just as old habits die hard, Dona Camila saw, in parallel, that such a festival of love was also a stage, indeed a very grand stage. She prepared herself enthusiastically, and the effect matched her efforts. At the church among the other ladies, and in her drawing room seated on the sofa (covered with upholstery which, like the wallpaper, was always dark, so as to accentuate Dona Camila's fair complexion), she was exquisitely dressed, with neither youthful whimsy nor matronly severity; a happy medium that served to highlight her autumnal graces, smiling and happy. In sum, the brand-new mother-in-law received the warmest of praise. Clearly a few shreds of the royal purple still hung from her shoulders.

Purple implies dynasty. Dynasty requires grandchildren. All that remained was for the Lord to bless the union, and He did so the following year. Dona Camila had gotten used to the idea, but abdicating her throne was so painful that she awaited the grandchild with a mixture of love and repugnance. Did the Earth really need this troublesome embryo, so puffed-up and curious about life? Evidently not, but it nevertheless appeared one day, along with the flowers of spring. During the most critical phase, Dona Camila had only to think of her daughter; once the danger had passed she had both a daughter and a grandson to think about. Only days later could she think of herself. Finally, she was a grandmother. No ifs, no buts, she was a grandmother. Neither her features, which were still perfection, nor her hair, which was still black (except for half a dozen stray hairs, carefully concealed), could by themselves betray reality, but the reality existed: she was, finally, a grandmother.

She wanted to hide away. To have her grandson nearby, she asked her daughter to come and live with her. But her house was no monastery, and the streets and newspapers, with their constant chatter, awoke in her echoes of times gone by. She therefore tore up the instrument of abdication and returned to the fray.

One fine day, I saw her standing beside a black nanny who was cradling a baby of five or six months. Dona Camila was holding up her little parasol to shade the baby. I saw her again a week later, with the same baby, the same black nanny, and the same parasol. Three weeks later, and again a month later, I saw her again, getting onto the streetcar with the black nanny and the baby. "Have you already fed him?" she asked the black woman. "Watch the sun. Don't trip. Don't hold him so tightly. Is he awake? Don't disturb him. Cover his little face." And so on.

It was, of course, her grandson. However, she paid such close and careful attention to the baby, so frequently and with no other lady in sight, that she seemed more mother than grandmother. Indeed, many people thought so. As to whether this was Dona Camila's intention, I cannot swear ("Swear not"—Matthew 5:34). I can only say that no mother could have been more vigilant than Dona Camila with her grandson; to assume he was her son was the most natural thing in the world.

PECUNIARY ANECDOTE

———

T HE MAN IN QUESTION is called Falcão. On that day—April 14, 1870—
anyone who came into his house, at ten o'clock at night, would have
seen him pacing up and down the parlor in his shirtsleeves, black pants, and
white necktie, muttering, gesticulating, and sighing to himself, evidently
greatly troubled. At times, he would sit, or stop and lean against the window, looking out at the shoreline in Gamboa. But whichever position or
pose he adopted, he didn't maintain it for very long.

"It was wrong of me," he kept saying, "very wrong of me. She was always
so kind to me! Such a sweet, loving creature! She was crying, poor thing! It
was wrong of me, very wrong . . . Well, I hope she may at least be happy!"

If I were to tell you that this man had sold one of his nieces, you would
not believe me. If I were to go so far as to state the price, ten *contos de réis*,
you would turn your back on me in scorn and indignation. And yet it is
enough to see his feline gaze and his two lips—those masters of calculation
that seemed to be counting something even when they were closed—to
guess immediately that our fellow's principal characteristic is his voracious
appetite for profit. Let us be perfectly clear: he believes in art for art's sake;
he does not love money for what it can give, but for what it intrinsically is.
No one can interest him in the pleasures of life. He has neither soft bed
nor fine table, neither carriage nor grandiose titles. "Money isn't earned to
be squandered," he says. He lives on crumbs; everything he accumulates
is for his private contemplation. He often goes to check his safe, which he

keeps in his bedroom, with the sole purpose of feasting his eyes on the neat stacks of gold coins and bundles of stocks and shares. At other times, out of a refined sense of pecuniary eroticism, he contemplates them from memory alone. In this regard, I can do no more than quote the man himself, in 1857.

By then already a millionaire, or almost, he encountered two boys in the street, who were well known to him and who asked him whether a five-*mil-réis* note their uncle had given them was genuine. There were some counterfeit banknotes circulating at the time, and the boys had remembered this on their way home. Falcão was with a friend of his. He took the note, trembling, and examined it carefully, turning it this way and that.

"Is it fake?" asked one of the boys impatiently.

"No, it's real."

"Give it here," said both boys.

Falcão slowly folded the note up, without taking his eyes off it. Then he gave it back to the boys, and, turning to his patiently waiting friend, he said with a look of utter candor on his face:

"It's always a pleasure to see money, even when it's not your own."

This was how much he loved money, even in disinterested contemplation. What other motive could have brought him to linger outside the money changers' windows for five, ten, or even fifteen minutes, salivating over the piles of sovereigns and francs, so neatly stacked and yellow? His shiver of alarm upon touching the five-*mil-réis* note was but a subtle manifestation of his abiding fear of fake banknotes. Nothing upset him as much as counterfeiters, not because they were criminals, but because of their detrimental and demoralizing effect on the genuine article.

Falcão's own words merit close study. So it is that one day, in 1864, returning from a friend's funeral and describing the splendor of the procession, he exclaimed enthusiastically: "There were three thousand *contos* carrying the coffin!" And, as one of the bystanders didn't immediately understand what he meant, Falcão assumed in astonishment that the man did not believe him, and itemized the pallbearers as follows: "You-know-who at the front is worth four hundred; the fellow beside him, six hundred. Yes, six hundred, mark my words; when he wound up that business with his father-in-law two years ago, it was worth more than five hundred, but let's call it five . . ." And on he went, adding them up one by one and concluding: "Three thousand *contos* exactly!"

He was not married. To marry was to throw money away. But the years passed, and, at forty-five, he began to feel a certain moral necessity, which he did not immediately understand, for that need was the longing to be a father. He didn't want a wife or relatives, mind you, but to have a son or daughter would be like receiving a precious gold coin. Unfortunately, this other kind of capital should have been accumulated a long time ago, and it was too late to start earning it now. All that remained was the lottery, and the lottery brought him the grand prize.

His brother died and then, three months later, so did his sister-in-law, leaving an eleven-year-old daughter. He was very fond both of this niece and another one, the daughter of a widowed sister; he bestowed kisses on them when he visited, and his enthusiasm even stretched, on several occasions, to taking them some cookies. He hesitated somewhat, but, finally, he took in the orphan; she was the daughter he had always wanted. He could scarcely contain his happiness; for the first few weeks, he barely left the house and was always at her side, listening to her stories and silliness.

Her name was Jacinta. She wasn't pretty, but she had a melodious voice and a gentle manner. She could already read and write, and was starting to learn music. Her piano came with her along with what she had learned and a few exercises; she couldn't bring her piano teacher, for her uncle thought it better to carry on practicing what she knew already, and one day, perhaps later . . . Eleven, twelve, thirteen—every year that passed was another tie that bound the old bachelor to his adopted daughter, and vice versa. At thirteen, Jacinta was running the household; by seventeen she was its true mistress. She did not abuse her power; she was naturally modest, frugal, and thrifty.

"An angel!" said Falcão to Chico Borges.

This Chico Borges fellow was forty years old and owned a warehouse. He played cards with Falcão in the evenings. Jacinta accompanied them when they played. By then she was eighteen; she was no prettier, but everyone said that she was "improving with age." She was petite, and the warehouse owner liked petite women. They wrote to each other, and courtship turned to passion.

"Right, let's get down to it," said Chico Borges as he entered the room one evening, shortly after dusk.

The card games were the two lovers' discreet parasol. The two men didn't play for real money, but Falcão had such a thirst for profit that he drooled over his worthless counters, and totted them up every ten minutes, just to see if he was winning or losing. When he was losing, a terrible look of dejection would come over his face, and he would withdraw into silence. If bad luck continued to pursue him, he would stop the game and rise to his feet, so absorbed in his own melancholy that his niece and Chico Borges could clasp each other's hand once, twice, or even three times, without him even noticing.

This was in 1869. At the beginning of 1870, Falcão offered to sell some shares to Chico Borges. He didn't yet own the shares, but his nose told him the stock market was about to crash, and he reckoned he could make thirty to forty *contos* from Chico Borges in one go. The latter replied delicately that he had been thinking of making the very same proposal to Falcão. Since they both wished to sell and neither wished to buy, why didn't they club together and offer to sell to a third party? They found just such a third party, and signed the contract with sixty days for delivery. On their way home from closing the deal, Falcão was in such good spirits that his partner opened his heart to him and asked for Jacinta's hand. Falcão stopped in his tracks, as stunned and bewildered as if Borges had suddenly started speaking Turkish. Hand over his niece? But . . .

"Yes, I confess that I would very much like to marry her, and she . . . I think that she, too, would very much like to marry me."

"What? Absolutely not!" said Falcão, interrupting him. "No, sir. She's still a child; I will not consent."

"At least think about it . . ."

"I will not think about it; I will not have it."

He arrived home feeling angry and afraid. His niece cajoled him into telling her what was the matter, and he ended up telling her everything, even calling her thoughtless and ungrateful. Jacinta turned pale; she loved both her uncle and Chico Borges, and thought them such good friends that she had never imagined this clash of affections. In her bedroom she wept profusely; then she wrote a letter to Chico Borges, begging him, for the love of Christ and His five Holy Wounds, that he neither make a fuss nor fight with her uncle; she told him she would wait, and swore eternal love.

The two friends did not fight, but Borges's visits naturally became fewer and chillier. Jacinta did not come down to the parlor, or else withdrew quickly. Falcão was petrified. He loved his niece with a dog-like devotion, the kind of dog that snaps at the heels of strangers. He wanted her for himself, not as a man, but as a father. Natural fatherhood provides its own strength for the sacrifice of separation, but his fatherhood was on loan, and, perhaps for that very reason, more selfish. He had never considered losing her; now, however, he took endless precautions: closing the shutters, warning the servants, mounting a perpetual vigil, spying on her every word and deed; in other words, a campaign worthy of Don Bartolo in *The Barber of Seville*.

Meanwhile, the sun, that model of public officialdom, continued punctually to serve the passing days, one by one, until the two-month period for delivery of the shares was up. By then the share price should have gone down, but, like lotteries and wars, the stock market scorns human calculations. In this particular case, scorn was met by cruelty, for the price neither fell nor stayed the same; it rose to such an extent that the expected profit of forty *contos* became a loss of twenty.

It was at this point that Chico Borges had an ingenious idea. That evening, while Falcão paced the room in silent, dejected disappointment, Chico Borges proposed that he would finance the whole of the shortfall if Falcão gave him his niece. Falcão was dumbstruck.

"You want me to—"

"Precisely," interrupted Chico Borges, smiling.

"No, certainly not."

He would not hear of it, and refused three or four times. His first reaction had been one of happiness at the ten *contos* he would save, but the idea of being parted from Jacinta was unbearable, and so he refused. He slept badly. In the morning, he reviewed the situation, and, weighing up all the factors, concluded that, in handing Jacinta over to Chico Borges, he wouldn't be losing her entirely, whereas if he didn't, the ten *contos* would be irretrievably lost. Furthermore, if she liked him and he liked her, who was he to keep them apart? All daughters get married, and their fathers content themselves with seeing them happy. He hurried over to Chico Borges's house, and they reached an agreement.

"It was wrong of me, very wrong," he bawled on the night of the wedding. "So kind to me! Such a sweet, loving creature . . . She was crying, poor thing! It was wrong of me, very wrong."

The terror of losing the ten *contos* had passed, but the tedium of solitude had just begun. The following morning, he went to visit the two newlyweds. Jacinta did not just treat him to a good lunch, she showered him with love and affection, but neither her affection nor the lunch restored his spirits. On the contrary, the newlyweds' happiness made him sadder still. When he returned to his own house he felt lost without Jacinta's gentle face. Never again would he hear her girlish songs; no longer would it be Jacinta who made his tea, nor, at night, when he wanted to read, would she be the one to bring him his well-thumbed old copy of *St. Clair of the Isles*, a gift from 1850.

"It was wrong of me, very wrong . . ."

To right the wrong, he moved the card games to his niece's house, and would go there, in the evenings, to play cards with Chico Borges. But when fortune decides to punish a man, she takes away all his winnings. Four months later, the young couple took themselves off to Europe; his solitude now stretched the entire width of the ocean. By this time, Falcão was fifty-four. He was reconciled to Jacinta's marriage and had even planned to go and live with them, either at no cost to himself or by making some small contribution, which, he had calculated, would still be far more economical than living alone. All these plans now crumbled into dust; there he was, back in the same situation as eight years before, with the difference that fate had snatched the cup away from him between sips.

Then, suddenly, another niece landed upon him. This was the daughter of his widowed sister, who, on her deathbed, had asked him to take care of her daughter. Falcão promised nothing, because a certain instinct told him not to promise anything to anyone, but he did in fact take in his niece, no sooner than his sister's body was cold. There was no reticence on his part; on the contrary, he opened the doors of his house to her with a feverish excitement, and almost gave thanks to God for his sister's death. Once again, here was the daughter he had never had.

"She'll be the one at my bedside when I die," he said to himself.

It wasn't easy. Virgínia was eighteen, a genuinely original beauty; she was both tall and attractive. To avoid the risk of anyone taking her away from him, Falcão picked up where he had left off the first time around: closed shutters, warnings to servants, rare outings, or only with him and with her eyes modestly lowered. Virgínia didn't seem bothered.

"I was never one for gazing out of windows," she would say, "and I think it's hardly becoming for a young lady to spend all her time wandering the streets."

Another of Falcão's precautions was never to bring card players to the house unless they were over fifty or married. In short, he stopped caring about falls in the stock market. But all of this proved unnecessary, because Virgínia didn't really care for anything except him and the house. Sometimes, as her uncle's sight was beginning to fail, she herself would read to him a page or two from St. Clair of the Isles. Since there was sometimes a lack of partners, she learned to play cards and, realizing that her uncle liked to win, she always made a point of losing. She went still further: when she was losing badly, she would pretend to be angry or sad, with the sole aim of increasing her uncle's pleasure. He would roar with laughter, make fun of her, say her nose was too big, and ask for a handkerchief to wipe away her tears, but he carried on adding up his counters every ten minutes, and if one fell on the floor (they used corn kernels), he would rummage around with the candle to find it.

Three months later, Falcão fell ill. It wasn't a serious or prolonged illness, but a fear of death nevertheless gripped his soul and it became clear then how very fond he was of his niece. Every visitor to the house was received coldly, or at least with indifference. Those closest to him suffered the most, for he would tell them brutally that he was not yet a corpse, that the flesh was still living, that the vultures had picked up the wrong scent, and so on. Virgínia, however, never saw in him the merest glimmer of bad humor. Falcão obeyed her in everything, with a childlike docility, and when he laughed, it was because she made him laugh.

"Come on, be good and take your medicine. You're my little boy now . . ."

Falcão would smile and sip the syrupy concoction. She sat beside the bed, telling him stories; she kept an eye on the clock for when it was time for his soup or chicken broth; she read to him from the everlasting and eternal St. Clair. Then came convalescence. Falcão went out for a few gentle strolls, accompanied by Virgínia. When she offered him her arm, her uncle was delighted to see the care with which she kept her eyes fixed firmly on the cobblestones, for fear of catching a man's gaze.

"She'll be the one at my bedside when I die," he repeated to himself. One day, he even thought it out loud: "Isn't it true that you'll be at my bedside when I die?"

"Don't talk such nonsense!"

Even though they were in a public place, he stopped and clasped her hands in gratitude, not knowing what to say. Had he possessed the ability to cry, his eyes would doubtless have grown moist with tears. When they arrived home, Virgínia rushed to her room to reread a letter that a certain

Dona Bernarda, an old friend of her mother's, had given her the day before. It was postmarked from New York, and the only signature was the name "Reginaldo." One passage read as follows:

> *I leave here by steamer on the twenty-fifth. Wait for me without*
> *fail. I don't yet know if I will be able to come and see you straight away.*
> *Your uncle may well remember me; he saw me at the house of my uncle,*
> *Chico Borges, on the day of your cousin's wedding . . .*

Forty days later, the same Reginaldo disembarked in Rio; he was a young man of thirty and with three hundred thousand dollars to his name. Twenty-four hours later, he visited Falcão, who received him courteously, but nothing more. Reginaldo, though, was shrewd and practical; he struck a chord with the other man, and it resonated. He regaled him with tales of the fortunes to be made in the United States, and the waves of money that washed from one ocean to the other. Falcão listened in amazement and wanted to hear more. Reginaldo then provided him with an extensive account of companies and banks, stocks and shares, public expenditure, private fortunes, the municipal revenues of New York; he described the mighty palaces of commerce . . .

"It truly is a great country," said Falcão from time to time. And after a few minutes' reflection: "But from what you tell me, there's only gold."

"No, not gold alone; there's lots of silver and paper money too; but, up there, paper and gold are the same thing. And as for coins from other countries, well, I must show you the collection I brought back with me. If you want to see what sort of place it is, you need look no further. I went there a poor man at the age of twenty-three; seven years later, I arrived back here with six hundred *contos*."

Falcão quivered. "At your age," he confessed, "I had barely one hundred."

He was captivated. Reginaldo said it would take him two or three weeks to tell him all the miracles of the American dollar.

"What's that you call it?"

"The dollar."

"You perhaps won't believe it, but I've never even seen a dollar."

Reginaldo took a dollar coin out of his vest pocket and showed it to him. Before touching it, Falcão devoured it with his eyes. As it was somewhat dark inside, he stood up and went to the window to get a good look at it—

from both sides. He then returned it, warmly praising how well it had been designed and minted, and adding that our old *patacas* were also rather fine.

The visits continued. Reginaldo resolved to ask for the young lady's hand. She, however, told him that he must first earn her uncle's blessing; she would not marry against his wishes. Undaunted, Reginaldo redoubled his efforts, overwhelming the uncle with tales of fabulous dividends.

"By the way," Falcão said to him one day, "you never did show me your coin collection."

"Come to my house tomorrow."

Falcão went, and Reginaldo showed him the collection, displayed in a magnificent glass cabinet. Falcão was flabbergasted; he had expected a little box with one specimen of each coin, and instead found mounds of gold, silver, bronze, and copper. At first Falcão gazed at them in universal and collective wonder; then he began to study them one by one. He only knew the pounds, dollars, and francs, but Reginaldo named all of them: florins, crowns, rubles, drachmas, piastres, pesos, rupees—the entire numismatics of toil, he concluded poetically.

"But what patience you showed in putting this collection together!" said Falcão.

"Oh, it wasn't me," replied Reginaldo. "The collection belonged to the estate of a man from Philadelphia. I bought it for a trifle—five thousand dollars."

In reality, of course, it was worth a great deal more. Falcão left Reginaldo's house with the collection embedded in his soul. He told his niece about it and, in his imagination, he untidied and re-tidied the coins, the way a lover tousles his sweetheart's hair just in order to smooth it down again. At night, he dreamt he was a florin, tossed by a lansquenet player onto the card table, and that he returned to the player's pocket with more than two hundred other florins. In the morning, as consolation, he went to examine the coins that he kept in his own safe, but nothing would console him. The finest possessions are those we don't possess.

A few days later, at home, in the parlor, he thought he saw some money lying on the floor. He bent down to pick it up; it wasn't money, just a letter. He opened it absentmindedly and read it in horror: it was from Reginaldo to Virgínia . . . But the reader interrupts me, crying:

"Enough! I can guess the rest. Virgínia married Reginaldo, the coins passed into Falcão's hands, and they turned out to be fake . . ."

No, dear reader, they were genuine. It would indeed be more moral if, to punish our man, they were counterfeit. But, alas! I am no Seneca; I am more like a Suetonius, who would recount the death of Caesar ten times over if that would bring him back to life, and yet Caesar would only return to life if he could also return to his empire.

FULANO

COME WITH ME, dear reader, to hear the will of my dear friend Fulano Beltrão. Did you know him? Now, stop sniggering; that's not his real name, of course, but does it really matter what the fellow was called? Anyway, he was nearly sixty years old and he died yesterday, January 2, 1884, at half-past eleven at night. You can't imagine the strength of mind he showed throughout his illness. He fell ill on Halloween, and at first we all assumed it was nothing to worry about, but the illness persisted and, just over two months later, death carried him off.

I must confess that I'm very curious to hear the will. It's bound to contain several provisions that are of both general interest and to his credit. It would not have been so prior to 1863, because, up until then, he was a man who kept very much to himself, living quietly on the road that leads to the Jardim Botânico, to where he would journey by omnibus or mule. He had a wife and son, and an unmarried daughter then age thirteen. It was in that year that he began to concern himself with other things besides his family, revealing a universal and generous spirit, although I cannot say why. I believe, however, that it began with a tribute from a friend on the occasion of his fortieth birthday. Fulano Beltrão read in the *Jornal do Commercio*, on March 5, 1864, an anonymous article in which many a fine and true thing was said about him: a good husband and father, a loyal friend, a worthy citizen, a pure and noble soul. To do him such ample justice was remarkable in itself; to do so anonymously was rare indeed.

"You'll see," said Fulano Beltrão to his wife, "it will be Xavier or Castro who's behind this; we'll unmask them soon enough."

Castro and Xavier were two regular visitors to the house, constant partners in games of ombre and old friends of my late friend. Kind words were always spoken on the occasion of his birthday on March 5, but this usually happened over dinner, in the intimacy of the family circle, between four walls; it was the first time he had been blessed with tributes in the press. I may be wrong, but I am of the opinion that this display of justice, the material proof that fine qualities and good deeds do not go unnoticed, was what first encouraged my friend to place himself in the public eye, to see and be seen, and to bestow on human society a few of the virtues he had been born with. He marveled to think that thousands of other people would be reading the article at the same time as him, and he imagined them commenting, querying, and confirming what they had read; indeed, thanks to a phenomenon of hallucination that science will someday explain, and which is not that uncommon, he really did hear, quite distinctly, several of those readers' voices. He heard them describe him as a good man, a worthy gentleman, a loyal friend, hardworking and honest: all the qualifications he had seen employed to describe others, and which in his quiet, reclusive life he had never presumed would be applied—typographically—to him.

"The printing press is a great invention," he said to his wife.

It was Dona Maria Antônia who unmasked the author; the article was indeed by Xavier. He declared that he was only admitting this out of consideration for the lady of the house, and added that the tribute had not been as fulsome as he had intended, because his plan had been for the article to be published in all the newspapers, but, in the end, he had only finished writing it at seven o'clock in the evening and there had been no time to make copies. Fulano Beltrão corrected this failing, if it could be called a failing, by having the article transcribed in the *Diário do Rio* and the *Correio Mercantil*.

Even if this event does not explain the change in our friend's life, the fact remains that, from that year onward, and, more precisely, from the month of March, Fulano began to appear more often in public. Until then, he had been a stick-in-the-mud who didn't attend society gatherings, didn't vote in political elections, and didn't go to the theaters, or to anything at all. But already by the end of March, on the twenty-second or twenty-third, he had presented the Santa Casa de Misericórdia Hospital with a Spanish lottery ticket, and received a dignified letter from the chairman, thanking him on behalf of the poor. He consulted his wife and friends as to whether he should publish the letter or put it away, being somewhat concerned that *not* publishing it might be seen as a discourtesy. And so, on March 26, the letter was sent to all the papers, one of which added an extensive commentary on the pious devotion of the donor. Of those who read the piece, many naturally remembered Xavier's article, and linked the two: "Why, it's that very same Fulano Beltrão who . . ." etc. Such are the foundations upon which a man's reputation is built.

It's getting late, and we have to go and hear the will, so I shan't give all the details now, but will simply say that the iniquities of life found in him an active and eloquent avenger, and that misery, particularly the dramatic sort, begotten of fire or flood, found in my friend the instigator of the kind of charitable relief that, in such cases, must be both immediate and public. There was no one like him when it came to that sort of thing. It was the same with freeing slaves. Before the Law of September 28, 1871, came into force, it was very common for slave-children to turn up in the Praça do Comércio begging the merchants to help them purchase their freedom. Fulano Beltrão would sign up for three-quarters of the contributions necessary, and with such success that within a few minutes the full price was covered.

The recognition he received further encouraged him, and even gave him ideas that might not otherwise have occurred to him. I won't even mention the ball he gave to celebrate the Battle of Riachuelo, because it was a ball planned long before news of the victory reached Rio, and he did no more than invest it with a higher purpose than mere family entertainment, placing the portrait of Admiral Barroso among a display of flags and naval trophies in the hall of honor, opposite the Emperor's portrait, and, during the supper, he offered several patriotic toasts, all as reported in the newspapers of 1865.

But here, for example, we have a typical case of the influence that the just recognition of others can have on our own conduct. Fulano Beltrão was returning one day from the Treasury, where he had gone to sort out some taxes. As he was passing the Lampadosa Church, he remembered that he had been baptized there; and no man can recall such things without going back through all the years and events of his life, curling up once more in his mother's lap, laughing and playing as he would never again laugh and play. Fulano Beltrão was no exception; he went up the steps and entered the church, so simple and modest, and yet to him so rich and beautiful. As he left, he made a resolution, which he put into action a few days later, to send the church a gift, a superb silver candlestick, engraved, along with the donor's name, with two dates: the date of the donation and the date of his baptism. The gift was reported in all the papers, not least since they received the news twice, because the church authorities understood (and with good reason) that it was also incumbent on them to disclose the donation to all and sundry.

Within three years or less, my friend had entered the public imagination; his name was remembered, even when no recent event suggested it, and not only remembered but endowed with adjectives. His absence was commented upon, his presence sought out. Thus, Dona Maria Antônia saw the biblical snake enter her Eden, not to tempt her, but to tempt Adam. Indeed, her husband had so many places to visit, so many things to take care of, as well as putting in frequent appearances outside Bernardo's Emporium on Rua do Ouvidor, that their former domestic intimacy became positively strained. Dona Maria Antônia told him so. He agreed, but assured her that it could not be otherwise, and that, in any event, if his habits had changed, his sentiments had not. He had a moral obligation to society; no man is an island and so on, hence his recent neglect of domestic duties. The truth is that their lives had been too secluded; it was neither right nor decorous. It was certainly not appropriate; their daughter was reaching the age of matrimony, and a closed house carries a whiff of the convent about it. A carriage, for example. Why on earth didn't they have a carriage? Dona Maria Antônia felt a brief frisson of excitement, but, after a moment's reflection, she protested.

"No. Whatever for? Certainly not. We don't need a carriage."

"I've already bought one," lied her husband.

But here we are at the probate office. No one else has arrived yet; let's wait at the door. Are you in a hurry? It'll only take twenty minutes at most. Anyway, it's true, he bought a fine carriage, a victoria, no less; and, for someone who, purely out of modesty, had for so many years traveled on the back of a mule or squeezed into a public omnibus, it was not easy to get used to this new mode of transport. To this I attribute his jutting, forward-leaning posture during those first few weeks, his eyes darting to left and right like someone looking for some particular person or house. Eventually he became accustomed to it and began to lean back in his seat, although without that air of indifference or nonchalance which his wife and daughter had in abundance, perhaps because they were women. As a matter of fact, the two ladies did not like going out in the carriage, but he was so insistent, regardless of whether or not they had any particular place to go, that they had no alternative but to obey. And so they became a well-known sight around the city; as soon as anyone caught so much as a distant glimpse of two ladies' dresses, along with a certain coachman on the driver's seat, everyone would immediately say: "Here comes Fulano Beltrão's family." And this, without perhaps him realizing it, made him even better known.

He entered politics in 1868. I remember the year because it coincided with the fall of the liberals and the return of the conservatives. It was only a month or two before this, in March or April 1868, that he announced he was joining the ruling party, not surreptitiously, but with a great fanfare. It was, perhaps, the lowest point in my friend's life. He was utterly devoid of political ideas; at best, he had one of those temperaments that is a kind of substitute for ideas, and gives the impression that a man is thinking when he is merely sweating. He gave in, however, to a momentary hallucination. He saw himself making pithy remarks in the Chamber, or leaning against the balustrade in conversation with the prime minister, who smiled at him with a grave, governmental intimacy. And it was there that the gallery, in the theatrical sense of the word, would gaze down upon him. He did everything he could to enter the legislature, but when he was halfway there, the government collapsed. Recovering from this shock, he had the presence of mind to tell Viscount Itaboraí the exact opposite of what he had said to the outgoing Zacarias, or perhaps it was the same thing; but, in any event, he lost the election and bowed out of politics. He behaved more wisely when he got himself involved with the prelates over the issue of freemasonry. He had kept quiet, at first; on the one hand, he himself was a Mason; on the other, he wanted to respect his wife's religious sentiments. But the dispute reached such proportions that he could no longer remain silent; he entered the debate with the same passion, enthusiasm, and publicity that he poured into everything; he held meetings at which he spoke at length about freedom of conscience and the Mason's right to don his apron; he signed petitions, representations, and letters of congratulations, and opened wide both his heart and his pocketbook.

His wife died in 1878. She had asked to be buried without pomp and ceremony, and he did precisely that, because he truly loved her and considered her final wishes a decree from heaven. He had already lost his son; and his daughter, by then married, had gone off to Europe. My friend shared his pain with the public at large, and, although he did bury his wife without any pomp and ceremony, he nevertheless sent to Italy to have a magnificent mausoleum made for her which the whole of Rio was able to admire for nearly a month, when it was displayed on Rua do Ouvidor. His daughter even came to attend the inauguration. I lost touch with them around four years ago. He fell ill recently and, just over two months later, that illness carried him off to a better place. Note that, until the final death throes set in, he never lost either his wits or his strength of mind. He would chat with his visitors, get them to tell him all the news, and was always sure to reveal the names of his previous visitors to the new arrivals, a pointless exercise, since a sympathetic newspaper always published the full list. He had the papers read to him even on the morning of the day he died, and in one of them a brief article about his illness seemed in some way to reinvigorate him. But as the day wore on, he weakened somewhat, and, in the evening, he died.

I can see you're getting bored. They really are taking their time. Wait, I think that's them. Yes, it is. Let's go in. Here's our magistrate, and he's starting to read the will. Are you listening? All this painstaking genealogy is hardly necessary, well beyond the usual notarial requirements; but I suppose the mere fact of listing the entire family since his great-great-great-grandfather is evidence of my friend's patient and meticulous nature. He certainly hasn't left anything out. The funeral ceremony he sets out is long and complicated, but beautiful. Now begins the list of legacies. They're all charitable; some industrial. You see laid before you the soul of my friend. Thirty *contos* . . .

Thirty *contos* for what? To open a public subscription for the purpose of erecting a statue of Captain Pedro Álvares Cabral. "We Brazilians must not forget Cabral," says the will, "for he was the precursor to our Empire." It recommends that the statue be made of bronze, with four medallions on the pedestal, viz., a portrait of Bishop Coutinho, president of the Constituent Assembly, one of Gonzaga, leader of the Minas Conspiracy, and portraits of two citizens of the present generation "noted for their patriotism and liberalism," to be chosen by the commission, which he himself appointed to complete the undertaking.

Whether or not it comes to anything, I can't say; we, of course, lack the determination of the first subscriber. However, should the commission carry out its task properly, and this South American sun of ours ever see the statue of Cabral erected, it would be an honor to us all if the distinguished features of my late friend were to appear on one of the medallions. Don't you agree? Ah, the magistrate has finished; we can go now.

SECOND LIFE

Monsignor Caldas interrupted the stranger's story:
"Would you excuse me? I'll just be a moment."

He stood up, made his way toward the kitchens, called for his old black manservant, and said in a low voice:

"João, go down to the police station, speak to the commander on my behalf, and ask him to come here with one or two men, to take a madman off my hands. Go on, hurry."

And, returning to the parlor:

"Right," he said, "where were we?"

"As I was saying, Reverend, I died on March 20, 1860, at forty-three minutes past five in the morning. I was sixty-eight years of age. My soul soared through space until it had lost sight of the Earth and left the moon, stars, and sun far behind. Finally, it entered a space where there was nothing at all, just a diffuse glow. I continued to soar ever higher, and began to see a brighter spot far, far in the distance. The spot grew and became a sun. I entered it, without getting burned, because souls are incombustible. Has yours ever caught fire?"

"No, it hasn't."

"Well, that's because souls are incombustible. I carried on upward; when I was forty thousand leagues off, I heard delightful music, and as soon as I reached five thousand leagues, a swarm of souls descended and bore me aloft on a palanquin of ether and feathers. Shortly afterward, I entered the new sun, which is the planet of the virtuous souls of the Earth. I am no poet, Monsignor, and I dare not describe to you the magnificence of that heavenly abode. Even if I were a poet, the language of mere humans would not suffice to convey the feeling of grandeur, bedazzlement, and joy, the rapturous melodies, the shimmering lights and colors, a thing both indefinable and incomprehensible. It has to be seen to be believed. Once inside, I discovered that my arrival completed another set of one thousand souls; this was the reason for the extraordinary celebrations they laid on for me, and which lasted for two centuries, or, by our reckoning, forty-eight hours. When the festivities were finally over, they invited me to return to Earth to take on a new life; it was a privilege granted to each thousandth soul. I thanked them, but refused; however, refusal was not permitted. It was an eternal law. The only liberty they allowed me was my choice of vehicle; I could be reborn either as a prince or a bus conductor. What was I to do? What would you have done in my shoes?"

"I couldn't possibly say; it would all depend . . ."

"Quite right; it all depends on the circumstances. But imagine that my circumstances were such that it gave me no pleasure to return to this world. I was the victim of inexperience, Monsignor, and, for that very reason, I had a terrible old age. Then I remembered what I had always heard my father and other old people saying when they saw some young man: "Oh, to be that age again, knowing what I know now!" With this in mind, I announced that I cared not a jot whether I was born a beggar or a prince, as long as I was born with experience. You can scarcely imagine the universal laughter this provoked. Job, who presides over the province of patient souls up there, told me that such a wish was sheer nonsense; but I insisted and I got my way. Shortly afterward, I slipped back through space; I spent nine months traversing the void until I plumped down into the arms of a nursemaid, and was named José Maria. Your name's Romualdo, isn't it?"

"Yes, it is. Romualdo de Sousa Caldas."

"Would you be any relation of Father Sousa Caldas?"

"No, I wouldn't."

"He's a fine poet, Father Caldas. Poetry is a gift; I myself could never compose so much as a sonnet. But let's cut to the chase. First I'll tell you what happened to me, then I'll tell you what I would like from you, Reverend. Meanwhile, do you mind, if I smoke . . . ?"

Monsignor made a gesture of assent, without losing sight of the cane lying on José Maria's lap. José Maria slowly rolled a cigarette. He was in his early thirties, rather pale, and with a gaze that, at times, was dim and dull, and, at others, bright and restless. He'd appeared just after the priest had finished lunch, and asked to speak to him on a grave and urgent matter. The monsignor asked him to come in and sit down; within ten minutes he could tell that the man was a lunatic. He could excuse the incoherence of his ideas and his astonishing imagination; indeed, they might even provide him with a useful case study. But the stranger seemed very angry, and this put the fear of God into the peaceable cleric. What could he and his equally elderly manservant do to defend themselves against a strong man who had clearly lost his mind? While waiting for the police to arrive, Monsignor Caldas was all smiles and nods, playing along with whatever emotion the man expressed, be it astonishment, dread, or joy—a useful policy with lunatics, women, and princes.

José Maria finally lit his cigarette, and continued:

"I was reborn on January 5, 1861. I'll spare you the details of my second childhood, because, at that stage, experience was purely instinctive. I suckled very sparingly and cried as little as I could so as not to be smacked. I began to walk rather late, for fear of falling, leaving me with a certain weakness in the legs. Running and tumbling, climbing trees, jumping over walls, trading blows, all of which have their uses, were things I steered well clear of, for fear of bruises and bleeding. To put it frankly, I had a dull childhood, and school was no different. They said I was foolish and lazy. In fact, I was simply avoiding everything. During all that time I don't believe I ever once slipped and fell, but then I never ran, either. I swear to God, Reverend, it was a terrible time, and, when I compare the bumps and bruises of my former life with the tedium of this one, I'd rather have the bumps and bruises. I grew up; I became a young man and entered the usual romantic phase . . . Don't be shocked, Reverend; I will be chaste, just like the first supper I attended. Do you know what a supper with young men and easy women is like, Reverend?"

"How could I possibly know that?"

"I was nineteen years old," José Maria went on, "and you can't imagine my friends' surprise when I announced that I was ready to go to such a supper. No one expected a thing like that from a cautious young man like myself, who balked at everything, whether it was going to bed late, oversleeping, or wandering alone in the dead of night, and who lived, so to speak, by feeling his way cautiously forward in the dark. Anyway, I went to the supper; it was held at the Jardim Botânico and was a splendid occasion. Food, wine, candles, flowers, the young men's high spirits, the ladies' eyes, and, above all, the appetite of a twenty-year-old. Would you believe it? I didn't eat a thing. The memory of three bouts of indigestion forty years earlier, during my first life, made me hold back. I lied, saying I was indisposed. One of the ladies came and sat on my right, to cure me; another also got up and came and sat on my left, with the same objective. 'You cure from one side and I'll cure from the other,' they said. They were jolly, vivacious, and wily, with a reputation for devouring young men's hearts and souls. I confess that I took fright and recoiled. They did everything, absolutely everything, but all in vain. I left in the morning, in love with both of them, but with neither of them on my arm, and almost faint with hunger. What do you make of that?" concluded José Maria, putting his hands on his knees, with his elbows sticking out.

"Well . . ."

"I won't say another word, Reverend; you can guess the rest. My second life is one of expansive, youthful impetuosity reined in by stiff, starchy experience. I live like Eurico, tied to my own corpse. No, it's not a good comparison. What does my life look like to you?"

"I'm not very imaginative. I suppose you live like a bird, flapping your wings and tethered by your feet . . ."

"Precisely. Not very imaginative, you say. Well, you've certainly found the right words there; you've hit the nail on the head, Reverend. A bird, a great big bird, flapping its wings, just as you say."

José Maria stood up, flapping his arms as if they were wings. As he got up, his cane fell to the floor, but he didn't notice. He continued flapping his arms as he stood facing the priest and saying, yes, that was exactly what he was, a bird, a great big bird. Each time his arms struck his thighs, he raised himself up on his heels, giving his body a rhythmic movement, his feet together, to show that they were tied. Monsignor nodded approvingly, at the same time straining his ears for the sound of footsteps on the stairs. Only silence. All he could hear were the noises from outside: buggies and carriages coming down the street, barrow boys hawking their wares, and a piano somewhere nearby. Finally, José Maria sat down again, after picking up his cane, and continued as follows:

"A bird, a great big bird. The adventure that brings me here will suffice to show just what a felicitous comparison that is. It was a matter of conscience, a passion, a woman: a widow by the name of Dona Clemência. She is twenty-six years old and has eyes that are just endless, not so much in size as in expression, and, to complete the picture, a downy upper lip. She is the daughter of a retired professor. Black dresses suit her so well that, at times, I tell her, with a smile, that she only became a widow so that she could wear mourning. Ha ha! Only joking! We met a year ago, at the home of a plantation owner from Cantagalo. We left there completely in love with each other. I know what you're going to ask me: Why don't we get married, since we're both free to do so?"

"Yes, quite."

"But good God, man! That's the very nub of the matter We're both free, we love each other, and we aren't getting married: such is the murky situation I have come to lay before you, Reverend, so that your theology, or whatever you want to call it, may explain it, if it can. We returned to Rio as sweethearts. Clemência was living with her elderly father, and with a brother who worked in commerce; I made the acquaintance of both men, and began to visit their house, on Rua de Matacavalos. Furtive glances, clasped hands, a word here, another there, then a sentence, two sentences, and before you know it we were lovers. One night, on the staircase landing, we exchanged our first kiss. Please excuse such lapses, Monsignor, and pretend that you're hearing my confession. I wouldn't even mention such matters if it weren't to explain how I left that place dazed and bewildered, with a vision of Clemência in my head and the taste of her kiss on my lips. I wandered about for nearly two hours, planning a life without equal; I decided to ask for her hand at the end of the week, and to be married within a month. I planned it down to the very last detail, even composing and embellishing the wedding invitations. I arrived home after midnight, when this whole phantasmagoria flew away before me, just like the changes of scenery in one of those old-fashioned plays at the theater. Can you guess how?"

"No, I can't."

"Just as I was taking off my vest, it occurred to me that love can end abruptly; it has happened before, after all. As I removed my boots, I thought of something even worse: it could turn to boredom. I finished my evening *toilette*, lit a cigarette, and, reclining on the sofa, reflected that domestic routine and harmony could yet save the day. But this was quickly followed by the thought that our inherent dispositions might be incompatible, and what was to be done with two incompatible but inseparable dispositions? Eventually I dismissed these questions, for, after all, ours was a great and violent passion. I imagined myself married, with a beautiful child . . . One? Or two? Six? Eight? Why, there might be eight or even ten of the little tykes, and some of them might be crippled. Some crisis might occur, two crises—lack of money, hardship, illness, or one of those spurious indiscretions that can so disrupt domestic harmony. I considered it from every angle and concluded that I would be better off not marrying. What I cannot describe is my despair; I have no words with which to tell you how I suffered that night . . . Do you mind if I smoke another cigarette?"

He didn't wait for an answer, but rolled the cigarette and lit it. Monsignor Caldas could not help but admire his handsome head, despite the disordered state of his mind; at the same time, he noted that the man spoke politely, and was well mannered, apart from his occasional unsavory outbursts. Who on earth could he be? José Maria carried on with his story, saying that, for six whole days, he stopped visiting Clemência's house, but could not resist her letters or her tears. After a week, he rushed to her side and confessed everything. She listened to him eagerly, wanting to know what she could do to allay his fears, what proof of love he wanted from her. José Maria's answer was a question.

"Are you willing to make a great sacrifice for me?" he asked. Clemência swore that she was. "Well, then, break with everything and everyone, both family and society. Come and live with me, and, after a trial period, we'll get married." I can understand your alarm, Reverend. Her eyes filled with tears, but, despite her feeling of humiliation, she agreed to everything. Come on, admit it, I'm a monster."

"No . . ."

"Why not? I am a monster. Clemência came to my house, and you cannot imagine how jubilantly I received her. 'I'm leaving everything,' she told me. 'You are the whole universe to me.' I kissed her feet; I kissed the heels of her shoes. You cannot imagine my contentment. The following day, I received a letter edged in black; it was news of the death of an uncle of mine in Santa Ana do Livramento, leaving me twenty thousand *contos*. I was furious. 'Now I understand,' I said to Clemência. 'You sacrificed everything because you'd heard about the inheritance.' This time Clemência did not cry; she stood up and left. I went after her, ashamed, asking her forgiveness; she refused. This went on for one day, two days, three days, but all in vain.

Clemência would not yield, nor even speak to me. Then I told her I would kill myself; I bought a revolver, and went and showed it to her. Here it is— this is the one."

Monsignor Caldas turned pale. José Maria showed him the gun, just for a few seconds, then put it back in his pocket and continued:

"I even managed to pull the trigger. Clemência was terrified; she took it off me and forgave me. We decided to bring forward the wedding date and, of my own accord, I set one condition: I would donate the twenty thousand *contos* to the National Library. Clemência threw herself into my arms and sealed her approval with a kiss. I donated the twenty thousand *contos*. You must have read about it in the papers. Three weeks later, we were married. You're sighing with relief, Reverend, as if we had reached the end of the story. As if! Now we come to the tragic bit. I can shorten some bits and leave others out entirely; I will restrict myself to Clemência. I won't tell you of other mutilated feelings, which are all mine, of sudden pleasures, plans torn asunder, tattered illusions, nor of that godforsaken bird . . . whoosh . . . whoosh . . . whoosh . . ."

And, with one leap, José Maria was once again on his feet, flapping his arms and rhythmically moving his body. Monsignor Caldas broke out in a cold sweat. A few seconds later, José Maria stopped, sat down, and continued his story, this time wilder, more frenzied, and clearly even crazier. He told of the state of dread in which he lived, his sorrows and his suspicions. No longer could he bite into a fig as he would once have done; the fear of a worm diminished the pleasure. He did not believe the happy faces of people passing by in the street: worry, hatred, desire, sadness, and other things seemed to lurk in three-quarters of them. He lived in fear that a child of his would be born blind, or deaf and dumb, or consumptive, or a murderer. He could not give a dinner party without becoming depressed at the thought that, as soon as the soup was served, a word from him, a gesture from his wife, or some blunder by the servants might provoke some flippant post-prandial jibe, outside in the street, under a lamppost. Experience had given him a horror of being mocked. He confessed to the priest that, in reality, he had never gained anything by this horror; on the contrary, he had lost, because he had even caused blood to be shed . . . He would tell the monsignor all about that too. The previous night he had gone to bed early, and dreamed . . . Who did the priest think he had dreamed of?

"I have no idea."

"I dreamed that the Devil was reading me the Gospel. When he reached the part where Jesus talks about the lilies of the field, the Devil picked some and gave them to me. 'Take them,' he said to me, 'they are the lilies of the Scriptures; as you know, not even Solomon in all his glory could match them. Solomon is wisdom. Do you know what these lilies are, José? They are your twenties.' I stared at them in wonderment; they were more beautiful than I could imagine. The Devil took them, sniffed them, and told me to sniff them too. I can barely bring myself to tell you; as soon as they reached my nose, I saw a repulsive, reeking reptile come crawling out of them. I screamed and threw the flowers away. Then, roaring with laughter, the Devil said: 'José Maria, these are your twenties.' His laughter was almost a cackle—ka, ka, ka, ka, ka . . ."

José Maria laughed uncontrollably, a laugh that was both shrill and diabolical. Suddenly he stopped. He stood up, saying that, as soon as he opened his eyes, he saw his wife standing before him, distraught and disheveled. Clemência's eyes were gentle, but he told her that even gentle eyes can wound. She threw herself at his feet. At this point, José Maria's face was so contorted that the priest, who, by now, was also standing, began to back away, trembling and ashen-faced. "No, you miserable wretch! No! You won't get away from me now," José Maria thundered as he lunged toward the priest. His eyes were bulging, his temples throbbing; the priest stepped back . . . and back . . . Coming up the stairs he heard the sound of rattling swords and pounding feet.

ADMIRAL'S NIGHT

———

Deolindo Big-Nose (his nickname aboard ship) left the Naval Dockyard and made his way along Rua de Bragança. The clocks were just striking three o'clock in the afternoon. He walked with a spring in his step and, what's more, he had a happy gleam in his eyes. His corvette had returned from a long training voyage, and Deolindo came ashore just as soon as he could obtain leave. His shipmates said to him, laughing:

"Ah! Big-Nose! You're in for a real admiral's night! Supper, guitar music, and the arms of Genoveva waiting to embrace you . . ."

Deolindo smiled. That was exactly it: an "admiral's night," as they call it, one of those magnificent admiral's nights, was waiting for him ashore. The passionate affair had begun three months before the corvette left. Her name was Genoveva, a charming dusky-skinned country girl, twenty years of age, clever, with dark, mischievous eyes. They had met at a friend's house and fallen head over heels for each other, to such an extent that they were on the verge of throwing caution to the winds, with him leaving the navy and the two of them running off to some tiny village in the back of beyond.

Old Inácia, who lived with Genoveva, dissuaded them, and Deolindo had no choice but to go off on his training voyage. He would be away for eight or ten months. As a guarantee of their feelings for each other, they decided they should take an oath of fidelity.

"I swear by God in heaven. And you?"

"Me too."

"Say it properly."

"I swear by God in heaven; may the light fail me at the hour of my death."

The contract was sealed. There was no doubting the couple's sincerity; she wept like a woman possessed; he bit his lip to disguise his feelings. Finally they parted; Genoveva went to see the corvette leave, and returned home with such a tight feeling in her chest that she thought she was, in her words "about to have a funny turn." Luckily, she didn't; the days passed, then weeks, then months, and after ten months the corvette returned, and Deolindo with it.

There he goes, along Rua de Bragança, through Prainha and Saúde, and on to Gamboa, where Genoveva lives. The house is just past the English Cemetery, a dark hovel, its wooden doorway cracked by the sun. Genoveva would surely be there, leaning out the window, waiting for him. Deolindo prepares what he will say to her. He has already decided upon, "I swore an oath and I've kept it," but now he's trying to think of something better. At the same time, he remembers the other women he saw in those distant lands of Christ: Italians and Turks, the ladies of Marseilles, many of them pretty, or so at least they seemed to him. Perhaps not all of them were entirely to his taste, but some were, and still he paid them no attention. He thought only of Genoveva. That little house of hers, so tiny, and its few sticks of rickety old furniture—that is what filled his mind when he gazed upon the palaces of distant lands. He scrimped and saved to buy a pair of earrings in Trieste, and he now carries them in his pocket along with a few other trinkets. And what will she have for him? Perhaps a handkerchief embroidered with his name and an anchor in the corner, because she was an expert with needle and thread. By this point he has arrived in Gamboa, passed the cemetery and found the house. The door was closed. He knocked, and a familiar voice answered; it was old Inácia, who came to open the door for him with loud exclamations of delight. Deolindo asked impatiently for Genoveva.

"Don't talk to me about that crazy woman," exploded the old woman. "I'm glad I gave you the advice I did. Imagine if you'd run off with her. She'll be with her lover now."

"But what happened? What on earth happened?"

The old woman told him to calm down, that it was nothing at all, just one of those things life throws at us; no point getting all worked up. Genoveva's head had been turned . . .

"But turned by what?"

"She's gone off with a peddler, José Diogo. Do you know José Diogo, the draper? Well, she's gone off with him. You can't imagine how smitten they are. And now she's crazy, mark my words. That's why we quarreled. José Diogo was always hanging around here; it was all talk, talk, talk, until one day I said to him, I said, I don't want my house getting a bad name. Ah! Father in heaven! That was a day of judgment, that was. Genoveva glowered at me with eyes as big as saucers, saying that she never gave nobody a bad name and didn't need no favors from anyone. What favors, Genoveva? All I'm saying is I don't want no more of these whisperings around the door all evening . . . Two days later, she'd moved out, and that's the last I heard of her."

"Where does she live?"

"Over at Praia Formosa, just before you reach the quarry, in a shack that's just been painted."

Deolindo didn't want to hear any more. Old Inácia, somewhat regretting she'd said so much, kept warning him to be careful, but he wouldn't listen and went on his way. I won't say what he was thinking, for he wasn't thinking anything at all. Ideas buffeted around his brain like a storm at sea, amid howling winds and shrieking whistles. In among them flashed his sailor's knife, bloodied and vengeful. By now he had passed through Gamboa, Saco do Alferes, and reached the shoreline at Formosa. He didn't know the house number, but he knew it was near the quarry and freshly painted, and with the help of some of the neighbors he would be able to find it. He had not counted on chance placing Genoveva at her window, sitting and sewing, at the very moment Deolindo passed by. He recognized her and stopped; she, seeing a man's figure, looked up and found the sailor standing before her.

"What's this?" she exclaimed in surprise. "When did you get back? Come in, Deolindo."

She stood up, opened the door, and let him in. So frank and sincere was the girl's manner that any other man would have been filled with hope; perhaps the old woman was mistaken, or lying; perhaps even the peddler's seductive song had come to an end. All this passed through Deolindo's head, without the precise form of reason or reflection, but in a tumultuous rush. Genoveva left the door open and offered him a seat; she asked about the voyage and said he'd grown fatter; but there was no excitement, no tenderness. Deolindo abandoned all hope. He might not have his knife with him, but he could still strangle Genoveva with his bare hands; she was a tiny slip of a thing, and, for the first few minutes, he could think of nothing else.

"I know everything," he said.

"Who told you?"

Deolindo shrugged.

"Whoever it was," she replied, "did they tell you I was in love with a young man?"

"They did."

"Well, it's true."

Deolindo lunged toward her; she stopped him with a look. Then she said that she had only invited him in because she took him to be a man of reason. She told him everything, how much she had missed him, then about the peddler's propositions, her refusals, until one day, without knowing how, she had woken up in love with him.

"Believe you me, I thought about you an awful lot. Ask Sinhá Inácia—she'll tell you how I cried and cried. But the heart changes, as mine did . . . I'm telling you all this as if I was telling the priest," she concluded, smiling.

It was not a smile of derision. She spoke with a mixture of candor and cynicism, insolence and simplicity, which I shall refrain from trying to define any better. Actually, I think even insolence and cynicism are wide of the mark. Genoveva wasn't excusing herself for making a mistake or breaking an oath; she wasn't excusing herself for anything at all; she had no moral compass for her actions. What she was saying, in brief, was that it would have been better if things hadn't changed; she had enjoyed Deolindo's affections—the proof being that she had wanted to run away with him. But once the peddler had supplanted the sailor, then reason was on the peddler's side, and it was only right to say so. What do you think? The poor sailor cited their parting oaths as imposing an eternal obligation, the condition on which he had agreed not to elope with her, but to rejoin his ship instead: "I swear by God in heaven; may the light fail me at the hour of my death." He had only embarked because she had sworn that oath. Upon those words of hers he had left, traveled, waited, and returned; they had given him the strength to live. I swear by God in heaven; may the light fail me at the hour of my death . . .

"All right, yes, Deolindo, that's true. When I swore it, it was true. It was so true that I wanted to run far, far away with you where no one would find us. God knows it was true! But then other things came along . . . This other young man came along and I took a shine to him."

"But that's exactly why people swear things; so that they don't fall in love with someone else."

"Oh, stop it, Deolindo. Are you telling me you thought only about me? Go on, pull the other one!"

"What time does José Diogo come home?"

"He's not coming home today."

"No?"

"No, he's over near Guaratiba trying to sell stuff; he's due back on Friday or Saturday. Why do you want to know? What harm has he ever done to you?"

Perhaps any other woman would have said the same thing, but few would have said it so candidly, not deliberately, but quite spontaneously. Note that here we are very close to unvarnished nature. What harm has he ever done to you? What harm has this falling stone ever done to you? Any physicist could explain about falling stones. With a despairing gesture, Deolindo announced that he wanted to kill the peddler. Genoveva looked at him scornfully, smiled faintly and tut-tutted. When he started talking about ingratitude and broken promises, she couldn't quite disguise her astonishment. What promises? What ingratitude? She had already said, over and over, that the oath was true when she said it. The Blessed Virgin, over there on top of the chest of drawers, knew if it was true or not. Was this how he repaid her for everything she'd been through? And as for him, going on and on about fidelity, had he thought about her in every single place he went?

His reply was to put his hand in his pocket and pull out the package he had brought with him. She opened it, pulled out the trinkets one by one, and finally came upon the earrings. They were not, they couldn't be, expensive; they were even rather tasteless, but they were really striking. Dazzled and contented, Genoveva picked them up, gazed at them from one side and then the other, close up and far away, and finally put them on. Then she went over to the cheap mirror hanging on the wall between the window and the door, to gauge their effect. She stepped back, then forward, turned her head from right to left and from left to right.

"Oh, they're lovely!" she said, thanking him with a deep curtsy. "Where did you buy them?"

He did not reply, nor was there time for him to do so, because she fired off another two or three questions, one after the other, so overwhelmed was she at receiving a gift in exchange for having forgotten someone. This lasted four or five minutes, or perhaps only two. She quickly took the earrings off, gazed at them again, and put them in the little box on the round table in the middle of the room. He, for his part, began to think that, just as he had lost her by his absence, the same thing might now happen to the other man; and Genoveva probably hadn't sworn anything at all to the peddler.

"Enough idle chatter," said Genoveva. "It's getting dark!"

Night was indeed falling fast. They could no longer see the leper hospital, and could barely make out Melões Island; the rowing boats and canoes, pulled up on dry land in front of the house, were now indistinguishable from the mud and earth of the shoreline. Genoveva lit a candle. Then she went to sit on the doorstep and asked him to tell her something about all the places he had been to. Deolindo refused at first; he said he was leaving, got up, and took a few steps across the room. But the demon of hope still gnawed at the poor fellow's heart, and so he sat down again to tell two or three tales from his travels. Genoveva listened attentively. When a neighbor popped her head around the door, Genoveva made her sit down as well, and listen to the "lovely stories Senhor Deolindo is telling me." There were no other introductions. The grand lady who stays up late to finish reading her book or chapter could not live the lives of the characters more intensely than the sailor's former sweetheart lived the scenes he described; she was fascinated and enthralled, as if, between them, there was nothing more than the telling of those tales. What does the grand lady care about the book's author? What did this girl care about the teller of the tales?

Hope, however, began to desert him, and he finally got up to leave. Genoveva would not hear of him going before her friend from next door had seen the earrings, and with great excitement, she went to show them to her. The other woman thought they were charming, and praised them lavishly; she asked if Deolindo had purchased them in France and begged Genoveva to put them on.

"They're really very pretty."

I imagine the sailor himself agreed with this opinion. He liked looking at them, thought they seemed made for her, and, for a few seconds, he savored the exquisite and exclusive pleasure of having given a good present. But it was only a matter of a few seconds.

As he said goodbye, Genoveva accompanied him to the door to thank him one more time for the gift, and probably to murmur some sweet and useless things to him. Her friend, whom she'd left behind in the room, heard only these words: "Don't be silly, Deolindo," and this from the sailor: "You'll see." She could not hear the rest, which was spoken in no more than a whisper.

Utterly downcast, Deolindo made his way slowly back along the shoreline; he was no longer the impetuous young man of earlier in the day, but had an ancient, sorrowful air about him, or, to use a nautical metaphor, he looked like a man "who has turned back to shore." Genoveva went inside a few moments later, happy and boisterous. She told her friend the story of her maritime romance, praising Deolindo's character and good manners; and her friend said she thought him very charming.

"He's a fine young man," insisted Genoveva. "Do you know what he said to me just now?"

"What?"

"That he's going to kill himself."

"Goodness!"

"Stuff and nonsense! He won't kill himself. That's just the way he is. He says things, but doesn't do them. You'll see; he won't kill himself. Poor thing, he's just jealous. But the earrings are really sweet."

"I've never seen anything like them around here."

"Nor have I," Genoveva agreed, examining them in the light. Then she put them away and invited the other woman to sew with her. "Let's do a bit of sewing; I want to finish my little blue camisole . . ."

It was true; the sailor did not, in fact, kill himself. The next day, some of his shipmates slapped him on the shoulder, congratulating him on his admiral's night, and asked about Genoveva, whether she was even prettier than before, whether she'd cried a lot while he was away, and so on. He answered everything with a discreet, satisfied smile, the smile of a man who'd had a wonderful night. It would seem he was ashamed of the truth and preferred to lie.

A SACRISTAN'S MANUSCRIPT

I

· · · · · · · · · · · · WHEN I SAW Father Teófilo speaking to a lady, both of them seated comfortably on a church pew, and the church deserted, I confess that I was shocked. They were speaking in such quiet, discreet voices that, however hard I strained my ears and however long I lingered over snuffing out the candles on the altar, I couldn't catch a word, not a single word. I had no choice but to draw my own conclusions, for I am a philosophical sacristan. No one should judge me by my crumpled, tattered surplice, or by my clandestine use of the Communion vessels. No, I am, as I say, a philosophical sacristan. I had some ecclesiastical training, but this was interrupted by illness and then abandoned entirely on account of a violent passion that reduced me to penury. Since the seminary always leaves its mark, however, I became a sacristan at the age of thirty, just to make ends meet. That's enough about me, though, let's get back to the priest and the lady.

II

Before going any further, I should say that, as I found out later, they were cousins, both born in the town of Vassouras. Her parents moved to Rio when Eulália (for that is her name) was seven. Teófilo came later. It was a family tradition for one of the sons to become a priest. One of Teófilo's uncles, still living up in Bahia, was a canon. Since, in this generation, it fell to Teófilo to don the cassock, in the year eighteen hundred and fifty something, he enrolled at the São José Seminary, which is where I met him. You will understand my discretion in not specifying the date.

III

At the seminary, the rhetoric teacher used to tell us:

"Theology is the head of the human species, Latin the left leg, and rhetoric the right."

Teófilo's weak point was that right leg. He knew a lot about the other things: theology, philosophy, Latin, church history; but he simply could not get rhetoric into his head. As an excuse, he used to say that the divine word needed no adornment. He was twenty or twenty-two years of age then, with the good looks of a Saint John.

By that time, he was already a mystic, finding hidden meaning in everything. Life was an eternal mass, in which the world served as altar, the soul as priest, and the body as acolyte; nothing conformed to external reality. He was keen to take holy orders so as to go out into the world and preach great things, awaken souls, summon men's hearts to the Church, and renew the human race. Of all the apostles, he especially loved Saint Paul.

I don't know if the reader shares my opinion, but I believe a man may be judged by his historical affinities; you will become more or less the same tribe as the people you truly love. I thus apply Helvétius's law: "The degree of intellect that pleases us gives an exact measure of the degree of intellect we possess." In our case, at least, the rule did not fail. Teófilo loved Saint Paul, adored him, studied him day and night, and seemed to live by that notable convert who wandered from city to city, pursuing the humble trade of spreading the good news to all men. Saint Paul was not his only role model; there were two more: Hildebrand and Loyola. From this you may conclude that he was born with a rebellious, evangelizing streak. He hungered for ideals and creation, viewing all worldly affairs as if peering over the head of this century of ours. In the opinion of a canon who used to attend the seminary, his love of the two latter role models tempered what might have been dangerous in the first. One day, the canon said to him gently:

"Don't fall into the sins of excess and exclusivity. Don't give the impression that by exalting Paul, you intend to diminish Peter. The Church, which honors them side by side, included both of them in the Creed, yet we revere Paul and obey Peter. *Super hanc petram . . .*"

The other seminarians liked Teófilo, in particular Vasconcelos, Soares, and Veloso, all three of whom were excellent rhetoricians. They were also fine young men, cheerful by nature, serious by necessity, and ambitious. Vasconcelos solemnly vowed that he would become a bishop; Soares contented himself with some other senior position; Veloso coveted a pulpit and the purple socks of a canon. Teófilo tried to share with them the mystical bread of his dreams, but soon realized that it was either too light or too heavy a morsel, and instead devoured it alone. So much for the priest; now let's turn to the lady.

IV

The lady. At the time I saw them whispering in church, Eulália was thirty-eight years of age. She was, I can assure you, still very pretty. She was not poor, for her parents had left her some money. Nor was she married, although she had turned down five or six admirers.

This latter point was never fully understood by her female friends. None of them would have been capable of repelling a suitor. Indeed, I believe that they asked for nothing else when they prayed before getting into bed, and on Sunday, at mass, at the moment of raising their eyes to God. Why did Eulália reject all comers? I will say now what I found out later. Her friends supposed, at first, that it was simply scorn on her part—too stuck-up, one of them said—but after the third refusal, they were inclined to believe there was some secret love affair, and this was the explanation that prevailed. Even Eulália's mother would accept no other. She didn't mind the initial refusals, but the more they went on, the more concerned she became. One day, sitting in their carriage on the way back from a wedding, she asked her daughter if it hadn't occurred to her that she would end up all alone.

"All alone?"

"Yes, one day I'll be gone. For now, everything is a bed of roses; I'm here to run the house, and all you need to do is read, daydream, play the piano, and amuse yourself. But I will die, Eulália, and you'll be left all alone."

Eulália clasped her hands, speechless. She had never thought about her mother's death; to lose her mother would be like losing half of her own self. Making the most of this moment of intimacy, her mother dared to ask Eulália if she was in love with someone who did not return her feelings, but Eulália said that she wasn't. She simply hadn't liked any of the candidates. The old lady shook her head; she spoke of her daughter's twenty-seven years, tried to terrify her with thirty, and told her that although not all the suitors were up to scratch, some of them were worthy of being accepted. Did it really matter if they didn't love each other? Conjugal love could be like that; it could grow later, as the fruit of companionship. She knew several people who had gotten married simply for family reasons, and ended up very much in love. Waiting for a great passion in order to marry was to risk dying waiting.

"Yes, of course, Mama. But just let me be . . ."

And, leaning back her head, she closed her eyes a little to see if she could spy someone, her hidden lover, who was not only hidden, but intangible. I agree that this is all somewhat obscure, and I do not hesitate to say that we are entering the realm of dreams.

Eulália was a strange creature, to use her mother's expression, or a romantic, to employ her friends' definition. She did, indeed, have a peculiar way of seeing things. She took after her father, who had been born with a love of the enigmatic, the dangerous, and the obscure; he died while preparing an expedition to Bahia to discover the "abandoned city." Eulália received this spiritual inheritance, modified or aggravated by her feminine nature. Her dominant characteristic was that of contemplation. Her abandoned cities were to be found in her head. Her eyes were set in such a way that they could not wholly capture life's contours. She began by idealizing things, and, if she did not end up denying them entirely, it is certain that her sense of reality grew thinner and thinner until it reached the fine transparency at which fabric becomes indistinguishable from air.

She rejected her first marriage proposal at eighteen, her reason being that she was waiting for someone else, an extraordinary husband whom she had seen and conversed with in her dreams and imaginings; the most radiant figure in the universe, the rarest and most sublime, a creature in whom there was no flaw or fault, a true grammar with no irregularities, a pure language with no solecisms.

"Excuse me," a lady says, "this suitor is not the exclusive invention of

Eulália. He is the husband of every seventeen-year-old virgin." Excuse me, I say to you, madam, there is one difference between Eulália and the others, which is that the others eventually swapped the desired original for an engraved copy, *avant ou après la lettre*, and sometimes for just a simple photograph or lithograph, whereas Eulália continued to wait for the original masterpiece. The engravings and lithographs came and went, some very well executed, the work of an artist or even a great artist, but for her they all carried the defect of being copies. She hungered and thirsted for originality. Ordinary life seemed to her an eternal copy. Persons of her acquaintance insisted on repeating each other's ideas, using the same words and even the same tone of voice, just as the clothes they wore were all of the same cut and style. If she had caught sight of a Moorish turban in the street, or even a fluttering ostrich feather, she might have forgiven the rest; but there was nothing, absolutely nothing, only a never-ending uniformity of ideas and vests. It was the mortal sin of objects. But, since she had the ability to live everything she dreamed, she continued to hope for a new life and a unique husband.

While she waited, one by one the other women got married. Thus she lost her three best friends: Júlia Costinha, Josefa, and Mariana. She saw them all as brides and then as mothers, first of one child and then of two, four, and five. Eulália visited them, joined them in their serene and happy daily lives, trivial and banal, with no dreams or dramas, and more or less content. The years went by, and Eulália turned thirty, then thirty-three, thirty-five, and, finally, thirty-eight, as she was when we saw her in the church, conversing with Father Teófilo.

V

On that particular day, she'd had a mass said for the soul of her mother, who had died a year earlier. She didn't invite anyone else, and attended the mass alone. She listened, prayed, then sat down on the pew.

After serving at mass, I returned to the sacristy, where I saw Father Teófilo, who had come up from the country two weeks earlier and was in search of a few masses, meals included. It seems he had heard from the other sacristan, or from the officiating priest himself, the name of the person being prayed for. Realizing that the deceased was his own aunt, he rushed to the church, where he found his cousin sitting on the pew. He sat down beside her, completely forgetting where they were and their respective positions, and the two of them talked entirely naturally about themselves. They had not seen each other for a long time. Teófilo had visited his aunt and cousin shortly after being ordained a priest, but then left Rio for a distant parish and never heard any more from them, or they from him.

As I said before, I couldn't hear a word. They sat there for nearly half an hour. The coadjutor priest came poking around, saw them, and was suitably scandalized. Two days later, news reached the bishop. Teófilo was warned by a friend, marched up to Conceição, where he explained everything: she was a dear cousin he hadn't seen for a very long time. When the coadjutor heard this explanation, he exclaimed, quite rightly, that the fact of being a relative neither changed her sex nor diminished the scandal.

I had known Teófilo at the seminary and was very fond of him; I, therefore, wholeheartedly defended him and made sure my testimony reached the bishop's palace. Teófilo was very grateful, and we became close friends. Since the two cousins could respectably meet at her house, Teófilo began to visit Eulália, and she was always pleased to receive him. A week later, she received me as well, and, within two weeks, I was part of the family circle.

Two compatriots meeting in a foreign land and finally exchanging words first learned at their mother's breast could not have felt a greater excitement than these two cousins, who were more than just cousins: spiritually, they were twins. He told her about his life and, as events inevitably evoked feelings, she peered into her cousin's soul and found it to be identical to her own. In substance, their lives were one and the same. The only difference was that she had waited quietly, while he had gone searching over hill and vale; other than that, it was the same misapprehension, the same conflict with reality, the same dialogue between Arab and Japanese.

"Everything around me is trivial and empty," he would say to her.

For he had, indeed, wasted his youthful vigor trying to spread an idea that no one understood. While his three closest friends at the seminary progressed, working and serving the Lord, in tune with the times—Veloso now a canon and preacher, Soares with a large parish, Vasconcelos almost a bishop—he, Teófilo, was the same mystic evangelist he had been in his early years, in the same Christian and metaphysical dawn. He lived very poorly, always courting hunger, thin bread, and the threadbare cassock; he had moments, hours, of sadness and dejection, all of which he confessed to his cousin.

"You too?" she asked.

And they clasped one another's hands: they understood each other. Failing to find a star in a watchmaker's shop was the watchmaker's fault; such was the logic they shared. They gazed at each other as fondly as ship-wrecked sailors—shipwrecked but not disillusioned—because their illu-sions were intact. On his desert island, Robinson Crusoe works and makes things; they did not; cast up on the island, they gazed out over the endless sea, waiting for the eagle that would come to fetch them with its great wings spread wide. One of them was the eternal bride without a bridegroom, the other the eternal prophet without an Israel; both punished, both stubbornly tenacious.

I've already said that Eulália was still pretty. I should add that Father Teófilo, at the age of forty-two, had graying hair and a worn face; his hands had neither the softness nor the scent of the sacristy; they were scrawny and callused and smelled of the outdoors. It was his eyes that retained their old fire, that spoke of his inner youth, and, it goes without saying, they alone were worth all the rest.

Our visits became more frequent. In the end, we were spending after-noons and evenings there, as well as Sunday dinners. Our companionship had two effects, even three. The first was that, in spending more time in each other's company, the two cousins each gave strength and life to the other; if you will excuse the familiar expression: they made a picnic of their illusions. The second is that Eulália, tired of waiting for a human bride-groom, turned her eyes to the divine one and, just as the desire to follow Saint Paul had inspired her cousin, so Eulália began to feel a desire to follow in the footsteps of Saint Teresa. The third effect is the one the reader will already have guessed.

You *have* already guessed, haven't you? The third was the road to Damascus—a topsy-turvy road, because the voice did not descend from Heaven, but rose up from Earth, and it was not calling them to praise God, but to praise man. Setting aside all metaphors, they were in love. Another difference is that this vocation did not happen suddenly, as it did for the apostle of the peoples; it was slow, very slow, murmuring, insinuating, gen-tly wafted along on the wings of the mystic dove.

Note that reputation preceded love. It had long been whispered that the priest's visits were not so much those of a confessor as those of a sinner. This was a lie; I swear it was a lie. I watched them, I sat with them, I observed those two temperaments, which were so spiritual, so wrapped up in each other, that they never once thought of reputation, or of the danger of appearances. One day, I saw in them the first signs of love. Call it what you will, a midlife passion, a pale autumn rose, but it was there, it existed, it grew, and it completely overwhelmed them. I considered warning Teófilo, for his sake rather than mine, but that would have been difficult, and possibly dangerous. Moreover, I was and am both a gastronome and a psychologist; to warn him would be to throw away a fine case study and lose those Sunday dinners. Psychology, at the very least, deserves a sacrifice; I kept quiet.

I kept quiet in vain. What I would not say, their hearts made public. If the reader has read me hastily, then he can finish the story for himself by joining the two cousins together. But if he has read me slowly, he will have guessed what happened. The two mystics recoiled; they had no horror of each other, nor of themselves, because that feeling was entirely absent from both of them. But they recoiled, nonetheless, shaken by fear and desire.

"I'm going back to the countryside," the priest told me.

"But why?"

"I'm going back to the countryside."

And he did go back to the countryside, never to return. She had clearly found the husband she was waiting for, but he turned out to be as impossible as the life she had dreamed of. I, the gastronome and psychologist, continued to go for dinner with Eulália on Sundays. If it is true, as Schiller would have it, that love and hunger rule the world, then I am of the firm opinion that something, either love or dinner, must still exist somewhere or other.

EX CATHEDRA

———

"You'll go blind like that, Godfather."

"What?"

"You'll go blind; you read as if there were no tomorrow. Go on, give me the book."

Caetaninha took the book from his hands. Her godfather turned on his heel and went into his study, where there was no shortage of books. He shut the door behind him and carried on reading. It was his vice; he read to excess—morning, noon, and night, at lunch and dinner, in bed, after his bath, while walking or standing up, in the house and in the garden; he read before reading and he read after reading. He read every sort of book, but especially law (for he was a law graduate), mathematics, and philosophy; recently, he had also taken up the natural sciences.

Worse than going blind, he went mad. It was toward the end of 1873, up in Tijuca, that he began to show signs of mental derangement. But since the episodes were few and insignificant, it was only in March or April 1874 that his goddaughter noticed the change. One day, over lunch, he interrupted his reading to ask her:

"What's my name again?"

"What's your name?" she repeated, shocked. "Your name is Fulgêncio."

"From this day forth, you shall call me Fulgencius."

And, once more burying his nose in the book, he carried on with his reading. Caetaninha discussed the matter with the house-slaves, who told her they had suspected for some time that he wasn't well. You can imagine the young lady's fears, but her fear soon passed, leaving only pity, which merely made her feel still fonder of him. Also, his mania was harmless enough, for it extended only to books. Fulgêncio lived for the written word, the printed word, the doctrinal and the abstract, for principles and formulas. Over time, he reached the point of theoretical hallucination, although not yet superstition. One of his maxims was that freedom would not die as long as there remained one piece of paper on which to declare it. One day, waking up with the idea of improving the condition of the Turks, he drafted a constitution and sent it to the British envoy in Petrópolis, as a gift. On another occasion, he applied himself to studying the anatomy of the eyes, to see if they really could see, and concluded that they could.

Tell me how, under such conditions, Caetaninha's life could possibly be happy? It's true that she wanted for nothing, because her godfather was a rich man. It was he himself who had brought her up from the age of seven, when he lost his wife; he taught her reading and writing, then French, a little history and geography (which is tantamount to saying almost nothing), and charged one of the house-slaves with teaching her embroidery, lace-making, and sewing. So much is true. But Caetaninha was now fourteen, and, if toys and slaves had once been enough to amuse her, she was reaching the age when toys lose their appeal and slaves their interest, and when no amount of reading and writing can make a paradise of a secluded house up in Tijuca. She sometimes went down to the city, but these were rare occasions, and always very rushed; she didn't visit the theater or go to dances, and she neither made nor received visits. Whenever she saw a riding party of ladies and gentlemen pass by on the road, her soul would jump up behind one of the riders, while her body stayed put by the side of her godfather, who carried on reading.

One day, when she was in the garden, she saw a young man stop at the front gate. He was riding a small mule, and he asked if this was Senhor Fulgêncio's house.

"Indeed it is, sir."

"May I speak with him?"

Caetaninha replied that she would go and see; she entered the house and went to the study, where she found her godfather ruminating over a chapter of Hegel with the most devoutly voluptuous expression on his face.

"A young man? What young man?" Caetaninha told him that it was a young man dressed in mourning.

"In mourning?" repeated the old man, snapping the book shut; it must be him.

I forgot to say (but there is time for everything) that a brother of Fulgêncio's had passed away three months earlier, up north, leaving an illegitimate son. Since the brother, a few days before dying, had written to Fulgêncio asking him to take care of the soon-to-be orphan, Fulgêncio sent for the boy to come to Rio de Janeiro. Upon hearing that a young man in mourning had arrived, he concluded that he must be his nephew, and concluded correctly. It was indeed him.

So far, nothing has happened that would seem out of place in any innocently romantic tale: we have an old lunatic, a lonely, sighing damsel, and now the unexpected arrival of a nephew. So as not to descend from the poetic sphere in which we find ourselves, I shall omit to mention that the mule on which Raimundo was mounted was led back by a slave to the place it had been hired from; I shall skim over the arrangements for the young man's accommodation, limiting myself to saying that since the uncle, by virtue of his devotion to reading, had entirely forgotten that he had sent for the boy, no preparations whatsoever had been made to receive him. However, the house was large and well appointed, and, an hour later, the young man was comfortably lodged in a beautiful room overlooking the kitchen garden, the old well, the laundry, copious lush greenery, and an immense blue sky.

I don't believe I have yet revealed the new guest's age. He is fifteen years old, with just a hint of fuzz on his upper lip; in fact, he's almost a child. So if Caetaninha quickly became flustered, and the slave-women began rushing hither and thither, peering around doors and talking about "the ole master's nephew come from far away," it's because nothing much happened in that house, not because he was a grown man. This was also Fulgêncio's impression, but here's the difference. Caetaninha was unaware that the vocation of such fuzz is to become a mustache, or if she thought of it at all, she did this so vaguely that it's not worth mentioning here. This was not the case with old Fulgêncio. He understood that here was material for a husband, and he resolved to marry the pair of them. But he also saw that, unless he took them by the hand and instructed them to fall in love, chance might move things in a different direction.

One thought begets another. The idea of marrying them combined with one of his recent opinions, viz., that calamities and setbacks in matters of the heart come from love being conducted in a purely empirical manner, with no scientific basis. A man and a woman who were aware of the physical and metaphysical reasons for such a sentiment would be more inclined to receive and nourish it effectively than a man and a woman who knew nothing of the phenomenon.

"My young charges are still wet behind the ears," he said to himself. "I have three or four years ahead of me, and I can start preparing them now. We shall proceed in a logical manner; first, the foundations, then the walls, then the roof . . . rather than starting with the roof . . . Someday we will learn to love just as we learn to read. When that day comes . . ."

He was dazed, dazzled, and delirious. He went to his bookshelves, took down various volumes on astronomy, geology, physiology, anatomy, jurisprudence, politics, and linguistics, opening them, leafing through them, comparing them, and taking a few notes here and there, until he had formulated a program of instruction. It was composed of twenty chapters, and included general concepts of the universe, a definition of life, a demonstration of the existence of man and woman, the organization of societies, the definition and analysis of passion, and the definition and analysis of love, along with its causes, needs, and effects. In truth, they were rather tricky subjects, but he knew how to tame them by using plain, everyday language, giving them a purely familiar tone, just as Fontenelle did when he wrote about astronomy. And he would say emphatically that the essential part of the fruit was the pulp, not the peel.

All of this was highly ingenious, but here is the most ingenious bit. He did not ask them if they wanted to learn. One night, looking up at the sky, he commented on how brightly the stars were shining; and what were the stars? Did they perhaps know what the stars were?

"No, sir."

From here it was but a short step to beginning a description of the universe. Fulgêncio took that step so nimbly and so naturally that the two youngsters were delighted and charmed, and begged him to continue the journey.

"No," said the old man. "We won't exhaust it all today; these things can only be understood slowly. Maybe tomorrow, or the day after . . ."

Thus, stealthily, he began to execute his plan. The two students, astounded by the world of astronomy, begged him every day to continue, and, although Caetaninha was a little confused at the end of this first lesson, she still wanted to hear the other things her godfather had promised to tell them.

I will say nothing about the growing familiarity between the two students, since that would be too obvious. The difference between fourteen and fifteen is so small that the two bearers of those respective ages had little more to do than take each other by the hand. This is what happened.

After three weeks, it was as if they had been raised together. This alone was enough to change Caetaninha's life, but Raimundo brought her still more. Less than ten minutes ago, we saw her looking longingly at the riding parties of ladies and gentlemen passing along the road. Raimundo put an end to such longings by teaching her to ride, despite the reluctance of her godfather, who feared some accident might befall her. Nevertheless, he gave in and hired two horses. Caetaninha ordered a beautiful riding habit; Raimundo went into the city to buy her gloves and a riding crop, with his uncle's money (obviously), which also provided him with the boots and other men's apparel he needed. It was soon a pleasure to behold them both, gallant and intrepid, riding up and down the mountain.

At home, they were free to do as they wished, playing checkers and cards, tending to the birds and the plants. They often quarreled, but, according to the house-slaves, these were silly squabbles that they got into just so that they could make up afterward. Such was the extent of their quarrels. Raimundo sometimes went into the city on his uncle's instructions. Caetaninha would wait for him at the front gate, watching anxiously. When he arrived, they would always argue, because she wanted to take the largest parcels on the pretext that he looked tired, and he wanted to give her the lightest one, claiming that she was too delicate.

After four months, life had changed completely. One could even say that only then did Caetaninha begin to wear roses in her hair. Before this, she would often come to the breakfast table with her hair uncombed. Now, not only did she comb and brush her hair first thing, she would even, as I say, wear roses—one or even two, which were either picked by her the previous night and kept in water, or picked that very morning by Raimundo, who would then bring them to her window. The window was high up, but, by standing on tiptoe and reaching out his arm, Raimundo managed to hand her the roses. It was at around this time that he acquired the habit of tormenting his incipient mustache, tugging at it, first on one side and then on the other. Caetaninha would rap him on the knuckles to make him desist from such an unseemly practice.

Meanwhile, their lessons followed a regular pattern. They already had a general notion of the universe, and a definition of life that neither of them understood. Thus they reached the fifth month. In the sixth, Fulgêncio began his demonstration of the existence of man. Caetaninha could not help giggling when her godfather asked if they knew that they existed and why; but she quickly became serious, and replied that she did not.

"What about you?"

"No, me neither," confirmed the nephew.

Fulgêncio began a general, and profoundly Cartesian, demonstration. The following lesson took place in the garden. It had rained heavily in the preceding days, but the sun now flooded everything with light, and the garden resembled a beautiful widow who has swapped her mourning veil for that of a bride. As if wanting to imitate the sun (great things naturally copy each other), Raimundo shot her a long, all-embracing gaze, which Caetaninha received, quivering, just like the garden. Fusion, transfusion, diffusion, confusion, and profusion of beings and things.

While the old man spoke—straightforward, logical, and plodding, relishing his words, and with his eyes fixed on nowhere in particular, his two students made strenuous efforts to listen, but found themselves hopelessly distracted by other things. First, it was a pair of butterflies fluttering in the breeze. Would you please tell me what is so extraordinary about a pair of butterflies? Admittedly, they were yellow, but this alone is insufficient to explain the distraction. Nor was their distraction justified by the fact that the butterflies were chasing each other—to the left, to the right, then up, then down—given that butterflies, unlike soldiers, never travel in a straight line.

"Man's understanding," Fulgêncio was saying, "as I have just explained . . ."

Raimundo gazed at Caetaninha, and found her gazing at him. Each of them seemed awkward and confused. She was the first to lower her eyes. Then she raised them again, so as to look at something else farther off, such as the garden wall; on their way there, given that Raimundo's eyes lay in their path, she glanced at them as briefly as she could. Luckily, the wall presented a spectacle that filled her with surprise: a pair of swallows (it was the day for couples) were hopping along it with the elegance peculiar to winged beings. They chirruped as they hopped, saying things to each other, whatever it might be, perhaps this: that it was a very good thing that there was no philosophy in garden walls. Suddenly one of them took off, probably the female, and the other, naturally the male, was not going to let himself be left behind: he spread his wings and flew off in the same direction. Caetaninha looked down at the grass.

When the lesson finished a few minutes later, she begged her godfather to continue and, when he refused, took him by the arm and invited him to take a turn in the garden.

"No, it's too sunny," protested the old man.

"We'll walk in the shade."

"It's terribly hot."

Caetaninha suggested they remain on the veranda, but her godfather said to her mysteriously that Rome was not built in a day, and ended up saying that he would only continue the lesson two days hence. Caetaninha retired to her room and stayed there for three-quarters of an hour, with the door closed, either seated or standing at the window or pacing back and forth, or else looking for something she was already holding in her hand, and even going so far as to imagine herself riding up the road alongside Raimundo. At one point, she saw the young man standing by the garden wall, but, on closer inspection she realized it was a pair of beetles buzzing through the air. One of the beetles was saying to the other:

"Thou art the flower of our race, the flower of the air, the flower of flowers, the sun and moon of my life."

To which the other replied:

"No one exceeds thee in beauty and grace; thy buzzing is an echo of divine voices; but leave me . . . leave me . . ."

"Why should I leave thee, O soul of these sylvan glades?"

"I have told thee, king of pure breezes, leave me."

"Do not speak to me like that, thou charm and ornament of the forest. Everything above and around us is saying that thou shouldst speak to me another way. Dost thou not know the song of blue mysteries?"

"Let us listen to it upon the green leaves of the orange tree."

"The leaves of the mango tree are lovelier."

"Thou art more beautiful than both."

"And thee, O sun of my life?"

"Moon of my being, I am whatever thou wilt have me be . . ."

This is how the two beetles were talking. She listened to them, engrossed. When they disappeared, she turned away from the window, saw what time it was, and left her bedroom. Raimundo had gone out; she went to wait for him at the front gate for ten, twenty, thirty, forty, fifty minutes. When he returned, they said very little; they met and parted two or three times. The last time it was she who took him to the veranda, to show him a trinket she thought she'd lost and had just found. Readers, please do her the justice of believing that this was a blatant lie. Meanwhile, Fulgêncio brought the next lesson forward and gave it on the following day between lunch and dinner. Never had he spoken so clearly and simply, which was just as it should be, for it was the lesson concerning the existence of man, a profoundly metaphysical chapter, in which it was necessary to consider everything and from every possible angle.

"Do you understand?" he asked.

"Perfectly."

And the lesson carried on to its conclusion. When it was over, the same thing happened as the day before. As if she were afraid of being alone, Caetaninha begged him to continue the lesson, or to take a turn about the garden with her. He refused both requests, patted her paternally on the cheek, and went and shut himself up in his study.

"Next week," the old man thought as he turned the key, "next week I will make a start on the organization of societies; all of next month and the one after will be devoted to the definition and classification of passion; in May we will move on to love . . . by then it will be time . . ."

While he was saying this and closing the study door, a sound echoed forth from the veranda—a thunderclap of kisses, according to the caterpillars in the garden. Mind you, to caterpillars the slightest noise sounds like thunder. As for the authors of the noise, nothing definitive is known. It seems that a wasp, seeing Caetaninha and Raimundo together at that moment, confused coincidence with consequence and deduced that it was them, but an old grasshopper demonstrated the absurdity of such a proposition, citing the fact that he had heard many kisses, long ago, in places where neither Raimundo nor Caetaninha had ever set foot. We may all agree that this latter argument was utter nonsense, but such is the prestige of good character that the grasshopper was applauded for having once again defended both truth and reason. And, on that basis, maybe it was indeed so. But a thunderclap of kisses? Let's imagine there were two; let's even imagine three or four.

GALVÃO'S WIFE

PEOPLE BEGAN TO MUTTER about the lawyer's affection for the brigadier's widow long before they had even passed the stage of initial flirtation. Such are the ways of the world. It is how some bad reputations are
made, and, absurd though it may seem, some good ones too. Indeed, there
are lives that have only a prologue, but everyone talks about the great book
that ensues, and the author dies with the pages left blank. In the present
case, the pages were written and formed a fat volume of three hundred
dense pages, not counting the notes. These were placed at the end, not to
enlighten the reader, but to remind him or her of the preceding chapters;
that is how these collaborative books work. The truth is, though, that they
were merely settling on a plan, when the lawyer's wife received this anonymous note:

> Madam, you cannot possibly allow yourself to be so scandalously
> deceived for a moment longer by one of your own friends, who seeks
> comfort in her widowhood by seducing other women's husbands, when
> it would be enough to keep her ringlets . . .

What ringlets? Maria Olímpia did not ask which ringlets these were;
they belonged to the brigadier's widow, who wore them for pleasure and
not for fashion. I believe this took place in 1853. Maria Olímpia read and
reread the note; she examined the handwriting, which appeared to be a

woman's, albeit disguised, and mentally she ran through the names of her closest friends, trying to think who the author might be. No one came to mind, and so she folded up the piece of paper and stared down at the carpet, her eyes falling on precisely the part of the pattern where two doves were teaching each other how to make one beak out of two. Some of these ironies of coincidence make you want to tear down the universe. Finally, she put the note in her pocket and turned to face her slave, who was patiently waiting, and who asked her:

"Don't you want to see the shawl no more, missy?"

Maria Olímpia took the shawl the slave was holding out for her and draped it over her shoulders in front of the mirror. She thought it looked much better on her than it would have on the widow. She compared her own charms with the other woman's. Neither eyes nor mouth bore any comparison; the widow had narrow little shoulders, a big head, and an ugly gait. She was tall, but what use was that? And thirty-five years old, nine more than her! While she was thinking these thoughts, she adjusted the shawl, pinning and unpinning it this way and that.

"This one looks nicer than the other," ventured the slave.

"I don't know," said the lady, moving closer to the window with both shawls in her hands.

"Put the other one on, missy."

Missy obeyed. She tried on five of the ten shawls that surrounded her, still in their boxes, from a shop on Rua da Ajuda. She concluded that the first two were the best, but here there was a complication—a minor one, really, but so subtle and so profound in its solution that I would not hesitate to recommend it to our thinkers of 1906. The question was to know which of the two shawls she would choose, given that her husband, a recently qualified lawyer, was asking her to be economical. She looked at them one after another, first preferring one, then the other. Suddenly she remembered her husband's perfidy, the need to punish him, to make him suffer, to show him that she was no one's patsy, nor some ragamuffin; and so, out of anger, she bought both shawls.

When four o'clock struck (being the time her husband was due home), there was no husband. Not at four, nor at half-past four. Maria Olímpia imagined all sorts of distressing things; she went to the window, then came back again, fearing an accident or a sudden illness; she also wondered if it might be a jury session. Five o'clock and still nothing. The widow's ringlets also loomed darkly before her, somewhere between the illness and the jury, in shades of dark blue, which was probably the devil's color. It really was enough to exhaust the patience of a young woman of twenty-six. Twenty-six, that's all she was. She was the daughter of a parliamentarian from the time of the Regency, who had died when she was still a child, and an aunt had given her a most unusual upbringing, not taking her to dances or spectacles before her time. She was a religious woman and took her first to church. Maria Olímpia's vocation was for the outside world, and at the processions and sung masses what she liked best was the hubbub and the pomp; her devotion was sincere, but tepid and absentminded. The first thing she saw on the church balcony was herself. She particularly enjoyed looking down from above, staring at the crowd of women, kneeling or seated, and the young men who, standing below the choir or at the side doors, enlivened the Latin liturgy with their passionate glances. She didn't understand the sermons, but the rest—musicians, song, flowers, candles, canopies, gold, people—all cast a peculiar spell on her. A meager faith, then, which became even more so after her first theatrical spectacle and her first ball. She didn't manage to see Candiani, but she saw Ida Edelvira, danced exuberantly, and gained a reputation for elegance.

It was half-past five when Galvão arrived. When she heard his footsteps, Maria Olímpia, who by then was pacing the drawing room, did what any other lady would do in a similar situation: she picked up a fashion magazine and nonchalantly sat down to read. Galvão entered, smiling and out of breath, asking her affectionately if she was angry, and swearing that he had a good reason for being late, a reason she would thank him for, once she knew . . .

"There's no need," she said coldly, interrupting him in midsentence.

She stood up and they went in to dinner. They spoke little, she less than he, but without appearing to be at all upset. Perhaps she had begun to doubt the anonymous letter; it may also be that the two shawls were weighing on her conscience. At the end of dinner, Galvão explained his lateness; he had gone, on foot, to the Teatro Provisório to buy tickets for a box that very evening: they were putting on *I Lombardi*. On his way back, he had gone to order a carriage—

"*I Lombardi?*" interrupted Maria Olímpia.

"Yes. Laboceta's singing, and Jacobson, and there's a ballet scene. You've never seen *I Lombardi?*"

"Never."

"Anyway, that's why I'm late. So what punishment do you deserve now? Perhaps I should cut off the tip of that turned-up little nose of yours . . ."

As he accompanied his words with a gesture, she drew back her head; then she finished her coffee. We really should have pity on the soul of this young lady. While the first chords of I Lombardi were already echoing inside her, the anonymous letter struck a lugubrious note, a kind of requiem. And might the letter not simply be a vicious calumny? Obviously it couldn't be anything else: some wild invention of her enemies, either to upset her or to set the couple quarreling. That was it. In the meantime, now that she was forewarned, she wouldn't let them out of her sight. Here an idea came to her: she asked her husband if he would send an invitation to the widow to join them.

"No," he replied. "The carriage only has two seats, and I have no intention of sitting up with the coachman."

Maria Olímpia smiled contentedly, and stood up. She had long wanted to hear I Lombardi. Let's go! Tra, la, la, la . . . Half an hour later, she went upstairs to dress. When Galvão saw her come down a short time later, ready to go, he was delighted. "My wife is beautiful," he thought, and made as if to clasp her to his chest. But his wife pulled back, telling him not to rumple her dress. And when he, playing the valet, tried to straighten the feather in her hair, she said to him, rather irritated:

"Stop it, Eduardo! Is the carriage here yet?"

They got into the carriage and set off for the theater. And who should be in the box next to theirs? The widow and her mother, of course. This coincidence—the daughter of fate—might lead one to believe there had been some prior arrangement. Maria Olímpia did, indeed, suspect as much, but the sensation caused by her arrival gave her no time to examine her suspicion. The entire audience had turned to look at her, and she drank in, in slow draughts, the milk of public admiration. Moreover, her husband had the Machiavellian inspiration to say in her ear: "Perhaps you should have invited her, then she would have owed us the favor." Any suspicion would evaporate at such words. Nevertheless, she took care not to let them out of her sight, a resolution she renewed every five minutes for half an hour, until, unable to remain vigilant, she allowed her attention to wander. Off the restless thing goes, heading straight for the bright lights, the magnificent costumes, lingering briefly on the opera itself, as if demanding from all those things some delicious sensation in which a cold, individual soul could luxuriate. And then back it came to her, to her fan, her gloves, the frills on her dress, which really was rather magnificent. Talking with the widow during the intervals, Maria Olímpia maintained her usual voice and gestures, uncalculated and effortless, not a trace of resentment, the letter entirely forgotten. And during the intervals her husband, of course, with a discretion rare among the sons of men, went off to the aisles or the foyer, looking for news about the government.

At the end, the two ladies left the box together and made their way down to the foyer. The modesty with which the widow was dressed may well have emphasized the magnificence of her friend. Her features, however, were not as the latter had described them while trying on shawls that morning. No, sir; the widow's features were charming, with a certain originality about them. Her shoulders were pretty and perfectly proportioned. She was not thirty-five but thirty-one; she was born in 1822, on the very eve of independence, so much so that her father, jokingly, began to call her Ipiranga, and the nickname stuck among her friends. Furthermore, the baptism registry was there for all to see in Santa Rita.

A week later, Maria Olímpia received another anonymous letter. It was longer and more explicit. Others followed, once a week for three months. Maria Olímpia read the first with some irritation, but she gradually became hardened to those that followed. There was no doubt that, unlike before, her husband often came home late from work, or he would go out in the evenings and return very late; but, according to him, he spent the time at Wallerstein's or Bernardo's, discussing politics. And this was true, but only for five or ten minutes, the time necessary to pick up some anecdote or novelty he could repeat at home as an alibi. From there he would go to Largo de São Francisco and catch the public omnibus.

It was all true. And yet, still she refused to believe the letters. Lately, she no longer bothered to take the trouble to reject what they said; she would read them just once and tear them up. As time passed, other, less vague signs began to appear, little by little, in the way that land gradually appears to sailors; but this Columbus stubbornly refused to believe in America. She denied what she saw; and when she could no longer deny it, she interpreted it; then she would recall some instance of a hallucination, a tale about illusory appearances, and on this soft and comfortable pillow she would lay her head and sleep. By now the law practice was prospering, and Galvão hosted card games and dinner parties; they went to balls, theaters, and horse races. Maria Olímpia was happy and radiant; she was beginning to be thought of as one of the foremost ladies of fashion. And she was frequently in the company of the widow, despite the letters, and to such an extent that one letter commented: "There seems little point in writing to you again, since you are evidently relishing this distasteful concubinage." What on earth was concubinage? Maria Olímpia wanted to ask her husband, but promptly forgot the word and thought no more about it.

Meanwhile, it came to the attention of her husband that his wife was receiving letters in the post. Letters from whom? This was a hard and unexpected blow. Galvão scoured his memory for all the people who came to their house, those they might meet at theaters and balls, and found many likely candidates. Indeed, she did not lack admirers.

"Letters from whom?" he repeated, biting his lip and furrowing his brow.

For seven days he was restless and irritable, spying on his wife and spending most of his time at home. On the eighth day, a letter arrived.

"For me?" he asked brightly.

"No, it's for me," replied Maria Olímpia, reading the envelope. "It looks like Mariana or Lula Fontoura's handwriting."

She didn't want to open it, but her husband told her to read it; it might be some grave news. Maria Olímpia read the letter and folded it up, smiling; she was about to put it away when her husband asked her what it was.

"You smiled," he said teasingly. "It must be some joke at my expense."

"As if! It's about sewing patterns."

"Then let me see."

"What for, Eduardo?"

"What's the matter? If you don't want to show me, there must be some reason. Give it here."

He was no longer smiling; his voice trembled. She again refused to hand over the letter, once, twice, three times. She even considered tearing it up, but that would only make matters worse, and she wouldn't be able to destroy it completely. It really was a rather peculiar situation. When she saw that there was no other solution, she decided to give in. What better occasion to read the expression of truth on his face? The letter was one of the most explicit; it talked about the widow in the crudest of terms. Maria Olímpia handed it to him.

"I didn't want to show you this," she said first, "just as I haven't shown you the others that I've received and thrown away. It's all silly tittle-tattle, designed to . . . Go on, read it, read the letter."

Galvão opened the letter and read avidly. She hung her head low, studying at close quarters the fringe on her dress. She did not see him turn pale. When, a few minutes later, he said a few words, his face was already perfectly composed and bore an inkling of a smile. But his wife, failing to divine his true feelings, replied with her head still bowed; she raised it only three or four minutes later, and not to look straight at him, but bit by bit, as if she feared finding in his eyes confirmation of the anonymous letter. Seeing, on the contrary, that he was smiling, she thought this was the smile of innocence, and changed the subject.

The husband redoubled his precautions; it would also seem that he could not help feeling a certain admiration for his wife. The widow, for her part, having been warned about the letters, felt deeply ashamed, but reacted quickly by becoming even more affectionate toward her dear, dear friend.

In the second or third week of August, Galvão became a member of the Cassino Fluminense club. This was one of his wife's fondest dreams. September 6 was the widow's birthday, as we already know. The day before, Maria Olímpia (accompanied by her aunt who was visiting the city) went to buy her a gift, as was their usual habit. She bought her a ring. At the same establishment she saw a charming piece of jewelry, a diamond hairpiece in the shape of a crescent moon, the emblem of Diana, which would suit her very well, pinned just above her forehead. Even when the symbol comes from Muhammad, anything with diamonds in it counts as Christian. Maria Olímpia naturally thought of the first night that they would be attending the Cassino, and her aunt, seeing that she wanted it, offered to buy it for her. Too late; it had already been sold.

The evening of the ball arrived. Maria Olímpia felt a thrill of excitement as she ascended the staircase at the Cassino. People who knew her at the time say that what she experienced when out in the world was a sense of being caressed by the public gaze, albeit at a distance; it was her way of being loved. Now that they were members of the Cassino, she would be gathering a veritable cornucopia of admiring looks. She was not mistaken, for this is precisely what happened, and from the highest echelons too.

It was at around half-past ten that the widow arrived. She looked really beautiful, impeccably dressed, and wearing the crescent moon of diamonds on her head. The wretched jewel suited her devilishly well, with its two points turned upward, emerging from among her dark hair. Everyone in the hall had always admired the widow. She had many female friends, some closer than others, and more than a few admirers, and she possessed the kind of personality that comes alive under the bright lights. The head of a certain legation simply would not stop recommending her to newer members of the diplomatic corps: "*Causez avec Mme. Tavares; c'est adorable!*" Thus it had been on other nights, and thus it was on this one.

"I've had hardly a moment to talk to you tonight," she said to Maria Olímpia, as midnight approached.

"It's only natural," said the other, opening and closing her fan. And, after moistening her lips, as if to prime them with all the venom she had in her heart: "My dear Ipiranga, tonight, you are a very charming widow . . . Have you come to seduce yet another husband?"

The widow turned pale and speechless. With her eyes, Maria Olímpia added something that humiliated the widow utterly, splattering her triumph with mud. For the rest of the night, they spoke little; three days later, they broke with each other for good.

THE ACADEMIES OF SIAM

———

Have you heard of the academies of Siam? All right, I know Siam never had any academies, but let's just suppose it did, and that there were four of them, and then listen.

I

Whenever they saw swarms of milky-hued fireflies rising up through the night sky, the stars would often say that these were the sighs of the king of Siam, who was amusing himself with his three hundred concubines. And, winking at each other, they would ask:

"Pray tell us, O regal sighs, what is the beautiful Kalaphangko up to tonight?"

To which the fireflies would reply gravely:

"We are the sublime thoughts of the four academies of Siam; we bring with us all the wisdom of the universe."

One night, there were so many fireflies that the stars took fright and hid in their bedrooms, and the fireflies took over part of outer space, where they stayed forever and called themselves the "Milky Way."

This enormous rising cloud of thoughts was the result of the four academies of Siam trying to solve a very peculiar puzzle: Why are there feminine men and masculine women? And it was the nature of their young king that led them to ask this question. Kalaphangko was virtually a lady. Everything about him breathed the most exquisite femininity: he had velvety eyes, a silvery voice, gentle, amenable manners, and an abiding horror of war. The Siamese warlords grumbled, but the nation lived very happily; everywhere there were dances, plays, and songs, following the example of the king, who cared for little else, which rather explains the stars' misinterpretation of those sighs.

Then, suddenly, one of the academies came up with a solution to the problem:

"Some souls are masculine, others are feminine. The anomaly we have before us is a case of mistaken bodies."

"I disagree," shouted the other three. "The soul is neuter; it has nothing to do with external differences."

Nothing more was needed for the alleys and waterways of Bangkok to turn red with academic blood. First came controversy, then insults, and finally fistfights. It wasn't so bad when the insults began; no one hurled abuse that was not scrupulously derived from Sanskrit, which was the academic language, the Latin of Siam. From then on, though, they lost all shame. The rivalry turned very nasty indeed, rolled up its sleeves, and descended into mudslinging, stone-throwing, punches, and vile gestures, until, in exasperation, the sexual academy (i.e., that which espoused the sexuality of souls) decided to put an end to the other three academies, and prepared a sinister plan . . . O winds that blow, scatter forth these leaves of paper, that I may not recount the tragedy of Siam! For—woe is me!—I can scarcely bear to write of such a dastardly revenge. They secretly armed themselves and went to find the members of the other academies, just as the latter, sitting hunched in thought over the famous puzzle, were dispatching a cloud of fireflies up to heaven. They gave no warning and showed no pity, but fell upon them, foaming with rage. Those who fled did not flee for long; pursued and attacked, they died on the riverbank, aboard barges, or in dark alleyways. Altogether there were thirty-eight corpses. An ear was cut off from each of the leaders, and these were made into necklaces and bracelets for their own victorious president, the sublime U-Tong. Drunk on victory, they celebrated the deed with a great feast, at which they sang this magnificent hymn: "Glory be to us, for we are the rice of science and the lamp of the universe."

The city awoke to this horrifying news. Terror gripped the masses. No one could forgive such a cruel and despicable act; some even doubted their own eyes. Only one person approved of it all: the beautiful Kinnara, the flower of the royal concubines.

II

Lying languidly at the feet of the beautiful Kinnara, the young king asked her to sing.

"I'll sing no other song than this: I believe that souls have a sex."

"What you believe is absurd, Kinnara."

"So, Your Majesty believes that souls are neuter?"

"That is equally absurd. No, I don't believe in the neuter soul, or the sexual soul, either."

"But then what does Your Majesty believe in?"

"I believe in your eyes, Kinnara. They are the sun and light of the universe."

"But you must choose: either you believe that souls have no sex, and must, therefore, punish the only surviving academy, or you believe that souls do have a sex, and must, therefore, pardon it."

"What a delightful mouth you have, my sweet Kinnara! I believe in your mouth; it is the very fount of wisdom."

Kinnara leapt angrily to her feet. Just as the king was the feminine man, she was the masculine woman—a buffalo in swan's feathers. Just now it was the buffalo that strode across the bedchamber, but, a moment later, it was the swan that stopped and, tilting her neck, asked and obtained from the king, between two gentle caresses, a decree in which the doctrine of the sexual soul was declared legitimate and orthodox, and the other doctrine absurd and perverse. On that same day, the decree was sent to the victorious academy, to all the pagodas and mandarins, and distributed throughout the kingdom. The academy hung out lanterns, and peace was restored.

III

Meanwhile, the beautiful Kinnara had an ingenious and secret plan. One night, while the king was studying some papers of state, she asked him if taxes were being paid on time.

"*Ohimè!*" he exclaimed, repeating a word he had heard from an Italian missionary. "Alas, very few taxes have been paid, but I didn't want to have the defaulters beheaded . . . No, not that . . . Blood? Blood? No, I want no blood . . ."

"And what if I were to find you a solution to all of this?"

"What solution?"

"Your Majesty has decreed that souls are masculine and feminine," said Kinnara, after first giving him a kiss. "Suppose that our bodies have been switched. All we need is to return each soul to the body that belongs to it. Let us exchange souls and bodies . . ."

Kalaphangko scoffed at the idea, and asked her just how they would achieve such an exchange. She replied that she would use the method of Mukunda, the king of the Hindus, who placed himself in the corpse of a Brahmin while a jester entered Mukunda's. It's an old legend passed down to the Turks, Persians, and Christians. Yes, but how was the invocation worded? Kinnara declared that she knew the wording, because an old Buddhist monk had found a copy of it in the ruins of a temple.

"What do you think?"

"I don't actually believe in my own decree," he retorted, laughing, "but go ahead; if it's true, let's switch. But only for six months, no more. At the end of six months, we'll change back."

They agreed to make the exchange that very night. While the city slept, they sent for the royal barge, stepped aboard, and let themselves drift away. None of the rowers saw them. When Dawn appeared, urging on the golden-red cows drawing her glittering chariot, Kinnara offered up the mysterious invocation. Her soul detached itself from her body and hovered in the air, waiting for the king's body to become vacant too. Her own body lay slumped on the rug.

"Ready?" asked Kalaphangko.

"Ready. I'm here in the air, waiting for you. Please excuse my undignified state, Your Majesty . . ."

But the king's soul did not hear the rest. Sprightly and shimmering, it left its physical vessel and entered Kinnara's body, while her soul took possession of the royal remains. Both bodies sat up and gazed at each other, and one can only imagine their amazement. It was the same situation as Buoso and the serpent in Dante's *Inferno*, but see here my audacity. The poet silences Ovid and Lucan, because he considers his metamorphosis worthier than either of theirs. I am silencing all three of them. Buoso and the snake never meet again, whereas my two heroes continue talking and living together after the switch—which, though I say so myself, is obviously even more Dantesque.

Kalaphangko said: "This business of looking at myself and calling myself 'Your Majesty' is very strange. Does Your Majesty not feel the same?"

Both of them were content, like people who have finally found their proper home. Kalaphangko luxuriated in Kinnara's feminine curves. Kinnara flexed her muscles in Kalaphangko's solid torso. Siam finally had a king.

IV

Kalaphangko's first action (from now on, it should be understood that "Kalaphangko" means the king's body and Kinnara's soul, whereas "Kinnara" means the body of the beautiful Siamese lady and Kalaphangko's soul) was to bestow the very highest honors upon the sexual academy. He did not elevate its members to the status of mandarins, for they were men given to philosophy and literature rather than action and administration, but he decreed that everyone must prostrate themselves before them, as was the custom with mandarins. He also presented them with rare and valuable gifts, such as stuffed crocodiles, ivory chairs, emerald tableware, diamonds, and sacred relics. Grateful for all these favors, the academy also requested the official right to use the title "Light of the World," which was duly granted.

Once this was done, Kalaphangko turned his attention to the public finances, justice, religion, and ceremonial matters. The nation began to feel the "heavy weight," to use the words of our distinguished poet, Camões— for no less than eleven tax dodgers were forthwith beheaded. The others, who naturally preferred their heads to their money, rushed to pay their taxes, and order was quickly restored. The courts and legislation were greatly improved. New pagodas were built, and religion seemed to gain a new impetus, since Kalaphangko, imitating the ancient Spanish arts, ordered the burning of a dozen poor Christian missionaries who were wandering those parts; the bonzes called this action the "pearl" of his reign.

What he lacked was a war. On a more or less diplomatic pretext, Kalaphangko attacked a neighboring kingdom, in what was the shortest and most glorious campaign of the century. On his return to Bangkok, he was greeted with splendid celebrations. Three hundred boats decorated with blue and scarlet silk went out to receive him. On the prow of each boat stood a golden dragon or swan, and all the boats were crewed by the city's finest inhabitants. Music and cheering filled the air. At night, when the festivities had ended, his beautiful concubine whispered in his ear:

"My young warrior, repay me for the pangs of longing that I felt in your absence; tell me that the greatest of celebrations is your sweet Kinnara."

Kalaphangko responded with a kiss.

"Your lips have the chill of death or disdain on them," she sighed.

It was true; the king was distracted and preoccupied, for he was plotting a tragedy. It was getting close to the time when they should return to their own bodies, and he was thinking of escaping that clause in their agreement by killing his beautiful concubine. He hesitated because he did not know if he, too, would suffer upon her death, given that it was his body, or even if he would have to succumb with her. Such were Kalaphangko's thoughts. But the idea of death cast a shadow over his brow, while, imitating the Borgias, he clutched to his breast a little vial of poison.

Suddenly he remembered the learned academy; he could consult it, not directly, but hypothetically. He summoned the academicians; they all came except their president, the illustrious U-Tong, who was ill. There were thirteen of them; they prostrated themselves and, in the Siamese manner, said:

"Mere despicable straws that we are, we hasten to answer the call of Kalaphangko."

"Arise," said the king benevolently.

"No, the place for dust is underfoot," they insisted, their knees and elbows on the ground.

"Then I will be the wind that lifts up the dust," replied Kalaphangko, and, with a gracious, tolerant gesture, he stretched out his hands to them.

He then started to talk about a variety of matters, so that the main topic of interest should appear to arise naturally of its own accord. He spoke of the latest news from the west and the Laws of Manu. Referring to U-Tong, he asked them whether he really was as great a sage as he seemed; when he received only a reluctant, mumbled response, he ordered them to tell him the whole truth. They confessed, with exemplary unanimity, that U-Tong was one of the most sublime idiots in the kingdom—a shallow, worthless mind who knew nothing and was incapable of learning. Kalaphangko was shocked. An idiot?

"It pains us to say so, but that is what he is; a shallow, withered intellect. He has, however, a pure heart, and a noble, elevated character."

When he had recovered from his shock, Kalaphangko told the academicians to leave, without asking them the question he had intended to ask. An idiot? He would somehow have to unseat him from the academy without offending him. Three days later, U-Tong was summoned by the king. The king inquired kindly after his health. He then said that he wanted to send someone to Japan to study some documents; it was a matter which could only be entrusted to a person of enlightenment. Which of his colleagues at the academy seemed to him most suitable for such a task? One can see the king's cunning plan: he would hear two or three names, and then conclude that he preferred U-Tong himself to all of them. But here's what U-Tong replied:

"My royal lord and master, if you will pardon my coarse language: the men you speak of are thirteen camels, except that camels are modest and they are not. They compare themselves to the sun and the moon. But, in truth, neither the sun nor the moon has ever shone on such worthless fools. I understand Your Majesty's surprise, but I would be unworthy of my position if I did not say this with all due loyalty, albeit confidentially . . ."

Kalaphangko's jaw dropped. Thirteen camels? Thirteen, thirteen! U-Tong's only kind word was for their hearts, all of which he declared to be excellent; no one was superior to them in terms of character. With an elegant, indulgent gesture, Kalaphangko dismissed the sublime U-Tong from his presence, and remained pensive. What his thoughts were, no one knew. What we do know is that he sent for the other academicians, but this time separately, to conceal his intentions and obtain a franker exchange of views. The first to arrive, although unaware of U-Tong's opinion, was entirely in agreement, with but one emendation, that there were twelve camels, or thirteen if one counted U-Tang himself. The second academician expressed the same opinion, as did the third and all the others. They differed only in style: some said camels, others used circumlocutions and metaphors that meant the same thing. However, none of them cast any aspersions on anyone's moral character. Kalaphangko was speechless.

But this was not the final shock to greet the king. Since he could not consult the academy, he attempted to make his own deliberations. He devoted two whole days to this, but then the beautiful Kinnara revealed that she was going to be a mother. This news made him recoil from the crime he had been planning. How could he destroy the chosen vessel of the flower that would bloom the following spring? He swore to heaven and earth that the child would be born and would flourish. The end of the week arrived, and with it the moment for each of them to return to their original bodies.

As on the previous occasion, they boarded the royal barge at night, and let themselves drift downstream, both of them against their will, not wanting to give up the body they had and return to the other. When the shimmering cows of Dawn's chariot began to tread slowly across the sky, they offered up the mysterious invocation, and each soul was returned to its former body. On returning to hers, Kinnara felt a maternal instinct, just as she had felt a paternal instinct when she occupied Kalaphongko's body. It even seemed to her that she was simultaneously mother and father of the child.

"Father and mother?" repeated the king, restored to his former self.

They were interrupted by delightful music in the distance. It was a junk or a canoe coming upriver, for the music was fast approaching. By then the sun was flooding the waters and green riverbanks with light, giving the scene an air of life and rebirth, which to some extent made the two lovers forget this return to their former selves. And the music kept coming closer, clearer now, until a magnificent boat appeared around a bend in the river, decorated with feathers and fluttering pennants. Aboard were the fourteen members of the academy (including U-Tong), all chanting in unison that old hymn: "Glory be to us, for we are the rice of science and the light of the world!"

The beautiful Kinnara (formerly Kalaphangko) was wide-eyed with astonishment. She could not understand how fourteen males, gathered together in an academy, could be both the light of the world, and yet, individually, a bunch of camels. She consulted Kalaphangko, but he could think of no explanation. If someone happens to find one, they would be doing a great service to one of the most gracious ladies in the Orient by sending it to her in a sealed letter, addressed, for greater security, to our consul in Shanghai, China.

ASSORTED STORIES

(1896)

My friend, let us always tell stories . . .
Time passes, and the story of life
comes to an end, unnoticed.

—*DIDEROT*

Author's Preface

The various stories that make up this volume are only a selection and could have been added to, had it not been advisable to keep the book within a reasonable length. This is the fifth collection I have published. The words of Diderot that appear as its epigraph serve as an apology to those who consider such a large number of stories to be excessive. They are simply a way of passing the time. They do not aspire to endure like the stories written by that same esteemed philosopher. They lack both the matter and the style that give Mérimée's tales the status of masterpieces and make Poe one of the greatest writers in America. It is, of course, quality rather than length that counts with this kind of story, and the mediocre short story has one quality that gives it an advantage over the mediocre novel: it is short.

M. de A.

THE FORTUNE-TELLER

———

Hamlet tells Horatio that there are more things in heaven and earth than are dreamt of in our philosophy. This was the same explanation that the lovely Rita gave to young Camilo, one Friday in November of 1869, when he scoffed at her for having gone to consult a fortune-teller the previous day, although she put it rather differently.

"Go on, then, laugh. You men are all the same; you don't believe in anything. But just so you know, when I went there, the woman knew exactly why I'd come even before I told her. As soon as she started laying down the cards, she said to me: "You love someone . . ." I confessed that I did, and then she carried on laying down the cards, and when she'd finished, she told me I was afraid you would forget me, but that this wasn't true . . ."

"Well, she was wrong there!" said Camilo, laughing.

"Oh, don't say that, Camilo. If you knew what I've been going through because of you, but then you do know; I've already told you, so don't laugh at me . . ."

Camilo clasped her hands and gazed earnestly into her eyes. He swore that he loved her deeply and that her fears were pure childishness; in any event, if she had any fears, he was the best fortune-teller to come to. Then he scolded her, telling her it was unwise to visit such places. Vilela might find out, and then . . .

"Oh, he won't find out. I made sure no one saw me going into the house."

"Where is the house?"

"Not far from here, on Rua da Guarda Velha. There was no one around. Don't worry: I'm not a complete fool."

Camilo laughed again:

"So you really believe in such things?" he asked.

It was then that she, not knowing she was translating Hamlet into every-day language, told him that there were many things in this world that are both mysterious *and* true. So what if he didn't believe her—the truth was that the fortune-teller had foreseen everything. What more did he want? Now she felt perfectly calm and contented, and *that* was the proof.

I think Camilo was about to say something, but stopped himself. He didn't want to destroy her illusions. He had been superstitious as a child and even for some time afterward, full of a whole arsenal of irrational beliefs that his mother had instilled in him, and which disappeared when he turned twenty. On the day he stripped away all this parasitical vegetation to reveal the bare trunk of religion, he, since he had learned both lessons from his mother, wrapped them in the same newfound skepticism and, soon after-ward, discarded them both. Camilo didn't believe in anything. Why? He couldn't say; he had no one reason, and so contented himself with rejecting everything. But even that isn't quite right, since rejection is itself a form of affirmation and he could not put his disbelief into words; in the face of such mysteries, he merely shrugged his shoulders and carried on regardless.

They parted in good spirits, he even more than she. Rita was sure of being loved; Camilo was not only sure of that, but also saw how she trembled and ran risks for him, for example, by resorting to visiting fortune-tellers. Though he scolded her, he couldn't help feeling flattered. Their meeting place was a house on the old Rua dos Barbonos, where a woman from Rita's home province was living. Rita walked down Rua das Mangueiras toward Botafogo, where she lived, and Camilo set off down Rua da Guarda Velha, glancing on his way at the fortune-teller's house.

Vilela, Camilo, and Rita: three names, one adventure, and no explana-tion whatsoever as to how we got there. So let me explain. The first two were childhood friends. Vilela took up a career as a local magistrate, while Camilo went into the civil service, much against the wishes of his father, who wanted him to be a doctor. However, his father died, and Camilo pre-ferred doing nothing at all, until his mother found him a government posi-tion. At the beginning of 1869, Vilela returned from the provinces, where he'd married a very beautiful, but empty-headed young woman. He had given up the magistracy and come back to the city to set up a law firm. Camilo found him a house near Botafogo, and boarded the steamer to welcome him home.

"Is it you, sir?" exclaimed Rita, holding out her hand to Camilo. "You cannot imagine how highly my husband values your friendship, for he is always talking about you."

Camilo and Vilela gazed warmly at each other. They were friends indeed.

Afterward, Camilo had to admit that Vilela's wife entirely lived up to her husband's letters. She really was both graceful and vivacious, with warm eyes and a delicate, inquisitive mouth. She was a little older than both of them: she was thirty, Vilela twenty-nine, and Camilo twenty-six. Vilela's grave demeanor, however, made him appear older than his wife, whereas Camilo was an innocent in all things practical and moral. He had acquired none of the knowledge that normally comes with the years, nor had nature endowed him with the "spectacles" it bestows on some almost at birth, giving them wisdom beyond their years; in short, he lacked both experience and intuition.

The three of them became inseparable. Proximity led to intimacy. Then Camilo's mother died, and in this disaster (for so it was) both Vilela and Rita gave proof of their great friendship for him. Vilela dealt with all the arrangements for the funeral, the mass, and the inventory of the deceased's belongings, while Rita took special care of his emotional needs, and no one could have done it better.

How they went from that to love, he never quite knew. He certainly enjoyed spending hours at her side; she was his spiritual nurse, almost his sister, but most of all she was a beautiful woman. *Odor di femmina*, the scent of a woman: that is what he breathed in from her and from the air about her, until it became part of his own self. They read the same books and went on walks together and to the theater. Camilo taught her chess and draughts, and they played every night, she badly, and he, wishing to make himself agreeable, not much better. I think you get the picture. Then came effects of a more physical nature: there were Rita's willful eyes persistently seeking his and consulting his even before her husband's; her strangely cold hands; the occasional unexpected exchange of glances. On his birthday, he received from Vilela the gift of a magnificent walking cane, and from Rita only a card with the plainest of greetings written in pencil. It was then that

Camilo learned to read his own heart, for he could not tear his eyes away from that little scrap of paper. Banal words, but some banalities are sublime, or at least delectable. The decrepit old hansom cab in which you and your ladylove first rode together entirely alone is as fine a thing as Apollo's chariot. Such is man, and such are the things that surround him.

Camilo genuinely wanted to escape, but it was too late. Rita, serpent-like, had encircled him, embraced him, squeezed him until his bones cracked and dripped venom in his mouth. He was dazed and defeated. Shame, fear, remorse, desire—he felt all of them, but the battle was brief and the victory divine. Farewell, scruples! It did not take long for the shoe to mold itself to the foot, and off they went on their merry way, arm in arm, skipping lightly over grass and pebbles, suffering nothing more than a few pangs of regret, for the moments when they were apart. Meanwhile, Vilela's trust and affection remained unchanged.

One day, however, Camilo received an anonymous letter calling him immoral and perfidious, and saying that the affair was public knowledge. Camilo was afraid and, hoping to divert suspicion, he began to visit Vilela's house less frequently. His friend commented on his absence. Camilo gave as his reason a frivolous youthful passion. Innocence bred ingenuity. Camilo's absences grew longer and longer, until his visits ceased completely. A little *amour propre* may have played its part too; a desire to escape the husband's kindnesses and thus alleviate the burden of his treachery.

It was around this time that Rita, feeling fearful and suspicious, went off to consult the fortune-teller about the real reason for Camilo's behavior. As we have seen, the fortune-teller entirely restored Rita's faith in Camilo, and Camilo scolded her for going there in the first place. Several weeks went by. Camilo received two or three more anonymous letters, so passionate that they could not be considered mere sanctimonious warnings, but rather the bitter outpourings of a rival. That was Rita's view, and she, somewhat less succinctly, formulated the following thought: "Virtue is niggardly and lazy, wasting neither paper nor time; only self-interest is spendthrift and diligent."

Not that this was of any comfort to Camilo; he feared the anonymous letter-writer would go to Vilela, and then catastrophe would be inevitable. Rita agreed that this was a possibility.

"Very well, then," she said, "I will take the envelopes home with me and compare them to the handwriting on every letter that arrives. If any arrive bearing the same handwriting, I'll tear them up."

No such letters appeared, but shortly afterward, Vilela grew suddenly somber and taciturn, as if he suspected something. Rita rushed to tell Camilo, and they pondered what to do. Rita felt that Camilo should begin visiting their house again and sound out her husband: it might well be that Vilela would confide in him some business matter that was troubling him. Camilo disagreed: appearing suddenly after so many months would only confirm any suspicion or accusation. Better to lie low and forgo each other's company for a few weeks. They agreed on how they would communicate in case of necessity, and separated tearfully.

The following day, at the department, Camilo received the following note from Vilela: "Come to our house immediately; I need to speak to you at once." It was already after midday. Camilo did not hesitate, but once in the street, it occurred to him that it would have been more natural for Vilela to summon him to his office—why to his house? Everything indicated that something grave had happened, and, although he may have been imagining it, the handwriting did look shaky. He put all this together with what Rita had told him the previous day.

"Come to our house immediately; I need to speak to you at once," he repeated to himself, his eyes fixed on the piece of paper.

In his imagination he sketched the climactic scene of a drama: Rita tearful and defeated, Vilela angrily grabbing his pen and scribbling the note, certain that Camilo would come, then sitting there waiting to kill him. Camilo shuddered. He felt afraid, but then he smiled through clenched teeth and carried on walking, for he found the idea of retreating utterly repugnant. On the way, it occurred to him to call in at home first—there might be a message from Rita explaining everything. There was no message and no messenger. Back in the street, the notion that they had been discovered seemed to him ever more plausible; the most likely thing was an anonymous informer, maybe even the same person who had threatened him previously. Perhaps Vilela knew everything. Calling off his visits, on only the flimsiest of pretexts, would only have confirmed what he now knew.

Camilo carried on walking, anxious and agitated. He didn't read the note again, but he knew the words by heart, they were there before his eyes, or, worse still, he could hear them whispered in his ear, in Vilela's own voice. "Come to our house immediately; I need to speak to you at once." Spoken like that, in the other man's voice, they had an air of mystery and menace. Come immediately—but why? It was nearly one o'clock. His agitation was growing by the minute. So vivid was his imagination of what would happen that he came to believe it and even see it there before him. By now he really was afraid. He began to think about taking a gun, since if it turned out there was no reason to worry he would still have nothing to lose, and it would be a sensible precaution. However, he quickly dismissed the idea, annoyed with himself for even thinking of it, and carried on, walking more quickly as he approached the cab rank in Largo da Carioca. He climbed in and told the driver to set off at full speed.

"The sooner I get it over with, the better," he thought. "I can't go on like this . . ."

But the horse's steady trotting only served to discomfit him further. Time was flying and very soon he would find himself face-to-face with danger. Almost at the end of Rua da Guarda Velha, the cab came to a halt, because the street was blocked by an overturned cart. Camilo privately welcomed the obstruction and waited. After five minutes, he noticed that just a few steps away, on the left-hand side of the street, stood the house of the fortune-teller—the same one Rita had once consulted. Never before had he wished so fervently to believe in what the cards had said. He looked up at the windows of the house, all firmly shut, while every other window in the street was flung wide and crammed with curious onlookers. It appeared every bit the home of indifferent Fate.

Camilo leaned back in his seat, not wanting to see any more. He was by now extraordinarily agitated, and rising up from the innermost depths of his moral being came his old beliefs and superstitions, the ghosts of times gone by. The cabdriver suggested they turn around and take the first side street; he, however, said he would rather wait, and again leaned forward to look up at the house. Then he made an incredulous gesture, unable to believe the thought that had just occurred to him, namely, the idea of consulting the fortune-teller, an idea that flapped past him in the far distance on vast gray wings, disappearing, then reappearing, and once again fading from view; then, moments later, the wings flapped past him again, this time circling ever closer . . . In the street, men were shouting as they struggled to move the cart:

"Push! Push! Keep going!"

Soon the obstruction would be cleared. Camilo closed his eyes, his mind on other things, but the voice of Rita's husband was whispering the words of the letter in his ear. "Come immediately . . ." And, trembling, he could see before him the twists and turns of the unfolding drama. The house was looking at him. His legs wanted to get out of the cab and go in. Camilo found himself confronted by a long, heavy veil; his mind rapidly reviewed the many things in life that defy explanation. His mother's voice gave him a long litany of extraordinary events, and that same saying of the Prince of Denmark echoed inside him: "There are more things in heaven and earth than are dreamt of in your philosophy." What did he have to lose . . . ?

He found himself on the sidewalk, outside the street door. He told the cabdriver to wait, darted into the hallway and went up the stairs. There was little light, the steps were badly worn, and the handrail sticky, but he didn't see or feel any of these things. He continued on up and knocked. When no one answered, he considered leaving, but it was too late, curiosity was beating in his veins, and his temples throbbed; he knocked again, once, twice, three times. A woman came; it was the fortune-teller. Camilo said he had come to consult her and she ushered him in. They went up to the attic, by way of a staircase even darker and more decrepit than the last. Upstairs there was a small room, poorly lit by a single window that looked out over the backs of the houses. The shabby furniture, stained walls, and the general air of poverty all served to increase rather than destroy the power and mystery of the place.

The fortune-teller told him to sit down at the table, while she sat on the other side with her back to the window, so that what little light entered the room fell on Camilo's face. She opened a drawer and took out a deck of long, grubby, dog-eared cards. As she rapidly shuffled the cards, she was studying him, not directly, but furtively from beneath heavy eyelids. She was a woman of about forty, an Italian, thin and swarthy, with large, sly, astute eyes. She turned over three cards on the table and said:

"First, we shall see what has brought you here. You are very afraid . . ." Camilo nodded in amazement.

"And you want to know," she continued, "whether or not something will happen to you . . ."

"To me and to her," he explained enthusiastically.

The fortune-teller did not smile; she simply told him to wait. She scooped up the cards and shuffled them again with her long tapering fingers, their nails untrimmed and neglected. She shuffled the cards thoroughly and cut the pack once, twice, three times; then she began to lay them out. Camilo watched her with anxious, curious eyes

"The cards tell me . . ."

Camilo leaned forward to drink in her words one by one. She told him he had nothing to fear. Nothing would happen to either of them; the third party suspected nothing. It was nevertheless vital to exercise caution, for there was much simmering envy and resentment. She spoke of the love that bound them, of Rita's beauty . . . Camilo was amazed. The fortune-teller finished, gathered up the cards, and locked them away in the drawer.

"You have restored my peace of mind," he said, reaching across the table and grasping her hand in his.

She stood up and laughed.

"Off you go then," she said, "*ragazzo innamorato* . . ."

Standing over him, she touched his forehead with her index finger. Camilo shuddered as if it were the hand of the Sibyl herself, then he, too, stood up. The fortune-teller went over to the chest of drawers, on which there stood a bowl of raisins. She picked up a handful and began eating the raisins, revealing two rows of white teeth in sharp contrast with the state of her nails. Even when doing something so ordinary, the woman had about her a most unusual air. Camilo was keen to leave, but had no idea how he should pay, or how much.

"Raisins cost money," he said at last, taking out his wallet. "How many do you want to send for?"

"The answer is in your heart," she replied.

Camilo took out a ten-*mil-réis* note and gave it to her. The fortune-teller's eyes lit up. The usual fee was two *mil-réis*.

"I can see you love her very much . . . And you're quite right, for she loves you very much too. Off you go, it will all be fine. Watch out on the stairs, though, it's dark. And put your hat on . . ."

The fortune-teller had already slipped the money into her pocket. She accompanied him down the stairs, talking with a slight Italian accent. Camilo said goodbye to her on the landing and went down to the street, while the fortune-teller, delighted with the ten *mil-réis*, returned to the attic, humming a Venetian *barcarola*. Camilo found the cab waiting; the traffic was moving again. He climbed in and they set off at a fast trot.

Everything seemed better now. Things took on a different aspect: the sky was clear and the faces about him beamed. He even managed to laugh at his own fears, which he now found puerile; he remembered the words of Vilela's letter and saw in them merely the familiarity of a close friend. What on earth had he found threatening about them? He also noticed the urgency of the message, and that he had been wrong to take so long: it could well be some terribly serious business matter.

"As fast as you can!" he said to the cabdriver, several times.

He thought up some story to explain the delay to his friend; it seems he also devised a plan to take advantage of the situation and resume his regular visits . . . Meanwhile, the fortune-teller's words still echoed in his soul. After all, she had foreseen the reason for his visit, his current predicament, the existence of a third party; why wouldn't she also be able to foresee everything else? After all, the unknown present is as much of an enigma as the future. And so, slowly but surely, his former beliefs and superstitions took hold of him once again, and mystery gripped him in its iron claws. At times he wanted to laugh, and he did laugh at himself, somewhat shamefacedly; but the woman, the cards, her brief yet reassuring words, her final exhortation—"Off you go then, *ragazzo innamorato*"—and finally, in the distance, her slow, lilting farewell *barcarola*, all these were the new elements which, combined with the old ones, formed the basis of a new and vigorous faith.

The truth is that his heart was cheerful and impatient, thinking about happy times gone by, and those to come. As he passed through Glória, Camilo gazed across the water, staring out to where sea and sky clasp each other in an infinite embrace, and he sensed before him a long, long unending future.

Shortly afterward, he arrived at Vilela's house. He got out of the cab and pushed open the iron gate into the garden. The house was silent. He climbed the six stone steps and barely had time to knock when the door opened and Vilela appeared.

"Sorry, I couldn't get here any sooner. What's happened?"

Vilela did not reply; he looked almost deranged. He beckoned to Camilo, and led him to a small room off the parlor. When he entered, Camilo could not suppress a terrified scream: there, on the sofa, lay Rita, dead and drenched in blood. Vilela then grabbed Camilo by the throat and, with two shots from his revolver, laid him out dead on the floor.

AMONG SAINTS

———

Whe n I was chaplain at the Church of São Francisco de Paula (an elderly priest told me), the most extraordinary thing happened to me.

I lived right by the church, and one night, I retired to bed rather late. I would never, of course, go to bed without first checking to see that the church doors were properly locked. And so they were, but beneath them I could see a light. Frightened, I ran to fetch the night watchman, and when I couldn't find him, I went back to the church steps and waited, not knowing what to do. The light wasn't very bright, but still far too bright for thieves; besides, I noticed that it shone with a steady, even glow rather than wandering from side to side, as would be the case with the candles or lanterns of persons intent on stealing. The mystery intrigued me, and I went home to fetch the keys to the sacristy (the sacristan having gone to spend the night in Niterói), then, having made the sign of the cross, I unlocked the door and went inside.

The passageway lay in darkness. Holding my lantern, I edged slowly forward, trying to make as little noise as possible. The first and second doors leading into the church were shut, but under them I could see that same light; indeed, it seemed even more intense than when seen from the street. I carried on until I came to the third door, which stood open. I set the lantern down in one corner and covered it with my handkerchief so that I wouldn't be noticed inside the church, and then I moved closer so as to find out what was going on.

Suddenly I stopped. It was only then that I realized I had come entirely unarmed, and that entering the church with only my two hands to defend myself could prove risky. Several more minutes raced by. The light from within remained unchanged—a steady, even milky glow, quite unlike candlelight. I could hear voices now, which I found still more troubling: they were neither whispering nor mumbling, but speaking in calm, clear, measured tones, as if they were conducting a normal conversation. At first I couldn't understand what they were saying, and as I listened, I was struck by a thought that made me shudder. At the time, corpses were often laid to rest inside the church, and I suddenly imagined that it might be the dead talking to each other. I shrank back in terror, and it took me some time to pull myself together and return once more to the doorway, telling myself that such ideas were mere foolish nonsense. Reality, however, was about to show me something even more astonishing than a dialogue of the dead. I commended myself to God, again made the sign of the cross, and, keeping very close to the wall, crept gingerly forward and went in. What I saw was truly extraordinary.

Two of the three saints on the opposite side, Saint Joseph and Saint Michael (on the right as you enter the church though the main door), had stepped down from their niches and were sitting on their respective altars. They were smaller than their statues, more the size of ordinary men. They seemed to be addressing someone on my side of the church, where the altars of Saint John the Baptist and Saint Francis de Sales were located. I cannot begin to describe what went through my mind. For quite some time (I have no idea how long), I stood rooted to the spot, covered in goose bumps and trembling. I was teetering on the very edge of the abyss of madness, and it was only by divine mercy that I did not actually topple in. What I can, however, confirm is that I lost all consciousness of myself and of any other reality beyond the new and utterly unique reality before my eyes; only thus can I explain the boldness with which, only moments later, I advanced farther into the church, in order to see the other wall. And there the same sight greeted my eyes: Saint Francis de Sales and Saint John, having stepped down from their niches, were also sitting on their altars and conversing with the other saints.

I was so astonished that I believe they continued talking without me even hearing the sound of their voices. Little by little, however, my senses returned and I realized that they had not once interrupted their conversation; I could clearly hear and distinguish their words, but, initially, could make no sense of them. When one of the saints addressed the high altar, I turned my head in that direction and saw that Saint Francis of Paola, the church's patron saint, had also stepped down from his niche and was joining in the conversation. They weren't speaking particularly loudly, and yet they were perfectly audible, as if the sound waves had somehow been endowed with a greater power of transmission. But if all this was astonishing, then so was the light: it seemed to come from nowhere, for the chandeliers and candlesticks were all unlit. It was as if moonlight had somehow found its way into the building, but with the moon itself hidden from sight; the comparison is even more exact when you consider that, if it really had been moonlight, some places would have been left in darkness, as indeed was the case, for it was in one of those dark corners that I sought refuge.

By then I was acting purely on instinct, and what I experienced on that night bore no relation to my life before or after. Suffice it to say that, confronted by this strange spectacle, I felt absolutely no fear; I lost all power of thought and could do little more than listen and look.

After a few moments, I realized that they were cataloguing and commenting on all of the day's prayers and petitions. Each of them had something to contribute. All of them, with terrifying psychological insight, had penetrated into the lives and souls of the faithful and picked apart the feelings of each and every one, just as anatomists dissect a corpse. Saint John the Baptist and Saint Francis of Paola, those harsh ascetics, were, by turns, angry and absolute. Unlike Saint Francis de Sales, who listened and gave his judgments with the same kindly indulgence to be found in his famous work *Introduction to the Devout Life.*

It was thus, each according to his own temperament, that they recounted and remarked on the day's events. Examples of pure, sincere faith, of indifference, of dissembling and double-dealing, had already been laid bare; the two ascetics grew ever sadder, but Saint Francis de Sales reminded them of the words of the Scriptures: "Many are called but few are chosen," by which he meant that not all who attended that church came with a pure heart. Saint John shook his head.

"I must tell you, Francis de Sales, I am developing a most unusual sentiment in a saint: I'm beginning to lose my faith in humankind."

"Now, don't exaggerate, John the Baptist," replied the saintly bishop. "Let's not get carried away. Look, something happened here today that made me smile, and yet the very same thing might well have filled you with indignation. Men are no worse now than they were in earlier centuries. Set aside all their bad qualities, and you'll find there are many good qualities left. Believe this and you will surely smile when you hear the tale I have to tell you."

"Me? Smile?"

"Yes, you, John the Baptist, and you as well, Francis of Paola; in fact, it will make all of you smile. And I can tell you about it now because I have already interceded with the Lord and obtained from Him the very thing for which this person was praying."

"Which person?"

"Someone far more interesting than your notary, Joseph, or your store-keeper, Michael—"

"That may be so," said Saint Joseph, breaking in. "But nothing could be more interesting than the adulteress who prostrated herself at my feet today, asking me to cleanse her heart of the leprosy of lust. Only yesterday she had argued with her lover, who vilely insulted her, and she had spent the whole night crying. In the morning, she resolved to leave him, and came here to seek the strength she needed to escape the demon's grasp. She began by praying earnestly, fervently even, but little by little I could tell that her thoughts were drifting back to those earthly delights. Her words gradually lost their vigor. Her prayers became lukewarm, then cold, then mechanical; her lips, accustomed to prayer, continued praying, but her soul, on which I was spying from above, was no longer present; it was with that other man. Finally, she crossed herself, stood up, and left without asking for anything."

"My story is better than that."

"Better than mine?" asked Saint Joseph curiously.

"Much better," replied Saint Francis de Sales, "and it isn't sad like the one about that poor soul tormented by base earthly desires, and who may yet be saved by the grace of our Lord. For why would He not save her as well? Anyway, here goes."

They all stopped talking and leaned forward attentively, waiting. Here I took fright, remembering how they, who see everything that goes on inside us as clearly as if we were made of glass—all our hidden thoughts, our devious intentions, our secret loathings—could easily have already spied within me some sin, or even the germ of a sin. But I had no time for further reflection; Saint Francis de Sales began to speak.

"My man is fifty years old," he said, "his wife is in bed, suffering from a deadly skin infection in her left leg. He's been beside himself with worry for the last five days, because the disease is getting worse and science has as yet failed to come up with a cure. See, however, how far public prejudice can go. Nobody believes in Sales's anguish (yes, he bears my name), nobody believes he loves anything but money, for as soon as news of his unhappiness began to spread, the whole neighborhood was awash with scurrilous jokes and jests; there were even those who believed that what was really upsetting him was the thought of how much her funeral would cost."

"That could well be true," said Saint John.

"But it wasn't. That he is usurious and miserly I do not deny; as usurious as life itself, and as miserly as death. Never has anyone so resolutely extracted gold, silver, paper, and copper from the pockets of others; never has anyone squirreled away money with more alacrity and zeal. A coin that falls into his hand rarely leaves it again, and anything that isn't invested in property resides in an iron chest always kept firmly under lock and key. Sometimes, in the dead of night, he opens the chest and contemplates his money for a few minutes, then quickly closes it again; but on such nights, he sleeps either badly or not at all. He has no children. He leads a mean and niggardly life, eating little and badly, just enough to keep body and soul together. His family consists of his wife and a black slave woman, one of two he bought many years ago, secretly, from smugglers. They say he didn't even pay for them, because the seller died shortly afterward and there was nothing written down. The other slave woman died a little while ago, and this is where you can decide whether or not this man is a genius when it comes to penny-pinching: he gave the corpse its freedom!"

And the saintly bishop paused to savor the reaction of his fellow saints.

"The corpse?"

"Yes, the corpse. He had the slave buried as a free pauper, so as not to incur any funeral expenses. Little enough, perhaps, but it was still something. And for him there is no such thing as little: it is with drops of water that whole streets are flooded. He's not interested in outward appearances or in aping aristocratic tastes; all those things cost money and, as he says, money doesn't grow on trees. He has no social life to speak of and no family amusements. He listens to and repeats tittle-tattle about other people's lives, for such pleasures come free."

"One can understand people's skepticism," said Saint Michael.

"I wouldn't disagree there, because the world never looks below the surface of things. The world doesn't see that, while Sales does indeed think of his wife as his carefully house-trained companion and confidante of twenty years, he really does love her. Don't be shocked, Michael. Even on the most inhospitable of walls a flower may bloom, colorless and without scent, but a flower nonetheless. The botany of love is full of such anomalies. Sales loves his wife; he's devastated at the thought of losing her. And so, in the early hours of this morning, not having slept for more than two hours, he began thinking about the impending catastrophe. Despairing of the Earth, he turned to God; he thought of us, and especially of me, since he bears my name. Only a miracle could save her, and so he resolved to come here. He lives nearby, and came running. When he entered, his eyes shone with hope; it could have been the light of faith, but, in fact, it was something quite specific, as I will explain. Now, here's where you all need to pay even closer attention."

I saw them lean even farther forward, and I myself could not resist the temptation to take another step closer. The saint's account was so long and detailed, his analysis so complicated, that I won't set it down here in full, but merely give the main points.

"When he thought of coming to ask me to intercede on behalf of his wife, Sales had an idea typical of a usurer: he would promise me a wax leg. It wasn't the believer seeking a symbolic reminder of a favor granted, but, rather, the usurer trying to force the hand of divine grace with the expectation of profit. And it wasn't only usury that spoke, but avarice too: by offering this vow he was showing that he truly wished to save his wife—a miser's intuition. Payment is proof: parting with ready cash is the test of whether you truly want something, or so his conscience whispered darkly to him. Well, you all know that such thoughts are not formed as others are; they are born deep within the bowels of character and linger on in the shadows of conscience. But I read all this in his mind the moment he came into the church, looking agitated, his eyes ablaze with hope. I read all these things, and waited for him to finish crossing himself and praying."

"At least he has some religious feeling," muttered Saint Joseph.

"Some, yes, but only in a very vague and parsimonious way. He never became a member of any confraternities or lay orders, because they do nothing but steal what belongs to the Lord. Or so he says, trying to reconcile devotion with his pocket. But I suppose we can't have everything; at least he fears God and believes in doctrine."

"So he knelt and prayed."

"Yes, he prayed, and while he was praying, I saw his poor suffering soul, although hope was already beginning to turn to instinctive certainty. God was sure to save the sick woman; He was bound to, thanks to my intervention, and I *would* intercede. That's what he was thinking as his lips mouthed the words of the prayer. When he had finished praying, Sales stayed for a short time gazing upward, his hands still clasped together. Finally, he spoke: to confess his pain and to swear that no other hand, beyond that of the Lord Himself, could stay the blow. His wife was dying . . . dying . . . dying . . . And he repeated the word, unable to escape it. His wife was dying. He went no further. Ready to formulate his request and give his promise, he could find no appropriate or even vaguely approximate words; he could find nothing at all, so unaccustomed was he to giving anything away. Finally, he spluttered out his request; his wife was dying and he was begging me to save her, to plead with the Lord on her behalf. The promise, however, simply would not come out. As his mouth tried to articulate the first word, avarice tightened its grip about his guts and stopped that promise from escaping his lips. 'Save her . . . Intercede for her . . .' he begged.

"The wax leg appeared to him, hanging in midair before his eyes, followed shortly by the vision of the coin that it would cost him. The leg disappeared, but the coin remained; a disk of purest yellow gold—solid gold, far better than the candlesticks on my altar, which are merely gilt. Whichever way he looked, he could see the coin spinning, spinning, spinning. From afar, he caressed it with his eyes, feeling the cold sensation of the metal and even the texture of the raised relief stamped upon it. It was her, his old friend of many years, his companion by day and by night; it was her, hanging in the air before him, spinning giddily, descending from the ceiling, rising from the floor, rolling across the altar from the Epistle to the Gospel, tinkling against the chandelier's crystal drops.

"By now the sadness and supplication in his eyes were more intense and entirely genuine. I watched his gaze reach up to me, full of contrition, humiliation, and pain. He mouthed some incoherent platitudes—God . . . the angel of the Lord . . . Christ's holy wounds . . .—tearful, tremulous words, as if hoping they would convince me of the sincerity of his faith and the immensity of his sorrow. But still no promise of a leg. At times, like someone steeling himself before leaping a ditch, his soul dwelled at length upon his wife's imminent demise and prepared to fling itself into the despair her death would bring him; but when he reached the edge of the ditch and the moment came to leap, he hung back. The coin rose up before him, and the promise stayed buried in his heart.

"Time was passing. The hallucination grew, because the coin, accelerating and multiplying its leaps and bounds, multiplied itself again and again until there appeared an infinite number of coins; his inner conflict reached tragic proportions. Suddenly the fear that his wife might be at death's door froze the poor man's blood and all he could think of was rushing off to be with her. She might be dying! Again he asked me to intercede for her, to save her . . .

"At this point, the demon of avarice suggested a new transaction—a change of currency, if you will—telling him that the value of prayer was of the highest rank and quality, far superior to that of mere earthly undertakings. And Sales, contrite, head bowed, hands pressed together, his gaze obedient, helpless and resigned, asked me once again to save his wife. And to save her he promised me three hundred—no less—three hundred Our Fathers and three hundred Hail Marys. He repeated this emphatically: three hundred, three hundred, three hundred . . . He went higher and higher: *five* hundred, then a thousand Our Fathers and a thousand Hail Marys. He could see this number written out in front of him, not in words but in numerals, as if this made the figure somehow more vivid and exact, the obligation greater, greater also its seductive power. One thousand Our Fathers, one thousand Hail Marys. And once again those tearful, tremulous words returned: the holy wounds, the angel of the Lord . . . 1,000, 1,000, 1,000. The four numerals had grown so tall that they now filled the church from top to bottom, and with them grew both the man's efforts and his confidence. The word came out loud and clear, ever faster, ever more urgent: 'thousand, thousand, thousand, thousand!' Come, now," said Saint Francis of Sales, "surely you can see the funny side. Go on, laugh! Laugh as much as you like."

And the other saints did indeed laugh; not the great guffaws of Homer's gods when they saw lame Vulcan serving at table, but a polite, pious, very Catholic laugh.

I heard nothing more after that. I fell to the floor in a dead faint. When I came to, it was broad daylight. I rushed to open the doors and windows of the church and sacristy, to let in the sun, that enemy of bad dreams.

HER ARMS

———

FLINCHING AT THE attorney's angry cries, Inácio took the plate being handed to him and tried to eat beneath the deluge of insults: "Good-for-nothing, blockhead, idiot, imbecile!

"How is it you never hear a word I say? I'll tell your father and he'll beat the laziness out of you with a good quince rod or some other big stick; you're not too old to get a beating, sonny, so don't go thinking you are. Idiot! Imbecile!

"He's the same out of the house as in," the attorney went on, turning to Dona Severina, a lady who had been living with him, matrimonially, that is, for many years. "He gets all my documents in a muddle, goes to the wrong house, visits one notary instead of another, mixes up the lawyers' names: he's a complete disaster! It's that endless sleeping of his that does it. You've seen what he's like in the mornings; you practically have to break his bones to get him out of bed . . . Well, just you wait; tomorrow I'll beat him out of bed with a broom handle!"

Dona Severina nudged him with her foot to stop. Borges spat out several more choice insults, then made his peace with God and men.

I won't say he made his peace with children, because our Inácio was not exactly a child. He was fifteen years old, and a good fifteen at that. He had a somewhat disheveled but handsome head, and the dreamy eyes of a young lad who wonders, and questions, and wants to know everything, but ends up knowing nothing at all. All this set atop a body that was not devoid of grace, albeit badly dressed. His father, a barber in Cidade Nova, had apprenticed him as an errand boy or clerk or whatever, to the attorney Borges, in the hope of seeing him one day practice at the bar, for he reckoned that even small-time attorneys made lots of money. All this took place in Rua da Lapa, in 1870.

For some minutes, nothing more was heard apart from the clink of cutlery and the sound of chewing. Borges stuffed himself with lettuce and beef, punctuating his munching with an occasional slurp of wine before continuing to eat in silence.

Inácio ate slowly, not daring to raise his eyes from his plate, not even to return them to where they had been resting before the formidable Borges began laying into him. Doing so now would be very risky indeed. He never could set eyes upon Dona Severina's arms without forgetting both himself and everything else.

The blame for this lay first and foremost with Dona Severina for showing off her arms like that. All the dresses she wore around the house had short sleeves, scarcely a few inches below the shoulder, leaving her arms bare for all to see. They were, it must be said, beautifully full and rounded arms in perfect harmony with their mistress—who was more plump than thin—and neither their color nor their softness suffered on being exposed to the air. However, it is only fair to explain that she did not display them out of vanity, but because all her long-sleeved dresses were too old and worn. When standing, she was a fine figure of a woman, and when she walked, she had a charming little wiggle; Inácio, however, hardly ever saw her except at the dining table, where he could scarcely see beyond her arms to look at her bust. She could not be said to be pretty, but nor was she ugly. She wore no jewelry and took little trouble with her hair, simply combing it back and fastening it on top of her head with the tortoiseshell comb her mother had left her. She wore a dark-colored scarf around her neck and no earrings at all—a sturdy twenty-seven-year-old in the full bloom of life.

When supper was over and coffee was served, Borges pulled four cigars from his pocket, compared them, squeezed them between thumb and forefinger, chose one, and put the others back. Once he had lit the chosen cigar, he planted his elbows on the table and talked to Dona Severina about a hundred and one things that were of no interest whatsoever to our Inácio. Still, for as long as the attorney talked, at least he wasn't scolding him, and he could let his mind wander freely.

Inácio lingered over his coffee as long as he could. Between one sip and the next, he smoothed the tablecloth, picked imaginary bits of skin from his fingers, or let his eyes wander over the pictures in the dining room, of which there were two: one of Saint Peter and one of Saint John, devotional prints brought back from church festivals and framed at home. He might just about be able to hide his thoughts from Saint John, whose youthful head brings cheer to Catholic imaginations, but the austere Saint Peter was too much for him. In his defense, young Inácio could plead only that he saw neither one nor the other; his eyes passed over them as if there were nothing there at all. He saw only Dona Severina's arms—either because he took the occasional stealthy sideways glance at them, or because they were emblazoned on his memory.

"Come on, man! Are you still not done?" bellowed the attorney suddenly.

There was nothing for it. Inácio downed the last drop of already cold coffee, and retired, as usual, to his room at the rear of the house. On entering, he made a silent gesture of anger and despair, then went over to lean at one of the two windows looking out to sea. After five minutes, the view of the water close by and the mountains far off brought back the confused, vague, restless feeling that both pained and comforted him, much as a plant must feel when its first flower blooms. He wanted to leave, but also to stay. He'd been there for five weeks now, and his life followed the same, unchanging routine: leaving the house every morning with Borges, hanging around the courts and notaries' offices, running here and there getting documents stamped and delivered, chasing after clerks and bailiffs. In the afternoon, he would return to the house, have his dinner, and go to his room until it was time for supper; after supper, he went straight to bed. Borges did not treat him as part of the family, which consisted solely of Dona Severina, whom Inácio saw only three times a day at mealtimes. Five weeks of solitude and drudgery, far from his mother and sisters; five weeks of silence, since he only spoke now and then to someone in the street, and in the house, not a word.

"Just you wait," he thought to himself one day, "I'll run away and never come back."

But he stayed; chained and shackled there by Dona Severina's arms. He had never seen such fresh, pretty arms. His upbringing would not allow him to look at them directly; at first it seems he even averted his eyes in embarrassment. Little by little, though, he did begin to look, especially when he realized that those arms were always unencumbered by sleeves, and thus he gradually began to discover, contemplate, and love them. By the end of three weeks they had become, spiritually speaking, the tent where he laid his weary head. He put up with the hard slog of mundane work, the melancholy of his solitude and silence, his boss's rudeness, for the reward of seeing, three times a day, that stupendous pair of arms.

The very same evening, as night fell and Inácio was stretching out in his hammock (for there was no other bed for him), Dona Severina, in the front room, was going over the episode at dinner and, for the first time, began to suspect something. She quickly rejected the idea—he was a child, for goodness' sake! But some ideas are like insistent flies: however often we brush them away, they still return to pester us. A child? He was fifteen years old; and she noted that between the lad's nose and lip were the fuzzy beginnings of a mustache. Was it so surprising that he had begun to fall in love? Was she not, after all, pretty? She did not reject this second observation, but rather cherished and embraced it. She recalled his listless demeanor, his lapses of concentration, his habit of staring into the middle distance—such small things, but symptoms nonetheless. Yes, she concluded, he must be in love.

"What's the matter with you?" asked the attorney after several minutes' silence, as he lay on the sofa.

"Nothing," she replied.

"Nothing? Everyone in this house seems half asleep! Well, just you wait; I know a good cure for sleepyheads . . ."

And on he went, in the same angry tone, firing off threats that he was quite incapable of carrying out, for he was more boorish than bad. Dona Severina interrupted several times to tell him he was mistaken, that she hadn't been sleeping, but rather thinking about Fortunata, her godson's mother. They hadn't been to see her since Christmas; perhaps one of these evenings they should pay her a visit. Borges retorted that he was tired, that he'd been working like a black, that he wasn't in the mood for social chit-chat, and then launched into a tirade against the mother, the father, *and* the godson, who at ten years of age still wasn't at school! By that age, he, Borges, could already read, write, and do his sums; not very well, of course, but still. Ten years old! Well, it was sure to end badly: he'd be picked up off the streets and marched off to war, that's what would happen. A soldier's billet would sort him out, one way or another.

Dona Severina tried to assuage him with excuses: the mother's poverty, the father's string of misfortunes. She caressed her husband, tentatively, for fear of irritating him further. It was now completely dark, and she heard the *tlic* of the streetlamp as the gas was lit, and saw its glow reflected in the windows of the house across the street. Borges, tired after his long day (for he really was a prodigiously hard worker), let his eyes close and drifted off to sleep, leaving her alone in the room, in the dark, alone with herself and this new discovery.

Everything seemed to tell her it was true; but this truth, once she had gotten over the initial shock, brought with it a moral dilemma she could only recognize by its effects, since she had no means of identifying exactly what it was. She could make no sense of herself, nor regain her equilibrium, and she even thought of telling the attorney everything so that he would send the young whippersnapper packing. But what was "everything"? Here she paused: in reality there was nothing but supposition, coincidence, and quite possibly delusion. No, not delusion. She began to piece together all the vague clues in the boy's behavior: his awkwardness, his absentmindedness, and rejected the idea that she might be mistaken. But shortly afterward (ah, capricious nature!), reflecting that it would be wrong to make groundless accusations, she admitted that she was perhaps fooling herself after all. Her sole aim, of course, was to watch the young man more closely and ascertain the true state of affairs.

That same evening, Dona Severina surreptitiously studied Inácio's every look and gesture. She could find nothing, because teatime was very short, and the boy scarcely raised his eyes from his cup. The next day she was able to observe him more closely, and even more so in the days that followed. She realized that, yes, she was both loved and revered—an adolescent and virginal love constrained by social proprieties and by a feeling of inferiority that prevented the young man from even acknowledging it to himself. Dona Severina saw that she need fear no impertinence on his part, and decided it was best to say nothing to her husband; she would be sparing both him and the poor child any unpleasantness. By now she was persuaded that he was indeed a child, and resolved to treat him just as coolly as before, or even more so. And so she did; Inácio began to notice that she avoided his looks and spoke sharply to him, almost as sharply as Borges himself. It's true that, on other occasions, her tone of voice was soft, even tender, very tender; in the same way, her gaze, generally so elusive, wandered so much around the room that, for a moment's respite, it would occasionally come to rest upon his head; but such moments were only fleeting.

"I've got to leave," he would say to himself in the street, just as he had in the early days.

He would arrive back at the house, though, and he wouldn't leave. Dona Severina's arms were a parenthesis in the long, tedious sentence of the life he was leading and this interpolated clause contained a profound and original idea, invented by Heaven solely for him. So he stayed and carried on as before. Finally, however, he did have to leave, never to return; here's the how and why.

For several days, Dona Severina had been treating him kindly. The severe tone had vanished from her voice, and now there was more than just softness, there was genuine care and affection. One day, she warned him to keep away from drafts, another day, she told him not to drink cold water after hot coffee—the advice, thoughts, and concerns of a friend and mother, all of which threw Inácio into an even greater state of confusion and consternation. He grew so confident, however, that he actually laughed at the table, something he had never done before. This time the attorney did not scold him, because it was the attorney himself who was telling a funny story, and no one punishes an appreciative audience. It was then that Dona Severina noticed that the young lad's lips, attractive when he was silent, were no less so when he laughed.

Inácio's turmoil grew and grew, and he could neither calm himself nor understand what was going on. He felt uncomfortable wherever he was. He would wake up at night thinking about Dona Severina. When out on his errands, he became even more likely to take a wrong turn or knock on the wrong door, and every woman he saw, from near or far, reminded him of her. He always felt a certain, occasionally intense, excitement when he returned from work and found her standing at the top of the stairs, peering down through the wooden banisters, as if she had rushed to see who it was.

One Sunday—a Sunday he would never forget—Inácio was alone in his room, at the window, looking out to sea, which spoke to him in the same obscure new language as Dona Severina. He was amusing himself watching the seagulls as they made wide circles in the air, or hovered above the water, or simply fluttered on the breeze. It was a magnificent day, not merely a Christian Sabbath, but an immense, universal Sabbath.

Inácio spent all his Sundays there in his room, either at the window or rereading one of the three cheap, slender books he had brought with him from home, stories of times gone by, purchased for a penny under the arches on Largo do Paço. It was two o'clock in the afternoon. He was tired; he had slept badly the night before, after having walked a lot the previous day. He stretched out in the hammock, picked up one of the books—*Princess Magalona*—and began to read. He could never understand why all the heroines in these old stories had the same face and figure as Dona Severina, but they did. After half an hour, he let the book drop and rested his eyes on the wall, from where, five minutes later, he saw the lady of his dreams emerge. He should, naturally, have been astonished, but he wasn't. Even though his eyes were shut, he watched her detach herself from the wall, pause, smile, and walk toward the hammock. It really was her; those really were her arms.

It is certain, however, that Dona Severina could not have emerged from the wall, even had there been a door or a crack in it, for at that very moment she was in the front room listening to the attorney's footsteps going down the stairs. When he reached the bottom, she went to the window to watch him leave the house, only withdrawing once he had disappeared into the distance, on his way to Rua das Mangueiras. Then she came back into the room and sat on the sofa. She seemed out of sorts, restless, almost manic; she stood up, went over to the sideboard, picked up a jug only to set it back down in the same place; then she walked to the door, paused, and turned back, for no apparent reason. She sat down again for five or ten minutes. Suddenly she remembered that Inácio had eaten very little at breakfast and had looked rather downcast; she wondered if he might be ill, perhaps even gravely ill.

She left the parlor and went straight along the hallway to the young man's bedroom. The door was wide open. Dona Severina stopped, peered in, and saw him lying in the hammock, asleep, one arm hanging loose and his book lying on the floor. His head was tilted slightly toward the door, so she could see his closed eyes, his tousled hair, and a wide, blissful grin on his face.

Dona Severina felt her heart pounding furiously, and drew back. The previous night she had dreamt of him; perhaps now he was dreaming of her. Ever since dawn, the lad's face had danced before her eyes like a devilish temptation. She took a further step back, then returned, and looked at him for two, three, five minutes or more. Sleep seemed to accentuate Inácio's youth, giving it an almost feminine, childlike expression. "A child!" she said to herself, in that wordless language we all carry around inside us. And this idea slowed her racing blood and somewhat calmed her turbulent senses.

"A child!"

She gazed at him unhurriedly, until she had had her fill: his head tilted to one side, one arm hanging loose; but, at the same time as she found him childlike, she also found him handsome, much more so than when he was awake; one of these notions either corrected or corrupted the other. Suddenly she jumped back in fear: she had heard a sound close by, in the linen closet. She went to investigate: a cat had knocked a bowl onto the floor. Creeping back to spy on Inácio, she saw that he was still sleeping soundly. He was certainly a deep sleeper! The noise that had made her jump out of her skin hadn't even caused him to stir. She stood there and watched him sleep—to sleep, perchance to dream.

Ah, if only we could see other people's dreams! Dona Severina would have seen herself in the boy's imagination; she would have seen herself standing by the hammock, smiling and quite still, then leaning toward him, taking his hands, raising them to her chest, and folding them in her arms, those stupendous arms. Even thus, in love with her arms, Inácio could still hear her words, which were beautiful, warm, and above all new—or, rather, they belonged to some language he did not know, although he understood it well enough. Two, three, and even four times, the figure faded only to return, swooping in from the sea or from up among the seagulls, or sailing down the hallway with her usual sturdy elegance. And each time she returned, she would lean toward him, take his hands once again, and fold them in her arms, until, leaning closer, much closer, she pursed her lips and kissed him gently on the mouth.

Here the dream coincided with reality, and the same mouths united both in his imagination and outside it. The difference is that the vision did not draw back, whereas the real person had no sooner kissed him than she fled to the door, ashamed and afraid. She went back to the front room, shocked at what she had done and staring blankly into space. Straining her ears, retracing her steps down the hallway, she listened for any sound of him waking, and it took quite some time before her fears subsided. The child really did sleep like a log; nothing would open his eyes, neither the nearby sound of things breaking nor real-life kisses. But while her fears subsided, her shame lingered and grew. Dona Severina could not believe what she had done; it seems she had swathed her desires in the notion that this was an adoring child lying blameless and unconscious there before her; and, half mother, half friend, she had leaned over and kissed him. Be that as it may, she felt confused, cross, and annoyed with herself and with him. The fear that he might have been feigning sleep troubled her soul and sent shivers down her spine.

In fact, he carried on sleeping for a long time and only awoke for dinner. He sat down gaily at the table. Although Dona Severina was as tight-lipped and stern as ever, and the attorney just as abrasive, neither the harshness of one nor the severity of the other could dispel the charming vision he still carried inside his head, or dull the sensation of that kiss. He didn't notice that Dona Severina was wearing a shawl covering her arms; he noticed later, on Monday, and then again on Tuesday, and every day until Saturday, which was the day on which Borges sent to tell the boy's father that he couldn't keep him on any longer. He did not act in anger, though, for he treated Iná-cio relatively well and even said to him as he left:

"If you ever need me for anything, you know where I am."

"Yes, sir. And Senhora Dona Severina . . . ?"

"She's up in her room, with a very bad headache. Come back tomorrow or the day after to say goodbye to her."

Inácio left, not understanding a thing. He didn't understand his dismissal, or Dona Severina's complete change of attitude, or the shawl, or any of it. She had seemed so contented! She had spoken to him so kindly! How, then, so suddenly . . . ? He thought and thought, and ended up imagining that some indiscreet look on his part, some thoughtless act, had offended her; yes, that must be it, and that would explain her scowling face and the shawl covering her lovely, lovely arms . . . Well, never mind; he still had his dream to savor. And down through the years, despite other love affairs, more real and lasting, he never felt anything that could match the sensation of that Sunday, in Rua da Lapa, when he was fifteen years old. He even sometimes exclaims, not knowing how wrong he is:

"And it was all a dream! Just a dream!"

FAME

———

"OH! SO YOU'RE PESTANA? said Sinhazinha Mota, raising her hands in surprise and admiration. And then, correcting her over-familiar tone, she quickly followed this up with: "You must forgive me for being so forward, but . . . is it really you?"

Embarrassed and annoyed, Pestana replied that yes, it was indeed him. He had just left the piano, mopping his brow with his handkerchief, and had nearly reached the window, when the young lady stopped him. It was not a ball, just an intimate gathering for a handful of guests, no more than twenty, all told, who had come to dine with the Widow Camargo at Rua do Areal on the occasion of her birthday, November 5, 1875. Such a kind and cheerful widow! She loved to laugh and have fun, even though she had just reached the fine old age of sixty; indeed this turned out to be the last time she did laugh and have fun, for she died during the first few days of 1876. Yes, such a kind and cheerful widow! Such spirit and enthusiasm: no sooner had they finished dinner than she launched into organizing the dances, asking Pestana to play a quadrille! She scarcely needed to finish her request, for Pestana bowed graciously and hastened to the piano. After the quadrille, she gave him barely time to draw breath before she bustled over once again to ask a very particular favor.

"Just say the word, madam."

"Would you play that polka of yours, *Keep Your Hands to Yourself, Mister?*"

Pestana grimaced, then, quickly disguising his displeasure, gave a stiff, silent bow, and returned, unenthusiastically, to the piano. On hearing the first few bars, a new wave of gaiety swept the room, the gentlemen rushed over to the ladies, and the pairs launched furiously into the latest polka. It was absolutely the latest thing, for it had been published only a couple of weeks earlier and there was hardly a corner of the city where it had not been heard. It had even attained that highest of accolades, being whistled and hummed in the streets at night.

Sinhazinha Mota had not for one moment thought that the Pestana she had seen at the dining table and then at the piano, with his snuff-brown frock coat and long black curly hair, his somewhat wary eyes and smoothly shaven chin, could possibly be the *composer* Pestana; a friend had only told her this when Pestana got up from the piano after finishing the polka. Hence her admiring question. As we have seen, he responded with some embarrassment and annoyance. Unperturbed, Sinhazinha Mota and her friend heaped so many extravagant compliments upon him that even the most humble of vanities would have been pleased. Pestana, however, received their words with growing annoyance until, pleading a terrible headache, he asked to be excused. Neither the young ladies nor his hostess could persuade him to stay. He was offered homemade remedies and a little rest, but would have none of it; he insisted on leaving, and he left.

Out in the street, he walked quickly away, afraid they might still call him back; he only slowed down once he had turned the corner of Rua Formosa. But there, too, his polka awaited him in all its jollity. From a smallish house on the right-hand side, only a few yards away, came the notes of his latest composition, played on a clarinet. There was the sound of dancing, too. Pestana paused for a few moments, considered turning back, but carried on walking, quickening his pace and crossing to the other side of the street. The notes faded into the distance, and Pestana turned into Rua do Aterrado, where he lived. As he reached his house, he saw two men coming toward him. One of them, almost brushing past Pestana, started whistling the same polka, *con brio*; the other man joined in and the two of them headed noisily and cheerily off down the street, while the tune's composer ran despairingly into his house.

Once inside, he breathed again. His old house, his old staircase, his old black manservant, who came to inquire whether he wanted any supper.

"No, no supper," Pestana bawled at him. "Just make me some coffee and go to bed."

He got undressed, put on a nightshirt, and went to the room at the back of the house. When the servant lit the gas lamp in the room, Pestana smiled and nodded his heartfelt greetings to the ten or so portraits hanging on the wall. Only one was an oil painting; it was a portrait of the priest who had raised him, taught him Latin and music, and who, if you believed idle gossip, was Pestana's father. He had certainly left him as an inheritance this old house, along with its bits and pieces of antique furniture, some dating from the reign of Pedro I. The priest had himself composed a couple of motets; he was mad about music, both sacred and profane, and this passion he instilled in the boy, or perhaps transmitted to him by blood, if those wagging tongues were right. However, as you will see, my story does not concern itself with such matters.

The other portraits were of classical composers: Cimarosa, Mozart, Beethoven, Gluck, Bach, Schumann, and three more; some of them were engravings, others lithographs, all badly framed and of differing sizes, but arranged on the wall like saints in a church. The piano was the altar and upon it lay open the evening gospel: a Beethoven sonata.

The coffee arrived; Pestana gulped down the first cup and went over to the piano. He looked up at the portrait of Beethoven and began to play the sonata, as if caught up in a kind of wild ecstasy, but with absolute perfection. He repeated the piece, then paused, stood up, and went to one of the windows. Then he returned to the piano; now it was Mozart's turn. He picked up a sheet of music and performed it in the same manner, his soul transported to another place. Haydn took him up to midnight and his second cup of coffee.

Between midnight and one o'clock, Pestana did little except stand at the window and gaze at the stars, or back at the portraits in the room. From time to time he went to the piano and, without sitting down, played a few random chords, as if searching for a thought. But the thought did not appear and he returned to the window. To him the stars resembled a host of musical notes fixed in the night sky waiting for someone to reach out and unstick them; a time would come when the sky would be empty, and the Earth would be a constellation of musical scores. Nothing, no image, no reverie or reflection reminded him of Sinhazinha Mota, who, at that very moment, was drifting off to sleep thinking about him, that famous composer of so many well-loved polkas. Perhaps the idea of marriage deprived that young lady of several moments of sleep? And why shouldn't it? She was about to turn twenty, and he was thirty, a good age. The young lady fell asleep to the sound of the polka, which she knew by heart, whereas its composer was thinking of neither the polka nor of her, but of the great classics of old, while he endlessly quizzed the heavens and the night, asking the angels and, as a last resort, the devil himself. Why could he not write just one of those immortal pages?

At times, the dawn of an idea seemed to rise up from the depths of his unconscious, and he would run to the piano in order to set it down whole, translate it into sounds, but in vain; the idea vanished. At other times, sitting at the piano, he would let his fingers run wild, to see what fantasias blossomed from them, as they had from Mozart's hands. But nothing, absolutely nothing; inspiration failed him, his imagination slumbered. If by any chance an idea did appear, fully formed and beautiful, it was merely the echo of another piece repeated from his memory, and which he thought he had invented. Then he would leap angrily to his feet and swear that he would give up his art, go and plant coffee or push a cart around the streets. But ten minutes later there he would be once again at the piano, with his eyes fixed on Mozart, trying to mimic his genius.

Two, three, four o'clock. Sometime after four he went to bed; he was weary, disheartened, dead with fatigue; he had to give lessons the following day. He only slept a little, awoke at seven, got dressed, and ate breakfast.

"Would Sir like the cane or the umbrella?" the servant asked, following orders, for his master was often distracted.

"The cane."

"But it looks like rain today, sir."

"Rain," Pestana repeated mechanically.

"Yes, sir. Seems so. The sky's quite dark."

Pestana looked at the servant vaguely, his mind elsewhere. Suddenly: "Wait right there."

He ran to the room with the portraits, opened the piano, sat down, and spread his hands over the keyboard. He began to play something of his own making, a real and spontaneous inspiration, a polka, a rambunctious polka, as the papers would say. The composer did not hold back: his fingers plucked the notes from the air, entwining them, shaping them; you could say his muse was simultaneously composing and dancing. Pestana forgot all about his lessons, his servant waiting for him with the cane and the umbrella, forgot even the portraits hanging gravely on the wall. He simply composed, at the keyboard or on paper, with none of the previous evening's vain efforts, no frustration, asking nothing of heaven or of Mozart's impassive eyes. No weariness at all. Life, wit, and novelty gushed from his soul like an unquenchable stream.

Soon the polka was finished. He made a few minor changes when he returned for dinner, but already he was humming the tune as he walked down the street. He liked it; the blood of his father and his musical vocation flowed through this new and original composition. Two days later, he took it to the publisher of his other polkas, of which there were already over thirty. The editor thought it delightful.

"It will be a huge success."

The matter of a title arose. When Pestana composed his first polka, in 1871, he had wanted to give it a poetical title; his choice was *"Drops of Sunshine."* The publisher shook his head and told him that titles must themselves be destined for popular tastes, either by allusion to some current event or some catchy expression. He suggested two: *"The Law of September 28,"* or *"Fine Words Butter No Parsnips."*

"But what does *'Fine Words Butter No Parsnips'* mean?" asked the composer.

"Oh, it means nothing at all, but soon enough it'll be all the rage."

Still new to the ways of the world, Pestana refused both titles and kept his polka, but it was not long before he composed another, and the itch of publicity led him to have both of them published, with whatever titles the publisher considered most attractive or appropriate. And thus the pattern was set.

Now, when the composer delivered his brand-new polka and they came to discussing the title, the publisher remembered that, for quite some time, he had been keeping one aside for the next tune Pestana brought him. It was intriguing and expansive, yet jaunty: *"Hey Missus, Hang On to Your Hamper."*

"And I've already thought up another good one for next time," he added.

The first edition sold out as soon as it appeared. The composer's fame was enough to guarantee sales, and in itself the tune was well suited to the genre, being original, danceable, and easily learned by heart. Within one week it was famous. For the first few days Pestana was truly in love with his new creation; he enjoyed humming it to himself, would stop in the street to listen to it being played in some house, and get annoyed when it was played badly. Soon the theater orchestras were playing it, and he even went to one of the performances. Nor was he displeased to hear it whistled, one night, by a shadowy figure coming down Rua do Aterrado.

The honeymoon lasted only a quarter moon. As on previous occasions, and even more quickly than before, the old masters in the portraits made him bleed with remorse. Angry and ashamed, Pestana raged against the muse who had so often consoled him, she with her impish eyes and warm embraces, so easygoing and so gracious. Back came his self-disgust and his loathing of anyone who asked him to play his latest polka, and he resumed his efforts to compose something along classical lines, even if it was only a page, just one, but one that would deserve to be bound between those of Bach and Schumann. A futile enterprise, a vain effort. He plunged himself into that Jordan, but emerged from it unbaptized. He wasted night after night, confidently and stubbornly convinced that it was only a matter of willpower, and that if he could only let go of the easy stuff . . .

"To hell with polkas; let the devil dance to them," he said to himself one morning, at dawn, as he was getting into bed.

But the polkas did not want to go quite that far. They came to Pestana's house, to the very room where the portraits hung, bursting in so profusely that he scarcely had time to set them down, have them published, enjoy them for a few days, get bored with them, and return to the same old well-springs whence nothing flowed. And thus his life swung between those two extremes until he married, and after he married too.

"Who's he marrying?" Sinhazinha Mota asked her uncle the notary, who gave her this news.

"A widow."

"Is she old?"

"Twenty-seven."

"Pretty?"

"No, but not ugly, either. Just so-so. I'm told he fell in love with her because he heard her sing at the last feast day of Saint Francis of Paola. But I also heard that she possesses another great gift, less rare and not as worthy: she has consumption."

Notaries should not attempt wit, or at least not the caustic sort. At this last piece of news, his niece felt a drop of soothing balm, which cured her twinge of envy. It was all true. A few days later, Pestana married a widow age twenty-seven, a fine singer and a consumptive. She would be the spiritual wife of his creative genius. Celibacy was doubtless the cause of his sterile, errant ways, he told himself; artistically he considered himself a wandering outcast of the dead of night; his polkas were merely his foppish fancies. Now, finally, he was going to beget a whole family of works that were serious, profound, inspired, and finely polished.

Such hopes had budded in the very first hours of love, and blossomed at the first dawn of married life. "Maria," his soul stammered, "give me what I could find neither in the solitude of night, nor in the turmoil of day."

Straightaway, to celebrate their union, he had the idea of composing a nocturne. He would call it *Ave Maria*. It was as though happiness brought with it the beginnings of inspiration; not wanting to say anything to his wife before it was ready, he worked in secret, which was difficult, since Maria, also a fervent music lover, would come and play with him, or simply listen, for hours and hours, in the room with the portraits. They even put on a few weekly concerts, with three of Pestana's musician friends. One Sunday, however, he could contain himself no longer and called his wife into the room to play her a passage from the nocturne; he did not tell her what it was, nor who it was by. Suddenly, stopping, he looked at her inquiringly.

"Don't stop," said Maria. "It's Chopin, isn't it?"

Pestana went pale, stared into space, repeated one or two passages, and stood up. Maria sat down at the piano, and, struggling slightly to remember, played the piece by Chopin. The idea and the motif were the same; Pestana had discovered them in some dark alleyway of his memory, that perfidious old city. Sad and despairing, he left the house and headed toward the bridge, in the direction of São Cristóvão.

"Why struggle?" he asked himself. "I'll stick to polkas . . . Long live the polka!"

Passersby hearing this stared at him as if he were mad. He carried on walking, delirious, tormented, an eternal shuttlecock between his ambition and his vocation. He passed the old slaughterhouse; when he came to the railroad crossing, he had the notion of walking up the tracks and waiting for the first train to come and crush him. The guard made him turn back. He came to his senses and went home.

A few days later—a clear, fresh morning in May 1876—at six o'clock in the morning, Pestana felt a familiar tingling in his fingers. He slipped slowly out of bed so as not to wake Maria, who had been coughing all night and was now sound asleep. He went to the room with the portraits, opened the lid of the piano, and, as quietly as he could, knocked out a polka. He had it published under a pseudonym; in the following two months he composed and published two more. Maria knew nothing about it; she carried on coughing and dying, until one night she passed away in the arms of her distraught and despairing husband.

It was Christmas Eve. Pestana's suffering was only made worse by the sounds of a dance nearby, where several of his best polkas were being played. The dancing was bad enough; hearing his own compositions gave it all a perverse air of irony. He heard the rhythm of the footsteps and imagined the accidentally salacious movements of the dancers, movements that some of his compositions quite frankly called out for; all this as he sat by her pale corpse, mere skin and bones, laid out on the bed. Every hour of the long night passed like that, fast or slow, moistened by tears and sweat, by eau de cologne and Labarraque's disinfectant, springing ceaselessly back and forth as if to the sound of a polka written by the great invisible Pestana.

After the burial, the widower had only one goal: to abandon his music forever once he had composed a *Requiem*, which he would perform on the first anniversary of Maria's death. Then he would take up some other job: clerk, postman, street peddler, anything that would make him forget his murderous art, so deaf to his aspirations.

He began the great work. He put everything into it: boldness, patience, thought, and even the occasional flight of fancy, as he had done in times gone by, imitating Mozart, whose *Requiem* he reread and studied. Weeks and months went by. The work, which at first went quickly, slowed its pace. Pestana had his good days and bad. At times he found the music lacking in some way, a sacred soul, ideas, inspiration, or method; at other times his spirits rose and he worked frantically. Eight, nine, ten, eleven months, and the *Requiem* was still not finished. He redoubled his efforts, neglected his teaching and his friends. He had reworked the piece many times, but now he wanted to finish it, no matter what. Two weeks, one week, five days to go . . . The anniversary dawned and he was still working on it.

He had to make do with a simple spoken mass, for him alone. It is hard to say whether all the tears that came stealthily to his eyes were those of the husband, or if some were the composer's. In any event, he never looked at the *Requiem* again.

"What for?" he asked himself.

Another year passed. At the beginning of 1878, the publisher came to see him.

"It's been two years," he said, "since you've given us one of your lively tunes. Everyone is wondering if you have lost your talent. What have you been doing with yourself?"

"Nothing."

"I know what a blow your wife's death must have been, but it's been two years now. I'm here to offer you a contract: twenty polkas over the next twelve months; the usual fee, and a higher percentage of the sales. And at the end of the year, we can renew it."

Pestana nodded his agreement. He was giving very few lessons, had sold the house to pay off debts, and daily necessities were eating up what little remained. He accepted the contract.

"But I need the first polka straightaway," explained the publisher. "It's urgent. Did you hear that the Emperor has dismissed the Duke of Caxias? The liberals have been summoned to form a government; they're going ahead with electoral reform. The polka will be called 'Hurrah for Direct Elections!' It's not political, just a good title for the occasion."

Pestana composed the first piece for the contract. Despite his lengthy silence, he had lost neither his originality nor his inspiration. It had the same touch of genius. The other polkas followed one by one at regular intervals. He had kept the portraits and their subjects' repertoire, but he avoided spending all his nights at the piano, so as not to fall into new temptations. Now he would always ask for a free ticket whenever there was a good opera or recital on; he would sit in a corner and simply savor the sounds that would never again blossom in his own mind. From time to time, on returning home, his head filled with music, the unsung maestro in him would awaken once again; he would sit at the piano and aimlessly play a few notes, then, twenty or thirty minutes later, go to bed.

And so the years passed, until 1885. Pestana's fame made him the undisputed master of the polka, but first place in such a village did not suffice for this Caesar, who would still have preferred not the second, but the hundredth place in Rome. He had the same mood swings regarding his compositions as before, the difference being that now they were less violent. No more wild enthusiasm during the first few hours, nor revulsion after the first week; just a degree of pleasure followed by a certain ennui.

That year, he caught a slight fever. After a few days, the fever rose, and became life-threatening. He was already in grave danger when the publisher appeared, unaware that Pestana was ill; he had come to give him the news that the conservatives were back in power, and to ask him to write a polka for the occasion. The nurse, an impoverished theater clarinetist, informed him of Pestana's condition, and the publisher realized it was best to say nothing. It was the patient himself who insisted that he tell him what he had come for; the publisher obeyed.

"But only once you're fully recovered," he concluded.

"Just as soon as the fever subsides a little," said Pestana.

There was a few seconds' pause. The clarinetist quietly tiptoed over to prepare the medication; the publisher stood up and took his leave.

"Goodbye."

"Look," said Pestana, "since it's quite likely that I'll be dead in the next few days, I'll do you two polkas straightaway; the other will come in handy for when the liberals are back."

It was the only joke he had made in his entire life, and it came none too soon, for he died at five minutes past four the following morning, at peace with his fellow men and at war with himself.

THE OBJECT OF DESIRE

———

"AH, COUNSELOR, now you're beginning to talk in verse!"
"All men should carry a lyre in their hearts, or else they're not men.
I'm not saying they should use it all the time or for no good reason, just
now and again, when recalling certain special moments. Do you know why
I sound to you like a poet, despite all my years as a lawyer and my graying
hair? It's because we're walking through Glória, past the foreign ministry . . .
There's the famous hill . . . And farther on, there's a certain house . . ."

"Let's keep walking."

"Yes, let's. Ah, the divine Quintília! The faces we pass are all different,
of course, and yet they speak to me of those times, as if they were the same
faces as before; the lyre has been plucked, and the imagination does the rest.
Divine Quintília!"

"Her name was Quintília, you say? I once knew a pretty girl by that
name, when I was at medical school. People used to say she was the most
beautiful girl in Rio."

"It must be the same one, for she did have that reputation. Tall and slim?"

"That's the one. What became of her?"

"She died in 1859. The twentieth of April. A day I'll never forget. I'm
going to tell you an interesting story, or at least it's interesting to me, and I
believe it will be to you too. See? There's the house. She lived with an uncle,
a retired naval commander. She had another house up in Cosme Velho.
When I met Quintília . . . What age do you think she was when I met her?"

"If it was in 1855 . . ."

"Yes, in 1855."

"She must have been twenty."

"She was thirty."

"Thirty?"

"Yes, thirty. She didn't look it, and even her rivals wouldn't have accused her of being that old. But she herself admitted it, even reveled in it. In fact, one of her friends contended that Quintília was no older than twenty-seven, but since they had both been born on the same day, she was only saying that to make herself seem younger."

"Now, now. No irony, please. Irony and nostalgia make poor bedfellows."

"What is nostalgia but the irony of time and fortune? You see? I'm beginning to sound pompous. Thirty years old, but she really didn't look it. You're quite right when you say she was tall and slim; she had eyes that, as I used to say back then, seemed cut from the very cloak of night, but although nocturnal, they held neither mysteries nor unplumbed depths. Her voice was soft with a very slight São Paulo accent; she had a generous mouth, with teeth that, even when she was talking, made her look as if she were laughing. She did laugh as well, and, for a time, it was the combination of her laughter and her eyes that caused me such pain."

"But you said her eyes held no mysteries . . ."

"Yes, so much so that I reached the point of supposing them to be the open gates of the castle, and her laughter the bugle call summoning the knights in shining armor. We already knew her, João Nóbrega and I; he and I shared an office when we were both bosom pals starting out at the bar, but it never occurred to us to woo her. She was then at the very pinnacle of society; she was beautiful, rich, elegant, and moved in all the best circles. But one day, standing in the aisle at the old Teatro Provisório, between two acts of Bellini's *I Puritani*, I heard a group of young men referring to her as an impregnable fortress. Two of them confessed to having tried to approach her, but with no success; all of them were amazed she was still single, which struck them as inexplicable. And they joked about it: one said she'd vowed to see if she got fat first; another that she was waiting for her uncle's second youth so she could marry him; another that she had probably summoned some guardian angel from heaven. I found such tittle-tattle irksome in the extreme and, coming as it did from those who claimed to have loved or courted her, I thought it rude beyond words. What they all agreed upon was her extraordinary beauty; about that they were utterly enthusiastic and sincere."

"Ah, yes, I remember! She was very pretty indeed."

"The following day, on arriving at the office, after two court cases had failed to turn up, I told Nóbrega what I'd heard the previous night. Nóbrega laughed at the incident, then grew thoughtful and, after pacing the room, he stopped in front of me and stared down at me in silence. 'Are you in love with her? Is that what it is?' I asked. 'No,' he replied, 'are you? I've just had an idea: why don't we attempt our own assault on the fortress? What have we got to lose? Either she throws us out on our ear, which is the most likely outcome, or she accepts one of us, and then so much the better for the other one, who will see his friend happy.' 'Are you serious?' 'Very.' Nóbrega added that it was not only her beauty that made her attractive. Note that he liked to think of himself as a practical type, whereas he was really a dreamer who spent all his time reading and concocting plots of a sociopolitical nature. According to him, what those young bucks at the theater had avoided mentioning was the lady's wealth, which was one of her most notable charms, and one of the likely causes of their disappointment and sarcasm. 'Listen here,' he said to me, 'money shouldn't be worshipped, but nor should we turn our backs on it; we shouldn't start thinking that money can buy everything, but we must allow that it can buy quite a few things—this watch, for example. So let's fight for our Quintília, mine or yours, but probably mine, since I'm so much better-looking than you.'"

"This is a grave confession, Counselor. Did it really start like that, as a joke . . . ?"

"Yes, that weighty undertaking started out as a joke, which still had a whiff of the student prank about it, one that could well have ended in nothing, but was to have serious consequences. It was a reckless beginning, almost a childish game, without an ounce of sincerity, but man proposes and the species disposes. We already knew her, although we had met her only occasionally. However, once we had embarked on this common endeavor, a new element entered our life, and within a month we had fallen out."

"Fallen out?"

"Well, nearly. We hadn't reckoned on Quintília herself, and she bewitched us both, completely and utterly. After a few weeks, we avoided talking about her or did so with feigned indifference, each trying to fool the other and hide our true feelings. That was how our friendship crumbled, after just six months, without rancor or struggle, or indeed any outward sign, for we still spoke when we happened to run into one another; but, by then, we'd set up our own separate offices."

"I'm beginning to get a first inkling of the drama."

"Tragedy, call it a tragedy; because shortly afterward, either because of some words of discouragement she may have given him, or simply because he despaired of ever winning, Nóbrega abandoned the field and left it to me alone. He got himself appointed district judge somewhere up in the backlands of Bahia, where he wasted away and died before four years were out. And I swear to you it wasn't Nóbrega's much-vaunted practicality that separated him from me; he, who had talked so much about the advantages of money, died as wracked by love as any young Werther."

"Only without the pistol."

"Poison also kills, and love for Quintília could be said to be something along those lines; that was what killed him, and what still pains me to this day. But I see from your remark that I'm boring you."

"Good God, man, certainly not! I swear it was just a silly joke of mine. Do carry on, Counselor; you were saying that you had the field to yourself."

"With Quintília, no one ever had the field to himself. This was not her doing, but there were always other men. Many came to sip an aperitif of hope, and then went on to dine elsewhere. She didn't favor anyone in particular, but she was always amiable and charming, with the kind of languid eyes that were not made for jealous men. I was bitterly, at times ferociously, jealous. I made many a mountain out of a molehill, and on every mountain sat the devil himself. Finally, I got used to seeing them merely as fleeting fancies. Others gave me more cause for concern: those who came holding the gloved hands of her female companions. I believe there were two or three attempts at such introductions, but without success. Quintília declared that she would do nothing without consulting her uncle, and her uncle always advised her to refuse—as, of course, she had already anticipated. The old man never liked any of her gentlemen callers, fearing that his niece would choose one and marry. He was so used to having her by his side, like a crutch for his crippled soul, and he feared losing her entirely."

"Might that not be the reason for the young lady's steadfast indifference?"

"No, as you will see."

"What I do see is that you were more persistent than the others . . ."

"Deluded, rather, at least to begin with, because, in the midst of so many ill-fated proposals, Quintília seemed to prefer me to all the other men, and always spoke to me far more freely and intimately, so much so that rumors spread of our impending marriage."

"But what did you talk about?"

"Oh, about all the things she didn't discuss with the others; indeed, it was astonishing that a person so keen on balls and promenades, on waltzing and laughing, could be so earnest and serious with me, so different from how she normally was or appeared to be."

"She obviously must have found your conversation less banal than that of the other men."

"Well, thank you, but the reason was deeper than that, and it grew more pronounced as time went on. When life down here in the city became too tedious for her, she would go up to Cosme Velho, and there our conversations were longer and more frequent. I cannot begin to tell you, for even you would not understand, how many hours I spent there, absorbing the vitality that flowed out of her. Many a time, I wanted to tell her how I felt, but the words took fright and stayed locked in my heart. I wrote letter after letter, but they all seemed to me too cold, long-winded, or pompous. Furthermore, she gave me no opportunity, always behaving as if we were merely old friends. At the beginning of 1857, my father fell ill in Itaboraí; I rushed to see him and found him close to death. This kept me away from the capital for around four months. I returned toward the end of May. Quintília was clearly saddened by my sadness, and I could see that my grief had reached her eyes too . . ."

"And what was that if not love?"

"That's what I thought, and I set my sights on marrying her. At that point, her uncle fell gravely ill. Quintília would not be left alone in the event of him dying, because, in addition to her many relations scattered here and there, a widowed cousin, Dona Ana, now lived with her, in the house on Rua do Catete. It was evident, however, that her chief emotional attachment was departing this world and, in that transition between her present and future lives, I might achieve what I most desired. The uncle's illness was brief and, assisted by old age, it carried him off within a fortnight. His death, I can tell you, reminded me of my own father's, and the sorrow I felt was almost the same. Quintília saw my suffering, understood its dual causes, and, as she told me afterward, took some consolation in the coincidence, since it had fallen on us both so inevitably and abruptly. Her words seemed to me an invitation to declare my hand; two months later, I decided to propose. Dona Ana was still living with her up in Cosme Velho. I went there and found them together on the terrace, close to the mountain. It was four o'clock on a Sunday afternoon. Dona Ana, who assumed there was an understanding between us, tactfully left us alone."

"At last!"

"There on the terrace, in that isolated and, may I say, rather wild place, I resolved that I would say my piece first, for fear that five minutes of conversation would sap me of my strength. Even so, you can scarcely imagine how much it took out of me: I would have found a pitched battle less exhausting, and I can assure you I was not born to be a soldier. But that slight, delicate woman held me in the palm of her hand like no other, before or since . . ."

"And what happened?"

"Quintília had guessed from my troubled expression what I was going to ask her, and she prepared her answer while I spoke. Her response was interrogative and negative. Whatever for? It was better for us to remain friends. I replied that for me friendship had been, for quite some time, the mere sentinel of love; now, no longer able to contain it, the sentinel had set it free. Quintília smiled at the metaphor, and, fool that I was, I found her smile painful; seeing the effect her words had on me, she again became serious and set out to persuade me that it was better not to marry. 'I'm old,' she said; 'I'm nearly thirty-three.' 'But I love you just the same,' I replied, and said many other things I could not possibly repeat now. Quintília reflected for a moment, then insisted again on friendship; she said that, despite being younger than her, I had the gravity of an older man and inspired her with a confidence no other man had. I paced the terrace in despair, then sat down again and told her everything. When she heard about my quarrel with my old friend from law school, and our subsequent estrangement, she felt hurt or annoyed, I'm not quite sure which. She blamed us both; things should never have gone that far. 'You're just saying that,' I told her, 'because you don't feel the same about me.' 'Have you lost your senses?' 'I believe I have. What I can assure you is that even now, if the need arose, I would do the same again a hundred times over, and I think I can safely say that he would too.' At this point, she looked at me in astonishment, as if at someone who has completely lost his mind. Then she shook her head and repeated that it had all been a terrible mistake, that it simply wasn't worth all that pain. 'Let us be friends,' she said, holding out her hand. 'That's impossible,' I replied, 'you're asking me for something I cannot give. I could never see you as only a friend; I don't want to impose on you; I'll even say that I will insist no further, because now I would accept no other answer.' We exchanged a few more words and I left. Just look at my hand."

"It's shaking . . ."

"And I haven't told you everything yet. I haven't told you about the pain I endured, or the lingering grief and resentment. I regretted it all bitterly, angrily even, for I should have brought matters to a head during those first few weeks. Hope was the culprit, a weed that had crowded out other, finer plants. After five days, I left for Itaboraí, summoned by certain matters arising from my father's will. When I returned home three weeks later, a letter from Quintília was waiting for me."

"Oh!"

"I tore it open: it was dated four days earlier. It was a long letter, alluding to recent events and saying things that were both tender and serious. Quintília assured me she had waited for me every day, unable to believe that I would be so selfish as not to return. And so she was writing to beg me to turn the page on my unrequited feelings, to remain her friend, and see her as mine. And she concluded with these rather peculiar words: 'Is it a guarantee you want? I promise you that I will never marry.' I understood that we were bound together by a moral sympathy, with the difference that what in me was a genuine passion, in her was merely a matter of temperament. We were two partners entering into the commerce of life with differing amounts of capital: I brought all that I possessed, she came with barely a penny. I replied to her letter along such lines, and declared that my obedience and love were such that I would submit to her wishes, but with bad grace, because after all that had happened between us, I was bound to feel humiliated. I had crossed out the word 'ridiculous,' which is what I had written initially, so that I could go and see her without that additional indignity; the other word was bad enough."

"And you yourself followed hard on the heels of the letter, I imagine? That's what I would have done, because, unless I'm much mistaken, that young lady was dying to marry you."

"Leave aside your usual theories; this is a most unusual case."

"Then let me guess the rest; her promise was some kind of mystical

encirclement from which only you, the recipient, could release her, on condition that you yourself would profit from the absolution. In any event, you
rushed to see her."

"No, I didn't rush; I went two days later. In the meantime, she replied
to my letter with an affectionate note, which concluded with this remark:
'Don't speak of humiliation when there were no witnesses.' I returned not
once but many times, and things went back to how they had been before.
Nothing was said; at first I found it very hard to pretend nothing had changed;
later on, the demon hope again took up residence in my heart and, without
ever saying anything, I entertained the thought that, one day, sooner or
later, she would come around to marrying me. And, given the situation I
found myself in, it was this hope that restored me in my own eyes. Rumors
of our impending marriage circulated widely. When they reached our ears,
I denied them formally and categorically, and she shrugged her shoulders
and laughed. This phase of our life was for me the most serene, except for
one brief incident involving a diplomat from Austria or somewhere, a strap-
ping fellow, elegant, redheaded, with large, seductive eyes, and a nobleman
to boot. Quintília behaved so amiably toward him that he thought he was
in with a chance, and tried to take things further. I believe some involun-
tary gesture of mine, or perhaps some finer perception bestowed on him
by heaven, soon disabused the Austrian legation of any misunderstanding.
Not long afterward, Quintília became ill, and it was then that our friendship deepened. She decided not to leave the house during her treatment, for
such were the doctors' orders. I spent many hours there every day. She and
Dona Ana would play the piano, or all three of us would sit at cards, or read
to each other; most of the time we just talked. It was then that I was able
to study her at length; listening to her read, I saw that books purely about
love were incomprehensible to her, and if they contained violent passions
she would cast the book aside out of boredom. This wasn't ignorance on her
part; she had a vague notion of such passions, and had witnessed them in
other people around her."

"What was her illness?"

"Something in her spine. The doctors said it had probably been there for
quite some time, and was now becoming dangerous. By then it was 1859.
From March of that year, her condition grew steadily worse; then there was
a brief respite, but by the end of the month the situation was hopeless. I
have never seen anyone so energetic in the face of imminent doom; by then

she was transparently, almost fluidly thin; she laughed, or rather smiled, and, seeing me hide my tears, she would clasp my hands in gratitude. One day, when we were alone with the doctor, she asked him to tell her the truth; he was on the point of lying, but she told him it was useless, that she knew she was done for. 'No, not done for,' murmured the doctor. 'Do you swear?' He hesitated, and she thanked him. Now that she was sure she was dying, she finally did what she had promised herself."

"She married your good self, I'll wager."

"Don't remind me of that unhappy ceremony; or rather, let me remember it for myself, because it brings me a breath of something from the past. She would hear nothing of my pleas or refusals; she wed me when she was at the very threshold of death. That was on April 18, 1859. I spent the final two days, until April 20, at the bedside of my dying bride, and when I embraced her for the first time she was already a corpse."

"All this is very strange indeed."

"I don't know what you and your theories will make of it. Mine, which are those of a mere layman, conclude that the young lady had a purely physical aversion to marriage. She married when she was half dead and at the gates of oblivion. Call her a monster, if you will, but add the word 'divine.'"

THE SECRET CAUSE

GARCIA WAS STANDING up, nervously picking at his fingernails; Fortunato, in the rocking chair, was gazing up at the ceiling; Maria Luísa, by the window, was finishing her needlework. Five minutes had passed without any of them saying a word. They had talked about the weather, which had been excellent, about Catumbi, where Fortunato and his wife lived, and about a private hospital, but more of that later. Since the three people here described are all now dead and buried, the time has come to tell the unvarnished truth.

They had also talked about something else apart from those three subjects, a matter so serious and so distasteful that it left them with little appetite for discussing the weather, the neighborhood, or the hospital. The conversation on this subject had been very awkward indeed. Even now, Maria Luísa's fingers still seemed to be trembling, while Garcia's face wore a stern expression, which for him was most unusual. The nature of what had happened was such that in order to understand it we must go back to the very beginning.

Garcia had qualified as a doctor the previous year, 1861. In 1860, while still at medical school, he had met Fortunato for the first time, at the entrance to the Santa Casa Hospital; he was going in as the other was leaving. Something about Fortunato impressed him, but he would have forgotten all about him had it not been for their second meeting a few days later. Garcia lived in Rua Dom Manuel. One of his few amusements was to go to the Teatro de São Januário, which was close by, between his street and the waterfront; he went once or twice a month, and there were never more than forty or so spectators in the audience. Only the most intrepid souls dared venture down to that part of town. One night, he was sitting in the stalls, when Fortunato appeared and sat right next to him.

The play was an old melodrama, stitched together with stabbings and bristling with curses and wails of remorse; but Fortunato watched it with unusual interest. During the most painful scenes, he was doubly attentive; his eyes leapt from one character to another so intently that Garcia suspected that the play stirred some personal reminiscences in his neighbor. The drama was followed by a farce, but Fortunato did not stay to see it; Garcia followed him out. Fortunato headed down Beco do Cotovelo and Rua de São José, as far as Largo da Carioca. He was walking slowly, shoulders hunched, stopping now and then to prod a sleeping dog with his cane; the dog would yelp, and Fortunato would carry on walking. At Largo da Carioca he got into a cab and headed off toward Praça da Constituição. Garcia returned home none the wiser.

Several weeks went by. He was at home one night when, at around nine o'clock, he heard the sound of voices on the stairs; he quickly left his attic lodgings and went down to the first floor, which was occupied by a man who worked at the War Arsenal. The man in question was being carried upstairs, soaked in blood. His black servant hurried to open the door; the man was groaning, the voices around him jumbled, the light dim. Once they'd laid the wounded man on the bed, Garcia said they should call a doctor.

"He's on his way," someone replied.

Garcia looked up: it was the same man he'd seen at the hospital and at the theater. He imagined him to be a friend or relative of the wounded man, but immediately rejected this idea when he heard him ask if the man had any family or next-of-kin. The black man said no, and the stranger took control of the situation, asking the others to leave, paying the porters, and giving some initial instructions regarding the patient. On learning that Garcia was a neighbor and a medical student, he asked him to stay and assist the doctor. Then he explained what had happened.

"It was a gang of ruffians. I was coming back from the Moura Barracks where I'd been to visit a cousin, when I heard lot of shouting, and then some sort of scuffle. It seems they also wounded another passerby, who fled down one of the alleyways; but I only saw this gentleman, who was crossing the street when one of the ruffians brushed past him and stabbed him with a knife. He didn't pass out immediately; he told me where he lived and, since it was only a few yards away, I thought it best to bring him here myself."

"Had you met him before?" asked Garcia.

"No, never laid eyes on him. Who is he?"

"He's a good man, works at the War Arsenal. His name is Gouvêa."

"Never heard of him."

The doctor and deputy superintendent arrived shortly afterward; bandages were applied and statements taken. The stranger gave his name as Fortunato Gomes da Silveira, a bachelor of independent means residing in Catumbi. The wound was deemed serious. While it was being dressed with Garcia's assistance, Fortunato played the role of servant, holding the basin, the candle, and the bandages, not in the least disturbed, looking coldly down at the wounded man, who groaned constantly. Afterward, he spoke privately with the doctor, accompanied him as far as the landing, and again assured the deputy superintendent that he stood ready to help the police with their inquiries. The doctor and deputy superintendent left; Fortunato and the student remained in the bedroom.

Garcia was astonished. He looked at the other man and watched him calmly sit down, stretch his legs, put his hands in his trouser pockets, and fix his gaze on the wounded man. His eyes were pale gray, the color of lead; they moved slowly and had a hard, cold, dry expression. His face was thin and pale, framed by a wispy, ginger chinstrap beard. He was probably around forty. From time to time, he would turn to the student and ask something about the wounded man, then turn back to look at the patient while Garcia answered. The young man's feeling was one of revulsion mixed with curiosity; he couldn't deny that he was witnessing an act of rare dedication, and if it was as selfless as it seemed, then he had to accept that the human heart was indeed a well of mysteries.

Fortunato left shortly before one o'clock; he returned during the days that followed, but the wound healed quickly, and, before it was completely healed, he disappeared without telling the object of his charity where he lived. It was Garcia who passed on Fortunato's name, street, and house number.

"I'll go and thank him for his kindness just as soon as I'm able to leave the house," said the convalescent.

And six days later, he hurried over to Catumbi. Fortunato received him with some embarrassment, listened impatiently to his words of thanks, replied somewhat irritably, and ended up playing with the tassels on his dressing gown. Sitting silently in front of him, Gouvêa fiddled with his hat and looked up from time to time, unable to think of anything else to say. After ten minutes he took his leave.

"Watch out for those ruffians!" his host said, laughing.

The unfortunate fellow left the house feeling humiliated and mortified, resentful of the disdainful way in which he had been received. He struggled to forget, to explain or pardon, so that only the memory of the kind deed would remain in his heart, but all in vain. Resentment, a new, exclusive lodger, entered his heart and kicked out the kind deed, which, poor thing, had no alternative but to clamber up into his brain and seek refuge there as a mere idea. Thus it was that the benefactor instilled in the beneficiary a feeling of rank ingratitude.

All this astonished Garcia. The young man had a nascent ability to decipher men and deconstruct characters; he loved analysis and possessed the gift, which he prized above all others, of being able to penetrate numerous emotional and spiritual layers until he grasped the inner secret of a human organism. His curiosity pricked, he considered going to see the man from Catumbi, but realized that he had received no formal invitation to call on him. At the very least he needed a pretext, and he could think of none.

Some time later, when he was a qualified doctor and living on Rua de Matacavalos, near Rua do Conde, he met Fortunato in a streetcar. He subsequently bumped into him on several more occasions, and the frequency of those encounters led to a certain degree of familiarity. One day, Fortunato invited him to come and visit him nearby, in Catumbi.

"You do know that I'm married?"

"No, I didn't."

"I got married four months ago, although it seems like four days. Come and dine with us on Sunday."

"Sunday?"

"Now, don't start making excuses. I won't hear of it. Come on Sunday."

Garcia duly went on Sunday. Fortunato gave him a good dinner, good cigars, and good conversation, in the company of his wife, who was an interesting woman. Fortunato's face had not changed; his eyes were the same sheets of cold, hard tin, and his other features were no more attractive, either. While his obliging manners did not entirely make up for his gruff nature, they were at least some compensation. Maria Luísa, on the other hand, was charming both in person and in manners. She was slim and elegant, with soft, submissive eyes; she was twenty-five years old, but looked not a day over nineteen. On his second visit, Garcia noticed that there was between the couple a certain disparity of character, little or no emotional affinity, and the wife's attitude toward her husband went beyond respect, bordering almost on subjection and fear. One day, when the three of them were together, Garcia asked Maria Luísa if she had heard about the circumstances in which he had met her husband.

"No," replied the young lady.

"Then you're going to hear the tale of a very handsome deed."

"There's really no need," said Fortunato, interrupting.

"I shall let you be the judge of that, senhora," Garcia insisted.

He described the events on Rua Dom Manuel. The young lady listened in astonishment, unconsciously reaching out her hand to grasp her husband's wrist, smiling in gratitude, as if she had just discovered that he did actually have a heart. Fortunato shrugged, but was clearly not unmoved. Afterward, he himself described the wounded man's visit, describing the look on his face, his gestures, his garbled words and awkward silences—a complete idiot, in fact. He laughed and laughed as he spoke. There was no guile in that laughter; guile is evasive and oblique; his laughter was jovial and frank.

"What a peculiar man!" thought Garcia.

Maria Luísa was saddened by her husband's mocking account, but Garcia restored her previous contentment by returning to the subject of Fortunato's dedication and rare qualities as a nurse: "So good a nurse," he concluded, "that if someday I were to set up my own private hospital, I would invite him to join me."

"Are you serious?" asked Fortunato.

"About what?"

"About setting up a hospital together?"

"No, not at all; I was joking."

"Well, we could give it a go, and for you, just starting out, it might not be a bad idea. I own a house that is about to become vacant, and that would be just the ticket."

Garcia refused then, and refused again the following day, but the idea had lodged itself in the other man's head and there was no going back. It would indeed make a good start to Garcia's career, and it could well become a profitable venture for them both. He finally accepted a few days later, much to Maria Luísa's disappointment. A nervous, fragile creature, she shuddered at the mere thought of her husband living in contact with human diseases, but she didn't dare oppose him, and so bowed her head. Plans were quickly laid and carried out. In fact, Fortunato paid little attention to anything else, either then or later. When the hospital opened, he himself became the administrator and chief nurse: he inspected everything and organized everything, from soups to storerooms, medicines to ledgers.

Garcia could see then that the dedication he had shown toward the wounded man on Rua Dom Manuel had not been an isolated event, but was grounded in the man's very nature. He watched him serve more willingly than any of the servants. He did not recoil from anything; no disease distressed or repelled him and he was always ready for anything, at any hour of the day or night. Everyone admired and applauded him. Fortunato read books, attended all the surgical operations, and it was he alone who applied the caustic lotions. "I have a lot of faith in caustic lotions," he used to say.

Their common interests strengthened their bonds of friendship. Garcia was a frequent visitor to the house; he dined there almost every day, observing Maria Luísa and her ever more apparent emotional isolation, an isolation that merely doubled her charms, he thought. Garcia began to feel a certain agitation whenever she appeared, when she talked, when she would sit silently sewing by the window, or play sad songs on the piano. Softly, gently, love slipped into his heart. When he realized this, he tried to drive it out, so that there would be no bond but his friendship with Fortunato, but he could not. He could only lock it away; Maria Luísa understood both his affection and his silence, but said nothing.

At the beginning of October, something happened that revealed to Garcia yet more of the young lady's plight. Fortunato had taken up the study of anatomy and physiology, and spent his free time dissecting and poisoning cats and dogs. Since the animals' squeals disturbed the patients, he moved his laboratory to the house, forcing his wife, with her nervous temperament, to endure their cries. One day, however, unable to bear it any longer, she went to see Garcia and begged him to ask her husband, on her behalf, to put an end to these experiments.

"But couldn't you yourself . . ."

Maria Luísa answered with a smile:

"He would no doubt think it very childish of me. What I would like is for you, as a doctor, to tell him that it's doing me harm; for, believe me, it most certainly is."

Garcia promptly persuaded Fortunato to end his live experiments. No one knew if he continued them elsewhere, but he may well have done. Maria Luísa thanked Garcia, for her own sake and that of the animals, for she could not bear to see them suffer. She coughed from time to time; Garcia asked if anything was the matter; she said there wasn't.

"Let me feel your pulse."

"There's nothing wrong with me."

She wouldn't let him feel her pulse, and left the room. Garcia became apprehensive. He thought there might indeed be something wrong with her, and that he would need to keep a close eye on her and warn her husband in good time.

Two days later—the very day on which we see them now—Garcia went to dinner with them. When he arrived, he was told that Fortunato was in his study and so he immediately made his way there. He had just reached the door when Maria Luísa rushed out in a state of terrible distress.

"What's the matter?" he asked.

"The mouse! The mouse!" exclaimed the young lady, gasping for air and rushing away.

Garcia remembered that the evening before he had heard Fortunato complaining that a mouse had chewed up an important document. He did not, however, expect to see what now appeared before him. Fortunato was sitting at the table in the middle of the study, and on the table sat a dish of alcohol. The liquid was alight. Between the thumb and forefinger of his left hand he held a piece of string, from which the mouse dangled by its tail. In his right hand was a pair of scissors. At the precise moment Garcia entered the room, Fortunato snipped off one of the mouse's legs; then he slowly lowered the poor creature into the flame, only briefly, so as not to kill it, and then prepared to snip the third leg, for he had already cut off the first before Garcia arrived. Garcia froze in horror.

"Kill it now!" he said.

"Just a moment."

And with a most peculiar smile, something that hinted at an inner satisfaction, the slow savoring of sublime sensations, Fortunato cut off the mouse's third leg, and for the third time lowered the mouse into the flame. The miserable creature writhed and squealed in agony, bloodied and scorched, but still did not die. Garcia turned away, then looked back and reached out his hand to stop the torture. But he did nothing, because this devil of a man, his face radiant and serene, filled him with fear. Only the last leg remained; Fortunato cut it very slowly, his eyes fixed on the scissors; the leg fell, and he continued to stare at the half-dead mouse. When he lowered it into the flame for the fourth time, he did so even more briefly than before, so as to salvage, if he could, whatever shred of life remained.

Standing in front of him, Garcia managed to overcome his repugnance at the spectacle and stared into the man's face. There was neither anger nor hatred there, simply an immense pleasure, quiet and profound, such as another man might get from hearing a beautiful sonata or gazing at an exquisite statue—something resembling a purely aesthetic sensation. It seemed to him, and indeed it was the case, that Fortunato had forgotten all about him. He could not, therefore, be pretending, and Garcia's analysis must be correct. The flame was dying down, and the mouse retained perhaps the faintest glimmer of life; Fortunato put this possibility to good use by cutting off the mouse's nose and, for the last time, lowering the exposed flesh into the flame. Finally, he let the dead body fall into the dish, and pushed the mess of charred flesh and blood away from him.

When he stood up, he saw Garcia and jumped. Then he put on a display of rage against the animal for having devoured his precious document, but his anger was clearly a sham.

"He punishes coldly and without anger," thought Garcia, "driven by the need for a pleasure that only another's pain can give him: that is his secret."

Fortunato stressed the importance of the lost document and the time he had wasted because of it; true, it was only time, but time was now so precious to him. Garcia listened without saying anything, without believing him. He recalled other things he had seen Fortunato do, both the serious and the trivial, and he found the same explanation for all of them. It was the same key change in all of that man's sensibilities, a peculiar form of dilettantism, a miniature Caligula.

When, shortly afterward, Maria Luísa returned to the study, her husband went up to her, chuckling, took her hands, and whispered gently: "You big softy!"

And, turning to Garcia, he said: "Would you believe she nearly fainted?"

Maria Luísa timidly defended herself, saying she was nervous, and a woman; then she went to sit by the window with her needles and threads, her fingers still trembling, just as we saw her at the beginning of this story. You will remember that, after talking of other matters, the three of them fell silent, the husband sitting, gazing up at the ceiling, the doctor picking at his fingernails. A little later, they sat down to dinner, but it was not a happy occasion. Maria Luísa brooded and coughed; Garcia wondered if the company of such a man might not, perhaps, expose her to some violent excess. It was only a possibility, but his love transformed possibility into certainty; he trembled for her and resolved to keep a close eye on both of them.

She coughed and coughed, and it wasn't long before the illness removed its mask. It was consumption, that insatiable old hag that sucks life to the core, leaving only a husk of bare bones. It came as a tremendous blow to Fortunato; he truly loved his wife, in his fashion; he was used to her and it would be hard to lose her. He spared no effort, doctors, medication, changes of air, resorted to every possible remedy and palliative. But all in vain. The illness was fatal.

During the final days, as Garcia watched the young lady's terrible suffering, her husband's inner nature prevailed over any other sentiments he may have had. He never left her side and watched with a cold, dull eye as her life slowly, painfully decayed, drinking in one by one the afflictions of that beautiful creature, now thin and transparent, devoured by fever and consumed by death. His raging egotism, hungry for sensation, would not let him miss one single moment of her agony, nor repay her with a single tear, public or private. Only when she died did the shock hit him. When he came to his senses again, he saw that once again he was alone.

That night, when a relative of Maria Luísa's, who had helped her while she was dying, left the room in order to rest, Fortunato and Garcia stayed, watching over the corpse, both of them deep in thought. But the husband was himself exhausted and Garcia told him to rest a little.

"Go and sleep for an hour or two; afterward, it will be my turn."

Fortunato went and lay down on the sofa in the adjoining room, and promptly fell asleep. Twenty minutes later he woke, tried to go back to sleep, dozed for a few moments, then got up and returned to the drawing room. He walked on tiptoe so as not to wake the relative, who was sleeping nearby. As he reached the door, he stopped in astonishment.

Garcia had gone over to the body, lifted the veil, and gazed for several moments at the dead woman's features. Then, as if death rendered all things spiritual, he leaned over and kissed her forehead. It was then that Fortunato reached the door. He stopped in his tracks; it could not be a kiss of friend-ship, but perhaps rather the epilogue to an adulterous novel. Note that he felt no jealousy; nature had formed him in such a way as to give him neither jealousy nor envy, but it had given him vanity, which is no less prone to resentment. He watched in astonishment, biting his lip.

Meanwhile, Garcia leaned over to kiss the corpse again, but this time he could no longer contain himself. That kiss became a sob, and his eyes could not hold back the tears that streamed down his face, tears of silent love and unquenchable despair. Still standing at the door, Fortunato quietly savored this outburst of spiritual pain, which went on, and on, for a deliciously long time.

TRIO IN A MINOR

———

I

ADAGIO CANTABILE

MARIA REGINA ACCOMPANIED her grandmother to her bedroom, said good night, and retired to her own room. Despite the familiarity that existed between them, the slave-woman who attended to her could not get a word out of her and left, half an hour later, saying that mistress was in a very serious mood. As soon as she was alone, Maria Regina sat down on the end of the bed, legs outstretched, ankles crossed, thinking.

Truth requires me to tell you that the young lady was thinking simultaneously and equally amorously about two men; one of them, Maciel, was twenty-seven, while the other, Miranda, was fifty. Quite abominable, I agree, but I cannot change the facts, nor can I deny that if the two men were both smitten with her, she was no less smitten with both of them. In short, a most peculiar young lady or, as her old school chums from the convent would have put it, a bit of a scatterbrain. No one would deny her excellence of heart and purity of mind; the problem lay in her imagination: an ardent, covetous imagination, insatiably so, a stranger to reality, superimposing its own inventions on everything around her, and from that flowed all sorts of curious consequences.

The visit of these two men (who had been courting her for only a short while) lasted around an hour. Maria Regina chatted gaily with them and played a classical piece, a sonata, on the piano, which sent her grandmother into a light doze. Later on, they all discussed music. Miranda made some pertinent comments about modern and not-so-modern music; the grandmother was devoted to Bellini and *Norma*, and she talked about the tunes from her youth: dreamy, delightful, and above all clear. The granddaughter sided with Miranda; Maciel politely agreed with everyone.

As she sat on the end of the bed, Maria Regina went over it all again: the visit, the conversation, the music, the discussion, the qualities of the two men, Miranda's words, and Maciel's beautiful eyes. It was eleven o'clock, the only light in her bedroom was a little night lamp, and everything lent itself to dreams and reveries. As Maria Regina reconstructed the evening's events, she saw the two men standing there before her, heard them, and spoke with them for quite some time, thirty or forty minutes, accompanied by the sound of the same sonata she had played earlier; da, da, dum . . .

II

ALLEGRO MA NON TROPPO

The following day, grandmother and granddaughter went to visit a friend in Tijuca. On the way back, their carriage knocked down a little boy running across the street. Someone who witnessed the incident grabbed the horses and, at much risk to himself, managed to hold them back and save the child, who was only slightly injured and had merely fainted from the shock. A crowd gathered and uproar ensued; the boy's mother rushed into the street in tears. Maria Regina got out of the carriage and accompanied the injured child into his mother's house, which was immediately opposite where the accident had happened.

Anyone familiar with the workings of destiny will already have guessed that the person who saved the little boy was one of the two men from the other night: Maciel. Once he and Maria Regina had made sure the boy had received proper treatment, he accompanied her back to the carriage and accepted the grandmother's offer of a ride into town (at this point they were in Engenho Velho). It was only in the carriage that Maria Regina noticed Maciel's bloodied hand. The grandmother kept asking if the little boy was badly hurt, if he would pull through. Maciel told her that his injuries were very slight. Then he described the incident in full: he had been standing on the sidewalk, waiting for a cab, when he saw the boy crossing the street in front of the horses; he realized the child was in danger and tried to prevent, or at least diminish, any risk of injury.

"But you're hurt," said the old lady.

"Oh, it's nothing."

"But you are, you are!" cried the young lady. "We should have bandaged you too."

"It's nothing at all," he insisted. "Just a scratch. I'll just use my handkerchief."

Before he could pull out his handkerchief, Maria Regina offered him hers. Touched by this offer, Maciel took the handkerchief, but was reluctant to dirty it. "Go on," she said, and, noting his diffidence, took the handkerchief from him, and she herself wiped the blood from his hand.

It was an attractive hand, as attractive as its owner, but he seemed less concerned about the wound than about his rumpled cuffs. As he spoke, he kept glancing down at them surreptitiously and trying to hide them. Maria Regina did not even notice, for she saw only him and, above all, the noble action he had just performed, and which had, in her eyes, bestowed on him a halo. She understood that the young man's generous nature had overcome his usual elegant reserve in order to snatch from death a child he didn't even know. They talked of nothing else until they reached the ladies' house; Maciel thanked them, but refused their offer of the carriage, and said that he would see them again that evening.

"Yes, till this evening!" called out Maria Regina.

She waited anxiously for him. He arrived at around eight o'clock, his hand wrapped in a black bandage. He apologized for his appearance; he had been told to put something on the wound, and had obeyed.

"You do seem much better!"

"I am indeed—it was nothing at all."

"Come over here," said the grandmother, from the other side of the room. "Come and sit next to me: you are a hero, sir!"

Maciel smiled. His generous impulse had passed, and he was now reaping the rewards of his sacrifice. The best of these was Maria Regina's admiration, so heartfelt and so great that she forgot entirely about her grandmother and the room. Maciel sat down beside the old lady, with Maria Regina facing them. While the grandmother, now quite recovered from her earlier shock, described the torments she had suffered, not knowing at first what had happened, and then imagining that the child had died, the two young people gazed at each other, at first discreetly, and then quite openly. Maria Regina wondered where she would ever find a better suitor. However, since there was nothing wrong with the grandmother's eyesight, she eventually found their doe-eyed gazing rather too much and, changing the subject, asked Maciel for the latest society gossip.

III

ALLEGRO APPASSIONATO

As Maciel himself would have said in French, he was *très répandu*. He plucked out of the air all kinds of interesting titbits, the most titillating of which was that the wedding of a certain widow had been called off.

"You don't say!" exclaimed the grandmother. "How has she taken it?"

"It seems that she herself put a stop to it: she was certainly in very high spirits at the ball the night before last, dancing and chatting. Oh, and aside from the news itself, what most caught my attention was the necklace she was wearing, with a magnificent—"

"Was it a cross made out of diamonds?" asked the old lady. "Yes, I've seen it; it's very becoming."

"No, not that one."

Maciel knew the one with the cross, which she had worn at the house of a certain Mascarenhas. No, it wasn't that one. This new one had been in Resende's only a few days earlier and was a thing of real beauty. And he described in detail the number, arrangement, and cut of the stones, and concluded by saying that it was the most splendid piece of jewelry at the ball.

"If she wants luxury like that she'd be better off marrying," the grandmother commented snidely.

"I agree that her fortune doesn't run to such things. Now, here's an idea—I'll go to Resende's tomorrow, just out of curiosity, to find out how much he sold it for. It wasn't cheap, it can't have been."

"But why was the wedding called off?"

"That I wasn't able to find out, but I'm dining with Venancinho Correia on Saturday, and he'll tell me everything. He's related to her in some way, you know. A fine fellow, but at daggers drawn with the baron, of course . . ."

The grandmother hadn't heard about this falling-out. Maciel told her the story from beginning to end, giving all the background and further aggravating circumstances. The last straw had been some scathing comment made at the card table about Venancinho's left-handedness. Venancinho got wind of it and broke off all relations with the baron. The best bit was that the baron's fellow cardplayers all accused each other of having spilled the beans. Maciel declared it was a rule of his never to repeat anything he heard at the card table, since it was a place where people often spoke somewhat too freely.

Then he gave a full account of Rua do Ouvidor the previous day, between one and four in the afternoon. He knew the names of all the fabrics and the latest colors. He described the latest outfits: first, that of Madame Pena Maia, a distinguished lady from Bahia, which was judged *très pschutt*. Second, that of Mademoiselle Pedrosa, the daughter of a São Paulo judge, acclaimed as *adorable*. He mentioned a further three, then compared all five and drew his conclusions. At times, he forgot himself and spoke in French; or perhaps he did so on purpose, for he knew the language well, spoke it fluently, and had once pronounced the following ethnological axiom: "Everywhere there are Parisians." Then he launched into an explanation of what to do in a card game if you were dealt a particular hand:

"Say you have five trumps, both spadille and manille, along with a king and queen of hearts . . ."

Maria Regina's admiration was slowly descending into boredom; she clung on as best she could, gazed at Maciel's youthful face, and recalled his noble actions earlier that day, but down and down she slipped, and it wasn't long before tedium overwhelmed her. There was no help for it. Then she resorted to an unusual expedient. She tried to combine the two men, the present and the absent, looking at one while listening to the other from memory. It was an extreme and painful way to proceed, but so effective that for some time she was able to contemplate one single, perfect creature.

At that moment, the other man arrived, Miranda himself. The two men greeted one another coolly. Maciel stayed for a further ten minutes, then left.

Miranda remained. He was tall and angular, with hard, icy features.

He looked tired, and his fifty years were evident in his grizzled hair and wrinkled, aging skin. Only his eyes retained something a little less decrepit. They were small, almost hidden beneath the enormous arch of his eyebrows, but deep down, when not lost in thought, they still sparkled with youth. As soon as Maciel left, the old lady asked Miranda if he had heard about the accident at Engenho Velho, and recounted the tale in elaborate detail, but Miranda listened to it all with neither admiration nor envy.

"Isn't that wonderful?" she asked, once she had finished.

"He may, of course, have saved the life of some worthless individual who, one of these days, not recognizing him, will stick a knife in his belly."

"Surely not!" the grandmother protested.

"Or even if he did recognize him," added Miranda, correcting himself.

"Now, don't be spiteful," retorted Maria Regina. "No doubt you would have done the same, had you been there."

Miranda smiled sardonically. The smile accentuated the harshness of his features. Egotistical and ill-spirited, Miranda distinguished himself in one aspect only: his intellect, which was unsurpassed. Maria Regina found in him the most marvelous and faithful translator of the clatter of ideas that battled vaguely within her, without form or expression. He was clever and refined, even profound, and always kept to the open plains of normal conversation rather than plunging into thickets of pedantry, for the true worth of things lies in the ideas they instill in us. Both men had the same artistic inclinations: Miranda had studied law only to obey his father; his true vocation was music.

Anticipating the sonata, the grandmother prepared herself for a little nap. Besides, she could not bear to let a man like Miranda into her affections, for she found him dull and disagreeable. After a few minutes, she fell silent. Then came the sonata, in the midst of a conversation that Maria Regina found perfectly delightful; indeed, it came entirely at Miranda's request, for he would gladly hear her play.

"Granny," she said, "now, do please bear with us . . ."

Miranda moved closer to the piano. Next to the glow of the lamp, his head revealed all the weariness of the passing years, while the expression on his face was all granite and spleen. Maria Regina noted the change in his demeanor and played without looking up at him—a difficult thing to do, because whenever he spoke, his words penetrated her soul so deeply that the young lady could not help but look up, only to find herself face-to-face with a decrepit old man. That was when she remembered Maciel in the flower of youth, his sincere, tender, warmhearted expression, and his actions earlier that day. A comparison just as unfair to Miranda as her earlier comparison of their respective intellects had been to Maciel. And the young lady resorted to the same expedient. She completed one man with the other: she listened to this one while thinking of the other one, and the music helped her with this fiction, which, hesitant at first, soon became intense and complete. Thus Titania, listening enamored to the weaver's song, admired his handsome figure, not noticing that he had the head of an ass.

IV

MINUETTO

Ten, twenty, thirty days passed after that night, and then another twenty, and then thirty more. The chronology is by no means certain, so it's best to keep things vague. The situation remained the same: the two men's same individual inadequacies, and, from the young lady's perspective, the same ideal conjunction of the two; resulting in a third man, whom she did not know.

Maciel and Miranda distrusted, indeed increasingly detested, each other, and they suffered greatly, especially Miranda, for whom this passion was a last throw of the dice. Eventually the young lady tired of them both. She watched them gradually retreat. There were a few hopeful relapses, but everything dies, even hope, and finally they left, never to return. The nights went by, and by . . . Maria Regina understood that it was all over.

The night on which she fully convinced herself of this was one of the most beautiful of the year: cool, clear, and bright. There was no moon, but our friend abhorred the moon—we don't entirely know why—either because it shines with a borrowed light, or because everyone else admires it, or perhaps for both reasons. It was one of her peculiarities. Here's another.

That morning she had read a short piece in the newspaper about double stars, and how they appear to us as one single star. And so, instead of going to sleep, she leaned out of her bedroom window and looked up at the night sky to see if she could spot one of them. All to no avail. Failing to find one in the heavens, she searched for its equivalent within herself, closing her eyes to imagine such a phenomenon—a cheap and easy form of astronomy, but not without its risks. The main disadvantage is that it appears to put the stars within easy reach, so much so that, when the person opens her eyes and sees the stars still shining high above, disappointment and disillusion will surely follow. This is precisely what happened here. Maria Regina saw in her mind's eye the double-yet-single star. Separately, they were worthy enough; together, they made a truly splendid star. And it was the splendid star that she wanted. When she opened her eyes and saw that the heavenly firmament remained as far away as ever, she concluded that creation was nothing but a flawed book full of errors, and she despaired.

Then she saw on the garden wall something like two cat's eyes. At first she was afraid, but quickly realized that they were nothing more than the external projection of the two stars she had seen within herself and which had remained imprinted on her retina. This young lady's retina projected all her imagined fantasies outward. When the breeze grew cooler, she withdrew, closed the window, and went to bed.

She did not fall asleep straightaway, on account of the two disks of opal embedded in the bedroom wall; realizing that it was still the same illusion, she closed her eyes and slept. She dreamed that she was dying, and that her soul, borne aloft, was soaring up toward a beautiful double star. The star divided in two and she flew toward one of its halves; not finding her initial feeling there, she hurled herself toward the other half, but with the same result. And there she remained, flitting back and forth between the two separate stars. Then a voice rose up from the abyss, speaking words she could not understand.

"This is your punishment, O soul in search of perfection; your punishment is to swing back and forth, for all eternity, between two incomplete stars, to the sound of this old and most absolute of sonatas: da, da, dum . . ."

ADAM AND EVE

———

SOMETIME BACK IN the 1700s, the mistress of a sugar plantation in Bahia, who had invited some intimate friends to dinner, announced to one of her guests, a man well known for his gluttony, that there was to be a rather special pudding. He immediately wanted to know what it was; the lady of the house told him not to be so curious. It took only a few minutes for the whole table to be arguing about curiosity, whether it was a masculine or feminine attribute, and who had been responsible for us being cast out of paradise, Adam or Eve. The ladies said it was Adam, the men said Eve, all except for the circuit judge, who said nothing, and Brother Bento, a Carmelite monk who, when quizzed by his hostess, Dona Leonor, replied with a smile: "I, madam, play the viola." He wasn't lying, either, for he was just as accomplished on the viola and the harp as he was in theology.

When asked, the judge replied that there was no basis on which to give an opinion, given that the expulsion from earthly paradise had happened somewhat differently from the account given in the first book of the Pentateuch, which was apocryphal. There was general astonishment, and a chuckle from the Carmelite, who knew the judge to be one of the most pious men in the city, but also an imaginative and jovial fellow, always fond of a good joke as long as it was within the bounds of decency and good taste; on serious matters, however, he was always very serious.

"Brother Bento," said Dona Leonor, "do please tell Senhor Veloso to be quiet."

"Certainly not," replied the monk, "because I know that nothing but the truth will fall from his lips."

"But the Scriptures—" began Colonel Barbosa.

"Let us leave the Scriptures in peace," said the Carmelite, interrupting him. "Senhor Veloso is doubtless acquainted with other books . . ."

"I know the authentic version," insisted the judge, accepting the plate of pudding offered to him by Dona Leonor, "and I'm ready to tell you what I know, unless you ask me not to."

"Go on, then, tell us."

"Here is what really happened. First of all, it wasn't God who created the world, but Satan."

"Goodness gracious!" exclaimed the ladies.

"Please do not utter that name in this house," begged Dona Leonor.

"Quite, it would seem that—" began Brother Bento.

"All right, the Evil One, if you prefer. It was the Evil One who created the world, but God, who could read his thoughts, gave him a free hand in the matter, taking it upon himself only to correct or modify the results, so that hope of salvation or good deeds would not be subsumed by the power of evil. And the divine Will soon manifested itself, for when the Evil One created darkness, God created light, and thus the first day was made. On the second day, when the waters were created, storms and hurricanes erupted, but then gentle afternoon breezes came down from the divine mind. On the third day, the earth was created, and from it sprang forth plants, but only thorny shrubs that bear no fruit or flower, and deadly weeds like hemlock; however, God then created trees that do bear fruit and plants that nourish and delight. And as the Evil One dug caves and chasms in the earth, God made the sun, the moon, and the stars; such was the work of the fourth day. On the fifth day, the beasts of earth, water, and sky were created. Now we come to the sixth day, and here I ask for your undivided attention."

He didn't need to ask; the whole table was watching him, rapt with curiosity.

Veloso carried on, saying that on the sixth day man was created, and soon afterward woman too; both were beautiful, but equipped only with base instincts and lacking a soul, which the Evil One could not give them. With one breath God infused them each with a soul, and then, with another breath, he gave them all that is noble and pure in spirit. And divine mercy did not stop there; He caused a garden of delights to grow and led them into it, giving them dominion over everything within it. Both of them fell at the Lord's feet, weeping tears of gratitude. "Here shall ye live," the Lord told them, "and ye shall eat of the fruit of every tree, except this one, which is the tree of the knowledge of good and evil."

Adam and Eve listened obediently, and, once they were alone, looked at each other in amazement, for they seemed to have changed utterly. Before God had instilled her with noble feelings, Eve had been planning to ensnare Adam in a trap, while Adam had felt an urge to beat her. Now, however, they were absorbed in peaceful contemplation of each other and the magnificent nature surrounding them. Never before had they known air so pure, water so fresh, or flowers so beautiful and fragrant; nor had the sun ever poured down in such torrents of light. Hand in hand they wandered through the garden, and during those first few days they were constantly laughing, because, until then, they had not known how to laugh. They had no sense of time. They did not feel the weight of idleness, for they lived by contemplation alone. In the evening, they would watch the sun set and the moon rise, and count the stars; they rarely reached a thousand, though, for counting made them drowsy and they would sleep like angels.

Naturally, the Evil One was furious when he found out. He could not enter paradise, where everything was against him, nor was he capable of taking on the Lord; however, hearing a rustling in a pile of dry leaves, he looked down and saw the serpent. Eagerly, he called to it.

"Come here, snake, you slithering piece of bile, venom of venoms; will you be your father's ambassador and restore his works?"

The serpent made a vague gesture with its tail, which seemed to be affirmative. Then the Evil One granted the power of speech to the serpent, who replied that, yes, it would go wherever it was sent—to the stars, if he would give it the wings of an eagle; to the sea, if he would tell it the secret of breathing underwater; to the depths of the earth, if he would teach it the talents of an ant. And so the evil serpent rambled on without stopping, its tongue running away with contentment. But the devil interrupted it:

"There'll be none of that. Neither air nor sea nor depths of the earth; just the garden of delights, where Adam and Eve live."

"Adam and Eve?"

"Yes, Adam and Eve."

"Those two beautiful creatures we saw not so long ago, walking tall and straight as palm trees?"

"Precisely."

"Oh, I hate them. Adam and Eve? No, no—send me anywhere but there. I really hate them! The mere sight of them makes me sick. You wouldn't by any chance want me to do them harm?"

"That's exactly what I want."

"Really? Then I will go; I will do everything you wish, my lord and father. Go on, then, quickly, tell me what you want me to do. You want me to bite Eve on the heel? I'll bite—"

"No," said the Evil One. "Quite the opposite. In the garden there is a tree, the tree of the knowledge of good and evil. They must not touch it or eat of its fruit. Go into the garden, coil yourself up in the tree, and when one of them passes by, call to them gently, pick a fruit from the tree, and offer it, saying it is the tastiest fruit in all the world. If they say no, you will insist, telling them that just by eating it they will know the secret of life itself. Go! Go!"

"I'm going. But I won't speak to Adam, I'll speak to Eve. Okay, I'm going. The secret of life itself—is that it?"

"Yes, the secret of life itself. Go, serpent of my entrails, flower of evil, and if you succeed, I swear that the best part of creation, the human part, will be yours, for you will have the heels of many Eves to bite and the blood of many Adams to infect with your venom. Off you go, then, and don't forget . . ."

Forget? The serpent had learned its lesson by heart. It went, it entered paradise, it slithered over to the tree of the knowledge of good and evil, it coiled itself up in the branches, and waited. Soon Eve appeared, walking alone, with the graceful confidence of a queen who knows that no one can take away her crown. Stung by envy, the serpent felt the venom rise to the tip of its tongue, but then remembered the Evil One's orders, and, with a honeyed voice, called out to her. Eve jumped.

"Who's that?"

"It's me. I'm up here, eating this fruit . . ."

"Shame on you! That is the tree of the knowledge of good and evil!"

"Exactly so. Now I know everything, the origin of all things and the meaning of life. Come, eat, and you will have great powers over the earth."

"Never, perfidious snake!"

"Fool! How can you refuse the glory of all the ages? Listen. Do what I say and you will be legion; you will found cities and your name will be

Cleopatra, Dido, and Semiramis; you will carry heroes in your belly and be Cornelia; you will hear the voice of heaven and be Deborah; you will sing and be Sappho. And one day, should God decide to come down to earth, he will choose your womb and you will be called Mary of Nazareth. What more could you want? Royalty, poetry, divinity—all of this you give up because you insist on obeying some silly rule. And that's not all. All of nature will make you ever more beautiful. The colors of green leaves, dark or pale, the colors of blue skies and deepest night, all of these will be reflected in your eyes. Even the night, in rivalry with the sun, will come and cast playful shadows on your hair. The children of your bosom will weave for you the finest garments, concoct the sweetest perfumes, and the birds will give you their feathers and the land its flowers; everything, everything shall be yours!"

Eve listened impassively. Adam arrived, listened to them both, and confirmed Eve's answer. Nothing was worth the loss of paradise, neither knowledge, nor power, nor any other earthly illusion. As they said this, they took each other by the hand and turned away from the serpent, who hurriedly left to report back to the Evil One.

God, who had heard everything, said to Gabriel: "Go, my archangel, descend to earthly paradise, where Adam and Eve dwell, and bring them here to eternal bliss, which they truly deserve for rejecting the Evil One's temptations."

And, placing on his head his diamond helmet, which glittered like a thousand suns, the archangel tore instantaneously through the air to Adam and Eve and said to them: "Hail, Adam and Eve. Come with me to paradise, which you truly deserve for having rejected the Evil One's temptations."

Astonished and confused, both of them bowed their heads in obedience. Then Gabriel took them each by the hand and the three of them ascended to the eternal abode, where hosts of angels awaited them.

"Come in! Come in!" the angels sang. "The earth you left behind is given over to the works of the Evil One, to cruel, fierce animals, to dangerous, poisonous plants, to filthy air and fetid swamps. The slithering, hissing, biting snake will reign over it, and no creature like you will ever sound a note of hope and compassion amidst such abomination."

And so it was that Adam and Eve entered the kingdom of heaven, to the sound of all the heavenly zithers, which joined together in a hymn to the two cast out from earthly creation.

When he had finished speaking, the judge handed his plate to Dona Leonor for a second helping of pudding, while the other guests looked at one another, flabbergasted; instead of an explanation, they had just listened to a tale that was highly enigmatic, or, at the very least, without any apparent meaning. Dona Leonor was the first to speak: "I was quite right when I said Senhor Veloso was pulling our legs. That wasn't what we asked of him at all, and of course nothing of the sort happened. Isn't that right, Brother Bento?"

"Only the honorable judge will know the answer to that," replied the Carmelite, smiling.

And, raising a spoonful of pudding to his lips, the judge replied: "On second thought, I don't believe that was what happened at all; on the other hand, Dona Leonor, if it *had* happened, none of us would be here enjoying this pudding, which is truly divine. Is it the work of that old pastry cook of yours from Itapagipe?"

THE GENTLEMAN'S COMPANION

———————

So you really think that what happened to me in 1860 could be made into a story? Very well, but on the sole condition that nothing is published before my death. You'll only have to wait a week at most, for I'm really not long for this world.

I could even tell you my whole life story, which contains various other interesting episodes, but that would require time, energy, and paper, and I only have paper; my energy is low and time for me is like the guttering flame of a night lamp. Soon the sun will rise on a new day, a terrible sun, impenetrable as life itself. Farewell, my dear friend; read on and wish me well, forgive anything that offends, and don't be surprised if not everything smells of roses. You asked me for a human document and here you have it. Do not ask me for the empire of the Great Mogul or a photograph of the Maccabees. Ask me, on the other hand, for my dead man's shoes, and they will be yours and yours alone.

As you know, these events took place in 1860. Sometime around August of the preceding year, when I was forty-two, I became a theologian—or rather, I began copying out theological tracts for a priest in Niterói, an old friend from school, who thereby tactfully provided me with room and board. During that month of August 1859, he received a letter from a fellow priest in a certain provincial town, who asked him if he knew of a discreet, intelligent, patient fellow who would be willing to go and serve as gentleman's companion to a Colonel Felisberto, in return for a decent wage. My friend duly consulted me, and I gladly accepted, for I was already becoming fed up with copying out Latin quotations and ecclesiastical formulas. I returned to Rio to say goodbye to a brother of mine, then set off for the provinces.

When I arrived in the town, I heard dire reports about the colonel. He was, it seemed, a quite unbearable man, eccentric and demanding; no one, it was said, could stand him, not even his friends. He had been through more gentleman's companions than medicines. Indeed, he had punched two of them in the face. I replied that I was not afraid of healthy folk, still less of the sick; and after discussing matters with the priest, who confirmed what I had heard and recommended an attitude of meekness and loving charity, I proceeded to the colonel's residence.

I found him stretched out in a chair on the veranda, breathing heavily. He did not receive me badly; at first he said nothing and merely fixed me with his eyes like a watchful cat. Then a malevolent smile spread across his harsh features. Finally, he told me that none of his previous gentleman's companions had been any use at all—always sleeping, answering back, chasing after the female slaves. Two of them had been downright thieves!

"Are you a thief?"

"No, sir."

Then he asked me my name. I told him and he looked startled. Colombo? No, sir: Procópio José Gomes Valongo. Valongo? He thought this a preposterous name and proposed calling me just plain Procópio, to which I replied that he could call me whatever he pleased. I'm telling you this detail not just because I think it gives you an idea of what he was like, but also because my reply made a very favorable impression on the colonel. He himself said so to the priest, adding that I was the most agreeable of all the gentleman's companions he'd had. The honeymoon lasted for seven days.

On the eighth day, my life became exactly the same as that of my predecessors. It was a dog's life, with no sleep, no thoughts of my own, and being constantly showered with insults, which, at times, I laughed at with an air of resignation and deference, for I had noticed that this was one way of mollifying him. His rudeness stemmed as much from his illness as from his temperament, for he suffered from a litany of complaints: an aneurism, rheumatism, and three or four lesser afflictions. He was nearly sixty, and from the age of five everyone had indulged his every whim. Had he been merely grumpy, that would have been fine; but he had a mean streak in him, and took pleasure in the pain and humiliation of others. At the end of three months I'd had enough and decided to leave; I waited only for the right opportunity.

It wasn't long in coming. One day, when I failed to give him his embrocation at the correct time, he grabbed his stick and struck me two or three times. That was the last straw; I quit there and then and went to pack my bags. Later, he came to my room and begged me to stay, saying that there was no need to take offense at an old man's bad temper. He was so insistent that I stayed.

"I'm in a terrible pickle, Procópio," he told me that night. "I won't live much longer. One foot in the grave, you might say. But you must go to my funeral, Procópio; I absolutely insist. You must go, and you must pray at my graveside. If you don't," he added with a chuckle, "I'll come back at night and torment you. Do you believe in spirits from the other world, Procópio?"

"Certainly not!"

"Why wouldn't you believe, you donkey?" he retorted excitedly, opening his eyes very wide.

If these were the truces, just imagine the wars! He stopped hitting me with the stick, but the insults were just as bad, if not worse. With time I became inured to them and stopped noticing; I was an ass, a dolt, an idiot, a good-for-nothing lazybones, everything under the sun. There wasn't even anyone to share these insults with me. He had no relatives; there had been a nephew up in Minas Gerais, but he had died of consumption sometime between the end of May and the beginning of July. His friends came by occasionally to flatter and indulge him; a five- or ten-minute visit, nothing more. So there was no one but me, just me, for an entire dictionary of expletives. More than once I resolved to leave, but each time, at the priest's insistence, I ended up staying.

Not only were relations between us becoming increasingly strained, I was also keen to return to Rio. At forty-two I wasn't yet ready to become a complete recluse tending to a petulant old invalid in the back of beyond. To get an idea of my isolation, suffice it to say that I didn't even read the newspapers; apart from the odd piece of news that reached the colonel, I was totally cut off from the rest of the world. I therefore decided to return to the capital at the first opportunity, even if it meant crossing swords with the local priest. Seeing as I'm making a general confession, I should perhaps add that, since I was spending nothing and saving up all of my wages, I was eager to come and squander them here in the city.

Such an opportunity seemed imminent. The colonel's health was steadily deteriorating and he had drawn up his will, managing to offend the notary almost as much as he had me. His manners became ever coarser, and the brief lapses of peace and affability were now rare. I had already lost the meager dose of pity that had made me overlook the sick man's excesses; inside, I was seething with hatred and revulsion. At the beginning of August, I resolved definitively to go; the priest and the doctor, while accepting my reasons, asked me to stay just a little longer. I granted them one month; at the end of the month I would leave, no matter what the patient's condition. The priest took it upon himself to find my replacement.

Now here comes the event itself. On the evening of the twenty-fourth of August, the colonel fell into a fit of rage and knocked me down, calling me all sorts of vile names, threatening to shoot me, even ending up by throwing a bowl of porridge at me because he said it had gone cold. The bowl hit the wall and shattered into pieces.

"You'll pay for that, you thief!" he bellowed.

He rumbled on in this manner for quite some time. At eleven o'clock he fell asleep. While he slept, I pulled from my pocket an old translation of a d'Arlincourt novel which I had happened to find lying about. I sat down in his room to read it, a short distance from the bed, since I would have to wake the colonel at midnight to give him his medicine. Whether it was the effects of tiredness or the book itself, before I had reached the end of the second page, I, too, fell asleep. The colonel's shouts woke me with a start and I sprang to my feet, still half asleep. He seemed delirious and kept on shouting, finally flinging the water jug at me. There was no time to duck; the jug caught me hard on the left cheek. Blinded by pain, I lunged at the invalid and grabbed him by the throat; we struggled, and I strangled him.

When I realized he had stopped breathing, I stepped back in alarm and cried out, but no one heard me. I shook him then, trying to bring him back to life, but it was too late; the aneurism must have burst, and the colonel was dead. I went into the adjoining room and for two hours did not dare return to the bedroom. I cannot even begin to describe what went through my mind during that time. I was in a complete daze, a kind of vague, vacant delirium. It seemed to me that the walls had faces, and I could hear muffled voices. The victim's cries, both before and during the struggle, continued to reverberate inside me, and whichever way I turned, the air seemed to shake with convulsions. Do not imagine that I'm simply making up colorful imagery for mere stylistic effect; I am telling you that I distinctly heard several voices crying: "Murderer! Murderer!"

Otherwise, the house was silent. The slow, staccato tick tick of the clock only emphasized the silence and solitude. I put my ear to the bedroom door hoping to hear a groan, a word, an insult, anything that would indicate that he was alive and restore some peace to my conscience. I would have willingly taken ten, twenty, a hundred blows from the colonel's fists. But nothing, absolutely nothing; all was silent. I began to pace the room once again; I sat down, my head in my hands, wishing I had never come to this place. "Damn and blast their wretched job!" I exclaimed. And I cursed the priest from Niterói, the doctor, the local priest, everyone who had gotten me the job and begged me to stay just a little longer. I clung to their complicity.

When I began to find the silence too terrifying, I opened a window in the hope of hearing the sound of the wind, but there was no wind. The night was utterly still and the stars shone with the indifference of those who remove their hats when a funeral passes by but carry on with their conversation. I leaned out of the window for some time, staring into the darkness, mentally reviewing my life in the hope that this might ease my present anguish. Only then can I say that I thought clearly about my possible punishment. A heinous crime weighed upon me and certain retribution awaited. At this point, fear was added to my feelings of remorse. I felt my hair stand on end. A few minutes later, I saw three or four human shapes peering in at me from yard, as if ready to pounce; I stepped back into the room, the shapes vanished into thin air; it was a hallucination.

Before day broke, I carefully cleaned the wound on my cheek. Only then did I dare return to the bedroom. Twice I drew back, but, finally, there was no avoiding it and I went in; even then I couldn't go near the bed. My legs shook, my heart pounded; I considered fleeing the scene, but that would be tantamount to confessing my guilt, when what I urgently needed to do was to remove all traces of it. I went over to the bed and looked at the corpse, at its staring eyes and open mouth, as if it were uttering those eternal, centuries-old words: "Cain, what hast thou done with thy brother?" I saw the marks of my fingernails on his neck; I buttoned his nightshirt as high as I could and drew the sheet up to his chin. Then I called one of the slaves, told him the colonel had died in the night, and sent word to the local priest and the doctor.

My first thought was to leave immediately, on the pretext that my brother was ill, for I had indeed received a letter from him a few days earlier saying he was not feeling well. But I realized that such a sudden departure might arouse suspicions, and so I stayed. I laid out the body myself, with the help of a shortsighted old Negro. I sat with the body, afraid others might notice something. I wanted to scrutinize their faces for some flicker of suspicion, and yet I dared not look at anyone. Everything made me jittery: the quiet footsteps stealing into the room, the whispers, the priest's rituals and mumbled prayers. When the time came to close the coffin, my hands trembled so much that someone commented pityingly to their neighbor:

"Poor Procópio! See how moved he is, despite all he had to put up with."

Fearing this might be an ironic remark, I was desperate to get it all over with. We moved outside. Passing from the half darkness of the house into the bright light of the street terrified me, convinced now that my crime would be impossible to hide. I fixed my eyes on the ground and kept walking. When it was all over, I breathed a sigh of relief. I was at peace with my fellow men, if not with my conscience; the next few nights were naturally ones of anxiety and affliction. I need hardly say that I came straight back to Rio de Janeiro and that I lived here in terror, even though I was far removed from the scene of the crime. I never laughed and barely spoke; I ate badly and suffered from hallucinations and nightmares . . .

"Let the dead rest in peace," people would say to me. "There's no reason to be so upset."

And I took full advantage of this illusion, singing the praises of the dead man, calling him a fine old fellow, a little rough around the edges, perhaps, but with a heart of gold. And as I praised him, I almost persuaded myself that this was true, at least for a few moments. Another interesting aspect, which may be of some interest to you, is that, although I wasn't a religious man, I had a mass said for the eternal rest of the colonel's soul, at the Church of the Blessed Sacrament. I didn't send out any invitations, or mention it to anyone; I went to hear it alone, kneeling throughout and crossing myself many times. I paid the priest double the usual amount and distributed alms at the door of the church, all in the name of the deceased. I wasn't trying to deceive anyone, the proof being that I went to the mass alone. I should also add that I never mentioned the colonel without saying, "God rest his soul!" And then I would tell a couple of lighthearted anecdotes about him and some of his more amusing outbursts.

Seven days after arriving in Rio de Janeiro, I received the letter from the priest that I showed you, telling me they'd found the colonel's will and that I was his sole heir. You can imagine my astonishment. I thought I had misread the letter; I showed it to my brother and some friends; they all interpreted it in exactly the same way. It was there in writing: I was the colonel's sole heir. I even wondered if it was a trap, but quickly realized that there were other means of ensnaring me if the crime had been discovered. Furthermore, I knew the priest to be an honest man and a most unlikely instrument for such a scheme. I reread the letter countless times; there it was in black and white.

"How much was he worth?" my brother asked me.

"I don't know, but he was rich."

"Well, he's certainly proved himself to be your friend."

"He has . . . yes, he has . . ."

Thus, by some strange irony of fate, all the colonel's worldly goods came into my possession. I considered refusing the inheritance. Taking even a penny from his estate seemed odious to me, worse even than being a hired killer. I thought about it for three days, and every time I bumped up against the argument that my refusal might arouse suspicion. At the end of the three days, I settled on a compromise: I would accept the inheritance and secretly give it all away, little by little. It wasn't just a matter of scruples; it was also a way of redeeming my crime through an act of virtue—by doing so, my accounts would be settled.

I made preparations and set off for the town. The closer I got, the more vividly I recalled the whole sad adventure; an air of tragedy surrounded the town, and the colonel's shadow seemed to loom out at me from every side. My imagination re-created every word, every gesture, the whole horrendous night of the murder . . .

Murder or self-defense? Surely the latter, for I had been defending myself from an attack, and in my defense . . . It was an unfortunate accident, just one of those things. I gladly seized upon this idea. And I weighed up all the aggravating circumstances, the blows, the insults . . . I knew very well that the fault lay not with the colonel, but with his illness, which had made him surly, even wicked. But I forgave him everything; nothing, though, could erase what had happened that fateful night. However, I took into account that the colonel could not in any event have lived much longer; he was clearly at death's door—he himself knew it and said so. How long would he have lived? Two weeks? One? Perhaps even less? It wasn't a life, it was a tattered old toe-rag of a life, if even that could describe the poor man's continual suffering. And who knows, perhaps our struggle and his death were simply coincidental? It was possible, even probable; indeed it could not have been otherwise. I seized upon this idea too.

When I reached the town, I felt my heart sink, and I wanted to turn back, but I pulled myself together and carried on. Everyone congratulated me. The priest explained the various provisions of the will, the usual charitable gifts and legacies, all the while praising my Christian patience and devotion in serving the colonel, a man who, for all his harsh behavior, had nonetheless shown his gratitude.

"Indeed," I said, looking away.

I was dumbstruck. Everyone praised my dedication and patience. The initial formalities of drawing up the estate detained me in the town for some time. I appointed a lawyer and everything proceeded smoothly. During this time, there was much talk of the colonel. People came to tell me things about him, in rather less moderate terms than the priest; I defended the colonel, pointing out his few virtues, yes, he could be stern perhaps . . .

"Stern, you say? Well, he's dead now and good riddance, but he was the very devil, that's for sure."

And they described incidents of extraordinary, even perverse, cruelty. What could I say? At first I listened with curiosity; then I began to feel a singular pleasure, which I made a genuine effort to drive out. I continued to defend the colonel, explain his actions, and attribute certain things to local rivalries. He was, I confessed, somewhat violent . . .

"Somewhat? He was a vicious snake-in-the-grass!" said the barber. The tax collector, the pharmacist, the notary, and everyone else agreed. Other stories followed, encompassing the entire life of the dead man. Older people recalled his cruelties as a little boy. And that secret, silent, insidious pleasure grew inside me like a kind of moral tapeworm, which for all that I tried to extract it, ring by ring, would always recover and keep on growing.

The legal formalities kept me busy, and, besides, since no one in the town had a good word to say about the colonel, I began to find the place less forbidding than I had at first. Once I took possession of my inheritance, I converted it into bonds and cash. Many months passed, and the idea of distributing it all in charitable gifts and worthy donations no longer held me in such a firm grip; I even began to consider this rather presumptuous. I trimmed back the initial plan; I gave something to the poor, new vestments to the parish church, and a donation to the Santa Casa Hospital: thirty-two *contos* in all. I also had a tomb built for the colonel, all marble, the work of a Neapolitan sculptor who was here in Rio until 1866, before going off to die, I believe, in Paraguay.

The years have rolled by and my memories have grown faded and gray. I still sometimes think about the colonel, but without the terror of those early days. I told several doctors about the colonel's illnesses and they all agreed that death would have been imminent; they were only surprised he hadn't succumbed earlier. I may have unwittingly exaggerated his ailments, but the truth is he was going to die, no matter what happened . . .

Anyway, farewell, dear friend. If you judge these scribblings of any value, then repay me with my own marble tomb, on which you may carve as an epitaph this little amendment I have made to the Sermon on the Mount: "Blessed are they that possess: for they shall be comforted."

MR. DIPLOMAT

————

THE BLACK SERVING WOMAN entered the dining room, approached the table where all the guests were seated, and whispered to her mistress. It must have been something urgent, because the lady of the house immediately got up.

"Shall we wait for you, Dona Adelaide?"

"Do carry on, Senhor Rangel; there's no need to wait. I'll take my turn when I get back."

Rangel was reading from the book of fortunes. He turned the page and read out another question: "Is someone secretly in love with you?" There was general fidgeting; the young ladies and gentlemen smiled at each other. The year was 1854, it was the eve of São João, and we were in a fine house on Rua das Mangueiras. João was also the name of the host, João Viegas, and he had a daughter named after him, Joaninha. Every year, the same group of friends and family gathered, a bonfire was lit in the garden, potatoes were roasted as custom required, and fortunes were told. There would be supper and sometimes dancing or parlor games to follow; it was all very convivial. João Viegas was a clerk at one of the civil courts in Rio.

"Come on, who's going to start the ball rolling?" he said. "Dona Felismina, surely. Let's see if you have a secret admirer."

Dona Felismina gave a somewhat forced smile. She was well into her forties and had neither money nor looks, and beneath her veil of piety she was constantly on the lookout for a husband. It was a rather cruel joke, but understandable. Dona Felismina was the perfect example of those gentle, forgiving creatures who seem to have been born to be the butt of other people's jokes. She picked up the dice and threw them with a patient but skeptical air. "Number ten!" cried two voices. Rangel ran his eyes down the page, found the corresponding box, and read: Yes, it was someone she should seek out at church on Sunday, when she went to mass. The whole table congratulated Dona Felismina, who smiled dismissively, but was secretly rather hopeful.

Others took the dice, and Rangel proceeded to read each person's fortune. He read in a pretentious, affected manner. From time to time, he removed his spectacles and wiped them very slowly with the corner of his cambric handkerchief—either simply because it was rather fine cambric or because it gave off a delicate scent of jasmine. His fondness for such airs and graces had merited him the nickname "Mr. Diplomat."

"Go on, Mr. Diplomat, *do* please continue!"

Rangel started; he was so absorbed in perusing the row of young ladies across the table from him that he had forgotten to read out one of the predictions. Was he in love with one of them? Let us take things from the beginning, step by step.

He was a bachelor, by virtue of circumstance rather than vocation. As a young man he had enjoyed several passing flirtations, but, as time passed, the itching for rank and status had set in, and it was this that prolonged his bachelorhood until he was forty-one, the age at which we now see him. He hoped for a bride superior to both him and the circles in which he moved, and he wasted his time in waiting for her. He even attended dances given by a rich and celebrated lawyer for whom he transcribed documents, and who made him his protégé. At these dances, however, he occupied the same subaltern position he held at the office; he would spend the evening wandering the hallways, peering into the ballroom, watching the ladies pass by, devouring with his eyes a multitude of magnificent shoulders and elegant figures. He envied the other men and imitated them. He would leave full of enthusiasm and determination. When there were no dances, he would attend religious processions, where he could feast his eyes on some of the most eligible young ladies in the city. He was also to be found in the courtyard of the imperial palace on gala days, watching the great ladies and gentlemen of the court, together with ministers, generals, diplomats, and high court judges; he recognized everyone and everything, both the individuals themselves and their carriages. He would return from church or palace just as he returned from a ball, feeling impetuous and passionate, ready to grasp the laurels of fortune.

The worst of it is that between hand and branch stood that wall of which the poet spoke, and Rangel was not a man to leap over walls. Everything that he did, from razing cities to carrying off their womenfolk, he did only in his imagination. More than once he imagined himself a minister of state, wallowing in a surfeit of salutations and decrees. One year, on the second of December, as he was returning from the birthday parade on Largo do Paço, he even went so far as to proclaim himself emperor; to this end he envisaged a revolution, in which some blood was spilled, but only a little, followed by a benevolent dictatorship, in which he merely took revenge for a few minor grudges from his days as a court clerk. However, all his daring deeds were but fairy tales. In reality, he was a quiet, discreet fellow.

By the time he reached forty, he had given up on his grandiose ambitions, but his essential nature remained the same, and, notwithstanding his desire to marry, he failed to find a bride. More than one lady would have accepted him willingly, but he lost them all because he was too cautious, too circumspect. One day, he noticed Joaninha, who was nearly nineteen and had a pair of eyes that were both beautiful and meek—undefiled by any masculine conversation. Rangel had known her since she was a child; he had carried her in his arms in the Passeio Público and to see the fireworks at Lapa. How could he speak to her of love? But, on the other hand, his relations with the family were such that a marriage should be easy to arrange; it was either her or nothing at all.

This time, the wall was not high and the branch within his grasp; he needed only to stretch out his arm with a modicum of effort and pluck it from its stem. Rangel had been engaged in this undertaking for several months. He would not, however, reach out his arm without first checking all around him to see that no one was coming, and if he spied someone, he would hide his intentions and continue on his way. Whenever he did reach out, a gust of wind would set the branch swaying or a little bird would make a rustling noise in the dry leaves, and that was all it needed for him to withdraw his hand. And so time passed and his passions deepened, giving him many hours of anguish, always followed by higher hopes. And so, on this very night, the Feast of Saint John, he is carrying with him his first love letter, ready to deliver. Two or three good opportunities have already presented themselves, but he keeps putting off the moment; the night is still young! Meanwhile, he carries on reading out fortunes with all the solemnity of a high priest.

Around him, everyone is cheerful and jolly. Some are whispering, others are laughing or talking over each other. Uncle Rufino, the joker in the family, is going around the table with a feather, tickling the ears of the young ladies. João Viegas is waiting impatiently for his friend Calisto, who is late. Where on earth has he got to?

"Everyone out! I need the table. Let's all go through to the drawing room."

Dona Adelaide had returned and it was time to lay the table for supper. All the guests migrated to the other room, and it was when she walked that the charms of the clerk's daughter could most truly be appreciated. Rangel followed her, besotted and puppy-eyed. She went to the window for a few moments, while a little parlor game was being set up, and he followed: it was his opportunity to slip her the letter.

In a large house across the street a ball was taking place, and the dancing had started. Joaninha was watching; Rangel watched too. Through the windows they could see the couples passing to and fro, swaying to the music, the ladies in their silks and laces, the gentlemen refined and elegant, some wearing medals. From time to time there was a flash of diamonds, swift and fleeting, amid the swirl of the dance. Couples talking, epaulets gleaming, men bowing, fans beckoning; all this could be glimpsed through the windows, which did not reveal the entire ballroom, but the rest could be imagined. He, at least, knew all of it, and described everything to the clerk's daughter. The demons of grandeur, which had seemed to be lying dormant, started once again to perform their prancing pantomimes in our friend's heart, and, lo and behold, began to seduce the young lady's heart too.

"I know someone who would be entirely at home over there," murmured Rangel.

"Why, you, of course," replied Joaninha, without a hint of guile.

Rangel smiled, flattered, and didn't know what to say. He looked at the footmen and liveried coachmen in the street, huddled in groups or leaning against the sides of the carriages. He began pointing out the various carriages to Joaninha: this one's the Marquis of Olinda's, that one belongs to the Viscount of Maranguape, and look, here comes another one, turning into the street from Rua da Lapa. It pulls up opposite: the footman jumps down, opens the carriage door, removes his hat, and stands at attention. From inside the carriage emerges a bald pate, a head, a man, two medals, then a richly dressed lady; they step into the entrance hall and ascend the grand staircase, carpeted and adorned with two large vases at its foot.

"Joaninha, Senhor Rangel . . ."

That blasted game! And just as he was formulating in his head some knowing comment regarding the couple ascending the stairs, from which he would have slipped naturally into giving her the letter . . . Rangel obeyed the summons and sat down opposite the young lady. Dona Adelaide, who had taken charge of the game, was collecting names; each person was to be a flower. Of course, Uncle Rufino, ever the jester, chose for himself the pumpkin flower. Rangel, wishing to avoid such trivialities, weighed up the potential of each flower and, when the lady of the house asked him for his, answered slowly and softly:

"Jasmine, senhora."

"What a shame Calisto isn't here!" sighed the court clerk.

"Did he actually say he was coming?"

"He did; indeed, he came to the office yesterday for the sole purpose of telling me he would be arriving late, but that he would definitely make it; he had to stop by first at some jolly down in Rua da Carioca."

"Room for two?" boomed a voice from the hallway.

"Thank goodness for that! Here he is, the man himself!"

João Viegas went to open the door; it was indeed Calisto, accompanied by an unknown young man, whom he presented to the general gathering: "This is Queirós; he works at the Santa Casa Hospital; no relation of mine whatsoever, although he does look awfully like me—people are always mixing us up . . ." Everyone laughed; it was one of Calisto's little jokes, for he was as ugly as sin, whereas Queirós was a handsome young man of twenty-six or twenty-seven, with dark hair, dark eyes, and a strikingly slender figure. The young ladies drew back a little. Dona Felismina unfurled her sails.

"We're playing a parlor game and you two gentlemen are very welcome to join us," said the lady of the house. "Will you play, Senhor Queirós?"

Queirós said he would be delighted and looked around at the other guests. He knew some of them, and exchanged a few words of greetings. He told João Viegas that he had been wanting to meet him for quite some time, on account of a favor his father owed him from many years before, concerning a legal matter. João Viegas had forgotten all about it, even when Queirós told him what the favor had been, but he enjoyed hearing such things said in public, and basked for a few minutes in quiet, smug contentment.

Queirós threw himself into the game. Within half an hour he had made himself one of the family. He was a lively fellow, who talked easily, and his manners were natural and spontaneous. He charmed the whole gathering with his vast repertoire of penalties, and indeed there was no one better than him at leading the game, rushing from one side to the other with such vivacity and animation, putting groups together, moving chairs, chatting with the young ladies as if they had all been playmates since childhood.

"Dona Joaninha sits here, on this chair; Dona Cesária stands over on that side, and Senhor Camilo comes in through this door . . . No, not that way. Look: like this, and then . . ."

Sitting stiffly on his chair, Rangel was speechless. Where had this hurricane blown in from? And the hurricane continued to blow, lifting the men's hats and tousling the ladies' hair, and all of them laughing merrily: Queirós here, Queirós there, Queirós everywhere. Rangel went from stupefaction to mortification. Slowly, the scepter was falling from his grasp. He didn't look at the other man, didn't laugh at anything he said, and answered him only curtly. Inside, he was seething with rage and cursing the man, one of those happy fools who knows how to amuse people and make them laugh, because that's what happens at parties. But not even telling himself these and even worse things restored his peace of mind. In the innermost depths of his self-esteem, he was really suffering. Worse still, the other man saw this, and, worst of all, knew he was the cause of it.

Just as he dreamt of future glories, Rangel also dreamt of revenge. In his head, he pounded Queirós to a pulp. Then he imagined some sort of disaster befalling his rival; a sudden pain would do, something serious enough to get rid of the interloper entirely. But no pain appeared, nothing at all; the wretch seemed to grow merrier by the minute, and the whole room fell under his spell. Even Joaninha, normally so timid, quivered with excitement in Queirós's hands, as did the other young ladies; all the guests, men and women, seemed to be at his beck and call. When he mentioned dancing, all the young ladies rushed over to Uncle Rufino and asked him to play a quadrille on his flute, just one, promising not to ask for any more.

"I can't, I've got a callus on my finger."

"The flute?" exclaimed Calisto. "Ask Queirós to play something and then you'll see what a flute can really do. Go and get your flute, Rufino. Come on, everyone, listen to Queirós. You can't imagine how hauntingly he plays!"

Queirós played "*Casta Diva*." "Utterly ridiculous," Rangel muttered to himself, "even the kids in the street are whistling that tune." He shot Queirós a sideways glance, trying to determine whether any serious man would ever stand with his arms like that, and concluded that the flute was indeed a grotesque instrument. He also looked at Joaninha and saw that, like everyone else, her eyes were on Queirós, enraptured, carried away by the sounds of the aria. He shuddered, although without quite knowing why. Joaninha's expression was no different from everyone else's, and yet he felt something which added a further complication to his dislike of the interloper. When Queirós finished playing, Joaninha clapped less loudly than the others, and Rangel was unsure whether to attribute this to her usual shyness or to some other emotion. He urgently needed to give her that letter.

Supper was served. The guests entered the dining room in no particular order and, happily for Rangel, he found himself opposite Joaninha, whose eyes were more beautiful than ever and so bright they scarcely seemed the same eyes at all. Rangel savored them in silence, and carefully pieced back together the dream that wretch Queirós had so abruptly shattered with a snap of his fingers. Once again he saw himself by her side, in the house he would rent for them, their little love nest, adorned with all the golden ornaments of his imagination. He would even win a prize in the lottery and spend it all on silks and jewels for his dear wife, the lovely Joaninha, Joaninha Rangel, Dona Joaninha Rangel, Dona Joana Viegas Rangel, or even Dona Joana Cândida Viegas Rangel—he couldn't leave out the Cândida.

"Come on, a toast, Mr. Diplomat. Give us one of your famous toasts!"

Rangel awoke from his reverie; the whole table joined in Uncle Rufino's request; Joaninha herself was begging him to propose a toast, just like last year's. Rangel promised to oblige, just as soon as he had polished off his chicken wing. There were general stirrings and murmurings of praise; when one of the young ladies confided that she had never heard Rangel speak, Dona Adelaide replied in astonishment:

"Really? Goodness gracious, you can't imagine how well he speaks: so very clearly, and with such well-chosen words, and such refinement!"

As he ate, he rehearsed a few thoughts and fragments of ideas that would form the basis of his fine phrases and metaphors. When he was ready, he stood up with an air of self-satisfaction. At last, they were coming knocking at his door. The merry-go-round of anecdotes and mindless jokes was over and they had come to him for something dignified and serious. He looked around and saw all eyes fixed expectantly on him. Not quite all; Joaninha's were turned toward Queirós, whose eyes met hers halfway, along with a cavalcade of promises. Rangel blanched. The words died in his throat, but speak he must; everyone was eagerly, silently waiting for him.

His efforts failed to impress. He merely toasted their host and his daughter. The latter he called "a divine inspiration, transported from immortality to reality," a phrase he had used three years earlier, but that should by now have faded from memory. He spoke also of the sanctuary of family, the altar of friendship, and of gratitude being the flowering of pure hearts. What it lacked in meaning, it made up for in empty grandiloquence. All in all, it was a speech that should have stretched to a good ten minutes, but which he dispatched in five, then sat down.

That wasn't the end of it. Queirós stood up two or three minutes later for another toast, and this time the silence was even more immediate and complete. Joaninha stared into her lap, embarrassed at what he might say. Rangel shuddered.

"Senhor Rangel, the illustrious friend of this house," said Queirós, "drank to the two people who share the name of the saint we commemorate today; I drink to the person who is a saint every day of the year, Dona Adelaide."

Loud applause greeted this worthy sentiment, and Dona Adelaide, greatly flattered, was congratulated by each and every guest. Her daughter did not stop at congratulations. "Mama! Dearest Mama!" she exclaimed, getting up from her seat and going over to hug and kiss her mother three or four times—a sort of letter, as it were, to be read by two people.

Rangel's anger turned to despondency and, as soon as supper was finished, he decided it was time to leave. But hope, that green-eyed demon, begged him to stay, and he stayed. Who knows? It might blow over, a St. John's Eve flirtation; he was, after all, a good friend of the family, held in high esteem, and the young lady's hand was his for the asking. Furthermore, that Queirós fellow might well not have the means to marry. What was that job of his at the hospital? Something menial, perhaps? He glanced at Queirós's clothes, running his eyes over the seams, scrutinizing the embroidery on his shirt, examining the knees of his trousers to see if they were worn from use, also his shoes, and he concluded that Queirós was a capricious young man who probably spent all his money on himself, whereas marriage was a serious business. Also, he might well have a widowed mother, unmarried sisters. Rangel had only himself to provide for.

"Play a quadrille, Uncle Rufino."

"I can't. After a meal, playing the flute always gives me indigestion. Let's play lotto."

Rangel declared he could not play lotto on account of a headache, but Joaninha came over to him and asked him to be her partner. "Half the winnings for you, half for me," she said, smiling; he smiled, too, and accepted. They sat down side by side. Joaninha talked, laughed, looked up at him with her beautiful eyes, and glanced restlessly around at her at the other guests. Rangel felt a little better, and in no time at all felt entirely better. He marked off the numbers randomly, missing some of them, which she pointed out with her finger—a nymph's finger, he said to himself, and his mistakes became deliberate, just so he could see her finger and hear her scold him: "You're not paying attention, Senhor Rangel; do watch out or we'll lose all our money!"

Rangel thought of slipping her the letter under the table, but since nothing had been said between them, she would be taken too much by surprise, and that would spoil everything. Best to say something first. He looked around the table: all the faces were bent over their cards, attentively following the numbers. Then he leaned to his right and looked down at Joaninha's cards, as if checking something.

"You have two squares left," he whispered.

"No, I haven't. I have three."

"Oh, yes, quite right. Three. Now, listen—"

"And you?"

"I have two."

"What do you mean, 'two'? You have four."

There were indeed four; she leaned closer as she pointed to them, almost brushing her ear against his lips; then she looked up at him laughing and shaking her head: "Oh, Senhor Rangel! Senhor Rangel!" Rangel listened with exquisite delight; her voice was so soft, her tone so amicable that he forgot everything, seized her by the waist, and launched them both into the eternal waltz of the chimeras. House, table, guests, all vanished as if they were mere fancies, leaving the two of them as the one true reality, turning and turning in space beneath a million stars that shone for them and them alone.

No letter, nothing. As dawn approached, they all went to the window to watch the guests leaving the ball across the street. Rangel recoiled in horror. He saw Queirós and the lovely Joaninha brush fingers. He tried to explain this away as a mere illusion, but no sooner had he demolished one such illusion than up sprang another and another, breaking over him like never-ending waves. He could scarcely believe that a single night, a few hours, could be enough to bind two creatures together like that, but the proof was there in their gestures, their eyes, their words, their laughter, and even in the regret with which they parted in the early hours of the morning.

He left, feeling bewildered. A single night! A few hours! When he arrived home late, he lay down on his bed, not in order to sleep, but to sob. Only now, alone, did all his affectations desert him; no longer was he the haughty Mr. Diplomat, he was the crazed madman, tossing and turning on his bed, screaming and bawling like a child, made truly miserable by his sad autumnal love. The poor devil, made of daydreams, indolence, and pretension, was, in substance, as wretched as Othello, and had met a still crueler fate.

Othello killed Desdemona; our lover, whose hidden passions went unnoticed by anyone, served as a witness when, six months later, Queirós married Joaninha.

Neither events nor the passing years changed his essential nature. When the Paraguayan War broke out, he often thought about enlisting as an officer with the volunteers, but he never did; although there can be no doubt that he won several battles and ended up a brigadier.

MARIANA

I

"I WONDER WHAT became of Mariana?" Evaristo asked himself as he crossed Largo da Carioca, after bidding farewell to an old friend who had reminded him of his old sweetheart.

The year was 1890. Evaristo had returned from Europe only a few days earlier, after an absence of eighteen years. He had left Rio de Janeiro in 1872, expecting to stay until 1874 or 1875 while he visited a series of famous or merely interesting cities, but the traveler proposes and Paris disposes. Upon reaching the City of Light in 1873, Evaristo allowed himself to stay on beyond his allotted timetable; he postponed his departure for a year, then another, then thought no more of leaving. He had lost all interest in the affairs of our country, latterly not even bothering to read the Brazilian newspapers; an impoverished student from Bahia would borrow his newspapers before he'd read them, and in return give him a summary of one or two of the more important items. Then, suddenly, in November 1889, a Parisian reporter came to his home and started talking about the revolution in Rio de Janeiro, and asking for political, social, and biographical information. Evaristo considered his response, then said:

"My dear sir, I rather think I should go there myself and find out."

Having neither party nor opinions, no close relatives, no financial interests (all his wealth being in Europe), it is difficult to explain Evaristo's sudden decision in terms of mere curiosity, and yet there was no other motive. He simply wanted to see the new state of affairs. He checked the date of an opening night at the Odéon, for a lighthearted play written by a friend, and calculated that if he left on the first steamship and returned three steamships later, he would be back just in time to buy a ticket and take his seat for the performance. He packed his bags, hastened to Bordeaux, and boarded the ship.

"Yes, I wonder what became of Mariana?" he thought again on his way down Rua da Assembléia. "Perhaps she's dead? Or if she's still alive, she must be very different; she'll be forty-five or so . . . No, forty-eight! She was about five years younger than me. Forty-eight, by Jove . . . She was a real beauty, absolutely marvelous! And a marvelous old time we had of it too!"

He wanted to see her. He inquired discreetly, and found out that she was still alive and living in the same house on Rua do Engenho Velho, but she hadn't been seen for several months, on account of her husband, who was ill and, according to some reports, dying.

"She's probably at death's door herself," Evaristo said to the acquaintance who gave him the information.

"Good Lord, no. The last time I saw her, she was as fresh as a daisy. You wouldn't think her a day over forty. Shall I let you in on a secret? There may be some delightful rosebushes around these parts, but when it comes to our stately cedars of 1860 to 1865, well, they just don't make them like that anymore."

"Ah, but they do! You just don't see them because you've stopped climbing Mount Lebanon," retorted Evaristo.

His desire to see Mariana had grown. How would they look to each other now? What bygone visions would return to transform the reality of the present? It goes without saying that the purpose of Evaristo's journey was not simply to amuse, but to cure. Now that the march of time had done its work, what would remain of the specter of 1872, the sad year when they parted, a separation that nearly drove him crazy, and nearly killed her?

II

A few days later, he stepped down from a cab at Mariana's front door, and handed his card to a servant, who showed him into the parlor.

While he waited, he looked around him and was moved by what he saw. All the furnishings were exactly as they had been eighteen years before. Although he had been unable to reconstruct them mentally during his absence, he recognized all of them instantly, along with their precise arrangement, which hadn't changed, either. They looked old and fusty. The artificial flowers in a large vase, placed on a side table, had faded with time. The room resembled a pile of scattered bones that the imagination could fit together once again to form a body, lacking only a soul.

But the soul was not lacking. Hanging on the wall, above the sofa, was Mariana's portrait. It had been painted when she was twenty-five; the frame, never re-gilded and peeling in several places, was in marked contrast with her fresh, cheerful face. Time had not tarnished her beauty. Mariana was there, dressed in the fashions of 1865, with the wide, pretty eyes of a woman in love. It was the only living breath in the room, but that was enough to give a fleeting youthfulness to the decrepit surroundings. Evaristo felt a surge of emotion. There was an armchair facing the portrait; he sat down in it and stared at that young woman from another time. Her painted eyes stared back at his real ones, perhaps surprised both at their meeting again and at the changes in him, because his real eyes did not have the warmth and humor of those in the portrait. However, this difference did not last long; the man's former life outwardly restored his youthful vigor, and they drank in each other's eyes and all their former sins.

Then, slowly, Mariana descended from the canvas and its frame, and came and sat opposite Evaristo. She leaned forward, reached out her arms to him, and opened her hands. Evaristo placed his hands in hers, and the four hands squeezed each other in cordial affection. Neither of them asked anything about the past, because as yet there was no past; they were both in the present, time had stopped so instantaneously and completely that it was as if they had spent the whole of the previous evening rehearsing for this single, unending, performance. All the clocks in the city and around the world had quietly broken their mechanisms, and all the clockmakers had found a new trade. *Adieu, vieux lac de Lamartine!* Evaristo and Mariana had dropped anchor in the ocean of time. And then came the sweetest words ever uttered by the lips of man or woman, and that includes the most ardent words, words never spoken, angry words, dying words, words of jealousy and of forgiveness.

"Are you well?"

"I am, and you?"

"I've been dying to see you. I've been waiting for you for the last hour, so filled with longing I almost cried; but as you can see I'm happy and cheerful now, and all because the very best of men has finally entered the room. What took you so long?"

"I was delayed along the way, and the second delay took much longer than the first."

"If you truly loved me, you would have spent only two minutes with either of them, then you'd have got here three-quarters of an hour ago. Why are you laughing?"

"The second delay was your husband."

Mariana trembled.

"It was just near here, around the corner," continued Evaristo. "We talked about you, he mentioned you first. I'm not entirely sure what he said, but he spoke kindly, almost affectionately. It dawned on me that it was a trap, a way of winning my confidence. Finally, we said goodbye. I waited, watching to see if he'd come back, but he didn't. That's the reason for my delay, and there you also have the cause of all my torments."

"Don't start again with those eternal suspicions of yours," said Mariana, smiling just as she had in the portrait a moment or two earlier. "What do you want me to do? Xavier's my husband; I'm not going to send him away, or punish him, or kill him, simply because you and I love each other."

"I'm not telling you to kill him, but do you love him, Mariana?"

"I love you and no one else," she replied, thus avoiding a negative answer, which seemed to her excessively cruel.

That was what Evaristo thought, but he couldn't accept the delicacy of that indirect answer. Only a plain and simple negative would satisfy him.

"You do love him, then," he insisted.

Mariana paused for a moment.

"Why must you rummage about in my soul and in my past?" she said. "For us, the world began four months ago and will never end—or only when you tire of me, for I shall never change . . ."

Evaristo knelt down, drew her arms toward him, kissed her hands, and buried his face in them; finally, he rested his head on Mariana's knees. The two of them remained like that for several moments, until, feeling her fingers growing moist, she raised his head and saw his eyes brimming with tears. "What is it?"

"Nothing," he said. "Goodbye."

"What on earth has got into you?"

"You love him," replied Evaristo, "and the idea both torments and ter-
rifies me, because I would be capable of killing him if I were sure you did
still love him."

"What a strange man you are," retorted Mariana, after drying Evaristo's
eyes with her hair, which she had hurriedly loosened, thus providing him
with the finest handkerchief in the world. "Do I love him? No, I don't love
him anymore. There—you have my answer. But now you will allow me to tell
you everything, because it is not in my nature to indulge in half confidences."

This time it was Evaristo who trembled, but curiosity so gnawed at his
heart that his fears had to give way to waiting and listening. With his head
still resting on her knees, he heard what she had to say, which was brief.
Mariana told him about her marriage, her father's opposition, her mother's
suffering, and her own and Xavier's perseverance. They waited resolutely
for ten months, she less patiently than he, because the passion that gripped
her was strong enough to withstand even the most violent decisions. What
tears she shed for him! What heartfelt curses she heaped on her parents, sti-
fled only by her fear of God, for she did not want such words, like weapons
of parricide, to condemn her to a fate even worse than hell: eternal separation from the man she loved. Perseverance triumphed, time disarmed her
parents, and the wedding took place some seven years later. Their passionate
courtship continued into married life. When time brought with it tranquility, it also brought affection. Their hearts were in tune; the memories of
their struggle still poignant and sweet. A serene happiness came and sat at
their door, like a sentinel, but then, suddenly, the sentinel departed, leaving
behind neither unhappiness nor even tedium, but apathy: a pale, motionless
figure who barely smiled and remembered nothing. It was around this time
that Evaristo appeared and stole her heart. He hadn't stolen her from the
love of another man, and for exactly that reason he had nothing to do with
her past, which remained a mystery and a potential source of regrets—

"Regrets?" he asked, interrupting her.

"You may well imagine that I have regrets, but I don't, and I never will."

"Thank you!" said Evaristo after several moments. "I'm grateful for your
confession. I will never speak of the matter again. You do not love him, and
that's what counts. How beautiful you are when you swear such an oath and
talk to me about our future! Yes, it's all over, and here I am, so love me!"

"You and only you, my love."

"Only me? Swear it once again!"

"By these eyes," she replied, kissing his eyes, "by these lips," she continued, placing her lips on his. "By my life and yours, I swear!"

Evaristo repeated the same words, accompanied by the same ceremony.
Then he sat down facing Mariana, just as he had been at the beginning. She
rose and went to kneel at his feet, resting her elbows on his knees. Her loose
hair framed her face so perfectly that he regretted not having the genius to
copy it and bequeath it to the world. He told her this, but she said nothing
in reply; her eyes were gazing yearningly up at him. Evaristo leaned forward,
his eyes fixed on hers, and there they stayed, their faces almost touching, for
one, two, three hours, until someone came to interrupt them:

"Please, follow me."

III

Evaristo jumped. Before him stood a man, the same servant who had taken
his visiting card. He stood up quickly; Mariana withdrew into the canvas
on the wall, where he could see her once again, dressed in the fashions
of 1865, hair neatly coiffed, face serene. As if in a dream, his thoughts,
gestures, and actions had occupied their own particular time, whereas in
reality everything had happened in five or six minutes, the time taken by
the servant to carry Evaristo's card to his mistress and to return with her
invitation. However, there was no doubting that Evaristo could still feel
the young woman's caresses, for he really had been back to the years 1869
to 1872, in a vision lasting three hours that had eluded ordinary time. The
whole story had come flooding back to him, his jealousy of Xavier, his own
words of forgiveness, and Mariana's reciprocal tenderness. The only thing
lacking was the final crisis, when Mariana's mother, when she found out
everything, had bravely intervened, and separated them. Mariana wanted to
die and even took poison; it was only her mother's desperation that brought
her back to life. Xavier, who, at the time, was visiting the surrounding province, knew nothing of the tragedy other than that his wife had narrowly
escaped death after taking the wrong medication. Evaristo had tried to see
her before embarking for Europe, but it proved impossible.

"After you," he said to the servant, who was waiting for him.

Xavier was in the adjoining study, lying on a sofa, with his wife and several visitors by his side. Evaristo entered in a state of high emotion. The light was dim, the silence deep; Mariana was clutching one of her husband's hands, watching him closely, fearing either death or some sort of crisis. She scarcely looked up at Evaristo to hold out her hand to him, immediately turning back to gaze at her husband, whose face bore the marks of long suffering, and whose labored breathing seemed like the prelude to that last great, infinite opera. Evaristo, who had barely seen Mariana's face, withdrew to a corner of the room, not daring to look at her or follow her movements. The doctor arrived, examined the patient, prescribed the same medication as before, and left, promising to come back that night. Mariana accompanied him to the door, asking him whispered questions and trying to read in his face the truth that his lips dared not speak. It was only then that Evaristo was able to look at her properly; suffering seemed to have bowed her more than the years. He recognized the unmistakable way she moved. This Mariana was stepping out not from a canvas as the other one had, but from time itself. Before she returned to her husband's side, Evaristo realized that he, too, should leave, and moved toward the door.

"Do please excuse me . . . I'm very sorry not to be able to speak with your husband at this moment."

"I'm afraid it's not possible; the doctor recommends complete rest and silence. Perhaps another time . . ."

"I would have come earlier, but I only just found out . . . and I haven't been back in Rio for long."

"Thank you."

Evaristo shook her hand and crept out, while she returned to sit beside the patient. Neither Mariana's hand nor her eyes had revealed any sort of feeling for Evaristo, and they parted almost as strangers. True, their love had ended long ago, her heart had aged with time, and her husband was on the point of dying. And yet, he thought, how could he explain that, after eighteen years of separation, Mariana could see before her a man who had once played such an important part in her life, without betraying the slightest shock, surprise, or embarrassment? Therein lay a mystery. A mystery indeed. Even now, on leaving, he had felt a pang, something that made his words stumble and threw all his thoughts into disarray, even the most banal expressions of sorrow and hope. She, on the other hand, had shown not the least emotion on seeing him. And, remembering the portrait in the parlor,

Evaristo concluded that art was indeed superior to nature, for the canvas had preserved both her body and her soul. All this came sprinkled with a dose of bitter resentment.

Xavier lasted one more week. On his second visit, Evaristo was present at the invalid's death, and could not detach himself from the inevitable emotions of the moment, the place, and the circumstances. Mariana, her eyes hollow from weeping and watching, sat at the bedside, her hair disheveled. When, after a long, drawn-out death agony, Xavier finally departed this life, the weeping of the gathered family and friends could scarcely be heard; it was Mariana's piercing cry that caught everyone's attention, followed by her fainting and falling to the floor. She lay unconscious for several minutes. When she came to, she rushed over to her husband's dead body, embracing him, sobbing uncontrollably, calling him by the most loving and tender names. They had not yet closed the corpse's eyes, and this provoked a painful, tragic scene, for she, covering his eyes with kisses, became convinced that he was still alive and cried out that he had been saved. However hard they tried to pull her away, she would not let go and pushed them off, screaming that they were trying to take her husband away from her. She fainted again and was quickly carried to another room.

When the funeral procession left the house the following day, Mariana was not present, despite insisting on saying her final farewell; her strength was no longer the equal of her desires. Evaristo accompanied the cortege. As he followed the hearse, he could hardly believe where he was and what he was doing. At the cemetery, he spoke to one of Xavier's relatives, offering him his deepest condolences.

"They clearly loved each other very much," he concluded.

"Oh, indeed," said the relative. "They married for love, you know; I wasn't at the wedding because I only came to live in Rio de Janeiro some years later, in 1874. Nevertheless, I found them to be as inseparable as newlyweds, and I have followed their lives together ever since. They lived for each other, and, frankly, I don't know if she'll be long for this world."

"1874," thought Evaristo. "Two years later."

Mariana did not attend the seventh-day mass; a relative—the same one he had met in the cemetery—represented her on that mournful occasion. Evaristo learned from him that the widow was not in a fit state to risk attending the commemoration of such a tragedy. He let several days pass and went to pay a visit of condolence, but, having given his card, he was told she was not receiving anyone. He then went to São Paulo, returned five or six weeks later, and prepared to embark for Europe. Before leaving, he thought once again about visiting Mariana—not so much for reasons of simple courtesy, but so as to take away with him a final image, albeit impaired, of their four-year passion.

She was not at home. He turned to leave, angry and annoyed with himself, considering his visit impertinent and in poor taste. A short distance from the house he noticed coming out of the Espírito Santo Church a woman in mourning, who looked like Mariana. It was Mariana. She was on foot, and as she passed by his carriage she looked up at him, pretended not to recognize him, and carried on walking, leaving Evaristo's greeting unanswered. Even at this point, he wanted to stop the carriage and say goodbye to her, right there in the street, just one minute, just a few words. However, he hesitated for too long and, by the time his carriage stopped, he had already passed the church, and Mariana was, by then, some distance away. He nevertheless stepped down from the carriage and made his way back along the street. However, whether out of respect or resentment, he changed his mind, climbed back into the carriage, and left.

"Three times she was sincere," he concluded, after several minutes of reflection.

Within a month he was back in Paris. He had not forgotten his friend's new play, whose opening night at the Odéon he had promised to attend. He made some inquiries; it had been a resounding flop.

"Well, that's theater for you," said Evaristo to the playwright, in an attempt to console him. "Some plays fail. Others run and run."

A SCHOOL TALE

———

THE SCHOOL WAS on Rua do Costa, a little two-story building with a wooden fence. The year was 1840. On that Monday in May, I hung around for a few moments on Rua da Princesa pondering where I would go and play that morning. I couldn't decide between the São Diogo hill and the Campo de Sant'Ana, which, back then, was not the park for fine gentlemen we know today, but a more or less infinite expanse of countryside, dotted with washerwomen, patches of grass, and untethered donkeys. Hill or field? That was the question. Suddenly I told myself I'd be better off going to school. And so I went. Here's why.

I had skipped class twice the previous week, and when I was found out, I received my just reward from my father, who gave me a good thrashing with a big quince stick. The beating hurt for quite some time. He was a former employee at the War Arsenal, and was strict and intolerant. He dreamed of a successful business career for me, and was keen that I should master the rudiments of commerce, reading, writing, and arithmetic, in order to get me started somewhere as a cashier. He was always reeling off the names of successful businessmen who had started behind the counter. So it was the recollection of that most recent punishment that carried me to school that morning. I was not a virtuous child.

I crept up the stairs so that the schoolmaster wouldn't hear me, and arrived just in time; he entered the classroom three or four minutes later. He padded softly in as usual, wearing leather slippers, a faded linen jacket,

ill-fitting white trousers, and a wide, drooping collar. His name was Policarpo and he was around fifty years of age, perhaps more. He sat down, took
his snuffbox and red handkerchief from his inside jacket pocket and placed
them in a drawer, then cast his eyes around the room. The boys, who had
stood up when he entered, had sat down again. Everything was in order;
work could begin.

"I need to speak to you, Pilar," the schoolmaster's son whispered to me.

He was called Raimundo, this little fellow, and although he studied
hard, he was rather dim and slow-witted. It would take Raimundo two
hours to grasp what others could master in thirty or fifty minutes; he overcame with time what his brain could not at first achieve. To this was added a
great fear of his father. A delicate child with a pale, sickly face, he was rarely
cheerful. He arrived at school after his father and left before him. His father
was even stricter with him than he was with us.

"What do you want?"

"Later," he replied, his voice trembling.

The writing lesson began. I hate to say that I was among the more
advanced pupils in the school, but I was. And although an understandable
and praiseworthy fastidiousness on my part makes me hesitate to say that I
was also one of the most intelligent, I cannot deny it. It should be noted that
I was neither pale nor sickly; I had a good complexion and muscles of iron. In
the writing lesson, for example, I would always finish before everyone else,
and would while away the time drawing noses either on a piece of paper or
on the desk, an entirely foolish, ignoble occupation, but innocent enough
nevertheless. That day was the same as any other; no sooner had I finished
than I began to draw the schoolmaster's nose, in five or six different poses,
of which I remember the interrogative, the admirative, the dubitative, and
the cogitative. I didn't call them by these names, poor student of rudimen-
tary letters that I was, but I instinctively gave them those expressions. One
by one, the other pupils finished, and there was nothing for it but for me to
finish, too, hand in my writing exercise, and return to my place.

If truth be told, I was sorry I had come. Now that I was trapped there, I
was aching to escape, and once again I thought of the field, the hill, and the
other young rascals, Chico Telha, Américo, and Carlos das Escadinhas, the
very flower of the neighborhood and of the human race itself. To compound
my despair, through the schoolroom window, floating in the bright blue sky
high above the Livramento hill, I could see a magnificent paper kite, long

and broad, dancing in the breeze on a long string. And there was I sitting in the classroom, with my reading book and my grammar book on my knees.

"I was a fool to come to school today," I said to Raimundo.

"Don't say that," he whispered back.

I looked at him; he seemed even paler than before. Then I remembered that he wanted to ask me something, and I asked him what it was. Again Raimundo trembled and hurriedly told me to wait; it was a private matter.

"Pilar . . ." he whispered a few minutes later.

"What?"

"You . . ."

"You, what?"

He glanced up at his father, then at some of the other boys. One of them, Curvelo, stared back at him suspiciously, and, indicating this with a nod of his head, Raimundo asked me to wait a few more minutes. I confess that, by this point, I was burning with curiosity. I looked at Curvelo and saw that he did seem to be watching us; it might have been mere curiosity, natural inquisitiveness, but it might also have been a sign that there was something between them. Curvelo was a mischievous devil. At eleven he was the oldest in the class.

What on earth did Raimundo want from me? I was getting increasingly restless, fidgeting and whispering insistently to Raimundo that he should tell me what it was all about, and that no one was watching either of us. Or if he couldn't tell me now, then maybe this afternoon—

"No, not this afternoon," he interrupted, "it can't be this afternoon."

"Well, then, why not now?"

"Papa is watching."

The schoolmaster was, indeed, staring at us. Since he was stricter with his own son, he often looked in his direction, the better to keep him under his thumb. But we could play at that game too; we stuck our noses in our books and carried on reading. Finally, he wearied of watching us and picked up one of three or four newspapers, which he proceeded to read slowly, chewing over the thoughts and passions therein. Don't forget that this was the end of the Regency, and feelings were running high. Policarpo doubtless had some political affiliation, although I was never able to confirm what it was. His worst affiliation, from our point of view, was with the strap. There it hung, to the right of the window, with its five devilish eyes. He needed only to raise his hand, unhook the fiendish strap, and brandish it with his customary and not inconsiderable vigor. It was conceivable, however, that his interest in politics would so engage him that we would be spared any punishment. On that particular day, at any rate, he seemed to be reading the newspapers with particular relish; he raised his eyes from time to time, or took a pinch of snuff, but quickly returned to the papers, devouring them avidly.

After some time—ten or twelve minutes—Raimundo put his hand in his trouser pocket and looked at me.

"Can you guess what I've got in here?"

"No."

"A silver coin Mama gave me."

"Today?"

"No, the other day, on my birthday."

"Real silver?"

"Yes, real."

He slowly pulled it out and showed it to me from a distance. It was a coin from the days of the king, twelve *vinténs* or two *tostões*, I can't quite remember which, but it was a coin nonetheless, and a coin that made my heart beat faster. Raimundo turned his insipid gaze on me, then asked if I wanted it. I said he must be joking, but he swore he wasn't.

"But then what would you do without it?"

"Mama will get me another one. She has lots that Grandpapa left her, in a little chest; some of them are gold. Would you like this one?"

In reply, and after a quick glance at the schoolmaster's desk, I surreptitiously held out my hand. Raimundo immediately withdrew his hand, smiling feebly. Then he proposed a deal, an exchange of services: he would give me the coin if I would explain to him a bit of our syntax lesson. He couldn't remember anything from the book, and he was afraid of asking his father. He concluded his proposal by rubbing the coin on his knee.

I had a very strange feeling. Not that I possessed anything like a grown-up notion of virtue; nor did I have any difficulty in indulging in childish lies. We both knew how to deceive the schoolmaster. The novelty lay in the terms of the proposal, in that exchange of lessons for money, a straightforward, honest transaction—tit for tat; and that was what caused that strange feeling. I sat staring at him, speechless.

As you can imagine, the lesson was a difficult one, and Raimundo, having failed to learn it, was resorting to what seemed to him a useful means of escaping punishment by his father. If he had asked me as a favor, I would have helped him just the same, as I had on previous occasions, but it seems it was the memory of such previous occasions, the fear that I might be reluctant or unwilling to help, or else not explain things very well—and it may even be that on some occasions I had told him the wrong answer—it seems that this was the motivation behind his proposal. The poor devil was desperate for me to do him a favor, but he wanted to ensure its efficacy, and so he resorted to the coin his mother had given him and which he kept like some holy relic or toy; he took it out again and rubbed it up and down on his knee, showing me, tempting me . . . It really was very pretty, slender, and bright, especially to my eyes, for if I carried any coins at all in my pocket, they were only ever of the thick, ugly, green-tinged copper variety.

I didn't want to take it, but it was a hard thing to refuse. I looked up at the schoolmaster, who was still reading with such intense interest that the snuff dripped from his nose. "Come on, take it," the son whispered to me. And the little silver coin sparkled between his fingers like a diamond. If the schoolmaster didn't notice, what possible harm could there be? And he would see nothing, for he had his nose buried in his newspapers, which he continued to read with fire and indignation.

"Go on, take it . . ."

I again glanced around the schoolroom, and saw that Curvelo was looking at us; I told Raimundo to wait. It seemed to me that Curvelo was watching, and so I pretended not to notice; but after a few seconds, I shot him another glance and—ah, how our desires delude us!—I saw he had turned away. My courage returned.

"Give it here."

Raimundo furtively passed me the coin; with an excitement I can barely describe I put it in my trouser pocket. There it was, pressed against my leg, all mine. It only remained for me to perform my side of the bargain by teaching him the lesson, and I lost no time at all in doing so. I didn't even give him the wrong answers, at least not intentionally; I passed them to him on a scrap of paper, which he very cautiously took from me and gave his full attention. You could sense that he was expending five or six times the effort needed to learn something so simple, but it didn't particularly matter, just as long as he escaped punishment.

Suddenly I looked over at Curvelo and jumped; he was looking straight at us, with a malicious grin on his face. I pretended not to have seen this, but when I turned back toward him a few moments later, I saw that he was still looking, and had the same malicious air about him, in addition to which he was now fidgeting impatiently in his seat. I smiled at him, but he did not smile back; on the contrary, he frowned, which gave him a distinctly menacing appearance. My heart was racing.

"We need to be very careful," I said to Raimundo.

"Just explain this bit here," he whispered.

I gestured to him to shut up, but he insisted, and the coin in my pocket reminded me of the contract between us. I gave him the answer, as surreptitiously as I could; then I turned to look at Curvelo, who was fidgeting even more, and the smile on his face, which had been wicked enough before, was now even more so. It goes without saying that I was desperate for the lesson to finish, but the hands on the clock seemed to be stuck and the schoolmaster wasn't paying the slightest bit of attention to anything around him; he was still reading the newspapers, article by article, punctuating them with exclamations, shrugs, and one or two little taps on the table. And there outside, in the blue sky, above the hill, the same eternal kite swooped and swerved, as if calling me to go and join it. I imagined myself sitting there with my books and my slate beneath the mango tree, the little silver coin in my trouser pocket; I wouldn't give it to anyone, not for anything in the world; I would keep it at home, telling my mother I'd found it in the street. I felt for it in my pocket, just to make sure it didn't get away, running my fingers over its surface, almost reading the inscription by touch, and desperately wanting to peek at it.

"Hey! Pilar!" shouted the schoolmaster, with a voice of thunder.

I started as if woken from a dream and jumped to my feet. I found the schoolmaster scowling at me, the newspapers thrown to one side. Standing next to his desk was Curvelo. He seemed to have understood exactly what was going on.

"Come here," barked the schoolmaster.

I went up and stood before him. He drilled into my mind with his pointy little eyes, then summoned his son. The whole class had stopped work; nobody was reading, nobody moved. I didn't take my eyes off the schoolmaster, but I could sense everyone's curiosity and fear.

"So, you take money for teaching the other boys their lessons, do you, Pilar?"

"I . . ."

"Give me the coin that your chum over there gave you!" he shouted.

I hesitated, but I couldn't refuse. I was still trembling uncontrollably. Policarpo again bawled at me to give him the coin, and I had no choice; I reached into my pocket, slowly drew out the coin, and handed it over. He examined it carefully, snorting with rage; then he stretched out his arm and hurled it into the street. He laid into us with a tirade of abuse, about how both I and his son had committed a despicable, unworthy, vile, base act, and that we were to be punished both for our own sakes and to set an example. At this, he reached out and took the strap down from its hook.

"I'm sorry, sir . . ." I sobbed.

"Sorry isn't good enough! Hold out your hand! Hold it out! Come on! Shameless rascal! Hold out your hand!"

"But, sir . . ."

"You'll only make matters worse!"

I held out my right hand, then the left, and I took the strokes one after the other, twelve in all, which left my palms red and swollen. Then it was his son's turn and there was no sparing him, either; two, four, eight, twelve strokes. When he'd finished, he preached us another sermon, calling us insolent good-for-nothings, a disgrace to the school, and swore that if we did it again, the punishment would be so harsh we would remember it for the rest of our lives. "Swine! Crooks! Swindlers!" he shouted.

As for me, I just stared down at the floor. I didn't dare look at anyone and I could feel the weight of everyone's eyes on us. I returned to my seat, sobbing, bludgeoned by the schoolmaster's insults. Fear stalked the classroom; I can assure you that no one would try the same thing that day. I believe even Curvelo was taken aback. I didn't look at him straightaway, but I swore to myself that, as soon as we were outside in the street, I would smash his face in, just as sure as two plus three makes five.

A little while later, I glanced over at him; he was looking at me, too, but instantly looked away, and I'm pretty sure he turned pale. He pulled himself together and began to read out loud; he was afraid, though. He began to move around, fidgeting distractedly, scratching his knees, rubbing his nose. Maybe he regretted telling on us; indeed, why had he done it? What had we ever done to him?

"You'll pay for this! And how!" I muttered to myself.

It was time to leave, and he hurried out ahead of me. I didn't want to fight him right there in Rua do Costa, outside the school; it would have to be in Rua Larga de São Joaquim. However, when I reached the corner, there was no sign of him; he'd probably scuttled down some alley or gone into a shop; I went into an apothecary's, peered into a few houses, and asked several people if they'd seen him, but no one could tell me anything. That afternoon, he skipped school.

Obviously, at home, I said nothing, and to explain my swollen hands, I lied to my mother, telling her I hadn't learned the lesson properly. As I fell asleep that night, I cursed both boys, the one with the coin and the blabbermouth. And I dreamed about the coin; I dreamed that when I went back to school the next day, I found it in the street and picked it up, without feeling a smidgen of fear or guilt . . .

In the morning, I woke early. The idea of going to look for the coin prompted me to get dressed quickly. It was a splendid May morning, a day of glorious sunshine and gentle breezes, not to mention the pair of new trousers my mother gave me, which, by the way, were yellow. All this *and* the little silver coin . . . I left the house like a prince about to ascend the throne of Jerusalem. I quickened my pace so that no one would get to school before me, but not so fast that I would crease my new trousers. Oh, but they were smart! I gazed down at them and carefully avoided any chance contact with people or with the rubbish in the street.

On my way, I met with a company of fusiliers, led by a drummer. When I heard the drumming, I just couldn't keep still. The soldiers were marching briskly along in perfect time—left, right, left, right—with the sound of the drum; they approached, passed by, and carried on. I felt an itching in my feet and an urge to follow them. As I said, it was a beautiful day, and then there was that drum too . . . I looked both ways; finally, I'm not entirely sure how, I, too, began marching to the drumbeat, even humming some tune or other: "*Rato na Casaca,*" I believe. I didn't go to school. I followed the fusiliers, then carried on down to Saúde, and ended the morning on the shore at Gamboa. I returned home with filthy trousers, and with no silver coin in my pocket and no resentment in my soul. Still, that little silver coin was very pretty and it was they, Raimundo and Curvelo, who had given me my first taste of corruption on the one hand, and betrayal on the other. And as for that naughty drum . . .

AN APOLOGUE

Once upon a time, there was a needle, who said to the reel of thread: "Why are you so full of airs and graces, all neatly rolled up like that, pretending you're worth something in this world?"

"Leave me alone, madam."

"Leave you alone? Why? Just because I tell you that you're being unbearably pompous? I'll say it now and I'll say it again every time it passes through my head."

"What head, madam? You are not a pin, you're a needle. Needles don't have heads. And what's it to you how I behave? Each to his own, I say. You mind your business and leave others to theirs."

"My, but you're a proud one."

"Indeed I am."

"And why would that be?"

"Well, that's a fine question! Because I sew. All our mistress's dresses and ribbons and all the rest of it, who sews them if it isn't me?"

"You? Oh, this gets even better. So it's you who sews? You seem to be overlooking the fact that I, and I alone, do the sewing.

"You make holes in the fabric, that's all; I'm the one who sews, joining one piece with another and making all the frilly bits flounce."

"Yes, but that's hardly the important bit. I'm the one who makes the holes, I go on ahead, pulling you behind me, and you do exactly as I do."

"The drummers also march ahead of the emperor."

"So you think you're an emperor, do you?"

"I'm not saying that. But the truth is that yours is just a supporting role; your job is only to show the way, like a low and humble servant. I'm the one who joins, fastens, and binds together."

That's where they had gotten to when the seamstress arrived at the baroness's. I don't know if I mentioned that this took place at the home of a baroness, who had her dressmaker come to her, rather than having to visit the shop. The seamstress arrived, picked up the fabric, picked up the needle, picked up the thread, threaded the needle, and began to sew. Between the seamstress's fingers—which, to give the story a poetic touch, were as agile as the hounds of Diana—the needle and thread marched proudly onward across the fabric, which was the finest of silks. And the needle said to the thread:

"So, then, Miss High and Mighty, do you still persist in what you were saying earlier? Can't you see that this fine seamstress cares only for me? Here I am between her fingers, inseparable from them, piercing the cloth up and down, up and down . . ."

The thread did not reply, but carried on. Every hole opened by the needle was promptly filled by the thread, silently, firmly, purposefully, oblivious to any foolish words. Seeing that no response was forthcoming, the needle, too, fell silent, and continued its work. Silence reigned in the little sewing room; nothing could be heard but the *plic-plic-plic-plic* of needle and fabric. As the sun began to set, the seamstress put away her sewing; the next day, and the day after, she carried on, until on the fourth day she finished her work, ready for the ball.

The night of the ball arrived and the baroness put on the dress. The seamstress, who helped her, had the needle pinned in her bodice, so as to make any adjustments should the need arise. And while she was fixing the fine lady's dress, pulling here, tucking there, smoothing, buttoning, hooking, and fastening, the thread mockingly asked the needle:

"Now, then, tell me this: Who will be going to the ball, clothing the baroness, inseparable from her dress, her elegance? Who will be dancing with ministers and diplomats, while you go back to the seamstress's sewing box, and from there to the basket the slaves keep their things in? Come on, tell me!"

It seems the needle said nothing, but a pin, with a big head and no less experience, whispered to the poor needle:

"Let that be a lesson to you, you silly old thing. You wear yourself out leading the way for her and she's the one who gets to enjoy life, while you stay there in the sewing box. Do as I do: I never lead the way for anyone. Wherever they stick me, I stay."

I told this tale to a professor of melancholy, who replied, shaking his head: "I, too, have served as needle to many a mediocre thread!"

DONA PAULA

SHE COULD NOT have arrived at a more opportune moment. Dona Paula entered the room just as her niece was drying her eyes, which were red with crying. The aunt's surprise is easy enough to understand, as is the niece's, given that Dona Paula lives up in Tijuca and rarely comes down to the city; the last time was at Christmas and we are now in May of 1882. She arrived yesterday afternoon and went straight to her sister's house in Rua do Lavradio. Today, as soon as she had breakfasted, she dressed and rushed over to visit her niece. When she reached the house, one of the slaves tried to go and warn her mistress, but Dona Paula ordered her to stay put, and, tiptoeing very slowly to keep her skirts from rustling, she opened the door of the drawing room and went in.

"Whatever's wrong?" she exclaimed.

Venancinha threw herself into her aunt's arms, and again burst into tears. Her aunt kissed her and embraced her tightly, saying many words of comfort, and begging her to tell her what the matter was. Was she ill, or—

"Oh, I wish I *were* ill! I wish I were dead!" said the young lady, interrupting her.

"Now, don't be so silly. What is it? Come on, what's happened?"

Venancinha dried her eyes and tried to speak. She got no further than five or six words before the tears returned, so abundantly and unstoppably that Dona Paula thought it best to let them first run their course. Meanwhile, she took off her black lace cape and removed her gloves. She was, for her age, still a beautiful, elegant woman whose large eyes must once have seemed infinite. While her niece wept, she prudently went over to shut the door, then returned to the sofa. After a few minutes, Venancinha stopped crying and told her aunt what had happened.

She'd had a terrible quarrel with her husband, so violent that they had even spoken of separation. The cause was jealousy. For some time now, her husband had harbored a dislike for a certain gentleman, but on the previous evening, at C.'s house, seeing her dance with said man twice and talk to him for several minutes, he had concluded that they were lovers. He sulked all the way home, and, in the morning, after breakfast, his anger exploded and he said some very harsh and bitter things, to which she had responded in kind.

"Where is your husband?" asked her aunt.

"He's gone out, probably to the office."

Dona Paula asked if his office was still to be found in the same building, and told her not to worry, that this was clearly a fuss about nothing, and in a couple of hours it would all have blown over. She quickly pulled on her gloves.

"Are you going to see him, Auntie?"

"I am indeed. Your husband is a good man, and this is just a minor tiff. Number 104, you said? Right, I'm off; wait for me here, so that the slaves don't see you."

All this was said with a kind and confident fluency. After her gloves, she put on her cape, helped by her niece, who kept repeating, indeed swearing, how, despite everything, she still adored Conrado. Conrado was her husband, who had been practicing as a lawyer since 1874. Dona Paula left, taking with her many kisses from the young lady. She really could not have arrived at a more opportune moment. As she made her way to Conrado's office, it seems that Dona Paula reflected upon the incident with curiosity and not a little suspicion, somewhat uneasy about what might really have happened; in any event, she was determined to restore domestic harmony.

Her nephew was not in his office when she arrived, but he soon returned. Despite his initial surprise at seeing her there, he did not need Dona Paula to explain the reason for her visit; he guessed what had happened. He admitted that he had gone too far in some respects, and while he did not actually believe his wife to be a wicked or depraved woman, she was something of a flibbertigibbet, too fond of men's gallantry, tender looks, and flattering remarks. Frivolity could itself be a doorway to vice. As for the man in question, he had no doubt that something was going on between them. Venancinha had only told Dona Paula about the previous night; she had not mentioned the four or five other incidents, the last of which had taken place at the theater, and had even turned into something of a scandal. He had no desire to assume responsibility for his wife's indiscretions. If she wanted to take lovers, then so be it, but it would be at a cost.

Dona Paula listened in silence, then she spoke. She agreed that her niece was somewhat flighty; it was only to be expected at her age. Pretty girls cannot go out into the street without attracting attention, and it was only natural for her to be flattered by the attentions of other men. It was also only natural that her response should appear, both to the flatterers and to her husband and to other people, as the beginnings of an affair: their foolishness and his jealousy explained everything. On the other hand, she, Dona Paula, had just seen the poor girl shed genuine tears; she had left her in a wretched state, completely distraught at what he had said to her, even saying she wanted to die. And if he himself only thought her frivolous, then why not proceed with caution and kindness, offering sage advice, avoiding as much as possible the occasions on which such incidents might arise and pointing out to her the harm that can be done to a lady's reputation by even the appearance on her part of any reciprocity, affection, or kindness toward other men?

The good lady spent no less than twenty minutes saying these soothing things, and so convincing were her arguments that the nephew felt his heart soften. He did, of course, put up some resistance. Not wishing to seem overly indulgent, he declared two or three times that it was all over between him and Venancinha. To stir his resolve, he brought to mind all the various grievances he held against his wife. The aunt, meanwhile, bowed her head to let the wave wash over, before again raising it and fixing him with her large, wise, perseverant eyes. Slowly and reluctantly, Conrado began to give way. It was then that Dona Paula proposed a compromise.

"Forgive her, make peace between you, and let her come and stay with me up in Tijuca for a month or two; call it a sort of exile. While she's with me, I will do my best to knock some sense into her. Agreed?"

Conrado agreed. As soon as she had his word, Dona Paula bade him good day and left to take the good news to her niece. Conrado accompanied her to the stairs and they shook hands; Dona Paula did not release his without first repeating her words of prudent, compassionate advice, then commented nonchalantly:

"And the pair of you will come to see that the man who caused all this trouble doesn't merit even a moment's thought."

"His name is Vasco Maria Portela."

Dona Paula turned pale. Which Vasco Maria Portela? An old man, a former diplomat, who . . . No, he had retired to Europe several years before and had just been made a baron. It was one of his sons, recently returned, a regular dandy . . . Dona Paula released Conrado's hand and hurried downstairs. Although there was no need to adjust her cape, she stood in the hallway for several minutes, fumbling with it, her hands trembling, and with a somewhat troubled look on her face. She even stopped and stared down at the floor, thinking. Then she left the building and returned to her niece, taking with her the reconciliation and its conditions. Venancinha agreed to everything.

Two days later, they left for Tijuca. Venancinha went rather less willingly than she had promised; it was probably the prospect of exile, or perhaps some lingering regrets. In any event, Vasco's name went with them up to Tijuca, if not in both of their heads, then at least in the aunt's, where it created a kind of distant echo, wafting gently down from the days of the great mezzo Rosine Stoltz when the Marquis of Paraná was in government. Power and fame are fragile things, and no less fragile than the bloom on a young girl's cheek. And where had those three eternities gone? They were buried beneath the ruins of the past thirty years, which was all that Dona Paula had within her and all that lay ahead of her.

The reader will by now have realized that the other Vasco, the older one, had also once been young and in love. For several years, in the shadow of their respective marriages, they had loved each other until they could love no more, and since the passing breeze does not record our human words, it is impossible to set down here what was said of the affair at the time. The affair ended; it had been a succession of sweet and bitter hours, of delights, tears, rages, and raptures—for such were the intoxications that filled this lady's cup of passion. Dona Paula drank deeply, down to the very last drop, then cast the cup aside, never to drink again. Surfeit led to abstinence, and, with time, her public reputation rested on that latter phase. Her husband died and the years passed. Dona Paula was now an austere and pious widow, held in the highest esteem and respect.

It was her niece who took her thoughts back to the past. The similarity of the situation, with a man of the same name and blood, awoke in her some old memories. Do not forget that the two of them were now up in Tijuca and would be living together for some time, one in obedience to the other; it was both a temptation and a challenge to memory.

"Are we really not going back to the city for several weeks?" asked Venancinha, laughing, the following morning.

"Are you bored already?"

"No, not at all, I could never be bored; I was just asking . . ."

Dona Paula, also laughing, wagged her finger and asked if she was already missing life down in the city. Of course she wasn't, said Venancinha, curling her lip in disdain or indifference. She did perhaps protest too much, like someone who reveals more than she should in her letters, and Dona Paula had the good sense not to read in haste, preferring to weigh each word and syllable so that nothing escaped her, and she found her niece's gesture somewhat excessive.

"They're in love!" she thought to herself.

This discovery reawakened the spirit of the past. Dona Paula struggled to shake off those importunate memories, yet back they came, meek and mild or bold and blowsy, like the young things they were, singing and laughing and generally causing mayhem. Dona Paula returned to the dances of her youth, to those endless waltzes that sent everyone into raptures, to the mazurkas, which she always held up to her niece as the most graceful thing in the world, to the theaters, the card games, and, more circumspectly, the kisses; but all of these things—and here's the nub of it—all of these things were like dry, dusty chronicles, mere skeletons of the story, lacking any soul. It was all in her head. Dona Paula tried to yoke her heart to her head, to see if she could feel anything beyond a purely mental reenactment, but, however hard she tried to revive those extinct emotions, none returned. Only bare stumps remained.

If she could only peer into her niece's heart, she might find her own image reflected there, and then . . . Once this notion entered Dona Paula's head, it somewhat complicated her task of cure and restoration. She was sincere in her concern for her niece's welfare, and wanted to see her reconciled with her husband. Steadfast sinners may well wish for others to sin as well, so as to have some company on the way down to purgatory, but in this case the sin was long gone. Dona Paula set out to her niece Conrado's superior virtues, but also the passions that could bring their marriage to a bad, indeed worse than tragic, end: he could disown her.

Conrado's first visit to them, nine days later, only confirmed her aunt's warnings: he was cold when he arrived and cold when he left. Venancinha was terrified. She had hoped that those nine days of separation would have softened her husband's heart, which indeed they had, but he concealed this on arrival and kept a tight lid on his feelings so as not to be seen to be giving in. This proved more salutary than anything else. The terror of losing her husband was the most important element in Venancinha's recovery. It was even more effective than exile.

Then, all of a sudden, two days after Conrado's visit, when aunt and niece were standing at the garden gate ready to go out for their customary stroll, they saw a man approaching on horseback. Venancinha stared at him, uttered a faint cry, and ran to hide behind the wall. Dona Paula understood at once, and remained where she was. She wanted to see the rider at closer quarters, and two or three minutes later she did just that: a handsome, elegant young man with gleaming boots and a firm seat in the saddle. He had the same face as the other Vasco, for he was indeed the son; the same tilt of the head, slightly to the right, the same broad shoulders, the same round, deep eyes.

That very night, once the first word had been pried out of her, Venancinha told her aunt everything. They had first seen each other at the races, soon after he returned from Europe. Two weeks later, he was introduced to her at a ball, and he looked so dashing, had such a Parisian air about him, that the following morning she mentioned him to her husband. Conrado had frowned, and it was precisely this reaction that planted in her mind an idea that had never occurred to her up until then. She began to enjoy seeing Vasco, and soon enjoyment turned to longing. He spoke to her respectfully and said nice things to her, that she was the prettiest and most elegant girl in Rio, that some of the ladies of the Alvarenga family, whom he had met in Paris, had already been singing her praises to him. He made witty, cutting remarks about other mutual acquaintances, but also knew how to speak from the heart, like no one else she had met before. He did not speak of love, but followed her with his eyes, and though she tried to look away, she could not do so entirely. She began to think about him, often and with great excitement, and her heart beat faster whenever they met; and he may well have seen in the look on her face the impression he made upon her.

Leaning toward her niece, Dona Paula listened to this account, which appears here in abbreviated form. Her whole life was there in her eyes; with her lips parted, she seemed to drink in her niece's words, eagerly, like a cordial. She asked for more, for her to tell her everything, absolutely everything. Venancinha's confidence grew. Her aunt looked so youthful, her very exhortations were so gentle and full of ready forgiveness, that Venancinha found in her a confidante and a friend, apart from the few harsh words that Dona Paula, out of unwitting hypocrisy, had felt obliged to mix in with other, kinder ones, for I wouldn't say this was intentional, given that Dona Paula was deceiving herself as well. We might compare her to a general invalided out of the army and who tries to rekindle some of his former ardor by listening to the tales of other men's campaigns.

"Now you can see that your husband was right," she said. "You've been reckless, very reckless . . ."

Venancinha agreed, but swore that it was all over.

"I'm afraid it might not be. Did you really love him?"

"Auntie!"

"So you do still love him!"

"I swear I don't. Not anymore, but I confess . . . yes, I confess I did. Oh, Auntie, please forgive me; don't say anything to Conrado. I'm truly sorry . . . As I said, at the beginning I was somewhat smitten . . . But what can you expect?"

"Did he make any declarations of love?"

"Yes, one night at the theater, the Teatro Lírico, as we were leaving. He had the habit of calling at our box to accompany me to my carriage. It was at the door to the box . . . just three little words . . ."

Dona Paula did not, for the sake of decency, ask Venancinha what the precise words of her lover had been, but she imagined the setting, the corridor, the couples leaving, the lights, the crowd, the chatter of voices. With this tableau before her, she was able to imagine some of her niece's feelings; astutely, and not entirely disinterestedly, she asked her to describe them.

"I don't know what I felt," replied the young lady, whose tongue was loosening with her swelling emotions. "I don't remember the first five minutes. I think I remained composed, though, and I certainly didn't respond. Everyone seemed to be looking at us, as if they'd overheard something, and when someone greeted me with a smile, I had the impression they were making fun of me. Somehow I made it down the stairs, and without really knowing what I was doing, I got into the carriage; when we shook hands I let my fingers go limp. I swear to you I wish I hadn't heard those words. Conrado told me he was sleepy and leaned back in the carriage; it was better that way, because I don't know what I would have said if we'd had to talk all the way home. I leaned back, too, but not for long; I couldn't keep still. I looked out of the window and could see only the glare of the streetlamps, and then not even that; I saw the corridors at the theater, the stairs, everyone standing there, him right beside me, whispering those words, just three little words, and I cannot say what I thought during all that time; everything inside me was mixed up and confused, like a kind of internal revolution . . ."

"And when you got home?"

"At home, as I undressed, I was able to gather my thoughts a little, but only a little. I slept poorly, and late. I woke in the morning feeling utterly confused. I can't say whether I was happy or sad; I remember thinking about him a lot, and to put him out of my mind I promised myself that I would tell Conrado everything, but the thoughts kept coming back. From time to time, I could almost hear his voice, and it made me tremble. Then I remembered that, when we said goodbye, I had let my fingers go limp, and I felt, I don't quite know how to put it, a sort of regret, a fear of having offended him . . . and that made me want to see him again . . . Forgive me, Auntie, but you did ask me to tell you everything."

Dona Paula nodded and squeezed her niece's hand tightly. Hearing those feelings so innocently expressed, she had at last rediscovered something from the old days. One minute her eyes were dull with the drowsiness of remembrance, the next instant they sparkled with warmth and curiosity; she listened to everything, day by day, encounter by encounter, the scene at the theater itself, which, at first, her niece had hidden from her. And then came the rest, the hours of anguish, of longing, fear, hope, the disappointments, the deceptions, the sudden impulses, all the turmoil of any young woman in such circumstances; nothing was spared the aunt's insatiable curiosity. It was not an entire book, not even one chapter of an adultery, but a prologue—interesting and disturbing.

Venancinha finished speaking. Lost in her own thoughts, her aunt said nothing. Then she stirred from her reverie, took her niece's hand, and drew it toward her. She still didn't speak; at first she just stared intently at all that restless, quivering youthfulness, the fresh mouth, the still-infinite eyes, and only came to herself when her niece asked once again for her forgiveness.

Dona Paula said to her everything that a tender, austere mother could say; she spoke of chastity, of love for her husband, of public reputation; she was so eloquent that Venancinha could not contain herself, and wept.

Tea was brought in, but after certain confidences tea is impossible. Venancinha quickly withdrew to her room and, now that more candles had been lit, she left the room with her eyes lowered so that the footman would not see how upset she was. Dona Paula remained at the table, as did the footman. She spent nearly twenty minutes sipping a cup of tea and nibbling a biscuit, and as soon as she was alone, she went and leaned against the window, which looked out over the garden.

A gentle breeze was blowing; the leaves stirred and whispered, and even though they were not the same leaves as in times gone by, they still asked her: "Do you remember the old days, Paula?" For that is the peculiar thing about leaves: each passing generation tells the next what it has seen, and so they always know everything and ask about everything. "Do you remember the old days?"

Yes, she did remember, but what she had felt only a short time earlier, a mere shadow, had now passed. In vain she repeated her niece's words, breathing in the sharp night air: it was only in her head that she found some remnants, mere reminiscences, bare stumps. Her heart had slowed once again and her blood was flowing at its normal pace. She lacked her niece's moral presence. And yet there she stood, staring into the night, which was just the same as all those other nights and yet had nothing in common with the days of Rosine Stoltz and the Marquis of Paraná; and there she stood, while inside the house the slave-women staved off sleep by telling stories and occasionally, growing impatient, saying to each other:

"My, but ol' missy don't never go to bed tonight!"

LIFE!

———

T HE END OF TIME. Ahasuerus, sitting on a rock, stares out at the distant horizon, across which two eagles are flying. He meditates, then dreams. The day draws slowly to a close.

AHASUERUS: And so I reach the end of time, for here lies the very threshold of eternity. The earth is deserted and forsaken; no other man breathes the air of life. I am the last; now I can die. Death! What a wonderful thought! For centuries upon centuries have I lived, weary and tormented, ever the wanderer, but behold, the centuries have come to an end, and with them, I, too, will die. Farewell, old nature! Blue sky, reborn clouds, roses of a single day and every day, everlasting waters, enemy earth who would not eat my bones, farewell! The wanderer will wander no more. God will forgive me, if he so wishes, but death consoles me. Jagged as my pain rises yonder mountain; the hunger of those passing eagles must be as desperate as my despair. Will ye, divine eagles, die too?

PROMETHEUS: All mankind must have died; the earth is bare of them.

AHASUERUS: And yet I hear a voice . . . A man's voice? Merciless heavens, am I not the last? Here, he approaches. Who are you? In your wide eyes there is something of the mysterious light of the archangels of Israel; you are not a man . . .

PROMETHEUS: No.

AHASUERUS: Are you, then, one of the divine race?

PROMETHEUS: You said it, not I.

AHASUERUS: I do not know you, but what does that matter? You are
not a man and so I can still die; for I am the last, and behind me I
close the door of life.

PROMETHEUS: Life, like ancient Thebes, has a hundred doors. You
close one, others will open. You say you are the last of your species? Another species will come, a better one, made not from the
same clay, but from the same light. Yes, O last of mankind, the
plebeian element will perish forever, and the elite will be what
returns to reign over the earth. The times will be set right. Evil
will end; the winds will no longer scatter the germs of death, nor
the weeping and wailing of the oppressed, but only the song of
everlasting love and the blessing of universal justice . . .

AHASUERUS: What do all these posthumous delights matter to the
species that will die with me? Believe me, you who are immortal,
to bones that rot in the earth, all the purple of Sidon is worthless.
What you are telling me is even better than the world dreamed of
by Campanella, in whose ideal city there was crime and sickness;
yours excludes all moral and physical injuries. May the Lord hear
you! But let me go now and die.

PROMETHEUS: Go, then, go. But why such haste to end your days?

AHASUERUS: It is the haste of a man who has lived for thousands of
years. Yes, thousands of years. Even men who lived for only a few
decades invented a term for that sense of weariness, *tedium vitae*,
which they could never truly have known, not at least in all its vast
and unyielding reality, because to acquire such a profound aversion to existence it is necessary to have walked, as I have, through
every generation and through every ruin.

PROMETHEUS: Thousands of years?

AHASUERUS: My name is Ahasuerus. I was living in Jerusalem when
they took Jesus Christ to be crucified. As he passed by my door,
he stumbled under the weight of the cross he was carrying, and I
drove him on, shouting at him not to stop, not to rest, but to go
on up to the hill where he would be crucified . . . Then a voice
from heaven told me that I would be condemned to wander ceaselessly until the end of time. So great was my sin, for I showed no

pity for the man who was going to die. I didn't even know why he must die. The Pharisees said the son of Mary had come to destroy the law, and that he must be killed; poor fool that I was, I wanted to show off my zeal, and that is what provoked my actions on that day. Later, as I made my way through all the ages and all the cities of the earth, how often did I see the same thing happen again and again! Whenever zeal entered a humble soul, it became something cruel or ridiculous. That was my unpardonable sin.

PROMETHEUS: A grievous sin indeed, but the punishment was generous. Other men read only one of life's chapters; you have read the entire book. What does one chapter know of another chapter? Nothing. But he who has read every chapter connects them all together and draws conclusions. If some pages are melancholy, others are jovial and happy. After bitter tears comes laughter, out of death springs life, storks and swallows change climate without ever abandoning it entirely; thus is everything reconciled and restored. You saw this, not ten times, not a thousand times, but every time; you saw the magnificence of the earth healing the affliction of the soul, and the joy of the soul overcoming the desolation of things. Such is the alternating dance of nature, which gives its left hand to Job and its right hand to Sardanapalus.

AHASUERUS: What do you know about my life? Nothing; you know nothing of human life.

PROMETHEUS: I know nothing of human life? Don't make me laugh! Come on, then, everlasting man, explain yourself! Tell me everything; you left Jerusalem . . .

AHASUERUS: I left Jerusalem. I began my pilgrimage through the ages. I traveled everywhere, encountered all races, beliefs, and tongues; I traveled in sunshine and in snow, among civilized peoples and barbarians, to islands and to continents; wherever mankind breathed, there breathed I. I never worked again. Work is a refuge, and I never again knew such a refuge. Every morning brought with it my daily coin . . . See? Here is the last one. Be gone with you, worthless thing! (*He hurls the coin into the distance.*) I did not work, only wandered, always, always, always wandering, day after day, year after year, down through all the years and all the centuries. Eternal justice knew what it was doing, for to eternity it added idle-

ness. Each generation bequeathed me to the next. Languages that
had died lay with my name embedded in their bones. With each
passing age everything was forgotten; heroes vanished into myths,
into a distant shade, and history slowly dissolved, retaining only
two or three faint and far-off outlines. And in one way or another
I saw it all. You spoke of chapters? Happy are those who read
their lives in only one chapter. Those who departed at the birth of
empires took with them an impression of their perpetuity; those
who died when those empires were declining were buried with
the hope of their restoration; but do you know what it is like to see
the same thing over and over again, the same alternation of prosperity and desolation, desolation and prosperity, endless funerals
and endless hallelujahs, sunrise after sunrise, sunset after sunset?

PROMETHEUS: But you did not suffer, I believe, and it is at least something not to have suffered.

AHASUERUS: Yes, but I saw other men suffer, and, toward the end,
cries of joy had much the same effect on me as the ramblings of
a madman. Calamities of flesh and blood, endless conflicts; I saw
everything pass before my eyes, to the point where night has made
me lose my taste for day, and I can no longer distinguish flowers
from weeds. To my weary retina everything looks the same.

PROMETHEUS: But nothing harmed you personally; it was I who, for
time immemorial, suffered the effects of divine wrath.

AHASUERUS: You?

PROMETHEUS: I am Prometheus.

AHASUERUS: You are Prometheus?

PROMETHEUS: And what was my crime? From mud and water I made
the first men, and then, out of compassion, I stole for them the fire
of heaven. That was my crime. Jupiter, who reigned over Olympus at the time, condemned me to the cruelest of tortures. Come,
climb up upon this rock with me.

AHASUERUS: This is a fable you are telling me. I know this Hellenistic
dream.

PROMETHEUS: Old man of little faith! Come and see these chains that
bind me; an excessive punishment, given that no crime was committed, but proud divinity is a terrible thing. Anyway, look, here
they are . . .

AHASUERUS: You mean that Time, which corrodes everything, did not want these chains?

PROMETHEUS: They were the work of divine hands: Vulcan forged them. Two messengers from heaven came and chained me to the rock, and an eagle, like that one over there flying across the horizon, pecked at my liver, without ever consuming it entirely. This I endured for countless ages. You cannot imagine the agony.

AHASUERUS: Is this a trick? You really are Prometheus? So it was not some dream concocted by the ancient imagination?

PROMETHEUS: Look at me; touch these hands. See if I exist.

AHASUERUS: So Moses lied to me. You, Prometheus, you created the first men?

PROMETHEUS: That was my crime.

AHASUERUS: Yes, it was your crime, you artificer of hell; it was a crime for which there is no possible atonement. Here you should have remained for all time, chained and being endlessly devoured; you who are the source of all the evils that afflict me. I lacked pity, it is true, but you, who brought me into existence, you, perverse divinity, were the original cause of everything.

PROMETHEUS: Your impending death clouds your reason.

AHASUERUS: Yes, it really is you; you have the Olympian forehead of a strong and handsome Titan: it really is you . . . Are these your chains? I see no sign of your tears.

PROMETHEUS: I shed them for your race.

AHASUERUS: It shed many more on account of you.

PROMETHEUS: Listen to me, O last of your ungrateful line!

AHASUERUS: What do I want with your words? I want to hear your groans, you perverse divinity. Here are your chains. See how I lift them up? Hear the clanking of the irons? Who unchained you?

PROMETHEUS: Hercules.

AHASUERUS: Hercules . . . Let us see if he performs the same service now that you will once again be chained.

PROMETHEUS: You must be mad.

AHASUERUS: Heaven gave you your first punishment; now earth will give you your second and last. Not even Hercules will be able to break these irons again. See how I shake them about in the air like feathers; for I represent the strength of millennia of despair. All of humanity is within me. Before I fall into the abyss, I will write the world's epitaph on this rock. I will summon the eagle and it will come; I will tell it that, on departing this life, the very last man is leaving it a gift from the gods.

PROMETHEUS: Poor ignorant man; you are refusing a throne! No, you cannot refuse it.

AHASUERUS: Now you are the madman. Come on, kneel. Let me bind your arms. Yes, like that, don't resist. Breathe, breathe deeply. Now your legs . . .

PROMETHEUS: Go on, go on! These are earthly passions that turn against me, but I am not a man and know nothing of ingratitude. You will not change one letter of your fate; it will be fulfilled in its entirety. You will be the new Hercules. I, who proclaimed the glory of the first one, also proclaim yours; and you will be no less generous than he.

AHASUERUS: Are you mad?

PROMETHEUS: The truth men do not know is the madness of whoever proclaims it. Go on, finish it!

AHASUERUS: Glory never pays for anything, and then it dies.

PROMETHEUS: This glory will never die. Go on, finish what you're doing; teach the sharp beak of the eagle how to devour my entrails, but listen . . . No, don't listen; you cannot understand me.

AHASUERUS: No, speak, speak.

PROMETHEUS: The passing world cannot understand the eternal, but you will be the link between the two.

AHASUERUS: Tell me everything, I'm listening.

PROMETHEUS: I will tell you nothing. Go on, tighten the chains on my wrists so that I cannot escape, so that you will find me here when you return. You want me to tell you everything? I have already told you that a new race will inhabit the earth, made from the finest spirits of the extinct race; the multitude of others will perish. A noble family, lucid and powerful, it will be the perfect blend of the divine and the human. A new era will be born, but between that old era and this a link is needed, and that link is you.

AHASUERUS: Me?

PROMETHEUS: Yes, you, the chosen one, the king. Yes, indeed, Ahasuerus, you shall be king. The wanderer shall find rest. He who was scorned by men shall govern them.

AHASUERUS: Cunning Titan, you wish to deceive me. Me, a king?

PROMETHEUS: Yes, you. Who else could it be? The new world needs something from the old world, and no one can explain those two worlds better than you. Thus there will be no break between the two humanities. From the imperfect will come the perfect, and your mouth will tell it of its origins. You will tell the new mankind of all the good and evil of the old. You will spring to life once again like the tree whose dead leaves have been removed to reveal only the lush green ones, but in this case the lushness will be eternal.

AHASUERUS: A shining vision! Can it really be me?

PROMETHEUS: Yes, really.

AHASUERUS: These eyes . . . these hands . . . a new and better life . . . Sublime vision! Well, it is only fair, Titan. The punishment was fair, but so is the glorious remission of my sin. I shall live? Me? A new and better life? No, surely you mock me.

PROMETHEUS: Well, then, leave me; one day you will return, when these immense heavens open for the spirits of new life to descend. You will find me here, at peace. Go.

AHASUERUS: Will I greet the sun again?

PROMETHEUS: This very sun which now is setting. Our friend the sun, eye of the ages, will never again close its eyelids. Gaze upon it, if you can.

AHASUERUS: I cannot.

PROMETHEUS: Later you will, when the circumstances of life have changed. Then your eyes will be able to gaze safely at the sun, because future mankind will be a concentration of all that is best in nature: robust and delicate, shimmering and pure.

AHASUERUS: Swear to me you're not lying.

PROMETHEUS: You will see if I am lying.

AHASUERUS: Speak, tell me more; tell me everything.

PROMETHEUS: Describing life is not the same as feeling it; you will have it in abundance. The bosom of Abraham described in your old Scriptures is none other than this perfect world beyond. There you will see David and the prophets. There you will tell the astonished multitudes not only the great events of the extinct world, but also the evils that they will never know: illness and old age, deceit, selfishness, hypocrisy, tedious vanity, unimaginable foolishness, and all the rest. The soul, like the earth, will have an incorruptible sheath.

AHASUERUS: I will once again see this immense blue sky!

PROMETHEUS: Look, how beautiful it is!

AHASUERUS: As beautiful and serene as eternal justice. O magnificent sky, more beautiful even than the tents of Kedar, I will see you again and forevermore; you will gather up my thoughts as in ages past; you will grant me clear days and friendly nights . . .

PROMETHEUS: Sunrise upon sunrise.

AHASUERUS: Speak, speak! Tell me more. Tell me everything. Let me loosen these chains . . .

PROMETHEUS: Unchain me, new Hercules, last man of one world and first of the next. That is your destiny; neither you nor I, nor anyone else, can change it. You are greater even than your Moses. From the heights of Nebo, ready to die, he gazed upon all the lands of Jericho that would belong to his posterity; and the Lord said unto him: "You have seen it with your eyes, but you will not cross into it." You will cross into it, Ahasuerus; you will reach Jericho.

AHASUERUS: Place your hand upon my head, look into my eyes; fill me with the reality and force of your prediction; let me feel something of this full, new life . . . King, you said?

PROMETHEUS: Chosen king of a chosen people.

AHASUERUS: It is no more than just amends for the utter scorn in which I have lived. Where one life spat mud at me, another will crown my head with a halo. Go on, tell me more . . . tell me more . . . (*He continues dreaming. The two eagles approach.*)

FIRST EAGLE: Woe is he, this the last man on earth, for he is dying and yet still dreams of life.

SECOND EAGLE: He only hated life so much because he loved it dearly.

THE CANON,
OR THE METAPHYSICS OF STYLE

———————

"COME FROM LEBANON, my spouse, come from Lebanon, come . . . The mandrakes give their smell. At our doors we have every breed of dove . . .

"I charge you, O daughters of Jerusalem, if ye find my beloved, that ye tell him I am sick of love . . ."

And so it was, to the melody of that ancient drama of Judah, that a noun and an adjective searched for each other inside the head of Canon Matias. Do not interrupt me, hasty reader; I know you won't believe anything I'm about to say. I will, however, say it, despite your little faith, because the day of public conversion will come.

On that day—sometime around 2222, I imagine—the paradox will take off its wings and put on the thick coat of common truth. At that point, this page will merit not just favor, but apotheosis. It will be translated into every tongue. Academies and institutes will make a little book out of it, to be used throughout the centuries, with bronze pages, gilt edges, letters of inlaid opal, and a cover of unpolished silver. Governments will decree that it be taught in schools and colleges. Philosophers will burn all previous doctrines, even the most definitive, and will embrace this, the one true psychology, and everything will be complete. Until then, I will pass for a fool, as you will see.

Matias, honorary canon and a preacher by trade, was composing a sermon when this psychic idyll began. He is forty years of age and lives in the Gamboa District surrounded by books. Someone came to ask him to

give a sermon at a forthcoming festival; at the time, he was enjoying reading a weighty spiritual tome that had arrived on the last steamer and so he
refused their request; but they were so insistent that he gave in.

"Your Reverence will rattle it off in no time at all," said the principal
organizer of the festival.

Matias smiled meekly and discreetly, as should all clerics and diplomats.
Bowing low, the organizers took their leave and went to announce the festival in the newspapers, with the declaration that Canon Matias, "one of the
ornaments of the Brazilian clergy," would preach the Gospel. The phrase
"ornaments of the clergy" quite put the canon off his breakfast when he read
the morning papers, and it was only because he had given his word that he
sat down to write the sermon.

He began unwillingly, but after only a few minutes he was already
working with passion. Inspiration, its eyes turned toward heaven, and meditation, its eyes turned to the floor, stand on either side of his chair, whispering a thousand grave and mystical things in his ear. Matias carries on
writing, sometimes slowly, sometimes quickly. The sheets of paper fly from
his hands, vibrant and polished. Some have a few corrections, others have
none at all. Suddenly, on the point of writing an adjective, he stops; he
writes another and scores it out, then another, which meets the same fate.
Here lies the nub of the idyll. Let us climb inside the canon's head.

Ouf! Here we are. Not that easy, was it, dear reader? So don't go believing those people who troop up to the top of Corcovado and claim that from
that great height man seems utterly insignificant. A false and hasty conclusion; as false as Judas and other such diamonds. Do not believe it, beloved
reader. No Corcovados or Himalayas are worth much when set beside the
head that measures them. Here we are. Notice that it is indeed the canon's
head. We have the choice of one or other cerebral hemisphere, but let's go
into this one, which is where nouns are born. Adjectives are born in the
other one, on the left-hand side. This is one of my own discoveries, possibly
the principal one, but it is a starting point, as we will see. Yes, sir, adjectives
are born on one side and nouns on the other, and the entire destiny of words
is based on sexual difference—

"Sexual difference?"

Yes, ma'am. Words have a gender. Indeed, I am currently in the process
of finishing my great psycho-lexico-logical dissertation, in which I expound
and demonstrate this discovery. Words are of different sexes . . .

"But do they then love each other?"

They do indeed. And they get married. Their marriage is what we call style. You must confess, ma'am, that you have understood nothing.

"I confess I haven't."

Well, then, join me inside the canon's head. Just now there is some whispering going on over there. Do you know who is whispering? It is the noun from just a few minutes ago, the one the canon wrote down on the piece of paper just before his pen hesitated. The noun is summoning a certain adjective, which fails to appear: "Come from Lebanon, come . . ." That is how it speaks, for it is inside the head of a priest; if it were in a layman's head, the language would be Romeo's: "Juliet is the sun . . . Arise, fair sun." But in an ecclesiastical brain, the language is that of Scripture. At the end of the day, though, what do such formulations matter? Lovers in Verona or in Judah all speak the same language, just as the thaler or the dollar, the florin or the pound, are all the same money.

So let us carry on through these circumvolutions of the ecclesiastical brain, on the trail of the noun seeking an adjective. Sílvio calls to Sílvia. Listen: in the distance it sounds like someone else is whispering; lo, it is Sílvia calling to Sílvio.

Now they can hear each other and they begin to seek each other out. What a difficult and intricate path this is, in a brain so chock-full of things old and new! There is such a hubbub of ideas in here that it almost drowns out their voices; let us not lose sight of ardent Sílvio over there, going up and down, slipping and jumping; when he stumbles, he grabs hold of some Latin roots over there, he leans against a psalm, yonder he climbs aboard a pentameter, and on he goes, carried along by an irresistible inner force.

From time to time, a lady—another adjective—appears to him and offers him her graces ancient or modern; but, alas, she is not the right one, not the one and only, the one destined *ab eterno* for this union. And so Sílvio carries on, looking for that special one. Pass by, ye eyes of every hue, ye shapes of every caste, ye hairstyles fit for Day or Night; die without an echo, sweet ballads yearningly played upon the eternal violin; Sílvio is not asking for any old love, casual or anonymous; he is asking for one specific love, named and predestined.

Don't be frightened, reader; it's nothing to worry about, it's just the canon standing up, going over to the window, and taking a break from all his labors. While he's there he forgets about the sermon and about everything else. The parrot on its perch beside the window repeats its usual words to him and, out in the courtyard, the peacock puffs himself up in the morning sun. The sun, for its part, recognizing the canon, sends him one of its faithful rays as a greeting. The ray arrives and stops in front of the window: "Illustrious canon, I bring you the compliments of the sun, my lord and father." Thus all of nature seems to applaud the return of that galley-slave of the mind. He himself rejoices, gazes up at the pure air and feasts his eyes on greenery and freshness, all to the sound of a little bird and a piano. Then he speaks to the parrot, calls to the gardener, blows his nose, rubs his hands, and leans forward. He has forgotten all about Sílvio and Sílvia.

But Sílvio and Sílvia have not forgotten each other. While the canon concerns himself with other things, they continue to search for each other, without him suspecting a thing. Now, however, the path is dark. We pass from the conscious to the unconscious, where the confused elaboration of ideas takes place, where reminiscences sleep or doze. Here swarms formless life, the germs and the detritus, the rudiments and the sediments; it is the immense attic of the mind. Here they slip and slide, searching for each other, calling and whispering. Give me your hand, madam reader; you, too, sir, hold tight, and let us slip and slide with them.

Vast and alien, *terra incognita*. Sílvio and Sílvia rush onward past embryos and ruins. Groups of ideas, deducing themselves in the manner of syllogisms, lose themselves in the tumult of memories of childhood and the seminary. Other ideas, pregnant with more ideas, drag themselves still more heavily along, assisted by other, virgin ideas. Things and men merge; Plato brings the spectacles of a scribe from the ecclesiastical court; mandarins of all classes distribute Etruscan and Chilean coins, English books, and pale roses; so pale that they do not seem the same as the ones the canon's mother planted when he was a child. Pious memories and family memories cross paths and commingle. Here are the distant voices of his first mass; here are the country rhymes he heard the black women sing at home; the tattered remnants of faded sensations, a fear here, a pleasure there, over there a distaste for things that arrived singly, but now lie in an obscure, impalpable heap.

"Come from Lebanon, my bride . . ."

"I charge you, O daughters of Jerusalem . . ."

They could hear each other growing ever closer. Here they reach the deep strata of theology, philosophy, liturgy, geography, and history, of ancient lessons and modern notions, all mixed together, dogma and syntax. Here the secret, pantheistic hand of Spinoza; there the scratch mark left by the Angelic Doctor's fingernail; but none of this is Sílvio or Sílvia. They plow on, carried along by an inner force, a secret affinity, through all the obstacles and over all the abysses. But sorrows will also come. Here are dark sorrows that did not linger in the canon's heart, like moral stains, surrounded by the yellow or purple tints of universal pain, the pain of others, if such pain has a color. They slice through all of this with the speed of love and desire.

Do you sway and stumble, gentle reader? Fear not, the world is not collapsing; it is the canon sitting down again. Having cleared his head, he returns to his desk and rereads what he wrote; now he takes up his pen, dips it in the ink, and lowers it to the paper, to see which adjective he will attach to the noun.

Now is precisely the moment when the two lovesick lovers will draw closest. Their voices rise, as does their enthusiasm, the entire *Song of Songs* passes their lips, tinged with fever. Joyous phrases, sacristy anecdotes, caricatures, witticisms, nonsense, mere foolishness, nothing holds their attention, or even makes them smile. On and on they go, while the space between them narrows. Stay where you are, blurred outlines of dunderheads who made the canon laugh and whom he has long since forgotten; stay, vanished wrinkles, old riddles, the rules of card games, and you, too, the germs of new ideas, outlines of conceits, the dust of what must once have been a pyramid; stay, jostle, hope, and then despair, for to them you are nothing. They have eyes only for each other.

They seek and they find. Sílvio has finally found his Sílvia. They see each other and fall into each other's arms, panting with exhaustion, but satisfied with their reward. They join together, arms about each other, and return, pulsating, from unconscious to conscious. "Who is this that cometh up from the wilderness, leaning upon her beloved?" asks Sílvio, as in the *Song*; and she, with the same erudite turn of phrase, replies that it is "the seal upon thine heart" and that "love is as strong as death itself."

At this the canon trembles. His face lights up. His pen, filled with emotion and respect, joins the adjective to its noun. Sílvia will now walk side by side with Sílvio in the sermon that the canon will one day preach, and hand in hand they will go to the printer's, if, that is, he ever gets around to putting together a collection of his sermons, which remains to be seen.

COLLECTED PAGES

(1899)

Author's Preface

Whatever various herbs you use,
they are all swallowed up beneath the name of salad.

—MONTAIGNE, *ESSAYS*, BOOK I, CHAPTER XLVI

Montaigne explains in his own way the variousness of this book. There is no point in repeating the same idea, nor would any other idea have the same elegance of expression as that in the epigraph. The only thing I need do is explain the origin of these pages.

Some are tales and short stories, figures that I saw or imagined, or merely ideas that it occurred to me could be reduced to language. They first appeared in the ephemeral pages of magazines, at various times, and were chosen from among many, because it was felt that they might still be of interest. All in all, it is an excuse to collect together stories I am fond of.

Machado de Assis

THE CANE

———

Damião ran away from the seminary at eleven o'clock on a Friday morning in August. I don't know which year it was exactly, but certainly before 1850. After only a few minutes, he stopped running, suddenly filled with embarrassment. He had not considered how people might react to the sight of a fleeing, frightened seminarian. Being unfamiliar with the streets, he walked aimlessly up and down, and finally stopped. Where could he go? He could not go home, because his father, after giving him a sound beating, would send him straight back to the seminary. He had not planned where exactly he might take refuge, because he had intended making his escape at some later date; however, a chance incident had precipitated his departure. Where could he go? There was his godfather, João Carneiro, but he was a spineless creature, incapable of doing anything on his own initiative. He had been the one to take him to the seminary in the first place, presenting him to the rector with these words:

"I bring you a great man of the future."

"We welcome great men," the rector said, "as long as they are humble and good. True greatness lies in simplicity. Come in, boy."

That had been his introduction to the seminary. Shortly afterward, he had run away. We see him now standing in the street, frightened, uncertain, not knowing where to turn for shelter or advice; in his mind he reviewed his various relatives and friends, but none seemed quite right. Then a thought occurred to him:

"I'll appeal to Sinhá Rita! She'll send for my godfather and tell him she wants me to leave the seminary. Perhaps that way . . ."

Sinhá Rita was a widow and João Carneiro's mistress. Damião had a vague understanding of what this meant, and it occurred to him that he might be able to take advantage of the situation. But where did she live? He was so disoriented that it took him a few minutes to find the house, which was in Largo do Capim.

"Good heavens! Whatever's the matter?" cried Sinhá Rita, sitting bolt upright on the sofa on which she was reclining

Damião had burst in unannounced, looking utterly terrified, for when he reached Sinhá Rita's house, he saw a priest coming down the street, and, in sheer panic, he violently pushed open Sinhá Rita's front door, which, fortunately for him, was neither locked nor bolted. Once inside, he peered through the shutters to watch the priest, who had clearly failed to notice him and walked on by.

"Whatever's the matter, Senhor Damião?" she said again, for she had recognized him now. "What are *you* doing here?"

Damião, who was trembling so much he could barely speak, told her not to be afraid, it was nothing very important, and he would explain everything.

"All right, sit down and explain yourself, then."

"First, I swear that I haven't committed a crime of any kind . . ."

Sinhá Rita stared at him in alarm, and all the young girls in the room— boarders and day pupils—froze over their lace-making pillows, their bobbins and hands suddenly motionless. Sinhá Rita earned her living largely from teaching lace-making, cutwork, and embroidery. While the boy was catching his breath, she ordered the girls to go back to their tasks, while she waited for Damião to speak. Finally, he told her everything, about how much he hated the seminary and how he was certain he would not make a good priest. He spoke with great passion and begged her to save him.

"But how? I can't do anything."

"You could if you wanted to."

"No," she said, shaking her head, "I'm not getting involved in family matters; besides, I hardly know your family, and they say your father has a very nasty temper on him!"

Damião saw that he was lost. In desperation, he knelt at her feet and kissed her hands.

"Please help me, Sinhá Rita. Please, for the love of God, by everything you hold most sacred, by the soul of your late husband, save me from death, because I will kill myself if I have to go back."

Flattered by the boy's pleas, Sinhá Rita tried to reason with him. The life of a priest was a very holy and pleasant one, she said; in time, he would see that it was best to overcome his dislike of the seminary and then, one day—

"No, never!" insisted Damião, shaking his head and again kissing her hands and saying it would be the death of him.

Sinhá Rita hesitated for a while longer. Then she asked why he could not speak to his godfather.

"My godfather? He's even worse than Papa. He never listens to me. I shouldn't think he listens to anyone . . ."

"Doesn't listen, eh?" Sinhá Rita responded, her pride wounded. "I'll show you if he listens or not."

She summoned a slave-boy and ordered him to go straight to Senhor João Carneiro's house, and if the gentleman wasn't at home, then he should ask where he could be found and run and tell him that she needed to speak to him urgently.

"Off you go."

Damião sighed loudly and sadly. To justify the authority with which she had issued these orders, she explained to him that Senhor João Carneiro had been a friend of her late husband and had brought her several new pupils. Then, when he remained leaning in the doorway, looking glum, she tweaked his nose and said, smiling:

"Don't you worry, my little priest, it'll all be fine."

According to her birth certificate, Sinhá Rita was forty years old, but her eyes were only twenty-seven. She was a handsome, lively woman, who enjoyed both her food and a joke; however, when she had a mind to, she could be extremely fierce. She tried to cheer the boy up and, despite the situation, this did not prove difficult. Soon they were both laughing; she was telling him stories and asking him to reciprocate, which he did with considerable humor. One particularly extravagant tale, which required him to pull funny faces, made one of Sinhá Rita's pupils laugh so much that she neglected her work. Sinhá Rita picked up a cane lying next to the sofa and threatened her:

"Remember the cane, Lucrécia!"

The girl bowed her head, waiting for the blow, but the blow did not come. It had only been a warning. If, by the evening, she had not finished her work, then Lucrécia would receive the usual punishment. Damião looked at her; she was a scrawny little black girl, all skin and bone, with a scar on her forehead and a burn mark on her left hand. She was about eleven years old. Damião noticed, too, that she kept coughing, quietly, as if not wanting to disturb their conversation. He felt sorry for her and decided to take her side if she did not finish her work. Sinhá Rita would be sure to forgive her . . . Besides, she had been laughing at *him*, so it was his fault, if being funny can be a fault.

At this point, João Carneiro arrived. He blanched when he saw his godson there, and looked at Sinhá Rita, who came straight to the point. She told him he had to remove the boy from the seminary, that the child had no vocation for the ecclesiastical life, and it was far better to have no priest at all than a bad priest. One could just as easily love and serve Our Lord in the outside world. For the first few minutes, João Carneiro was too taken aback to reply; in the end, however, he did open his mouth to scold his godson for coming and bothering "complete strangers" and threatened him with punishment.

"What do you mean, 'punishment'!" Sinhá Rita broke in. "Punish him for what? Go on, talk to his father."

"I can't promise anything; in fact, I think it's highly unlikely, if not impossible . . ."

"Well, I'm telling you that it has to be possible. If you really try," she went on in a rather insinuating tone, "I'm sure you can sort something out. You just have to ask nicely and he'll give in. Because, Senhor João Carneiro, your godson is not going back to the seminary."

"But, senhora—"

"Go on, off you go."

João Carneiro did not want to go, but neither could he stay. He was caught between two opposing forces. He really didn't care if the boy ended up being a cleric, a lawyer, or a doctor, or something else entirely, however useless, but he was being asked to do battle with the father's deepest feelings and could not guarantee the result. If he failed, that would mean another battle with Sinhá Rita, whose final words had a threatening note to them: "your godson is not going back to the seminary." Either way, there was sure to be a ruckus. João Carneiro stood there, wide-eyed, his eyelids twitching, his chest heaving. He kept shooting pleading glances at Sinhá Rita, glances in which there was just a hint of censure. Why couldn't she ask him for something else, anything? Why couldn't she ask him to walk in the rain all the way to Tijuca or Jacarepaguá? But to persuade a father to change his mind about his son's career . . . He knew the boy's father well, and knew that he was perfectly capable of smashing a glass in his face. Ah, if only the boy would just drop down dead of an apoplectic fit! That would be a solution—cruel, yes, but final.

"What do you say?" demanded Sinhá Rita.

He made a gesture as if asking for more time. He stroked his beard, looking for some way out. A papal decree dissolving the Church or, at the very least, abolishing all seminaries, that would do the trick. João Carneiro could then go home and enjoy a quiet game of cards. It was like asking Napoleon's barber to lead the Battle of Austerlitz . . . Alas, the Church was still there, so were the seminaries, and his godson was still standing waiting by the wall, eyes downcast, with no convenient apoplectic fit in sight.

"Go on, off you go," said Sinhá Rita, handing him his hat and cane.

There was nothing for it. The barber put away his razor, buckled on his sword, and went off to battle. Damião breathed more easily, although, outwardly, he remained grave-faced, eyes fixed on the floor. This time, Sinhá Rita pinched his chin.

"Come on, don't be so glum, let's have something to eat."

"Do you really think he'll succeed?"

"He has to," retorted Sinhá Rita proudly. "Come along, the soup's getting cold."

Despite Sinhá Rita's natural joviality and his own naturally playful self, Damião felt less happy over supper than he had earlier on. He had no confidence in his spineless godfather. Nevertheless, he ate well and, toward the end, was once again telling jokes as he had in the morning. Over dessert, he heard the sound of people in the next room, and asked if they had come for him.

"No, it'll be the ladies."

They got up and went into the drawing room. The "ladies" were five neighbors who came every evening after supper to have coffee with Sinhá Rita and stayed until nightfall.

Once the pupils had finished their supper, they returned to their lace-making pillows. Sinhá Rita presided over this gaggle of women, some of whom were resident and others not. The whisper of bobbins and the chatter of the ladies were such worldly sounds, so far removed from theology and

Latin, that the boy let himself be carried along by them and forgot about everything else. At first the ladies were a little shy, but soon recovered. One of them sang a popular ballad accompanied on the guitar by Sinhá Rita, and the evening passed quickly. Before the soirée ended, Sinhá Rita asked Damião to tell them the story she had particularly liked. The same one that had made Lucrécia laugh.

"Come on, Senhor Damião, don't play hard to get. Our guests are just about to leave. You'll really love this one, ladies."

Damião had no option but to obey. Despite the expectation created by Sinhá Rita's words—which rather diminished the joke and its effect—the story did nevertheless make the ladies laugh. Pleased with himself, Damião glanced over at Lucrécia to see if she had laughed as well, but she had her head bent over her work, intent now on finishing her task. She certainly wasn't laughing, or perhaps only to herself, in the same way she kept her cough to herself.

The ladies left, and darkness fell. Damião's heart also grew blacker with the onset of night. What would be happening at his father's house? Every few minutes he went over to peer out of the window, but returned each time feeling more discouraged. No sign of his godfather. His father had doubtless sent him packing, then summoned a couple of slaves and gone to the police station to demand that a constable come with him to arrest his son and take him back to the seminary. Damião asked Sinhá Rita if there was a back entrance to the house and ran out into the garden to see if he could climb over the wall. He also asked if there was an escape route down Rua da Vala or if she could perhaps speak to one of her neighbors, who might be kind enough to take him in. The problem was his cassock: could Sinhá Rita lend him a jacket or an old overcoat? Sinhá Rita did indeed have a jacket, left behind by João Carneiro, either as a souvenir or out of sheer absentmindedness.

"I have an old jacket of my husband's," she said, laughing, "but why are you so frightened? It will all work out, don't you worry."

At last, when night had fallen, a slave arrived bearing a letter for Sinhá Rita from his godfather. No agreement had yet been reached; the father had reacted furiously and tried to smash everything in the room; he had roared out his disapproval, saying that if his lazy rapscallion of a son refused to go back to the seminary, he would have him thrown in jail or sent to the prison ship. João Carneiro had battled very hard to persuade Damião's father not to rush into a decision, but to sleep on it and ponder deeply whether it was right to give the Church such a rebellious, immoral child. He explained in the letter that he had only used such language as a way of winning the argument. Not that he considered the argument won, by any means, but tomorrow he would go and see the man again and try to win him around. He concluded by saying that, meanwhile, the boy could stay at his house.

Damião finished reading the letter and looked at Sinhá Rita. She's my last hope, he thought. Sinhá Rita ordered a bottle of ink to be brought, and she wrote this response on the bottom half of João Carneiro's letter: "My dear Joãozinho, either you save the boy or you'll never see me again." She sealed the letter with glue and gave it to the slave for him to deliver with all speed. She again tried to cheer up the reluctant seminarian, who had again donned the monkish hood of humility and consternation. She told him not to worry, that she would sort things out.

"They'll see what I'm made of! No one's going to get the better of me!"

It was time to collect in the lace work. Sinhá Rita examined each piece, and all the girls had completed their daily task. Only Lucrécia was still at her lace-making pillow, furiously working the bobbins, even though it was too dark to see. Sinhá Rita went over to her, saw that the work was unfinished, and flew into a rage, seizing her by one ear.

"You lazy girl!"

"Please, senhora, please, for the love of God and Our Lady in Heaven."

"You idler! Our Lady doesn't protect good-for-nothings like you!"

Lucrécia broke away and fled the room. Sinhá Rita went after her and caught her by the arm.

"Come here!"

"Please, senhora, please forgive me!"

"No, I won't forgive you!"

And they came back into the room: Lucrécia dragged along by her ear, struggling and crying and pleading; and Sinhá Rita declaring that she must be punished.

"Where's that cane?"

The cane was next to the sofa. From the other side of the room, Sinhá Rita, not wanting to let the girl go, shouted to Damião.

"Senhor Damião, give me that cane, will you?"

Damião froze. Oh, cruel moment! A kind of cloud passed before his eyes. Had he not sworn to help the young girl, who had only fallen behind with her work because of him?

"Give me the cane, Senhor Damião!"

Damião began to walk over to the sofa. The young black girl begged him by all that he held most sacred, his mother, his father, Our Lord . . .

"Help me, sir!

Sinhá Rita, face aflame, eyes bulging, was demanding the cane, still not letting go of the girl, who was now convulsed by a coughing fit. Damião was terribly touched by her plight, but . . . he had to get out of that seminary. He went over to the sofa, picked up the cane, and handed it to Sinhá Rita.

THE DICTIONARY

ONCE UPON A TIME, there was a demagogic barrel-maker called Bernardino, who, in the field of cosmography, professed the view that the world is a vast vat of quince jelly, and, in the field of politics, called for the masses to be enthroned. In order for this to happen, he took up a big stick, roused the people to revolution, and overthrew the king; however, on entering the palace, acclaimed as victor, he saw that there was only room on the throne for one person, and got around this little difficulty by sitting on the throne himself, declaring in a booming voice:

"You see in me the masses enthroned. I am all of you, and all of you are me."

The first act of the new king was to abolish barrel-making, immediately rewarding the other barrel-makers, who threatened to overthrow him, with the title of the Magnificent Ones. His second act was to declare that, in order to lend greater luster to the person and position of king, he would, henceforth, be called by the grander name of Bernardão, rather than by the more diminutive Bernardino. He commissioned a great expert in matters of genealogy, who, in no time at all, had traced his ancestry back to some Roman general from the fourth century, Bernardus Barrelius—a name that gave rise to great controversy, which continues to this day, with some saying that King Bernardão must once have been a barrel-maker, and others that this was all a silly confusion arising from the name of the founder of the family. As we have seen, this second view is the only true one.

Having been bald ever since he was a young man, Bernardão decreed that all his subjects should be equally bald, either naturally or with the help of a razor, and he based this act on a purely political idea, namely, that the moral unity of the state depended on all heads looking the same. A further, equally wise act was one that ordered every left shoe to have a small hole cut in it next to the little toe, thus giving his subjects another opportunity to resemble him, for he had a corn on that very toe. The use of spectacles throughout the kingdom can also only be explained by an eye infection that afflicted Bernardão in the second year of his reign. The illness cost him the sight of one eye, and this was the moment when Bernardão's poetic vocation was first revealed, because, when one of his two ministers, called Alpha, commented that the loss of one eye made him equal to Hannibal—a comparison he found deeply flattering—the second minister, called Omega, went still further, and remarked that he was superior even to Homer, who had lost the sight of both eyes. This compliment was a revelation, and since this leads us neatly to the matter of his marriage, let us move swiftly on.

Marriage was, to be honest, a way of securing the Barrelius dynasty. There was no shortage of brides for the new king, but none pleased him as much as a beautiful, rich, illustrious young woman called Estrelada. This lady, who cultivated music and poetry, was much sought-after by certain gentlemen, but remained faithful to the old dynasty. Bernardão plied her with rare, sumptuous gifts, while her family screamed at her to remember that a crown on the head is worth more than any affair of the heart, urging her not to bring shame on them when the illustrious Bernardão was tempting them with a principality, reminding her that thrones were few and far between, etc., etc. Estrelada, however, resisted these temptations.

She did not resist for very long, but neither did she give in entirely. Since among her suitors she secretly preferred one young man who was a poet, she declared that she was willing to get married, but only to the man who was deemed to have written the best madrigal in a competition created for that purpose. Mad with love and full of confidence, Bernardão accepted this condition; he did, after all, have one eye more than Homer and had achieved homogeneity among feet and heads.

Twenty suitors took part in the competition, with the entrants' names kept entirely secret. One madrigal was judged to be better than all the others, and it was written by the poet she loved. Bernardão decreed the competition null and void, and ordered another to be held; then, in a moment of Machiavellian inspiration, he decreed that only words more than three hundred years old could be used. None of the other competitors had studied the classics, and so this seemed a certain way of defeating them.

He still did not win, though, because the beloved poet had quickly read as many of the classical writers as he could, and his madrigal was again judged to be the best. Bernardão once more declared this second competition to be null and void, and, seeing that in the winning madrigal the use of ancient turns of phrase gave a remarkable elegance to the poem, he decreed that only modern, fashionable terminology could be used. A third competition ended in a third victory for the poet.

Furious, Bernardão confided in his two ministers, asking them to come up with a swift and energetic remedy, because, if he did not win Estrelada's hand, he would order three hundred thousand heads to be cut off. The ministers spent some time in discussion, then returned with this proposal:

"We, Alpha and Omega, are, by virtue of our names, responsible for all matters linguistic. Our idea is that Your Sublimeness should order all dictionaries to be confiscated, and we will then compile a new vocabulary that will ensure your victory."

Bernardão did as they proposed, and the two ministers remained closeted in the palace for three whole months, after which they placed in his august hands the finished work, a book they entitled the Dictionary of Babel, because it really was no more than a jumble of letters. No word bore any resemblance to the spoken language; consonants climbed on top of other consonants, vowels dissolved into other vowels, words of two syllables now had seven or eight and vice versa, everything was muddled up and switched around, with no verve, no elegance—a language of fragments and scraps.

"Your Sublimeness has only to impose this language by decree, and our job is done."

Bernardão rewarded them each with an embrace and a large pension, and decreed that this new vocabulary would, from then on, be the official vocabulary. He also declared that there would be one final competition to win the hand of the lovely Estrelada. The jumble in the dictionary was transferred to people's minds; everyone lived in a state of utter confusion. Jokers would greet each other in the street, using the new phrases; for example, instead of saying: "Good morning, how are you?" they would say: "Pflerrgpxx, rouph, aa?" Fearing that her beloved poet would finally lose the competition, the young lady herself suggested that they elope together.

He, however, answered that, first, he would see what he could do. Entrants were given ninety days to compose their poem, and again there were twenty entries. The best of these, despite that barbarous new language, was the one written by the poet. Half mad with rage, Bernardão ordered the hands of his two ministers to be cut off, but that was his only act of revenge. Estrelada was so wonderfully beautiful that he did not dare to harm her, and so he gave in. Greatly displeased, he shut himself up for a week in the library, reading, pacing, and thinking. It seems that the last thing he read was a satire by the poet Garção, in particular these lines, which seemed as if made to order:

> It was not the paints that made them eternal,
> Those three rare, inimitable artists—
> Apelles, Rubens, and Raphael—
> But the elegant way they blended them.

A WANDERER

T HE DOOR OPENED . . . No, let me tell the tale as if it were a novel, said
Tosta to his wife when, a month after they were married, she asked
him about the man she had seen in an old photograph on her husband's
desk. The door opened, and that same man appeared, tall and serious,
rather dark-complexioned, and wearing a vast snuff-brown overcoat, which
the lads called his cope.

"Here's Elisiário's cope again."

"Come in, cope!"

"No, keep the cope out and let Elisiário in instead, but, first, he must
complete a rhyming couplet. Who has a first line ready?"

No one. The "house" was merely a room, sublet by a tailor, who lived in
the back of the house with his family; Rua do Lavradio in 1866. It was only
the second time Elisiário had gone there, at the invitation of one of the regu-
lars. You simply cannot imagine what that room and that life were like, or
only if you can imagine some bohemian outpost, all disorder and confusion;
for, apart from a few battered bits of furniture belonging to the tailor, there
were two hammocks, a laundry basket, a coat stand, a tin trunk, books, hats,
and shoes. Five young men lived there, but were often joined by a motley
assortment of other young men: students, translators, editors, philanderers,
who, nevertheless, still found time to produce a political and literary magazine, which was published every Saturday. Ah, the long debates we had!

We regularly demolished the very foundations of society, discovered new worlds, new constellations, new freedoms. Everything was spanking new.

Finally, one of the lads said:

"I've got one. 'Such was the scope of Elisiário's cope . . .'"

Standing in the doorway, Elisiário closed his eyes for a few moments, then opened them, mopped his brow with the screwed-up ball of a handkerchief he was carrying, and instantly improvised a second line. We all laughed long and loud; I, who had no idea that he really was improvising, thought, at first, that it was one he'd made up before and that they were merely trying to impress me. Elisiário removed his overcoat, raised it up on one end of his cane, and walked triumphantly twice around the room before hanging it on a nail in the wall, because the coat rack was full. Then he threw his hat into the air, caught it, and went over to place it on the sideboard.

"Room for one?" he said at last.

I hurriedly surrendered the sofa to him, and he lay down, knees bent, and asked what the latest news was.

"Supper looks unlikely," said the chief editor of the magazine. "Chico went out to see if he could get some subscription money in, and, if he succeeds, then he'll bring supper straight back here. Have you already eaten?"

"I have, indeed, and very well too," answered Elisiário. "I dined at a local restaurant. But tell me, why don't you just sell Chico? He's a handsome Negro. True, he's not actually a slave, but I'm sure he'd understand that if he allowed himself to be sold as a slave, then you'd be able to pay his wages. Will two *mil-réis* be enough? Romeu, have a look in my overcoat pocket. There must be two *mil-réis* in there."

There was only one and half *mil-réis*, but they proved unnecessary. Five minutes later, Chico returned, bearing a tray containing their supper and what remained of a week's subscription.

"Amazing!" cried Elisiário. "A subscription! Come here, Chico. Who paid you? What did the man look like? Was he short? No, he can't have been short; no short man would be capable of making such a sublime gesture. He was tall, wasn't he? Or at the very least of medium height. He was, wasn't he? Good. What's his name? Guimarães? Lads, let us have that name engraved on a bronze plaque. I assume you didn't give him a receipt, Chico."

"I did, sir."

"A receipt! But you must never give a paid-up subscriber a receipt, because if you don't give him a receipt, you can always gull him into paying again. Hope springs eternal, Chico."

All of this, when spoken by him, was far wittier than it sounds. I can't begin to describe his gestures, his eyes, the unique laugh that wasn't a laugh, but left his face utterly impassive and afforded not a glimpse of teeth. That was his least attractive feature, but everything else, his voice, his ideas, and, above all, his youthful, fertile imagination, out of which flowed sayings, anecdotes, epigrams, poems, descriptions, now serious, almost sublime, now familiar, almost humble, but always original, yes, everything about him drew you in. He was unshaven, his hair cut very short, his high forehead marked by two vertical lines. When silent, he appeared to be deep in thought, but he fidgeted constantly, getting up from the sofa, sitting down again, lying back. He was still there when I left at nine o'clock that night.

I became a regular visitor to the house in Rua do Lavradio, but initially there was no sign of Elisiário. I was told he was a very unreliable guest. He went through phases, sometimes joining us every day, then disappearing for one, two, or even three weeks or longer. He worked as a Latin teacher and mathematics tutor. He had no qualifications, even though he had studied engineering, medicine, and law, always moving from faculty to faculty and leaving behind him the same reputation, that of a highly talented student who lacked application. He would have been a fine prose writer if he could have made himself sit down for more than twenty minutes and write; he was an improviser of poems, but never put pen to paper, and although others who heard these verses would set them down and give him copies, he would usually lose these. He had no family, although he did have a protector, a certain Dr. Lousada, a surgeon of some renown, who owed Elisiário's father many favors and wished to repay these through the son. He could be prickly, too, because he was extremely sensitive to any perceived slight. In that house in Rua do Lavradio, though, he was on good terms with everyone. He was thirty-five, whereas the oldest of the other lads was only twenty-one. His relationship with them resembled that of uncle and nephews, with a little less authority and a little more freedom.

After a week had passed, Elisiário finally turned up again at Rua do Lavradio. He wanted to write a play and needed to dictate it to someone. I was chosen because I could write quickly. This mental and manual collaboration went on for two and half nights. He wrote one whole act and the first few scenes of the second, but then refused to finish it. At first he said he would do so later on, that he was feeling unwell, and then he simply changed the subject. In the end, he declared that the play was no good anyway. This statement was greeted with general amazement, because we had all thought the play excellent, and I still think so now. The author, however, disagreed and demonstrated that the writing was feeble and the rest of the plot useless. He spoke as if he were speaking of someone else. We argued back, and I, in particular, thought it a crime and repeated that word with real feeling and fire—I genuinely did think it a crime not to finish the play, which really was first-rate.

"No, no, it's worthless," he said, smiling kindly at me. "How old are you, boy?"

"Eighteen."

"Ah, everything is sublime when you're eighteen. Wait until you grow up. The play is a failure, but don't worry, we'll write another in a few days' time. I already have an idea for a plot."

"Really?"

"Yes, a very good idea," he went on, a dreamy look in his eyes. "An idea that really could make quite a decent play. Five acts, possibly in verse. That would suit the subject matter perfectly."

He never again mentioned the idea, but that first fragment of a play brought us slightly closer together. Whether it was genuine sympathy or satisfied pride when he saw how violently I reacted to his decision to abandon the play—something I even condemned as a dereliction of duty—or whether it was for some other reason unknown to me and which I see no point in trying to fathom out, Elisiário began to pay more attention to me. He asked about my parents and asked me what I did. I told him I had no mother, but that my father was a farmer in Baturité, that I was studying for my university entrance exams, in between writing popular verses, and that I had ideas for a poem, a play, and a novel. Indeed, I already had a list of subscribers for my popular verses. It seems that something—perhaps those literary ambitions of mine or perhaps my youthful enthusiasm—sparked his interest. He suggested helping me with my studies, by teaching me Latin, French, English, and history. Bursting with pride and rather touched, too, I made some flattering comment, to which he responded gravely:

"I want to make a man of you."

We were alone at the time, and I said nothing about this remark to the others, so as not to cause any ill feeling, although they may not even have noticed any change in Elisiário's attitude toward me. Not that the change was particularly marked, and his plan "to make a man of me" went no further than kindness and sympathy. He did teach me a few things when I asked him for help, but that was not very often. I wanted only to listen to him, then listen some more. You cannot imagine how eloquent he was, he could speak warmly and forcefully, gently and sweetly, and the images he came out with, the ideas, the startlingly elegant turns of phrase! We were often left alone in Rua do Lavradio, with him talking and me listening. Where did he live? The others said vaguely that he lived somewhere over toward Gamboa, but he never invited me there, and no one knew his actual address.

If you met him in the street, though, he seemed slow, upright, and circumspect. There was not a hint of the gawky, ebullient man I knew from Rua do Lavradio, for, if he spoke at all, he spoke very little. At first, if we ever did meet in the street, he showed no pleasure or excitement, he would simply listen to me intently, make some brief reply, then shake hands and go on his way. He walked everywhere; he could be found in the most disparate places, in Botafogo, São Cristóvão, Andaraí. When he felt like it, he would take the boat over to Niterói. He said of himself:

"I'm a wanderer, and the day I stop wandering, you can be sure I'll be dead."

One day, I met him in Rua de São José, and when I told him I was going to Castelo to see the Jesuit church, which I had never visited before, he said:

"Let's go together, then."

We walked up the hill, found the church open, and went in. While I was looking at the various altars, he talked, but it took only a matter of minutes for him to become the one thing worth looking at, a living spectacle, as if everything had been reborn as it once was. I saw the city's first churches, the Jesuit priests, monastic life, and secular life, all the key names and climactic moments. When we left the church and went over to the wall, looking out over the sea and part of the city, Elisiário carried me two centuries back. I saw the French being driven off, as if I had been commander-in-chief and had myself joined battle with them. I breathed the air of colonial Brazil, saw people long since dead. Elisiário's great gift was his ability to evoke the past, breathing life into things extinct and reality into mere inventions.

But his knowledge extended beyond local history or his own imaginings. You see that little statuette over there? It's a miniature of the Venus de

Milo. Once, I went to an art exhibition, and there I found Elisiário, walking gravely up and down in his vast overcoat. He joined me, and as we entered the sculpture hall, I spotted a copy of that same Venus. It was the first time I had seen the statue, and I recognized it at once because of its missing arms.

"How wonderful!" I cried.

Elisiário began telling me about that lovely, anonymous work, in such astonishingly abundant, penetrating detail that my amazement only grew. The things he told me about the Venus de Milo, and about Venus too! He spoke about the position of the statue's arms, the gesture they would have been making, and what a difference that would have made, and he came up with all kinds of elegant, natural hypotheses. He spoke about aesthetics, about the great artists, about Greece and Greek marble and the Greek soul. He appeared to me then as a pure Greek, as if he were transporting me from some wretched, narrow street and depositing me in front of the Parthenon itself. Elisiário's cope became a chlamys, the language he spoke was that of the Hellenes, even though I knew nothing of such things, then or now. That extraordinary man was a veritable magus.

We left and went to Campo da Aclamação, which was not the park it is today and was policed only by Nature, which covered it in rough grass, and by the washerwomen soaping and scrubbing their laundry outside the barracks. My mind was still full of all the things Elisiário had told me, and he walked along beside me with bowed head and pensive eyes. Suddenly I heard someone say softly:

"Hello, there, Ioió!"

The person who spoke was a woman selling sweets, a black woman from Bahia, or so she seemed to me, given the lavish amount of embroidery and lace on her skirt and blouse. She was walking up from Cidade Nova across Campo da Aclamação. Elisiário responded, saying:

"Hello, Zeferina."

He stopped and turned to me, smiling without smiling, and then, after a few seconds, he said:

"Don't look so surprised, boy. There are many different kinds of Venus. However, no one could say of this Venus that she lacks arms," he went on, still gazing appreciatively at the sweet-seller's arms, which looked still blacker against the short white sleeves of her blouse. I was too embarrassed to say anything.

I said nothing about this episode to the other denizens of Rua do Lavradio because it might have gotten Elisiário into trouble, and I didn't want to appear indiscreet. I felt a kind of veneration for him, which familiarity did nothing to diminish. We even had supper together a few times, and visited the theater. What he found hardest about being in the theater was having to sit for so long in the same seat, squeezed in between two other people, with people in front and behind. On nights when the performance was sold out, and they had to put benches in the aisles, he would become quite agitated at the thought that he wouldn't be able to leave in the middle of an act if he so chose. On one occasion, at the end of the third act (the play had five), he told me that he could stand it no longer and had to leave.

We went and had tea at the nearest café, and I stayed there with him until closing time, having forgotten all about the play. We talked about journeys; I told him about my life in the *Sertão*, the backlands of Ceará; he listened and told me of his many plans to travel throughout the *Sertão*, over hills, fields, and rivers, by mule and canoe. He would collect all kinds of things: plants, legends, songs, turns of phrase. He described the life of the country people there, he spoke of Aeneas, quoted Virgil and Camões, to the astonishment of the waiters, who stood staring, openmouthed.

"Do you fancy walking to São Cristóvão—now?" he asked when we were out in the street.

"Possibly."

"No, you're tired."

"I'm not. Let's go."

"No, you're too tired," he said at last. "I'll see you later."

I really was very tired and needed to sleep, but just as I was about to turn and set off home, I wondered where he would go all alone at that late hour and decided to follow him for a while from a distance. I caught up with him in Rua dos Ciganos. He was walking slowly, his cane under his arm, his hands either clasped behind him or plunged in his trouser pockets. He walked across Campo da Aclamação into Rua de São Pedro and then up Aterrado. When I reached Campo, I felt like turning back, but curiosity drove me on. Perhaps the wanderer was heading for some secret love nest? Discarding such a prurient thought, I decided to punish myself by abandoning the chase; curiosity, however, had banished my tiredness and lent vigor to my legs. I continued to follow Elisiário, and thus we reached the bridge, which we crossed, ending up in Rua de São Cristóvão. He would sometimes stop to light a cigar or for no reason at all. The city was deserted, apart from the occasional police patrol or the odd cab trotting sleepily past, otherwise there was no one. We reached the harbor at Igrejinha. Asleep on the water were the boats that, during the day, took people to Saco do Alferes. It was low tide, and all we could hear was the gentle lapping of the waves. After a few minutes, when I felt sure he was about to retrace his steps, he woke the oarsmen who happened to be sleeping in their boat, and asked them to row him over to the city. I don't know how much money he offered them, but I saw that, after some reluctance, they agreed.

Elisiário got into the boat, which immediately set off, the oars plying the water, and away he went, my Latin teacher and mathematics tutor, until he was lost in the night and the sea. I was lost, too, far from the center and utterly exhausted. Fortunately, I found a cab crossing Campo de São Cristóvão as wearily as me, but, equally fortunately, the driver took pity on me, and no doubt needed the money.

"It's a shame you didn't come with me to São Cristóvão the other night. You don't know what you missed; it was a beautiful night and a lovely walk. When I got as far as the harbor at Igrejinha, I took a boat over to Saco do Alferes, which was quite a way from home, and so I stayed in a cheap hostel in Campo de Santa Ana. I was attacked by a dog in Saco, and by two more in Rua de São Diogo, but I didn't even notice the fleas in the guesthouse because I slept the sleep of the just. What about you?"

"Me?"

Not daring to lie in case he noticed and not daring to confess that I'd followed him, either, I replied briefly:

"Me? Oh, I, too, slept the sleep of the just."

"*Justus, justa, justum.*"

We were at the house in Rua do Lavradio. Elisiário had a coral pin in his shirtfront, which was the object of great surprise and excitement on the part of the other lads, who had never seen him wearing any kind of jewelry before. I was even more surprised later on when the others had left, for, hearing me mention that I didn't have enough money to buy a new pair of shoes, Elisiário removed the pin and told me to buy some shoes with the proceeds from that. I roundly refused, but, in the end, was obliged to accept. I didn't sell it or pawn it, however; instead, the following day, I asked for an advance from my father's agent, bought some new shoes, and took the ferryboat back so that I could restore the pin to its rightful owner. You should have seen the disconsolate look on Elisiário's face!

"But didn't you tell me the other night that it was a present from some-one?" I said when he urged me to keep it.

"Yes, I did, and it's true, but what use are coral pins to me? I think they look far better on others. Then again, since it was a present, I'll keep it. You're sure you don't want it?"

"Certainly not if it was a present."

"A birthday present, actually," he went on, staring absentmindedly at the pin. "I've just turned thirty-five. I'm getting old, my boy. I'll soon be claiming my pension and crawling off to die in some hole somewhere."

He had replaced the pin in his shirtfront.

"You mean it was your birthday and you didn't tell me?"

"Why should I? So that you could come and visit me? I never receive guests on my birthday. I usually have supper with my old friend Dr. Lousada, who also writes the occasional poem, and the other day he pre-sented me with a sonnet printed on blue paper. I've got it at home. It's not bad, actually."

"Was he the one who gave you the pin?"

"No, it was his daughter. One line of his sonnet is very similar to one by Camões. My old friend knows his classics, and he's a fine doctor, too, but the best thing about him is his kind heart."

I heard that two politician friends of his had once encouraged Elisiário to become a deputy, thinking that he would make a fine orator in the Chamber. He didn't refuse, exactly, but the project foundered amid much laughter when he asked his friends if they could possibly lend him a few political ideas.

I like to think that it wasn't that he lacked ideas, rather that he had too many, and all so contradictory that they never amounted to an opinion. His thoughts depended on the mood of the moment, whether he felt himself to be an exalted liberal or a monarchy-loving conservative. The main rea-son for his refusal to become a deputy was his complete inability to obey a party, a leader, or any rules and regulations. If he had been free to change the hours when the deputies were in session, to have one session in the morning, another at night, another in the early hours, depending on when he felt like attending, with no order of business, but free to discuss anything from the rings of Saturn to the sonnets of Petrarch, then my wanderer would gladly have accepted the post, as long as he was not actually obliged to do anything, whether that meant remaining silent or speaking when he was called upon.

Anyway, that was the man captured in that photograph in 1862. He was, in short, a good and very talented man, a fascinating conversationalist, a gentle, restless soul, distrustful and impatient, with no future and no past, with no nostalgia for what was or ambitions for what might be, in short, a wanderer. Except . . . but I've been talking for far too long without the benefit of a cigar. Do you mind? And while I'm lighting my cigar, please take another look at that photo, but ignore the eyes, which haven't come out well at all; they look like the piercing eyes of an inquisitorial cat, as if they wanted to drill into our consciousness. And yet they weren't like that at all: he tended to look more inward than outward, but when he did turn his gaze outward, he seemed to see everything everywhere.

Except on that one evening, at around seven o'clock, when it was already dark, and my friend Elisiário turned up at my boardinghouse. I hadn't seen him for three weeks, and since I was studying for my exams and spending more time closeted in my room, I hadn't really noticed his absence. Besides, by then I was accustomed to his occasional eclipses. I was just about to go out and had extinguished my candle, leaving the room in darkness, when the tall, lean figure of Elisiário appeared in the doorway. He came in, went straight over to a chair, and I sat down near him, asking where he had been. Elisiário embraced me, sobbing. I was so surprised, I said nothing, but returned his embrace. Finally, he dried his eyes on the handkerchief he usually carried screwed up in one hand and gave a long sigh. I think he continued to weep quietly, though, because now and then he would again dab at his eyes. Feeling more and more alarmed, I waited for him to tell me what was wrong, then, at last, I murmured:

"What is it? What's happened?"

"I got married on Saturday, Tosta . . ."

My amazement grew still greater, but I didn't have time to ask for any further explanation, because Elisiário immediately went on to say that he had married out of gratitude, not love. Disastrous. I didn't know how to respond to this confidence, barely able to believe what he was saying, and mainly because I didn't understand why he was so downcast, so sad. As I realized later on, I did not know then who the real Elisiário was. I thought there must be some other reason apart from his marriage; perhaps his wife was an idiot or a consumptive, but who would have forced him to marry an invalid?

"Disastrous!" he muttered to himself. "Disastrous!"

When I stood up, saying I would light a candle, Elisiário grabbed the tail of my frock coat.

"No, don't embarrass me by lighting a candle. I'd rather tell you about this whole disastrous business in the dark. Yes, married! Disastrous. Not because she doesn't love me; on the contrary, apparently she's been madly in love with me for seven years. She's twenty-five . . . A kind creature! Just disastrous!"

The word "disastrous" kept recurring throughout the conversation. I was so eager to know the rest of the story that I was almost holding my breath; but I learned very little more, because, after he had stammered out a few more disconnected words, he stopped. All I could glean from him was that his wife was the daughter of Dr. Lousada, his protector and friend, the same woman who had given him the coral pin. Elisiário suddenly fell silent, and, after a few moments, as if filled with regret or embarrassment, he begged me not to tell anyone else what had taken place in that room.

"You know me better than that . . ."

"Yes, I do, which is why I came here. I could think of no one else I could confide in. But I'll go now and say nothing more, there's no point. You're young, Tosta, and if you feel no real vocation for marriage, then don't marry, either out of gratitude or out of self-interest. It will be utter torment. Good-bye. I won't tell you where I live, because I live with my father-in-law now, so don't come looking for me."

He embraced me again and left. I stood watching from the door of my room. By the time it had occurred to me that I should have shown him out, it was too late; he had already reached the last few steps. The oil lamp barely lit the stairs, and he was descending them very slowly, clinging to the banister, his head bowed and his vast, once-jolly overcoat looking distinctly sad.

I did not see him again until ten months later. Initially, this was because I had gone to Ceará to see my father during the holidays. When I returned, I heard that he had left for Rio Grande do Sul. Then one day, over lunch, I read in the newspapers that he had arrived back in Rio de Janeiro the previous day, and I hurried off in search of him. I found him in Santa Teresa, in a tiny house, with a garden not much bigger. He embraced me warmly; we spoke about the past, and I asked about his poetry.

"I published a volume of my poems in Porto Alegre. I didn't want to, but my wife was so insistent that, in the end, I gave in. She copied them out herself. It still contains a few errors, though, so I'm going to get a second edition published here."

Elisiário gave me a copy of the book, but wouldn't allow me to read any of the poems there and then. He wanted only to talk about times past. He had lost his father-in-law, who had left him a little money, and he was planning to take up teaching again, to see if he could reawaken old emotions. Whatever happened to the lads who used to live in Rua do Lavradio? He recalled former pleasures, long nights full of noisy talk and laughter, which, in turn, sparked similar memories in me, and thus we spent a good two hours. When I stood up to leave, he asked me to stay for supper.

"You haven't met my wife yet," he said. And, going over to the door, he called: "Cintinha!"

"Coming!" a sweet voice answered.

Dona Jacinta appeared immediately afterward. She was twenty-six, short rather than tall, plain rather than pretty, but with a kind, serious face and a very serene manner. When he told her my name, she looked at me, startled.

"He's a good-looking lad, isn't he?"

She agreed, nodding modestly. Elisiário told her I would be dining with them, and she left the room to inform the cook.

"She's a good woman," he said, "devoted and helpful and, it would seem, she adores me. I never have any buttons missing off my jackets now, which is a shame, really. The missing buttons were far better. Do you remember that old overcoat of mine? 'Such was the scope of Elisiário's cope . . .'"

"Of course I remember."

"I think it lasted me five years. I wonder where it is now. I should really dedicate a funeral ode to it, with an epigraph from Horace!"

We had a very jolly supper, although Dona Jacinta said little, leaving me and her husband to spend all our time reminiscing. As in the old days, he, of course, gave a few eloquent speeches, to which his wife listened enraptured. Elisiário forgot about us, and she forgot about herself, and I found in his words the same strong, vibrant voice. When he finished one of these speeches, he always tended to remain silent for a while. Digesting what he had just said? Continuing to think about it all? Allowing himself to be carried away by the sheer music of his own words? I really don't know, but he had retained that habit of remaining briefly silent, oblivious to anyone else there with him. When he did this, his wife fell silent, too, gazing at him, filled not with thoughts, but with admiration. This happened twice that evening, and on both occasions she looked almost pretty.

After coffee, Elisiário announced that he would walk down with me to the city.

"Is that all right, Cintinha?"

Dona Jacinta smiled at me, as if to say that such a request was quite unnecessary. She also mentioned her husband's book of poetry.

"Elisiário's so lazy. You must help me to get him to work harder."

Half an hour later, he and I were walking down the hill. Elisiário admitted that, since he had married, he'd had little opportunity to recall his bachelor days, and when we reached the center, he suggested we go to the theater.

"But you didn't say anything about that to your wife."

"Oh, I'll tell her later. Cintinha's very good. She won't mind. Which theater shall we choose?"

In the end, we chose none of them, but spoke of other things, and at nine o'clock he set off back home. I returned to Santa Teresa a few days later, but he wasn't in. His wife, though, urged me to wait, saying that he wouldn't be long.

"He's gone to visit someone just around the corner. He'll be really pleased to see you."

While she spoke, she discreetly closed the book she was reading and placed it on one end of the table. We talked about her husband, and she asked me if I considered him to be a great intellect, a great poet, a great orator, in short, a great man. She didn't use quite those words, but it amounted to the same thing. Since I genuinely did admire him, I agreed absolutely, and the pleasure with which she heard me say this was reward enough for the effort I put into giving due emphasis to my words.

"You're quite right to have him as your friend," she concluded. "He's always spoken very warmly about you and said you were a very serious young man."

There were fresh flowers in the study and a bird in a cage. All very orderly, everything in its place—clear evidence of his wife's hand. Elisiário arrived shortly afterward; he was clean-shaven and looking very smart and fresh, complete with a carefully tied cravat. It was only then that I noticed the difference between this Elisiário and the old one. The slight incoherence of his gestures was far less marked now, almost nonexistent. All his former restlessness and awkwardness had vanished. As soon as he entered the room, his wife left us so as to order some coffee to be brought, then returned shortly afterward, carrying some sewing.

"No, senhora, first we must do our Latin," Elisiário roared.

Dona Jacinta blushed scarlet, but obediently went to fetch the book she'd been reading when I arrived.

"You can trust Tosta," Elisiário went on. "He won't say anything to anyone."

Then, turning to me, he added:

"It wasn't my idea, you know. She was the one who wanted to study Latin."

I didn't believe him, and wanted to spare her the Latin lesson, but she herself gaily took up her grammar book. Once she'd recovered from her embarrassment, she did her lesson like any good pupil. She listened attentively, took pleasure in pronouncing the words, and was clearly keen to learn. When they'd finished their Latin, Elisiário wanted to move on to history, but this time she refused, not wanting to get in the way of our conversation. I was astonished and heaped praise on them both, although, in fact, I found that conjugal Latin lesson so preposterous that I could find no explanation for it, nor did I dare ask for one.

My visits became more frequent. I would occasionally dine with them, but on Sundays I only ever had lunch there. Dona Jacinta was perfect. You can't imagine how delightful she was in every way, and yet she never lost her composure and always talked very gravely and sensibly. She was skilled at all kinds of needlework, despite the Latin and history her husband was teaching her. She dressed very simply, her hair combed smoothly back, and she never wore any jewelry; this could have been an affectation, but she was so sincere in everything she did that it seemed as natural in her as did everything else.

On Sundays, we lunched in the garden. I would find Elisiário waiting eagerly for me at the front door. His wife would be putting the finishing touches to the flowers and foliage that would adorn the table, and she always drew up a menu decorated with poetic emblems and with each course named after one of the muses. Since she and her husband were not rich and our appetites not that large, there was never room for all the muses, but those who could duly joined us for lunch. It was over lunch that, in the early days, Elisiário would improvise, usually poems with ten-line stanzas—his preferred length; later, he reduced the number of stanzas and they rarely went beyond one or two. Then Dona Jacinta asked him to begin composing sonnets, and she and I would copy them down in pencil, making any corrections he asked for. He would laugh and say: "But what do you want with these poems?" In the end, to his wife's great sadness and to mine, too, he got out of the habit. They were good poems, and they came easily to him. All they lacked was the old fire.

One day, I asked Elisiário why he didn't publish a new edition of his poems, which, he had told me, contained a number of errors; I would, I said, gladly help with the proofreading. Dona Jacinta enthusiastically seconded this proposal.

"All right," he said. "I will one day. We could even start on Sunday."

On Sunday, when Dona Jacinta was alone with me for a moment, she asked me not to forget our proposal.

"No, don't worry, I won't."

"And don't waver if he tries to put off starting work," she went on. "He'll probably suggest postponing it for another time, but you must dig your heels in, and say no, that you'll be angry and never come back . . ."

She squeezed my hand very hard, and I was astonished to find that her hand was trembling, like the hand of a lover. I did as she asked, and she backed me up, but, even so, it took half an hour before he would sit down to work. In the end, he asked us to wait while he went to fetch the book.

"This time, we have victory," I said.

Dona Jacinta looked doubtful and her mood switched from joy to despair.

"Elisiário is terribly lazy. We never manage to finish anything. Haven't you noticed that he only composes poems if we insist, and that now he hardly composes any? He could write prose as well, even if it was only those improvised speeches of his, but even they are getting few and far between. I'm always offering to write down whatever he dictates. I get out pen and paper and I wait, but he just laughs, makes a joke, and says he's not in the mood."

"Well, he probably isn't always in the mood."

"Maybe not, but then I say that I'm ready for whenever inspiration strikes, that he just has to call me, but he never does. He's always full of plans, and I get all excited about them, but they never go beyond being plans. And yet the book he published in Porto Alegre was well received. You could encourage him."

"Encourage him? He doesn't need encouragement; all he needs is his enormous natural talent."

"I know," she said, coming closer, her eyes aflame. "But it's a terrible shame to see such talent wasted!"

"We'll find that talent again. I'll have to start treating him as if he were younger than me. We should never have let him fall into such idleness."

Elisiário returned with a copy of the book, but without pen or paper, and Dona Jacinta went off to fetch those. We began the work of revision; the plan was to amend not just any typographical errors, but the text itself. The novelty of the exercise kept our poet engaged for nearly two whole hours, although, to be honest, most of that time was filled by him telling us the stories that lay behind the poems or about the various dedicatees, of whom there were many, for a large proportion of the poems were dedicated to friends or to men in the public eye. Inevitably, we got very little done, twenty pages at most. Elisiário announced then that he was tired, and so we stopped working and never returned to it.

Dona Jacinta even asked her husband to leave it to us to make the corrections; he could check the amended version afterward and that would be that. Elisiário refused, saying that he would see to everything, we just had to wait, there was no hurry. But, as I said, we never returned to that book. He rarely improvised now, and since he lacked the patience to write anything down, he composed fewer and fewer poems. Those he did compose were feeble and repetitive. We nevertheless tried to suggest bringing out another book, collecting together what poems there were, and before we even proposed this to him, she and I actually put together an anthology. All that it needed then was for him to correct it. Elisiário agreed to do this, but, as before, our project came to nothing. He rarely made speeches now. His pleasure in language was dying. He spoke pretty much as we all speak; he was now not even a shadow of that cornucopia of ideas, images, phrases, which revealed the poet behind the orator. In the end, he hardly spoke; he received me cordially, but unenthusiastically. He became deeply bored. After only a few years of marriage, Dona Jacinta found herself with a husband who was orderly and quiet, but cold and uninspired. She began to change, too, no longer urging him to write new poems or to correct old ones. She became as dull as him. Suppers and lunches at their house were like those in any other unlettered household. Dona Jacinta was careful not to touch on a subject that was painful to her and to her husband; I did the same. When I graduated from university, Elisiário wrote a sonnet in my honor, but he found it very hard work, and it wasn't nearly as good as the sonnets that the old Elisiário used to write.

Dona Jacinta was not so much sad as disenchanted, and the reason for this would be hard to understand without some knowledge of what had led her into marriage.

As far as I could gather and observe, she never truly loved the man she married. Elisiário thought she loved him and said as much, because her father had always believed it to be true love. The truth is, though, that what Dona Jacinta felt for him was merely admiration. She had always nursed a purely intellectual passion for him, and, initially, had never even considered marriage. Elisiário's visits to Dr. Lousada's house were the high points of her life, listening to his seemingly endless supply of poems, new and old, those he knew by heart and those he improvised on the spot. And even when he wasn't reciting poetry, she was content simply to listen to and admire him. Elisiário, who had known her since she was a child, would talk to her as if to a younger sister. Then he realized that she was more intelligent than most women, and had a real feeling for poetry and art, which marked her out as far superior. He genuinely respected her, but it went no further than that.

And so the years passed, until Dona Jacinta came up with a plan to dedicate her life to him. She knew about the wasted days, the staying up into the small hours talking or walking, the incoherence and disorder of a life that seemed doomed to end in futility. He lacked all drive or ambition, but Dona Jacinta believed in Elisiário's genius. He had many admirers, but none of them shared her brightly burning faith or deep, silent devotion. Her plan was to marry him. Once they were married, she would give him the ambition he lacked, the drive, the habit of regular, methodical, and, of course, abundant work. Instead of wasting his time and inspiration on futile things or idle conversations, he would compose brilliant works when he was at his inspired best, which he nearly always was. The great poet would at last be revealed to the world. Once she had decided on marrying him, she easily persuaded her father to collaborate, although without admitting the secret, underlying reason, which would have been to admit to him that she wasn't marrying for love. Indeed, she told him that she really did love Elisiário.

True, there was something romantic about her plan, but it was more an act of mercy, with its roots in her deep admiration for him; it could even be seen as a sacrifice. She may have had other suitors, but she had never thought about marriage, until that one generous idea occurred to her, to seduce the poet. And he, as we know, married out of gratitude.

The result was quite contrary to all her hopes. Far from being crowned with laurels, the poet donned a monkish cowl and sent poetry packing. He became a mere nothing. In the end, he didn't even read great works of literature. Dona Jacinta suffered greatly; she saw her dream vanishing, and although she did not lose, but rather gained Latin, she lost the sublime language in which she hoped to speak to the ambitions of a great mind. The conclusion she reached was still less consoling. She concluded that marriage had killed an imagination that could only find inspiration in bachelor freedom. She was filled with remorse. And, as well as failing to find the pleasures of marital life with Elisiário, she lost the one advantage of her intended sacrifice.

She was, of course, wrong. For me, Elisiário remained the same wanderer he had always been, even though he appeared to be entirely settled; but his was a talent that could not last; it would have died even if he hadn't married. It wasn't order that took away his inspiration. True, disorder was better suited to someone so restless and solitary, but peace and method would not have destroyed him as a poet if the poetry in him had not been merely a youthful fever . . . Indeed, in my own case, poetry turned out to be nothing more enduring than an adolescent cold. So, concluded Tosta, kissing his wife, ask me for my love and you shall have it, but don't ask me for poetry, which I abandoned long ago.

ETERNAL

"**D**ON'T TELL ME," I said, going into his room. "It's that business with the baroness, isn't it?"

Norberto dried his eyes and sat on the edge of the bed, his legs dangling. I sat astride a chair, resting my chin on the chair back, and gave the following brief speech:

"How often must I tell you, you little fool, to give up on this ridiculous, humiliating passion of yours? Yes, 'ridiculous' and 'humiliating,' because she doesn't even know you exist. Besides, it's dangerous. You don't agree? Well, you'll find out soon enough when the baron starts to suspect you of setting your cap at his wife. He certainly doesn't look like the sweetest-tempered of men."

Norberto clutched his head in despair. Having waited for me in the street until nearly one o'clock in the morning, opposite the boardinghouse where I lived, he had finally written a letter, begging me to go to him and offer comfort and advice; in the letter he told me he hadn't slept, that he'd received a terrible blow; he even talked of drowning himself. Despite the terrible blow that I, too, had received, I went to see my poor friend. We were both the same age, both of us studying medicine, the only difference being that I was currently repeating my third year, which I had failed out of sheer idleness. Norberto was still living with his parents; I was less fortunate, having lost both of mine, and I lived on an allowance from an uncle in Bahia, and on the debts that this good old man paid off for me every six months.

He would then write me a letter full of invective, which always concluded by saying that I must continue my studies and become a doctor. But why? I asked myself. If neither the sun, the moon, the girls, nor the best Ville-gas cigars were doctors, what was the point in my becoming one? And so I laughed and played and let the weeks and the creditors roll by.

I've just mentioned receiving a terrible blow of my own. This came in a letter from that same uncle, and arrived at the same time as Norberto's, on the same morning. I opened my uncle's letter first and read it, horri-fied. He no longer addressed me in his usual familiar way, but stiffly and formally: "Senhor Simeão Antônio de Barros, I have had enough of throw-ing my money away on you, sir. If you wish to finish your studies, then come and enroll in a university up here and live with me. If not, then you must find your own money, because you will receive nothing more from me." I crumpled up the letter, stared hard at a very bad lithograph of the Viscount of Sepetiba—which had always been there in my boardinghouse room, hanging from a nail on the wall—and called him every name under the sun, from madman downward. I bawled at him that he could keep his money, that I was twenty years old, which was the very first of the rights of man, and took precedence over uncles and all other social conventions.

My imagination—always my mother and my friend—immediately came up with endless possible sources of income, which would mean I could dis-pense with the paltry amount doled out by a miserly old man; however, after that initial defiant response, I reread the letter and began to see that the solution was not as easy as it seemed. Those other possible sources might be good and even reliable, but I had grown so accustomed to visiting Rua da Quitanda to collect my monthly allowance and then spend it twice over, that I would find it very hard to adopt any other system.

It was then that I opened my friend Norberto's letter and ran straight to his house. You already know what his letter said and saw him clutch his head in despair. What you do not know is that, having made that gesture, he eyed me gravely and said he had hoped to hear rather different words of advice from me.

"Such as?"

He did not respond.

"Should I tell you to buy a pistol or a lockpick, or perhaps some narcotic or other?"

"Why are you making fun of me?"

"To make a man of you."

Norberto shrugged, and one corner of his mouth lifted slightly in scornful sneer. What kind of man? What did it mean to be a man if not to love the divinest creature on earth and to die for her?

The Baroness of Magalhães, the cause of this madness, had recently arrived from Bahia with her husband, who, before he became a baron—a title acquired to please his fiancée—had been just plain Antônio José Soares de Magalhães. They were newly married; the baroness was about twenty-four, some thirty years younger than the baron. She really was very beautiful. Her childhood name had been Iaiá Lindinha, the Pretty Young Miss. The baron was an old friend of Norberto's father, and the two families were immediately thrown together.

"Die for her?" I said.

Norberto swore that he truly was capable of killing himself for her sake. She was such a mysterious creature! Her voice seeped into his very bones. And, saying this, he writhed about on the bed, pummeling his head and biting the pillows. He would stop occasionally, panting, then resume these convulsions, muffling his sobs and cries so that no one would hear him on the next floor.

Since the arrival of the baroness, I had grown accustomed to my friend's tears, and so I waited for them to cease. When they did not, I left my chair, went over to the bed, and yelled at him that he was behaving like a child, and that I was leaving. Norberto grabbed my hand to make me stay and explained that he had not yet told me the worst part.

"That's true. What is it?"

"They're leaving. We visited them yesterday, and I heard them say they were taking the boat to Bahia."

"To Bahia?"

"Yes."

"Then they'll be on the same boat as me."

I told him about my uncle's letter, and how he had ordered me to enroll in a Bahian university and live with him. Norberto listened in astonishment. In Bahia? Then we could go together; we were close friends, his parents would surely not refuse this favor to our youthful friendship. Despite the many tears that she would shed to lose her son, his mother gave in more quickly than we had imagined. His father, however, would not agree. No amount of pleading and persuading could change his mind; I had managed to get the baron involved in our plan, too, but even he could not get his old friend to allow his son to go with him, not even with the promise that he would take him into his own house and watch over him. Norberto's father proved utterly immovable.

You can imagine my friend's despair. I spent Friday night at his house with his family, and stayed until eleven o'clock. On the pretext of spending my last night in Rio together, he came back to my boardinghouse, and the tears he wept were so many and so bitter that I could neither doubt his passion nor presume to console him, it being the first passion he had experienced. Up until then, we had both known only the small change of love; and, alas for him, the first really valuable coin he had found was made not of gold or silver, but of iron, hard iron, like that of old Lycurgus, forged in the fire, then cooled in the same vinegar bath.

We did not sleep at all. Norberto wept and moaned, calling for death to come, making absurd and terrifying plans. As I was packing my bags, I kept trying to console him, but this only made matters worse; it was like inviting a gimpy leg to a dance. I managed to get him to smoke a cigar, then another, and he ended up smoking dozens of them, but never finishing one. At around three o'clock in the morning, he was talking about running away from Rio de Janeiro, not immediately, but in a few days' time, on the first steamship that would take him. I managed to dissuade him from this, purely in his own interests.

"If it would be of any use, then, fine," I said, "but not if you have no idea how you will be received when you simply turn up on her doorstep, because if she doesn't care for you, she might well guess the reason behind your journey and refuse to see you."

"How do you know?"

"I don't. But there's no guarantee that she'll welcome your visit. Do you think she really cares for you?"

"Possibly, possibly not."

He described incidents, gestures, words, all either ambiguous or insignificant; then came another tearful interlude, more breast-beating, more anguished cries, and I began to feel his pain and to suffer with him; reason gave way to compassion, and we melted into a single sorrow. And that is why I made this promise:

"I have an idea. I'll travel to Bahia with them; after all, since we know each other already, I'll probably visit them there. If so, I'll try to sound her out. If I see that she doesn't care for you one jot, then I'll write to you, advising you frankly that you should look elsewhere; however, if I detect so much as a tiny tremor of affection, I'll let you know, and only then, for good or ill, can you get on that boat."

Norberto was thrilled with this plan. It was, at least, a hope. He made me swear that I would keep my word, that I would fearlessly observe her, and he, for his part, swore that he would not waver for an instant. He urged me not to miss a thing, saying that sometimes the smallest gesture could be worth its weight in gold, that a single word could be a whole book; and he asked me, please, if I could, to tell her of the despairing state in which I had left him. To further shore up my determination, he said that disappointment would kill him, because his love, being eternal, would find rest only in death and eternity. I couldn't bring myself to tell him that this was tantamount to obliging me to send only good news. At the time, though, all I could do was to weep with him.

Dawn witnessed our immoral pact. I would not allow him to come on board to say goodbye, and I left. Let us not talk about the voyage . . . O epic seas of Homer, whipped up by Eurus, Boreas, and violent Zephyrus, you may buffet brave Ulysses all you like, but whatever you do, do not afflict him with seasickness. That is best left to our modern-day seas, and especially for those that carried me from Rio to Bahia. Only when we had nearly reached our destination did I dare to appear before our magnificent lady, who was as calm and composed as if she had merely taken a longer-than-usual walk.

"Do you miss Rio?" I asked as an introit.

"Of course."

The baron joined us to point out to me the places we could see from the ship, or the location of others that remained out of sight. He invited me to their house in Bonfim. My uncle came on board, and, despite his attempt to maintain a stern demeanor, I could tell that he had a good heart and that he saw in me his late sister's only child, and saw, too, that I was prepared to be obedient. My first impressions could not have been better. Ah, divine youth! These new things were more than enough to compensate for the old things I had left behind.

I spent the first few days getting to know the city, but it was not long before I received a letter from my friend Norberto, reminding me of his plight. I duly went to visit Bonfim. The Baroness—or Iaiá Lindinha, the name by which everyone still knew her—received me with such good grace, and her husband was so kind and hospitable, that I felt ashamed of my mission. That shame was short-lived, though, for I could feel my friend's despair, and the need either to console or to undeceive him was more important than anything else. Oddly enough, now that they were separated, I confess that I began to hope that she did actually like him, which was precisely what I had always refused to believe earlier. Perhaps it was a desire to see him happy, or perhaps merely the promptings of vanity, that made me hope I would prove victorious and save the poor unfortunate.

Inevitably, we talked about Rio de Janeiro. I told her the things I missed most, we spoke of familiar sights, the streets that were almost part of my very being, the faces I saw every day, the houses, the friendships. Ah, yes, friendships were what bound one most closely to a place. I had friends, Norberto's parents, for example—

"Two angels!" she said, interrupting me. "My husband, who has known the gentleman for many years, has told me some interesting things about him. Did you know that he was passionately in love with his wife when they married?"

"That doesn't surprise me. The son is clearly the fruit of that love. Do you know my poor Norberto well?"

"Yes, he often came to our house."

"No, I'm afraid you don't know him at all well."

Iaiá Lindinha frowned slightly.

"Forgive me for contradicting you," I went on urgently. "But you don't know the kindest, purest, most ardent soul in God's creation. You might think me somewhat biased because he's my friend, but the truth is, he is the person who binds me closest to Rio de Janeiro. Poor Norberto! He is a man made for two careers at once, archangel and hero—born both to tell the earth about the delights of heaven and, if necessary, to carry our human lamentations up there too . . ."

Only when I finished this speech did I realize how ridiculous it was. Iaiá Lindinha either didn't think it ridiculous or pretended not to; she said only that I clearly valued my friend greatly, but that while he had seemed a very nice person, he was not exactly cheerful company or else appeared to suffer from frequent bouts of melancholia. People told her that he studied a great deal . . .

"Oh, yes, he does."

I did not insist so as not to rush things, but, please, dear reader, do not condemn me out of hand. I know the part I played was not exactly a pretty one, but this did all happen twenty-seven years ago. I put my trust in Time, that most noble of alchemists. Give Time a dollop of mud, and it will turn the mud into diamonds, or, at the very least, grit. It's the same when a statesman writes and publishes an utterly unscrupulous volume of memoirs, omitting nothing, not even private conversations or government secrets, not even love affairs of an extremely personal and unconfessable nature. The scandal that ensues! People will—quite rightly—say that the author is a cynic, unworthy of the men who put their trust in him and of the women who loved him. A perfectly sincere and legitimate outcry, because public life imposes many barriers; the politeness and respect one owes to the women one has loved both demand silence . . .

However, allow the years to fall, drip by drip, into the bucket of a century, and once the century is full, the book becomes a historical document, psychological, anecdotal. It will be read purely as a study of the private lives and loves of our age, of how governments were built up and torn down, of whether women at the time were more forward or more discreet, how elections and flirtations were conducted, whether people wore shawls or cloaks, what vehicles we used, whether we wore our pocket watches on the right or the left, along with a multitude of other interesting details about our public and private history. That is why I hope not to be condemned outright by the consciences of my readers. After all, it was twenty-seven years ago!

I spent more than six months knocking at the door of that heart to see if I might find Norberto in there, but no one answered, not even the husband. Nevertheless, the letters I sent to my poor friend somehow managed to convey neither hope nor despair. Some were actually more hopeful than despairing. The affection I felt for him and for my own pride combined forces to arouse in her at least some curiosity and intrigue about that remote, possible mystery.

By then I had become firm friends with the couple, and often visited them. When three whole nights passed without my going to their house, I would be filled with torment and unrest, and when I rushed to see them on the fourth night, she would be waiting for me at the door, calling me all kinds of ugly things, ungrateful, idle, indifferent. This name-calling eventually ceased, but the person would still be there waiting, her sometimes tremulous hand ready to squeeze mine, or was it my hand that trembled?

I'm not sure. Sometimes, when the moment came to say good night, I would stand beneath a window and say softly:

"I won't be able to come tomorrow."

"Why?" she would ask.

And I would explain either that I had to study or that I had promised to help my uncle. While she never tried to dissuade me, she was clearly disappointed. My letters to Norberto became less frequent and, when I did write, I hardly mentioned Iaiá Lindinha, as if I rarely went to her house. I used various different formulas: "Yesterday, near the palace, I bumped into the baron, who told me that his wife is well." Or: "Do you know who I saw at the theater the other night? The baroness." To avoid coming face-to-face with my own hypocrisy, I never reread my letters. For his part, Norberto also wrote less often, and then only briefly. His name was never spoken between me and her; we silently agreed that he had died, a sad death with none of the usual funeral pomp.

We skirted around the abyss, both of us insisting that it was merely a reflection of the celestial dome—a contradiction in terms for those who are not in love. Death finally solved the problem by carrying off the baron with an attack of apoplexy, on the twenty-third of March, 1861, at six o'clock in the evening. He was an excellent man, and his widow repaid him with prayers for the love she had failed to give him.

When, three months later, once the period of mourning was over, I asked her to marry me, Iaiá Lindinha was neither surprised nor outraged. On the contrary, she said yes, but not yet. She imposed one condition, that I must first finish my studies and qualify as a doctor. And she said this with lips that seemed to be the one book of the world, the universal book, the best of academies, the school of schools. I argued my case, but she heard me unmoved. The reason she gave was that my uncle might think that, once married, I would interrupt my studies.

"And he would be right," she concluded. "I will only marry a doctor."

We both kept that promise. For a while, she went traveling in Europe with one of her sisters-in-law and the latter's husband; and I missed her so much that those feelings became my hardest taskmasters. I studied patiently and abandoned all my former idle occupations. I graduated on the eve of our wedding, and I can say, without a hint of hypocrisy, that I found the priest's Latin far superior to the graduation address.

Some weeks later, Iaiá Lindinha asked if we could visit Rio de Janeiro.

I agreed to her request, but confess that I felt distinctly uncomfortable. We would be sure to run into my friend Norberto, always assuming he still lived there. We had not written to each other for three years, and our last letters had been brief and rather dull. Would he know about our marriage? Or about what led up to it? We went to Rio, and I said nothing to my wife of these anxieties.

What would be the point? It would, I told myself, mean owning up to a secret act of treachery. When we arrived in Rio, I wondered whether I should wait for him to visit me or if I should be the one to seek him out; I chose the second option, in order to explain the situation to him. I dreamed up certain special, curious circumstances engineered by Providence itself, the threads of whose web are always hidden from mankind. This was not a joke, you understand; in my mind, these were all serious justifications.

Four days later, I learned that Norberto was living near Rio Comprido; he was married. So much the better. I hurried to his house. In the garden, I found a wet nurse suckling a baby, and another child of about eighteen months was crouched on the ground, picking up pebbles.

"Master Bertinho, go and tell your mama that a gentleman is here, asking to speak to your Papa."

The child obeyed, but before he could return, my old friend Norberto came in through the garden gate. I recognized him at once, despite the thick sideburns he was wearing. We embraced each other warmly.

"What are you doing here? When did you arrive?"

"Yesterday."

"You've grown positively plump, my friend! Plump and handsome. Let's go inside. And what's wrong with *you*?" he said, bending down to Master Bertinho, who had his arms clasped about one of his legs.

He picked the boy up, lifted him into the air, and showered him with a profusion of kisses, then, holding him perched on one arm, he pointed to me:

"Do you know this young man?"

Master Bertinho regarded me in alarm, one finger in his mouth, as his father explained that I was a very old friend of Papa's, from the days when Grandma and Grandpa were still alive . . .

"Oh, so your parents are dead?"

Norberto nodded and turned back to his son, who now had his little hands pressed to his father's face, begging for more kisses. Then Norberto turned to the baby, and, without picking her up, spoke to her tenderly and called me over to see her. He gazed at her adoringly. She was five months old, he said, but if I came back in fifteen years' time, I'd find a big, strong, healthy girl. What arms! What fat fingers! Unable to resist, he bent over and kissed her.

"But come in and meet my wife. Stay for dinner."

"No, I'm afraid I can't."

"Mama's watching," said Master Bertinho.

I looked up and saw a young woman standing and waiting for us at the parlor door, which opened out onto the garden. We went up five steps and into the parlor. Norberto clasped her hands and kissed her twice. She tried to draw back, but, unable to escape, she blushed deeply.

"Don't be embarrassed, Carmela," he said. "Do you know who this gentleman is? He's Simeão Barros, the medical student I've often spoken to you about. By the way, Simeão, why did you never respond to our wedding invitation?"

"I never received it," I said.

"Well, I definitely put it in the post."

Carmela was listening to her husband admiringly, and, seeing this, he went and sat down next to her and secretly took her hand. I pretended not to notice, and I spoke about our university days, about mutual friends, politics, the war, anything to avoid him asking me if I was married. I was already regretting my visit; what would I say if he mentioned marriage and asked my wife's name? He said nothing, so perhaps he already knew.

The conversation dragged on, but, in the end, I insisted that I had to leave and got up to go. Carmela bade me a very friendly goodbye. She was very beautiful, and her eyes lent her face an almost saintly glow. Her husband clearly adored her.

"Did you look at her closely?" he asked me at the garden gate. "I won't even attempt to describe the love that binds us together, those are things that one feels but cannot put into words. What are you smiling at? Do you think me a child? I think I probably am, an eternal child, just as my love is eternal."

I got into my cab, promising that I would have supper with them one day soon.

"Eternal!" I thought. "Just like the love he once felt for my wife."

And, turning to the driver, I asked him:

"Is there anything that's truly eternal?"

"If you'll forgive me, sir," he said, "I think the tax collector who lives in my street is eternal, a right old rascal he is, sir. I'd give my soul to smack him in the face just once. He's definitely eternal, clinging on like a limpet, and he's got useful connections, too, apparently—well, that's what people say. Not that it's any of my business, really, but, yes, if I could smack him in the face just once . . ."

I didn't hear the rest. I sat absorbed in my own thoughts, lulled by the driver's voice droning on and on. Before I knew it, we had arrived in Rua da Glória. And the wretch was still talking. I paid him and walked down to Glória Beach, then along Rua do Russel to Flamengo Beach, where the sea was quite rough. I slowed my pace, and stood looking at the waves rising and falling. Like a line from a song, the question I had asked the driver kept repeating inside me: "Is there anything that's truly eternal?" The waves, more discreet than him, said nothing of their private troubles, but merely rose and fell, rose and fell.

I reached the Hotel dos Estrangeiros as dusk was coming on. My wife was waiting for me to have supper. On entering our room, I clasped her hands and asked her:

"Is there anything that's truly eternal, Iaiá Lindinha?"

She sighed and said:

"Why, you ungrateful boy! My love for you, of course."

I dined with no feelings of remorse; indeed, I felt serene and cheerful. Time! Give it a dollop of mud and it'll turn mud into diamonds . . .

MIDNIGHT MASS

I'VE NEVER QUITE understood a conversation I had with a lady many years ago, when I was seventeen and she was thirty. It was Christmas Eve. Having arranged to attend midnight mass with a neighbor, I had agreed that I would stay awake and call for him just before midnight.

The house where I was staying belonged to the notary Meneses, whose first wife had been one of my cousins. His second wife, Conceição, and her mother had both welcomed me warmly when, months before, I arrived in Rio de Janeiro from Mangaratiba to study for my university entrance exams. I led a very quiet life in that two-story house on Rua do Senado, with my books, a few friends, and the occasional outing. It was a small household, consisting of the notary, his wife, his mother-in-law, and two slave-women. They kept to the old routines, retiring to bed at ten and with everyone sound asleep by half-past. Now, I had never been to the theater, and more than once, on hearing Meneses announce that he was going, I would ask him to take me with him. On such occasions, his mother-in-law would pull a disapproving face, and the slave-women would titter; he, however, would not even reply, but would get dressed, leave the house, and not return until the following morning. Only later on did I realize that the theater was a euphemism in action. Meneses was having an affair with a lady who was separated from her husband and, once a week, he slept elsewhere. At first Conceição had found the existence of this mistress deeply wounding, but, in the end, she had resigned herself and grown accustomed to the situation, deciding that there was nothing untoward about it at all.

Good, kind Conceição! People called her "a saint," and she did full justice to that title, given how easily she put up with her husband's neglect. Hers was a very moderate nature, with no extremes, no tearful tantrums, and no great outbursts of hilarity. In this respect, she would have been fine as a Muslim woman and would have been quite happy in a harem, as long as appearances were maintained. May God forgive me if I'm misjudging her, but everything about her was contained and passive. Even her face was average, neither pretty nor ugly. She was what people call "a nice person." She never spoke ill of anyone and was very forgiving. She wouldn't have known how to hate anyone, nor, perhaps, how to love them.

On that particular Christmas Eve, the notary went off to the theater. It was around 1861 or 1862. I should have been in Mangaratiba on holiday, but I had stayed until Christmas because I wanted to see what midnight mass was like in the big city. The family retired to bed at the usual time, and I waited in the front room, dressed and ready. From there I could go out into the hallway and leave the house without disturbing anyone. There were three keys to the front door: the notary had one, I would take the second, and the third would remain in the house.

"But Senhor Nogueira, what will you do to fill the time?" Conceição's mother asked.

"I'll read, Dona Inácia."

I had with me a novel, *The Three Musketeers*, in an old translation published, I think, by the *Jornal do Commercio*. I sat down at the table in the middle of the room, and by the light of an oil lamp, while the rest of the house was sleeping, I once again climbed onto D'Artagnan's scrawny horse and set off on an adventure. I was soon completely intoxicated by Dumas. The minutes flew past, as they so rarely do when one is waiting; I heard the clock strike eleven, but barely took any notice, as if it were of no importance. However, the sound of someone stirring in the house roused me from my reading: footsteps in the passageway between the parlor and the dining room. I looked up and, soon afterward, saw Conceição appear in the doorway.

"Still here?" she asked.

"Yes, it's not yet midnight."

"Such patience!"

Conceição came into the room, her bedroom slippers flip-flapping. She was wearing a white dressing gown, loosely tied at the waist. She was quite thin and this somehow lent her a romantic air, rather in keeping with my adventure story. I closed the book, and she went and sat on the chair next to mine, near the couch. When I asked if I had unwittingly woken her by making a noise, she immediately said:

"No, not at all. I simply woke up."

I looked at her and rather doubted the truth of this. Her eyes were not those of someone who had been asleep, but of someone who had not yet slept at all. However, I quickly dismissed this observation—which might have borne fruit in someone else's mind—never dreaming that I might be the reason she hadn't gone to sleep and that she was lying so as not to worry or annoy me. She was, as I said, a kind person, very kind.

"It must be nearly time, though," I said.

"How do you have the patience to stay awake while your neighbor sleeps? And to wait here all alone too. Aren't you afraid of ghosts? I bet I startled you just now."

"I was a little surprised when I heard footsteps, but then you appeared immediately afterward."

"What were you reading? Don't tell me, I know: it's The *Three Musketeers*."

"Exactly. It's such a good book."

"Do you like novels?"

"I do."

"Have you read *The Dark-Haired Girl*?"

"By Macedo? Yes, I have it at home in Mangaratiba."

"I love novels, but I don't have much time to read anymore. What novels have you read?"

I began listing a few titles. Conceiçao listened, leaning her head against the chair back, looking at me fixedly through half-closed eyelids. Now and then, she would run her tongue over her lips to moisten them. When I finished speaking, she said nothing, and we sat in silence for a few seconds. Then, still gazing at me with her large, intelligent eyes, she sat up straight, interlaced her fingers, and rested her chin on them, her elbows on the arms of the chair.

"Perhaps she's bored," I thought. Then, out loud, I said:

"Dona Conceição, I think it must be nearly time, and I—"

"No, no, it's still early. I just looked at the clock and it's only half-past eleven. You still have time. If you ever do miss a night's sleep, can you get through the next day without sleeping at all?"

"I have in the past."

"I can't. If I miss a night's sleep, I'm no use for anything the next day and have to have a nap, even if it's only for half an hour. But then I'm getting old."

"What do you mean, 'old,' Dona Conceição?"

I spoke these words with such passion that it made her smile. She usually moved very slowly and serenely, but now she sprang to her feet, walked over to the other side of the room, and paced up and down between the window looking out onto the street and the door of her husband's study. Her modestly rumpled appearance made a singular impression on me. Although she was quite slender, there was something about that swaying gait, as if she were weighed down by her own body; I had never really noticed this until then. She paused occasionally to examine the hem of a curtain or to adjust the position of some object on the sideboard; finally, she stopped in front of me, with the table between us. Her ideas appeared to be caught in a very narrow circle; she again remarked on her astonishment at my ability to stay awake; I repeated what she already knew, that I had never attended midnight mass in Rio and did not want to miss it.

"It's just the same as mass in the countryside, well, all masses are alike, really."

"I'm sure you're right, but here it's bound to be more lavish and there'll be more people too. After all, Holy Week is much prettier in Rio than it is in the countryside. Not to mention the feasts of Saint John or Saint Anthony . . ."

She gradually leaned forward, resting her elbows on the marble table-top, her face cupped in her outspread hands. Her unbuttoned sleeves fell back to reveal her forearms, which were very pale and plumper than one might have expected. This was not exactly a novelty, although it wasn't a common sight, either; at that moment, however, it made a great impression on me. Her veins were so blue that, despite the dim light, I could count every one. Her presence was even better at keeping me awake than my book. I continued to compare religious festivals in the countryside and in the city, and to give my views on whatever happened to pop into my head. I kept changing the subject for no reason, talking about one thing, then going back to something I'd mentioned earlier, and laughing in the hope that this would make her smile, too, thus affording me a glimpse of her perfect, gleaming white teeth. Her eyes were very dark, almost black; her long, slender, slightly curved nose gave her face an interrogative air. When I raised my voice a little, she told me off:

"Ssh! You might wake Mama!"

Much to my delight, though, she didn't move from where she was, our faces very close. It really wasn't necessary to speak loudly in order to be heard; we were both whispering, I even more softly than her, because I was doing most of the talking. At times, she would look serious—very serious—even frowning slightly. She eventually grew tired and changed position and place. She walked around to my side of the table and sat down on the couch. I turned and could just see the toes of her slippers, but only for the time it took her to sit down, because her dressing gown was long enough to cover them. I remember that the slippers were black. She said very softly:

"Mama's room is quite some way away, but she sleeps so very lightly, and if she were to wake up now, it would take her ages to get back to sleep."

"I'm the same."

"What?" she asked, leaning forward to hear better.

I went and sat on the chair beside the couch and repeated what I'd said. She laughed at the coincidence of there being three light sleepers in the same house.

"Because I'm just like Mama sometimes: if I do wake in the night, I find it hard to go back to sleep, I toss and turn, get up, light a candle, pace up and down, get into bed again, but it's no use."

"Is that what happened tonight?"

"No, not at all," she said.

I couldn't understand why she denied this, and perhaps she couldn't, either. She picked up the two ends of her dressing-gown belt and kept flicking them against her knees, or, rather, against her right knee, because she had crossed her legs. Then she told some story about dreams, and assured me that she had only ever had one nightmare, when she was a child. She asked if I ever had nightmares. The conversation continued in this same slow, leisurely way, and I gave not a thought to the time or to mass. Whenever I finished some anecdote or explanation, she would come up with another question or another subject, and I would again start talking. Now and then she would hush me:

"Ssh! Speak more softly!"

There were pauses too. Twice I thought she had dropped asleep, but her eyes, which had closed for an instant, immediately opened again with no sign of tiredness or fatigue, as if she had merely closed them in order to see more clearly. On one such occasion, I think she became aware of my rapt gaze, and she closed her eyes again, whether quickly or slowly I can't recall. Other memories of that night appear to me as truncated or confused. I contradict myself, stumble. One memory does still remain fresh, though; at one point, she, who I had only thought of as "nice-looking" before, looked really pretty, positively lovely. She was standing up, arms folded; out of politeness, I made as if to stand up, too, but she stopped me, placing one hand on my shoulder and obliging me to sit down again. I thought she was about to say something, but, instead, she shivered, as if she suddenly felt cold, then turned and sat in the chair where I had been sitting when she entered the room. From there, she glanced up at the mirror above the couch and commented on the two engravings on the wall.

"They're getting old, those pictures. I've already asked Chiquinho to buy some new ones."

Chiquinho was her husband. The pictures exemplified the man's main interest. One was a representation of Cleopatra, and I can't remember the other one, but both were of women. They were perhaps rather vulgar, but, at the time, I didn't think them particularly ugly.

"They're pretty," I said.

"Yes, but they're rather faded now. And frankly I would prefer two images of saints. These are more suited to a boy's bedroom or a barber's shop."

"A barber's shop? But you've never been in one, have you?"

"No, but I imagine that, while they're waiting, the customers talk about girls and love affairs and, naturally, the owner brightens up the place with a few pretty pictures. The ones over there just don't seem appropriate in a family home. At least, that's what I think, but then I often have strange thoughts. Anyway, I don't like them. In my prayer niche I have a really beautiful statuette of Our Lady of the Conception, my patron saint, but you can't hang a sculpture on the wall, much as I would like to."

This talk of prayer niches reminded me of mass, and it occurred to me that it might be getting late, and I was just about to mention this. I did, I think, get as far as opening my mouth, but immediately closed it again to listen to what she was saying, so gently, touchingly, softly, that my soul grew indolent and I forgot all about mass and church. She was talking about her devotions as a child and as a young girl. She then moved on to stories about dances, about outings she'd made, memories of Paquetá, all woven almost seamlessly together. When she grew tired of the past, she spoke about the present, about her household duties and the burdens of family life, which, before she married, she had been told were many, but which were not, in fact, burdensome at all. She didn't mention that she was twenty-seven when she married, but I knew that already.

She was no longer pacing up and down as she had been to begin with, but stayed almost frozen in the same pose. She no longer kept her large eyes fixed on me, but glanced around at the walls.

"This room needs repapering," she said after a while, as if talking to herself.

I agreed, simply in order to say something and to try to shake off that strange, magnetic sleep or whatever it was trammeling my tongue and my senses. I both wanted and didn't want to end that conversation; I made an effort to take my eyes off her, and I did so out of a sense of respect, but then, fearing that she might think I was bored, when I wasn't at all, I quickly brought my gaze back to her. The conversation was gradually dying. Out in the street, utter silence reigned.

We sat without speaking for some time, I don't know for how long. The only sound came from the study, the faint noise of a mouse gnawing away at something, and this did at last rouse me from my somnolent state; I tried to speak, but couldn't. Conceição appeared to be daydreaming. Then, suddenly, I heard someone banging on the window outside, and a voice shouting:

"Midnight mass! Midnight mass!"

"Ah, there's your friend," she said, getting up. "How funny! You were the one who was supposed to wake him up, but there he is waking you. Off you go. It must be time."

"Is it midnight already?" I asked.

"It must be."

"Midnight mass!" came the voice again, accompanied by more banging on the window.

"Quick, off you go. Don't keep him waiting. It was my fault. Good night. See you tomorrow."

And, with the same swaying gait, Conceição slipped silently back down the corridor. I went out into the street, where my neighbor was waiting.

We set off to the church. More than once during mass, the figure of Conceição interposed itself between me and the priest, but let's put that down to my seventeen years. The following morning, over breakfast, I described the mass and the congregation, but Conceição showed not a flicker of interest. During the day, she was her usual natural, benign self and made no mention of our conversation the previous night. At New Year, I went home to Mangaratiba. By the time I returned to Rio in March, the notary had died of apoplexy. Conceição was living in Engenho Novo, but I neither visited her nor met her again. I later heard that she had married her late husband's articled clerk.

CANARY THOUGHTS

––––––––––

A KEEN ORNITHOLOGIST, Macedo by name, once told some friends a story so extraordinary that none of them believed him. Some even thought Macedo had lost his mind. Here is a summary of that tale.

I was walking down a street at the beginning of last month—he said—when a cab came careering past and almost knocked me over. I escaped by jumping into the doorway of a junk shop. Neither the clatter of horse and cab nor my sudden irruption into his shop roused the owner, who was in the back, dozing in a folding chair. He was a ruin of a man, with a grubby, straw-colored beard and, on his head, a tattered cap that had doubtless failed to find a buyer. He appeared to be a man without a past, unlike some of the objects he was selling, and yet he did not exude the air of austere, embittered sadness you might expect of a man who did once have a life.

The shop was dark and crammed with the bent, broken, grimy, rusty objects one usually finds in such places, and all in the state of semi-disorder one would expect. However banal, though, this motley collection of detritus was not without interest. Filling the area around the shop door were pots without lids, lids without pots, buttons, shoes, locks, a black skirt, straw hats and fur hats, picture frames, a pair of binoculars, tailcoats, a fencing foil, a stuffed dog, slippers, gloves, various nondescript vases, some epaulets, a velvet bag, two coat racks, a catapult, a thermometer, some chairs, a lithograph of a portrait by Sisson, a backgammon set, two wire masks for some future carnival, as well as other things I either didn't even see or have forgotten, all leaning or hanging or on display in equally ancient glass cases. Farther in there was still more shabby merchandise, mostly larger pieces of furniture, dressers and chairs and beds piled one on top of the other, lost in the gloom.

I was just about to leave when I spotted a cage hanging in the doorway. Like everything else, it was very old, and, in keeping with the general desolation, it should really have been empty, but it wasn't. A canary was hopping about inside. The little creature's color, animation, and grace lent a touch of life and youth to the surrounding junk. He was the last surviving passenger from a shipwreck, washed up on that shore, happy and unscathed. As soon as I saw him, he began to jump from perch to perch, as if to say that in the midst of that cemetery there was at least one ray of sunlight. I do not attribute that image to the canary, and I use it only because I am speaking now to rhetorically minded people; as he told me later on, he knew nothing of either cemeteries or sunlight. Carried away by the sheer pleasure he gave me, I felt indignant at his fate and murmured bitterly:

"What base owner could have had the heart to sell him for a few coins? Or what indifferent servant, not wishing to keep this, his late master's companion, gave him away for free to a small boy, who, in turn, sold him on so that he could buy a lottery ticket?"

The canary paused on the perch and trilled:

"Whoever you are, you're clearly not in your right mind. I had no owner, nor was I given to a child who then sold me on. Those are the imaginings of a sick mind; go cure yourself, my friend—"

"What?" I asked, interrupting him, without even having time to feel amazed. "So your owner didn't sell you to this shop? And it wasn't poverty or idleness that brought you to light up this cemetery like a ray of sunlight?"

"I don't know what 'sunlight' or 'cemetery' mean. If the other canaries you've known used the first of those words, so much the better, because it's a lovely word, but I think you're wrong."

"Excuse me, are you saying you came here of your own accord, without anyone's help, unless, of course, that man sitting over there is your owner?"

"My owner? That man is my servant, he gives me food and water every day and with such regularity that if I had to pay him for his services, it would cost me a pretty penny, but canaries don't pay their servants. Indeed, since the world belongs to canaries, it would be ridiculous for us to pay for something that already exists in that world."

Astonished by these responses, I didn't know which to find most amazing, his language or his ideas. His words emerged from him as charming trills, but entered my ears as if couched in our human language. I looked around to make sure I was indeed awake; yes, it was the same street, the same sad, damp, gloomy shop. Still hopping back and forth, the canary was waiting for me to speak. I asked him then if he didn't miss the infinite blue sky . . .

"My dear fellow," trilled the canary, "what does 'infinite blue sky' mean?"

"Tell me, then, what you think of this world. What *is* the world?"

"The world," responded the canary with a somewhat professorial air, "the world is a junk shop, with a small, square wicker cage hanging from a nail; the canary is the master of the cage he inhabits and of the surrounding shop. Everything else is illusion and lies."

At this point, the old man woke up and came shuffling over to me. He asked if I wanted to buy the canary, and I asked him if he had acquired it in the same way he had acquired the other things he was selling, and he told me that, yes, he had bought it from a barber, along with a set of razors.

"The razors are in very good condition," he said.

"No, I only want the canary."

I paid the asking price, took the canary home with me, bought a vast, circular cage made of wood and wire, which I ordered to be painted white and placed on the veranda, from where the bird could see the garden, the fountain, and a scrap of blue sky.

I intended to make a long study of this phenomenon, but would say nothing to anyone else until I had reached the point where I could dazzle the whole century with my extraordinary discovery. I began to alphabetize the canary's language, to study its structure, its links with music, the creature's aesthetic feelings, his ideas and memories. Having completed this initial philological and psychological analysis, I immersed myself in the history of canaries, their origins, their early history, the geology and flora of the Canary Islands, whether he had any knowledge of navigation, and so on. We talked for long hours, with me taking notes, and him waiting, hopping about, and trilling.

Since I had no other family than my two servants, I had ordered them not to interrupt me, not even with a letter or an urgent telegram or an important visitor. They both knew about my scientific interests and so found these instructions perfectly normal and did not suspect for a moment that the canary and I could understand each other.

Needless to say, I slept very little, waking two or three times in the night to pace aimlessly, feverishly about. Finally, I would return to my work, rereading, expanding, and amending my thoughts. I had to correct more than one of the canary's observations, either because I had misunderstood or because he had not expressed himself clearly enough. His definition of the world was one such example. Three weeks after he came to live in my house, I asked him to repeat his definition of the world.

"The world," he said, "is a fair-sized garden with a fountain in the middle, a few flowers and shrubs, a little grass, clear air and a scrap of blue up above; the canary, who is the master of this world, lives in a vast white circular cage, from which he views all these things. Everything else is illusion and lies."

The language he used underwent a few changes, too, and I realized that certain of my conclusions, which I had thought quite straightforward, were, in fact, positively rash. I could not yet write the article I intended to send to the National Museum, to the Historical Institute, and to various German universities, not because I lacked material, but because I still needed to compile and confirm all these observations. Latterly, I did not even leave the house or answer letters and I had no time for friends or relatives. I was pure canary. Each morning, one of the servants was tasked with cleaning the cage and giving the canary his food and water. The canary said nothing to him, as if he knew that the servant lacked any scientific training. Besides, the servant carried out this task in a very summary fashion, for he was not a lover of birds. One Saturday, I woke up feeling ill, my head and back aching. The doctor ordered complete rest; I had been overtaxing my brain and must neither read nor think; I must not even attempt to find out what was going on in the city and the world. I remained like this for five days, and on the sixth, I left my bed, only to discover that the canary had escaped while the servant was cleaning out its cage. My first impulse was to strangle my servant; overcome with rage, I slumped into a chair, my head spinning, unable to speak. The servant defended himself, swearing that he had taken every possible care, but that the bird had cunningly escaped . . .

"Didn't you look for him?"

"We did, sir. At first he flew up onto the roof, and I went after him, then he flew over to a tree and hid. I've been asking everywhere, the neighbors, the local farmers, but no one has seen him."

You can imagine my anguish. Fortunately, though, I had by then recovered from my exhausted state and, after only a few hours, I was able to go out onto the veranda and into the garden. Not a sign of the canary. I made inquiries, I went here, there, and everywhere, I advertised, but all in vain. I had already compiled my notes for the article, however truncated and incomplete, when I happened to visit a friend, who lived in one of the largest and most beautiful mansions in the area. We went for a stroll in the garden before supper, when I heard a voice trill out this question:

"Hello, Senhor Macedo, where did you disappear to?"

It was the canary. He was perched on the branch of a tree. You can imagine my feelings and what I said to him. My friend thought I had gone mad, but what did I care what my friends thought? I addressed the canary tenderly, begging him to come back and resume our conversation, in our world composed of garden, fountain, veranda, and white circular cage . . .

"What garden? What fountain?"

"The world, my dear friend."

"What world? I see you have lost none of your bad professorial habits. The world," he concluded solemnly, "is an infinite blue space, with the sun up above."

I indignantly retorted that, if he was to be believed, the world was everything and anything; it had even been a junk shop . . .

"A junk shop?" he trilled mockingly. "Do such things exist?

XERXES'S TEARS

LET US SUPPOSE (because everything is mere supposition) that before
Friar Lawrence married Juliet and Romeo, they had the following curious conversation:

JULIET: One person?
FRIAR LAWRENCE: Yes, child, and as soon as I have made one person of
the two of you, no power on earth can separate you. Come, now,
let us hasten to the altar, the candles are being lit. (*They leave the
cell and walk down the passageway.*)
ROMEO: Why do we need candles? Give us your blessing here. (*He
stops beside a window.*) Why do we need an altar and candles?
The sky is our altar, and it won't be long before the angels light
the eternal stars, although the sky is an altar even without stars.
Besides, the church is open to all, and someone might see us.
Come, give us your blessing here.
FRIAR LAWRENCE: No, let us go into the church. It won't be long
before everything is ready. But you must keep your head bowed,
child, so that you will not be seen by any prying eyes, should there
be any.
ROMEO: A vain hope, for there is not in the whole of Verona a figure
to equal that of my lovely Juliet; no other lady could ever be mis-

taken for her. What's wrong with this spot here? The altar is no
better than the sky.

FRIAR LAWRENCE: But it is more effective.

ROMEO: How so?

FRIAR LAWRENCE: Everything blessed at the altar endures. The candles
you will see burning there will sputter out long before the bride
and groom and the priest who is about to unite them in matrimony; I have seen infinite numbers of candles die; but the stars . . .

ROMEO: What about them? They will still burn; indeed, they were
only lit to make the heavens as beautiful as the Earth. Yes, my
divine Juliet, the Milky Way is like the luminous dust of your
thoughts; all those distant, lofty jewels and lights are here embod-
ied in your person, because the placid moon is merely an imitation of your benevolence, and Venus, when it shines, is like the fire
of your imagination. Marry us here and now, Father. What other
formality need you ask of us? We need no outward formality, nor
anyone's consent. Only love and desire. We are separated by the
hatred of others, but united by our love.

FRIAR LAWRENCE: Forever.

JULIET: Yes, unite us—forever. What more do we need? Your hand
will stop the hours. In vain will the sun pass from one sky to
another, in vain will it come and go, for it will not take with it the
time that lies at our feet like a tame tiger. Friend and father, repeat
those lovely words.

FRIAR LAWRENCE: Forever.

JULIET: Forever! Eternal love! Eternal life! I swear to you that I know
no other language than that. I swear to you that I do not even
understand my own mother's language.

FRIAR LAWRENCE: It may well be that your mother didn't understand
her mother's language, either. Life is a Babel, child, and each of us
is a nation.

ROMEO: Not in our case, Father. She and I are two provinces of the
same language, which we intermingle in order to say the same
prayers, with the same alphabet and but one meaning. Nor is there
any other meaning worth having on Earth. Now, who taught us
that divine language, neither of us knows; perhaps it was a star.

Look, maybe it was that star up there, the first to appear in the sky tonight.

JULIET: What celestial hand lit that star? Perhaps the Archangel Raphael's or yours, beloved Romeo. O magnificent star, will you be the star of my life, you, who mark the moment of my marriage? What is that star called, Father?

FRIAR LAWRENCE: I know nothing of astronomy, my child.

JULIET: You must know. You know both the divine and the human languages, the very herbs that grow, those that kill and those that cure. Tell me, tell me . . .

FRIAR LAWRENCE: Ah, eternal Eve!

JULIET: Tell me the name of the celestial torch that will light my nuptials, and marry us here and now. The stars are far superior to any earthly torches.

FRIAR LAWRENCE: No, they're not. You ask me what that star is called. I don't know. My astronomy is not like that of other men. (*After a pause for thought.*) I know what the winds told me, though, the winds that blow from here and there, from above and below, from one age to another, and they know a great deal, because they see everything. They remain united when dispersed, and find constancy in change.

ROMEO: And what did the winds tell you?

FRIAR LAWRENCE: Harsh things. Herodotus describes how, one day, Xerxes wept, but that is all he says. The winds told me the rest, because they were standing next to Xerxes, and caught every word . . . Listen, they've begun to grow agitated; they must have heard us speaking and are murmuring . . . Howl, friendly winds, howl as you did in your young days at Thermopylae.

ROMEO: But what did they tell you? Quick, tell us.

JULIET: No, Father, speak when you feel ready. We will wait for you.

FRIAR LAWRENCE: Gentle creature. Learn from her, my boy, learn to tolerate the excesses of an old lunatic. What did they tell me? It would be best not to repeat it, but if you insist on me marrying you here, by the light of the stars, I will tell you the origin of the one star that appears to rule over all the others. Come, we still have time, the altar awaits . . . No? How stubborn you are. I will

tell you, then, what the winds told me, the winds blowing around
Xerxes when he came to destroy Hellas with his countless troops.
The troops marched ahead of him, under the lash, because that
crude man was particularly fond of the lash and used it often,
without hesitation and without remorse. Even the sea, when it
dared to destroy the bridge he had ordered to be built, received
three hundred lashes. This was perhaps fair punishment, but,
wishing to be not only fair but brutal, Xerxes ordered the behead-
ing of all those who had built the bridge and failed to make it
indestructible. The whip and the sword; beatings and blood.

JULIET: Brutal indeed!

FRIAR LAWRENCE: Brutal, but strong. Strength has its value, and the
proof is that the sea ended up accepting the yoke imposed on it
by the great Persian. Now, one day, on the banks of the Hellespont, curious to see the troops he had gathered there, on sea and
land, Xerxes climbed a sacred hill, from which he could enjoy a
clear view in all directions. Imagine how proud he felt. He saw
countless people, the sweetest milk drawn from the Asian cow,
hundreds of thousands alongside hundreds of thousands more, different squadrons and different peoples, diverse colors and diverse
clothes, all mixed up together, arrow and sword, crown and helmet, goat's hair, horse's hair, panther skin, an infinite clamor of
things and men. He saw and he laughed; he could sense victory.
What other power could possibly oppose him? He felt invincible.
And he stood there laughing and looking with greedy, happy eyes,
a bridegroom's eyes, like yours, my young friend . . .

ROMEO: There's no comparison. Even the greatest despot in the universe is a miserable slave if he is not the master of the most beautiful eyes in Verona. And the proof is that, despite all his power,
he wept.

FRIAR LAWRENCE: Yes, he did weep, you're right, the moment he
stopped laughing. His face suddenly clouded over, and great, irre-
pressible tears poured forth. An uncle of the warrior standing
nearby was shocked and asked him the reason for his tears; Xerxes
replied sadly that he was crying at the thought that, in a hundred
years' time, not one of those thousands and thousands of men at
his command would exist. That is as far as Herodotus goes, but

listen now to the winds. The winds were astonished. They were asking each other if that proud, cruel man had ever cried before in his life and had concluded that this was impossible, since he knew nothing of compassion, only injustice and cruelty. And it was compassion that was filling the tyrant's tears and filling his throat with sobs. They roared their amazement, then gathered up Xerxes's tears. What would you have done with them?

ROMEO: I would have dried them so as not to dishonor human pity.

FRIAR LAWRENCE: They chose not to do that; instead, they gathered up all his tears and flew off into space, calling out: Look, look! Here they are, the first diamonds from the barbarian's soul! The entire firmament was in uproar; for a moment, everything stopped. Not a single star wanted to believe the winds. Tears from Xerxes? Impossible! Such a plant could never grow in such stony ground. But there they were for all to see; the winds showed them around, telling the curious story about the laughter that had provided the shell for those pearls, those words; then the constellations had no choice but to believe that hardhearted Xerxes had indeed wept. The planets gazed for a long time on those unlikely tears; there was no denying that they contained both the bitterness of pain and the salt tang of melancholy. And when they considered that the heart that had shed those tears was particularly fond of the lash, they cast a sideways glance at the Earth, as if wondering at such contradictions. One of them told the winds to return the tears to the barbarian, so that he could drink them, but the winds refused and paused to deliberate, for it is not only men who disagree with each other.

JULIET: You mean the winds do too?

FRIAR LAWRENCE: They do. The north wind wanted to turn the tears into violent, destructive storms, like the man who had shed them; but the other winds could not accept this idea. Storms always pass, and they wanted something lasting, a river, for example, or a new sea. Unable to reach an agreement, they went to talk to the sun and the moon. You know the moon, don't you, child?

ROMEO: She herself is the moon; as I said just a while ago, good father, both she and the moon are the serene image of compassion and love.

JULIET: No, don't believe anything he says, Father; the moon is my rival, the rival who lights from afar the handsome face of gallant Romeo, lending him an opalescent glow when he walks down the street . . .

FRIAR LAWRENCE: You are both right. The moon and Juliet could be the same person, which is why they both love the same man. But if you are the moon, my child, you should know what she said to the winds.

JULIET: I've no idea.

FRIAR LAWRENCE: The winds went to see her and asked what they should do with Xerxes's tears, and her response was the most compassionate response you can imagine. Let us crystallize these tears, said the moon, and make of them a star that will shine down all the centuries with the light of compassion, a place where all those who left the Earth will reside, finding there the perpetuity that eluded them in life.

JULIET: Yes, I would say the same thing. (*Looking out of the window.*) Ah, eternal light, cradle of renewal, world of continuing, infinite love, we were just hearing your lovely story.

FRIAR LAWRENCE: No, no, no.

JULIET: No?

FRIAR LAWRENCE: No, because the winds also went to talk to the sun, and, while you may know the moon, my child, you do not know the sun. The winds took Xerxes's tears to the sun, explained their origin, and told him what the moon had advised, and they spoke of how beautiful that special new star would be. The sun listened to them and replied, saying, yes, they should, indeed, crystallize the tears and turn them into a star, but not the kind of star the moon had asked for, nor one with the same purpose. It must be bright and eternal, he said, but if you want compassion, there's quite enough of that in the moon and her sickly sweet poetry. No, that star made of tears prompted by a proud man's realization of the brevity of life will hang in the sky as the star of irony, where it will shine down on all the multitudes passing by, believing them-selves to be immortal, and on anything built in defiance of time. Wherever weddings sing a hymn to eternity, it will send down one of its lightning bolts, one of Xerxes's tears, to scribble a message of extinction—instant, total, and irremissible. Every epiphany will receive that same sarcastic note. I don't want melancholy—the faded roses of the moon and her ilk—I want irony, uttered by hard, cold, sardonic lips . . .

ROMEO: You mean, that splendid star . . .

FRIAR LAWRENCE: Exactly, my child, and that is why the altar is better than the sky. On the altar, the blessed candle burns quickly and dies before our eyes.

JULIET: What a lot of hot air!

FRIAR LAWRENCE: No, no, it isn't!

JULIET: Or a lunatic's horrible dream. An old lunatic, you said a little while ago, and that is what you are. An empty, nasty dream, like your winds, and your Xerxes, and your tears, and your sun, and that whole parade of imaginary figures.

FRIAR LAWRENCE: My child . . .

JULIET: Father, you clearly do not know that there is at least one immortal thing, which is my love, and another, too, which is the incomparable Romeo. Take a good look at him, and tell me if you see in him one of Xerxes's soldiers. No, you don't. Long live my beloved, who was not at the Hellespont, who paid no heed to the ravings of those night winds, unlike you, a friar, who is both friend and enemy. Be but our friend and marry us. Marry us wherever you like, here or there, before the candles or beneath the stars, be they ironic or compassionate, but marry us, marry us, marry us . . .

OLD LETTERS

BROTERO IS A DEPUTY. It is two o'clock in the morning, and he has just arrived home in a somber, agitated mood, speaking sharply to the houseboy, who keeps asking if he wants this or that, until, finally, he orders the boy to stop pestering him. Once alone, he takes off his jacket, slips on his dressing gown, and, cigar in mouth, lies down on the couch in his study, where he gazes up at the ceiling, muttering and trembling, unable to think clearly. After a while, he sits up, gets to his feet, and walks over to one of the windows, where he paces back and forth, before stopping in the middle of the room and stamping his foot; at last, he decides he will try to sleep, and goes into his bedroom; he undresses and climbs into bed, where he lies tossing and turning; unable to sleep, he again gets dressed and returns to his study. No sooner has he sat down on the couch than the clock strikes three. A profound silence follows, then, since a fundamental principle of clock-making is that clocks never agree, all the other clocks in the vicinity begin to chime at irregular intervals: one, two, three. When the mind is troubled, the most insignificant thing seems to contain a hidden intention, a humiliating message from fate. And Brotero began to feel precisely as if those three short chimes, cutting through the night silence, were like the voices of time itself, calling to him: Go to sleep. Then they stopped, and he felt free to ponder and reach a decision, finally springing to his feet, crying:

"There's no alternative, that's what I must do."

Having said this, he went over to his desk, picked up his pen and a sheet of paper, and wrote this letter to the president of the Council of Ministers:

Dear Sir,

Everything I am about to say is sure to seem strange to you, but, however strange it may seem both to you and to me, extraordinary situations sometimes call for extraordinary measures. I do not wish to vent my feelings on street corners, on Rua do Ouvidor, or in the corridors of the Chamber. Nor do I wish to address the Chamber tomorrow or at some later date, when you present your government's program; that would be the dignified thing to do, but it would also imply complicity with an order of things I entirely repudiate. I have only one alternative: to resign from my position as deputy and return to private life.

I do not know, even so, if you would describe me as resentful. If you did, I think you would be right. However, I must draw your attention to the fact that there are two kinds of resentment, and mine is of the very finest quality.

Do not think I am withdrawing because of certain influential appointments, nor that I felt wounded by A.'s intriguing, or by all of B.'s connivings to get C. a post in the cabinet. Mere trivia. What bothers me is loyalty, not political but personal loyalty; what bothers me, sir, is you. You were the one who obliged me to break with the former administration earlier than had been my intention, and possibly earlier than suited the party. You, sir, were the one who, once, standing by a window in Z.'s house, told me that my diplomatic training made me a natural candidate for the post of Foreign Minister. You will recall my answer: that such promotions mattered little to me as long as I could serve my country. You responded: "That's all very well, but the government wants only the top talents."

In the Chamber, as I continued to rise up the ladder and to be showered with distinctions, it was said, indeed, assumed, that I would be appointed a minister at the earliest opportunity; and when you summoned me yesterday to organize the new cabinet, that belief remained. Various lists were drawn up, and my name appeared on all of them. Well, everyone knew how kind you had been to me, had seen various memoranda in which you praised me to the skies, had heard your oft-repeated invitations, etc. And I confess that I shared that widely held view.

However, the widely held view was mistaken, as was I. I have been excluded from the cabinet, and since I consider that exclusion to be an irreparable stain on my reputation, I have decided to bequeath the post of deputy to someone more capable and, more importantly, more docile. I am sure you will have no problem finding such a person among your numerous admirers.

With the greatest esteem and respect,
Your Excellency's former friend,
Brotero

Real politicians will say that the only believable thing about this letter is the resentment it contains, while the decision taken by the writer is completely unbelievable. However, these politicians are, I feel, unaware of two things. They have not read Boileau's words, warning us that, in matters of art, the truth may not seem probable, and, as defined by one of the fathers of our language, politics is the art of all the arts; they also do not know that Brotero's soul had received another blow. As if his exclusion from the cabinet were not enough to explain his resignation, a further loss had given him a firm nudge in the same direction. You already know about the political crisis; you know that the Emperor charged Counselor *** with forming a new cabinet, and that, thanks to the machinations of B., he managed to slip in C., who ended up with the post of foreign minister. The secret aim of these machinations was to provide a place in the public gallery for Widow Pedroso. Only days before, this lady—as lovely as she was rich—had chosen the new minister as her husband. This would not have been so very bad if Brotero had not coveted both ministry and widow, and coveting them, courting them, and losing them without being left with even one to console him for the loss of the other, well, is that not enough to explain our friend's angry response?

Brotero reread his letter, folded it up, put it in an envelope, and addressed it; then he tossed it to one side, intending to send it off the next day. The die was cast. Caesar had crossed the Rubicon, only in the opposite direction. Rome could keep her new consuls and rich, fickle patrician ladies! He was returning to the land of the obscure and forgotten. He did not want to waste good steel in empty, futile, demeaning shows of force. He leaned back in his chair and covered his face with one hand. When he stood up, his eyes were red, and the reason he stood up was that he heard the house clock chime four, followed by a repeat of that cruel, infuriating, monotonous procession of other clocks. One, two, three, four . . .

He did not feel at all sleepy; he did not even return to bed. He began his pacing again, pacing, planning, thinking. As he drifted from memory to memory, he revisited past illusions, and, comparing then and now, he felt as if he had been robbed. A voluptuary even in matters of pain, he scrutinized those lost illusions, the way an old lady scrutinizes photographs from her youth. He remembered a friend saying that, even in the most difficult of times, one must always look to the future. But what future? He could see none at all. He went over to his desk, where he kept all his letters from friends, lovers, and political allies. And since he would not now be able to sleep, he decided to reread those old letters. After all, people often reread old books.

He opened the drawer, took out a few bundles, and untied them. Many of the letters had grown yellow with age. Not all the signatories were dead, but, even so, the letters did have a whiff of the cemetery about them, which rather implies that, in a certain sense, the senders were all dead and buried. And he began to reread the letters, one by one, those that were ten pages long as well as the briefest of notes, plunging into that dead sea of faded memories, matters private and public, a play, a ball, a loan, an intrigue, a new book, a speech, a confession of love. One of the letters signed by Vasconcelos made him shudder:

L. [the letter said] *arrived in São Paulo the day before yesterday. I had the devil's own job getting her to give me your letters, but I succeeded, and, in a week's time, you'll have them back again. I'll bring them myself. As for what you say in the letter you wrote from H. . . . , I hope you've abandoned that grim idea; quite absurd. We'll talk when we meet.*

That brief passage brought with it a swarm of memories. He decided to read all of Vasconcelos's letters. He and Vasconcelos had been friends in their student days, and Vasconcelos was now governor of the state of Piauí. In another letter, written long before that first one, he wrote:

So L. has really got her claws into you. And why not? She's a nice, quiet girl. And very pretty, too, you lucky so-and-so! As for Chico Sousa, I don't think you need worry; you're not friends, after all, just acquaintances. Besides, there's no adultery involved. After all, he who builds a house on another man's land . . .

Thirteen days later:

All right, I withdraw what I said about another man's land. I will say, rather, on land that by divine, human, and diabolical right belongs to my friend Brotero. Satisfied?

Another letter, two weeks later:

I give you my word of honor that I intended no disrespect; I was joking, not realizing that you were that serious about her. Let's forget I said it. It's easy enough to take back one's words, far harder to lose a friend like you . . .

Another four or five letters referred to further amorous effusions on his part. In the interval, Chico Sousa found out about the affair and left L., and our friend reported this to Vasconcelos, declaring how happy he was to have her all to himself. Vasconcelos congratulated him, but added a word of warning:

I think you're being too demanding, too persnickety. Having lost a man to whom she owed a great deal and who gave her a certain status in society, it's only natural that she should be somewhat upset by that loss. Her missing him, you say, is tantamount to infidelity, and that really is too much. All it proves is that she's grateful for past kindnesses. As for you ordering her to get rid of anything and everything that he ever bought her, from a chair to a comb, I don't quite understand. You say you made this demand out of a sense of dignity, and I can believe that, but isn't it also a form of retrospective jealousy? I think so. If missing someone is a form of infidelity, then a fan given as a gift is a kiss, and you want nothing of that sort in the house. Well, that's certainly one way of looking at things . . .

Brotero continued to read about the affair, a whole chapter of his life, not very long, it's true, but still warm and vivid. The letters covered a period of ten months, and the tantrums, arguments, and threats to leave her began in the sixth month. He was jealous, and she said that jealousy meant he didn't trust her; she even went so far as to repeat that commonplace, enigmatic saying: Zealous, yes, but never jealous. And she would simply shrug whenever her lover proved suspicious or interrogated her. Then he would go too far, provoking angry scenes, reproaches, threats, and, finally, tears. Brotero would occasionally storm out of the house, swearing that he would never come back, only to return the following day, meek and contrite. Vasconcelos scolded him from a distance, and, on the subject of those comings and goings, he said once:

> A bad policy, Brotero. Either read the book to the end or put it down once and for all; opening and closing it over and over is a danger- ous tactic, because then you always have to reread the previous chapter to pick up the thread again, and if you do that, you'll never finish.

Brotero agreed and promised to mend his ways; besides, he and L. were getting along famously now, like two angels in heaven.

Then the angels fell out again. It seems that angel L. grew weary of this perpetual antiphony, and, hearing Daphnis and Chloe singing down below, she flew off to see what those two innocent creatures were saying in such melodious tones. The new Daphnis was wearing a frock coat, had a medal pinned to his chest, and a touch of rouge on his cheeks. He was also a bank manager. The angel taught him, as Chloe had been taught, that the only cure for love was kissing; well, you can guess the rest.

During this period, Vasconcelos's letters were full of consoling words and philosophy. Brotero recalled what he had suffered, his reckless behav- ior, his mad outpourings, all on account of losing that woman, who had him in the palm of her hand. He tried everything to get her back, but in vain. Gripped by a sudden desire to read the letters he had written to her at the time, and which Vasconcelos had managed, later on, to retrieve, he went back to the drawer where he kept them along with the others. The bundle was tied with a black ribbon. Smiling at this detail, Brotero untied the rib- bon and read the letters. He did not skip a single word or date or comma; he read everything, justifications, curses, pleadings, promises of love and peace, all written in a humiliatingly garbled style. Everything was there in those letters—the infinite, the abyss, eternity. One such eternity, scribbled on the back of a sheet of paper, was now illegible, but one could guess what it said. The sentence ran as follows: "Just one minute of your love, and I would be prepared to suffer for all . . ." A silverfish had eaten the next word, devouring eternity and leaving only the minute. It is impossible to know to what one should attribute this, whether to the voracity of the silverfish or to their philosophy. Probably the former, because, as everyone knows, silverfish do have voracious appetites.

The last letter spoke of suicide. When Brotero read this banal word, he felt an indefinable shudder run through him, which one could perhaps put down to a sense of having narrowly escaped ridicule. If he had killed himself, he would not be suffering this present political and personal upset, but what would the idlers on Rua do Ouvidor have to say? It would all come out and more, and they would call him weak, foolish, libidinous, before the talk turned to something else, an opera, for example.

One, two, three, four, five, the clocks began to say.

Brotero gathered up the letters, putting them back in their envelopes one by one, tying them into neat bundles again, and returning them to the drawer. While he was doing this, and even for a few minutes afterward, he devoted himself to the interesting task of reviving those lost emotions. He had reconstructed the episode in his head, and now he wanted to reconstruct the feelings, too, with the aim of comparing cause and effect and trying to establish if the idea of suicide had been a natural product of that crisis. Logically, this would appear to be true, but Brotero was keen to judge not with his reason but with his emotions.

Imagine a soldier whose nose has been shot off and who, once the battle is over, returns to the battlefield to look for that unfortunate appendage. Let us suppose he finds his nose among a heap of arms and legs; he picks it up and examines it to make sure it's his. But is it a nose or merely the corpse of a nose? If the owner placed the finest Arabian perfumes before it, would the nose be able to smell them? No. That ex-nose will never again bring him any smells, either good or bad; he could take the nose home with him and preserve or embalm it; nothing will change. He will never again be able to fully grasp the act of blowing his nose, even though he can see and understand that same action in others; he will never be able to recall the touch of handkerchief on nose. He will know it rationally, but not sensorially.

"Never more?" thought Brotero. "I will never again be able to . . ."

Incapable of reviving that lost sensation, he wondered if it would be the same with his current feelings of pique, if this personal and political crisis would, one day, seem as footling as old diary entries in which he described the appointment of the new cabinet and the widow's marriage. Brotero decided that it would indeed seem just as footling. The sky was growing light. He got to his feet, picked up the letter he had written to the president of the Council of Ministers, and held it to the candle flame, only to draw back just in time.

"No," he said to himself, "let's add it to those other old scraps of paper. One day, it, too, will be an ex-nose."

RELICS FROM
AN OLD HOUSE

(1906)

Author's Preface

A house often contains its own relics, souvenirs of other times, of past sadness, lost happiness. Imagine that the owner of said house should, for your and my amusement, decide to expose those relics to the light of day. Not all of them will be interesting, a few may prove frankly dull, but if the owner chooses carefully, he can select those few that deserve an airing.

Call my life a house and give the name of "relic" to these hitherto unpublished, unprinted tales—ideas, stories, histories, dialogues—and you will have an explanation for both book and title. They will not perhaps enjoy the same imagined good fortune of others I did not choose, and not all of them will merit being brought out into the light. That is for you to judge, dear reader, and to forgive me if I have chosen badly.

Machado de Assis

FOR CAROLINA

My dearest, to this your final resting place,
In which you take repose from this long life,
I come and will come, my poor belovèd,
To bring you a companionable heart.

It beats with the same true affection
That, despite the usual human struggles,
Made ours an existence to be envied
And in one small corner built a world entire . . .

I bring you flowers—remnants plucked
From the earth that saw us live united
And leaves us separated now by death;

And if I, in my mortally wounded eyes,
Still harbor thoughts drawn from that life,
Those thoughts are of what was and is no more.

FATHER AGAINST MOTHER

LIKE MANY OTHER social institutions, slavery brought with it certain trades and implements. I will mention only a few of those implements because of their connection with a particular trade. There was the neck iron, the leg iron, and the iron muzzle. The muzzle covered the mouth as a way of putting a stop to the vice of drunkenness among slaves. It had only three holes, two to see through and one to breathe through, and was fastened at the back of the head with a padlock. Along with the vice of drunkenness, the muzzle also did away with the temptation to steal, because slaves tended to steal their master's money in order to slake their thirst, and thus two grave sins were abolished, and sobriety and honesty saved. The muzzle was a grotesque thing, but then human and social order cannot always be achieved without the grotesque or, indeed, without occasional acts of cruelty. The tinsmiths would hang them up at the doors of their shops. But that's enough of muzzles for the moment.

The neck iron was fitted to slaves who made repeated attempts to escape. Imagine a very thick collar, with a thick rod either to the right or the left that extended as far as the head and was locked from behind with a key. It was, of course, heavy, but was intended not so much as a punishment as a sign. Any slave who ran away wearing one of these would instantly be identified as a repeat offender and quickly recaptured.

Half a century ago, slaves often ran away. There were large numbers of them, and not all enjoyed enslavement. They would sometimes be beaten, and not all of them liked being beaten. Many would merely receive a reprimand, either because someone in the household would speak up for them or because the owner wasn't necessarily a bad man; besides, a sense of ownership moderates any punishment, and losing money is not itself without pain. There were always runaways, though. In a few rare cases, a contraband slave who had just been bought in the Valongo slave market would immediately escape and race off down the streets, even though he didn't know the town at all. Those who stayed put—usually the ones who already spoke Portuguese—would arrange to pay a nominal "rent" to their master and then earn their living outside the house as street vendors.

A reward was offered to anyone who returned a runaway slave. Advertisements were placed in the local newspapers, with a description of the fugitive, his name, what he was wearing, any physical defects, the area where he had last been seen, and the amount of the reward. When no amount was given, there would be a promise: "will be handsomely rewarded" or "will receive a generous reward." The advertisement would often be accompanied at the top or the side by a drawing of a black figure, barefoot and running, with, on his shoulder, a stick with a small bundle attached. It also carried a warning that anyone sheltering the runaway would feel the full force of the law.

Now, pursuing fugitive slaves was one of the trades of the time. It might not have been a very noble profession, but, since it involved helping the forces who defend the law and private property, it had a different sort of nobility, the kind implicit in retrieving what is lost. No one took up that trade in the pursuit of entertainment or education; other reasons lay behind such a choice for any man who felt tough enough to impose order on disorder: poverty, a need for money, a lack of any other skills, pure chance, and, occasionally, the desire to be useful, at least to one of the parties.

Cândido Neves—known to his family as Candinho—is the person caught up in this tale of an escaped slave; he had already sunk into poverty when he began recapturing fugitive slaves. He had one grave fault: an inability to hold down any job or trade; he had no staying power, although he himself put this down to bad luck. He started out wanting to be a typographer, but soon saw that it would take a long time to become really good, and that even then he might not earn enough, or so, at least, he told himself. Then a career in commerce seemed a good idea, and he eventually found a job as a clerk in a notions store. However, being obliged to attend to and serve all and sundry wounded his self-esteem, and, after five or six weeks, he left of his own volition. Bookkeeper to a notary, office boy in a department attached to the Ministry of Internal Affairs, postman, and other positions were all abandoned shortly after he took them up.

When he fell in love with Clara, all he had were debts, although not as yet that many, for he lived with a cousin, a wood-carver by trade. After several attempts to get work, he decided to take up his cousin's trade, and had already had a few lessons. It was easy enough to get his cousin to give him a few more, but, because he wanted to learn quickly, he learned badly too. He never made anything very fine or complicated, just claw-and-ball feet for sofas or mundane carvings for chair backs. He wanted to be working when he eventually married, and marriage was not far off.

He was thirty years old, and Clara was twenty-two. She was an orphan and lived with her Aunt Mônica, with whom she made a living as a seamstress. Her work was not so arduous that she had no time for flirtations, but none of her potential suitors proved serious. Whole evenings passed with her looking at them and with them looking at her, until it grew dark and she had to return to her sewing. What she noticed was that she did not really miss any of them and none filled her with desire; she didn't even know the names of some. She did, of course, want to marry, but, as her aunt said, it was like fishing with a rod and waiting for a fish to bite, but all the fish swam straight past, apart from the occasional one who stopped, swam around the bait, looked at it, sniffed, then swam away to inspect other bait.

Love, however, always recognizes its intended recipient. When she saw Cândido Neves, she felt at once that he was the husband for her, the one, true husband. They met at a dance; this—to take an image from Candinho's first job as a typographer—was the opening page of that book, one that would leave the presses badly composed and even more badly bound. The marriage took place eleven months later, and it was the most splendid party their relatives had ever attended. More out of envy than out of friendship, Clara's friends tried to dissuade her from the path she was about to take. They did not deny that her husband was a decent enough fellow, nor that he loved her, nor even that he had certain other virtues, but, they said, he was rather too fond of having a good time.

"Thank heavens for that," retorted Clara, "at least I'm not marrying a corpse."

"No, not a corpse, but . . ."

The friends did not explain further. After the wedding, the newlyweds moved into some shabby lodgings with Aunt Mônica, who spoke to them about the possibility of their having children. They wanted only one, even though it would, of course, be an added burden.

"If you have a child, you'll all die of hunger," her aunt said to her niece.

"Our Lady will provide," said Clara.

Aunt Mônica should have issued this warning or, rather, threat when Candinho came to ask for Clara's hand in marriage, but she, too, liked a good time, and the wedding would, after all, be an opportunity for a party, which it was.

All three of them enjoyed a laugh. The couple, in particular, would laugh at almost anything. Even their bright, snow-white names—Clara, Neves, Cândido—were the subject of jokes, and while jokes might not put food on the table, they did make them laugh, and laughter is easily digested. Clara took in more sewing, and Cândido did odd jobs here and there, but never found any fixed employment. They still did not give up their dream of having a child. The child, however, unaware of their hopes, was still waiting, hidden in eternity. One day, though, it did finally announce its presence, and regardless of whether it was male or female, it would be the blessèd fruit that would bring the couple the happiness they sought. Aunt Mônica was horrified, but Cândido and Clara laughed at her anxieties.

"God will help us, Auntie," insisted the mother-to-be.

The news spread from neighbor to neighbor. All that remained now was to wait for the great day to dawn. Clara worked even harder than before, well, she had no choice, since, on top of her paid work, she was also busily making the baby's layette out of odds and ends. Indeed, she thought of little else, measuring out diapers, sewing dresses. What little money they earned was slow to come in. Aunt Mônica did help, but only reluctantly.

"You're in for a wretched life, you'll see," she would sigh.

"But other people have children, don't they?" Clara would ask.

"They do, and those children are always guaranteed to find food on the table, too, however scant . . ."

"What do you mean, 'guaranteed'?"

"I mean because their father has a guaranteed job, trade, or occupation, but what does the father of this poor unfortunate creature do with his time?"

As soon as Cândido Neves heard about this conversation, he went to see the aunt, not in anger, but nonetheless rather less meekly than usual, and he asked if, since living with them, she had ever once gone hungry.

"The only time you've fasted was during Holy Week, and that's only because you chose not to have supper with us. We've never gone without our salt cod . . ."

"I know, but there's only the three of us."

"And soon we'll be four."

"It's not the same thing."

"What would you have me do, beyond what I'm already doing?"

"Something that would bring in a steady wage. Look at the cabinetmaker on the corner, or the haberdasher, or the typographer who got married on Saturday, they all have guaranteed employment. Now, don't be angry. I'm not saying you're lazy, but your chosen trade is so uncertain. There are some weeks when you don't earn a penny."

"Yes, but other nights make up for that entirely, or even more so. God is by my side, and any fugitive slave knows I mean business. They rarely resist and some give themselves up straightaway."

He was proud of this, and spoke of hope as if it were money in the bank. Then he laughed and made the aunt laugh, too, for she was, by nature, a cheerful soul and was already looking forward to another party when the child was baptized.

Cândido Neves had abandoned his job as a wood-carver, as he had so many others before, both better and worse. Catching runaway slaves had a certain charm. He was not obliged to spend long hours sitting down, and all the job required was strength, a quick eye, patience, courage, and a length of rope. He would read the advertisements, copy them down, stick the piece of paper in his pocket, and set off in search of fugitives. He had a keen memory too. Once he had fixed in his mind the features and habits of a slave, it did not take long to find him, secure him, tie him up, and bring him back. Strength and agility were what counted. On more than one occasion, he would be standing on a corner, chatting, and along would come a slave, looking no different from any other slave, and yet Cândido would recognize him at once as a runaway, his name, his master, his master's house, and the size of the reward; he would immediately interrupt the conversation and set off after the villain. He wouldn't stop him there and then, but would wait for the right place to nab both slave and reward. Occasionally the slave would fight tooth and nail, but, generally speaking, Candinho emerged from such encounters without a scratch.

One day, though, his earnings began to dwindle. Runaway slaves no longer surrendered themselves only to Cândido Neves's hands. There were newer, more skillful hands around. As the business grew, other unemployed men took themselves and a length of rope and went off to the newspapers to copy out the advertisements and go hunting. Even in his own neighborhood, he had more than one competitor. In short, Cândido's debts began to grow, and, without the instant or almost instant reward he had garnered before, life became much harder. They ate poorly and on credit; they ate late. The landlord would send around for the rent.

Clara was so busy sewing for other people that she barely had time to mend her husband's clothes. Aunt Mônica helped her niece, of course, and when Cândido arrived home in the evening, she could tell from his face that he had earned nothing. He would have supper, then go straight out again, on the trail of some fugitive or other. On a few rare occasions, a blindness brought on by necessity caused him to pick the wrong man and pounce on a loyal slave going about his master's business. Once, he captured a free black man, and although he apologized profusely, he was soundly beaten by the man's relatives.

"That's all you need!" cried Aunt Mônica when she saw him and after he had told them about his mistake and its consequences. "Give it up, Candinho, find another way of earning a living, another job."

Candinho would have much preferred to do something else, although not for the same reasons, but simply for the sake of variety; it would be a way of changing skins or personality. Alas, he could find no job that could be learned quickly.

Nature continued to take its course, the fetus was growing and was soon a weight in its mother's belly. The eighth month came, a month of anxieties and privations, then the ninth, but I won't go into that. It would be best simply to describe its effects, which could not have been crueler.

"No, Aunt Mônica!" roared Candinho, rejecting a piece of advice I find painful even to write down, although not as painful as it was for Candinho to hear. "Never!"

It was in the last week of the final month when Aunt Mônica advised the couple that, as soon as the baby was born, they should take it to the foundling wheel at the convent on Rua dos Barbonos, where they took in abandoned babies. Abandoned. There could have been no crueler word for those two young parents expecting their first child, looking forward to kissing and caring for it, watching it laugh and grow and prosper and play . . . In what sense would that child be abandoned? Candinho stared wild-eyed at the aunt and ended up thumping the table hard with his fist, so hard that the rickety old table almost collapsed. Clara intervened.

"Auntie doesn't mean any harm, Candinho."

"Of course I don't," retorted Aunt Mônica. "I'm just saying what I think would be best for you. You owe money for everything; you've no meat in the house, not even any beans. If you're not bringing in a wage, how is the family to grow? After all, there's still time. Later on, when you've found some steadier job, any future children will receive as much care and attention as this one, possibly more. He'll be well cared for, he'll lack for nothing. Giving him to the foundling hospital isn't like abandoning him on the shore or on a dung heap. They don't kill children there, no child dies of neglect, whereas here, living in poverty, he's sure to die . . ."

With a shrug, Aunt Mônica turned and went to her room. She had hinted at such a solution before, but this was the first time she had spoken with such candor and such passion, or so callously, if you like. Clara reached out her hand to her husband, as if to comfort him; Cândido Neves pulled a face and muttered something about her aunt being mad. This tender scene was interrupted by someone banging on the street door.

"Who is it?" asked Cândido.

It was the landlord, to whom they owed three months' rent, and who had come in person to threaten his tenant. His tenant invited him in.

"That won't be necessary . . ."

"No, please, come in."

The landlord came in, but would not accept the proffered chair; he glanced around at the furniture to see if there was anything worth pawning, but found very little. He had come for the unpaid rent and could wait no longer; if they didn't pay up in the next five days, he would put them out in the street. He hadn't worked hard all his life just to give others an easy time of it. To look at him, you would never think he was a landlord, but his words gave the lie to his face, and, rather than argue, poor Cândido Neves chose to say nothing. He gave a slight bow, which was both promise and plea. The landlord would not be swayed.

"Pay me in five days, or you're out!" he repeated, reaching for the door handle and leaving.

Candinho also left. At such moments, he never gave in to despair. He always relied on being able to get some loan or other, even though he didn't know how or from whom. He also went back to check the newspaper advertisements. There were several, some already old, but he had looked for all those runaways before with no success. He spent a few profitless hours, then returned home. At the end of the fourth day, he had still not managed to scrape together any money, and so he decided to try his luck with friends of the landlord, but all he received was that same order to quit the house.

The situation was critical. They couldn't find alternative lodgings or anyone who might take them in; they would definitely be out on the street. They had not, however, counted on Aunt Mônica. She had somehow or other found accommodation for the three of them in the house of a rich old lady, who promised to let them have the use of four rooms, behind the coach house and looking out onto a courtyard. Even more astutely, Aunt Mônica had said nothing to the couple, so that, in his despair, Cândido Neves would be forced to take the baby to the foundling wheel and find some steadier way of earning money; so that he would, in short, mend his ways. She listened patiently to Clara's complaints, but without offering her any consolation, either. On the day they were evicted, she would surprise them with the news of this gift and they would sleep far better than expected.

And so it was. Once evicted from their house, they went straight to the new lodgings, and, two days later, the baby was born. Cândido felt both enormously happy and enormously sad. Aunt Mônica insisted that they take the child straight to the foundling hospital on Rua dos Barbonos. "If you don't want to do it, I'll take him." Cândido begged her to wait, promising that he would take him later. Yes, the baby was a boy, just as his parents had wanted. Clara quickly gave the child some milk, but then it began to rain, and Candinho said that he would take the baby to the foundling wheel the next day.

That night, he went over all the notes he had taken about runaway slaves. Most of the rewards were mere promises; some did specify an amount, but it was always some very paltry sum. One, though, offered a hundred *mil-réis*. The slave in question was a mulatta; there was a description of her face and clothes. Cândido Neves had looked for her before, but given up, imagining that perhaps some lover had taken her in. Now, though, he felt encouraged both by the thought of that generous reward and by the desperate straits he was in. The next morning, he went out to patrol Rua da Carioca and the adjoining square, as well as Rua do Parto and Rua da Ajuda, which was the area where, according to the advertisement, she had last been seen. He found no trace of her, but a pharmacist on Rua da Ajuda recalled having sold an ounce of some drug three days before to a woman answering that description. Playing the part of the slave's master, Cândido Neves politely thanked the pharmacist. He had no better luck with any of the other fugitives for whom the reward was either unspecified or low.

He returned to their rather gloomy, temporary lodgings. Aunt Mônica had made some food for Clara, and had the baby all ready to be taken to the foundling hospital. Although Candinho had agreed to this, he could barely conceal his grief. He could not eat the food Aunt Mônica had kept for him; he simply wasn't hungry, he said, and it was true. He thought of a thousand ways that would allow him to keep his son, but none of them worked. He thought about the slum in which they lived. He consulted his wife, but she seemed resigned. Aunt Mônica had painted a picture for her of what awaited their child—still greater poverty and with the child possibly dying as a result. Cândido Neves had no option but to keep his promise; he asked Clara to give the child the last milk he would take from his mother. Once fed, the little one fell asleep, and his father picked him up and headed off toward Rua dos Barbonos.

More than once, he considered simply taking him back to the house; he also kept him carefully wrapped up, kissing him and covering his face to protect him from the damp night air. As he entered Rua da Guarda Velha, Cândido Neves slowed his pace.

"I'll delay handing him over for as long as possible," he murmured.

However, since the street was not infinite in length, he would soon reach the end; it was then that it occurred to him to go down one of the alleyways connecting that street to Rua da Ajuda. He reached the bottom of the alleyway and was about to turn right, in the direction of Largo da Ajuda, when, on the opposite side, he saw a woman: the runaway slave. I will not even attempt to describe Cândido Neves's emotions, because I could not do so with the necessary intensity. One adjective will have to suffice; let's say "overwhelming." The woman walked down the street, and he followed;

the pharmacy we mentioned earlier was only a few steps away. He went in, spoke to the pharmacist, and asked if he would be so kind as to look after the baby for a moment; he would return soon.

"Yes, but—"

Cândido Neves did not give him time to say anything more; he left at once, crossed the street, and continued on to a point where he could arrest the woman without making too much of a scene. At the end of the street, when she was about to head off down Rua de São José, Cândido Neves drew nearer. Yes, it was definitely her, the fugitive mulatta.

"Arminda," he called, for that was the name given in the advertisement.

Arminda innocently turned around, and it was only when he removed the length of rope from his pocket and grabbed her arms that she realized what was happening and tried to flee. By then it was too late. With his strong hands, Cândido Neves had bound her wrists together and was ordering her to walk. She tried to scream, and she did perhaps call out more loudly than usual, but saw at once that no one would come to free her; on the contrary. She then begged him, for the love of God, to let her go.

"I'm pregnant, sir!" she cried. "If you yourself have a child, I beg you for the love of that child to let me go. I'll be your slave and serve you for as long as you like. Please, sir, let me go!"

"Walk on!" repeated Cândido Neves.

"Let me go!"

"Look, I don't have time for this. Walk on!"

There was a struggle at this point, because she, heavy with her unborn child, kept moaning and resisting. Anyone passing by or standing in a shop doorway would have realized what was going on and would, naturally, have done nothing to help. Arminda was telling him that her master was a very bad man and would probably beat her, and in her present state that would be even harder to endure. Yes, there was no doubt about it, he would have her beaten.

"It's your own fault. Who told you to get pregnant and then run away?" Cândido Neves asked.

He was not in the best of moods because he had his own child waiting for him at the pharmacy, and, besides, he had never been a great talker. He continued to drag her down Rua dos Ourives toward Rua da Alfândega, where her master lived. On the corner, she struggled still more fiercely, planting her feet against the wall and trying vainly to pull away from him.

All that she achieved, though, with the house now so near, was to delay her arrival a little. They did at last arrive, she reluctant, desperate, panting. Even then, she knelt down, but again to no avail. Her master was at home and ran out to see what all the noise and shouting were about.

"Here's your runaway," said Cândido Neves.

"So it is."

"Master!"

"Come on, in you come!"

In the hallway, Arminda stumbled and fell. And there and then her master opened his wallet and took out two fifty-*mil-réis* notes, which Cândido Neves immediately pocketed, while the master again ordered Arminda to come into the house. Instead, on the floor where she lay, overcome by fear and pain, she went into labor and gave birth to her now-dead child.

That unripe fruit entered the world amid the cries and moans of the mother and the despairing gestures of the master. Cândido Neves watched the whole spectacle. He had no idea of the time, but whatever the hour, he urgently needed to go back to Rua da Ajuda, which is precisely what he did, quite indifferent to the consequences of the disaster he had just witnessed.

When he arrived at the shop, he found the pharmacist alone, with no son to return to him. Cândido's first instinct was to throttle the man. Fortunately, the pharmacist quickly explained that the child was inside with the family, and when both men went in, Cândido Neves furiously snatched up the baby, much as he had grabbed the runaway slave a little earlier—a very different fury, of course, the fury of love. He brusquely thanked the pharmacist; then, with his son in his arms and the reward in his pocket, he raced off, not to the foundling hospital, but back to their temporary lodgings. When Aunt Mônica heard his explanation, she forgave him for bringing the child back, given that he also brought with him the hundred *mil-réis*. She did have a few harsh words to say about the slave-woman, though, both for running away and for having miscarried. Kissing his son and shedding genuine tears, Cândido Neves, on the other hand, blessed the fugitive and gave barely a thought to her dead child.

"Not all children make it," his heart told him.

MARIA CORA

Chapter I

I ARRIVED HOME one night feeling so tired that I even forgot to wind my watch. My forgetfulness may have had something to do with a certain lady I had met at the comendador's house, but those two reasons, of course, cancel each other out. Thinking keeps you from sleeping, and sleeping stops you from thinking, so only one of those reasons can be the real one. Let's just say that neither of them was, and concentrate on the main point: my stopped watch and me waking in the morning to the sound of the house clock chiming ten.

At the time (1893), I was living in a boardinghouse in Catete. There were many such residences in Rio at the time. Mine was small and tranquil. With my four hundred *mil-réis* I could have afforded a house all to myself, but, firstly, I was already living in the boardinghouse when I won that money at cards, and, secondly, I was a forty-year-old bachelor so accustomed to boardinghouse life that I would have found it impossible to live alone. Marriage was equally impossible. Not that there was any shortage of candidates. Since the end of 1891, more than one lady—and not of the plainer variety, either—had looked at me with tender, friendly eyes. One of the comendador's daughters was particularly attentive. I didn't encourage any of them, though; the bachelor life is my very soul, my vocation, my habit, my destiny. I would only love if ordered to or for my own amusement.

A couple of adventures a year are quite enough for a heart half inclined toward sunset and night.

Perhaps that is why I did pay some attention to the lady I had seen at the comendador's house on the previous evening. She was a strong, dark-haired creature, between twenty-eight and thirty, and somberly dressed; she arrived at ten o'clock, accompanied by an old aunt. Since it was the first time she had been there—it was my third—she was greeted with rather more ceremony than the other guests. I asked someone if she was a widow.

"No, she's married."

"Who to?"

"The owner of a large estate in Rio Grande do Sul."

"Name?"

"Him? He's Fonseca, and she's Maria Cora."

"Didn't her husband come with her?"

"No, he's in Rio Grande."

That was all I could glean; but what intrigued me most were her physical attractions, the very opposite of what romantic poets and seraphic artists would dream of. I spoke to her for a few minutes about matters of no importance, but long enough to hear her very singsong voice, and to learn that she had republican leanings. I didn't like to admit that I had no leanings at all, and so mumbled something suitably vague about the future of the country. When she spoke, she had a way of moistening her lips with her tongue; whether this was intentional, I don't know, but it was both charming and piquant. Seen from close up, her features were less perfect than they had seemed at a distance, but they were also more hers, more original.

Chapter II

In the morning, I found that my watch had stopped. When I reached town, I walked down Rua do Ouvidor as far as Rua da Quitanda, and, as I was about to turn right to go to my lawyer's office, I glanced at my watch, forgetting that it had stopped.

"Oh, what a bore!" I cried.

Fortunately, to the left, on Rua da Quitanda, between Rua do Ouvidor and Rua do Rosário, was the shop where I had bought that watch, and by whose clock I always set my own. Instead of going in one direction, I went in the other. It was only half an hour out of my way; I wound my watch, set it to the right time, exchanged a few words with the clerk at the counter, and, as I was leaving, I saw, standing outside a novelty shop opposite, the somberly dressed lady I had met at the comendador's house. I greeted her, and she returned my greeting somewhat hesitantly, as if she did not immediately recognize me, and then she continued on up Rua da Quitanda, still on the other side of the road.

Since I had a little time to spare (slightly less than thirty minutes), I started following Maria Cora. I'm not saying I was already in the grip of some violent force, but I cannot deny giving in to an impulse of curiosity and desire, a remnant from my lost youth. Watching her walking along, wearing the same somber colors she had worn the night before, I found her even more impressive. She kept up a pace that was neither fast nor slow, but certainly one that allowed me to admire her lovely figure, which was more perfect than her face. She walked up Rua do Hospício to an optician's, where she went inside, remaining there for ten minutes or so. I kept a safe distance, furtively watching the doorway. Then she left and set off briskly, turning down Rua dos Ourives toward Rua do Rosário, then up to Largo da Sé; from there, she walked on to Largo de São Francisco de Paula. You will think all these details unnecessary, not to say tedious, but they fill me with a particularly intense feeling, as the first steps on a long and painful road. You'll have noticed that she avoided walking up Rua do Ouvidor, which is the route everyone and anyone would take at that or any other hour in order to go to Largo de São Francisco de Paula. She crossed the square in the direction of the Escola Politécnica, but, halfway there, was met by a carriage, which was waiting for her outside the college; she got in, and the carriage left.

Like other earthly paths, life has its crossroads. At that moment, I found myself at a particularly complicated one, except that I didn't have time to choose a direction—neither time nor opportunity. I still don't know how it was that I found myself in a cab, telling the driver to follow her carriage.

Maria Cora lived in a part of Rio called Engenho Velho, in a good, solid, fairly old house surrounded by a garden. I could tell that she lived there, because her aunt was looking out of one of the windows. When she stepped from the carriage, Maria Cora told the driver (my cab happened to be passing hers at that point) that she would not be going out again that week, but asked him to come for her on Monday at noon. Then she walked straight into the garden, as if she were the mistress of the house, and paused to talk to the gardener, who began earnestly explaining something to her.

I turned back once she had gone into the house, and only farther down the hill did I think to look at my watch; it was almost half-past one. I reached Rua da Quitanda at a trot, and got out at the door to my lawyer's office.

"I thought you weren't coming," he said.

"I'm sorry. I met a friend who insisted on recounting some tiresome business or other."

This was not the first time in my life that I had lied, nor would it be the last.

Chapter III

I often met Maria Cora after that; first, at the comendador's house and, later, at other houses. Maria Cora was not a complete recluse, but occasionally went on outings and visited friends and acquaintances. She also received visitors, not on any fixed day, but every now and then, although these gatherings only ever consisted of five or six close friends. The general view of her was that she was a person of strong feelings and austere habits. Add to this her sharp, brilliant, virile nature and her capacity for dealing with difficulties and hard work, not to mention quarrels and struggles; in the words of a poet and regular visitor, she was: "one part pampa and one part *pampeiro*," a reference to the icy wind that blows across the pampas in southern Brazil. The original line rhymed, but I took from it only the underlying idea. Maria Cora liked to hear herself described like this, although she didn't always display those qualities, nor did she dwell on stories of herself as an adolescent. Her aunt, on the other hand, did sometimes lovingly tell the occasional anecdote, saying that her niece was exactly like her when she was a girl. Justice demands that I declare, here and now, that her aunt, although ill, was still full of life and vigor.

It did not take long for me to fall in love with the niece. It doesn't pain me to admit this, because it is the one page in my life that merits any interest. I will make my story brief; and I will invent nothing and tell no lies.

I loved Maria Cora. I didn't tell her how I felt straightaway, but, like all women, she probably realized or guessed how I felt. Even if she had made this realization before my visit to the house in Engenho Velho, there are still no grounds for disapproving of her for inviting me there one evening. She may have been completely indifferent to my state of mind; she may also have enjoyed feeling loved, even though she had not the slightest intention of reciprocating that love. The fact is that I went there on that first evening and on other evenings too; her aunt took a liking to me and my ways. The silly, gabby poet who also visited said once that he was tuning his lyre in readiness for the aunt's marriage to me. The aunt laughed, and, wanting to stay in her good graces, I had to laugh, too, and, for about a week, the topic provided material for much banter. By then, though, my love for her niece had reached new heights.

Shortly afterward, I learned that Maria Cora was separated from her husband. They had married eight years before, and it had been a real love match. For five years, they lived very happily together. Then, one day, her husband had an affair that destroyed their domestic peace. João da Fonseca fell in love with a circus performer, a Chilean woman, Dolores, who did stunts on horseback. He left house and estate and went after her. Six months later, he returned, entirely cured of love, but only because Dolores had fallen in love with a newspaper editor without a penny to his name, and for whom she left Fonseca and all his wealth. His wife had sworn never to take him back, and this is what she said to him when he returned:

"It's all over between us. We must separate."

At first João da Fonseca agreed, but he was a proud forty-year-old, for whom such a suggestion was in itself an affront. That same evening, he began making the necessary arrangements; however, the following morning, his wife's beauty again stirred his heart and—not imploringly, but rather as if he were forgiving her—he suggested that they wait for six months. If, at the end of that period, the feelings that had provoked the separation remained unchanged, then they would part. Maria Cora did not want to accept this emendation, but her aunt, who lived in Porto Alegre and had gone to spend a few weeks with them, acted as go-between. Three months later, they were reconciled.

"João," his wife said to him on the day after their reconciliation, "as you can see, my love is greater than any feelings of jealousy, but you have to understand that if you deceive me again, I will never forgive you."

João da Fonseca's conjugal passion was reborn; he promised his wife everything and more. "I'm forty years old," he said, "I'm hardly going to have such an affair again, especially one that had such painful consequences. You'll see, this is forever."

They resumed their life together and were as happy as they had been at the start, he would have said even happier. So strong was his wife's passion for him that he came to love her as he had before. They lived like this for two years. By then his ardor had waned, and a few fleeting love affairs came between them. Contrary to what she had said, Maria Cora forgave him these minor flings, which, besides, were not as long-lasting or as important as the Dolores affair. They did have quarrels, though, major ones. There were violent scenes. It seems that, more than once, she even threatened to kill herself; but, although she didn't lack the necessary courage to do so, she made no actual attempt on her life, because it would have grieved her to leave the very cause of her distress, namely, her husband. João da Fonseca realized this and possibly exploited the power he had over his wife.

Politics further complicated this situation. João da Fonseca was on the side of the revolution, knew several of its leaders, and personally detested some of their opponents. Because of certain family ties, Maria Cora was against the Federalists. These opposing views were not enough to cause them to part, nor can it be said that it soured their life together. She, who was passionate about everything, was no less passionate in condemning the revolution, calling its leaders and officials by the very coarsest of names; and he, equally given to excess, responded with equal loathing, and yet these political tiffs would merely have added to their numerous domestic disagreements had not a new Dolores appeared on the scene—this time a woman called Prazeres, who was neither Chilean nor an acrobat—thus reviving the bitter times they had lived through before. Prazeres had connections with the rebels, not only political, but sentimental, for she was married to a Federalist. I met her shortly afterward, and she was, indeed, a beautiful, elegant woman; and since João da Fonseca was a handsome, seductive man, they seemed fated to fall passionately in love, and so it was. Various other things happened, some graver than others, until one decisive incident brought about the couple's final separation.

They had been discussing this for some time, but, despite Maria Cora having sworn to the contrary, a reconciliation was still not impossible, again thanks to her aunt's intervention. She had suggested to her niece that she go and live for a few months in Rio or São Paulo. Then something very sad occurred. In a moment of madness, João da Fonseca threatened Maria Cora with a whip. According to another version, he tried to strangle her. I prefer to believe the first version, and that the second was invented to cast a coarse, depressing light on João da Fonseca's violence. Maria Cora did not speak to her husband again. The separation was immediate, and she traveled to Rio de Janeiro with her aunt, having first, quite amicably, sorted out the couple's financial affairs. Besides, the aunt herself was very rich.

João da Fonseca and Prazeres went on to live a life full of adventures, which I will not go into here. Only one event impinges directly on my story. Some time after the separation, João da Fonseca had enlisted with the rebels. However strong his political passions, they would not have been enough to make him take up arms had Prazeres not issued a kind of challenge; that, at least, is what his friends say, although the matter remains obscure. According to their version, Prazeres, exasperated with their troops' repeated losses, told Fonseca that she was going to disguise herself as a man, don a soldier's uniform, and go and fight for the revolution, and she would have been perfectly capable of doing this too. Fonseca told her this was utter madness, and then she proposed that he should go in her stead; that would be a real proof of his love for her.

"Haven't I given you enough proof?"

"Yes, but that would be a far greater proof than all the rest, and would keep me bound to you until death."

"Are you not already bound to me until death?" he asked, laughing.

"No."

That may be what happened. Prazeres was, indeed, an impulsive, imperious woman and knew how to bind a man to her with bonds of steel. The Federalist, whom she abandoned for João da Fonseca, did everything he could to get her back, then moved east, where, it's said, he lives a wretched life, that his hair has turned gray and he has aged twenty years, and wants nothing more to do with women or politics. In the end, João da Fonseca gave in; she even begged him to let her go, too, and, if necessary, to fight alongside him; but he refused. The revolution would soon triumph, he said; once the government forces had been vanquished, he would return to the estate in Rio Grande, where she would wait for him.

"No," she said, "I'll wait for you in Porto Alegre."

Chapter IV

Just how long it took for me to fall in love is of no importance, but not very long. My love grew rapidly and vigorously and eventually became so all-consuming that I could not keep it to myself and, one night, I resolved to declare my love to her; however, her aunt, who could normally be relied on to doze off after about nine o'clock (she woke at four), did not fall asleep at all and, even if she had, I would probably not have said anything; I could not speak and, once out in the street, I felt as dizzy as I had when I fell in love for the very first time.

"Be careful not to fall, Senhor Correia," said her aunt when I went out onto the veranda, having said my goodbyes.

"Don't worry, I won't."

I had a bad night and slept for, at most, two hours, and then only fitfully. By five o'clock I was up and awake.

"I must put an end to this now!" I cried.

The truth is that, with me, Maria Cora was always kind and understanding, but never anything more, but then that is precisely what made her so attractive. All the other loves in my life had been so easy. I had never met with any resistance, nor left with any regret, or only a little sadness, perhaps, a touch of nostalgia. This time I felt I was in an iron grip. Maria Cora was so full of life; beside her, it seemed as though the chairs themselves could walk and the figures on the carpet could move their eyes. Add to this a strong dose of tenderness and grace. The finishing touch was her aunt's evident fondness for her, which made of Maria Cora an angel. A banal comparison, I know, but I have no other.

I decided to take drastic action and to keep away from Engenho Velho, and I did so for many long days, for two or three weeks. I tried to distract myself and forget her, but to no avail. I began to experience her absence as one would that of a loved one; and yet still I resisted and did not go back. The longer the absence, though, the deeper my love, and so I decided that I would return one night, although I might not have done so had I not met Maria Cora in the same shop on Rua da Quitanda where I had gone with my stopped watch.

"Oh, so you come here too?" she said when she came into the shop.

"I do."

"I need to have my watch repaired. But why haven't you been back to see us?"

"Yes, why haven't you been back?" echoed her aunt.

"Business affairs," I murmured, "but I was thinking of coming this evening."

"No, don't come this evening, come tomorrow," said Maria Cora. "We're out tonight."

I seemed to read in those last words an invitation to declare my love, and in her first words some indication that she had missed me. And so the next day I went to Engenho Velho. Maria Cora welcomed me as warmly as ever. The poet was there, telling me in verse how the aunt had sighed for me. I again became a frequent visitor, and resolved to declare myself.

I mentioned earlier that she had probably understood or guessed my feelings, just as any other woman would. Now she must definitely have understood, and yet she did not drive me away. On the contrary, she seemed to enjoy the feeling of being deeply loved.

Shortly after that night, I wrote her a letter before going to Engenho Velho. She seemed slightly withdrawn; her aunt explained that she had received troubling news from Rio Grande. I did not connect this with her marriage, and tried to cheer her up. She, however, responded merely politely. On the veranda, before I left, I handed her the letter and was about to say, "Please read it," but my voice failed me. I could see that she was slightly embarrassed, and, to avoid saying what was best said in writing, I merely bowed and walked away through the garden. You can imagine the kind of night I spent, and the day that followed was, of course, the same, until evening came. Nevertheless, I did not immediately go back to her house; I decided to wait three or four days, not in the expectation that she would write to me, but to give her time to consider her response. I was sure her response would be a positive one, for, lately, she had treated me in a friendly, almost inviting manner.

I did not last the full four days; indeed, I barely managed three. On the evening of the third day I went back to Engenho Velho. I would not be lying if I said that I was trembling with emotion when I arrived. I found her at the piano, playing for the poet; her aunt, seated in her armchair, was deep in thought, and I was so giddy with excitement that I barely noticed her.

"Come in, Senhor Correia, but don't fall on top of me."

"Oh, I'm so sorry."

Maria Cora did not stop playing, but when she saw me, she said:

"Forgive me for not shaking your hand, but I'm acting as muse for this gentleman here."

Minutes later, she came over and shook my hand so warmly that I saw in that a response to my letter and was almost on the point of thanking her. A few minutes passed, fifteen or twenty. Then, saying that there was a book she wanted to ask me about, we both went over to where she had left it lying on top of the sheet music on the piano. She opened it, and, inside, was a piece of paper.

"When you were here the other night, you gave me this letter. Could you tell me what it says?"

"Can you not guess?"

"I might guess wrongly."

"No, you have guessed correctly."

"Yes, but, even though I'm separated from my husband, I'm still a married woman. You love me, don't you? Well, you may assume that I love you, too, but, as I say, I'm still a married woman."

Having said this, she returned the letter to me unopened. Had we been alone, I might have read it out to her, but the presence of the other guests stopped me. Besides, there was no need. Maria Cora's answer was definitive, or so it seemed to me. I took the letter and, before I put it away, asked:

"So you don't want to read it?"

"No."

"Not even to see what I said?"

"No."

"What if I were to go and fight your husband, kill him, and then come back?" I said, growing ever more frantic.

"Would you actually do such a thing?"

"Why not?"

"I don't believe anyone could ever love me that much," she concluded with a smile. "But, be careful, people are looking at us."

With that, she moved away and joined her aunt and the poet. I stood there for a few seconds with the book in my hand, as if I really were studying it, then I put it down and went and sat opposite them. They were talking about what was happening in Rio Grande, about the battles between Federalists and Legalists and their varying fates. What I felt then cannot be put into words, not, that is, by me, for I am no novelist. It was a kind of vertigo, a delirium, a horrible, lucid image, a battle followed by victory. I imagined myself on the battlefield, alongside other men, fighting the Federalists and finally killing João da Fonseca, before returning to Rio and marrying his widow. Maria Cora had contributed to this seductive thought. After her refusal to read my letter, she seemed to me more beautiful than ever, especially as she did not seem annoyed or offended, but treated me as affectionately as before, possibly even more so. I could have drawn from this a double and contradictory impression—either tacit acquiescence or complete indifference—but I saw only the first of these and left the house in a state of utter madness.

What I decided to do then really was the act of a madman. Maria Cora's words—"I don't believe anyone could ever love me that much"—were still ringing in my ears like a challenge. I thought about them all night and the following day, I went back to Engenho Velho. As soon as the opportunity arose to tell her of my resolve, I did so.

"I'm leaving everything I care about, including peace, with the sole aim of proving to you that I love you and want you solely and purely for myself. I am going off to fight."

Maria Cora looked utterly astonished. I understood then that she really did love me with a genuine passion, and that if she were widowed, she would not marry anyone else. I swore again that I was going off to the war in the South. Deeply moved, she held out her hand to me. This was pure romanticism. When I was a child, my parents believed that such actions were the only real proof of love, and my mother would tell me stories in verse of knights-errant who, out of love for their faith and for their lady, journeyed to the Holy Land to liberate Christ's tomb. Yes, pure romanticism.

Chapter V

I traveled south. The battles between Legalists and rebels were continuous and bloody, and this encouraged me. And yet, since no political passion prompted me to enter the fight, I must confess that, for a moment, I felt discouraged and hesitant. I wasn't afraid of death, you understand, but I nevertheless loved life, which is, perhaps, a synonymous state; whatever it was, it was not so overwhelming as to cause me to hesitate for very long. In the city of Rio Grande I met a friend, to whom I had written saying that I was going there for political reasons, although without specifying what those were. He wanted to know more.

"My reasons are, of course, secret," I responded, trying to smile.

"Fine, but there's one thing I should know, just one, because I have no idea of your views on the matter, since you've never told me. Whose side are you on: the Legalists' or the rebels'?"

"Oh, really! I would hardly have written to you if I wasn't on the side of the Legalists. I would have come here under cover."

"Have you some secret commission from the marshal?"

"No."

He could get nothing more out of me, but I had to tell him what my plans were, if not my motives. When he found out that my intention was to enlist with the volunteers fighting the rebels, he didn't believe me and perhaps suspected that I really had been charged with some secret plan. I said nothing that could have suggested such a thing, but he wasted no time in trying to dissuade me; he himself was a Legalist and spoke of the enemy with anger and loathing. Once he had recovered from his surprise, however, he accepted my decision, which he found all the nobler because it was not inspired by party politics. He said many fine, heroic words on the subject, words that would raise the spirits of anyone already eager for a fight. I was not such a one, or only for personal reasons, which had now grown more urgent. I had just received a letter from Maria Cora's aunt, sending me their news and her niece's best wishes, all expressed in very general terms, but imbued, I thought, with genuine affection.

I went to Porto Alegre, where I enlisted and set off to join the campaign. I said nothing about myself that might arouse any curiosity, but it was difficult to conceal my social status, where I came from, and my journey there in order to fight the rebels. A legend soon sprang up around me. I was an extremely wealthy republican, an enthusiast for the cause, ready to give my life for the republic a thousand times over—if I had that many lives—and certainly resolutely prepared to sacrifice the one life I had. I allowed these rumors to grow and off I went. When I asked in which of the rebel forces João da Fonseca could be found, someone interpreted this as a desire for some act of personal revenge; someone else thought I was a spy for the rebels hoping to enter into secret communication with Fonseca. Those who knew about his relationship with Prazeres imagined I was an old lover of hers wanting to exact revenge. All these suppositions died, leaving only a belief in my political fervor. The rumor that had me down as a spy was more problematic, but, fortunately, it was the product of two men's nighttime lucubrations and soon vanished.

I took with me a picture of Maria Cora, which she herself had given me one night shortly before my departure, complete with a charming little dedication. As I said before, this was pure romanticism; once I had taken that first step, the others followed of their own accord. Add to this my male pride, and you will understand how an ordinary, indifferent citizen of Rio could become a hardened soldier in the Rio Grande campaign.

I won't describe any battles, though, nor write about the revolution, which was of no interest to me, except for the opportunity it gave me, and for the odd blow I dealt it in my own small way. João da Fonseca was my rebel. After taking part in the Battle of Sarandi and Cochila Negra, I heard that he had been killed in some skirmish or other; later, I heard that he was fighting alongside Gumercindo, and had been taken prisoner and sent to Porto Alegre; but even this was not true. One day, I became separated from my regiment, along with two comrades, and we came across another Legalist regiment that was just setting off to defend Encruzilhada, which had been under attack by the Federalist forces; I introduced myself to the commander and joined his company. There I discovered that João da Fonseca was among those Federalists; the other men told me all about him, about his love affairs and how he was separated from his wife.

The idea of killing him in the hurly-burly of battle had something fantastical about it; I didn't even know if such duels were possible in battle, when one man's strength should be part of a single force obedient to one commander. It also often occurred to me that I was about to commit a personal crime, and, believe me, this was not something I took lightly. However, the thought of Maria Cora bestowed on me something like an encouraging blessing, absolving me of guilt. I threw myself into combat. I did not know João da Fonseca; apart from what others had told me, I could only remember a portrait I had seen of him in Engenho Velho; if he had not greatly changed, it was likely that I would recognize him in a crowd. But would such an encounter be possible? The battles I had already been involved in made me think that it would certainly not be easy.

It was neither easy nor brief. In the Battle of Encruzilhada, I think I bore myself with the necessary courage and discipline, and I should point out that I was becoming accustomed to life in this civil war. The hate-filled words I heard were very potent. Both sides fought with great ardor, and the passion I sensed in those on my own side began to infect me too. I had heard my name read out in a report of the day's fighting, and had received personal praise as well, praise which, then and now, I felt was well deserved. But let's get back to what really matters, which is to finish this tale.

In that battle, I felt rather like Stendhal's hero at the Battle of Waterloo, the difference being that it was a much smaller arena. For this reason—and also because I don't wish to linger over facile memories—I will say only that I did succeed in killing João da Fonseca in person. It's true, too, that I escaped being killed by him. I still bear the scar on my head from the wound he inflicted on me. The fight between us was short-lived. If it doesn't seem too much like something out of a novel, I would say that João da Fonseca understood my motives and foresaw the result.

After a few minutes of hand-to-hand combat in one corner of the town, João da Fonseca fell prostrate to the ground. He tried to and did fight on for a while; I gave him no opportunity to retaliate, as this, I reasoned, would lead to my own defeat, if "reason" is the right term to use, for I was not thinking rationally at all. I was blinded by the blood in which I had bathed him, and deafened by the clamor and tumult of battle. Amid the killing and screaming, our side quickly became masters of the field.

When I saw that João da Fonseca was well and truly dead, I returned briefly to the fray; my intoxicated state had somewhat diminished, and my primary motivation came back to me, as if it were the one and only. Maria Cora's face appeared before me like an approving, forgiving smile; it all happened very fast.

You have probably read about the three or four women who were captured too. One of them was Prazeres. When battle was done, Prazeres saw her lover's body, and her reaction filled me with a mixture of loathing and envy. She lay down on the ground and put her arms around him; the tears she shed, the words she spoke, made some of those present laugh; others, if not moved, were surprised. As I say, I was filled at first with both envy and loathing, but that dual feeling also disappeared, leaving not even surprise, and I, too, ended up laughing. After honoring her lover's death with her grief, Prazeres remained the Federalist she was; she had not put on a soldier's uniform, as she had said she would when she challenged João da Fonseca, but she wanted to be taken prisoner along with the other rebels and to remain with them.

Obviously, I didn't leave the government forces at once, I went on to fight a few more battles, but eventually my prime reason for being there prevailed, and I put down my weapons. During the time I was enlisted, I wrote only two letters to Maria Cora, one shortly after taking up that new life, the other after the Battle of Encruzilhada; in that last letter, I said nothing about her husband, nor about his death, nor even that I had seen him. I announced only that the civil war was likely to end soon. In neither of those letters did I make the slightest allusion to my feelings or to the motive for my actions; nevertheless, for anyone who knew about either, the meaning would have been clear. Maria Cora replied only to the first letter, serenely, but not indifferently. It was clear—at least to me—that, although promising nothing, she was grateful, or, if not grateful, admiring. Gratitude and admiration could lead to love.

I did not say—and I still don't know quite how to say it—that at Encruzilhada, after João da Fonseca had died, I attempted to cut off his head, but I didn't really want to, and, in the end, I didn't. My object was quite different, more romantic. Any genuine realists among you must forgive me, but there was a touch of reality in this, too, and I acted in accordance with my state of mind: instead, I cut off a lock of his hair, as the proof of his death that I would take to his widow.

Chapter VI

When I returned to Rio de Janeiro, many months had passed since the Battle of Encruzilhada. However hard I tried to avoid all publicity and to disappear into the shadows, my name had appeared not only in official reports, but also in telegrams and letters. I received various letters of congratulations and inquiry. Please note that I did not return to Rio de Janeiro at once; I preferred to stay in São Paulo and avoid any possible celebrations. One day, when least expected, I took the train to Rio and went straight to the boardinghouse in Catete.

I didn't immediately seek out Maria Cora. It seemed best that she should learn of my arrival from the newspapers. I had no one who could tell her, and I couldn't bring myself to go to some editor's desk and announce my return from Rio Grande; I wasn't a passenger newly disembarked, whose name would appear on the ship's list. Two days passed; on the third day, I opened a newspaper and saw my name. The article announced that I had come from São Paulo after being involved in the fighting in Rio Grande; it mentioned certain battles, and generally praised my conduct, and, finally, mentioned that I was once again living in the same boardinghouse in Catete. Since my landlord was the only person to whom I had spoken briefly about my experiences, he could have been the one who submitted these facts, although he denied this. I began to receive a few visitors. They all wanted to know everything, but I said very little.

Among the various visiting cards, I received two from Maria Cora and her aunt, who both sent words of welcome. Nothing more was needed; all that remained was for me to go and thank them, and I prepared to do so; however, on the very day I had decided to visit them in Engenho Velho, I was filled with a sense of foreboding . . . but why? How to explain my feelings of apprehension whenever I recalled Maria Cora's husband, who had died by my hand? The mere thought of what I would feel in her presence overwhelmed me. Given my main motive for enlisting, such reticence may seem hard to comprehend, but, to understand the unease that made me keep postponing the visit, you have only to consider that, even though I had been defending myself against her husband and had killed him in order not to be killed myself, he was still her husband. Finally, though, I plucked up courage and went to her house.

Maria Cora was dressed in mourning. She received me kindly, and both she and her aunt repeated their congratulations. We spoke about the civil war, about life in Rio Grande, and a little about politics, but nothing more. Not a word was said about João da Fonseca. When I left, I wondered if Maria Cora would now be disposed to marry me.

"I don't think she would refuse, although she certainly doesn't single me out for special attention. In fact, she seems rather less friendly than before. Can she have changed?"

Such were my vague thoughts, and I attributed her altered mood to widowhood, as was only natural. I continued to visit her, ready to allow the first stage of mourning to pass before formally asking for her hand in marriage. There was no need to make any new declaration; she knew how I felt. She continued to welcome me. She asked not a single question about her husband, nor did her aunt, and we spoke no more about the revolution. For my part, I reverted to the way things had been before and, not wishing to waste any time, I played the role of suitor to the full. One day, I asked if she was considering going back to Rio Grande.

"Not for the moment, no."

"But you will go?"

"Possibly, but I have no definite plans. It's merely a possibility."

After a brief silence, during which I eyed her questioningly, I finally asked if, before she left—assuming she did leave—she would change anything in her life.

"My life has already changed completely . . ."

She obviously hadn't understood me, or so I thought. I tried to explain myself more clearly and wrote her a letter in which I reminded her of that first letter of mine, which she had refused to open and in which I had asked for her hand. Two days later, I gave her this new letter, saying:

"I'm sure you won't refuse to read this one."

She did not refuse and took the letter. This happened as I was leaving, at the door to the parlor. I think I even saw in her face a slight hopeful flicker of excitement. She did not reply in writing, as I had hoped. Three days passed, and by then I was so anxious that I resolved to return to Engenho Velho. On the way there, I imagined all kinds of possible responses: that she would reject me, accept me, put me off, and, if not that second option, then I was prepared to make do with the third one. Alas, she had gone to spend a few days in Tijuca and was not at home. I left, feeling slightly annoyed. It seemed to me that she really didn't want to marry, but then wouldn't it be easier for her to say so or to write a letter telling me as much? This thought aroused new hopes in me.

I still remembered what she had said when she returned that first letter to me and I spoke of my love: "You may assume that I love you, too, but I am still a married woman." It was clear that she cared for me then, and there was no real reason now to believe the contrary, even though she had grown somewhat cool toward me. Lately, I had come to think that she did still love me, out of vanity, perhaps, or fondness or possibly gratitude too; or so it seemed to me. And yet she did not reply to my second letter, either. When she returned from Tijuca, she was less expansive, possibly sadder too. I was the one who had to raise the matter. Her answer: she was not, for the moment, ready to marry again.

"But will you marry one day?" I asked after a short silence.

"By then I'll be too old."

"So it won't be for years?"

"My husband might not be dead."

I was astonished by this remark.

"But you're dressed in deep mourning."

"I read and was told that he was dead, but it might not be true. I've seen other certain deaths later proven to be false."

"If you want absolute certainty," I said, "I can give it to you."

Maria Cora turned very pale. Certainty. Certainty about what? She wanted me to tell her everything—everything. The whole situation had become so painful to me that I hesitated no longer, and, having confessed that it had been my intention to tell her nothing and that I had told no one else, either, I promised to do so now, purely in obedience to her request. And I told her about the battle, in all its phases, the risks taken, the words spoken, and, finally, the death of João da Fonseca. She listened in a state of terrible anguish and distress. She nevertheless managed to master her emotions and ask:

"Do you swear that you're telling the truth?"

"Why would I lie? What I did is enough to prove my sincerity. Tomorrow I will bring you further proof if proof is needed."

I took her the lock of hair I had cut from the corpse's head. I also told her—and I admit that my object was to turn her against the memory of her late husband—I told her of Prazeres's utter despair and grief. I described her and her tears. Maria Cora listened to me with wide, wild eyes. She still felt jealous. When I showed her the lock of hair, she snatched it from me, kissed it, and wept and wept and wept. I felt it was best if I left—for good this time. Days later, I received a response to my letter; she would not marry me.

Her answer contained a word that is the sole reason for writing this story: "Please understand that I could not accept the hand of the man who, even out of loyalty, killed my husband." I compared this with that other word she said to me earlier, when I decided to go into battle, kill him and come back: "I don't believe anyone could ever love me that much." And that one word had taken me off to war. Maria Cora now lives as a recluse, paying for a mass to be said for her husband's soul once a year on the anniversary of the Battle of Encruzilhada. I never saw her again, and, rather less painfully, I never again forgot to wind my watch.

FUNERAL MARCH

———————

ONE AUGUST NIGHT in 186*, Deputy Cordovil simply could not get to
sleep. He had come home early from the Cassino Fluminense, once
the Emperor had left, and, during the ball, he had not felt in the least bit
indisposed, either mentally or physically. On the contrary, it had been an
excellent evening, made even more excellent by the fact that an old enemy
of his, with a weak heart, had died just before ten o'clock, with news of his
death reaching the Cassino shortly after eleven.

You will naturally conclude that he was overjoyed at the man's death,
this being the only kind of revenge available to weak, malicious hearts. Well,
there you are wrong; it was not joy, it was relief. This death had been dragging on for months, the kind of death that seems never-ending, grinding,
chewing, crushing, and gnawing away at the poor human creature. Cordovil knew of his enemy's sufferings, for, to console Cordovil for various past
insults, certain friends would come and tell him what they saw or knew
of the dying man, who was permanently confined to an armchair, enduring long, agonizing nights, with the dawn bringing him no respite and the
evening no hope of recovery. Cordovil repaid these friends with the occasional compassionate word, which the bringers of good news would adopt
and repeat, rather less sincerely than him. The man's suffering had ended at
last, hence the feeling of relief.

Such a feeling was not dissimilar to human charity, and, indeed, Cordovil took no pleasure in other people's woes, except in the world of politics. When he prayed each morning, "Our Father which art in heaven, hallowed be Thy name. Thy kingdom come, Thy will be done in earth, as it is in Heaven. Give us this day our daily bread. And forgive us our debts, as we forgive our debtors . . ." he was not like a friend of his who mouthed the same words but never forgave his debtors; indeed, the friend would usually demand more than was owed, by which I mean that if he ever heard anyone speak ill of another man, he would learn the slander by heart, embellish it, and repeat it to whoever would listen. The next day, though, Jesus's beautiful words would emerge from those same lips with dutiful charity.

Cordovil was different; he was always ready to forgive. He may have been somewhat slow in offering his forgiveness, but never obviously so. And besides, slowness has its virtues. It's no bad thing to mitigate the power of evil. Don't forget, it was only in the world of politics that the deputy took pleasure in another's woes, and his dead enemy had been a personal, not a political, enemy. I've no idea what the cause of that enmity was, and the man's name died with him.

"Poor devil, at least he's at peace now," said Cordovil.

They had gone on to speak of the deceased's long illness and discussed other deaths in this world. Cordovil thought that Caesar's death had been by far the best, not because it involved knives, but because it was quick and unexpected.

"*Tu quoque?*" asked a colleague, laughing.

And, picking up the allusion to Caesar's words, Cordovil retorted:

"No, but if I had a son, for example, I would want to die at his hands. Parricide is so unusual that it would make the tragedy still more tragic."

And the conversation continued in this same sprightly vein. Cordovil left the ball feeling very sleepy and dozed off in his carriage, despite the bumpy ride. When they were almost at his house, he felt the carriage stop and heard the murmur of voices. A man had died, and two policemen were picking him up from where he lay on the ground.

"Was he murdered?" Cordovil asked the footman, who had climbed down to find out what was happening.

"I don't know, sir."

"Well, find out."

"That fellow over there knows what happened," said the footman, pointing to a man who was talking to some other people.

The young man came over to the carriage window and, without being asked, briefly told Cordovil what he had seen.

"We were both walking along. He was ahead of me and I was just behind. He was whistling a polka, I think. Anyway, just as he was about to cross the street and head off toward the canal, he seemed to stumble, keel over, then fall to the ground unconscious. A doctor came out of a house nearby, examined him, and said that he'd simply dropped down dead. A crowd began to gather, and the police took ages to arrive. They've only just come for him now. Do you want to have a look?"

"No, thank you. Can we get through now?"

"Yes, of course."

"Thank you. Come on, Domingos."

Domingos climbed back onto his seat, the driver chivied the horses into action, and the carriage continued on to Rua de São Cristóvão, where Cordovil lived.

Along the way, Cordovil was pondering the death of that stranger. In itself, it was a good death, and compared to that of his personal enemy, an excellent one. The man had been walking along whistling, thinking about who knows what past delights or future hopes, perhaps reliving something already experienced or anticipating some entirely new experience, when death snatched from him both delight and hope and carried him off to his eternal rest. He died painlessly, or, if he did feel any pain, it was probably very brief, like a lightning flash that leaves the darkness still darker.

He imagined himself in that same situation. What if it had happened to him at the Cassino? He would not have been dancing; at forty, he no longer danced. It could be said that he had only danced until he was twenty. He wasn't a ladies' man, and had known only one great love in his life, when he was twenty-five. He had married and been widowed five weeks later, never to marry again. Not that he had lacked for admirers, especially after his grandfather died, leaving him two country estates. He had sold both and, from then on, lived alone; he had made two trips to Europe, and continued his political and social life. Lately, he had seemed rather bored with both, but, having nothing better to do, had not yet abandoned either. He had been appointed minister once, of the navy, I believe, but lasted only seven months in the post. The appointment brought him no glory and his dismissal no regret. He wasn't ambitious, and was more given to inaction than action.

But what if he had died suddenly in the Cassino, during a waltz or a quadrille, alive one moment, dead the next? It could have worked out really well. Cordovil imagined the scene, with him lying prone or prostrate, all gaiety extinguished and the dancing at an end . . . or perhaps not. There would be a brief moment of shock, perhaps, or alarm, with the men reassuring the women, and the orchestra continuing to play on for a few moments despite the confusion. There would be no shortage of strong arms to carry him into another room, dead, totally dead.

"Just like Caesar's death," he told himself.

Then he added:

"No, better than that: no threats, no weapons, no blood, just a fall and it's over. I wouldn't feel a thing."

Cordovil found himself laughing or smiling, anything to drive away the terror and leave only the sense of freedom. Well, better to die like that than after long days or months and years, like the enemy he had lost a few hours before. It wasn't even like dying; it was like tipping one's hat, with the gesture lost in the air along with the hand and mind that had made it. Like nodding off into eternal sleep. He found only one thing wrong with it—the showiness of it. That death in the middle of a dance, in front of the Emperor, to a waltz by Strauss, described, painted, and exaggerated in the newspapers, that death would seem made to order. Never mind, as long as it was quick.

It could also, he thought, happen in the Chamber, the following day, at the beginning of the debate about the budget. He had the floor; he was already spouting figures and statistics. No, he didn't want to imagine the scene, there was no point, but it refused to go away and appeared of its own accord. The Chamber, rather than the Cassino, with no ladies present or only a very few in the public gallery. A vast silence. Cordovil, on his feet, would begin his speech, then glance around the room, at the minister and the prime minister: "I thank you, gentlemen, for your time. I will be brief and, I hope, fair . . ." A cloud would pass before his eyes, his tongue would stop, his heart, too, and he would suddenly collapse. Chamber, gallery, benches would freeze. Many deputies would rush to help him; one, who was a doctor, would declare him dead; he wouldn't say he had simply dropped down dead, as the doctor in the street earlier had put it, but would use some more technical term. Work would be halted, there would be a few words from the prime minister, and a group would be chosen to accompany the dead man to the cemetery . . .

Cordovil tried to laugh off these imaginings about what would happen after death, the crowds and the funeral, the obituaries in the newspapers, which he quickly had by heart. He tried to laugh, but would have far preferred simply to nod off; however, his eyes, sensing that they were now so close to home and bed, preferred not to spoil their night's sleep and remained wide awake.

And that same death—which he had imagined happening at the ball or the following day in the middle of the debate—now entered the carriage. He imagined the footman opening the door and finding his corpse. He would thus leave a very noisy night for a peaceful one, with no conversations, no dances, no meetings, no struggle or resistance. A sudden jolt made him realize this wasn't true. The carriage had proceeded up the drive to his house and stopped, and Domingos had sprung down from his seat to come and open the door for him. Cordovil climbed out with his legs and soul alive and went in by the side door, where his slave Florindo was waiting for him with a candle. He went up the stairs, and his feet felt that those steps were definitely of this world; had they been of the next world, they would, of course, have been going down. Upstairs, he went into his bedroom and looked at the bed; it was the same bed where he had spent many a long, tranquil night asleep.

"Any callers?"

"No, sir," said the slave distractedly, then corrected himself: "I mean, yes, sir. The doctor who had lunch with you last Sunday, he came to see you."

"Did he leave a message?"

"He said he had some good news and left a note, which I put at the foot of the bed."

The note announced the death of his enemy; the doctor was one of the friends who had kept him updated on the progress of his enemy's illness. He had wanted to be the first to tell him the great news and sent his very best wishes. So the blackguard had died. The friend didn't actually use that word, but it amounted to the same thing, and he added that this had not been his only reason to call. He had come to spend the evening with him, only to be told that Cordovil had gone to the Cassino. He had been about to leave, when he remembered their mutual enemy's death and asked Florindo to let him leave a brief message. Cordovil read the note and again felt the dead man's pain. He made a melancholy gesture and muttered:

"Poor wretch! Yes, long live sudden deaths!"

Had Florindo made a connection between the doctor who left the note, that gesture, and those words, he might have regretted taking the trouble to pass on the note, but this never even occurred to him. He helped his master undress, received his final orders, and said good night. Cordovil then climbed into bed.

"Ah!" he sighed, stretching out his weary body.

Then he had an idea: What if he were to wake up in the morning dead? This hypothesis—the best of the lot, because it would catch him when he was already half dead—brought with it a thousand other fantasies that drove sleep from his eyes. In part, these were a repetition of the earlier ones, his speech to the Chamber, the prime minister's words, the funeral cortege, and all the rest. He heard the sad words of friends and servants, read the obituaries, all either flattering or fair. He began to suspect that he was already asleep, but he wasn't. He brought himself back to the room, to the bed, to himself: he was awake.

The lamp lent more substance to reality. Cordovil dismissed these gloomy ideas and waited for happier ones to take over and dance him to sleep. He tried to vanquish one vision with another. He even did one rather ingenious thing: he summoned up all his five senses, whose memories were still sharp and fresh, and evoked long-extinct incidents and episodes. Certain gestures, social and family gatherings, panoramic vistas, and many other things he had seen, resurfaced from distant, diverse times. He once again savored a few favorite titbits as if he were eating them now. His ears heard footsteps, light and heavy, songs, cheerful and sad, and words in all their many guises. Touch and smell played their part, too, and he quite lost track of time.

He tried to sleep and firmly closed his eyes. But he couldn't sleep, not on his right side or his left, not on his back or his front. He sat up and looked at his watch; it was three o'clock. Unthinkingly, he pressed the watch to his ear to see if it had stopped; it hadn't; it was fully wound. Yes, he still had time to have a good sleep; he lay down again and covered his head with the sheet to block out any light.

It was then that sleep tried to enter, silently, soundlessly, cautiously, just as death would if it wanted to carry him off suddenly and for good. Cordovil again squeezed his eyes tight shut, but the effort involved in this only increased his longing to sleep; he managed then to relax his eyelids, and this worked, for sleep, which had been about to retreat, returned and came and lay down next to him, wrapping him in the simultaneously light and heavy arms that deprive a person of all movement. Cordovil could feel them and tried to return their embrace and snuggle up still closer. That is not a good image, but I have no better one at hand and no time to go and find another. I will describe only the result of that gesture, which was to drive away sleep, much to the annoyance of that giver of rest to the weary.

"What has he got against me tonight?" sleep would have asked if it could speak.

As you know, sleep is essentially silent. When it does seem to speak, it is a dream opening the dreamer's mouth; sleep is as silent as a stone, although even a stone can speak if struck, as the road-menders are doing right now outside in my street. Every blow awakens in the stone a sound, and the regularity of those blows makes a noise like the soul of a clock. People talking or selling something, carriage wheels, footsteps, a window blown shut by the wind, none of the things I can hear now enlivened Cordovil's street or his night. Everything favored sleep.

And Cordovil was, at last, falling asleep, when the idea of waking up dead reappeared. Sleep drew back and fled. This toing and froing went on for some time. Just as sleep was sealing his eyes shut, the thought of death would open them, until, in the end, he threw back his sheets and leapt out of bed. He opened the window and leaned on the sill. The sky was trying to grow light, a few dark shapes were walking down the street, workers or merchants making their way into town. Cordovil shivered, but whether from cold or fear, he didn't know; he went and put on a cotton dressing gown and returned to the window. Yes, it must have been the cold, because he had stopped shivering.

People continued to pass and the sky continued to lighten; a whistle from the station indicated that a train was about to leave. Men and things emerged from their night's rest, the sky frugally extinguished the stars as the sun arrived for its shift. Everything made one think of life, and the idea of death gradually slipped away and vanished entirely, while our man, who had sighed for death in the Cassino and wished for it the following day in the Chamber of Deputies, who had come face-to-face with it in his carriage, now turned his back on it when he saw it enter along with sleep, death's elder brother, or, who knows, its younger one.

When he did eventually die, many years later, he asked for and received not a sudden death, but a gradual one, the death of a slowly decanted wine, which leaves one bottle and enters another, with all its impurities filtered out. Only the dregs would go to the cemetery. Now he understood the philosophy of death; the wine remained in the bottles, until, drop by drop, it was all decanted into the second bottle. As for what a sudden death meant, he never did grasp that.

A CAPTAIN OF VOLUNTEERS

———

As he was about to set sail for Europe, immediately following the proclamation of the republic, Simão de Castro collected together all his old letters and notes, and tore them up. The only thing to survive was the story you are about to read; he gave it to a friend to publish as soon as he had crossed the bar. That friend declined because he felt the story might cause some upset, and he said as much in a letter. Simão replied saying that he could do as he wished. Since he himself had no literary ambitions, he really didn't care if the story was published or not. Now that both men have died, and there is less need for such scruples, the story can at last be sent to the printers.

At the beginning there were four of us, two young men and two young women. The other man and I used to go there, initially out of habit or boredom and, finally, out of friendship, for I became friends with the owner of the house, and he with me. In the evenings, after supper—people dined early in 1866—I would go there to smoke a cigar. The sun would still be coming in through the window, from which you could see a hill with some houses at the top. The opposite window looked out over the sea. I won't name the street or the district, although I can name the city: Rio de Janeiro. I will conceal the name of my friend too; let's call him X. And she, one of the girls, was called Maria.

When I arrived, X. would already be sitting in his rocking chair. The room was very sparsely furnished and decorated; it was all very simple. X.

would hold out his large, strong hand to shake mine, and I would go and sit by the window, looking now at the room and now out at the street. Maria would either already be in the room or appear later on. We meant nothing to each other, and were bound together purely by our affection for X. The three of us would sit and talk; I would go back to my own house or for a walk; they would stay behind and, later, go to bed. We would sometimes play cards, and, toward the end, that was where I spent most of my evenings.

I found everything about X. imposing. First of all, his physique, for he was robust whereas I was a weakling; my feeble, feminine grace disappeared in the presence of his manly vigor, his broad shoulders and hips, powerful thighs, solid feet, and firm step. Imagine me with a thin, sparse mustache; imagine him with long, thick, curly side-whiskers; one of his habitual gestures, when he was thinking or listening, was to run his fingers through those whiskers, leaving them even curlier. His eyes completed the picture, not just because they were large and beautiful, but because they smiled even more, and more brightly, than his lips. Add to this his age: X. was forty years old, whereas I was not yet twenty-four. And add to that his experience of life: he had lived a great deal, and in another milieu entirely, from which he had escaped to hide himself away in that house with that young lady; I had experienced nothing and never lived with anyone. Finally—and this characteristic is crucial—there was about him a Spanish quality, a drop of the blood that flows through the pages of Calderón, a moral attitude that, without wishing to diminish him or make fun, I would compare to a Cervantes hero.

How had they met and fallen in love? That went back a long way. Maria was already twenty-seven, and seemed quite well educated. I heard that they had first met at a masked ball in the old Teatro Provisório. She had been wearing a short skirt and dancing to the sound of a tambourine. She had admirable feet, and either they or fate caused X. to fall in love with her. I never asked about the wedding ring she wore; I know only that she had a daughter, who was at school and never came to the house; her mother would always go and see her. We treated each other with the greatest respect, and that respect included accepting their situation unquestioningly.

When I first began visiting, I was not yet employed at the bank. I only started working there a couple of months later, but this did not interrupt our friendship. Maria would play the piano; sometimes she and her friend Raimunda would manage to drag X. along to the theater, and I would go too. Afterward, we would take tea at someone's house, and, occasionally, if there was a full moon, we would end the night taking a cab to Botafogo.

Barreto did not join us on those occasions; he only became a regular visitor later, but he was good company, cheerful and lively. One night, as we were leaving, he turned the conversation to the two women, and suggested that he and I try to seduce them.

"You choose one, Simão, and I'll choose the other."

I shuddered and stood stock-still.

"Or, rather, I've already chosen," he went on. "I've chosen Raimunda. I really like her. You choose the other one."

"Maria?"

"Who else?"

I was so taken aback by this tempting idea that I could find no words to reject it, no words and no gestures. It all seemed to me perfectly natural and necessary. And so I agreed to choose Maria; she was only three years older than me, but old enough to teach me the ways of love. Barreto and I embarked on our conquests with ardor and tenacity. Barreto did not have to try very hard; his chosen one had no lover, for she had recently been jilted, with her lover going off to marry a girl from Minas. She soon allowed herself to be consoled. One day, when I was having my breakfast, Barreto came to announce that he had received a letter from her, which he showed to me.

"So you're a couple, then."

"We are. What about you?"

"No, not me."

"So when will you be?"

"We'll see. I'll tell you later."

I felt rather annoyed. With the best will in the world, I could not bring myself to tell Maria how I felt, not that I was in love, you understand, I was merely curious. Whenever I saw her youthful, slender figure, all warmth and life, I was filled with a mysterious new energy; on the one hand, I had never actually been in love, and, on the other, Maria was my friend's companion. I say this, not in order to explain my scruples, but simply so that you can understand my diffidence. They had been living together for some years and were devoted to each other. X. trusted me completely, telling me about his business dealings and about his past life. Despite the age difference, we were like students in the same year at college.

Given that I was always thinking about Maria, she had probably guessed

my new state of mind from my face; the fact is that, one day, when I shook
her hand, I noticed that she allowed her hand to linger a little longer than
usual in mine. Two days later, when I went to the post office, she was there
buying a stamp for a letter to Bahia. Did I mention she was from Bahia?
Well, she was. She spotted me first and came to speak to me. I waited while
she put the stamp on her letter, then we said goodbye. At the door, as we
were leaving, I was about to say something, when I saw X. standing there
before us.

"I was just sending a letter to Mama," Maria stammered.

She said goodbye and went home, while he and I set off in the opposite
direction. X. took this opportunity to praise Maria to the skies. He did not
go into any detail about how they had met, but assured me that they had
both fallen equally in love with each other and would stay together forever.

"I won't get married now, but we live together as man and wife, and I
will die at her side. My only regret is that I'm obliged to live apart from my
mother. My mother knows, though," he said, and, for a moment, he stopped
walking. Then he went on: "She knows, of course, and has even alluded to it,
in a very vague, remote way, but I understood. I don't think she disapproves.
She knows Maria is a kind, serious-minded girl, and as long as I'm happy, she
wants nothing more. That's all I would gain from marriage."

He said many other things, which I barely heard, for my heart was
pounding furiously and my legs had turned to jelly. I could not find the
right response, and any words I tried to say got stuck in my throat. After a
while, he noticed this and misinterpreted my feelings, assuming that I found
his confidences boring. Laughing, he remarked on this, and I told him very
earnestly:

"No, not at all, I'm very interested. After all, the people you're talking
about are worthy of great consideration and respect."

I think now that I was unconsciously giving in to a necessary hypocrisy.
The age of passions is a confusing one, and in that situation, I cannot really
identify what my feelings were or their precise causes. On the other hand, it
is not beyond the bounds of possibility that I was trying to drive any flicker
of distrust from X.'s mind. And he heard my words with a look of gratitude
on his face. He enfolded me in the gaze of his large, childlike eyes, and when
we said goodbye, he shook my hand energetically. I think he may even have
said: "Thank you."

I did not feel frightened when I left him, nor full of anticipated remorse.

My initial reaction to what he had confided in me vanished, leaving only the story itself, and I felt curiosity bubbling up inside me. X. had spoken of Maria as a chaste wife; he had made no allusion to her physical charms, but my youth required no direct references. Alone in the street, I summoned up her youthful figure, her gestures, at once robust and languid, and I felt more and more excited. Once at home, I wrote her a long, rambling letter, only to tear it up half an hour later. Then I went to supper, and afterward to X.'s house.

Dusk was coming on. He was sitting in his rocking chair, and I occupied my usual place, looking now at the room, now at the hill opposite. Maria arrived later than usual, and seemed so exhausted that she took no part in our conversation. She sat down in a chair and nodded off. Then she played the piano a little and left the room.

"Maria woke this morning determined to collect money for the war," X. said. "I pointed out that not everyone would necessarily share her views. Fortunately, she must have thought better of it. She gets these crazy notions sometimes . . ."

"But why shouldn't she collect money?"

"Because she shouldn't! Besides, the war with Paraguay, well, I'm not saying it isn't like other wars, but I'm really not that keen. At first I was, when López captured the *Marquês de Olinda*, yes, I was angry to begin with, then that feeling faded, and now, frankly, I think we would have been much better off allying ourselves with López against the Argentinians."

"I prefer the Argentinians."

"Oh, I like them, too, but, in the interests of our own people, it would have been better to stick with López."

"I almost enlisted as a volunteer."

"Not me. I wouldn't enlist, not even if they made me a colonel."

He said other things too. I didn't respond immediately or very clearly or coherently because I had my ears cocked, listening for Maria's footsteps. I muttered the occasional word, still listening. But that wretch of a girl didn't come back. I imagined they had quarreled. In the end, I suggested we have a game of ombre.

"All right," he said.

We went into his study. X. put the deck of cards on the table and went to call Maria. I heard a few whispered exchanges, but could only really make out the following words:

"Come on. It's only for half an hour."

"Do I have to? I'm really not feeling very well."

Maria entered the study, yawning. She said she would only play for half an hour, that she had slept badly and had a headache and was hoping to have an early night. She slumped down wearily at the table, and we began the game. I regretted having torn up my letter; I could remember a few passages, which would have explained my feelings with the necessary persuasive warmth. If I had kept it, I would have given it to her then, for she often came out onto the landing to say goodbye and to close the door. That would have been the perfect opportunity and a solution to my crisis.

After a few minutes, X. got up to fetch some tobacco from a tinplate box on his desk. Maria then did something I can barely put into words. I was sitting on her left, and she suddenly raised her cards to cover her eyes, then, turning to me, she lowered the cards and opened her eyes so wide and with such passion and feeling, that I don't know how I didn't step right into them. It all happened very quickly. By the time X. returned, rolling a cigarette, Maria was carefully studying her cards, calculating their value. I must have been shaking, and yet, despite having lost the power of speech, I still managed to make my calculations too. She then calmly uttered one of the usual words of the game, "pass" or "renege."

We played for nearly an hour. In the end, Maria really was falling asleep, and X. himself said she had better go to bed. I said good night and went out into the hallway, where I had left my hat and cane. Maria was waiting at the door to the parlor for me to leave, in order to accompany me to the door and close it after me. Before I could go down the stairs, though, she put one arm about my neck, drew me to her, and pressed her lips to mine in a quick, passionate silent kiss. I felt her slip something into my hand.

"Good night," she said, closing the door.

I don't know how I remained standing. I went down the stairs, with that kiss still on my lips, my eyes on hers, and my hand instinctively clasping whatever it was she had given me. I waited until I was at a safe distance, then, in the first lit street I came to, I went straight over to a streetlamp to see what it was. It was a card from a draper's shop, an advertisement, with these words written in pencil on the back: "Wait for me tomorrow at the Niterói ferry, at one o'clock."

I was in such turmoil that I have no memory of what I did during those first few minutes. My emotions were too many and too tumultuous, and had followed so close upon one another that I barely knew what to think. I walked as far as Largo de São Francisco de Paula. I reread the message on the card; I quickened my pace, then stopped again, and a couple of policemen on patrol may well have suspected that I was up to no good. Fortunately, despite those tumultuous feelings, I also felt hungry and went to dine at the Hotel dos Príncipes. I didn't fall asleep until dawn and was up again at six. The morning passed as slowly as certain slow deaths. I reached the ferry at ten minutes to one, and found Maria already waiting for me, swathed in a cape and wearing a blue veil over her face. A boat was just about to leave and so we went on board.

The sea welcomed us warmly. There were few passengers at that hour. Other boats and birds passed, and the bright sky seemed to be celebrating our first meeting. What we said was so rushed and so confused that I can only remember half a dozen words, and none of them was the name of X. or even a reference to him. However, we both felt that we were traitors: I was betraying my friend and she her friend and protector. However, even if we hadn't felt like traitors, I don't think we would have mentioned him, we had so little time for what really mattered to us. Maria seemed quite different from the woman I thought I knew as she talked about me and about her, as tenderly as was seemly in a public place, but certainly as tenderly as possible. We clasped each other's hands, devoured each other with our eyes, and our hearts were doubtless beating at the same frantic pace. That at least was my impression when we parted, after the round trip to Niterói and São Domingos. I invited her to disembark at both those points, but she refused; on the way back, I suggested taking a closed cab: "What kind of woman do you think I am?" she asked with a modest look that quite transformed her. And so we said goodbye, having, first, arranged to meet again, and with me swearing that I would, as usual, come to see them both that night.

Since I have not taken up my pen in order to describe my happiness, I will leave aside the most delightful part of the affair, with its meetings and letters and conversations, as well as the dreams and hopes, the infinite longings and resurgent desires. Such affairs are like almanacs, which, for all their changes, always bring us the same days and months, with their never-changing names and saints. Our almanac lasted only three months, with no third quarters or sunsets. Maria had many lovely qualities; she was all life, all movement. She was, as I said, from Bahia, but had been brought up in Rio Grande do Sul, in the countryside, near the frontier. When I asked

about her first meeting with X. at the Teatro Provisório, where she had
danced to the sound of a tambourine, she said it was true, that she had gone
there dressed as a Spanish *señorita* and wearing a mask; and when I asked
her to dress up like that for me, minus the mask, or simply put on a Bahian
costume to dance a *lundu*, she spoke like someone warning of a great danger:

"It might drive you crazy."

"X. didn't go crazy."

"But he's still not quite in his right mind," said Maria, laughing. "I would
only have to do this . . ."

And, standing up in one quick movement, she gave a single gyration of
her hips, which was enough to make my blood seethe.

The three months soon ended, as is the way with such quarterly peri-
ods. One day, Maria failed to turn up for our rendezvous. She was usually
so punctual that I felt quite dizzy with anxiety when the appointed time
passed. Five, ten, fifteen minutes; then twenty, then thirty, then forty . . . I
won't say how many times I paced up and down, in the parlor, in the hallway, watching and listening, until it became clear that she would not come.
I'll save you a description of my despair, of how I rolled about on the floor,
babbling, screaming, crying. When I grew tired, I wrote her a long letter and
hoped that she would write to me as well, explaining her absence. I did not
send my letter, and that night I went to their house as usual.

Maria explained that she had failed to meet me as arranged because she
was afraid of being seen and followed by someone who had been pursuing
her for some time. Indeed, I had already heard about some neighbor or other
who was determinedly courting her; she told me that once he had followed
her right to the door of my house. I believed this and suggested a different
meeting place, but she thought this unwise. It would, she felt, be best to
abandon our meetings until all suspicions had died down. She would stay at
home. At the time, I did not grasp the simple truth, namely, that her initial
ardor had faded. Maria changed completely then. You cannot imagine how
different that lovely creature became, for she contained both fire and ice,
and could be hotter and colder than anyone I know.

When I realized that it was all over, I decided not to go back to the
house, but still I did not lose hope. For me, it was a question of mental
effort. Imagination, which has the ability to make past pleasures present
again, easily convinced me that it really was possible to recover those first
few weeks. Five days later, I returned, feeling unable to live without her.

X. welcomed me with his broad, childlike smile, his pure eyes, and his firm, sincere handshake; he asked why I had not been to see him. I blamed this on a slight fever and, in order to explain my still-visible unease, claimed that it had left me with a faint headache. Maria understood what lay behind this, but showed me no affection, no pity, and, when I left, she did not accompany me to the door as she used to.

All this only increased my anguish. I considered suicide and, out of romantic symmetry, thought of taking the ferry to Niterói—the scene of our first lovers' tryst—and jumping overboard in the middle of the bay. I did not pursue this or any other such plan. Chancing to meet my old friend Barreto, I immediately told him everything. I needed someone as a sounding board. I swore him to secrecy and asked him most especially not to say anything to Raimunda. That same night, she knew everything. Raimunda was an adventurous soul, fond of plans and projects. She did not perhaps particularly care about me or her friend, but she saw the situation as providing her with a mission, an occupation, and was determined to reconcile us; or so at least I found out later, and that is what gives rise to this document.

She spoke to Maria several times. At first Maria denied everything, but ended up confessing, saying that she now regretted her foolishness. She doubtless used various circumlocutions and synonyms, vague, truncated phrases, sometimes mere gestures. I only know what Raimunda told me, for she summoned me to her house and recounted her efforts and was clearly very pleased with herself.

"But don't lose hope," she concluded. "I told her you might kill yourself."

"And I might."

"But don't do it just yet. Wait."

The following day I saw in the newspaper a list of the citizens who had gone to the army headquarters the previous day to sign up as volunteers to fight for their country, and on that list was X.'s name, with the rank of captain. I couldn't believe this at first, but all the newspapers said the same thing, and one of the papers referred to X.'s family, to his father, who had been an officer in the navy, and to the new captain's distinguished, manly figure. It was definitely him.

My first reaction was one of pleasure; Maria and I would be left alone. She was hardly likely to become a camp follower and head south with him. Then I remembered what he had said to me once about the war, and I found it very strange that he should enlist, even though this could be explained by his love of generous acts and his innate nobility of spirit. He had told me that he wouldn't go even if he was made a colonel, and now here he was accepting the rank of captain. And what about Maria? How could he, who loved her so much, suddenly be parted from her, when there was no strong sense of patriotism leading him off to war?

I hadn't been to their house for three weeks. The news of his enlistment was justification enough for an immediate visit and spared me having to make any excuses. I had breakfast and set off. Before going in, I put on a suitably grave face. After a few minutes, X. joined me in the parlor. His grim, withdrawn expression gave the lie to his words, which attempted to be light and cheery, and he looked dreadfully pale. He held out his hand, saying:

"So you've come to see the captain of volunteers?"

"I've come to hear you tell me it's not true."

"What do you mean? It *is* true. I don't quite know why, maybe it was just the latest news from the front . . . Why don't you come with me?"

"So it *is* true."

"It is."

After a few moments of silence, I managed to speak, and my hesitation was in part sincere, because I really didn't know quite what to say, and in part feigned, in the hope that I would convince him of my genuine concern. I said something about it being much better if he didn't go, that he must think of his mother. X. replied that his mother heartily approved; she was, after all, the widow of a military man. He tried to smile, but his features remained stiff and stony. He could not bring himself to look at me, and his eyes did not rest on anything for very long. We talked very little, and then he stood up and said he had some business to deal with, but asked me to come back and see him. At the door, he said rather awkwardly:

"Come and have supper one evening, before I leave."

"Yes, I will."

"Come tomorrow."

"Tomorrow?"

"Or today, if you like."

"No, tomorrow."

I was about to ask him to remember me to Maria, as was only natural and necessary, but I could not get up the courage. Downstairs, I wished I had. I reviewed our conversation, and thought how embarrassed and hesitant I must have seemed; he, on the other hand, had come across as cold and rather arrogant. There was something else too. Both when he greeted me and when we said goodbye, his handshake had not been as firm as it usually was.

That same night, Barreto came to see me, stunned by that morning's news and asking me what I knew. I said I knew nothing, but told him about my visit to X., about our conversation, but not my suspicions.

"It might just be a misunderstanding," he said after a moment.

"What do you mean?"

"Raimunda told me today that she had spoken to Maria, who, at first, denied everything, then confessed and declared that she had no intention of resuming her relationship with you."

"Yes, I know."

"But it seems that the third time this happened, he was listening in the small room next door. Maria ran to tell Raimunda that he had changed completely, and Raimunda said she would sound him out, but I told her not to; then I read the list in the newspapers. Later, I saw him walking down the street, and, although he didn't seem his usual serene self, he was striding out as energetically as usual."

I was very shaken by this news, which confirmed my own impression, but I decided nevertheless to go to supper the following evening. Barreto wanted to come, too, but I realized that he simply wanted to keep me company, and so I put him off.

X. had said nothing to Maria. I found them both in the parlor, and I cannot recall a more uncomfortable situation. I shook them both by the hand, but avoided her eyes, as I think she avoided mine. He certainly didn't look at either of us. He struck a match and lit a cigarette. Over supper, he chatted as naturally as he could, but struggled to shake off his coldness. His face looked more strained than it had the previous day. To explain his possible nervousness, he told me that he was due to embark at the end of the week and that, as the time approached, he felt less and less inclined to leave home.

"Once I've crossed the bar, though, I'll be myself again, and on the battlefield I'll be the man I have to be."

He spoke in a rather stiff, emphatic way. I noticed that Maria had dark shadows under her eyes; I found out later that she had wept profusely and, the night before, had pleaded with him not to go. She had only learned of his decision from the newspapers, which proved that his reasons went beyond mere patriotism. She did not speak during supper, and her grief would have been enough to explain her silence, rather than any other personal guilt. X., on the contrary, talked a great deal, chattering on about the battalions, the new officers, the likelihood of victory, and telling countless, disconnected anecdotes and rumors. He occasionally tried to laugh, but he looked so gloomy when he made a joke about how he would, of course, return from the war a general, that he did not attempt another. The supper ended miserably; we smoked a cigarette, and he began again to talk about the war, but, by then, the topic was exhausted. Before leaving, I invited him to come and have supper with me.

"No, I can't. All my evenings are taken up."

"Come and have lunch, then."

"No, really, I can't. I will do one thing, though. I'll reserve the third day after my return from Paraguay entirely for you."

I still believe that those words meant that his first two days at home would be reserved for his mother and for Maria; and this should have dispelled any suspicions I had about the secret reasons behind his decision. It did not. He asked me to choose a souvenir, a book, for example. I chose instead a recent photograph of him, taken at his mother's request, showing him in his captain's uniform. Hypocritically, I asked him to sign it, which he did: "A gift from X., captain of volunteers, to his loyal friend Simão de Castro . . ." His face had grown still stonier, his gaze still grimmer. He nervously smoothed his mustache, and with that, we said goodbye.

He embarked on the Saturday. He left Maria enough to live on whether she chose to stay in Rio, Bahia, or in Rio Grande do Sul. She chose Rio Grande and set off three weeks later, to await his return from the war. I did not see her again; she had closed her door to me, just as she had closed her face and heart.

Before a year was out, I learned that he had died in combat, where he bore himself with more courage than skill. I heard it said that he had already lost an arm, and that his shame at being left a cripple probably lay behind his decision to hurl himself on the enemy's weapons, like someone eager for death. This might be true, because he was quite vain about his handsome appearance, but the cause was doubtless more complicated than that. I also heard that Maria, on her return from Rio Grande, died in Curitiba; others said that she died in Montevideo. Her daughter was only fifteen.

I stayed in Rio with my feelings of remorse and nostalgia, which, later, became only remorse, and have since become admiration, a particular kind of admiration, which isn't in itself very considerable, but enough to make me feel small, for I was incapable of doing what he did. I never really knew anyone quite like X. But why persist in calling him by that letter? Let us call him by the name he was christened with, Emílio, gentle, strong, simple Emílio.

INTO THE MIRE!

———

ONE NIGHT, many years ago, a friend and I were strolling about on the
terrace of the Teatro de São Pedro de Alcântara, between the second
and third act of *The Sentence, or Trial by Jury*. I only remember the title of
the play, nothing more, but it was the title that started us talking about
juries and about a story that has stayed with me ever since.

"I was always opposed to trials by jury," my friend told me. "Not the
institution itself, which is very liberal, but because I hate the idea of condemning anyone, and because of those words in the Gospel: 'Judge not, that
ye be not judged.' And yet I've twice served on a jury. The court was located
in what used to be Rua do Aljube, at the end of Rua dos Ourives and the
beginning of Ladeira da Conceição.

"I felt so uneasy about passing judgment that, with just two exceptions,
I absolved all the prisoners. I really did feel that the other cases had not been
proven satisfactorily, and a couple of the trials were very badly handled.
The first prisoner I condemned was a previously law-abiding youth, who
was accused of having stolen a rather small amount of money by forging a
document. He didn't deny the fact, nor could he, but he did deny that the
crime had been his idea or initiative. Someone, whom he did not name, had
suggested it as a way of meeting an urgent financial need; but God, who sees
into all our hearts, would ensure that the real criminal received his just deserts. He said this unemphatically, sadly, in a barely audible voice, his eyes
dull, his face pitifully pale. The prosecutor saw this pallor as a confession of

guilt. The defense lawyer, on the other hand, demonstrated that the fellow's pale, downcast face was proof of innocence maligned.

"I have rarely witnessed a more brilliant debate. The prosecutor's speech was brief but powerful, and given in a voice apparently filled with indignation and hate. The defense lawyer was clearly very gifted, and yet it turned out that this was his first appearance in court. The court was packed with relatives, colleagues, and friends, all waiting to hear his first speech, and they were not disappointed, for it was admirable and would have saved the prisoner if he could have been saved, and if his guilt had not been plain for all to see. That lawyer died two years later, in 1865. Who can say what we lost with his death! You know, I find it harder to accept the death of a talented young man than that of an old man. But to return to my story. The prosecutor gave his argument and the defense lawyer his counterargument. The judge gave his summing-up, and, having read out all the questions for the jury, handed these over to the foreman, who happened to be me.

"I won't say what happened in the secrecy of the jury room, and it doesn't really matter in this particular case, which, I admit, is best left untold. I'll be brief, though; the third act will be starting soon.

"One of the jury members, a burly, red-haired man, seemed more convinced than anyone of the prisoner's guilt. The trial was duly discussed, the questions to the jury read out, and votes cast (eleven to one); only the red-haired man seemed uneasy about the outcome. In the end, though, since the vote ensured that the prisoner would be condemned, he declared himself satisfied, saying that it would have been an act of weakness, or worse, if we had let the man off. One of the other jury members, doubtless the only naysayer, offered a few words in the young man's defense. The red-haired fellow—Lopes by name—responded angrily:

"'What are you talking about, sir? The man's obviously guilty.'

"'Look, let's stop this debate, shall we?' I said, and everyone agreed.

"'I'm not debating, I'm defending my vote,' Lopes went on. 'His guilt has been proven beyond doubt. He denies it, because all criminals do, but the fact is that he committed a forgery, and what a pathetic forgery it was! All for the wretched sum of two hundred *mil-réis*. I mean, if you're going to commit a crime, then plunge into the mire! If you're going to get muddy, then into the mire with you!'

"'Into the mire!' I must confess I was astonished, not that I understood quite what he meant; on the contrary, I neither understood nor approved, which is why I was so shocked. In the end, I got up and knocked on the door of the jury room. The door was opened, I went over to the judge's table, gave him our verdict, and the prisoner was found guilty. The defense lawyer appealed, but whether the verdict was confirmed or the appeal granted, I don't know. It was no longer my business.

"When I left the court, I kept thinking about what Lopes had said, and I seemed to understand then. 'Into the mire' was tantamount to saying that the thief was worse than a thief, because he was a worthless thief, a thief of nothing at all. I came up with this explanation on the corner of Rua de São Pedro, while I was still heading down Rua dos Ourives. I even retraced my steps a little, to see if I could find Lopes and shake his hand, but there was no sign of him. The following day, when I read the newspapers, I saw his name among the other jury members, but there was no point in seeking him out, and I soon forgot his name altogether. That's what the pages of life are like, as my son once said in the days when he wrote poetry, adding that the pages turn one after the other, and are dead as soon as they're read. The whole poem rhymed like that, but that's the only rhyme I can remember.

"A long time after that, he told me, in prose this time, that I must not attempt to avoid the jury service for which I had again been summoned. I insisted that I wouldn't go and once more quoted those words from the Gospel. He declared that it was my duty as a citizen, a service that no self-respecting person should deny to his country. And so I went and sat through three trials.

"One involved an employee of the Banco do Trabalho Honrado—the Bank of Honest Toil—the teller, in fact, who was accused of embezzlement. I had heard about the case, which had been reported in the press, although not in much detail, and, besides, I didn't usually bother reading the crime reports. The accused entered the court and sat down on the prisoner's bench. He was a thin, red-haired man. I looked at him closely and shuddered, for I seemed to see before me my fellow jury member from that trial years before. I didn't immediately recognize him because he was so much thinner, but his hair and beard were the same color, and he had the same air about him, and, when he spoke, the same voice and name: Lopes.

"'Will you please state your name?' said the judge.

"'Antônio do Carmo Ribeiro Lopes.'

"I had forgotten the first three names, but the fourth was the same, and everything else confirmed my suspicions; he really was the man I had met

all those years ago. I have to say that this realization prevented me from following the interrogation very closely, and I missed many details. By the time
I was able to concentrate, the trial was almost over. Lopes stoutly denied
everything he was asked or else answered in a way that only complicated
the whole process. He looked around him with not a hint of fear or anxiety;
there was possibly even the suggestion of a smile on his lips.

"The charges were read out. Forgery and the embezzlement of one hundred and ten *contos de réis*. I won't say how the crime or the criminal were
discovered, because it's getting late, and the orchestra is tuning up. What I
will say with certainty is that I was very impressed by the reports that were
read out, the questions, the documents, the teller's attempt to escape, and
a series of other aggravating factors, and, finally, the witness statements. As
I listened to statements being read out or to evidence from the witnesses, I
kept my eyes trained on Lopes. He was listening, too, but with his head held
high, looking calmly around, at the court reporter and the judge, at the ceiling and the people who were going to judge him, among them myself. When
he looked at me, he didn't recognize me; he just stared at me for a while and
smiled, as he did at the other jury members.

"Both prosecution and defense leapt upon these gestures, just as they
had years before on that other man's very different gestures. The prosecutor saw in them a clear display of cynical disdain, the defense lawyer
declared that only innocence and the certainty that he would be absolved
could explain such composure.

"While the two lawyers were speaking, I was thinking how odd it was
that the same man who had condemned that other fellow should find himself sitting on the very same bench, and, needless to say, I murmured to
myself the words from the Gospel: 'Judge not, that ye be not judged.' I confess that, more than once, a shiver ran down my spine. Not because I myself
might one day embezzle money, but what if, in a fit of rage, I were to kill
someone or find myself falsely accused of embezzlement? The man who had
passed judgment before was now also being judged.

"Alongside those words from the Gospel, I suddenly recalled the words
spoken by Lopes: 'Into the mire!' You can't imagine how this shook me. I
recollected the whole story, just as I've told it to you now, including the
little speech he gave in the jury room, and those words of his: 'Into the
mire!' I saw that he wasn't a worthless thief, a thief of nothing at all, but a
thief of great value. The words defined the action. 'Into the mire!' He meant

that you should only carry out such an act for a really large sum of money There's no point muddying your name for the sake of a few pennies. If you want to muddy your name, then into the mire with you, up to your neck!

"Ideas and words went rolling around in my head, and I missed the judge's summing-up entirely. The trial was over, he read out the interrogatories, and then we withdrew to the jury room. Just between you and me, I can say that I voted 'guilty,' because his embezzlement of those one hundred and ten *contos* seemed beyond dispute. Among the other documents, there was a letter from Lopes that made this clear. Yet it seems that not everyone saw things as I did. Two other jury members voted with me. However, the nine others believed Lopes to be innocent; a verdict of not guilty was read out, and the accused walked from court a free man. That majority vote made me doubt myself. Perhaps I had been wrong. Even today I feel the odd twinge of conscience. Fortunately, if Lopes really didn't commit the crime, at least he didn't go to prison because of my vote, and that consoles me for any possible error of judgment. My conscience still troubles me, though. Judge not, that ye be not judged. Plunge into the mire up to your knees or up to your neck, that's your choice, but don't judge anyone else. Oh, the music's stopped, it's time we went back to our seats."

THE HOLIDAY

A SLAVE CAME into the room to say that someone wished to speak to the schoolmaster.

"Who is it?"

"He says you don't know him, sir," answered the slave.

"Ask him to come in."

I don't know exactly how many of us children there were at the school then, but there was a general turning of heads toward the door through which the stranger would enter. Shortly afterward, a rough, weather-beaten figure arrived; his long hair had clearly never seen a comb, his clothes were all creased and crumpled, and I can't now even recall what color they were or what fabric they were made from, but they were probably some sort of dun-colored cotton. We all waited to hear what the man had come to say, especially me, because he happened to be my uncle, and lived in Guaratiba. His name was Uncle Zeca.

He went over to the teacher and spoke to him very quietly. The teacher asked him to sit down, then glanced across at me, and I think he must have asked my uncle something, because Uncle Zeca then launched into a long explanation. The teacher questioned him further, and my uncle answered, and, finally, the teacher turned to me and said:

"Senhor José Martins, you may leave."

My sense of pleasure overcame any feelings of fear and confusion. I was only ten years old and I loved having fun and loathed school. Being summoned home by my uncle, my father's brother, who had arrived the previous day from Guaratiba, must indicate some celebration or outing, or something of the sort. I ran to fetch my hat, stuffed my exercise book into my pocket, and went down the steps of the school—a two-story building in Rua do Senado. In the corridor, I kissed Uncle Zeca's hand, and once we were out in the street, I trotted along beside him, looking up at his face. He still said nothing, and I didn't dare ask any questions. Shortly afterward, we reached my sister Felícia's school; my uncle told me to wait, went up the school steps, and eventually they both emerged, and the three of us set off home. I was feeling even more excited now. I was sure some celebration awaited us, because both of us were there, walking ahead of my uncle, exchanging questions and conjectures. Perhaps it was Uncle Zeca's birthday. I turned to look at him; he had his eyes fixed on the ground, probably so that he wouldn't stumble.

On we walked. Felícia was a year older than me. She was wearing flat shoes tied on with ribbons that crisscrossed her instep and ended in a bow around her ankles. I was wearing a pair of very worn cheap leather boots. Her bloomers just reached the ribbons on her ankles, whereas my baggy cotton pants reached down to my feet. Once or twice we stopped, she to admire the dolls displayed outside the notions stores, while I paused any-where that had a parrot bobbing up and down on a perch to which it would be attached by a metal chain. It was usually a parrot I'd met before, but, to a ten-year-old, parrots are always of unfailing interest. Uncle Zeca would drag us away from all these commercial or natural spectacles. "Come on," he would say in a gruff voice. And we would continue walking, until some other curiosity made us stop. The main thing was the party awaiting us at home.

"I don't think it can be Uncle Zeca's birthday," Felícia said.

"Why not?"

"He seems rather sad."

"No, he's not sad, he's just a bit grumpy."

"All right, grumpy, but if it was his birthday, you'd expect him to look really cheerful."

"Perhaps it's my godfather's birthday, then . . ."

"Or my godmother's . . ."

"But in that case, why did Mama send us to school today?"

"Perhaps she didn't know."

"There's bound to be a big supper. . . ."

"And puddings . . ."

"And maybe dancing . . ."

We finally agreed that it could be a party even if it wasn't anyone's birthday. A big lottery win, for example. It occurred to me, too, that it could be election time. My godfather was a candidate for alderman, and although I didn't really know what "candidate" or "alderman" meant, I'd heard so much talk about his imminent victory that I assumed it was already done and dusted. I didn't know that elections were always held on a Sunday, and today was Friday. I imagined music bands and cheering and people clapping, with us kids leaping about and laughing and eating coconut candy. There might be some sort of performance later on. I felt positively dizzy with excitement. I had been to the theater just once and had fallen asleep on the way home, but the following day I was so happy that I longed to go again, even though I hadn't understood a word of what I'd heard, because I'd seen a lot of things: fancy chairs, thrones, long spears, scenes that changed before your eyes, going from parlor to forest and from forest to street. And all the characters were princes. At least that's what we called the ones wearing silk breeches, buckled shoes or boots, swords, velvet capes, and plumed caps. There was dancing too. The dancers, male and female, spoke with their feet and hands, changing position all the time and with a permanent smile on their lips. Then the audience started shouting and clapping . . .

That's the second time I've mentioned "clapping" now, but that's because I knew about clapping. When I told Felícia about the possibility of some kind of performance, she didn't seem so keen, nor did she reject it entirely, either. She wouldn't mind going to the theater. Or perhaps the performance would be at home, maybe a puppet show. We were still engaged in these conjectures, when Uncle Zeca told us to stop while he talked to someone.

We waited. The idea of a party, of whatever kind, still excited us; well, more me than her. Myriad possibilities sprang up in my imagination, all of them incomplete, because they came into my head so quickly and in such confusion that I couldn't actually grasp them; some may even have appeared more than once. Felícia pointed out two houseboys wearing scarlet skullcaps, who were walking past carrying canes, and that reminded us of the feast nights of Saint Anthony and Saint John, which were both long gone. Then I told her about the bonfires we lit in the playground, about the Roman candles and Catherine wheels and firecrackers we set off, and how we boys danced together. Perhaps it would be something like that . . . Then I suddenly remembered that you were supposed to throw your schoolbook on the fire; she could throw hers, too, the one containing all the different stitches she was learning.

"I'm not burning my book," said Felícia.

"Oh, I'd happily burn mine."

"Papa would just buy you another one."

"Before he did, though, I could stay at home and play. School is so boring!"

We were still talking about this when Uncle Zeca and the stranger came over to join us. The stranger gently raised our faces to him and regarded us gravely, then he left, saying:

"Nine o'clock, is it? I'll be there."

"Come along," Uncle Zeca told us, when the man had gone.

I wanted to ask him who the man was; he seemed vaguely familiar. Felícia thought the same, but neither of us could put a name to his face; however, his promise to be there at nine o'clock struck home. It *must* be a party or a dance, because we were usually sent to bed at nine o'clock. Given the exceptional circumstances, though, we would still be awake. When we reached a muddy puddle, I grabbed Felícia's hand, and we both leapt over it, so energetically that my schoolbook almost fell out of my pocket. I glanced at Uncle Zeca to gauge his reaction; he was shaking his head disapprovingly. I laughed and Felicia smiled and we continued on down the sidewalk.

It was a day for meeting strangers. The next two strangers were riding donkeys, and one of them was a woman. They had come from the fields. Uncle Zeca went out into the street to talk to them, having first told us to wait. The donkeys stopped, and I said that they had done so of their own accord because they knew Uncle Zeca, too, an idea that Felícia hotly rejected, and which I defended, laughing. I wasn't really serious; it was all in good fun. Anyway, we waited, studying those two country folk. They were both very thin, the woman even more so than the man, and she was younger too; he had gray hair. We didn't hear what they said, the man or Uncle Zeca, but we saw the husband eyeing us curiously and saying something to his wife, who then also looked at us, this time with something like pity in her eyes. Then they moved on, Uncle Zeca rejoined us, and we set off again for the house.

Our house was in the next street, near the corner. As we turned that corner, we were horrified to see that all the doors on our house were draped in black cloth. We instinctively stopped and turned to Uncle Zeca. He came over to us, took us each by the hand, and was about to say something, but the words stuck in his throat. He walked on, taking us with him. When we arrived, the doors were both ajar. I don't know if I mentioned before that the house was a notions store. Inquisitive onlookers were standing in the street. The windows opposite and on either side were filled with heads. There was a sudden buzz of voices as we approached. Needless to say, Felícia and I could not believe what we were seeing. Uncle Zeca pushed open one of the doors, we all went in, and then he shut the door behind us, and led us down the hallway to the dining room and the bedroom. Inside, next to the bed, sat my mother, her head in her hands. When she realized we were there, she leapt to her feet and came to embrace us, weeping and crying:

"My children, your father is dead!"

The shock was enormous, even though confusion and uncertainty partially numbed my ability to grasp this news. I couldn't move; indeed, I felt afraid to do so. Dead? How? Why? I ask those questions now in order to move the action along, because, at the time, I asked nothing of myself or of anyone else. I could hear my mother's words echoing inside my head, along with her loud sobbing. She clung to us and dragged us over to the bed, where her husband's body lay, and she made us kiss his hand. I felt so removed from it all that, despite everything, I did not, at first, understand, although the sadness and silence of the people around the bed helped make it clear that my father really had died. It wasn't a saint's day, full of fun and play, it wasn't a party, we wouldn't be allowed to idle away the hours, long or short, far from the torments of school. I cannot honestly say whether that fall from such a delightful dream increased my childish grief or not; best not think about it. My father was lying there dead, with no leaping, no dancing, no laughter, no music bands, all of which were also dead. If I had been told when Uncle Zeca came to the school why they had come looking for me, joy would never have entered my heart, from which it was now being soundly beaten out.

The funeral took place the next day at nine o'clock in the morning, and the friend my Uncle Zeca had met in the street was probably there, too, the one who had said goodbye with a promise to be there at nine. I didn't see the ceremony; I remember only a few figures, not many, all dressed in black. My godfather, who owned an import-export business, was also present, as was his wife, and she took me to a room at the back of the church to show me some engravings. When we left, I heard my mother's cries, the muffled sound of footsteps, a few murmured words from the people taking hold of the coffin handles, something like: "turn to the side . . . slightly more to the left . . . that's it, hold on tight . . ." Then, in the distance, I saw the hearse followed by the closed carriages . . .

There went my father and the holiday! A day off from school, but no rest! It wasn't just one day, either, it was eight, eight days of grief, during which I occasionally thought about school. My mother would weep as she made our mourning clothes, in between visits from people offering their condolences. I cried too; I didn't see my father when I would usually see him, didn't hear his voice at the table or at the counter, or the tender words he addressed to the birds, for he was a great lover of birds, and kept three or four of them in cages. My mother barely spoke, or, when she did, it was only to outsiders. That is how I learned that my father had died of apoplexy. I heard this over and over, because visitors always asked how he had died, and she would tell them everything, the hour, the expression on his face, the circumstances; he had gone to get a drink of water, and was just filling his glass and standing at the window that looked out onto the courtyard. I learned the story by heart just from hearing her tell it so often.

And yet, even so, my schoolfellows still came to peer inside my mind. One of them even asked when I would be back.

"On Saturday, my dear," said my mother, when I repeated this imagined question. "Although, since the mass will be on Friday, perhaps it would be best if you went back on the Monday."

"I'd prefer Saturday," I said.

"As you wish," she said.

She didn't smile, but if she'd been able to, she would have smiled with pleasure to see that I actually wanted to return to school earlier. And since she knew how I hated school, I wonder what she made of this sudden eagerness on my part. She probably attributed some loftier meaning to it, a message from heaven or from her husband. And if you're reading this with a smile on your face, I certainly wasn't idle during that time. No, I had no rest, because my mother made me study, and I not only hated studying, I hated having to be seated, with the book in my hands, in a corner or at the table. I cursed the book, the table, and the chair. I resorted to something that I heartily recommend to other idle boys: I left my eyes on the page and opened the door to my imagination. I ran to snatch up skyrockets, to listen to hurdy-gurdies, to dance with girls, to sing, to laugh, to have fights, whether pretend or in play, whichever is the more appropriate term.

Once, when my mother found me in the parlor without my book, she told me off, but I explained that I'd been thinking about my father. This explanation made her cry, and it wasn't a complete lie on my part, either, for I had been remembering the last little gift he gave me, and I could see him with it in his hand.

Felícia lived as sadly as I did, but, I must confess, the main cause of her sadness was not the same as mine. She liked to play, too, but she didn't really miss playing, she spent all her time with our mother, sewing with her, and, once, I even saw her wiping away her tears. Slightly annoyed, I considered imitating her, and put my hand in my pocket to take out my handkerchief. My hand entered my pocket with no real feeling and, finding no handkerchief there, withdrew with no real regret. I think that my gesture lacked not only originality, but sincerity too.

Don't think badly of me. I was genuinely sad during those long, silent, reclusive days. Once, I decided to go into the store, which had opened again immediately after the funeral, and where the clerk continued to work. I could talk to him, watch him selling cotton and needles, measuring out ribbons, or I could go to the door, out onto the sidewalk, even as far as the street corner . . . My mother smothered that dream soon after it was born, sending the slave-woman to fetch me and bring me back into the house to study. I tore at my hair, clenched my fists like someone about to land a punch, and, possibly, even wept with rage.

The book I was studying reminded me of school, and the image of school consoled me. I was really missing it by then. I could see from afar the faces of the other boys, the silly expressions we all put on as we sat at our desks, and our sheer glee as we gamboled home. I felt on my face one of those little paper pellets we used to provoke each other with, and I made one of my own and threw it at my imaginary provoker. As often happened, the pellet hit someone else's head, and he soon took his revenge, although when it hit one of the shyer boys, he would merely pull a face. It wasn't proper fun, but it was enough. The exile I had so blithely abandoned when Uncle Zeca came to fetch me seemed to me now like a remote heaven, and I was afraid of losing it. There was no gaiety at home, hardly a word spoken, barely a movement made. It was around this time that I started drawing endless cats in the margins of my schoolbook, cats and pigs. They didn't exactly cheer me up, but they were a distraction.

The seventh-day mass restored me to the street. As it happened, I didn't go back to school on the Saturday, I went to my godfather's house, where I was free to talk a little more, and on the Sunday, I was allowed to stand outside the shop door. This wasn't complete happiness, though. Complete happiness came on Monday, at school. I arrived all dressed in black and the other boys eyed me curiously, but it felt so different to be back beside my schoolfellows that I forgot that joyless holiday and discovered instead a different joy, with not a holiday in sight.

EVOLUTION

———————

M Y NAME IS Inácio and his is Benedito. I won't give our last names out of a sense of decorum, which I'm sure all people of discretion will appreciate. Inácio is quite enough to be going on with, and you'll have to make do with Benedito. It's not much, but it's something, and chimes with Juliet's philosophy: "What's in a name?" she asked of her lover. "That which we call a rose by any other name would smell as sweet." Let us move on to Benedito's particular smell.

And let us state at once that he was the most unlikely Romeo in the world. He was forty-five when I met him, although I won't say precisely when we met, because everything in this story is going to be mysterious and incomplete. As I say, he was forty-five and endowed with a lot of black hair; and any hair that wasn't black he treated with a chemical substance so effective that you couldn't tell black from black—except when he got out of bed, but when he got out of bed, there was no one to see him. Everything else was entirely natural: legs, arms, head, eyes, clothes, shoes, watch chain, and cane. Even the diamond tie pin—one of the loveliest I've ever seen— was natural and genuine, and had cost him a fair penny too; I myself saw him buy it at . . . ah, but I nearly gave the name of the jeweler; let's just say it was on Rua do Ouvidor.

Morally, he was entirely himself. No one really changes his character, and Benedito was of good character, or, rather, he was a quiet soul. Intellec- tually, he was less original. He could be compared to a popular inn, where ideas of all kinds and from all over would visit and sit down at the table along with the family. Sometimes two enemies would be staying there or else people who simply disliked each other; they would not quarrel, though, for the landlord imposed on his guests a reciprocally indulgent attitude. Thus he was able to reconcile a vague kind of atheism with the two fraternities he had founded, possibly in Gávea or Tijuca or Engenho Velho. He thus made promiscuous use of devotion, irreligion, and silk socks. Not that I ever saw his socks, but he had no secrets from his friends.

We met on a trip to Vassouras. We had left the train and got into the cab that would take us from the station to the city. We exchanged a few words and were soon conversing freely, borne along on the circumstances that had brought us together, even before we really knew each other.

Naturally, the first topic of conversation was the enormous progress brought to us by the railroads. Benedito recalled the days when every journey was made by donkey. We told a few anecdotes then, mentioned a few names, and agreed that the country's progress was conditional on the existence of the railroads. Only those who have never traveled can possibly be ignorant of the value of these exchanges of grave, solid banalities, which help to dissipate the tedium of a journey. One's mind breathes more freely, one's very muscles revel in that pleasant interchange, the blood flows easily, one feels at peace with God and with mankind.

"Even our children won't see this country crisscrossed by railroads," he said.

"No, you're right. Do you have children yourself?"

"No, none."

"Nor do I. Anyway, it'll be another fifty years before we get the railroads we need, and yet it's what we most need. I always compare Brazil to a child who is only at the crawling stage, and who will only begin to walk when we have a whole network of railroads."

"What a fine image!" cried Benedito, his eyes shining.

"I don't know about fine, but it is, I hope, at least fitting."

"It's both fine and fitting," Benedito said warmly. "You're quite right. Brazil is only at the crawling stage, and will only begin to walk when we have a whole network of railroads."

We reached Vassouras, and I made my way to the house of the municipal judge, an old friend of mine, while Benedito was only staying in Vassouras for a day before traveling into the interior. A week later, I returned to Rio de Janeiro, alone this time, and he returned shortly afterward. We met at the theater and talked at length, exchanging news; Benedito ended by inviting me to have lunch with him the following day, and he gave me a lunch fit for a prince, followed by good cigars and animated talk. I noticed, however, that his conversation made less of an impression on me than it had during the journey, where it had refreshed the mind and left us both at peace with God and with mankind; but maybe the lunch was to blame for that. It really was magnificent, and it would be quite wrong to place Lucullus's lavish table in Plato's modest house. Between the coffee and the cognac, he leaned one elbow on the edge of table, gazed at his lit cigar, and said:

"On my recent journey, I had occasion to see how right you were about Brazil still being only at the crawling stage."

"Really?"

"Yes, it's exactly as you were saying in the carriage that took us to Vassouras that day. We will only start to walk when we have a proper network of railroads. That is so true."

And he spoke of many other things, about life in the interior, how difficult things were there, how backward, although he also remarked on the kindness of the people and their hopes for progress. Unfortunately, the government was not responding to the needs of the country; indeed, it seemed intent on holding the country back, keeping us lagging behind the other American nations. However, we had to convince ourselves that principles are everything and mankind nothing. The people are not made for the government, the government is made for the people, and *abyssus abyssum invocat*. Then he showed me the other rooms, all of which were furnished impeccably. He showed me his collections of paintings, coins, antiquarian books, stamps, and weapons, including swords and rapiers, while admitting that he knew nothing about fencing. Among the paintings, I noticed a lovely portrait of a young woman, and when I asked who she was, Benedito smiled.

"Say no more," I said, smiling too.

"No, I won't deny it," he went on. "She was a young woman of whom I was very fond. She's pretty, isn't she? You can't imagine how beautiful she was in the flesh. Her lips were carmine-red, and her cheeks like roses, and her eyes as dark as night. And her teeth! Like pearls they were. Sheer perfection."

We then went into his study. It was vast and elegant, but somehow rather banal, although it lacked for nothing. There were two bookcases full of beautifully bound volumes, a mappa mundi, and two maps of Brazil. The desk was made of exquisitely turned ebony, and lying casually open on the desk was a copy of *Laemmert's Almanac*. The inkwell was made of crystal, "rock crystal," he informed me, explaining this as he had explained all the other furnishings. In the next room, there was an organ, which he himself played, for he was a great lover of music and spoke about it with enthusiasm, citing his favorite operas and their best arias. He added that, as a boy, he had learned to play the flute, but had soon abandoned it, which, he concluded, was rather a shame, since the flute is the most nostalgic of instruments. He ushered me into still more rooms, then we went out into the garden, which was truly splendid, with art working hand in hand with nature, and nature crowning art. There were roses, for example, of every type and from every region. "There's no denying," he said, "that the rose is the very queen of flowers."

I left feeling utterly charmed. We met on other occasions, too, in the street, at the theater, in the houses of mutual friends, and I grew quite fond of him. Four months later, I traveled to Europe on business that would require me to be absent for a whole year; he had an election to deal with, for he wanted to be a deputy. In fact, I was the one who encouraged him in this ambition, albeit without any real political intention, but simply to be agreeable; if you'll forgive the comparison, it was rather as if I had complimented him on the cut of his vest. He took up the idea and duly stood for election. One day, as I was crossing a street in Paris, who should I bump into but Benedito.

"What are you doing here?" I cried.

"I lost the election," he said, "and so decided to visit Europe instead."

He did not leave my side then, and we traveled together for what remained of our stay. He confessed that, despite losing the election, he was still keen to get into parliament, indeed, he was even keener. He told me of his grand plan.

"You could be a minister," I told him.

Benedito was not expecting this remark, and his face lit up, although he quickly disguised this delight.

"Oh, I don't know about that," he said. "Although, if I were to become a minister, I would want to work solely with industry. People are tired of party politics; we need to develop the vital energies of our country, its great resources. Do you remember what we talked about on our way to Vassourae, about how Brazil is only at the crawling stage, and will only begin to walk once there's a proper railroad network . . . ?"

"Yes, you're right," I said, slightly alarmed. "And why do you think I came to Europe? To make arrangements for a railroad to be built. That's what I was doing in London."

"Really?"

"Yes."

I showed him the documents, and he gazed at them as if dazzled. I showed him the various notes, statistics, bulletins, reports, and contracts for industrial materials that I had accumulated, and he declared that he wanted to collect such things too. And to this end, he visited ministries, banks, and trade associations, requesting all manner of notes and pamphlets, which he stuffed into his luggage. He did this with great ardor, but the ardor was short-lived, on loan, as it were. He was far keener on collecting political axioms and parliamentary terminology. He had a whole arsenal of them in his head and often trotted them out in conversation, as if speaking from long experience; he believed them to be highly prestigious and of inestimable value. Many came from the English tradition, and he preferred these to any others, as if they brought a little touch of the House of Commons with them. He enjoyed them so much that I'm not sure he would even have accepted real freedom if he could not deck it out with all that verbal apparatus; no, I don't think he would. I think that, given the choice, he would have chosen those brief, convenient sayings, some of them satisfyingly pithy, some high-sounding, and all of them axiomatic, requiring no thought, filling the void, and leaving people at peace with God and with mankind.

We journeyed to Brazil together, but I disembarked in Pernambuco, before going back to London, and only returned to Rio a year later. By then Benedito was a deputy. I went to see him and found him preparing his maiden speech. He showed me his notes, excerpts from reports, and books on political economy, some with the pages marked with strips of paper labeled thus: "Exchange Rates," "Land Taxes," "Cereal Crops in England," "John Stuart Mill's Opinion," "Thiers' Erroneous Views on Railroads," etc. He was sincere, painstaking, and passionate. He spoke to me about these things as if he had just discovered them, laying it all out before me, *ab ovo*; he was determined to show the practical men of the Chamber that he, too, was practical. Then he asked me about my business dealings, and I brought him up to date.

"In a couple of years, I hope to be opening the first stretch of track."

"What about the English investors?"

"What do you mean?"

"Are they pleased? Hopeful?"

"Of course they are."

I told him a few technical details, to which he listened rather abstract-edly, either because what I told him was too complicated, or for some other reason. When I finished speaking, he said how glad he was to see me so involved in the industrial movement, which is precisely what the country needed, and a propos of this, he did me the favor of reading me the intro-duction to the speech he would be giving in a few days' time.

"It's still only in draft form," he said, "but the main ideas are there." He began thus:

"In an age of growing anxiety, when partisan shouting drowns out the voices of legitimate interests, allow me to give expression to a plea from the nation. Gentlemen, it is time to concentrate exclusively—and I mean exclusively—on the material improvements this country requires. Oh, I know what you will say, you will say that a nation is not merely a stomach for digesting food, but a head to think with and a heart to feel with. I say that all these things would be worth little or nothing if they had not legs to walk on; and I will repeat here what I said to a friend of mine a few years ago, on a journey into the interior of the country: Brazil is a child who is still only at the crawling stage, and will only begin to walk once it is crisscrossed by a network of railroads . . ."

I heard nothing more, but sat there, deep in thought. Or, rather, not deep in thought, but utterly astonished, staring wild-eyed into the abyss that psychology was digging beneath my feet. This man is completely sincere, I was thinking, he believes what he has written. And so I went down into that abyss to see if I could find some explanation for the various processes through which his memory of our trip to Vassouras had passed. I found (and forgive me if I'm being presumptuous), I found further proof of the law of evolution, as defined by Spencer. Well, either Spencer or Benedito, one of the two.

PYLADES AND ORESTES

QUINTANILHA BEGAT GONÇALVES. At least that was the impression they gave when you saw them together, even though they did not resemble each other. On the contrary, Quintanilha had a round face and Gonçalves a long face, the former was short and dark, the latter tall and fair; all in all, they could not have been less alike. I should add that they were almost the same age. The idea of paternity sprang from the way in which the former treated the latter, for a father could not have been more affectionate, caring, and thoughtful.

They had studied law together, shared lodgings, and graduated in the same year. Quintanilha did not pursue a career in law or the judiciary, but instead became involved in politics. However, after being elected provincial deputy in 187*, he served just one term, then left when he inherited all his uncle's wealth, which gave him an income of thirty *contos de réis*. He returned to Rio to see his friend Gonçalves, who was working as a lawyer there.

Even though he was wealthy, young, and enjoyed the friendship of that one close friend, it could not be said that Quintanilha was entirely happy, as you will see. I will set aside the unhappiness that came along with his inheritance, an unhappiness that was due entirely to his other relatives' furious reaction, so furious that he came close to giving up the inheritance entirely. He only did not do so because his friend Gonçalves, who advised him on many matters, had convinced him that this would be utter madness.

"It's not your fault your uncle valued you more than he did his other relatives. You didn't write the will, nor did you fawn on him, as they did. If he left you all his money that's because he thought you were better than them. Keep the money, since that was your late uncle's intention, and don't be so foolish."

In the end, Quintanilha did as he advised. Some of the other relatives subsequently tried to make peace with him, but his friend warned him of their ulterior motives, and Quintanilha did not open his door to them. One of his relatives, seeing him so bound to his old university friend, told all and sundry:

"He's abandoned his blood relatives in favor of a complete outsider. Well, we all know where that will lead."

Quintanilha was furious when he heard this, and ran to tell Gonçalves. Gonçalves smiled, told him not to be so silly, and generally soothed his anxieties, saying there was no point getting worked up over mere tittle-tattle.

"I ask just one thing," he went on, "that we separate, so that no one can say—"

"Say what? It would really come to something if I had to choose my friends according to the whim of some shameless ne'er-do-wells!"

"Don't talk like that, Quintanilha. Don't speak so coarsely about your relatives."

"Wretched creatures! Am I supposed to live only with people chosen by half a dozen frauds whose one desire is to get their hands on my money? No, Gonçalves. I'll do anything else you want, but not that. I am the only one who can choose my friends, I and my heart. Unless, of course, you're bored with me . . ."

"Me, bored? Really!"

"Well, then."

"But if they—"

"Ignore them."

The two friends could not have formed a more united pair. Quintanilha's first thought when he woke up was of Gonçalves, and after breakfast he would immediately set off to see him. Later, they would dine together, visit a mutual friend or two, go for a stroll, and end up at the theater. If Gonçalves had work to do in the evening, Quintanilha would gladly help him, looking up legal texts, marking them, copying them, carrying books. Gonçalves was always forgetting something: an errand, a letter, his shoes, his cigars, his papers. Quintanilha was his memory. Sometimes, on Rua do Ouvidor, while watching the girls pass by, Gonçalves would suddenly recall some document or other that he had left in the office. Quintanilha would rush off to find it and, having found it, would race back, smiling and exhausted, as excited as if he had retrieved a winning lottery ticket:

"Are these the papers you needed?"

"Let me see, yes, those are the ones. I'll take them, shall I?"

"No, it's all right, I'll carry them."

At first Gonçalves would sigh:

"Honestly, I'm such a bother to you!"

But Quintanilha would laugh so fondly that Gonçalves, not wishing to hurt his friend's feelings, would say no more and accept his help without a murmur. Over time, helping his friend became Quintanilha's full-time occupation. Gonçalves would say: "Now, today you must remind me to do this and this." And Quintanilha would make a mental note, or write a list if there were too many. Some tasks had to be performed at a particular time, and it was a delight to see Quintanilha sighing anxiously as he waited for the appointed hour, so that he would have the pleasure of reminding his friend what he needed to do. He would bring him his letters and papers, rush off to get some urgently needed response, meet clients, even wait for them at the station and make trips into the interior. On his own initiative, he would search out good cigars, good restaurants, and good plays for his friend to enjoy. Gonçalves could not even mention a book, however new or expensive, without finding a copy waiting for him at home. He would scold Quintanilha, saying:

"You're such a spendthrift."

"Spending money on literature and science is hardly money ill-spent!" retorted Quintanilha.

At the end of the year, Quintanilha urged his friend to take a vacation. Gonçalves finally accepted, which pleased his friend enormously. They went up to Petrópolis. On the way back, they got to talking about painting, and Quintanilha remarked that they had no portrait of the two of them together. He immediately commissioned one. When he showed it to Gonçalves, the latter had no compunction in telling him that it was quite dreadful. Quintanilha was speechless.

"It's utter trash," insisted Gonçalves.

"But the painter told me—"

"Look, Quintanilha, you know nothing about painting, and the painter took advantage of your ignorance to cheat you. I mean, do you call that a face? And is my arm really all twisted like that?"

"The thief!"

"No, he's not to blame. He was just doing his job. You're the one who has no feeling for and no experience of art, and you were well and truly duped. I know you meant well, but . . ."

"Yes, I did."

"And I suppose you've already paid him?"

"I have."

Gonçalves shook his head, called him an ignoramus, but ended up laughing. Quintanilha stared angrily at the canvas, then took out a penknife and slashed the painting from top to bottom. As if that vengeful gesture were not enough, he returned the picture to the artist with a note in which he passed on to him some of the rude names he himself had been called and added that of "jackass." Life is full of such trials. Shortly afterward, Quintanilha had his "revenge" when a promissory note issued by Gonçalves fell due and Gonçalves was unable to pay it. Indeed, they almost quarreled, for Gonçalves decided it would be best to reissue the note, whereas Quintanilha, who had guaranteed the note, felt that it was hardly worth reissuing for such a small sum of money (one thousand five hundred *mil-réis*); he suggested lending him the money, with Gonçalves paying him back when he could. Gonçalves refused this offer and, instead, renewed the note. When payment fell due again, the most he would agree to was accepting a loan from Quintanilha at the same rate of interest.

"Don't you see how shameful that is for me, Gonçalves, receiving interest from you?"

"You either agree or the deal's off."

"But, my dear friend . . ."

He had no alternative but to agree. They were so very close that one lady dubbed them "the newlyweds," and a more literary gentleman called them "Pylades and Orestes." The two friends laughed at these epithets, of course, but when Quintanilha laughed, his eyes grew moist with tender tears. The other difference was the note of enthusiasm in Quintanilha's feelings for his friend, something that was completely lacking in Gonçalves; and enthusiasm cannot be invented. The latter, of course, was more capable of inspiring enthusiasm in the former than the other way around. In truth, Quintanilha was extremely sensitive to praise, it took only a grateful word or look to inflame his heart. A gentle pat on the shoulder or the belly, intended to show approval or to emphasize their closeness, was enough to make him melt with pleasure. He would talk about such gestures and the circumstances that provoked them for two or three days afterward.

He could often be angry or stubborn or even rude to people, but he laughed a lot, too, and sometimes that laughter was all-compassing, flowing forth from mouth, eyes, head, arms, legs, so that he was all laughter. He may have harbored no great passions, but he was certainly not without emotions.

When Gonçalves's loan fell due six months later, Quintanilha was determined not to accept payment and decided to dine in some other part of town so as not to see his friend, for fear that he might ask him to renew the loan. Gonçalves put paid to this plan by turning up at his house early in the morning to bring him the money. Quintanilha's initial response was to reject the money, telling him to keep it, saying that he might need it; the debtor, however, insisted on paying and, indeed, paid.

Quintanilha observed Gonçalves and saw how hard he worked, how zealously he defended his clients, and he was filled with admiration. Gonçalves was not a great lawyer, but, within his limitations, he was a distinguished one.

"Why don't you marry?" Quintanilha asked him one day. "A lawyer ought to marry."

Gonçalves laughed. He had an aunt, his only relative, whom he loved dearly, and who died when the two friends were in their thirties. Days later, he said to his friend:

"Now I only have you."

Quintanilha felt his eyes welling up, and did not know what to say. By the time he had thought of a response—that he would stay with him till death did them part—it was too late. Instead, he redoubled his affections, and one day woke up with the idea that he should make his will. Without saying a word to his friend, he named him as his executor and sole heir.

"Keep this document for me, Gonçalves," he said, handing him the will. "I feel perfectly well, but death could come at any time, and I don't want to entrust just anyone with my final wishes."

It was around this time that the following incident occurred.

Quintanilha had a second cousin, Camila, who was twenty-two and a modest, well-brought-up, pretty young woman. She wasn't rich; her father, João Bastos, worked as a bookkeeper for a coffee exporter. Quintanilha and

Bastos had fallen out over his uncle's inheritance, but Quintanilha had subsequently attended the funeral of João Bastos's wife, and this act of piety
had brought them together again. João Bastos easily forgot all the crude
names he had called his cousin and called him other, far sweeter names,
and invited him to come and dine with him. Quintanilha went and went
again. He listened to his cousin praising his late wife, and, on one occasion
when Camila had left the room, João Bastos heaped still more praise on
his daughter's rare qualities, which, he claimed, were her mother's moral
legacy to her.

"I would never say such a thing to her, of course, and please don't tell
her I did. She's very modest, you see, and if we were to start praising her,
it might go to her head. For example, I'll never say she's as pretty as her
mother was when she was her age because she might become vain. The
truth is, though, she's even prettier, don't you think? She even plays the
piano well, which her mother never did."

When Camila returned to the dining room, Quintanilha felt like telling
her everything, but restrained himself and merely winked at her father. He
then asked her if she would play the piano for them, but she replied sadly:

"Ah, no, not yet. Mama only died a month ago. I'd prefer to allow a little
more time to pass. Besides, I play very badly."

"Really?"

"Yes, very badly."

Quintanilha again winked at her father and suggested that he could
only know if she played well or badly if she sat down at the piano. As for
the time that had elapsed since her mother's death, it was true that it was
only a month since her passing, but it was also true that music was a natural and lofty distraction. And she could always play a sad tune. João Bastos
approved of this way of looking at things and reminded Camila of a particularly elegiac piece she knew. Camila shook her head.

"No, no, I would still have to play the piano, and the neighbors could
easily lie and say that they heard me playing a polka."

Quintanilha thought this rather amusing and laughed. Then he bowed
to her wishes and waited for a further three months to pass. Meanwhile,
he saw her several times, and his last three visits were more prolonged
and closer together. When he did finally hear her play, he greatly enjoyed
it. Her father confessed that, at first, he hadn't really liked that German
music, but, with time and habit, he had come to appreciate it. He called his

daughter "my little German," a nickname that was adopted by Quintanilha, who simply changed it to a plural: "*our* little German." Possessive pronouns add intimacy, an intimacy that soon existed among the three of them—or four, if we count Gonçalves, who was introduced to father and daughter by Quintanilha—but let's stick with three for now.

As I'm sure you, wise reader, will already have guessed, Quintanilha ended up falling in love with the girl. How could he not, when Camila had such large, fatally beautiful eyes? Not that she often directed them at him, and if she did, she did so with a certain degree of awkwardness at first, like a child reluctantly obeying orders from her teacher or father; but she did sometimes look at him, and those eyes, however unintentionally, inflicted a mortal wound. She also smiled a great deal and spoke very charmingly. At the piano, even when obliged to play, she played well. In short, Camila did not voluntarily weave a spell, but she was no less a sorceress for that. One morning, Quintanilha realized that he had been dreaming about her all night, and that same night he realized he had been thinking about her all day, and he concluded from this discovery that he loved her and was loved. He found this idea so intoxicating that he felt like publishing it in all the newspapers. At the very least, he wanted to tell his friend Gonçalves, and so he hurried to his office. Quintanilha's affection for Gonçalves was mingled with respect and fear. As soon as he opened his mouth, he immediately swallowed his secret again. He didn't dare to tell him either that day or the next. He knew that he ought to speak, to declare himself and be done with it, but he put off telling him for a whole week. Then, one evening, he went to supper with his friend and, after much hesitation, told him everything, that he loved his cousin and was loved in return.

"Do you approve, Gonçalves?"

Gonçalves turned very pale, or at least grew very serious, but with him seriousness and pallor were often one and the same. But, no, he really did turn pale.

"So you approve?" asked Quintanilha again.

After a few seconds, Gonçalves opened his mouth to reply, only to close it again, then he fixed his eyes "on yesterday" as he used to say of himself whenever he sat staring off into the distance. In vain did Quintanilha try to find out what was wrong, what he was thinking, if he thought this love of his was sheer nonsense. He was so used to hearing Gonçalves pronounce these words that it no longer wounded or offended him, even regarding such

a delicate, personal matter as this. Gonçalves finally surfaced from his meditation, shrugged indifferently, and, in a barely audible voice, he said:

"Don't ask me any more questions, just do what you like."

"Gonçalves, what's wrong?" asked Quintanilha, anxiously clasping his
friend's hands.

Gonçalves gave a great sigh, which, had it had wings, would still be flying
now. That, at least, was Quintanilha's impression, although not expressed in
the same paradoxical form. The clock in the dining room struck eight, and
Gonçalves declared that he had to pay a visit to a magistrate, and so Quintanilha said good night.

He stood out in the street, too stunned to move. He could not understand his friend's gestures, his smile, his pallor, the whole mysterious effect
that the news of his love had provoked in him. He had arrived and spoken,
ready to have his friend hurl one of his usual fond epithets at him—idiot,
dupe, nincompoop—but had heard none of them. On the contrary, there
had been something almost respectful in Gonçalves's manner. He could
think of nothing he had said during supper that could have offended him;
his friend had only become distressed when he told him of these new feelings for his cousin Camila.

"But that's impossible," he thought. "Why on earth would Camila not
make a good wife?"

He stood outside the house for more than half an hour. He realized then
that Gonçalves had not, as he had announced, left the house. He waited
another half an hour, but still no Gonçalves. He was tempted to go back in
again, to embrace his friend and question him, but he didn't have the courage. He set off down the street in a state of despair. He went to João Bastos's
house, but Camila had retired to her room with a cold. He wanted to tell
her everything, and I should explain here that he had not yet declared his
feelings to his cousin. It was true that she certainly did not now avoid his
gaze, but that was all, and this might well have been mere flirtatiousness.
This, though, was the perfect moment to clarify the situation. Revealing
what had just happened with his friend would give him a chance to disclose
his love for her and his intention to ask her father for her hand. It would
have been some consolation in the midst of all that anguish. Fate, however,
denied him this chance, and Quintanilha left the house feeling worse than
when he had arrived. He went straight home.

He did not get to sleep until at least two in the morning, not that this brought him any rest, it only increased his anxiety. He dreamed that he was about to cross a very long, old bridge between two mountains, when, half-way across, rising up from below, a figure appeared and stood before him. It was Gonçalves. "Wretch," Gonçalves said, his eyes ablaze, "why have you come to take from me my heart's belovèd, the woman whom I love and who is mine? Why not take my whole heart and be done with it?" And with a rapid gesture he wrenched open his chest, tore out his heart, and thrust it into Quintanilha's mouth. Quintanilha tried to remove this piece of his friend's viscera from his mouth and put it back in Gonçalves's chest, but this proved impossible. His jaws locked tight. He tried to spit the thing out, but that only made matters worse, for his teeth only sank deeper into the heart. He tried to speak, but how could he speak with his mouth stuffed full like that? Finally, his friend reached out his arms and hands to him as if to curse him, a gesture Quintanilha recalled from the melodramas of his youth. Two vast tears flowed from Gonçalves's eyes, filling the whole valley with water; then Gonçalves threw himself off the bridge and disappeared. Quintanilha woke, struggling for breath.

The nightmare had seemed so real that he again put his hands to his mouth, as if to remove his friend's heart. He found only his own tongue. He rubbed his eyes and sat up in bed. Where was he? What was he? And where was the bridge? And Gonçalves? Finally, he came to his senses, realized that it had all been a dream, and lay down again for another bout of insomnia, fortunately briefer than the first, falling asleep at around four o'clock.

During the day, going over what had happened the previous night, both reality and dream, he reached the conclusion that Gonçalves was his rival, that he loved his cousin and was perhaps loved by her. Yes, that was it. Two very painful hours passed. In the end, he got a grip on himself and went to Gonçalves's office determined to learn the whole truth, and if it was true, then, yes, if it was true . . .

Gonçalves was drafting a statement for the defense. He stopped what he was doing and looked at Quintanilha for a moment, then he stood up, opened the safe where he kept confidential documents, took out the will, and handed it to Quintanilha.

"What's this for?"

"You're about to marry, aren't you?" said Gonçalves, sitting down again.

Quintanilha heard how his voice almost broke when he said this, or so it seemed to him. He asked him to put the will away, saying that he was still its natural depositary, but the only response he received was the scratching of his friend's pen racing over the paper. Actually, Gonçalves's pen stumbled rather than raced, his writing was shaky, with far more emendations than usual, the dates doubtless wrong. And when he consulted one of his books, he did so with a look of such melancholy that it saddened even his friend. Sometimes he would stop everything—writing and consulting books—and fix his eyes "on yesterday."

"I understand," Quintanilha said suddenly. "She will be yours."

"Who?" Gonçalves was about to ask, but his friend was already flying down the stairs like an arrow, and Gonçalves continued his scribbling.

No need to guess what happened next, it's enough to know the ending. You won't guess or even believe what happened, but the human soul is capable of doing great things, both for good and ill. Quintanilha made another will, leaving everything to his cousin, on condition that she marry his friend. Camila would not accept the will, but was so happy when Quintanilha told her of Gonçalves's tears that she accepted both Gonçalves and the tears. Then Quintanilha felt that the only remedy was to draw up a third will, leaving everything to his friend.

The end of the story was spoken in Latin. Quintanilha was best man to the groom and godfather to the couple's first two children. One day, during the disturbances of 1893, when he was crossing Praça Quinze de Novembro to take some sweets to his godchildren, he was hit by a stray bullet, which killed him almost instantly. He is buried in the cemetery of São João Batista; the grave is a simple one, with an epitaph that concludes with this pious phrase: "Pray for him!" And that is also the end of my story. Orestes is still alive, feeling none of the remorse felt by his Greek counterpart. And, as in Sophocles's play, Pylades is completely silent. Pray for him!

THE TALE OF THE CABRIOLET

"THE CABRIOLET'S HERE, sir," said the slave who had been dispatched to the mother church of São José to summon the priest to give the last rites to not one but two individuals.

Today's generation witnessed neither the arrival nor the departure of the cabriolet in Rio de Janeiro. Nor will they know about the days when the cabriolet and the tilbury filled the role of carriage, public and private. The cabriolet did not last very long. The tilbury, which predates both, looks likely to last as long as the city does. When the city is dead and gone and the archaeologists arrive, they will find a skeletal tilbury waiting for its usual customer, complete with the skeletons of horse and driver. They will be just as patient as they are today, however much it rains, and more melancholy than ever, even if the sun shines, because they will combine both present-day melancholy with that of the spectral past. The archaeologist will doubtless have some strange things to say about the three skeletons. The cabriolet, on the other hand, had no history, and left only the tale I'm about to tell you.

"Two?" cried the sacristan.

"Yes, sir, two: Senhora Anunciada and Senhor Pedrinho. Poor Senhor Pedrinho! And Senhora Anunciada, poor lady!" said the slave, moaning and groaning and pacing up and down, quite distraught.

Anyone reading this with a darkly skeptical soul will inevitably ask if the slave was genuinely upset, or if he simply wanted to pique the curiosity of the priest and the sacristan. I'm of the view that anything is possible in this world and the next. I believe he was genuinely upset, but then again I don't *not* believe that he was also eager to tell some terrible tale. However, neither the priest nor the sacristan asked him any questions.

Not that the sacristan wasn't curious. Indeed, he was more than curious. He knew the whole parish by heart; he knew the names of all the devout ladies, knew about their lives and those of their husbands and parents, their talents and resources, what they ate, drank, said, their clothes and their qualities, the dowries of the unmarried girls, the behavior of the married women, the sad longings of the widows. He poked his nose into everything, and, in between, helped at mass and so on. His name was João das Mercês, a man in his forties, thin, of medium height, and with a sparse, graying beard.

"Which Pedrinho and Anunciada does he mean?" he wondered, as he accompanied the priest.

He was burning to know, but the presence of the priest made any questions impossible. The priest walked to the door of the church so silently and piously that he felt obliged to be equally silent and pious. And off they went. The cabriolet was waiting for them; the driver doffed his hat, and the neighbors and a few passersby knelt down as priest and sacristan climbed into the vehicle and headed off down Rua da Misericórdia. The slave hurried back on foot.

Donkeys and people wander the streets, clouds wander the sky, if there are any clouds, and thoughts wander people's minds, if those minds have thoughts. The sacristan's mind was filled with various thoughts, all of them rather confused. He was not thinking about Our Holy Father, although the sacristan knew how He should be worshipped, nor about the holy water and the hyssop he was carrying; nor was he thinking about the lateness of the hour—a quarter past eight at night—and, besides, the sky was clear and the moon was coming up. The cabriolet itself—which was new in the town, and had replaced, in this case, the chaise—even that did not occupy the whole of João das Mercês's mind, or only the part that was preoccupied with Senhor Pedrinho and Senhora Anunciada.

"They must be young people," the sacristan was thinking, "staying as guests in someone's house, because there are no empty houses to be had near the sea, and the number he gave us is Comendador Brito's house. Relatives, perhaps? But I've never heard any mention of relatives. They could be friends or possibly mere acquaintances. But in that case why would they send a cabriolet? Even the slave is new to the house; he must belong to one of the two people who are dying, or to both."

Such were João das Mercês's thoughts, although he didn't have much time to think. The cabriolet stopped outside a two-story house, which was indeed the house of the comendador, José Martins de Brito. There were already a few people waiting outside, holding candles. The priest and the sacristan stepped out of the cabriolet and went up the stairs, accompanied by the comendador. On the landing above, his wife kissed the priest's ring. Grown-ups, children, slaves, a murmur of voices, dim light, and the two people who were dying, each waiting in their respective rooms at the back.

Everything happened as it always does on such occasions, according to rules and customs. Senhor Pedrinho was absolved and anointed, as was Senhora Anunciada, and the priest left the house to return to the church with the sacristan. The latter just had time to ask the comendador discreetly if the two were relatives of his. No, they weren't, said Brito; they were friends of his nephew, who lived in Campinas; a terrible story. João de Mercês's wide eyes drank in those three words and said, without actually speaking, that they would return to hear the rest—perhaps that same night. All this happened very quickly, because the priest was already going down the stairs, and he had to follow.

The fashion for the cabriolet was so short-lived that this one probably never took another priest to administer the last rites to anyone else. All that remained was this brief, insubstantial tale, a mere bagatelle that I'll have finished in no time. Not that its substance or lack of it mattered to the sacristan, for whom it was another welcome slice of life. He had to help the priest put away the Communion wafers, take off his surplice, and do various other things, before they could say good night and go their separate ways. When he was finally able to get away, he walked along by the shore as far as the comendador's house.

On the way, he reviewed the comendador's life, before and after he had received that title. He began with his business—which was, I think, that of ship's supplier—then moved on to his family, the parties he had given, the various parish, commercial, and electoral posts he had held, and it was only a step or two from that to sundry rumors and anecdotes. João das Mercês's vast memory stored away every fact and incident, however large or small, so vividly that they might have happened yesterday, and so completely that not even the people involved could have recounted them in such detail. He knew these things as he knew the Our Father, that is, without having to think about the words—indeed, he would pray as if he were eating or chewing the prayer, which emerged unthinking from his mouth. If the rule was to say three dozen Our Fathers on the trot, João das Mercês would do so without even counting. So it was with other people's lives; he loved knowing about them, finding out about them, and memorizing them so that he would never again forget them.

Everyone in the parish loved him, because he never meddled or gossiped. With him it was a case of art for art's sake. Often it wasn't even necessary to ask any questions. José would tell him about Antônio's life and Antônio about José's life. What he did was ratify or rectify one version with the other, then compare their two versions with Sancho's, then Sancho's version with Martinho's and vice versa, and so on and on. This is how he filled his empty hours, of which there were many. Occasionally, while at mass, he found himself thinking about some tale he had heard the previous evening, and the first time this happened, he asked God's forgiveness, but immediately canceled this request when he realized that he had not missed a single word or gesture of the holy sacrament, so consubstantiate were they with him. The tale he had briefly relived was like a swallow flitting across a landscape. The landscape remains the same, and the water, if there is water, murmurs the same song. This comparison was of his own invention and was more fitting than he imagined, because the swallow, even when it's flying, is part of the landscape, and the tale was part of him as a person; it was one of the ways in which he lived his life.

By the time he had reached his destination, he had told every rosary bead of the comendador's life, and he entered the house with his right foot first for luck. He had decided that, despite the sadness of the occasion, he would stay there for some time, and luck was on his side. Brito was in the front room, talking to his wife, when he was told that João das Mercês was asking after the two people who had received the last rites. His wife withdrew, and the sacristan entered, apologizing profusely and saying that he would not stay long. He had just been passing and wondered if they had already gone up into heaven or were still in this world. He was, naturally, interested in anything that affected the comendador.

"No, they haven't died, and may yet live, although I think it highly unlikely that she will survive," said Brito.

"They both seemed to be in a very bad way."

"Oh, yes, especially her, because she's the worst affected by the fever. They fell ill here, in our house, soon after they arrived from Campinas a few days ago."

"So they were already here?" asked the sacristan, astonished that he had known nothing of their arrival.

"Yes, they arrived nearly two weeks ago. They came with my nephew Carlos, and caught the fever here—"

Brito suddenly broke off, or so it seemed to the sacristan, who adopted the expression of someone eager to know more. Brito, however, sat for a moment biting his lip and staring at the wall, and did not notice the expectant look on the sacristan's face, and so both sat on in silence. Brito ended up walking the length of the room, and João das Mercês thought to himself that there was clearly more to this than a mere fever. He wondered, at first, if perhaps the doctors had made a wrong diagnosis or prescribed the wrong medicine; or if there was some other concealed illness, which Brito was calling a fever in order to cover up the truth. He kept his eyes fixed on the comendador as he paced up and down the room, treading very softly so as not to disturb anyone else in the house. From within came the occasional faint murmur of conversation, a call, an order, a door opening or closing. None of this would have been of any importance to those with their minds on other things, but our sacristan had but one thought, to find out what he did not already know. At the very least, some information about the patients' family, their social position, whether they were married or single, some page from their lives; anything was better than nothing, however removed it was from his own little parish.

"Ah!" cried Brito, stopping his pacing.

There seemed to be in him a great desire to recount something, the "terrible story" he had mentioned to the sacristan shortly before, but the sacristan did not dare ask him and the comendador, not daring to tell the sacristan, resumed his pacing.

João das Mercês sat down. He knew that, in the circumstances, the polite thing would be to leave, proffering a few kind, hopeful, comforting words, and then to return the following day. He, however, preferred to sit and wait, and saw no sign of disapproval on the other man's face; indeed, the comendador stopped pacing for a moment and stood before him, uttering a weary sigh.

"Yes, it's a very sad business," said João das Mercês. "And they're good people, too, I imagine."

"They were going to be married."

"What, to each other?"

Brito nodded in a melancholy way, but there was still no sign of the promised terrible story, for which the sacristan continued to wait. It occurred to him that this was the first time he had heard about the lives of people unknown to him. All he had seen of these people, shortly before, were their faces, but his curiosity was no less intense for that. They were going to be married. Perhaps that *was* the terrible story; to have fallen mortally ill on the eve of a new life, that was terrible indeed. About to be wed and about to die.

Someone came to summon the comendador, and he excused himself so hurriedly that the sacristan had no time to take his leave. The comendador disappeared for about fifty minutes, at the end of which time the sacristan heard something like muffled sobbing coming from the next room. The comendador returned shortly afterward.

"What was I saying just now? That she, at least, would die. Well, she's dead."

Brito said this unemotionally, almost indifferently. He had not known the dead woman very long. The sobbing the sacristan had heard came from Brito's nephew from Campinas and a relative of the dead woman who lived here in Mata-porcos. It took only an instant for the sacristan to imagine that the comendador's nephew must have been in love with the dying man's bride, but this idea proved short-lived, for the nephew had, after all, traveled to Rio with both of them. Perhaps he was to have been the best man. As was only natural and polite, he asked the name of the dead woman. However, either because he preferred not to say or because his thoughts were elsewhere—or perhaps for both those reasons—the comendador did not give her name, nor that of her fiancé.

"They were to be married . . ."

"May God receive her and keep her safe, and him, too, if he should die," said the sacristan sadly.

And that was enough to draw forth half of the secret that seemed so eager to leave the comendador's lips. When João das Mercês saw the look in his eyes, the gesture with which he beckoned him over to the window, and the promise he exacted from him, he swore on the souls of all his loved ones that he would listen and say nothing. He was not a man to divulge other people's confidences, especially those of honorable persons of high rank like the comendador, who, satisfied with these assurances, finally plucked up the courage to tell him the first half of the secret, which was that the engaged couple, who had been brought up together, had come to Rio in order to get married, when that same relative from Mata-porcos had given them some dreadful news . . .

"Which was?" João das Mercês prompted, sensing some hesitation on the part of the comendador.

"That they were brother and sister."

"What do you mean? Blood relatives?"

"Yes, they had the same mother, but different fathers. Their relative did not explain in detail, but she swore this was the truth, and for a day or more, they were both in a state of shock . . ."

João das Mercês was no less shocked, but he nonetheless determined not to leave without hearing the rest of the story. He heard ten o'clock strike and was prepared to hear the clock chime throughout the night and to watch over the corpse of one or both, as long as he could add this page to his other parish pages, even though these people were not from the parish.

"So was that when they fell ill with the fever?"

Brito clenched his jaw as if he would say nothing more. However, when he was once again summoned, he hurried off and returned half an hour later, with the news of the second death, news to which the sacristan had already been alerted by the sound of weeping, quieter this time, although not unexpected, since there was no one from whom it needed to be concealed.

"The brother, or bridegroom, has just passed away too. May God forgive them! I'll tell you the whole story now, my friend. They loved each other so much that, a few days after learning of the natural and canonical impediment to their marriage, they decided that, since they were only half-siblings, they would elope, and they fled in a cabriolet. The alarm was given, and the cabriolet was stopped on its way to Cidade Nova. They, however, were so distraught and angry at being captured that they both fell ill with the fever from which they have now died."

It is impossible to describe the sacristan's feelings when he heard this tale. He managed, with some difficulty, to keep it to himself for a while. He found out the names of the couple from the obituary in the newspaper, and supplemented the details the comendador had given him with others. In the end, without feeling he was being indiscreet, he divulged the story—without naming names—to a friend, who told it to another, who told it to another, and so on and so forth. More than that, he got it into his head that the cabriolet in which the couple had attempted to elope could well have been the same one that had carried him and the priest to offer them the last rites; he went to the coach house, chatted to an employee, and discovered that it was indeed the same one, which is why this story is called "the tale of the cabriolet."

ABOUT THE AUTHOR

JOAQUIM MARIA MACHADO DE ASSIS was born in 1839. His paternal grandparents were mulattoes and freed slaves. His father, also a mulatto, was a painter and decorator, his mother a washerwoman, a white Portuguese immigrant from the Azores. His mother died of tuberculosis when Machado was only ten and he lived with his father and stepmother until he was seventeen, thereafter earning his own living, first as an apprentice typographer and proofreader, and, only two years later, as a writer and editor on the *Correio Mercantil*, an important newspaper of the day. By the time he was twenty-one, he was already a well-known figure in intellectual circles. During all this time he read voraciously in numerous languages, and between the ages of fifteen and thirty he wrote prolifically: poetry, plays, librettos, short stories, and newspaper columns. In 1867 he was decorated by the Emperor with the Order of the Rose, and subsequently appointed to a position in the Ministry of Agriculture, Commerce, and Public Works, where he served for over thirty years, until just three months before his death. Fortunately, this job left him ample time to write: nine novels, nine plays, over two hundred stories, five collections of poems, and more than six hundred *crônicas*, or newspaper columns. In 1897, he was unanimously elected the first president of the newly established Brazilian Academy of Letters. He was fortunate, too, in his marriage to Carolina Augusta Xavier de Novais, to whom he was married for thirty-five years. Following her death in 1904, at the age of seventy, Machado fell into a deep depression, and published only one more novel and a collection of stories dedicated to her. On his death in 1908, he was given a state funeral, and to this day is considered Brazil's greatest writer.

ABOUT THE TRANSLATORS

MARGARET JULL COSTA has been a literary translator for over thirty years and has translated works by novelists such as Eça de Queiroz, José Saramago, Javier Marías, and Bernardo Atxaga, as well as poets such as Sophia de Mello Breyner Andresen and Ana Luísa Amaral. ROBIN PATTERSON has translated works by José Luandino Vieira and José Luís Peixoto. Their co-translation of the Brazilian novelist Lúcio Cardoso's *Chronicle of the Murdered House* won the 2017 Best Translated Book Award.